# THE PLAN COMMENCES

## THE RISING SERIES
### BOOK TWO

## KRISTEN ASHLEY

ROCK CHICK
PRESS

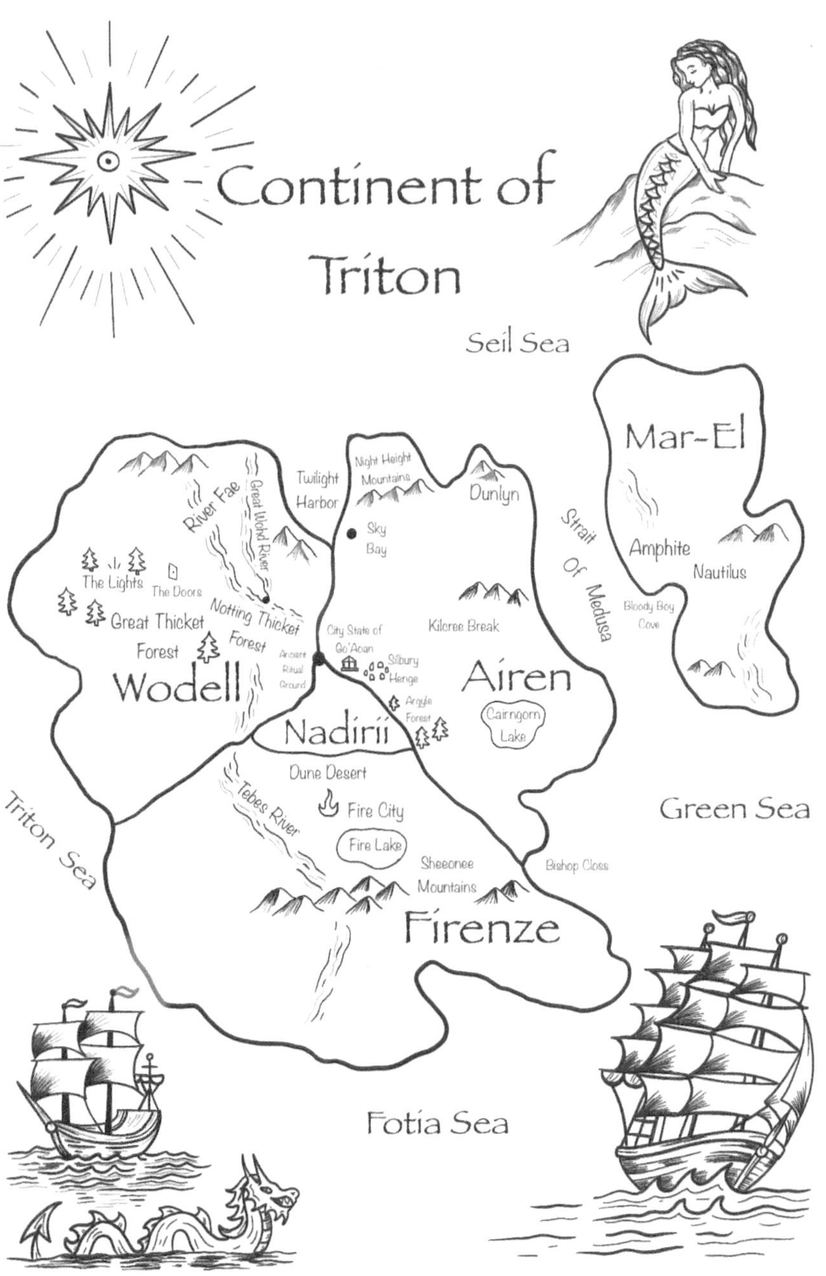

Continent of
Triton
Seil Sea
Mar-El
Twilight
Harbor
Night Height
Mountains
Dunlyn
River Fae
Great World River
Sky
Bay
Strait Of Medusa
Amphite
Nautilus
The Lights
The Doors
Notting Thicket Forest
Great Thicket Forest
Wodell
Kilcree Break
City State of Qo'Aoan
Ancient Ritual Ground
Silbury Henge
Airen
Bloody Boy Cove
Nadirii
Argyle Forest
Cairngorm Lake
Green Sea
Dune Desert
Tebes River
Fire City
Fire Lake
Triton Sea
Sheeonee Mountains
Bishop Closs
Firenze
Fotia Sea

THE RISING

# the Plan Commences

A LOVE IS EVERYTHING SAGA BY

# KRISTEN

*NEW YORK TIMES* BESTSELLING AUTHOR

# ASHLEY

# 36
## THE GRIEVING

***Prince True***
*Guest Suite, Second Floor, East Corridor, Catrame Palace, Fire City*
*FIRENZE*

"We should give her another sleeping draught," Queen Elpis said fretfully. "The last is clearly not working."

True did not even attempt to hide the censure in his gaze when he looked from the weeping beauty that was in his arms to the Queen of Firenze standing at the side of the foot of Farah's bed.

Elpis was as far from them as she could get at the same time staying close.

Her wont these past days when it came to Farah and her now-dead mother, Sofia.

Elpis's eyes were swollen and bloodshot from her own tears.

Too little.

Too bloody late.

Elpis flinched when she caught his gaze.

"You may leave," True rumbled.

"But, I—" Elpis started.

"You. May. *Leave*," True said lower and slower.

Her head jerked before she lifted her chin and stated, "This is my palace. She is my subject. I am queen and I—"

"For thirteen more hours," he interrupted her to note. "Then my cousin will be the Queen of Firenze and you will be naught but Relict Queen."

She gasped in affront.

True did not give a gods-damn.

"You leave, or my men will remove you," True warned.

"You cannot—"

"Leave, Your Grace, or my men will remove you," True repeated, and Florian made a move toward the queen.

"They have no authority here," she snapped.

"I am their prince, which means I will be their king and Farah will be their queen. Ask your son what authority that gives me," True retorted.

He immediately noted she took his meaning.

Then again, after the attack on the palace that occurred not two hours before had been quashed, Mars—her son, her king—had not allowed Silence, his intended, to climb down from his back where he held her as he battled their assailants.

It was safe, and still Mars kept Silence as close to him as he could without absorbing her, something he could not do, or he would have done that instead.

Yes.

Elpis took his meaning.

Her face softened, and her gaze moved to Farah, who was in his arms, silently crying, her head turned toward True's body, even if she was not holding him in return. Something that alarmed him and something he wished to address with his betrothed.

It was just that he'd do that when the bloody queen left.

"I am glad she has you," Elpis whispered.

"It would have been good if she'd had *you*," True retorted. "If they'd *both* had you."

Pain sharpened her features.

Pain and regret.

But Farah tightened in his arms.

This was upsetting his intended.

Therefore, this had to end.

"Go," he ordered the queen.

Elpis seemed to crumble before his eyes and True wished he didn't care about that either.

But he understood regret.

The woman could not know her friend would take hundreds of bites from poisonous emerald oil asps and die in her bed under a pile of them before they could find their way back to a friendship that had been torn apart by treason and murder.

However, now he didn't have time for Queen Elpis.

He needed to see to his future queen.

Fortunately, Elpis knew the only one who could look after Farah was in her bed holding her.

Thus, she gave up the fight and moved slowly from the chamber.

The door latched shut behind her.

"Leave us," True ordered Florian, Bram and Alfie, the members of his guard who were in the room. The others, Luther and Wallace, were guarding it elsewhere. One, Luther, in the hall. The other, Wallace, outside, under the window.

"True—" Alfie began.

"Leave," True said.

Alfie looked to Farah then to True.

"Magic," he replied quietly.

Indeed.

The asps that had killed Sofia had been very real.

They had also been transported to her bedchamber through magic.

A bedchamber that had been Farah's before her mother and she had switched in order to place Sofia farther away from Elpis's room.

True knew all this.

As did Alfie and his other lieutenants.

But he could have fifty swords in that room.

They wouldn't be able to fight magic.

"I'll want you in here, guarding her after I leave. But now, we need privacy," True told his friend.

"I think—"

"Go, Alfie," True demanded.

Alfie hesitated before he nodded then he jerked his head to Florian and Bram and they walked out of the room.

The instant the latch clicked, True turned his attention to Farah, pulling her deeper into his arms.

Hers remained resting limp at her sides, her body lax, her tears silent, but still tracking down her face.

"Sweets," he murmured. "Do you wish another sleeping draught?"

He offered it, for her sake, but he didn't like the idea. They'd already given her a strong one.

"I need to rise, dress," she told him, her voice dull and remote.

True grew more alarmed at her tone.

And her words.

Pain, he could understand.

Withdrawal was an additional concern.

"That's the last thing you need, Farah. You need to rest. Sleep," he refuted.

"I need to be in attendance at the procession."

"The wedding won't be for hours, love," True murmured. "Regardless, it would be understood if you didn't attend. And Mars might postpone it altogether after—"

Her head tipped back and True saw her eyes were just as remote as her voice.

This was not Farah.

Not his beautiful Farah with her shining topaz eyes that were always keen and alert and emotive.

"The torture procession," she explained.

True blinked down at her.

"The what?"

"Did they take any assailants alive?" she asked.

"Yes," he answered.

"Then Mars will torture them, and all affected will go to the necropolis by the pit in order to watch them walk to their deaths. They will go by procession so the people will know those who attacked our palace, our king, will have no mercy."

True grew even *more* alarmed.

"All?" he queried.

"All," she asserted.

"Even Silence?"

"Especially Silence."

Gods-damn it.

"She cannot—" True started.

"She must." Farah made to move. "And I must."

True tightened his arms. "You're going nowhere."

She stilled in his hold. "I must, True."

"You must if you're Firenz," he declared. "But you are no longer Firenz. You are Dellish. And the Princess of Wodell does not attend a procession to watch torture after she lost her mother...or ever. You'll take another sleeping draught and you'll rest. And when you wake, I'll be here, and I'll help you mourn."

She turned her head away.

True jostled her. "Farah."

She looked at him again. "I am Firenz."

"You are Dellish," he asserted.

"I am not."

"You are mine and I am Wodell."

"I am not yours," she whispered. "I am not anybody's. Not any longer. I'm now actually of no one and nowhere. I am not Firenz. I am not Dellish. I am nobody."

True's alarm increased exponentially.

"You belong to me, sweets," he said softly. "And I belong to you."

"For either of those to be true, you have to wish it to be true, and you do not, Your Grace."

Your Grace?

She hadn't called him that since the first day they met, and he asked her not to.

"Farah—"

She turned away from him, pulling out of his arms.

"Bring me the draught. As you wish, I shall sleep."

She slid down into the bed, settled on the pillow, her back to him, her knees pulled up to her chest.

True placed his hand on her hip and leaned toward her.

He tried again, "Farah—"

"Shall I call a servant for the draught?" she asked her pillow.

True didn't move or speak. He stayed right where he was, gazing at her profile in the lamplight.

And doing this, he decided she needed time.

She also, as he had noted, needed sleep.

After that, she would need him.

Even if she did not think she did.

And she would have him.

All of him.

He took his hand from her hip, pulled her hair away from her neck and then he tugged the silks up to her shoulder.

Through this, she didn't even twitch.

He then leaned ever closer and spoke in her ear.

"You grieve and speak through that grief. And I am at your side. You will sleep and you will wake, still in grief, and I'll be at your side. I'll see you through your grief, Farah, and I'll do it at your side. I will see you past your grief, also at your side. I will remember your mother as kind and loving, and

I will do it at your side. And then we will carry on with our lives, our marriage, building a family, and through it all, I'll be at your side. You do belong to me, Farah. My future princess. My future wife. And in return, darling, I belong to you."

He got ever closer, dipped his voice lower and finished.

"And as yours, I will avenge your mother, my sweetling. The one that caused your hurt will know his own pain. That is my vow to you as my friend, my betrothed, my future princess, my future queen and just *mine*."

Through his speech, her body got tighter and tighter.

It stayed that way when he bent low and brushed her temple with his lips.

He pulled an inch away and murmured, "I'll have a draught brought up."

Then he exited the bed, moved to the door, opened it and walked through it.

"Get her another sleeping draught," he ordered Florian after he closed the door. "Go in and sit with her," he ordered Bram after Florian moved down the hall to the stairs. "But be silent and keep distant. She needs time with her thoughts."

Bram nodded and entered Farah's room.

True gave Luther a look and Luther remained where he stood outside Farah's door as True started toward the stairs with Alfie at his side.

They did this dodging servants who were sweeping up plaster from the quake.

And mopping up blood from the bodies that had been removed.

"Do you know of this procession?" True asked the captain of his guard.

"I didn't, until Basil came up but moments before you came out and summoned you to Mars's study."

"Aramus will not allow Ha-Lah to take part in it," True guessed. "I wish to ask her to sit with Farah until I can return to her."

"Ha-Lah is not leaving Aramus," Alfie replied.

True looked to his man. "He can't possibly—"

"They had a guard under their window. Catedrais was killed in the attack."

This stood to reason. The assailants had breached the palace through the windows. And there had been a great number of them.

He thought it had been a miracle that all on their side had survived.

But True had learned a long time ago that miracles didn't happen.

Especially in battle.

"Bloody hell," True muttered, turning to walk down the stairs.

"The Mar-el are as us," Alfie continued. "As brothers. Aramus is not in a good state, losing his man. His wife is remaining close."

"And Mars?" True asked, now jogging down the stairs, Alfie doing the same.

"I do not know."

"Silence?" True went on.

"I do not know that either, though Luther shared, as far as he's heard, she's not left Mars's side," Alfie told him as they made the first-floor landing.

"Has not left his side or he has not let her away from his side?" True inquired.

"The latter," Alfie answered.

"Bloody hell," True repeated.

They spoke no more as they made their way to Mars's study.

Basil and Kyril stood outside it.

But the hall, both the east and west corridors, was laden with Firenz warriors as well as those from Airen, Wodell and the Nadirii.

Basil opened the door for them and True walked through while Alfie remained behind.

Only for True to stop dead.

Silence sat in Mars's chair behind his desk. She was curled into herself, thighs to her chest, arms around her calves.

And she was still wearing her nightgown, which was stained thoroughly with dried blood. So much so, only streaks of white could be seen through the rust. There was dried blood on her arms. In fact, the only bit of her that had been cleaned was her face.

And her neck, which was mottled an angry purple with bruising.

At the sight, True felt his heart begin to race, his blood heating in his veins.

Mars was behind her, pacing, his angry energy almost a physical thing in the room.

All the others were there. King Aramus and Queen Ha-Lah. Prince Cassius and Princess Elena. Queen Ophelia and Princess Serena. Queen Elpis. King Gallienus. Select members of each guard. And a variety of barons of Firenz clans and chieftains of Firenz tribes.

True's parents, King Wilmer and Queen Mercy, were also there.

But True was pleased to see his father's counsellor, Carrington, was not.

Lorenz, the captain of Mars's Trusted, was standing in front of his king's desk, reporting.

"Those who were not found dead were found asleep or unconscious, draughts for the former, blows for the latter. The sergeant for this eve realized swiftly half the unit had not reported for duty at the changing of the guard. He sent warriors to discover why, and as you know, died on the palace steps, most likely on his way to Chu to raise the alarm."

Mars kept pacing as he rapped out, "It's my understanding the hour for the changing of the guard is modified daily so this exact occurrence would not happen."

"It is," Lorenz answered.

"So tonight's hour was known to the assailants."

"It was."

Mars stopped moving abruptly and pinned his captain with dark eyes. "We have a traitor."

Lorenz's jaw was tight as he forced out, "We do."

"Have they been worked?" Mars asked.

"They have."

"Has the traitor been identified?"

"He has."

"And?" Mars prompted

Lorenz hesitated but a moment to give his king a meaningful look.

But he did not speak.

Mars clearly read this meaningful look for his face turned to granite.

"He and the rest are being marched to the pits?" Mars queried through clenched teeth.

"They are," Lorenz assured.

Mars seemed to realize then that True was with them and his gaze sliced his way.

"My sister?" he demanded of True.

"Your sister?" True asked in return.

"Farah," Mars snarled, and True noticed Silence curling deeper into herself.

His attention returned to the king.

"My princess," he corrected.

"Semantics," Mars spat impatiently.

But True suspected he was less patient.

Farah in her state, Sofia gone, the attackers coming in through his cousin's window, and his earlier thought proven untrue for it was a certain miracle Silence had survived.

Thus, he shared his impatience immediately.

"Absolutely fucking *not* semantics," he bit out.

He sensed Silence's, and everyone's, attention sharpening on him, but he didn't break eye contact with the Firenz king.

"I take it this means you're finally claiming her in a way that matters," Mars bit back.

"Do not try me, Your Grace," True warned. "Not with my cousin sitting in a bloodstained nightgown in your chair with her neck black-and-blue and my future wife in her bed so deep in her mourning, she's disavowed her country...*both* of them."

A vein in Mars's temple pulsed.

It took a moment before Mars declared quietly, "She will heal."

"She will. Because *I* will see to it," True returned. "In other words, Mars, she's a bloody mess. She's also not taking part in this procession."

"As you've claimed her, that's yours to decide," Mars allowed.

"My cousin isn't either," True declared.

The atmosphere of the room became heavy.

He was surprised to hear his mother's voice come first through the tense silence.

And he heard it when she simply said a warning, "True."

True ignored her and kept his gaze to the Firenz king.

"As I keep telling you, she is not of your realm."

"If she wasn't, she will be within the hour," Mars returned.

"I do not know what you intend to do. I just know you should not force Silence to witness it," True retorted.

"That is mine to decide," Mars rejoined.

"Actually, it should be Silence's to decide," Ophelia declared.

True looked to the Nadirii queen.

She had her gaze on Silence.

Therefore, True turned his attention to his cousin.

"Silence?" he called when she seemed to be lost in her study of the top of Mars's desk.

"*Mia piccolina*," Mars murmured, crouching beside her chair.

Silence turned her head to Mars.

"I go with you, my king," she whispered.

Mars's face lit with pride and triumph.

"Gods-damn it," True muttered.

"Can she at least bathe and clothe herself appropriately?" True's mother asked in a way it sounded more of a demand.

Mars straightened but he did it plucking Silence out of his chair and holding her to his chest but for a moment before he sat where his bride had been, now with her in his lap, still held close to his chest.

Once seated, he looked to Queen Mercy and answered, "No. My people see her covered in the blood of the vanquished, alive and noble in victory."

"That's frankly barbaric," True's father snapped.

"It's frankly Firenz," Mars retorted. "Which Silence will be, officially, this eve. But it is what my people, *her* people will see, the now. And something I wish to happen, soon, so we can see this matter concluded and I can wed my bride without delay tonight."

"You can hardly see an attempted coup concluded within hours," King Wilmer returned.

Mars slid his gaze to Lorenz.

True watched Lorenz tip his head to the side.

Mars returned his attention to True's father.

"It seems I can."

"Prisoners have rights," Wilmer stated.

"Not if those prisoners are traitors," Mars replied. "Not in Firenze."

"You surely must hold tribunals," Wilmer retorted.

"They wear the black, they storm the palace, they march to the pits under the eyes of their people, endure the necropolis, and sink in the tar," Mars declared. "Do not worry, Wilmer. Their time in the necropolis will be short. They planned fortuitously. I don't wish to dally in the necropolis. I wish to be wed."

"So you're saying you intend to wed my niece just hours after she suffered what she suffered in her chambers *and* you forcing her to watch you torture some of your citizens, then put them to death?" Wilmer asked in shock.

"I'm not forcing my Silence to do anything," Mars drawled. "*Mia bellezza* made her choice and wielded her own dagger rather than running from the fight. She makes her choice now, seeing this matter through to the end, instead of hiding in her chamber. If I did not know differently due to the color of her skin and the stature of her frame, I would think she *was* Firenz."

True studied his cousin as she sat silent in the lap of her betrothed.

She did not worry her lip, wring her hands or appear anxious, agitated or disturbed in any way.

She also did not seem relaxed and at her ease.

She simply seemed... dignified.

Or as dignified as a being could be, sitting in an enormous man's lap.

This sent True's gaze to the Firenz barons and chieftains.

At what he saw, he almost smiled.

Silence, enduring what she'd endured that night, sitting in a bloodstained nightgown in a barbarous king's hold, crafty enough to use this moment to advance her station.

That was his cousin.

Nobody's fool.

Fit to be queen.

Yes, he almost smiled.

True's thoughts were turned from this when Aramus spoke.

"I will know vengeance, Mars."

"What is your wish?" Mars asked, his tone no longer swaggering, but conciliatory.

"How many were caught?" Aramus asked.

"Seven," Lorenz answered.

"My men and I will have three," Aramus decreed, and Ha-Lah, who was already close to her husband's side, got closer and took his hand.

Aramus's fingers wrapped tight around his wife's. Too tight. True saw it. She winced at the pain.

But she said nothing.

"You shall have your pick," Mars murmured.

True turned again to Mars. "The snakes were another matter."

True saw the lick of flame in Mars's eyes before it extinguished, and he inclined his head.

"Is their aught known about that?" True asked.

"Nandra tried to trace the magic," Lorenz answered. "She failed. It's cloaked."

"Leave us," Mars ordered abruptly.

His attention was on his barons and chieftains.

True stepped out of the way as the men started to file out, and Mars commanded, "You ride in procession to the pits behind me and your future queen."

He received nods and chin lifts before the men disappeared behind the door.

"You leave us too," Mars demanded.

That, True noted, was directed to his mother and father.

"Just us?" Mercy asked.

"You and Gallienus. Yes," Mars answered.

"Whyever would we alone be left out?" True's father queried peevishly.

"You are neither soldier nor witch nor directly involved in the vanquishing the Beast," Mars answered.

"We represent Wodell," Wilmer returned.

"So does your son, far better than you. Now, I explained why you are to leave my study, when I did not need to. Don't test my patience further. There are things to do and one of them is not answering to you," Mars replied.

"I—" Wilmer began.

"My king, let us go," his mother urged, taking Wilmer's hand and shifting toward the door.

"I'm happy to leave," Gallienus declared. "All this talk of the injustice of Airen? Hypocrisy." He stopped at the door and leveled his eyes on Mars. "Even a traitor I'd give a tribunal."

"Sadly, I cannot ask any descendants of the women your ancestor put to death after the Night of the Fallen Masters as they were put to death without tribunal, therefore they have no descendants," Mars noted drolly.

Gallienus sniffed before he stormed out.

Wilmer and Mercy followed him.

When the door closed behind them, True turned again to Mars.

"When the sorcery behind the asps is uncovered, they are given to me," he decreed.

"They killed my second mother," Mars said quietly.

"They killed my mother-in-law, the grandmother my children will never know, but their intent was to kill my princess," True retorted. "Thus, whoever killed Sofia will be given to me."

"For tribunal?" Mars asked.

"Yes," True answered. "And then he'll be given a torch and the length of time it takes for it to burn out before he'll find himself covered in snakes in a different kind of pit in Wodell. It'll be Farah's decision if she wishes to watch. But I shall do so. Until the end."

Mars's lips twitched before he stated, "I find this acceptable."

"I don't very much care," True muttered.

"I find that acceptable too," Mars shared.

"Oh, for fuck's sake, can we move this along?" Cassius entered the conversation.

"It's clear, with the attack of the asps, Farah was the target," Ophelia noted.

No one spoke to that.

"They try to break the prophecy," the Nadirii queen continued.

"Perhaps, regardless of our grave losses this evening, we can take heart in understanding they fear the prophecy enough to try to do something about it," Ha-Lah noted.

"Your sisters, along with Nandra, must cast over this palace," Mars said to Ophelia.

"Protection spells will be done while you're at the pits," Ophelia agreed.

"And cast over the women," Cassius added.

"Ah yes, seeing as, due to you having a magical appendage, you need no protection spell cast on you," Elena clipped to her betrothed.

True studied her, feeling something strange, but his mind was consumed with so many other things, the most important being getting to Farah and checking on her before he had to attend this bloody procession, he couldn't put his finger on what that feeling was.

"We'll cast over the men too," Ophelia put in quickly, before Cassius could reply, as he'd opened his mouth to do.

Cassius wisely shut his mouth and a muscle danced in his cheek.

Elena turned away from her intended and crossed her arms angrily on her chest.

"I need a moment with my bride," Mars decreed.

Excellent.

Mars would see to Silence.

True could go up to look in on Farah.

He turned to do so but stopped when he caught sight of Aramus.

The king felt his regard and shifted his attention to True.

"My deepest sympathies, my brother," he said quietly.

Ha-Lah got even closer to her husband.

Aramus simply glowered at him before jerkily lifting his chin.

True left the room, made his way to the stairs, up them, and to Farah's room.

Thank the gods, she was asleep when he arrived.

Even so, he sat on the bed and stroked her soft hair.

He then tried to find his way to where she was in her mind.

He had no brothers or sisters, and she had no brothers or sisters.

But he had something she did not.

He had cousins, the closest of which was Silence. He could not say she was close as a sister, but he cared deeply for her, and she for him. And if something happened to him, she would be there for him, as he would for her.

He had a weak father and she had the weakest of fathers there could be.

But his father was alive.

Her father's bones were preserved in the tarpits of Fire City after he'd committed regicide and left her and her mother to bear the consequences of his actions while still breathing.

Her mother had been loyal and loving.

His mother was the same, the latter in a somewhat cold way that was often calculating, but that was for the betterment of husband and son.

She was also alive.

Thus, True could not put himself in Farah's place. He could not understand how alone she felt.

All he could do was whatever he needed to do to make her feel not alone as well as loved.

Mars would assist with this, obviously.

As would Silence, as was her way.

And if Farah could forgive her, True would as well, so she would have Elpis.

But his mother would be there for his bride too.

He knew Queen Mercy had no respect for his betrothed.

She also had no reason for her intolerance.

She would need to find her way past that.

Immediately.

Or she'd find herself without a son.

For True would soon have a wife, the mother to his children, the future queen of his country.

He'd realized that night that she was the most important thing in his life.

And she always would be.

His mother would know that, and she'd know it soon.

As would his Farah.

**King Mars Laches**
*King's Study, First Floor, East Corridor, Catrame Palace, Fire City*
*FIRENZE*

WHEN THE DOOR closed behind Lorenz, the last one out, Mars turned to his Silence, still curled in his lap.

"*Amore*," he called.

She tipped her head back to look up at him.

He ignored her garments. The skin of her arms crusted with blood. The visions in his head of her being dragged to the open window by her glorious hair.

And he especially ignored the bruising at her neck.

He had to ignore these things, or the rage would return, and the fullness of his vengeance would not be meted out for he'd set her aside and find the men still left and dispatch them far more quickly than they deserved.

Instead, he looked into her silver eyes.

"We need words," he murmured.

"I'm quite all right, Mars," she assured.

But she was not.

Her demeanor had changed, and it was not due to shock or fear.

Or perhaps it was, as she was locked away.

He'd seen her like this only once before. When she'd walked in his thronal room the moment he first saw her.

Except then she had been guarded and locked away and it took but a few words to draw her out.

Now she simply seemed...

Extinguished.

"You have endured a lot, my monkey," he reminded her. "And now, alone, just you and I, I will know your feelings about going to the pits."

"I'm going."

"You've said this," he replied. "This is not what we're discussing. As I noted, I will know your *feelings* about this and then I will decide if you will go or you will stay."

"Will Queen Elpis go?" she asked.

"She will. But you are not my mother," he answered.

"I will be queen," she returned. "And thus, it will be expected."

"Silence—"

"I'm going," she repeated.

Mars allowed his gaze to roam her face.

She was there, in his arms, but he could not shake the sensation that she was gone.

"When things such as this happen," he started carefully, "it's important to talk about them."

"I'm fine."

"You are changed."

"I will likely change a lot over the course of our years together, battling the Beast, you besting coup attempts, clan clashes, tribal wars. It's the nature of being, especially in Firenze."

"And we will talk about it," he declared.

"Yes," she agreed instantly.

"Honestly," he added.

She hesitated before she repeated, "Yes."

He did not like the hesitation.

Her light was out.

"Silence—"

She pushed against him to start to get up, asking, "Should we not go?"

"We have something else to discuss."

She settled in and gazed at him patiently.

He fought grinding his teeth at the loss of inquisitiveness, attentiveness and what he now knew, since it was gone, was constant awareness of and interest in him that was no longer a part of her expression.

"What else must we discuss?" she prompted when Mars did not speak.

"I'll have your vow, right now, if aught like this happens again, which it will not, but if it does, when you are made safe by a warrior, and told by that warrior to run, that you bloody do as you're told and *run*."

She stared up at him, a mercurial shifting of the silver of her eyes the only indication she gave she did not like his words.

"They're still counting body parts, but at least a hundred men attacked this palace," he went on. "If it was not for the might and skill of those who were close to your chamber, you could have easily been killed."

"Earlier, you bragged about me taking up a dagger," she remarked.

"Earlier, my barons and chieftains were here, and you desire to impress them, so I bragged of something that would mean something to you as it would mean something to them. However, it means something entirely different to me."

She shook her head. "I'm not certain it was safe for me to escape."

"Serena reported Elena told you to run, something she would not do if it was not safe for you to run. Instead, you attacked an opponent Elena easily dispatched."

"I was right here, Mars. I heard Serena report that. And just to say, I was *there*, and it wasn't that long ago. I remember what happened."

"It is not wise for you to be flippant in this moment, *piccolina*," he warned.

She fell silent.

"Do I have your vow you will not act so foolishly again?" he pressed.

"I will not act so foolishly again, Mars."

He did not like her tone. The rote manner in which her words came.

Not as if she did not mean them.

As if it meant nothing to her saying them, even if in saying them they meant a good deal to him to know his bride would keep herself safe.

In response to this, Mars pulled her closer and whispered, "There is a great change in you, *mia bellezza*."

"I'm bloodied, tired, Sofia is lost, she was a kind soul who touched mine too short of a time, yesterday was long, this night longer, and thus this day looms longest of all."

"And we will be wed at the end of it."

"Of course," she said, as if he'd told her they would sup together at the end of it.

He decided not to address that.

"And I have lost a woman I have known the whole of my life who means a great deal to me."

It was that which moved her.

She lifted a hand to his jaw, her face softening, and she said gently, "I'm so sorry, Mars."

He studied her, noted the softening of her face set the silver of her eyes to a liquid and that made him turn his head and kiss the skin of her palm.

When he turned back, he shared, "It is with darkness in my heart that the first official occasion you will stand at my side as my queen that is not our wedding will be the funeral of the woman who helped raise me. But we will give her the rite she deserved as to her place in this palace, her place in my father's heart and her place in mine."

"It will be with a sad heart, but still my honor to stand at your side for that, my king,"

And that was his Silence.

Mars dipped to touch his mouth to hers.

When he pulled back, he asked, "You are sure you wish to attend the procession?"

Silence nodded.

"If you need to leave, I will have you escorted back."

"That will not happen."

"You do not have to become my mother in one day, Silence."

"Yes, I do, Mars."

Mars studied her again.

Yes, this was his Silence.

And by the gods, she pleased him.

Every day, in new ways, this came more and more.

She was correct. Yesterday had been eventful, that night fraught, and there was much happening that day.

Perhaps she was conserving energy to endure it.

This was wise.

This was Silence.

He should not be concerned. His bride was clever. He knew that already.

She simply continued to prove it.

He stood, holding her to him as he did.

He only let one part of her go when he was on his feet.

After her legs swung toward the floor, he held her close, her toes brushing the tops of his feet.

"Then let us get this done," he muttered.

His bride nodded.

Mars then put her on her feet, took her hand, tucked it to his chest, and moved them to the door.

He would ride to the pits barefoot and bare-chested.

She would ride before him on his mount, barefoot, bloodied, but entirely intact, healthy and resplendent in their victory.

And his people would see, much more than any fetching red dress could show them, the great strength and trueness of the woman who would very soon be their queen.

~

**G'Seph**
*Catacombs, Go'Doan Temple, Fire City*
*FIRENZE*

IN A RAGE, G'Seph sent the clay pots flying.

They crashed against the empty sepulchers of the walls, carved out and waiting to bear the shrouded bones of dead priests, the ash of the spent incense in the pots dusting the air.

"*How could it bloody fail?*" he screeched.

"My liege," one of the men behind him murmured.

Seph turned, doing it lifting his arm and backhanding the soldier. As the man's head jerked to the side, Seph neared him, putting his hands on his shoulders and lifting his knee covered in the dark robes of The Rising and catching the soldier sharply in his groin.

The man's hands went to his crotch, he bent forth and coughed.

Seph cuffed him again with full fist on the side of his head and the man went down to a hip.

It was then, he kicked him with his sandaled foot right in his face.

Seph stepped back, staring at the cut that had opened up on the man's cheekbone that was oozing blood and he did this breathing heavily.

No other soldier dared to speak.

G'Seph looked to one of his other lieutenants. "Were any taken alive?"

His lieutenant did not answer his question.

And yet he did.

He advised, "We must flee the city, my liege."

"How did this happen?" Seph hissed. "They had few guards. Our men outnumbered them ten to one at *least*. And our squad were all bloody *Firenz*. They're beasts!"

"We...we don't...we don't know, sir," his lieutenant stammered.

"Word is spreading through the city," Seph spat. "Those men didn't even manage to kill the Dellish *waif*. She can't weigh fifty kilos! How can *she* best a one hundred and fifteen kilo Firenz? How the bloody hell can she best *one hundred of them*?"

"We...I'm sorry, we don't know, sir," the lieutenant repeated.

Seph shook his head in disgust.

"Tonight was meant to see the end of her. The end of True. The end of Ophelia," he ground out. "Pitting Wodell against Firenze in vengeance for their prince and their Countess of the Arbor. Weakening the Nadirii as it would pass on to the older sister, who wouldn't know an act of diplomacy if it struck her in the face. Which in turn would mean the younger would need to dispute the new reign. And as that played out and the older weakened her warrior nation, she would turn *all* against the Nadirii. We cannot *wait* for that sick queen to meet her end! Sister needs to be pitted against sister for the Nadirii to fall."

He did not know why he was explaining the plot to them. They all bloody knew it as well as he.

*"By Go'Bedi!"* he shrieked. *"How did we bloody fail?"*

"Sir, I must beseech you to make the order for the soldiers of The Rising to flee the city immediately," another lieutenant begged. "Some of our recruits were captured. We may be exposed."

"And why is that?" he demanded. "Those caught know to speak nothing of The Rising."

"We cannot assume they will do as instructed. They will be tortured, if they haven't been already, and marched to the pits. They could share of our sacred mission in hopes of mercy."

"They all knew this would be an eventuality if they failed," Seph returned.

"We did not, none of us, expect them to fail," his lieutenant replied.

This was true.

For it shouldn't have failed.

There was a significantly reduced guard at the palace. They'd seen to that. They should have dispatched the waif silently and gone on to the others without an alarm being raised, and then escaped unscathed, or at least with minor losses due to their vastly superior number, for Go'Vicee's sake.

Seph drew breath into his nose.

"Thus, we also cannot assume that they will share this is naught but another Firenz coup against their sitting king," the lieutenant went on.

"We cannot flee the city," Seph declared.

"But, my liege—"

Seph leaned forward and bellowed, "*We will not leave the city!*"

He leaned back, took another deep breath and calmed himself.

"If we did, they would suspect. G'Dor nor any of the men he recruited spoke even a word of The Rising. Mars and his men investigated that thoroughly. Even entering the hallowed confines of this very temple...*thrice*...to search for some evidence of Go'Doan collaboration." He shook his head. "No. A man can and will say anything under torture. It is rarely the truth. And Mars knows this."

"I fear we are still vulnerable," his man murmured.

"Then we will strengthen again," Seph returned. "And we will start to do that by not showing our hand by bloody *fleeing*."

No one replied which was all well, for Seph tired of this conversation.

And further, there was much to do.

Distractedly, he looked through them before he would dismiss them.

But he went still.

"Where is G'Drey?" he asked.

"My liege?" one of his lieutenants queried in return.

"Where's G'Drey?" he demanded, louder and sharper.

There was a shuffling of feet that made the heated blood in Seph's body feel like it would boil before a man in the back spoke.

"He was in an accident on his way to the school."

Seph's chin jerked into his neck. "I beg your pardon?"

"He was in an accident, my liege."

"Come forward," G'Seph ordered.

The man shifted through the bodies around him, doing it hesitantly, but he came forward.

"What of Drey?" Seph asked quietly when the soldier was standing before him.

"Apparently, my liege, on his way to school, he turned a corner as a horse was riding down the street. He gave the horse a fright, it reared and struck him in the head with a hoof. He received a headwound and was taken to a Firenz infirmary. A Firenz city guard came and reported it yesterday afternoon."

It was at that, Seph's blood ran cold.

For they might be treating a headwound.

But in so doing, they would undoubtedly find his other injuries.

And questions would be asked.

Not to mention, Seph had whipped that weak-willed priest.

G'Drey was devout to The Rising. No one who knew of the plot had not been vetted and thus known to be faithful to their righteous cause.

But Drey was weak-willed.

This story could be a ruse. Drey could have gone to the Firenz and shared the plot.

For the stupid twat was getting fucked by Mars's top general, and he didn't even know it.

Dear *Bedi*.

"And why wasn't this reported to me?" Seph asked.

"Why?" the man queried stupidly in return.

"Yes, why?"

"Well, my liege, you instructed us to be wary of G'Drey and not—"

Seph turned, finding the handle of whichever instrument was closest, instruments that were kept there for times such as these, and others besides.

It was a crop.

Perfection.

He then lifted it and brought it down violently on the man's cheek. And again. And again. Again. Again. And again. Until the soldier fell to a hand and his knees, lifting his other arm to stave the blows that Seph kept raining on him.

G'Seph tired of the crop, tossed it aside and kicked him in the face, taking him to his back.

And he did this again.

Again.

And again.

When the soldier was curled into himself, his arms over his head, Seph stopped and squealed, "*Disrobe him!* Bind him to the slab, fifty lashes. And someone go to that bloody infirmary, find *bloody* G'Drey and bloody *bring him back! Immediately!*"

Men moved to the soldier on the floor or out of the room, but Seph moved his eyes to his lieutenants.

"We do *not* flee," he declared. "The Go'Doan had naught to do with this coup no matter what one of those infidels might say."

"Sir, we lost over one hundred foot soldiers to that—"

"We will replace them," Seph stated offhandedly.

"This is our second failed—"

Oh yes.

He tired of this conversation.

"Silence," Seph whispered. "Recruitment goes unabated in schools and hospitals. Firenz, Dellish, even Airenzian are brought to their bloody knees in gratitude for healing of loved ones and the promise of a bright future for their children. It's ludicrous, but we all know how very well it works. And it will continue to do so. The Rising has had a setback, but we will recover, we will regroup, and we will rise again. Much more swiftly this time. So swiftly, they will not expect it."

He turned to another of his soldiers.

"Send a bird to G'Fenn in Go'Doan. Report these events. Share our defeat but that we are not defeated. I will see to it that I ride with the cavalcade when they leave Firenze. We will rise again in Wodell."

The man nodded and moved to push through those behind him.

Seph waited until the whipping started.

But he did not wait to see it end.

He wished to.

But he could not.

He had much to do.

# 37
## THE MORTAL BLOW

***Prince Cassius***
*Guest Suite, Second Floor, East Corridor, Catrame Palace, Fire City*
*FIRENZE*

His intended whirled on him the minute he closed the door behind them after following her into her bedchamber.

"Did I invite you into my chamber?" Elena asked.

"Where's Theodora?" Cassius queried in return.

She crossed her arms on her chest and tilted up her chin. "The palace is no longer safe. I sent her to the Nadirii camp. With my sisters. They have might and they have magic. They won't allow anything to harm her."

"This is a good decision," he murmured.

"I don't care you think it is, or it is not," she retorted.

His princess was in a snit.

This was not news. She'd been in that state since the attack ended.

Or, precisely, some moments before.

It was simply that Cassius was tiring of it.

"Elena—" he started on a sigh.

"You may leave. I must get kitted for the procession," she interrupted him, dropping her arms and turning away, dismissing him.

He didn't know what "kitted" meant. She'd already changed into her Nadirii tunic. Something he would have thought was a boon, considering she'd fought in a miniscule nightgown with thin straps and a hem that barely covered her arse. A garment that forced Cassius to the understanding that her long, shapely legs were miraculous, considering he wanted them wrapped around his back even if they were coated in blood.

Though, he knew what she wore under that tunic. And his brain had been seared with images of her stretching in the garden wearing nothing but her body stocking.

So it wasn't the boon he'd wish it to be.

"I think it's more important we discuss your pique," he replied.

That saw the return of her attention.

And she did this twisting her neck to look at him with narrowed eyes.

"My...*pique?*"

"Allow me to take us back to yesterday morning, at the fountain," he began.

Her mouth got tight.

"To yesterday afternoon, our chat after the Go'Doan spoke to you," he continued.

Her entire frame got tight.

"And last night, in my chamber," he finished quietly.

All of these occasions had been promising.

With last night, prior to the attack, the most promising of all.

They had spent some time together in his chamber after dinner the night before.

Most of it, they had talked, Cassius sharing the many issues that had been discussed and decided around the diplomatic table, a great number of them affecting her as Princess of the Nadirii, but mostly as his betrothed, the soon-to-be Princess to the Regent of Airen—and eventually Airen's queen.

He had been surprised her mother had not apprised her of these decisions.

However, in the end, he'd been gladdened, for he was able to share the fullness of them, further strengthening their burgeoning communication, establishing trust, and using both to draw her closer to him.

They had ended this interlude embracing for some time on a divan in his chambers.

Although she had heated for him quickly, like their few times before, unlike those times, the longer they shared intimacy, the more nervous she became.

Cassius understood this had to do with his declaration that he had given her a climax in the garden that morning, but that had not been reciprocated, and he wished for it to be so.

He'd thus gently ended their time together, deciding such would need to be led up to, come naturally, not announced it would occur, and then be taken.

However, for the most part, she responded to him beautifully.

One could definitely say they had chemistry. She roused him, he roused her.

But she was still virgin, and they'd known one another but days.

He had to tread cautiously, apparently in all things, and give her time to get used to him.

Hearteningly, the impossible seemed to be occurring. They were learning to come to accord and doing it swiftly.

A Nadirii and an Airenzian.

Unbelievable.

But it was true.

Until now.

"Let us go back to how we were in those times," he suggested.

Elena turned fully to him.

"With your hand between my legs?" she asked sarcastically. "Or with your tongue in my mouth?"

"I meant us speaking to each other and listening to each other in a civilized manner," he replied, seeking patience.

"We did this before you behaved in the manner in which you behaved during the fight," she retorted.

"Elena—"

"I do not know who those assailants were, but they were untrained. Easily dispatched. They factored surprise, numbers and brawn higher than skill and strategy. This is always a faulty play, as it was last night. I was in no danger."

"I disagree, my princess, for the minute I entered that room, you were moments away from receiving a mortal blow."

"And did this happen?" she queried.

"No," he gritted. "But only because True interceded."

"I did know he was near, Cassius," she spat. "Any warrior in any battle knows where her allies are."

She wished to speak of this?

They would speak of it.

The *fullness* of it.

"And of course it was True who was near," he returned.

"He was fighting to Silence."

She might be right.

She was still wrong.

"He was fighting to *you*."

She shook her head. "You cannot say that as you'd just arrived."

"I can say that because he's besotted with you."

"He didn't seem besotted with me not long ago, when he clashed with Mars over Farah."

"And does that wound you, my future wife?" he drawled.

She blinked rapidly three times before her eyes stayed open and they did this wide.

"I am no longer True's," she snapped.

Oh no.

Bloody *no*.

Those words did not just leave her mouth.

He leaned forward and bit back, "You were *never* True's."

Her eyes again narrowed. "You cannot know what True and I had."

"I know he never had his hand between your legs."

She gasped, and her cheeks flushed.

He had not known that. Not with certainty.

But he knew it then.

And he was absurdly gratified knowing it.

Thus, Cassius wasn't finished. "That is solely mine and *will be* solely mine *forever*."

"You may leave now," she hissed.

"Has he had his tongue in your mouth?" he demanded.

She stared at him in disbelief before declaring, "You cannot possibly be jealous."

"You know naught of men. *Real* men. You cannot know what I am, or I am not," he retorted. "Now answer me, has he had your mouth?"

She turned from him, muttering, "I'm not participating in this conversation."

"You bloody are," he contradicted.

She whirled again to him. "Is that why you carried me bodily from the fray *not* like I am what I am, trained warrior, but like I'm some damsel in distress who needs a *man* to keep her safe? Because you were jealous True and I were battling side by side?"

"You aren't answering my question, Elena."

"You aren't answering mine," she returned.

"You can't know of me and not know precisely why I carried you out of harm's way," he told her.

"You can't know *of me* and not know I do not *need* you to carry me out of harm's way." She took a step toward him. "We have not met in battle, Cassius, but by the goddess, you must know that I don't dither in my tree-home making wicker baskets. I patrol. I don't use my bow only for parade. I don't use my staff simply to keep my arms trim. There isn't a single patrol where I don't clash with brigand or sorcerer attempting to breach The Enchantments. And this might not often be hand to hand, but it is certainly often sword to sword."

Cassius felt a tightening in his chest.

And it was painful.

A pain he had to stop.

"Cease speaking," he growled.

She did not cease speaking

"You don't know women like me and I'll warn you now and urge you heed this warning. You need to have a care in dealing with a woman like me. It is all well and good, and I not only applaud your efforts, I shall champion them in the progress you desire to make for the females of your realm. But I am not one of them."

She was not.

But she would be.

"That will be your last battle, Elena," he decreed.

At that, her eyes grew enormous.

"And I'll repeat what I've informed you of before. You will significantly limit any time you spend with True. This being you spend time with him only when I'm with you," he concluded.

"You cannot tell me who I can spend time with."

"I just did."

She studied him a long moment before she whispered, "Are you mad?"

"I am not. I am Prince Regent. I will be king. But for you, most importantly, I will be *husband*."

Elena was still whispering when she said, "You *are* mad."

Cassius didn't deign to respond.

He was marrying a Nadirii.

He knew that.

But she was marrying an Airenzian.

She knew that too.

They would make compromises in their life together.

However, these would not be among them.

Her voice was vibrating with fury when she declared, "You need to leave now."

"No True," he stated. "And you will hang up your bow unless you use it for parade or to teach our daughters how to string theirs for interest and the fullness of their education. That is all. But in the now, you will kit yourself out, however that needs to be, while I wait, and we will walk together to join the procession."

"Get out," she demanded.

"Get sorted," he returned.

"Get out or I'll force you out."

"You couldn't manage that," he scoffed.

Her voice was chilling when she replied, "You do not wish to try that."

Cassius held his arms out to the side. "Again, you cannot know that."

She didn't hesitate.

She attacked.

Her attack was a surprise, even if it was not.

What was truly a surprise was that, in no time, she had him down on a knee and almost had his arm up his back in a way it would be difficult, and painful, to extricate himself.

And might even break a bone.

Or at the very least dislocate his shoulder.

Therefore, he had no choice but to use her hold on him to swing her around.

This took her off her feet, but before she hit ground, he surged up and caught her in his arms.

He then tossed her to the bed.

She bounced up instantly with grace borne of knowing every inch of her body and how to use it. She thus gained her feet on the mattress and launched herself back at him, front to front.

He caught her again, and she used her arms and legs around his torso to wrench him into a painful twist.

Thus, he was forced to move with the rotation, and he did. After, he backed toward her bed, dropped to it, and rolled onto her.

"Enough," he clipped when he'd subdued her.

She bucked under him at the same time she tried to find purchase on his hair.

And this meant he had to catch both her wrists and hold them to the bed over her head.

Gods bloody damn it, she felt good under him.

And her smell...

"*Enough*," he barked in her face. "You cannot possibly win hand to hand which is my *bloody* point."

"Get your broadsword and we'll see about your *bloody* point," she retorted, breathing heavily from exertion and fury, which did not make it any easier to lie atop her and not grow hard, something he was struggling mightily with already.

"We'll continue to discuss this later when you've calmed the fuck down," he growled.

"We won't be discussing *anything* at *any time*. We're done, Cassius. You are Regent. You will be king. You can do anything with your realm. Including allowing your daughter to assume your throne. You need no heir. You have an heir. I will be your wife. We will battle the Beast. And then I will live in my treehome in The Enchantments with Dora and carry on with my life as I wish, and *you* will do whatever you will, just without *me*."

His chest did not feel tight with her declaration.

It burned.

"We've already made our bargain, my warrior," he reminded her.

"No, *you* made your decree. Heed this, *my warrior*, you may be able to best me hand to hand, but you will never cow me to your whim."

"Do you wish to test that?" he asked.

"I think that question is better asked of you," she retorted.

He dipped closer and whispered, "I can smell your excitement."

Her chin dipped into her neck and he saw the truth of his statement flash fleetingly in her eyes.

Cassius did not relent.

"You like sparring, verbally, physically. You like my weight. You want my mouth on you. You want my hands on you. You yearn for it, Elena. I can feel it. I can *smell* it."

"That's absurd," she hissed, but her breath was coming even faster.

"So you wish to test that."

"Get off me," she snapped.

"I see," he murmured, studying her mouth. "You don't wish to test it for you know I'm right."

"Get off me, Cassius."

He looked to her eyes. "Has True had your mouth?"

"Yes," she bit.

"Liar," he whispered.

She turned her head to the side and he watched her swallow.

It looked painful.

He didn't like that for her.

Therefore, it was then he relented.

He kept hold on her wrists, but he did it using his thumbs to stroke the apples of her palms.

She swallowed again, for a different reason this time, and he spoke.

"Not even a stolen kiss, my lamb?" he asked gently.

"I am not your lamb."

Oh, but she was.

Playful and frisky in sparring.

Soft, innocent and dewy-eyed after climax.

Skittish and stubborn pretending she didn't want him as badly as he did her.

"Yes, you are."

She shook her head, still turned away. "Please, get off me."

"True is a gentleman."

"And you are not."

He didn't need to be.

He would be her husband.

"True was not meant to be," he told her quietly. "If he was, he would have had you. And you would have had him. We barely know one another, my princess, but we cannot keep our hands off each other. There is a reason for that. There is a reason you feel as you feel right now with my weight upon you. What I feel, with the softness of you under me, the smell of you in my nose. We were meant to be. This means you are mine, Elena. Do you not see that?"

She did not look at him when she stated, "I will not be cowed."

"I cannot believe you can even begin to think I wish to cow you, my warrior," he whispered, and her head turned, her eyes coming to his. "I cannot believe you can even begin to think I'd wish to take away any part of what makes you."

"And you reconcile this how, Cassius?" she demanded. "Catching me up and throwing me bodily from the fray. That is taking a very large part of me away, my prince."

She wished this?

She would have it as well.

"My dead wife was warrior," he returned, his voice gritty.

Elena went completely still beneath him.

"There are different kinds, my princess," he shared. "And she battled mightily. In a manner, she won. She gave me our daughter. They both did not perish to the fight. She fought, she did it bravely, and she succeeded in her goal. She also died doing it. And she did that happily. I know this because the last thing she did on this earth was smile at me as I held Aelia in my hands but moments after she slipped from her mother's womb. Now, ponder this, Elena. Do you think I tossed you bodily from the fray because I did not trust in your capabilities? Or do you think in a million millennia that I wish to lose another warrior to a battle beyond my control?"

"Cassius," she breathed, her face having softened, her eyes having warmed.

And there was his lamb.

But it was too late.

He might not have won the argument, but he won his point.

However, in forcing him to win it, she'd drawn blood.

And she had to learn that was no way to win between lovers.

Thus he pushed up at her wrists, angling from her and taking his feet.

She got up to her elbows but took one look at his face as he scowled down at her, and she made no other movement and said no further words.

"I shall meet you at our horses," he declared.

"Of course," she whispered, knowing she'd wounded her opponent, and conceding graciously. "I'll be down directly."

With that, he turned and left her chambers.

He had no desire to join a procession that would lead to witnessing torture and execution, this before he had to prepare to join the masses and watch his friend take his marital chain and give his new wife hers.

He wanted whiskey, an orgasm and sleep.

In that order.

All with Elena.

Even after their episode.

Which meant perhaps she was correct.

He was mad.

But that was what he wished.

However, he did not have a choice.

Instead he had torture, death, marriage and a stubborn bride on his hands who was born warrior who he did not want to die warrior.

No one was mentioning it, but the last quake that occurred but hours before shared explicitly the Beast was not only closer to the surface, it was angry.

And Cassius feared he was not going to convince Elena to use naught but her formidable magic as her part in quelling it.

So his chest was tight again and his heart felt heavy as he took the steps that would lead him to the front of the palace in order for him to mount his steed and await his bride.

He took these steps thinking of the tarot card he'd turned the morning before.

The warrior card he'd turned had had his head bowed.

His armor was intact. His body not bloodied.

But he'd tasted defeat all the same.

Cassius knew that taste.

It was vile.

And he would not experience it again.

Unless he had no choice.

He was now bloody Regent.

Even so, it seemed he still lived a life of limited choices.

A life marked with profound loss.

Both that of the past.

And as the warrior card was swept from his memory, and the vision he saw charging into the conflict but hours before of Elena under a raised sword filled his brain...

He knew it was a real possibility loss would scrape deep through his future.

**Queen Ha-Lah**
*Guest Suite, Second Floor, East Corridor, Catrame Palace, Fire City*
*FIRENZE*

"I GO WITH YOU."

"You do not."

"My king, I would go with you," I beseeched.

"You will not," he denied.

"We will surely be protected."

"It matters not."

"I know it might be difficult to witness, but I would be at your side through this."

"I do not need you at my side, Ha-Lah."

"Aramus," I whispered.

"Xi and Nis will stay behind, both in this room, where you will remain, wife."

After he issued that order, he started to move to the door.

I followed him.

Swiftly.

"I would wish to help you in your grief," I told my husband, reaching out, nearly touching his back.

But my hand fell when he spun around and pinned me with a glower so ferocious, I felt my breath catch in my throat.

"And how would you do that, my queen?" he asked caustically. He then tipped his head to the side, his black eyes flashing with derision. "Ah yes. I forget. You know me so well. You knew Cat so well. With all the interest you take in me. My men. These months of our marriage. These weeks when you sailed with me. With us. With them. With *him*. Traveled with me. Us. Them. *Him*. They kept you guarded and safe. You have come to know us all so very well?"

"That isn't fair, Aramus, and you know it," I replied softly.

Though, uncomfortably, I had to admit, he had a point.

"It isn't?" he asked, his brows rising. "You spent a good deal of energy spouting your defense of whales and dolphins, how do you feel about the loss of the life of *men*?"

He was right.

I did spend that energy in defense of my friends.

But that was even less fair.

And he had to know that too.

I chanced a step closer, considering putting my hand on his chest in a conciliatory matter.

I decided against it and simply said, "I'm very, very sorry you lost your friend, my husband."

"I am as well," he replied. "He will have no wife. He will have no children. He will have no grandchild carry anything of his from home to home just to keep him close, even if they had never met him but they knew of him and they knew he was beloved. He will be but a memory for me, Tint, Bond, Oreti, Xi, Nis, Nav, and when we are gone, he will be gone, for there will be no heart that bears him any longer."

I nodded, feeling my eyes prickle and wishing fruitlessly I had come to know this man at the same time deciding from that point on to make a concerted effort to get to know the others.

"You loved him a great deal," I whispered, and I loved this a great deal, this capacity for emotion my husband was demonstrating.

Even if the occasion for which he was demonstrating it rent my heart.

"He was my brother," Aramus confirmed. "And now he will be shrouded, borne through this bloody heat, rotting along the way—"

"Don't say that," I urged gently. "Don't even think of that."

He continued as if I didn't speak.

"Taken aboard a ship and carried home, only to have the black rocks of Mar-el piled upon what's left of him without his brothers at his side for we're traipsing across Triton attending fucking *weddings*."

He was in pain.

Such pain.

"Would you please let me come to you?" I asked, even if there was but a few feet of space between us, it felt like miles.

"Do you think I need your comfort?" he queried with contempt.

I blinked at his tone.

But he did not stop there.

Alas, my husband did not stop.

"You have given me nothing in this marriage. Not a thing, Ha-Lah. What little I have you made me earn. The barest scrap of your attention, your history, any part of you. I should likely praise Triton *and* Medusa both that you did not make me scrape and beg for morsels of you. But I fear I'm in no mood to praise our gods right now, my queen. There are ankles to noose and throats to slit."

I winced.

"Absolutely," he spat decisively when he caught my reaction. "You don't have the stomach to be queen." He leaned toward me. "In all this change, my wife, that I will bear on my realm after this bloody ludicrous journey is through, there will be one more. When I get my heir, *he* will not be saddled with the greatest beauty of the land. He will pick who he wishes. She can be ugly of visage as long as she's kind of heart and lustful for his cock and desirous of his company and supportive of his thoughts. What he will *not* have is he will not be burdened with a queen the likes of *you*."

At that, I flinched and took a step away.

It looked as if his lip would curl as he watched me do this, but he caught it before he did.

And instead, he dealt his mortal blow.

"We will battle this fucking Beast. I do not know of destiny, of the supposed power of these unions of man and wife, except it seems naught but nonsense. But when it is done, we will sever ties, you and me. And then I will find a queen that suits *me*. A queen that suits *Mar-el*. And *she* will give me an heir. Then I will change the laws of our land so my son will know nothing but happiness."

On that, he spun again and stalked to the door.

"King Aramus," I called.

He twisted at the waist and barked, "*What?*"

"I am truly very sorry for the loss of a man you cared for so deeply."

"This I believe," he bit.

"And I am further sorry for the loss of you, for I was falling in love with you, my king, and your brother died an honorable death, protecting his king and queen. I will carry him in my heart as well, for as long as I am breathing, grateful for the sacrifice he made for you and for me. But in the fury of your grief, you killed something not as precious, but it was coming to be precious to me. And I will mourn its loss, not as you clearly mourn, but I shall do it all the same."

As I spoke, he turned fully to me, his neck inclining, the rage seeping out of his expression.

It was then I turned away from him and moved toward the bath and my dressing room.

"Ha-Lah," he called.

I kept walking.

"Ha-Lah," he repeated.

I did not miss a step.

"My queen, come back to me," he issued his command, albeit gently.

At that, I stopped, turned only my head to him and looked him in the eye.

Mine were brimming.

At the sight, *he* flinched.

"Never," I whispered.

And with that vow, I walked away from my king.

~

**The Priest**
*Cell of a Go'En, Go'Doan Temple, Fire City*
*Firenze*

Sitting cross-legged upon a pentagram surrounded by sacred symbols drawn on the floorboards in chalk, black candles lit all around him, the priest closed his eyes, felt the whoosh in his stomach, and in astral form, his spirit left his body and he soared the astral plane.

Gleeful.

Joyous.

Victorious.

The Beast was almost there.

And he was angered that a ritual had taken place without his master in attendance.

As it should be.

All of it was just as it should be.

Thus, the priest was smiling when he took astral form in the chambers of his lover, Rupert.

His smile died instantly.

For what he saw was Rupert abed.

Inside a *woman*.

He was grunting and sweating, his cock thrusting in her cunt, his tongue in her mouth.

And when they broke the connection of their lips, his Rupert, his lover, his chosen one, his favorite, smiled with lust and bliss and *love* at the female.

In his body in Firenze, the priest felt fire blaze in his stomach, as his eyes in his astral form narrowed.

And as his lover bent his head back to the woman to take her mouth, the creatures the priest brought forth through magic slithered across the floor.

At his command they waited.

He'd give his lover one last thing.

And after the priest endured the revulsion of watching her cry out her ecstasy, he endured the heartbreak of watching Rupert throw back his head and shout his climax, thrusting deeply inside her through it as he would do the same when he took his priest.

That was when the asps struck.

His thigh.

Her ankle.

There were gasps.

Then Rupert pulled free and rolled, his eyes growing large as he stared at the snake slithering over his lover.

He brushed it off as she bolted up and screamed.

Many bites of the asps brought near-instant death.

One bite, it took a bit longer.

And Rupert was far from stupid.

He did not take a blade to himself or his female to slice it across the punctures and try to draw out the poison.

It was far too late for that.

As she started to pitch in agony when the venom reached her veins, Rupert's eyes searched his chamber.

And he found his priest.

"Why?" he asked.

It was then, the priest grew perplexed.

"Why?" he queried in return.

Rupert had no answer for he was curling into himself as the pain struck his system.

She was already writhing.

"*Why?*" Rupert cried, his face beginning to contort.

"You are mine," the priest answered. "Or were."

"Yes," he pushed out feebly. "I was."

The priest blinked.

But he had seen...

The female rolled off the bed.

Dead.

Well, that didn't take long.

"We would..." The priest looked back to his lover as he spoke again, Rupert's eyes to the vision of him, no attention to the woman, "rule the world."

"I will now, without you," the priest told him.

Rupert shook his head, but seized, his much larger frame taking longer for the venom to vanquish it.

"You...you..." Rupert forced out, awkwardly indicating a snake slithering over the bedsheets, "are weak. You do not...do not...understand loyalty."

"This is not loyalty," the priest sneered.

"There was naught but you," Rupert whispered.

The priest stared.

"He will...he will consume you," Rupert wheezed, spasming into himself. "And you will...you won't...have that first ally. You will...be alone and he will...be master."

The priest's corporeal form in Firenze felt a frisson of fear trace up the back of its neck.

"Emerald oil asps?" Rupert rasped. "You fool," he whispered.

And these were his last words.

His chosen one's eyes open, the priest saw the light of life blink out.

But Rupert was correct.

Rupert's chamber was in his manor in Airen.

There were no emerald oil asps in Airen. They were only in Firenze.

And they had a particular bite, a bite that left a unique mark. One that, if observed by someone knowledgeable in the subject, was easily recognized.

If those bite marks were identified ...

And then there were those asps that had killed the Dellish prince's intended that very night...

And if these were connected...

"Blast!" the priest cried, spiriting the asps back to their realm and speeding his way through the astral plane to his body, his eyes opening with a snap.

He stared at the walls of his cell, his body unmoving.

He could jump atop a horse and ride like blazes, but it'd still take at least two weeks to get to Rupert's manor.

His body and perhaps the nature of those bites would be discovered long before.

The priest could send no bird. There had probably already been dozens of birds and messengers dispatched, sharing the news the Dellish prince's betrothed had perished to the venom.

If the connection was made, if inquiries into Rupert commenced, all before they'd brought the Beast to the surface, it could be disastrous.

Not to mention, the others would be furious at this juncture in the raising of the Beast that he'd taken one of their own. They were close, but they couldn't know how long it would take to complete the rising.

They'd need to replace Rupert.

Train the replacement.

This would take weeks.

More likely months for the priest was weeks away from even bloody *getting to them*.

And the priest did not wish to even consider what Thom would say about all this.

"What have I done?" he whispered.

*There was naught but you.*

"How could that be?" he moaned.

No.

No, he had been betrayed.

You did not betray your master.

This was naught but a setback.

And the prophecy had fallen with the death of Farah.

They had time.

All the time they needed.

He would leave that day.

They would advance a new conspirator. It did not take long to train a man to rape and kill.

At such, they were naturals.

All would be well.

A delay.

They had no one to fight them now.

When the Beast rose, all would be theirs.

Or his.

And the Beast would be his new chosen one.

He did not need Rupert.

It was as it should be.

Or it would be.

Soon.

# 38

# THE NEW QUEEN

***The People of Firenze***
*Fire City*
THE DAY OF THE MAJESTIC NUPTIALS OF THEIR KING

On their way to the pits, Silence of the Dellish sat before their king on his steed known as Hephaestus, a horse revered as one of the strongest, fastest, most graceful mounts in the realm, as his father was, as the mare he sired was.

The mare, known as Epona, having been given to their future queen by their king.

She was the one who trotted beside them as she did to the parade, riderless.

Silence of Wodell was bloodied, shockingly so.

But her chin was up, and her eyes remained straight, her shoulders squared, as their king held her tight to his body, protection in his grip, pride in his bearing.

She entered the necropolis with no apparent trepidation.

And all who saw her watched.

Closely.

Her skin was so pale naturally, it could not be known how she fared when she left the necropolis hours after.

What was seen, as the people of Fire City crowded the stands around the tarpits to watch the death march of the latest traitors, was King Mars taking the royal podium with his bride.

He then lifted her—arse to the stout railing that guarded the podium from the tar, her back to the pits.

But he moved into her, sliding his arm around her waist to steady her on her perch, pressing his hip to the side of her leg, and she cuddled into him, twisted to face the tar.

While all others stood—for there were no chairs anywhere around the pits, the stands, or even on the royal podium—their king found a way to make his bride comfortable.

This, many thought odd.

Some thought it sweet.

Though others did not.

However, they would eventually discover why he did as such.

She showed no emotion as the four men walked (or more aptly limped, trudged or dragged themselves) into the pit.

She continued to show no emotion as they sunk, so very slowly, and writhed, awkwardly, and eventually cried out as the tar burned and their desperate, useless struggles pulled them deeper.

Until the blackness covered their faces, the last part of them to disappear, as they frenziedly tried to draw in air before their lungs would be filled with nothing but pitch.

Though she was caught, on more than one occasion, yawning.

And also, it appeared her brows drew together (as did her future husband's, in a much more ominous way) when one of the condemned shouted, "Long live The Rising!" before taking his first step into the tar.

The three final traitors were hung by one ankle from a hastily erected apparatus that looked like a yardarm, but on land.

Their throats were then slit.

There they drained of lifeblood and there they remained, even after that lifeblood was gone, and it was whispered they were to be left there to be fed from by the raven and crow, eagle and falcon, hawk, vulture and owl.

And the Mar-el king had his vengeance away from the sea.

As the King of Firenze had his vengeance as usual.

At the pits.

With his bride at his side appearing bored, but it would prove (as she fell asleep against her king in his arms on the ride home), she was simply tired.

This explained a number of things.

The people of Firenze found this understandable.

She'd had a grueling night.

~

IT WOULD BE AN EXCITING, busy day for the populace of Fire City and all its many visitors who had journeyed to the city for a glimpse of their king on the day of his majestic nuptials and the celebrations that would happen after. For they had little time to make their way from the pits to jockey for position along the parade route, up the foothills, into the crags and around the mesa in the Sheeonee Mountains that overlooked the city and the enormity of the glassy, smooth surface of Fire Lake.

Many thought it a great shame their future queen's neck was stippled with purple, for her gown was resplendent.

Stark white.

Well off the shoulder.

The bodice that cut just above her breasts was decorated in an intricate pattern of gold beads. The sheer white sleeves that fell at the wrists in panels so long, when she was standing, if she didn't have her arms raised, they trailed the ground, were trimmed also with these beads. And the high waistband under her breasts was also patterned in elaborate gold beading.

The floating train at the back of the gown weighed heavily on the high slit at her left leg, completely exposing that extremity after King Mars spanned her tiny waist with his large hands when he took her from Hephaestus and put her on her gold-sandaled feet.

This before he walked her up the mountain path set everywhere from dust to high branches of trees with bunches of bright red blooms and streaming crimson ribbons.

This path also smoked with burning coils of incense that scented the air amber. This for their Muse god (who would spark creativity, clear-headedness and elevate them). Then there was the scent of rose and cedar, for their Grace god (who commanded love and assisted positive energy). And last, cinnamon, for their Spirit god (who established balance and offered enlightenment).

While watching, from palace to altar, it would be determined by mothers and daughters in a manner that meant in the following days and months a rush on white silk and gold beading was had in the marketplaces. Thus, not dozens, but hundreds of brides wore much the same to their own nuptials.

As many had already worn (or soon would) versions of the red dress Silence of Wodell had worn days before to the parade.

At the end of their marital march, King Mars led his bride to the long panels of crimson and gold silk sheers that were twisted in the high canopies of cedar trees to form an altar above the bride and her groom. They stopped atop a bed of cedar needles that had fallen to the ground naturally and was now entirely covered in red rose petals.

There, only large coils of cedar and rose incense burned in brass plates around them, significantly heightening the smell of cedar in the air, the rose of the pedals they trod on, scenting devotion to Grace and worshiping love, lust and good energy.

As it should be at any wedding.

Silence of Wodell stood at her king's side in her white and gold gown, her hand held in his pressed to the side of his bared chest (bared, except the leather straps crossing it, of course). Their backs were to their guests and his people. Their gazes were to the trees through which the lake could be seen, the snowy tips of the Sheeonee reflected in its surface.

Her shoulders were covered in the fall of black curls that went to her waist.

The muscles of his broad, brown back were also covered in his thick, dark hair and crossed with his kingly swords that bore rubies and emeralds in their hilts.

The black-robed priest to the Grace intoned in front of them until it was time for their now Relict Queen to approach them with the ebony box of marital chains.

Their king chained his wife first, and it would be oo'ed and ah'ed over for the next days, weeks, indeed done so in a way it would continue for years, the memory of their tall, mighty king bent to their small, dainty queen, the grin playing about his lips as he threaded the gold and diamonds and onyx and rubies through her marital hoops.

And it would be clucked and cooed over for the next days, weeks (and possibly years), the memory of their small, dainty queen hesitantly, but reverently—and those close caught sight of (and later shared wide) the tears trembling in her eyes—while their tall, mighty king stayed bent so his new wife could chain her husband.

But most, it was sighed and whimpered over when she'd latched the end of her chain to the hoop at his lip, gaining his honesty for their entire marriage, and to a gasp from his audience, he'd immediately caught her at the back of her head.

There he'd fisted her shining curls in his long fingers and shoved her face in his wide chest as he bowed his back and roared his triumph to the cedars, the snow-capped mountaintops, the lake, the city, and the nation of Firenze.

Their king was pleased with his new queen.

As it should be.

This he did before he pulled her head back by her hair, rounded her with his other arm, scraped her bodily up his frame, held her tight to him with her feet dangling above the ground, and took her mouth in a ravenous (and very long) kiss.

This last had the rest of the assemblage roaring.

And they did this in a way that it carried on and on, down the long mountain path, along the parade route into the city, all the way back to the palace, even if thousands of them had no idea why they were cheering.

Proudly wearing her chain, with his Dellish-no-more bride at his side bearing his, King Mars then lifted her ever farther, to her surprised cry, to seat her on his shoulder, curling his long, powerful arm around her curvy white thighs.

And as such, he carried her back down the mountain to their waiting steeds, the blades of his kilt swaying, the heels of his sandals steady on the rocky earth.

The people of Firenze would talk much about the majestic nuptials, but little about their king deciding to wear more traditional gear to his wedding.

They liked the new leathers he and his men had been displaying.

They'd always liked the kilt.

However, they suspected (what they did not know was rightly) that he wore his kilt to honor his father.

And the people definitely approved of that.

Once King Mars had his queen down the mountain path, only then did their king finally seat their new queen on her own mount.

Surrounded by their Trusted, with her white skirts trailing down the flank of her horse, her shapely, pale legs bared to all eyes, skillfully settled in her saddle, dark hair streaming down her back, their new queen alongside their king galloped to the palace amongst loud cheers and shouts, floating red petals, coins tossed at the hooves of their horses and lit arrows scoring through the sky and popping cheerfully mid-air.

The people of Firenze were heartened to see their queen was a good horsewoman.

But that was not the only reason it was cried by thousands of voices all along the route, *"Long live King Mars and Silence, our new queen!"*

And many of the people of Firenze meant these words.

For only a true Firenz queen would yawn at the pits, cuddled into her king, wearing the blood of the vanquished as if it was naught but a shift of raw silk, watching the death throes of traitors as if they were the vaguely interesting flights of bumblebees.

And only a true Firenz queen would race down a mountain on her steed with her silk flowing, her skin exposed and glowing, her hair streaming in the wind, her husband close to her side.

It was also watched by a certain few.

A few who did so silently.

And these few had altogether different ideas.

# 39
## THE MARITAL BED

**Queen Silence**
*Royal Palace Gardens, Catrame Palace, Fire City*
FIRENZE

It would be hours into our reception before I was finally separated from Mars.

And I did not wish to be such, but I could not deny I was glad of it.

I needed a moment.

A sip of water.

Some quiet.

Solitude.

Time to process what I'd experienced that day.

Time to process what I'd seen.

Time to think.

I could do none of that as Mars guided me from person to person, group to group.

He did this with open pride, which was rather charming.

But there were things...

Such *things* about him that I had learned.

Things...

I straightened my spine as I moved through the guests, being sure to keep my chin up, catch eyes, smile or nod.

Elpis had warned me, and it stood to reason that this would be a highly-attended affair.

And she had not told a lie. It was not just the guests in the palace, the barons, clansmen, chieftains, tribes.

There were wealthy merchants (and their wives). High-ranking warriors (and their wives). Esteemed teachers and healers. Philosophers. Priests. Poets. Artists. Writers. Even (I was shocked to learn, not to mention meet) respected madams and traders in smoke, *ashesh* and *koekah*.

The front and back gardens and the entryway of the palace were opened up, decorated in red blooms, red ribbons and glowing lanterns with many tables laden with food and dozens of servants bearing heavy trays filled with drink.

It had long since grown loud and even rowdy. The din in the palace rivaling that which could be heard pitching ever and ever higher coming from the city.

The people of Firenze were celebrating.

And I saw, in the gardens of the palace, as the baths (and even some of the bigger fountains) got more and more crowded with naked bodies, and men and women (or men and men or women and women) disappeared behind shrub or tree or frond, that the tales of just how thoroughly the Firenz enjoyed a celebration were not exaggerated.

Aunt Mercy and King Wilmer had gone to their chamber ages ago.

As had my mother, and I assumed, my father.

As for me...

I had to stay.

But I needed escape.

At least for a moment.

Not due to all that was going on around me, I found that fascinating.

No.

I was tired. I was overwhelmed.

And I was queen.

*Queen.*

Although I could never know I would need to do so, I was seeing then I should long ago have paid more attention to Aunt Mercy.

This was because, that day, I felt the shift toward me by the barons and chieftains.

Apparently, if you wear a blood-soaked nightgown, witness your very soon-to-be husband and his men emotionlessly causing pain to screaming prisoners, watching those condemned die in more than one way, then be wed, all of this on top of what had happened the night before (*all* of it)...

Then wear a gown they approve of at your wedding...

And demonstrate you can ride a horse...

That was all the men needed.

The shift in attitude was almost entirely complete.

Add how they favored my taking in of smoke with Elpis (the best part of the evening so far, outside how proud and charming Mars was being, however, the smoke I'd taken in had sadly worn off). Or laughing at something bawdy Jasmine said. Or allowing my new husband to touch me, kiss me, clutch me, swing me around, all at whim.

And the men were won.

The women, however.

There were, I was realizing, two kinds.

The first, like my mother, who could be won by wedding gowns and accepting very public affection from my new husband as that was his wont, so it should be mine.

And the others, I suspected the ones like Aunt Mercy, who absolutely were not won by these things.

I would need to work much harder and much longer to turn them.

And I would need to do this, for even if the male approved Mars bending me over his arm and smiling wolfishly in my face before he claimed my mouth for all to see, that male's wife might have his ear only five minutes later, and with whatever she said, that would be the end of that.

I did not know for I had not paid attention to how Aunt Mercy handled these things.

But I was wishing I had.

And from there on, I would.

In that moment, however, I knew the last thing I should do was escape.

I should stay until the bitter end, even if I was dead on my feet and often, if I didn't keep close control of it, visions would enter my head, words would be remembered, and I'd feel my hands shaking or my lips quivering.

So I needed a moment to gather my wits and pull myself together.

A moment to find somewhere private, pull forth my shadow, and find some peace.

On this thought, I ran into something.

"My daughter."

I turned to what I'd run into and saw my father standing there.

He had not gone up with Mother, then.

Surprising.

"My beautiful Silence," he murmured, looking at me like a mourner at a funeral staring at the body on the pyre.

I did not have to ask when I became his "beautiful Silence," something he'd never called me.

I was queen now. Queen to a very powerful, very wealthy, exceptionally violent and apparently pitiless king.

This made me powerful.

This made me wealthy.

And this made me beautiful to my father.

"Father," I murmured in reply.

"You need to be abed," he declared. "How much sleep have you had? But thirty minutes? And this only on the ride back from those *appalling* pits."

"I am quite fine," I lied.

He shook his head. "You cannot be. The air is rife with that dreadful smoke. I'm getting fuzzy-headed just breathing it in. And how on earth can these people not only breathe through it, but also that shocking incense? They can't possibly think it smells good. It's heavy and cloying. I've been sick to my stomach since I walked up that mountain path to that 'altar.' If one can call such an altar. The view was stunning, of course, but my daughter wasn't wed in a bloody temple. Instead she was wed on a bloody *mountain*. Do their gods even sanctify such a thing?"

In all I did not have patience for in that moment, my father complaining about all things Firenz was quite suddenly on the top of the list.

"Father—"

"Allow me to find your mother." He craned his neck to look beyond me, as if she had not escaped all things Firenz at least an hour before. "She'll take you up to our rooms. Order you some tea. We brought some of your favorite. It will calm you and help you sleep."

I knew we'd brought my favorite tea, because Tril had packed it.

My father had no idea what my favorite tea was.

And he seemed to be forgetting it was my wedding night and there was a very good likelihood that sleep was not on the agenda. Not for some time.

Or maybe he did not forget.

"And if she hasn't already, she should talk to you about...your...your... well, your wedding night," he went on.

Balls and bloody begorrah.

"Father," I snapped.

His gaze turned hawkish on me. "Unless, last night…"

"Last night and tonight are not your concern," I told him.

"He's a large man."

Oh bloody *faith*.

"Would you please—?" I tried.

"And it is—"

"Father, please—"

"Utterly reprehensible—"

"Can we *please*—?"

Suddenly he bent and put his face in mine.

"It's *villainy*," he hissed. "Callous *villainy*. Not a realm in Triton carries on thus. Even the bounden of Mar-el and females of Airen have more rights than those poor souls Mars put to death this morning. And *forced* my *daughter* to watch him *do it*."

He did not force me.

It was my choice.

But he did do it.

Mars absolutely did just that.

"They came through my window with the intent to kill me, Father," I reminded him.

"And yes. Of course. They should be executed. After *tribunal*, for the gods' sakes."

"They were caught in the act."

He shot back to straight. "You cannot possibly—"

I didn't wish to start this conversation.

And now I needed to finish it.

"I need a sip of water and a moment to myself."

He rearranged his face instantly and muttered, "Of course. I'll see to this. Would you like to use your mother and my chamber?"

"I can see to myself, but I thank you."

"Please, Silence, allow me to see to you."

He then changed his expression again. We were back at my funeral. Even if I stood before him living and breathing, for some reason my father was desirous of making me think I was dead to him in some way.

And he did not bide his time to share what way that was.

"You're aware I won't see you at all after the royal weddings are through. Your new husband forbids it."

I stared up at my sire. "He…forbids it?"

He nodded curtly. "Yes. Of course. He told me I was never to see you again once he had you to himself in Firenze. You might see your mother, if he allows it. But me, not ever again. Surely he's shared this with you."

He had.

Of a sort.

I just didn't know he'd shared the same with Father.

And I was under the impression I had some say in this.

"And your mother obviously will never come to see you without me," Father continued. "And your king will not allow you back to Wodell."

He wouldn't?

He'd said nothing about that.

"I'll talk to him about this," I murmured.

"I wouldn't," he replied swiftly. "Please, do naught to anger him, my darling child. He is…today he has…." He shook his head. "Tread very cautiously, my Silence. I cannot say I've ever had a great deal of respect for Gallienus."

It shocked me he said this. He'd never said much about Gallienus except such as, "All are too hard on him. We cannot know the strains of rule."

Father carried on, "And you know my thoughts about your uncle."

One could say I did that, or at least I knew he didn't think much of our Dellish king.

"But this king," he continued, shaking his head. "I would have you wed to Cassius or even True, I'd pay the same dowry a hundred times over to do it, to save you from the likes of this king."

I tried not to appear sickened at the very idea of marrying True, who was not only my cousin, but like a brother to me.

But I could not say, after what I'd witnessed Mars do last night and this morning, not to mention the fact that he had no intention of staying true to me, at least not physically, that for once, my father was wrong.

"Really, Father, this is my matrimonial celebration. And I am now queen. I need to return to my king, but before, I need a moment to collect myself, for, as you say, it's been a very long day and I've not had much rest."

He nodded, fervently. "Of course, of course, my Silence. I will leave you to it." He reached out as if to touch me but dropped his hand forlornly. "And I would hope, considering you'll be lost to me at the end of it, that in our travels to Notting Thicket, and then Sky Bay, if I'm asked to join the royal company when you journey to Airen, you find moments to share with me." His face brightened. "We'll go riding together."

We would?

"And perhaps, share our favorite books."

Books?

"I've long wanted to do these things with you," he explained. "But as you know, business, overseeing Bower Manor, the farmers, the shepherds, the foresters, I'm always too busy."

This was true.

What was also true was that in those times, his daughter had not been queen.

I found it expedient in that moment to say, "We will find time, Father."

He reached to my hand, took it, and laid his other upon it, smiling down at me.

"This gladdens my heart, daughter. You cannot know how much."

I couldn't know, 'twas true.

I might not believe, that was true too.

I forced myself to smile up at him.

He let me go with a return smile and melted into the revelers.

I sought a place of darkness and quiet, which was not easily found.

But once I found it, I drew my shadow over myself so I would have privacy.

Fortunately, those who passed close, or stopped close, only to stumble away, didn't need me to have my shadow shrouding me. They were lost to inebriation (and smoke, and possibly even *ashesh* or *koekah*).

But I felt safe in my magical cloak.

And in it, I leaned against a broken column (that I decided was designed that way, for it was fetching, partially covered in vines) and wished I'd found a glass of cool water or juice to enjoy in my moment of calm.

I had much to think on.

Not only all I'd suffered since I awoke last night to villains climbing into my rooms.

But also the fact that Cassius seemed angry with Elena, and Elena seemed watchful and repentant to Cassius (which was quite a turnabout with those two, not that Cassius ever seemed repentant, but when it came to Elena, he was definitely watchful).

Not to mention poor, beautiful Farah had lost her lovely mother and had been abed all day, with True consistently going up to attend her.

Indeed, my cousin had practically bowled my new husband and I over, he'd raced down the mountain after our ceremony so fast. We'd barely walked over the threshold into the palace before True was charging up the steps to get back to his intended.

And then there was Aramus and Ha-Lah.

In fact, there was *especially* Aramus and Ha-Lah.

Something was *very* wrong there.

Dreadfully wrong.

But Ha-Lah was so closed off, regardless of the stunning gown she wore, you didn't approach (and her gown, one could argue, was even more beautiful than mine—a froth of white tulle at her ankles from which rose a swirl of silver sequins that seem to crest like a wave over her breasts, the rest sheer (you could see her white panties!) with thin straps and drop shoulders into poofs that led to sleeves with more silver beads and sequins dancing like tributaries and small islands on her arms—it was exquisite!).

But her demeanor made it seem she was not wearing the most gorgeous gown (outside mine) of the day.

It seemed she was wearing spines and bristles.

And her eyes held pain.

I should talk to her.

I could not talk to her.

For the last thing on my mind was the fact that I faced my marital bed.

And my marriage.

To a man who could...

A man who could...

A man who could slice another man in half, cuddle me as men sunk to their deaths, and what he and his men did in the necropolis.

And then, one day in the future, he would share me, and I would be forced to share him, and our marital bed would be a marital bed no more.

Not really.

"Silence."

My head jerked up and I stared at my king striding toward me with purpose.

I had been standing there, I had no idea how long. It was probably only minutes, and it was dark and private, but there were many people about.

And I was shadowed.

So no one saw me.

No one who walked (or drunkenly ambled) past saw me.

But my husband was walking right to me.

Oh no.

My shadow had not been faulty the other eve in his bedchamber.

He could see through it!

How could this be?

Balls!

I dropped it before he arrived and as I was very quickly becoming accustomed, now that I was his, officially, legally, in the eyes of his gods (and probably mine, even if we had not been wed in a temple), he did not hesitate to lay his hands on me.

This he did by cupping my jaw in both of his big palms and dipping his face right into mine.

"Are you well?" he asked.

I stared through the moonlight and lamplight and lanternlight at his handsome visage.

I wondered how he got those scars since I had seen him wield a sword, and no one got remotely close enough with even a tip, before they perished.

"Silence," he growled, the rumble filled with concern.

I opened my mouth, but he straightened. Catching me in the curve of an arm, he shifted his other hand back so it sifted through my hair as he drew me to his body.

"This is too much. You've had no rest. A frightening night. A trying day. A long evening. It's time we're to bed."

Oh gods.

"I could...I probably should—" I began.

"No, my wee monkey," he said, curling his fingers in my hair and using his knuckles to stroke my scalp. "Have you had time with Piccola today?"

I shook my head.

"She'll miss her mama," he murmured. "Go up. Have your woman bring her to you. Prepare for bed. I'll tell Mama we're retiring. She's adept at clearing those who would make nuisances of themselves by outstaying their welcome, doing this without communicating they're outstaying their welcome. As the crowd thins out, guests of the palace will find their beds."

I would eventually have to watch Elpis do this for I had a feeling with the Firenz this would be an important skill to have.

"But now, you go up," he ordered.

"These are my guests too, Mars," I reminded him.

He sent one of those smiles my way that did things to my belly (and regions south). Things that, after recent events, I found confusing.

"You prepare for your new husband to meet you in our chambers, my queen, they will think nothing of you retiring without farewells."

"Of course," I muttered, dropping my eyes to his chest.

"Silence."

I lifted my gaze to Mars again.

He dipped closer to me.

"I would have liked tonight to have been much different for you and me. Not just tonight, today as well. I have no power over that. It was how it was and the only thing I can say about it is that it is done. And now, we've both had trying days. As I told you last night, we will do as you wish, *only* what you wish. But most importantly for me, for this night, is that my wife gets some rest."

He slid his hand out of my hair so he could run the pad of his thumb gently under one of my eyes.

"I do not like these shadows, my queen," he finished on a whisper.

That was the Mars that I knew, now, I was coming to love.

But the Mars I knew *now* was also someone to fear.

He could cut a man in half with one swing of his sword.

And he did not hesitate to climb over bodies of dead.

He had told me I would know what it was like to be Firenz.

Now I knew.

It scared the daylights out of me.

And was vastly confusing.

For there was that Mars.

And there was this one right before me.

"Silence," he called, and I focused on him again. "You're drifting, *amore*."

"I'm tired," I mumbled.

"Then upstairs." He bent and touched his lips to mine, pulling not far away. "Time with your pet. Your woman. And then your husband. No?"

I nodded.

He smiled, and it was not wolfish.

It was kind and doting.

Why could this not be the only Mars?

And why could this Mars not be only mine?

"I will see you up there," I told him.

"This is an absolute," he replied, humor being added to the kind and doting.

I gave him a small smile back.

He hugged me (a barbarian, *hugging*) before he let me go.

I looked back at him as I walked away and saw him standing there, watching me.

Most assuredly doting.

What had I done to earn that?

I could not battle, like Elena and Serena.

I could not clear guests without seeming impolite, like Elpis.

I could never wear a gown that showed my knickers and had swirls of silver sequins that claimed me the queen of an entire country through just a garment and do it with grace and majesty, like Ha-Lah.

And yet there he was.

Doting on me.

I was caught only thrice by royal guests on my way to the stairs, and when I turned at the first landing, I realized that Elpis (or possibly Mars, or alternately Tril) had a servant boy waiting for me.

I knew this because he caught one glance at me and took off running.

Thus, by the time I moved through the door to Mars's bedchamber, Tril was dashing toward me.

"I watched through the windows, love," she cried. "It's all so terribly exciting."

Hmm.

"And so beautiful. Queen Elpis has a skilled hand with celebration décor. It seemed tasteful but still dazzling," Tril continued, grasping both my hands and walking backwards, pulling me toward the chamber where Mars's bed was. "I studied how she did that and I think it was the lanterns. She's a dab hand with placing those decorative lanterns. The light they radiate through those little holes. That's décor in and of itself."

"Tril—"

She stopped abruptly and shook my hands.

I shut my mouth when I saw the tears in her eyes.

"She had a special place for me," she whispered.

"I'm sorry?" I whispered back.

"Queen Elpis. She knows..." I watched her swallow before she went on, "She knows what we mean to each other and an officiant at the wedding found me when I arrived and took me to a special place, one close to you and your king, so I could see everything."

"Oh my goodness," I kept whispering.

I very much had to thank Elpis for that extraordinary kindness.

"You couldn't see me. You had other things on your mind. And you were... Oh, Silence!" Tril pulled me into her arms and held me close. "You were so beautiful. So dignified. So *regal*." She caught my upper arms and gave them a firm squeeze, pulling away and grinning teary-eyed at me. "And your king. If he hasn't already taken the plunge, my love, he's teetering on the precipice. He's utterly *smitten* with you."

To my shock, I could not argue that.

Her smile got wider as her eyes got brighter with tears.

"Just days. You've known him but *days* and he's roaring to the heavens at claiming you as his queen. I swear, my love, I've never seen anything so romantic in my *entire life*."

"That *was* rather lovely," I murmured.

"Lovely!" she hooted. "Darling girl, I think I saw about five Firenz girls faint, and a dozen more looked about ready to do so when he did that."

"Truly?" I asked.

She laughed aloud, tucked my hand in her elbow and moved me toward my new dressing room.

"Truly," she confirmed when she'd ceased laughing. "I cannot tell you," she drew the sheer black curtain aside, "how much I love this for so many reasons. Most specifically how very little your father has to do with any of it."

One could say that Estrilda was not fond of my father. Then again, she'd been my lady's maid for seven years and my friend since practically the first day we met. The way my father was with me, for a friend, that would happen.

However.

"Tril," I chided.

She pushed me to the daybed and waved a hand in the air. "Please, I'm maidservant to *a queen*. I can talk about Lord Johan as I like now."

I pressed my lips together and felt my eyes get big, because I was suddenly desperately in need of laughter and I wasn't sure it was appropriate, or it wouldn't spring forth hysterical.

"I'll get Piccola," she offered without me requesting, moving toward the door that led to what was now her room. "Do you want the white lace? Or the white satin and lace?"

Oh faith.

She was talking about wedding nightgowns.

One Tril had sewn on the way to Firenze. An upper of exquisite lace with short sleeves, a deep V at the front, falling into an elegant, wide skirt of satin and ending in a deep edge of more lace that was at least three inches longer than the length of my frame.

Acres of fabric.

The other I'd had made while we were there.

All lace. Very much see-through. Shorter sleeves that were almost winged. A ruched cross at my midriff and another deep V at the bodice.

The first was elegant and Dellish.

The other was sultry and Firenz.

"The satin," I declared at the same time Tril said, "The lace."

She stopped while opening the door to her rooms and looked at me.

I shot her an expression that said, *Eep!*

Piccola pranced out of Tril's room, across the dressing room floor, and I bent to her as she dashed into my hands.

"Allo, my darling," I cooed and brought her up to my face.

She chirruped an excited hello.

"Shall we beg Tril for some treats?" I asked her.

She chirruped an excited yes.

"Treats before satin, Tril, don't you think?" I said to my friend.

"I think lace, my love," she replied quietly.

I looked into her eyes and cuddled my wee monkey to my neck. "I'm not ready for lace and Mars tells me he will be ready when I am."

Surprise, relief and joy washed over her features before smugness entered them.

"Smitten," she declared and moved to the shelves that she had wasted no time in populating with my things. "*Deeply*," she concluded, pulling at the satin and flinging it so it soared in the air anchored to her fingers before taking an elegant fall.

"Extraordinary," a deep voice came, after which there was a startled chirrup and Piccola crawled up into my hair at the same time Tril emitted a strangled scream.

This was because Mars had flung back the sheers and was sauntering into my dressing room.

"I, uh...Your Grace, um...Your Majesty...uuuuuumm, my new king," Tril stammered bobbing up and down in a half curtsy, half bow that was so clumsy, I feared she'd topple out of it.

"I am King Mars, yes?" Mars stated, tossing his huge body into a full lounge on the daybed beside me. "Two syllables. Easy to remember," he teased Tril and then fell slightly back so he could lift a long arm at the end of which was a hand that he used to extricate Piccola from my hair.

"Very easy, uh, King Mars," Tril replied.

"And no bobbing," Mars went on. Having taken hold of my monkey, he was now allowing Piccola to grasp one of the thick leather straps across his chest. "It's awkward in a home. Parts of this palace are governmental, but this chamber is a part that's home."

"I...yes, it is," Tril whispered.

Mars lifted his dark gaze to my friend.

"And it's my understanding you are family, no?"

Oh, by the gods.

Was I...

*Melting?*

I stared at my new husband who was lounging at my side, his head nearly in my lap, his gaze still on my Tril.

"I...I love your queen very dearly, King Mars," Tril said quietly.

"Then this is decided," Mars murmured, removed Piccola from his strap and brought my wee thing to his face "How do you feel about this, Piccola?" he asked.

Oh yes.

I was melting.

Piccola chirruped.

"Very smart," Mars agreed then returned my monkey to me, his head tipping far back so he could catch my eyes. "Don't be long, *bellezza*. It's time to do something about those shadows under your eyes."

"All right, Mars," I whispered.

"I'm sending a boy for passionflower mint tea. Anything else you desire?" he asked, pushing up from the daybed.

"I—"

"Sir, uh, King Mars, my lady likes chamomile before bed," Tril put in.

I held my breath after my Tril said this, contradicting a king.

He did naught but look at me. "Do you prefer this, Silence?"

"I've never had passionflower mint. Why don't I try both?" I replied, only for him to smile largely.

"My queen. A diplomat. Over tea," he muttered. "It'll be done."

Then he turned, but instead of moving aside the sheers, he twisted back to look at Tril.

"Did you enjoy the wedding?" he asked.

"I...yes, it was beautiful, King Mars. And that view was stunning. I've never seen the like. Please, thank your mother for, um...seeing to me."

"My mother," he murmured pensively. "I'll be sure to do that."

And with that, he swept aside the sheers and strode out.

But with that, I knew, it might have been Elpis who had seen to Tril having a special place at our wedding.

But she did it at her son's request.

This did not make me feel like I was melting.

This did not make me feel afraid.

This made me feel as I had felt but twenty-four hours earlier.

Like I was falling in love.

I looked to Tril. She was staring at the sheers clutching lace and satin to her chest.

She'd realized the same thing.

"Tril," I called.

She turned to me. "Now *I'm* smitten. *Deeply*."

I could not hold it back.

And yes, it was partially hysterical.

But it felt good to giggle.

Tril giggled with me as she approached, saying through her laughter, "Let us get you ready for bed. Then treats for Piccola. By then, your *tea* will be ready."

We giggled more over her emphasis on tea.

And then we did as she said.

The tea arrived after I had changed and was sitting with Piccola crawling about my person while Tril brushed out my hair.

I tried both teas.

I preferred the passionflower mint.

When I told this to Tril, she simply mumbled, "I do not find this the least surprising."

Though she said these words with a big grin on her face.

The tea was relaxing, as was the hair brushing, and I could hear that the din outside was regressing, but then it was time for me to meet my husband at our marital bed.

Mars had made it clear it was my decision what tonight would bring.

But all I wished was to sleep so I would be refreshed and tomorrow, perhaps tackle some of the many things that plagued my thoughts.

Therefore, I hoped he spoke true.

When Tril was finished with my hair, she set aside the brush, caught both my shoulders from where she stood behind me and bent to my ear.

"I am happy for you. I am proud of you. And I wish you all the joy in the world in the life you will share with your king," she whispered there.

I turned my head and knew I had tears in my eyes when I caught hers.

She had tears as well.

We simply gazed at each other for a long moment before she squeezed my shoulders, let me go, took hold of Piccola and started to blow out the lamps in the dressing room.

I got up, took in a breath and walked to the black sheers.

I drew them aside and moved through, only able to take two steps before I stopped.

There were naught but two lamps lit, one on either side of the bed.

A bed my husband was on.

He was wearing nothing but a pair of his satin pants. These a deep red. And he was lying with his back up on pillows, his shoulders and head resting against the padded headboard.

His eyes were closed.

Was he asleep?

If he was asleep, this would make things easy.

It would also, I admitted to myself, be disappointing.

I approached the bed but stopped, the lace at the hem of the satin floating around my feet, when his head came up from the headboard and his eyes opened and fell on me.

Though, it would be more accurate to say his eyes opened and traveled the length of me.

"This was the perfect choice, my queen," he declared. "You look beautiful."

Everything about me warmed.

"You look, erm, beautiful too," I told him.

A smile flirted with his lips before he ordered, "Come to your husband."

My husband.

That man was my *husband*.

I moved to him slowly.

He curled up to sitting, and my feet were on the furs that carpeted the podium on which the bed sat before he reached with his long arms, caught my hips and pulled me down on him.

He lay back against the headboard again.

I lay on him.

Oh faith.

"I like the sound of your laughter with your woman," he murmured, his gaze now trailing over my face.

"We do it often," I told him.

"I do not know if I've ever heard you laugh like that, Silence," he remarked.

Was this true?

"I-I'm sorry," I replied.

His brows drew together before he asked, "Why are you sorry?" But he did not expect an answer for he kept talking. "It is me who should feel remorse for I have not made you laugh like this."

Yes, this was the Mars I could fall in love with.

"We've not had much time together, Mars," I reminded him.

"You've made me laugh."

I had. Not purposefully, but it could not be denied I found a thrill in doing so.

"Well—" I began.

His arms curled tighter around me, and he dragged me slightly up his frame so my face was closer to his.

And when he got me in position, he declared, "It will be my reason for being, after we leave Sofia to her rest, to make you laugh often, my wife."

I slid my hand that was lying on his warm chest up to his neck, whispering, "Mars."

"I do not wish to do so in this moment, but it's important so I'm sorry to say I must remonstrate you again," he shared.

I blinked into his face at his swift change in topic.

"I set Kyril on you," he continued. "Before I found you earlier and you came up to our chamber, he'd found me and reported that you'd disappeared in the garden."

Oh no.

Had Kyril seen my drawing over my shadow?

"You set Kyril on me?"

"Silence, you were attacked last night. But regardless, you are queen. You'll now have a guard everywhere you go for the rest of your life."

Well then.

That made sense.

It was unnerving.

But it made sense.

And further, all this proved that Mars could see through my shadow because Kyril, apparently, could not.

I wondered if this had anything to do with the prophecy.

Obviously, I wasn't going to discuss this with him. Not right then.

Instead, I had a thornier topic to discuss.

I did not get to broach it.

"I must command you not to disappear like that again," Mars said. "It's not safe."

He was right, in a manner, so I nodded.

It was then, his hand came up to my face and he touched the hoop in my nostril lightly, murmuring, "Your woman did not take your chain."

And it was then I noticed he was no longer wearing his.

"I—"

"This I like," he decreed. "Of a night, every night, if we retire together, and even if we don't, I shall come up with you and take your chain and you shall take mine."

I was surprised.

"You don't wear them to bed?"

He smiled tenderly at me. "No, my Silence. They would catch on pillows and might cause harm. We will wear them when we make love. We will remove them after."

As this was the thornier subject I had intended to broach, the fact I didn't wish to do that tonight, I felt my heart start beating harder, and Mars surely felt it too, as I was lying atop him. But, with some expertise, he unhooked the chain at my lip and upper ear and carefully unthreaded it from the hoops.

He then set it aside on his nightstand, and I gasped when he immediately rolled me—and rolled *over me*—but he did this to blow out the lamp on the other side of the bed. He rolled us again and he blew the lamp out there.

Directly after, he pulled the hides and silks out from under us. He drew them over us and arranged our bodies so mine was in the curve of his, my bottom in his lap, my back pressed to his chest, the backs of my legs riding the fronts of his thighs.

He held me close at the waist and I felt his breath stir the hair on the top of my head.

I had never—in my life—slept thus with *anyone*.

And it was...

It felt...

*Lovely*.

I stared into the dark and heard a lone female laugh drifting up from the gardens below.

Someone was dallying.

"Sleep, Silence," Mars said into my hair.

But I was no longer sleepy.

"Did you see to it that Tril had a special place to watch our ceremony?" I asked in order to confirm my earlier thought.

He squeezed me with his arm lightly and then it relaxed.

"Yes."

I closed my eyes tight.

And saw the inside of the necropolis and all that had happened there in a grisly flash.

I opened my eyes.

"That was very kind," I whispered. "Thank you."

"You will have more friends," he decreed. "You will have a fuller life. You will be revered by our people. You will be cherished in our home. But she will always be yours, the only thing of worth you brought from your country of birth. And thus, she earned where she stood this eve."

Without me willing it to do so, my body pushed back into his.

When it did, his arm again tightened, and he leaned into me so he was partially covering me.

He was so big. So warm.

Another hundred men could come surging through the windows, and in that moment, I felt not a one of them would get near me.

That was lovely too.

"Now sleep," he urged.

"You are very...*skilled* with your sword," I noted. "This being so, how did you get those scars on your face?"

"Silence?"

"Yes?"

"My queen." He squeezed me again, this time hard. "*Sleep.*"

Oh dear.

Was that a sensitive subject?

Had I mucked things up?

"Do you not want to, erm...talk about that?"

"No. I will share anything with you. I will tell you all you wish to know about me. You but need to ask, and it's yours. Though in the now, I want you to sleep, and I do it hoping you do not move much while in slumber, as if you do, we'll both be hopelessly caught up in satin and I'll likely have to call for my sword to slice through it to extricate us."

I giggled.

"Thank the gods," he whispered in a manner that I did not think he was referring to gratitude he'd made me laugh.

Therefore, I asked, "What?"

"This morning you were not yourself," he answered. "It troubled me. All day, you were withdrawn. And it was not simply that you were weary, grieving Sofia, or times were trying. It seemed your light was out." He fell deeper into me so I was nearly buried under him. "But your light is not out. And for that, I thank the gods."

I'd tried but knew I had not fully hidden where my mind was all day, this being everywhere and none of it was good.

I did not know I had "a light."

I found it both promising and disconcerting that he was as attuned to me as he was.

And simply lovely he thought I had "a light."

"You're not sleeping," Mars noted.

"Well—"

"Your arse is in my groin. Your perfume in my nostrils. Our time in this bed last night fresh in my mind." He gave me yet another squeeze, this time with a warning. "You need to sleep, Silence."

Yes.

One could say with that warning I did, indeed, need to find sleep.

"All right, Mars," I muttered, sighed, and closed my eyes.

I tried to even my breathing.

I tried to still my mind.

I thought I accomplished the first, but I did not accomplish the last.

So I focused on the Mars who made sure Tril was seen to during the most important occasion in my life. I focused on how very proud he was to claim me as his queen. I focused on the fact he did not like shadows under my eyes and wanted to devote himself to a lifetime of making me laugh. I focused on him telling me I would have a full life and be cherished. I focused on the fact that we were in our marital bed hours after I'd been made his wife, and he was holding me and admonishing me to sleep because he wanted me to have rest.

And doing that, being in the arms of *that* Mars, I fell asleep.

# 40

## THE TREMBLING

***Farah***
*Guest Suite, Second Floor, East Corridor, Catrame Palace, Fire City*
Firenze

I was not asleep when True came back.

Again.

He had returned repeatedly that day.

However, since the morning, he had not spoken to me except, after he returned from the necropolis, he asked if I'd had some luncheon.

I had not and told him this.

He'd looked disapproving, but he didn't press the matter.

Mars had come as well, after True had left.

His visit was brief, and he'd said only two things while standing by my bed looking down at me.

"Do not get up."

And.

"Sofia will be avenged, my little sister."

The red was in his eyes, but it warred with the heartache on his face.

Even seeing that, I felt no better.

It was not that I wanted him to hurt. Obviously, I did not for I didn't want anyone to hurt, especially Mars and especially why he was hurting.

It was just that a curious cold had stolen over me and I was beginning to feel like I would never feel anything.

Not ever again.

I had heard the cheers floating to the palace from the city. I'd heard the revelry at the palace after Mars and Silence returned.

But I had no interest even to rouse myself to open a window and look down in hopes of catching my king and my new queen celebrating their marriage.

Therefore, I did not get up.

I laid in bed and let my mind float on the chilly numbness that had overtaken me.

And this was my state when True came again just now, likely to check on me before bidding me goodnight.

I did not care he was there. I did not care that the celebrations were over for the noise outside was abating. I did not care that my country had a new queen. I did not care that in but days, we would be leaving my land to travel to a place I'd never been, never wanted to go, this so I could wed its future king, a man who did not want me, but had no choice but to have me.

I simply did not care.

About anything.

As these thoughts drifted through my mind, I realized that True had entered my room some minutes ago, but he had not approached the bed.

But I did not care enough to lift my head to see where he was.

I just stared at nothing as the lamplight danced in the room.

And I continued to do so when it started to dim as True moved about the room, extinguishing it.

Though something stirred in me when I felt the bedcovers behind me move.

And something else stirred when I felt the sensation of a body hitting the mattress.

Last, I felt my own body grow taut when my intended fitted himself to my back and snaked an arm around my belly.

This was highly unlike True.

I knew he wished to comfort me.

However...

"True—"

"Quiet."

I blinked into the dark at his word and the tone he'd used to utter it.

He pulled me tighter to his warmth. Warmth that was, first, very warm, and second, I could tell he did not have his usual clothing on. Shirt. Trousers. Waistcoat. Obviously no boots as he was under the silks with me.

I didn't know what he wore for I had my nightgown on.

But I could feel skin against skin at my shoulders.

He was silent for a long time and I thought he was going to sleep.

I was surprised he intended to sleep with me.

But apparently, he did.

Though, I was wrong about him being asleep for he spoke again.

"Tomorrow, you will eat. You may lie in bed. You may keep others away, except me. But you will eat, is this understood, Farah?"

Now I was surprised he was being domineering.

He'd never been domineering.

His arm gave me a shake.

"Farah?"

"Tomorrow, I will eat," I said simply to say what he wished to hear.

"Elpis is making arrangements for your mother's death ceremony. If you wish to be involved in that, you'll need to say so and I will make certain that your wishes are adhered to."

"What is Elpis planning?" I asked.

"I've no idea. Do you wish to know?"

I felt a flare of anger at such an offensive question and snapped, "Of course I do."

"Then I shall bring Elpis to you tomorrow, you will share how we'll say our final goodbyes to Sofia, and I'll see to it that your wishes are seen to."

"Thank you."

"After that," he went on as if I didn't speak, "after tomorrow, you must get up. You must take fresh air. You must have activity. You will, of course, continue to grieve. But it is not healthy hiding in the dark, lying abed."

I had no reply to that.

"After your father's actions, your mother carried on," he remarked, and my anger flared again, hotter this time. "She continued to live. She looked after you."

"It is not your right to say such things," I retorted. "Things you know nothing about. *She* did not endure that and what came after then lose her daughter."

"I did not know her well, this is true, but can you say with a hint of honesty that she would be fine with her daughter lying abed and feeling sorry for herself?"

I twisted my neck to look at him, and as I did, his head came up to look down at me through the shadows.

"If it pleases you, Your Grace, she's been dead only a day," I began sarcastically. "May I feel sorry for myself for *a day* without having to endure a prince's lecture?"

"Farah," he growled, and at his tone, one I'd never heard from him, I stared in shock through the dark as his face got closer to mine and the timbre of his voice remained just as aggravated, "if you call me 'Your Grace' one more time…"

He let that trail.

"What?" I snapped.

"It will hurt me, and it will harm us. I am not that to you. It did not start that way between us and it will never be that way between us, unless you make it so."

I shut my mouth.

I opened it again to state, "You have no idea how this feels. Until, and may the gods make this time long, you lose your own mother, as far as I'm concerned, you have nothing to say on the matter of how I grieve my own."

"Even when Queen Mercy dies, I will not feel the same as you," he retorted. "I have great love for my mother, and she me, but we never shared warmth. She is queen and I am to be king and for as long as I remember, she treated me entirely in the manner she saw fitted the rearing of the next king. It was not my father who saw to my schooling, the depth of it, the breadth of it, the concentration of it, and the expectation I should excel at it. It was my mother. It was not my father who saw to my military training, it was my mother. It was not my father who demanded from when I was age nine that I attend tribunals, disputes, and when my father sat as magistrate. It was my mother. And it was my mother, after, who whispered in my ear what decisions she felt were right, or those that were wrong, and eventually asked me how I felt and made me defend my positions."

I lay there, still, staring into his face, astonished by this.

Also fascinated.

And lastly, saddened.

"If I were sent into exile, and my mother went with me," True continued, "she would not help me to build the new life we would need to build and then set about living it. She would plot and she would connive to find a way that we were both, especially me, put back in our rightful place. Even if it meant her, or my, death. So I do not know warmth and smiles and understanding from my mother. When she dies, I will miss her. I will mourn her. I will forever be grateful that she spent so much energy crafting me into the honorable and just king I hope to become. I did not have what I saw you had from your mother. Though if I did, one thing I know, I would miss it more."

"True," I whispered.

His arm around me disappeared in order that he could wrap his fingers around the side of my neck.

"And you will not be the queen my mother is," True whispered back harshly. "I will see to it there will be no need for that to become you. You will provide our children with smiles and warmth and understanding. You will be the mother your mother was. And that way, she will live on through you. There will be peace and joy and family in the royal quarters of Birchlire Castle. That will be my gift to you. And that will be your gift to Sofia. But I cannot give it, and you will not have it, if I am *Your Grace*. I am *your betrothed*, Farah. I'll be *your husband*. The father of your children. Those come first. And the last will always be your king."

I was lying beside him in the dark, unmoving, and yet breathing as if I was running.

"You must feel your sorrow, sweets, of course," he said in a softer tone. "It is an honor to your mother. But I do not know what we face. We've barely left this palace and we've had two casualties—"

"Two?" I interrupted him to ask.

"Aramus lost a man."

I didn't know that.

"Oh no," I said quietly.

"Yes, Farah," he replied, now stroking my throat with his thumb. "There will be times when you will need to be weak, and I will be strong. There will be times when that's the other way around. But we have no idea what we're going to face. So when you are weak, I will persist in helping you to find your strength. And I will need you to do the same for me."

"I miss her," I blurted.

"Farah," he whispered, his hand coming up to cup my jaw.

My voice was getting thicker. "I ca-cannot believe that the sun will rise tomorrow, like it did today, and I-I will not s-see her."

"Darling," he murmured.

"I-I d-do not wish to c-cry again," I stated before a sob forced its way up my throat.

True turned me in his arms and pulled me close, gliding his fingers through my hair as I wept into his bare chest.

"I'm angry," I sobbed into his skin.

"Of course you are."

"At Elpis. At my father. At whoever sent those snakes. At everyone."

"You've the right."

"And...and, my chest...it burns, True. The pain is...if I allow myself to think on it, it's unbearable."

"Weep, sweets, that may help put out the fire," he urged.

"I hate the world," I told him.

"As you should, the world is behaving like it hates you."

At these words, I let out a snagged laugh and tipped my head back to look at him.

His hand came to my cheek and he ran a thumb over the wet.

"Why are you here?" I asked.

"Because you need me."

"In bed?" I pushed.

"Farah, you will not sleep alone for the rest of your days."

I felt my lips part.

I wouldn't?

"There are forces at work," he carried on. "And you will not be unguarded. Even in sleep. After we best those, you will be my wife. So naturally you will not be alone in sleep for you'll sleep at my side."

"But...*now?*"

"Yes, now."

"It is not very...Dellish of you to lay with the woman who is to be your wife before she's your wife, is it?"

"I know many a Dellish man who, in understanding their women, wives or no, are under threat, they would be abed with them too."

"Oh," I mumbled.

"Have you slept too much today and so you're awake now without hope of sleep?" he asked.

"I...well, I don't know. I've been feeling too sorry for myself to think what else I might be feeling," I admitted.

He tucked my face back into his chest and murmured, "Then try, for I'm weary. If you find you cannot sleep, don't descend into maudlin thoughts. Wake me. We will go find food, or wine, or both. Or simply talk until you're sleepy."

"I couldn't wake you," I muttered in return.

"If you do not, and I wake in the morn, and you are haggard from spending a sleepless night, I will be cross."

I continued to mutter. "I wouldn't wish to make you cross."

"Then don't."

I closed my eyes.

*Peace and joy and family in the royal quarters of Birchlire Castle.*

My mother would never see that. Never know it. Never meet my children.

And True wanted that, wanted it from me. Not as his love, his life, a woman he had chosen for his own to be at his side the rest of his days.

Instead, as friends. As partners.

He wished us to love our family and support each other through whatever befell us.

Through this, however, I would never belong to him. With my mother gone, I would never belong to anyone.

But in thinking on it, I decided this wouldn't be so bad.

It could be worse.

And I knew one thing, if True could, he'd always try to make it better.

It just would never be...*everything*.

"Farah?" True called as if he knew the turn of my thoughts.

"I'll wake you if I can't sleep, True."

"All right, love," he murmured, rounding me with both arms and holding me to his body.

True did not fall asleep quickly.

I did not either.

But he fell asleep.

And when he did, his presence, his warmth, the steadiness of his breath...

Meant I did too.

~

### King Aramus
*Guest Suite, Second Floor, East Corridor, Catrame Palace, Fire City*
*FIRENZE*

ARAMUS APPROACHED the bed his wife lay in, her back to his side of the mattress, the lamp at her nightstand blown out.

He did not sigh with discouragement.

He also did not hesitate.

He blew out his lamp and slid in beside his wife.

He then turned to his side and slid toward his wife, for the first time touching her in their bed by taking her in his arms. He then forced her rigid body into the curve of his.

"I was upset earlier," he said into her curls when he settled with his arm holding her close.

She made no reply.

"I spoke in hurt and anger," he admitted.

Ha-Lah said nothing.

"I said things, many of them I regret," he told her.

His queen remained silent.

"Deeply," he stressed.

She still had nothing to say.

"And the things I regret, deeply, are the things I said that hurt you."

She still had no reply.

He pressed closer to her. "Wife, speak to me. Shout at me. Curse at me. Scratch at my eyes. *Something.*"

There was nothing but a stiff form in his arm, and in his nose, the scent of the oil in her hair.

"We began to bridge the chasm separating us," he murmured. "Do not let pride force it to spread between us again."

"I was taken from my home," she said softly.

Thank Medusa.

She was speaking.

She'd said not a word to him since that morning.

Aramus pushed ever closer to her, at the same time pulling her closer to him.

"I was taken from my family, my friends, my village, all that I knew," she continued.

And now, if her tone was aught to go by, he was learning how she felt about that.

Not the optimal time, considering. Especially with the words she was saying and how she was saying them.

But he would be glad to know it.

"My wife," he whispered.

"I was not asked if this was something I wished. I was given no choice. I was then wed to a man. A king. The ultimate power in our realm. I was made queen. But I held no power. I had no voice."

It was Aramus who was quiet then.

"But even without it, I used it," she carried on. "I used my voice. I told you my thoughts. I told you what was important to me. You did not listen."

"Ha-Lah—"

"You railed at me and left me to sleep alone on my wedding night. I should not have minded. It was not my choice to be in that marital chamber. But it was the only wedding night I would have. And I slept alone."

"My wife—"

"Though, once you're rid of me, if you allow me to take another husband, I suppose I'll have another wedding night."

"Do not speak thus," he growled.

She fell silent.

"I lashed out. I regret it. I admitted that. And now you *do* have a choice," he informed her. "It is your choice if we again grow apart or if we move on together. But I warn you, don't allow your pride to make that decision."

"But don't you see?" she asked. "I have nothing. Pride, as empty as it is, is the only thing I possess."

Aramus growled again, this time with no words, as he stared through the dark at her curls on the pillow.

"I would thank you not to touch me," she declared.

"I would get used to me touching you, wife," he ground out. "For I will use touch, and any other manner at my disposal to win you again."

"Against my will?"

"It will not be against your will. You cannot be falling in love with a man of a morning and in that same morning stop doing this very thing."

"Yes, Aramus," she said quietly. "Yes, you can."

By Triton, she was right.

He'd made that so.

He could not go back there, to that morn, remember the words that came out of his mouth, the words that came from hers telling him he'd been earning her love, but he had put an end to that.

And he could not bear to remember the look on her face.

Instead, he did what he'd desired to do time and again since the first time he laid eyes on her.

He buried his face in her abundance of soft curls.

"I will miss my man," he told her.

"And I feel badly for you."

"Do not make me lose a man and my wife on the same day."

"It was not your doing, the loss of Catedrais. The other..."

She did not finish her statement.

It was still clear.

"I can only share my regret, what else would you have of me?" he asked.

"This is our problem."

He slid his head back to listen, closely, but she did not go on.

"What is our problem?" he prompted.

"Words, they have awesome power. Awesome power to wound. However, sadly, once that is done, they lose their power if you attempt to use them to heal."

Aramus wished this wasn't true, but he feared it was.

His wife was not finished speaking.

"It is worse. Worse for us. For you don't understand. It's impossible for you to understand. To understand who I am and how I am and what means something to me and why. To understand what has made me and how. To understand how your words would so thoroughly kill what was budding between us."

"Make me understand."

"It's impossible."

"Nothing is impossible, Ha-Lah."

Suddenly, she whispered, "I need the sea."

"We will leave tomorrow. We will take the fastest route. We will wade in the shores. You will swim with the dolphins. We will meet the others later or not at all. They can battle this Beast. We will return to Mar-el and reign side by side."

She shook her head on her pillow.

"Please, talk to me, my Ha-Lah," he pleaded.

"My father grieves my mother still," she said.

"You've shared this with me," Aramus replied.

"Every man in the village wanted her as his wife. Wanted to put babies in her belly. Wanted to live his life at her side."

Aramus remained quiet and listened.

"My auntie, she said all the women thought it was because she was so beautiful. 'But really,' she told me, 'she was. Though it was a beauty you could not see.'"

"So she was kind," Aramus guessed.

"And lively. And amusing," Ha-Lah added.

"She has given you this."

Her head moved on the pillow again, negatively. "No. My father says I'm too serious. He says if I were a man, I'd take up a sword and be a crusader. It wouldn't matter what cause. I just need a crusade."

From what Aramus knew of his wife, he could not dispute this.

"He won her," she said so low, Aramus barely heard her.

"He won her?" he asked to make certain that was what she said.

"Auntie Ha-Zahlah told me that if Momma told my father, to win her heart, he had to travel into the night sky and bring back a star, he would have found a way. And somehow, he found his way to prove this to her."

It was at that, Aramus's body went solid.

"He grieves her still," she whispered.

"I will bring you a star," he whispered back.

"You do not wish to win me, Aramus. You want a queen. A wife to give you sons. And the partner who will help all defeat the Beast. You regret your words because it takes you further from these goals. You do not regret your words because they harmed me."

"You are very wrong," he stated firmly.

She sighed. "You will never understand."

"You're correct," he agreed, and finished, "if you don't explain it to me."

"There will never be a time when you don't have power. I was not free to leave my rooms today, because you bid it."

"For your safety."

"I was not free to see to my husband because you did not wish it."

"And I regret that."

"I am not free."

Aramus's entire frame jerked.

"No. You will never understand," she declared.

"And do you wish for me to set you free, wife?" he asked cautiously, disturbingly, for if she wished that, and to win her, he'd need to give her that, how would he keep her safe as she made her way back to him?

For he couldn't think of an option that did not include him again going about earning her love.

She had to come back to him, for she was earning his.

"I would wish that would be the last thing on your mind, especially if you're hurting."

She'd wanted to comfort him.

She *had* been comforting him.

Since the attack was over, she had not left his side.

He was such a bloody fool.

"Ha-Lah," he murmured, again burying his face into her hair.

"I was torn from my home to be your queen. I did not make you earn anything from me. I wanted nothing but your respect. And then you disrespected me. And I cannot say, in your anger, no matter the regret you feel now, that the words you spoke, you did not speak true, from the heart, what you are feeling. Now, here we are. And here I'm afraid is where we will stay."

"Because you cannot forgive me."

"Because I have no worth to you."

"You cannot possibly think that's true."

"*He will not be burdened with a queen the likes of you,*" she quoted, and he ground his teeth at hearing the words that had come out of his own mouth. "I cannot possibly think it is not."

They were getting nowhere.

"Perhaps we should talk about this in the morning," he suggested.

"As you wish," she replied.

He didn't like the way she said that, but he'd learned, not easily, to keep his mouth shut in matters such as that. At least until he'd found the right words to say.

She lay in the curve of his arm, no less tense, but he did not leave her be.

She was his wife.

He was her husband.

They would disagree. They would fight. They might even wound each other (again).

But from then on, at the end of the night, they would fall asleep in each other's arms.

Or, in this case, she would fall asleep in his.

"It is odd, do you not think, that this destiny before us would bring me a crusader?" he asked.

"I do not wish to prolong our discussion, but I feel I must warn you that flattery isn't effective with me."

"I am not flattering you, my queen. I'm pondering. I'm sure another man would very much wish to have a beautiful, kind, lively, amusing wife. But I need a warrior. I need a wife who would stand strong and refuse to admit defeat. Even if she's defending herself."

That made her entire frame jerk.

Finally, he was getting somewhere.

"I regret what I said," he carried on. "I am not a man of words. I am a man of deeds. So I do not have the skill to express how deeply I regret wounding you. But I did not speak true, Ha-Lah. Mar-el got the queen it needed. Triton did. This planet did. And I did. And if you do not believe that to be in my heart, I will simply have to prove it to you."

"May I sleep, my king?" she asked.

"As you wish," he answered.

At that, he felt her body twitch.

Then she sighed.

He did not smile even if he felt his point had been made and he had eventually found a way to heal some of the damage he'd inflicted on his wife.

Or at least give her something to think about.

But Catedrais was dead.

The palace had been besieged last night.

A plot to assassinate Farah, and thus foil the prophecy, killed Sofia. And this came from magic.

Not to mention, the quake they'd experienced was by far the worst and he did not like to think not only what that meant, but what kind of tidal that forced on his realm.

And his wife was more distant to him than she'd ever been.

Therefore, there was naught to smile about.

But they would leave tomorrow.

They would ride like there was a siren on their heels.

And he would take his wife to the sea.

They would meet the others in Wodell.

Now, he had to see to his queen.

~

**Princess Elena**
*Guest Suite, Second Floor, East Corridor, Catrame Palace, Fire City*
*Firenze*

I blew out the lamps in my dressing room after I'd changed into my nightgown.

As I wandered into the bathing area on my way to bed, I wished Dora was with me.

Or I was with Dora.

It wasn't safe in the palace, so she was with my sisters at the camp.

But Mother had decreed I stay close, stating this was due to needing as many warriors in the palace as possible to keep all safe.

But I knew it was more.

She wanted her daughters close.

As I wanted Dora close, I understood this.

And as I saw that day that the events of last night, and the busyness of the day, had had a significant effect on my queen, making her look more drawn, lines beginning to form around her mouth due to the constant tightness that I imagined was her fighting pain, I wanted to be close to my mother.

These thoughts heavy on my mind, as well as what had happened with

Cassius that morning, and how, even if I was very right, I had gone about communicating that very wrongly, I entered my bedchamber.

And stopped short.

Cassius was standing by a divan in the corner, shedding his leather shirt.

"What—?" I began.

His head turned to me. "Which side of the bed do you sleep on?"

My mind as frozen as my body at his presence in my chamber, automatically, I replied, "The middle."

"Bloody perfect," he muttered, turning and sitting, shirtless, on the divan in order to take off his boots.

His tattoos spanned his side, shoulder and most of his arm.

They were, as ever, fascinating.

I shook myself free of my fascination and took two steps deeper into the room.

"Cassius, what are doing here?" I demanded to know.

"We sleep together," he declared, having taken off one boot, he was pulling off the other.

But again, I was frozen.

"We do?" I asked through stiff lips.

"Villains attacked the palace last night, Elena."

"I do remember this."

"Farah was targeted, Sofia lost."

"I haven't forgotten this either."

His boots and socks gone, he stood and put his hands to the buttons of his trousers, his eyes on me.

"I'm not taking any chances."

"So you intend to...to...*sleep with me?*" I asked, the end of that statement going up in pitch drattedly high.

"In terms of sleeping, as in actual slumber, yes. I'm fatigued, and as things have been going, tomorrow will likely not be less beset than today." His gaze grew intense on me. "However, if you have something else in mind, I have no doubt I'll be able to rally."

I could not even begin to think of that something else that might be on my mind (and was, altogether too often).

"I don't wish you to sleep with me, Cassius."

"I don't very much care, Elena," he muttered, unbuttoning his leather pants.

"I don't *need* you to sleep with me, Cassius," I carried on, beginning to feel not a small amount of desperation, not to mention something else.

What did he have under those trousers?

I wished to see.

Anxiously.

And I very much did not.

Determinedly.

"I can take care of myself," I finished.

"Well, you won't need to, as I'll be here to help you with that," he retorted.

"Cassius!" I snapped.

He started to pull down his trousers.

I averted my gaze so strongly, my entire torso jerked to the side in the effort to do it.

"I sleep in the nude," he announced.

Oh, by the mercy of the goddess.

"Cassius, you need to leave," I told the wall.

I watched the lamplight dim as he blew one out somewhere in the room.

He was walking naked around my bedchamber!

"Cassius—"

"Elena, you can stand there all night for all I care. But I'm going to bed."

He spoke truth for I heard bedclothes rustle.

Damn the man.

I could not bodily remove him.

Well, maybe I could.

I'd attacked in anger that morning (Melisse would be very cross with me if she knew), and thus had been bested humiliatingly quickly. If I gave it a moment's thought, considered my strategy, I might prevail.

However, I was not keen to physically struggle with a naked man.

A large naked man.

A large naked man with fascinating tattoos.

A large naked man with fascinating tattoos who was Prince Regent of Airen, my betrothed.

Bloody hell.

I stomped to two lit lamps and blew them out before, not looking at the man in my bed, I tramped there.

I pulled back the silks, slid in, stretched to blow out the lamp beside the bed, casting the room dark, and then wiggled, at length and hopefully irritatingly, into the mattress and pillows to find the best comfort.

Cassius's deep voice sounded into the dark.

"Your movements, along with the smell of you, the vision of you in your brief nightgown and your proximity, are making me hard."

I ceased moving immediately.

"Just so you will not be surprised in future," he went on, "we shall be sleeping together from now on."

That made me turn his way.

"What?" I cried. "For the goddess's sake, why?"

"Peace of mind."

"It won't give *me* peace of mind."

"You'll get used to it," he muttered.

I clenched my teeth.

"Go to sleep, Elena," he ordered.

"The only reason I'm not throwing you out bodily right now is because I, too, am fatigued. But after tonight, I won't be sleeping with you, Cassius."

"We'll discuss this in the morning."

"We won't."

"We will. Now sleep."

"You cannot order me to sleep. And we won't!"

Suddenly his hand was wrapped around the back of my neck, I was across the silks and pressed to the length of his frame, his hand still at my neck, his other arm wrapped tight around me.

"I would have you safe," he gritted.

Oh heavens.

We were here again.

I'd brought him here again.

Regrettably.

I held my breath as he carried on.

"And I will keep you safe how I see fit, woman, no matter how you argue, if you fight. I will not lose you. Dora will not lose you. When she meets you and becomes attached to you, Aelia will not lose you. I'll see to it. Is this understood?"

"Cassius," I started cautiously, "I think we need to talk."

"In the morning and along the bloody trek to Notting Thicket. We'll have fucking weeks to come to some accord, my princess. And this we'll *fucking* do. And not only to have an accord, but for there to be a time, hopefully very soon, where I'll do a variety of other vastly more enjoyable things with you when we're abed. But now...*sleep*."

I felt it prudent at that moment to give in.

So I did and I did it saying, "All right. Now, will you let me go?"

"No."

I stared at his shadowed jaw. "No?"

That jaw tipped down and I caught his eyes through the darkness.

"No," he confirmed.

"Cassius—"

"Elena, you feel good and you feel *alive*. Give me that without a bloody argument. Especially tonight. I beg you, please."

I felt alive.

Unlike, very obviously, his dead wife.

I closed my mouth.

Thoughts tumbled through my head, the most imperative of which was what happened between us that morning.

Therefore, I opened my mouth.

"I should have thought things through…er, this morning," I declared. "Discussed those issues with a clearer head and without anger."

"Yes, you should have," he agreed.

Hmm.

"Though I'll state now we should discuss those eventually and have an understanding."

His chin tipped back but his hand at my neck moved so he could wrap his arm around my shoulders, and both arms squeezed as he muttered to the headboard, "Oh for the gods' sakes."

"I'm simply saying—"

His chin tipped down again. "I heard you. Now bloody sleep."

"But tomorrow, are we going to—?"

"Elena, you can be quiet and sleep or I'll kiss you quiet then I'll kiss you elsewhere in a way you will not be quiet, but you won't be speaking words, at least not lucidly, and after, we'll both sleep. My guess, most thoroughly."

I fell quiet.

It was then, it occurred to me I'd never lain in the arms of a man.

Well, I had, after Cassius and my activities at the fountain.

But not in a bed.

He felt good too. Solid. Warm.

Good goddess.

I was quite certain there was no way I'd find slumber, but I'd had very little of it the night before, a full day, and he was warm.

His arms were also strong, even lying abed.

I'd relaxed into him after sliding an arm around his waist (for comfort only) when he muttered, "Too bloody good."

"Sorry?" I mumbled.

"You feel."

I blinked repeatedly at his chest.

He stroked my back and I could not deny it, it felt marvelous.

"Go to sleep, my princess," he murmured.

"You're very annoying," I told him.

"As are you. The perfect match," he returned.

I sighed.

But within minutes, I fell asleep.

Not long after, Cassius followed me.

AND NOT LONG AFTER THAT, four lovers abed in each other's arms, the earth trembled.

# 41
## THE REINFORCEMENTS

**Dax Lahn**
*Residence of the Dax, Korwahn*
KORWAHK, THE SOUTHLANDS

"We have to cross the Green Sea," Circe, his beloved *Dahksahna*, was informing him.

"We will not be crossing the Green Sea," he returned.

"We really should cross the Green Sea," Queen Cora of the country of Hawkvale in The Northlands mumbled.

Lahn heard a deep sigh and turned his eyes to King Noctorno, Cora's husband, Lahn's friend, who was standing, leaning his shoulders against the wall and looking what Lahn felt.

Beleaguered.

The sun shining through the windows, they were in what Circe called their "family room."

None of them had taken a cushion on the floor. All of them were standing.

Mostly because their conversation was annoying, and it was clear the women did not intend to give in.

Which made their conversation all the more annoying.

"I'm having visions, Lahn," Circe told him something she'd told him a number of times before, once the tremors of the earth started a few months ago, getting stronger each time.

Though Circe had told him she'd felt them even before, when he had not.

However, he did not hold magic, and his wife did.

"We are not crossing the Green Sea," he reiterated, staring directly into the eyes of his queen.

"I have a bad feeling, Tor," Cora said to her husband.

"You have mentioned that, my love," Tor muttered, and when Lahn looked his way, he saw Tor spear his wife with a glance. "Repeatedly."

"Well?" Cora threw up both her hands.

"I thought bringing you down here for a visit with our friends would take your mind off things," Tor returned. "Apparently, it has not."

"Did you *feel* the quake this morning?" she demanded.

Tor had. They all had.

It meant nothing.

Or Lahn hoped to his Tiger god it meant nothing.

"And anyway, you didn't come down here just so I could hang with Circe," Cora continued, using the kind of vernacular Lahn's queen did, something none of the women from that other world had lost, even after the years slid by where they remained where they were meant to be.

In this world with the men who loved them.

"You came to trade Valerian steel for Korwahkian jewels," Cora finished.

"There was also that," Tor muttered, his lips twitching.

"Lahn," Circe said quietly, and his gaze went to his wife.

Not a single measure of beauty had she lost in all these years.

In truth, his golden queen was more beautiful today than she'd ever been.

And tomorrow, as he knew from experience, she'd be even more beautiful.

"Circe," he said quietly as well, "that voyage is treacherous, and we will not be taking it. I am sorry, *kah rahna fauna*, I simply cannot allow either of us to risk it."

"But—" she tried.

"No."

"You can't—"

He took a chance, one that rarely to never worked, and stated resolutely, "I have spoken."

It wasn't going to work this time. He knew it when her face grew hard.

"I—" she began.

She said no more as they all turned their attention when Jacanda, Circe's closest maid, came rushing in and skidded to a halt.

"I can't...you don't...you won't believe...it's fantastical..." She drew in a deep breath and cried, "*The roof!*" and then she rushed out.

All moved after her.

Lahn's and Tor's legs were longer, but that didn't mean there was not some jostling as the men tried to keep their women belowstairs while they made their way to the roof.

But when Lahn alighted at the top, he saw all of Circe's servants standing there, gaping toward the Majestic Rim of Korwahn.

He turned and looked that way as well.

Then he felt his frame grow solid and his jaw get tight.

Tor stopped beside him and muttered, "Bloody hell."

"Holy *crap*," Cora breathed.

"See?" Circe asked, and Lahn knew this was addressed to him.

Dax Lahn, the warrior king of Korwahk, drew a sharp breath into his nose as he stared at the enormous dragon sitting on the grand, rocky ledge of the Majestic Rim, its powerful tail drifting idly, its forked tongue could be seen lolling even from their distance, its scales and wings glistening in the sun.

Its message clear.

Fucking Frey.

As if noting they'd made the roof and saw it, the dragon's mighty haunches bunched, and it soared gracefully into the air, great rocks falling from the rim at the power of that beast taking flight.

With only a few flaps of its wings, it was gone from sight.

"I suppose we sail the Green Sea," he said to Tor under his breath.

"Bloody hell," Tor repeated.

～

***Frey Drakkar***
*Aboard* The Finnie, *300 Miles East of Mar-el*
THE GREEN SEA

FREY, standing on the deck of his galleon, his head tipped back, took his eyes from the dragon's approach, the beast naturally falling into formation with all the others that soared above the ship.

He turned his gaze to the man who had come to stand beside him.

"I take it that means the message has been delivered," Apollo noted, also gazing at the night sky.

"Yes," Frey confirmed.

Apollo looked to him.

"Bloody things can fly fast," he said. "Too bad we can't put Tor and Lahn on the back of one. They'd be here now."

Viktor had tried riding one of their dragons once.

Once.

"They're not fond of passengers," Frey replied.

"How much chance do you think Lahn and Tor have of convincing Circe and Cora to remain behind?"

"Are Finnie and Maddie right now in my quarters, drinking ale and playing tuble with my men?" he asked as answer.

Apollo sighed.

"None," Frey finally answered him. "None at all. The queens will be in attendance." His voice lowered. "All the women will."

The men fell silent.

Apollo broke it.

"I do not have good feelings, Frey," he said quietly.

Frey didn't either.

The Finnie had survived the swell that had caught them late last night, but barely. They'd almost capsized and took on so much water, the men had been bailing it from belowdecks all day.

He'd have his dragons, Apollo's tactical skills, Tor's significant talents with a horse and a blade and Lahn's sheer brute strength, not to mention the combined women's magic.

But he would not have the elves. They did not leave the realm of Lunwyn.

And they faced an unknown enemy that, if myth proved true, was unstoppable.

"Let's get past this first obstacle," he muttered. "We enter pirate waters."

"Fantastic," Apollo replied.

"The flag of the Drakkar holds some power, even here, and especially with the beasts above us. We'll sail past Mar-el and make Airen."

"At least there's that," Apollo said.

Yes.

At least there was that.

Frey tipped his head back to study the bulk of the beasts that flew above, blotting out the moon, the strong flapping of their wings having been the constant accompaniment of their journey.

And at least they had them.

"We were not beaten before, we will not be beaten this time," Frey declared.

"I hope you're right, Frey," Apollo returned. "I very much hope you're right."

The Finnie sailed through the waves.

The dragons flapped overhead.

And as they did, Frey hoped he was right as well.

# 42
## THE VISION

***Marian***
*Lesser Thicket Forest*
WODELL

As with the times before, it took no effort to talk her Go'En, G'Ry, into allowing Marian to "visit her sick mother."

Marian's mother was indeed sick.

In the head.

And she was thus in a way Marian never wished to see her again.

She did not even know if the woman was still alive.

Though, she hoped she was not.

Ry didn't need to know any of that, and even if she shared it, he probably wouldn't listen.

Her Go'En was a Go'Nis, a Keeper of the Records. He was elderly. Stooped. Quite bald. Spotted all over with age. And he spent his days bent over tomes, carefully recording news about Triton so that it was beautifully calligraphied (and later would be sent to a Go'Nis who drew in illustrations or ornamentation around chapters and subheadings).

He was thoughtful and quiet and preferred solitude.

He expected his Go'Ella to draw his baths, clean his clothes, tidy his cell, cook and bring him food, remove the tray after, and sometimes sit and listen when he told stories of the history of Triton or spoke the latest news he was recording.

She liked doing this. It was perfect before finding her pallet of an eve. After Ry did this, she went right to sleep.

He wasn't like her former Go'En, a Go'Tec who thought his shite smelled of gardenias.

It did not, and she knew this because she oft found herself with the duty of cleaning his privy.

This if she did not suck his cock precisely to his liking. Or did not moan as he desired and share how virile and handsome he was (he was neither) while he pumped away at her.

Not terribly sadly, her former Go'En had come to an untimely demise. The other Go'En were still scratching their heads about it. A thirty-nine-year-old high priest simply slumping over his breakfast one morning, dead.

For Marian, it had taken months of poisoning his wine, small doses of concentrated *taibac* that she steadily increased so he'd get used to the flavor, and then finally, his heart stopped.

That had been a good day.

Not simply because he was gone, a fact that was good enough on its own, but because she, as with her fellow Go'Ella who served him, went to the cloisters for three months of solitude to "grieve."

That had been the best three months of her life.

Serving Ry was not terrible.

It was just that her time was not her own. Her actions hers to decide. When she would sleep, eat, bathe, what she would read, having time to teach herself the things she needed to know instead of catching snatches to herself and away from her fellow Go'Ella to perform her rituals and test her instincts.

Idyllic.

So much so, she considered killing Ry as well.

However, she suspected questions would be asked as she was his only Go'Ella who'd also served the other one.

Regardless, G'Ry was seventy-two years old. Time would do that duty, and likely not take much of it.

There was also the fact she'd grown rather fond of him.

Though, none of that mattered any longer.

The quakes were occurring and Ry had been decidedly loquacious about those.

And as he was dedicated to the act of recording history, he had an active interest in the subject. So when Marian asked questions, no matter how many, he answered.

At length.

And when Marian asked to read the tomes about the Beast, he'd been surprised, but he'd readily, even giddily procured them for her.

Often, he'd have to wait, as others were poring over them to try to understand the tremors.

But as Ry shared he would be doing that too, they'd handed them over with little complaint, and she, and he, had pored over them as well, spending quite some time doing this and discussing what they thought about it.

So she knew.

She knew everything.

Which meant many months ago, her mother suddenly became most poorly, necessitating Marian request a leave of absence to go visit her in order to tend her.

These visits happened regularly.

After the quakes.

Ry did not put this together.

G'Fenn, who was too clever for his own good, and too prying, as well as far too interfering, had asked some questions when he'd been visiting Ry on an eve that was an eve after a similar eve G'Fenn had been visiting, which was prior to her leaving in the morn to visit her mother.

Directly after a quake.

But Ry had shooed off his queries and did so with rather an unusual vigor.

Then again, no Go'Doan priest liked when another questioned what he did with his Go'Ella.

Apparently, Ry was no different.

It was actually unusual for any priest that he let her go without an escort...or at all.

In one of the very few fortunate occurrences in her entire life, Marian had a Go'En who did not question her request. He simply granted it.

It was even more fortunate now.

In this time of greatness.

Marian read this as what the visions she was seeing in her meditations and bowl readings and colorful dreams were telling her.

It was all coming together.

Her destiny.

So now she was riding swiftly after stopping at a brothel for a rubbing of her back, neck and shoulders and a hot scented bath then taking a nice meal at her leisure in a pub (Ry was also generous with his travel tithe, though Marian preferred to think of it as it actually was: him paying her for her bloody service, something no Go'Ella received).

She needed to be there in the night and the Ancient Ritual Ground was close to Go'Doan, less than a full day's ride away.

But after she spent the part of the day she'd have to spend waiting for the night if she got there too early (she'd learned that right away), she took the route quickly for the ride was rife with concerns.

This was partly due to the fact it was also close to the edge of The Enchantments, and there were all manner of men who regularly journeyed there for whatever purpose they got in their heads to go.

Over two hundred years, and not a one of them got in.

Men did not learn speedily. In some aspects it took centuries.

Even millennia.

Not to mention there were Zees.

Marian had no squabble with the Zees. She understood them traveling in their bright caravans, keeping themselves to themselves and very much not liking when anyone poked their nose in their business.

The problem was, they were known to set upon travelers. They didn't tend to harm them, just steal their possessions, including their horses.

And Marian needed her horse to get to the Ritual Grounds and then get back to Go'Doan. Ry could be downright fatherly when his mind was turned from his writings. If he knew Marian had been harassed by Zees, he might demand a G'Tish accompany her.

And that would not do.

She set her sights on her destination, settling the small dagger she had more firmly in her belt.

The pixies were out, their zip and buzz could be seen all through the dark of the trees with a light like a firefly's, except far less leisurely and they were lit constant. That was, when they were in motion. When they landed on something, their light dulled.

They'd soon be fewer and fewer. They disliked the cold, but more, the trees when they were naked of their leaves. They'd forage for food and go to share with others of their kind. But they would not dash and soar for flying's sake in abundance as they did in the summer.

And it was growing cold.

The next quake (which she hoped would come sooner, and not be delayed as the last, something that had alarmed her greatly), instead of the light cloak she now wore, she'd need fur robes to keep her warm.

Wodell had a wet chill that seeped into the bones in the autumn and winter (and a good part of the spring, especially up north). Something, as she'd come from the north, she was glad to see the back of when she made the mistake-slash-blessing of leaving behind her cruel mother, her often-times vexing profession of a prostitute, and going where many of her ilk went when there was no other choice.

Go'Doan.

It could get cold in the Dome City as well. But not near as cold as the north of Wodell. Not to mention, Ry kept the fire in his Go'Ella's cell blazing.

Marian rode on, thinking of this and deciding, when she met her destiny, she would be kind to G'Ry, as he had been to her.

And she was nearing. She knew it by her location but also by the quickening.

She'd need no fur robes as she got closer.

No.

And she sensed all would happen soon. After the power of the last quake, and that plaintive cry, it could be nothing else.

She finally reached her destination and her skin felt flush all over to the point it was heated.

And thus, she wasted no time in doing as she'd done the many times before, first divesting herself of the Dellish garments that Ry insisted she wear for her own protection when she left Go'Doan.

She also wasted no time, wearing nothing but her white Go'Ella sheer, in laying herself upon the ground.

She did this on her back with arms over her head and legs spread wide.

Like all the others.

Without the tethers.

Marian smelled the blood. The sweat. Centuries of it permeating the dirt.

But some of it was so very fresh.

She closed her eyes as saliva filled her mouth at sensing the struggle. The cries. The pleadings. The sobs. The eventual despair and capitulation. The prolonged death. Sensing it so strongly, with each passing moment that sensation growing to the point she could hear the cries and see the struggles...

And watch the death.

She would find them.

Oh, she would.

She would *find them all* and the things she'd do.

The things *they* would do.

It came, not as normal—a hum, like a lullaby, soothing her mind and soul, but further heating her skin.

Instead, it was a small trembling, not the likes of what was felt in the beginning of the quakes.

Something different.

Something Marian fancied was not about her destiny.

Or perhaps it was.

Something she did not like in the slightest.

That trembling came and was gone so fast, it was almost like it did not happen at all.

And then...

Nothing.

Moments fell into minutes and more and more of them ticked by and there was still nothing.

No hum.

No lullaby.

As she waited even longer, she grew concerned.

Was he angry at her?

On this thought, suddenly, she cried out as she found her waist captured in a strong grip on either side.

This hold coming from below.

But by what?

She could not then find an answer to that question as she was instead finding herself drawing dirt into her throat instead of air.

She closed her mouth, her eyes, as she went down when there was no down to go.

But she was going.

Down, into the earth, the roots of trees scraping her flesh.

Down deeper, her lungs beginning to burn at holding her breath, her eyes shut tight, her lips drawn in and pressed together by her teeth to keep her mouth closed and not scream in terror.

She did not writhe in the hold on her. She had far more prevalent concerns. And they weren't simply that she could not breathe.

Primarily, the weight of the dirt on top of her the deeper she fell—or was *pulled*—was bearing greatly on her.

Like it would crush her bones.

Crush her entire body.

And then she was in free fall and she did cry out, spluttering and spitting out dirt as her body was jarred with a landing.

However, she did not fall to the ground.

She was being held.

Held to...

She shook the dirt from her face, turned her head, opened her eyes and abruptly found herself on her feet as the creature before her took two steps back.

He was very tall.

Lean of frame, but broad of shoulder.

He had golden hair and bright blue eyes.

Winged dark brows and pleasing angular features.

Like her visions.

Just like her dreams.

That gilt head bent, and his voice rumbled forth toward her.

"*Patrona*."

Marian's skin came alive.

"*Me Brutum*," she whispered.

He lifted his head and stared directly at her.

Her vision.

Her dream.

Her destiny.

*Her Beast.*

Yes.

It was happening.

# 43

## THE SETBACK

***The Priest***
*Ancient Ritual Ground, Lesser Thicket Forest*
*Wodell*

He had to join them via the astral plane.

Which he did.

When he arrived, he saw the others were not happy.

They couldn't possibly know it was he who killed one of their own.

"You are most lucky you're not actually you," his least favorite spat the moment the priest took astral form.

They knew.

"Beware, my brother," the priest warned.

"Beware?" the man asked, throwing both of his arms wide in fury. "Beware of you setting a Firenz asp on me? Do you think we were foolish enough not to have consumed the antidote every morn since we heard how Rupert expired?"

Less clever brothers should have been chosen.

"The news is everywhere," another of the men joined in. "We must cease. We shouldn't even be here. If anyone deduced what we've deduced," he indicted the two men at his side with a hand, "investigators from four realms will be set upon us and the Go'Doan won't keep their noses out of it. With but a few tomes reviewed, at the very least, this sacred site will be breached. *You* know that best of all, being a bloody Go'Doan yourself."

"You can't possibly imagine my brothers in the Go'Doan haven't been poring over those tomes already and yet, we have not been discovered," the priest noted.

"That was *before* the Beast roared in conjunction with three people in two different realms losing their lives in the same but uncommon way," the second man returned.

"No one will put it together," the priest assured.

"The night of the mightiest quake where a roar could be heard across Triton, a life was taken at the king's palace in Firenze, and within hours, a member of Airen's landed gentry dies the same way, an *unusual* way, especially considering a Firenz asp, a creature that doesn't leave the sand, was the result of all the slayings," his least favorite summed things up snidely. "You don't think anyone will put that together?"

"Why did you kill the woman at the palace?" the third man asked.

The priest couldn't tell them he'd made a mistake. He'd meant to kill the betrothed of Prince True. He'd meant to put an end to the prophecy before it began.

Learning that he'd failed, after he'd seen to the death of his Rupert and Rupert's slut, was equally bad news that sorry day some weeks before. A day that should have been joyous.

"It was not me," he lied.

"Bullshite," his least favorite bit. "What are you playing at?" he demanded. "That mess and now we cannot perform rituals, we don't have the men, and furthermore, we have to lie low in case anyone adds Rupert to that Firenz woman to the Beast and gets *us*. But before that, you demanded we reduce our rituals, when we should have bloody doubled them, and then you rode to Firenze to quell some magical prophecy we've never bloody heard of so we couldn't even perform them at all."

"It wasn't only that. I'm part of a diplomatic envoy," the priest spat. "I couldn't demur. History is being made. It would be suspect if I declined. Especially as the Go'Doan know *why* history is being made with these marital alliances. We will resume our rituals, on schedule, once we recruit a new brother."

"Why is Rupert dead?" the third man asked.

"We will recruit another brother," the priest repeated.

"You didn't answer my question," the man returned. "Why is Rupert gone?"

Before the priest could answer, his nemesis did it for him. "Because he was fucking some wench and not fisting his own cock with thoughts of that one's," he jerked his head toward the priest, "arse." The man looked to him. "They were found together, naked, after intercourse. You caught him with a woman. And in a fit of jealousy, you killed them both."

"It doesn't matter," the priest muttered.

"You killed one of *us*," the man retorted. "It *does* matter."

"I don't answer to you," the priest clipped.

"We don't answer to you either," the man fired back.

The second man joined in, stating, "You realize, Rupert was loyal to you."

The priest had no response for he had seen with his own eyes he was *not*.

"We do not like you," the first said. "We don't trust you. The only reason we put up with you was because Rupert had great things to say about your magic. Because he told us, without you, it would not be in our generation that the Beast was roused. If it were not for Rupert, it would be *you* who would no longer have the ability to perform the rituals."

"You threaten me?" the priest whispered.

The man shook his head. "You find a man. You train a man. *Not* one you want to fuck. One who will get the job done. And we all renew our vows and the rituals begin again, no. If you do none of these things..."

He didn't finish.

And yes.

It was a threat.

The priest did not like to be threatened.

"I am currently on my way to Notting Thicket for Prince True's wedding," the priest sniffed.

"You better find your way to get your arse *here*," the second man demanded. "If you don't, we'll carry on without you."

"The Beast does not rouse for you," the priest snapped. "As you know, the rituals must go on as prescribed or they're meaningless."

"Would you like to test that?" the third man queried.

The priest looked amongst them.

He needed them.

He needed all of them.

He could not recruit *four* men. Not do that and retain his guise as a Go'Doan emissary.

And if they all fell prey to some "accident," how would he explain that to the Society?

He needed them until he was free to replace them.

All of them.

"I've received a missive from the Society," he said. "They know of Rupert's demise and they've informed me they've planned for such an occurrence. There is one always ready to join our ranks. I will dispatch a message to them and have him brought to me. I will interview him. If he's suitable, I will train him, I will bring him to you and I will come with him."

"And what if *we* don't find him suitable?" the second man asked.

"You will," the priest gritted.

"And how long will this take?" the first man inquired.

"The ride from Notting Thicket to the Ritual Ground is but a week. We've been delayed in leaving Firenze due to the death of that woman and the ostentatious ceremony King Mars bestowed on her. And the King of Mar-el demanded a further delay as he, for some reason, must take his wife and men to the sea. In other words, there is an interruption in the prophecy fulfilling itself. With our setback, we've been granted a boon."

"Without our setback, and this delay, the Beast might be here already, and Triton would be ours," his antagonist noted.

The priest said nothing.

"Fix it," the man hissed.

"It will be done," the priest returned haughtily, and before they could annoy him more, he returned across the astral plane to his physical form in the forest of southern Wodell, sitting atop his pentagram drawn in the dirt, the candles about him in a circle lit.

He extinguished them immediately. He was not near to the camp. He was also not far enough for his liking. He'd taken a chance lighting them. Now that he was safely back, he could risk it no longer.

And he sat in the dark, staring into the shadowy trees, giving the wax in the chilly clime time to harden so he could gather his implements, and he did this trying to keep his thoughts calm.

"This is but a setback," he eventually murmured and stood, reclaiming the candles and putting them in his sack.

He used his foot to erase the pentagram.

"Just a setback," he decreed.

With that, he made his way back to camp.

# 44
# THE INCOMPLETE CIRCLE

***The Great Coven***
*Silbury Henge, Argyll Forest*
AIREN

In the clearing of the forest, the first flash of light came before the first of the five standing stones.

The light was green.

The next came and it was marine blue.

The next was bright white.

And the next was crimson.

"We must—" Rebecca, the most powerful witch of Wodell started speaking urgently.

Nandra of Firenze interrupted her. "Not until we're all here."

"We must speak of Ophelia," Rebecca stated stubbornly.

"She is right," Lena of Mar-el agreed.

Fern of Airen drew breath into her nose but said nothing.

"I feel the veil absorbing her," Rebecca declared.

Nandra stared at her fellow witch.

Lena looked to the ground.

Fern drew in both her lips and bore down on them with her teeth.

"And all of you feel it too," Rebecca accused.

"There is naught we can do about it," Nandra said.

"As much as I hate to say this about my sister, my friend, a woman I respect greatly, she must be replaced. This is a burden on her," Rebecca told the coven. "And times are rife. We need this circle to be complete."

"'Tis true, our power is reduced if but one of us is not at her best," Fern said quietly. "And in this time especially, we need this circle at full strength."

"And who would you have replace her?" Nandra demanded to know. "Serena is a menace and Elena is caught up in the prophecy."

"Melisse," Rebecca stated.

Fern looked away.

Lena caught the movement and noted, "Melisse is an excellent suggestion."

Fern took her time looking back at her sisters before she admitted, "I've had a vision."

"Oh goddess," Nandra murmured.

"What vision?" Lena inquired.

"It is not good for...Melisse," Fern told them.

"Are you mad?" Nandra snapped.

Fern straightened her shoulders and Rebecca retorted, "Nandra. Calm down."

Nandra didn't calm. "When did you have this vision?"

"Not long ago," Fern shared.

"Unless it was fifteen minutes ago, it was too long not to inform the rest of us. Does she perish?" Nandra asked.

Fern shook her head. "It's murky."

"Of course," Lena mumbled.

"I cannot make a vision sharper if it doesn't want to come in that manner," Fern bit at Lena. "And you know this for you can't either."

"What was the vision?" Rebecca queried.

"There is great danger in Wodell for the Nadirii," Fern informed them. "Particularly Melisse."

"This doesn't surprise me. She's too clever and even-minded for her own good. It is always those who find grave ends," Nandra muttered.

"She must be warned," Lena stated.

"We'll tell Ophelia when she arrives," Rebecca replied.

"And Elena?" Nandra asked Fern.

Fern shook her head. "All those prophesied are shadowed. But I have a sense there is another."

"Another?" Lena inquired. "Another what?"

"Another threat."

"Wonderful," Nandra murmured. "And you didn't share this either."

"I've tried, but I cannot lock on it," Fern told them. "So there was naught to share. It is simply a feeling, not a vision."

"You must keep trying," Rebecca urged her fellow witch.

"Of course," Fern agreed and looked amongst them. "Have any of you felt it?"

All shook their heads.

"I wonder why it is only me," Fern said, as if to herself.

"Let us hope we don't discover the answer to that after it's too late," Nandra replied.

No one said anything further.

And because of this, they came to realize that some time after their appointed arrival had passed and Ophelia was still not there.

"Do you—?" Fern began.

"I will seek her," Rebecca stated, and moving to a standing stone, she touched it, and in a flash of green, she disappeared.

The others shuffled around uncomfortably.

But in little time at all, Rebecca had returned.

Her face was pale in the moonlight.

"Ophelia won't be joining us," she said quietly.

"Bloody hell," Lena whispered.

"How bad?" Nandra asked, her eyes sharp on the Dellish sorceress.

"She travels back to The Enchantments," Rebecca answered. "It is onerous, and the visit to Firenze was vigorous, thus she is weak. Once she arrives home, it will be good for her to be in the lap of magic and sisterhood. She'll be home in a week. We'll reconvene a week after."

"We need a replacement," Lena said softly.

"My king asked me to remain behind to assist his captain and provide magical aid if needed due to concerns after the attack on the palace. Rebecca can ride out to meet the travelers and there, talk to Melisse who rides with them," Nandra noted, then looked to the Airenzian witch. "Fern, you must join her in order to add your power."

"I don't have leave of my king to travel from Airen," Fern reminded her.

"How a powerful witch needs bloody leave from a king, I cannot understand," Nandra snarled.

"I have magic, but I still need breath in my body in order to use it, and a noose hinders that," Fern spat back.

"We must not quarrel amongst ourselves," Rebecca said quickly.

Nandra ignored her and instructed Fern, "Spirit away if they should try to detain you."

"And spirit where?" Fern demanded. "Wodell, where, if found, they will return me on demand? Mar-el, who do not abide strangers very well? The Dome City, where, if I ask for asylum, I might be pressed into being an acolyte? Or Firenze, who is on the verge of war with just about everybody, including themselves, at any moment."

"The Enchantments, of course," Nandra retorted.

"And how do I help my people from The Enchantments, Nandra?" Fern asked. "There is not much I can do, but what I can do, I do it, and it is needed. A little, in a land where there is not much for the sisterhood, is a lot. I toe a line in the Airenzian soil that has not been drawn in your sand and I do it with a purpose. You are not in a position to judge for you know nothing of this. I'm glad of it for you. But in return, it would be nice, if you can't understand, you can at least empathize."

Nandra made no response.

Rebecca changed the subject.

"I will speak with Melisse. But for now, without a complete circle, there is naught we can do. We will meet again soon."

"There is naught we could do even if we had a complete circle. What is taking these warriors and their women so long?" Nandra demanded to know. "It is far from hard to copulate."

"Matters of the heart are never easy," Rebecca returned.

"I fight the instinct every day to slip each one of them a love potion," Nandra muttered.

"Do not do that!" three witches stated sharply.

"It must be natural, organic," Lena remonstrated.

Nandra sighed deeply for she knew this too well.

"We have felt it in the veil, there is promise," Lena reminded them.

They had felt it.

There was promise.

What they could not know, was if it would come to fruition.

And if it did...

If it would be enough.

# 45
## THE GAME

**Queen Silence**
*Fifty Miles Inside the Southern Border*
WODELL

I stood in the opened flap of the large red tent I shared with my husband and I looked to the top of the swell of the moor where Mars stood with Farah.

His dark, handsome head was bent to her.

It was night, and although there were many torches around the expansive camp, the distance and the lack of light hid his expression from me.

But he stood very close to her, had his arm about her waist, and that spoke volumes.

My husband had spent a good deal of time with Farah during our journey.

Not to mention, he did the same before it, when we remained in Firenze as the death ceremony for Farah's mother, Sofia, was being arranged and then carried out.

I knew they were close. She had been sitting at his side on a stack of cushions beside his throne the first moment I laid eyes on him. Their manner to each other spoke of it as well.

However, I was wondering at this closeness now for it did not seem simply close.

It seemed *close*.

And as was the Firenz way, a man could have a wife and be very, *very* close to another woman.

Indeed, as close as he could get.

I felt a presence at my side, thus I turned my head and looked up.

Kyril, one of Mars's Trusted, one of *my* Trusted, our personal guard, stood beside me.

I had found, on our journey, and even before that Kyril was most often the one who was nearest to me.

I did not know if this was of my husband's design, or happenstance.

I also did not ask.

I was just glad of it.

Kyril was the youngest of the Trusted and the most jovial. I liked them all. But I felt an affinity with Kyril.

"I'm not sure how my king will get to know my queen better, he on the rise with his childhood playmate, you skulking at the folds of your tent," Kyril noted, his eyes, too, on the swell of the moor.

"I'm not skulking," I retorted.

He looked down at me, but said nothing.

"I was refreshing myself after our journey," I told him.

"We ceased moving two hours ago, and in between time, had dinner, which I will note, you took with Elena and Melisse, not your husband."

I huffed and looked away in order to stare off into the distance.

"My queen—"

"Silence!" my father's voice interrupted whatever Kyril was about to say and I felt my guard tense at my side as I turned my attention in my sire's direction. "Come, sit with your mother and me in our tent for an evening sherry."

I detested sherry.

"Heed my words, do not be in that tent when your husband returns, my queen," Kyril said under his breath.

I looked to the rise of the moor.

The light was poor.

I could still see Farah was now fully in my husband's arms.

She was betrothed to another. When we were but betrothed, Mars wouldn't allow my own cousin to hold my hand, much less embrace me.

But he had no issue, in front of the whole camp, which included Farah's intended, and Mars's *wife* (that being *me*), holding her *in his arms*.

I looked again to where my father was standing, waiting for an answer.

"I'll be there in a moment," I called.

He smiled, nodded and moved toward his and my mother's tent while I listened to Kyril emit a grunt of displeasure.

I tipped my head back to catch his gaze. "If my husband returns, please tell him I'm with my mother and father."

"I'm escorting you there, my queen," he replied.

"It's three tents away and we're surrounded by Dellish, Airenzian and Firenz soldiers. I'm quite safe to wander three tents down the line."

"I'm...*escorting*...you there, my queen," he repeated, mush less patiently this time, and the last time had not been all that patient.

I made a move to proceed, murmuring, "Then let us go."

"You should leave word with someone where you are so they can tell our king when he arrives," Kyril instructed.

I stopped and again looked to him. "You know where I'll be. You can tell him. And if my husband wishes to find me, he can seek me."

"I will not be leaving you," he reminded me.

This was true. He was my escort often and when he was done escorting me somewhere, he didn't go off to play a game of tuble.

His tone was much changed—quieter, softer—when he went on to advise, "Don't play these games, Silence."

"I'm not playing any games," I denied.

"You are."

"I am not. I'm having a sherry with my parents. We do that in Wodell, and as you know, we're now in Wodell. Sherry or brandy or port. Though I prefer a wee dram of Benedictine."

Kyril glowered down at me.

"My mother and father are waiting," I prompted.

"He tires of this distance, my queen. You do not know him well. He's very taken with you and thus has been courting you. But I advise you not to test him."

This was not news to me.

Since our wedding night some weeks prior, a night when Mars was very thoughtful and allowed me to rest after an intensely trying time, rather than expecting me to consummate our marriage, things that had been very promising between my new husband and I had deteriorated.

And of late, Mars was letting it be known that he was not fond of it.

This was, I would admit only to myself, my doing.

For Kyril was right, I did not know Mars very well.

However, what I did know was that he was indeed taken with me and he could be very affectionate and loving.

He could also be vicious and ruthless.

He had not been these things to me, but I'd witnessed them as he'd tortured and taken men's lives, in battle and by executing them.

I had spoken to no one of what I'd seen and how it made me feel.

I was now queen.

Queen of a land where traitors were put to death without trial.

*Tortured* and put to death.

My dreams were filled of these things. Remembering them and conjuring new images.

These new images included Mars torturing my father.

Mars torturing my friend and maid, Estrilda.

Mars torturing *me*.

This meant I woke with a start, with heart racing and skin chilled.

This I kept to myself as well, though my husband knew as I slept in his arms every night.

It was just that he had quit asking about it and cooing me back to sleep when I said it was naught but anxiety after the attack and the last quake made by the Beast.

He now, I suspected, knew it was more.

He just tired of attempting to make me talk about it.

A queen kept her chin raised, her eyes steady, her feelings hidden. I knew. I had been watching my Aunt Mercy, Queen of Wodell, and Elpis, Mars's mother, Queen of Firenze, since it occurred to me my present might include a new husband and whatever my part was in the prophecy to defeat the Beast.

But my future and the rest of my existence included being queen.

Queens did not get squeamish.

Queens did not complain.

Queens did not have nightmares that they brought into the day.

Queens were smart, quiet, and most of all, they carried on.

I would some day, I knew, need to come to terms with this in some manner and find my way to accept my husband as he was in our lives, as my ruler, and in our bed.

It was just that now I was finding ways to...delay that.

And it must be said that as the days passed, and his attention did not divert from Farah even as it was clear True was quite determined to be the strong shoulder for her to lean on in this time of grief, this did not help matters.

For my husband was not mine.

He was not my king (not really, I was Dellish, though officially that had changed, I'd never *not* be Dellish even if I was Queen of Firenze).

And he had been forced to wed me.

He did not select me. He did not fall in love with me.

But even if he had, he would not ever truly be my husband.

Not after, as he said we would, we took others to our bed.

This meant I had to share him in all ways.

And I did not wish to do this.

I didn't consider it selfish to chafe at this.

The matter of him being king obviously was not at issue. What he did at the necropolis in Firenze was something I had to come to rights with in my head...somehow.

But sharing *my husband*?

I wasn't sure I could come to terms with that.

Though I had to do that too.

Because it was the Firenz way.

And I might not be of Firenze.

But I was their queen.

I just needed time in order to do it.

And my mother and father, Elena, her mentor Melisse, Tril, my pet monkey, Piccola, and any number of other things I could latch onto were giving me ample opportunity to give myself that time.

Like now.

"I told my father I would attend him," I prompted. "We must go."

Kyril stared at me for some time before he sighed.

He then looked right, caught someone's attention and called, "Our queen is having a drink with her parents."

I looked in that direction and saw Basil, another of our Trusted, nod.

He appeared disapproving too.

I really didn't know what to say.

If I told them their ways were foreign to me, foreign and alarming and perhaps even abhorrent (in the case of torture and execution) and harmful (in the case of open infidelity in marriage), it would be insulting.

These people and these ways were of what was now my land, my people.

And I had to find it in me to live with it.

~

"You stayed too long," Kyril muttered two hours later (all right, perhaps two and three quarters of an hour later), as we made our way back to the royal tent.

I did not think we stayed too long.

I had a rather lively, and shockingly interesting, discussion with my father during those two hours.

We disagreed over our liking of a book.

I liked it.

He did not.

However, in the end, I believed I swayed his thinking for he'd told me he would reread it with what I'd said in mind and we'd discuss it again.

I had never, not in my life, had a lively or interesting tête-à-tête with my father.

I had never, not in my life, swayed my father's thinking.

And thus, I thought it'd been a rather pleasant night.

But regardless, no matter how petulant it might sound, my husband knew precisely where we were in those hours.

Therefore, if he wished my company, he could have had it.

"I'm most tired, Kyril," I replied. "Can we not have another disagreement?"

"I will grant you that, my queen," he returned. "For you're fatigued, so what energy you have, you'll need for my king."

I twisted my neck to look up at him to see his eyes aimed in the direction of the royal tent.

I aimed my eyes there as well, in time to see my husband disappearing around the corner toward the entry flaps that were hidden from my current vantage point.

Had he been coming to get me?

My heart jumped.

When we arrived at the tent, Kyril preceded me, pulled open the flap, peered inside but a scant second, then turned to me.

He made a small bow and instead of wishing me a good eve, he murmured, "Good luck."

I did not think that boded well.

I moved through the flap Kyril still held open.

I was correct.

That did not bode well.

I stopped several feet in and heard the tent flap swish closed behind me.

"Husband," I said tremulously to the large, dark man standing in the middle of our enormous tent.

A tent where the inside fabric was patterned in golds and greens against the reds, the ground covered in silk rugs and scattered with cushions, the soft mattress on which we slept placed on a platform and ensconced in red and gold sheers hanging from poles. Said bed was also strewn with silks, velvets, hides and patterned pillows.

There were even potted plants.

This was set up every night.

In fact, the servants' caravan with tents and accoutrements left hours before the rest of us did as we finished up breakfast under the late-rising sun and dallied to our horses so they could be at our destination prior to us arriving in order that we could immediately refresh and rest in luxury.

This was not the Dellish way. In a caravan, we all rode together. And when the party stopped, the gentry sat atop blankets and had a wine or some cool tea to refresh while the servants saw to diner and accommodations, which were not nearly this elaborate.

It was the Firenz way, where sumptuousness and extravagance and indulgence were priority and servants existed to see to that priority without fail.

"Ah," Mars spoke. "This heartens me. You remember who I am."

"Of course I do," I said softly.

"Mm," was his only reply as he stood, unmoving, his arms crossed over the sand-colored leathers on his wide chest, his black gaze locked on me irritably.

Even if he did look every bit what he was known as, a barbarian king, I gathered my courage.

For I knew he was also Mars.

I just had to settle into how he was both and neither belonged to me.

"Did Basil not tell you?" I asked. "I was with Mother and Father, enjoying a drink."

"Basil shared your whereabouts," he confirmed.

"Well, I, erm..."

I knew not what else to say.

I also knew I couldn't get to bed because, first, he was barring my path, and second, he was in the tent so Tril couldn't attend me to help me change clothes in order to sleep.

That gave me something to say.

"Has Tril been 'round?"

"Indeed," Mars answered. "I sent her to her pallet."

I blinked at my husband. "But I need her assistance with preparing for bed."

"If you need your laces loosened, Silence, my fingers work."

Oh *balls*.

"We...you and I usually—" I stammered.

"I have given you that, yes," he interrupted me to say. "I felt you needed time to get used to your husband and the closeness we will share throughout our lives together. Thus, I have absented myself while your maid helps you prepare for bed. However, as I'll be seeing you out of your clothes, as well as in them, and doing this with great frequency during our years of marriage, there's no reason when you're late to bed that your maid must remain awake when I can help you out of them."

I swallowed.

"Are you ready for bed, Silence?" Mars asked with faux courtesy.

"I feel like I need more time, Mars," I told him carefully.

He took but a second to think on this before he jerked up his bearded chin in assent.

I was about to sigh with relief, though even considering that, I wasn't sure I felt relief for it seemed with that gesture my husband was quite all right to continue this distance from me.

However, he didn't wait even a second to speak again.

"Before I leave to allow you to send for Tril, I'll share that Basil will replace Kyril as your personal guard. You'll be in Kyril's presence only when you're with me."

I felt my lips part in surprise and not because I now understood that Kyril had been assigned to me, something my husband had not openly shared with me.

No, because he'd given me Kyril.

And now he was taking him away.

Mars continued talking.

"You will also limit any time you spend with your father to time when I can attend him with you."

What?

"But...why?" My question came as a shocked whisper.

"Your father uses you for some purpose I have yet to understand. Until I understand it, I will be at your side when you're with him."

"We were talking about books," I told him.

"Of course you were," he murmured.

"What does that mean?" I asked.

He didn't explain what it meant.

He stated, "It will be done, my queen."

I closed my mouth.

He started toward the tent flaps, and as I was directly in his path and he clearly did not wish to adjust his course in order not to run into me, I scooted out of his way.

He stopped and turned again to me before exiting the tent.

"You were conscious during the piercing ceremony, no?" he asked oddly.

"Y-yes," I answered.

"And it was spoken in your language," he noted.

I nodded.

"You told me you were moved by it."

"I was," I whispered.

"I'm curious. What, my new wife, moved you?"

"I, well..."

I stared at him.

He didn't look curious.

He looked annoyed.

He was a king.

He was also my husband.

And I had to remember, I was his wife.

But I also was a queen.

*His* queen.

I lifted my chin and finished, "All of it."

"There are two piercings in the ear for a reason, Silence," he retorted.

I felt my body give an involuntary twitch as his meaning dawned on me.

He carried on, "You do not sleep well. You avoid my presence. My intended was lush and hot and wet in my arms and in my bed when my mouth and hands were on her. My wife is remote and prefers the company of her guard and her father. The latter of whom treated her with callous neglect the entirety of her life but is now her chosen companion."

"Mars—"

"Forcing my body on yours does not appeal," he continued, and I clamped my mouth shut for I'd never entertained the idea he would do as such and was shocked that he had. "I also cannot force you to speak. I have made it more than clear I will listen to whatever it is that has taken you from me. You've denied me that privilege. I will not beg."

I didn't want him to beg.

I wanted what I could not have.

I wanted to go back to how we were when we first met when he was but a beautiful man who made me feel beautiful too for the first time in my life and the promise of *us* was and always would be just...*us*.

"Now," he kept speaking, "I must consider my options. In considering these, I've realized those options are limited, which is something I do not like. But I will need to select one, and as matters as they are between us are vexing, I'll need to do that in short order. In the meantime, I'll protect you as best I can, by limiting your time with your father. And I'll protect our marriage, such as it is, by limiting your time with Kyril."

"Kyril is just a friend," I shared.

"Kyril is not your friend," he retorted. "He is a Trusted One. His life is yours. But more, his life is *mine*. Do not misconstrue who he is to you, Silence. He is your guard and I'll allow a rapport. If I do not like where that goes, he will cease being one of the premier soldiers of his realm and will spend the rest of his enlistment cleaning latrines."

I gasped.

Mars had one response to my stunned surprise.

He turned his back to me, slapped the tent open and strode out.

I stood, watching the flap settle into place, feeling a heat in my eyes and a prickle in my throat.

Now, in a way, my husband was taking my father from me and I felt not a vague sense of alarm for my father had made mention Mars intended to do just that.

And Kyril, who I felt was becoming a friend, was for all intents and purposes lost to me too.

I had few friends and Mars knew that.

It just seemed now, in a kingly pique, he did not care.

On our wedding night, he had told me he wanted to fill my life with laughter.

He was failing spectacularly at that and doing so without much of an effort to succeed.

And for all those reasons, and a number more, I felt like weeping.

However, I could not do that.

I was queen.

Queens did not weep.

Queens carried on.

And sadly, this made me need to weep all the more.

I did not do that.

I went to the tent flap, peeked out and saw Basil there.

I asked him to send for Tril.

I needed to prepare for bed in order to attempt to sleep in preparation for taking on another day as wife of Mars Laches.

But mostly as Queen of Firenze.

~

I HAD LEFT the lamps glowing on the squat tables on either side of our bed for Mars's return.

But I was abed, in my nightgown, one that Tril brought with a stubbornness that was disquieting, which meant it was one Tril refused to go back to my trunk in her tent to exchange for another that was more to my liking.

Not that I didn't like it. It was beautiful.

A bodice made entirely of lace (and thus you could see through it, not completely, but you didn't have to look hard get a clear-ish picture) with a skirt that fell to my knees, was somewhat sheer, but provided full coverage. That was, it did in the sense of material. The slits at the front of either leg went all the way up to some satin bows at the edge of the lace at either hip, and they exposed a good deal.

If I moved, that good deal was *everything*.

It was mauve.

The color complimented my skin.

It was nothing of the like I'd ever worn before I was married.

The lace was a bit scratchy so it wasn't all that comfortable.

And it was an invitation I did not want to give.

Tril, who was less patient with the distance growing between Mars and I than Kyril was, essentially demanded her queen wear it.

However, for Tril, I was not queen.

I was instead, and always would be, Silence. Tril was my only true friend and had been the only one I could faithfully count on my entire life.

Thus, half fearing Mars would return before we were done, and half not wanting to have an argument with another being who meant something to me, I'd donned it.

And wearing it, I had one more obstacle to climb before being able to go to sleep so I could be refreshed to take on whatever came on the morrow.

That obstacle had arrived, I knew, when I heard the tent flap open.

I lay in bed, my back to Mars's side, and I did it with my entire body tense.

I heard him moving about. I heard his leathers drop to the rugs. I heard the swish of him pulling on the silks he slept in. And finally, I felt the mattress shift as he laid his great bulk on it.

Only then did I brace to face what was next.

What always happened right before we went to bed. What I both looked forward to with wistfulness for what I'd hoped it could be but never would, and I dreaded because it never would be what I needed it to be.

My husband and I taking off each other's marital chains.

To do this, I sat up, twisted and looked to Mars.

He was in bed, but twisted as well, to the lantern, exposing his broad, brown-skinned, muscled back to me. He appeared as if he intended to blow the lamp out.

The fastenings were small on our chains, I needed the light to release his, as he would need it to release mine as well.

"Mars," I called.

Before blowing out the light, he turned his head to me.

His chain was gone.

I stared at him.

He'd taken off his chain.

*My* chain.

*Our* chain.

And he'd done it himself.

We had grown distant, but every night, like he'd said we would, my husband took the chain he gave me, and I, his wife, took his.

And as that was all I really had of him, something no other would have, not ever, it meant a great deal to me.

I had no idea why, but his chain being gone was too much.

I couldn't...

"Of course," I whispered and turned my head away, lifting my hands that felt peculiarly like they weighed five times more than they normally did to the links in my ear. "I'm sorry," I finished nonsensically.

"Silence?"

"Mm?"

Even my hum was husky. My eyes were burning, and I had no idea how to control the tears. I didn't feel like I could breathe too deeply in the quiet around us, for he'd hear it and know, and I didn't want him to know. But I did not know another way to keep them at bay.

The bed moved, and I heard a much firmer, "Silence," before my wrist at my ear was circled with his long fingers.

I twisted my neck to look up at him.

His gaze was at my ear, but it came to my eyes when I gave them to him and I watched his face freeze.

"I'll just see to this and…" I looked away and tried to pull from the hold he still had on my wrist, "blow out the lamp and we can sleep."

"Allow me," he murmured.

I evaded his gaze, and even with his hand still on my wrist, tried to catch a fastener with my nail.

"No. I've got it."

"Silence."

That was a rumble.

Which meant it was an order.

I dropped my hands and kept my eyes averted.

He released my wrist that was now in my lap and I felt his fingers at my ear.

I held my breath and felt the chain loosen as Mars whispered, "Turn more to me, *mia bellezza*."

I turned more to him even if I didn't wish to. I wished more to have this done. So I did it hoping he did not see my lip quivering.

"My Silence," he said softly.

He saw my lip quivering.

He released the chain at the hoop there and gently slid it out of the others, leaning into me to toss it on the table at the side of the bed.

I instantly began to turn away from him so I could settle in and maybe muffle the deep breaths I needed to control my emotion with my pillow.

Mars foiled this plan by catching the side of my neck in one hand, my waist in the other, and using his thumb at my jaw to force me to look up at him.

"I'm tired, Mars," I said to the empty hoops in his ear.

"I did not know it meant that much to you to take my chain from me," he shared quietly.

I did not reply.

"I will not make that mistake again, my beautiful wife," he murmured.

I simply nodded, still staring at his ear.

I would think on it much after it happened, whether it was fortunate, or unfortunate (and I'd lean heavily toward unfortunate) that in that moment, my husband dipped his head and touched his mouth to mine.

And I would think on it much after it happened, what prompted my response.

But the truth was, he had not kissed me in days.

In weeks.

Since our wedding.

And I loved his kisses.

Thus, feeling the touch of his lips, I pushed up into him, into *them*, and slid my tongue out to taste them.

I barely got a nuance for his mouth opened and my tongue slid inside.

So much better.

I made a hungry mew at having his essence, the warm wet of his mouth, the taste of some liquor and Mars, as I turned into his arms, eager for more.

He fell to his back and I fell on him.

Feeling him under me, I wanted so much, all of him, all at once.

But as I couldn't have it all at once, I focused on his mouth, our kiss, and greedily taking more of that.

Mars, on the other hand, was able to give that and much, much more.

His hands moving on me, on the lace, on the silk of my skirt, on my skin, he quickly found the slit in the chiffon and put it to use, stroking the inside of my thigh that I'd wantonly flung across his hip.

That felt lovely.

He adjusted us, I felt his hardness press against me and I made another mew, bearing down into it.

He groaned, and his big hand cupped the back of my head, holding my mouth to his (not that I would take it away), as his other hand slid over my thigh, up, and I felt the tips of his fingers glide just under the edge of my panties at my hip.

*So* lovely.

"Mars," I whispered against his lips.

He lifted his head from the pillow and took mine again, his tongue surging into my mouth, drinking, dancing, the stud in it teasing, his fingers slid over my behind, still at the edge of my panties, and then slid back.

Even more lovely.

I ground into his hardness.

His fingers retraced their path, going farther this time, farther, and I felt them tickle the wetness between my legs.

I pressed into them, seeking more.

They retreated. They were there, tantalizing, but not *there*, giving me what I needed.

"Mars," I begged, our mouths brushing.

His fingers skittered through my folds as he murmured hoarsely, "My wife is very wet."

"I—"

He rested his head on the pillow, taking his lips from mine, as his fingers went from between my legs and clamped on the back of my thigh, right under the cheek of my bottom. He held firm, locking me on him and *against* him, his maleness hard, hot, thick and pressing into me.

He then moved my head so my face was shoved into his neck, his beard grazing my forehead.

"Let this be a lesson learned, Silence," he murmured.

A...

*What?*

I stared at his neck.

"Tonight you will sleep as I have slept, every night since our wedding, in need of the body so close to mine, unable to have it, unable to find release," he declared.

I had no idea he slept as such.

I also had no idea why he would make me do it because I already knew it was wholly disagreeable.

"If you want something, my wife, you ask your husband for it," he instructed. "If you need something, you request it." His hands at my thigh and neck squeezed in a manner that was a clear rebuke even as his next words confirmed just that. "If something matters to you, you communicate it. I'm understood, yes?"

He was talking about the marital chain.

He was *punishing* me for having a response to *him* taking off his marital chain when it was *he* who had proclaimed we'd take off the other's every night for the rest of our lives.

This angered me.

But I could not think on my anger.

I needed to squirm.

I could not squirm.

I needed to shout my desires.

I could not shout my desires.

All I could do was mumble, "Yes."

"Good," he muttered, giving me another squeeze, this one affectionate. "Now we will sleep with the lamps lit. Perhaps that will chase your bad dreams away."

I did not think this was a possibility.

The sleeping part, that was.

Mostly because he was hard and ready against me, still. I was wet and ready atop him, definitely still.

And he seemed completely immune to both.

Like he was in the necropolis when the men he'd tortured begged him to stop.

Apparently, torture came in many forms.

And my husband was a master at all of them.

"I must admit," he muttered, "I do not like your Dellish clothes."

Well!

My Dellish gowns were lovely.

And they were *warm*.

I couldn't very well wear silk and sheers in a Dellish autumn clime, for goodness sake.

"But I do very much like this nightgown, my new wife," he finished, running his hand along the material at the slit before moving it back to claim my thigh.

I was burning it on the morrow.

After a spell, Mars seemed to relax under me.

I did not do the same even when his fingers at my neck started to stroke its side.

Eventually, he advised, "You need to ease, my Silence."

"Can I roll off?"

"No."

I tensed further.

He started to stroke my thigh.

That did not help.

"What did I tell you?" he whispered, his voice gentle.

Which thing he told me was he referring to?

"What did you tell me?" I asked.

"You do not run from me," he answered, and at that, I blinked at his neck. "You've been avoiding me in a manner that is the same as running, my queen, and I'll not have it. You do what I do not like, there will be conse-quences. These are your consequences. You'll sleep right here." He gripped my thigh again. "Tonight. And every night. Until you give yourself back to me, and after, you will likely fall asleep right here regardless, but due to me exhausting you. But for now, ease, Silence. And sleep."

He had indeed warned me never to run from him.

I just did not know the kind of consequences I would face if I did.

Now I knew.

I tried to force myself to ease.

It was difficult.

Mars did not fall asleep under me before I found slumber.

But eventually, my body demanded what my mind wished to refuse it.

And I fell asleep atop my king.

# 46
## THE GALE

**Princess Elena**
*Fifty Miles Inside the Southern Border*
WODELL

I was pacing my tent, waiting.

He would come.

He always came.

Because I was staying up, it was getting later and later when he would arrive.

But he always did.

The last two nights, it had gotten so late, I'd given up and gone to bed, only to wake when his weight shifted the pallet beneath me as he joined me on it.

He did not touch me or hold me in his arms as he had that first night he'd slept with me.

But he slept with me.

Every night since that first.

He just didn't touch me.

Or speak to me.

Prince Cassius, my future husband and I were not getting along.

Granted, I started it. I was big enough to admit that.

And apologized for it (of a sort).

It was known by all he greatly loved his deceased wife, and although she'd died some years earlier, I'd brought that loss to the fore in a manner that was innocent, but nevertheless thoughtless.

That said, it was *he* who ordered my ward, Theodora, to be sent home with my mother by making an arrangement to do just that *with* my mother prior to the Nadirii warriors commencing their return to The Enchantments.

He did this without discussing it with me.

Mother then took Dora without discussing it with me.

And I had lost my mind.

Rightly.

She was *my* ward.

*I* made the decisions of where she went and with whom.

I would admit, he *might* be right about where Dora would be safest. The attack at Catrame Palace. The strength of Beast's last quake. Sofia and Catedrais perishing in two separate assaults that came on the same night.

Every sister in The Enchantments was a witch. Even the new ones who arrived started their initiations into the ways of the craft shortly after they were settled. The very earth there was permeated by magic after the Fire King, Sky King and Green King spent their magic there millennia ago and then the Nadirii brought their magic there centuries later. Even if the Beast had risen, I would reckon the safest place on Triton would be in our charmed forest.

Indeed, Cassius had also changed the course of his daughter's journey, making another deal with my mother that Aelia, who he had sent the order to have brought directly to him, would go to my mother in The Enchantments.

He still did not discuss any of this with me.

Mother was gone. On her way home. She knew better then to take Dora without my knowledge (or consent). And probably for this reason and the fact she was ill and weak and needed to be home in order to rest and perhaps gather some strength, she did not approach me to discuss it for she knew that conversation would be contentious.

Though in the end, she was Queen of the Nadirii. What she said went.

In other words, I'd have to do what she wished regardless.

But my mother was my mother and my queen.

Cassius was my future husband.

He didn't get to take these decisions without discussion.

Something I had shared with him.

All right, perhaps it was something I had *shouted* at him.

And it could not be denied I'd learned instantly never to do that again for he'd stood there, staring at me in that brooding way of his (that was ridiculously attractive, and I wished it was *not*). He did this silently. And when I'd blown through my anger (something that happened quickly, it was difficult to keep yelling at someone who did not yell back), he'd waited what had to be at least a full minute, as if allowing me that time to carry on yelling at him should I have more to say, before he'd said not one word and he'd walked away.

He'd never mentioned it again.

I hadn't either.

Then again, we'd barely spoken since.

And the cold draught that had started gusting between us when I'd thoughtlessly (albeit, I would repeat, innocently) reminded him of the loss of his wife flourished into a chilly gale that seemed to be blowing us further apart with each passing day.

This was a problem and not simply because he was to be my husband, and after he became that we needed to fight side by side to save Triton from the clutches of an unknown but entirely feared entity.

But because I liked him.

Yes, I, a Nadirii, in fact, a Nadirii *princess*, liked him.

A man.

An Airenzian man.

Our mortal enemy.

Indeed, *the* Airenzian man for he was not only prince and future king of that realm, he was prince regent, thus essentially acting king.

But I liked him.

He was brooding, and when he wasn't that, he was wry.

But he was also a very good kisser and not hard at all to look upon and something about being around him, regardless if we hadn't had much time together and nearly the entirety of it we quarreled, I felt...

*Alive.*

Alive in the way I'd never felt before.

I had not had that feeling for long.

But it was such that not having it any longer, I missed it.

Therefore, these past days I'd become brooding.

And in that brooding I'd formed a plan.

Tonight, I would follow through with it.

I considered extinguishing the lanterns, which I suspected he waited for me to do before coming to the tent. However, I thought this was a tactic

I should not employ for it was a falsity, lying in wait to spring my plan on him, making him think I was asleep before I did that.

Due to Aramus and Ha-Lah taking a detour to the sea, we were riding so slowly to Notting Thicket, it wasn't like we needed hours of solid rest before enduring a grueling trek the next day.

But everyone needed sleep.

And obviously it got late enough even Cassius was ready for his bed. I knew this when the coral flap of my tent was slapped back, and his tall, be-leathered body, bent at the waist in order to clear the top, moved through it.

I drew in a breath of preparation and courage.

He straightened, allowing the flap to fall closed behind him.

My tent was not as large as Mars and Silence's. Nor King Wilmer and Queen Mercy's or King Gallienus's, nor my mother's, wherever she was in her journey home.

But it was not small.

His very presence dwarfed it.

Not simply because he was a large man.

His *presence* dwarfed it.

He looked how I thought a king should look.

As Mars did. Aramus as well. And the same with True.

Cassius was the second son. Only the death of his older brother brought him in direct line to ascend.

But everything about him screamed he was born to rule.

I liked that about him too.

"Cassius—" I attempted to launch my plan.

And immediately failed.

His deep voice interrupted me. "I'm weary, Elena."

He could not be weary. We'd done nothing all day but sit on horses, stop and eat, then sit on horses, then stop and eat and hang about visiting while waiting to go to sleep.

He began to move toward the pallet, doing this with his fingers to the buttons of his shirt.

"I wish for you to come with me," I told him.

He stopped moving and turned his head to the side to look down at me.

I also liked how tall he was.

Goddess help me.

"Come with you where?" he asked.

"To visit with the pixies," I answered.

He turned fully to me and dropped his hands from his shirt.

"Why would we do that?"

"We're in Wodell, and outside The Enchantments, the pixies are most populous in Wodell," I told him something he probably already knew.

I then went on telling him other things he probably knew.

"They don't exactly hibernate, but they don't often come out in the cold when the leaves are gone from the trees, and the leaves are falling. It's rare I have time to commune with them. But it's enjoyable when I do. And I have...that is, *we* have an opportunity to do that before they seek their holes."

He made to move to the pallet again, stating, "Then go, but take your lieutenants with you."

"They're already abed."

He ceased moving and drew an audibly beleaguered breath through his nose before again shifting to face me.

"I'm not going to visit with pixies," he denied.

I took a step toward him, stopped and inquired, "Have you ever visited with them?"

"No."

I gave him a small, encouraging smile. "Aren't you curious?"

"No."

Hmm.

"It'll only take an hour, at most, two," I coaxed.

He resumed unbuttoning his shirt "I have no desire to meet pixies, Elena."

All right.

It was clear this strategy was not working. Me maneuvering us out of the tent, out of the camp, into nature and amongst magical creatures. And thus us being mostly alone (because pixies were lovely, they could be mischievous, but they weren't chatterboxes when it came to communing with humans).

Cassius and I would have to talk.

Which would (I'd decided) lead to sorting a few things out.

However, since this was not working, I had to try a different tack.

Now.

Before he got to the point of taking off his pants, something I took pains not to witness when he disrobed around me because of the strength of my desire actually *to* witness what might be exposed in that act. Something that I had a feeling I would like very much, seeing as I liked the rest of him as much as I did. Something also that I would have in future, but now I was sensing I could not.

"You were right," I blurted. "About Dora," I explained. "She's much safer in The Enchantments."

He stilled, fingers at his buttons, but they were now down about his stomach.

"Though I would have liked to say farewell to her," I muttered.

"Ah." He turned away. "The Nadirii caveat."

"I'm sorry?"

He continued unbuttoning, repeating, "The Nadirii caveat."

"What do you mean by that?"

He again shifted to face me, doing this shrugging his shirt off his broad shoulders and exposing his wide chest with its fascinating adornments of ink on one side, a vision that was beyond titillating. Something I now allowed myself to admit fully. Something, now that I'd allowed myself to admit it fully, was frustrating as, before our estrangement, I could have done something about it, and now, I could not.

"I am right," he said, taking my attention from his chest and tattoos in order to look at his face. "*Though*," he stressed that word. "You should not have said or done something...*but*. Though. But. The Nadirii caveat. I cannot just be right, and you cannot simply be wrong. There seems always to be a caveat that makes *you* right and me the one who has done wrong."

I realized that it would not be beneficial in this situation to lose my temper.

But sadly, I was losing my temper.

I mean truly?

The *Nadirii* caveat?

"I'm being honest," I said tightly.

"This is regrettably the truth," he muttered, moving his hands to his pants.

That didn't make me angry.

That stung.

"Ow," I whispered.

His eyes caught mine.

When they did, if it could be credited (which I was in no place to credit it in that moment), I would have sworn I saw a minuscule flinch.

I took a step back, saying, "Jasmine will likely still be awake. She'll visit the pixies with me."

"Elena—"

I was moving to the tent opening but looked to him as I did and assured in a flat voice, "We won't be long."

"I've been unkind and spoke insensitively," he admitted. "Please stay. We need to talk."

I stopped at the flaps and queried, "It doesn't feel good, does it?"

"Pardon?"

"Speaking insensitively and having the person you did it to not allowing you to make up for it. And more, even if you aren't very good at that, they don't give you credit for trying."

His hard, handsome face grew soft.

"Elena," he said gently.

It must be noted, Cassius speaking thus with his expression gentling was a beautiful thing. Of a man who was beauty head to foot, that might be the most beautiful thing I'd experienced from him.

"Goodnight," I bid and moved through the flaps.

I did not want to be the kind of female who made a dramatic statement by swanning away from an unpleasant discussion in the hopes that the male who had caught her eye came chasing after her.

But I could not lie and say it didn't hurt worse that not only did I arrive at Jasmine's tent without Cassius even calling out to me to return, he did not waylay us at any time after I discovered she was awake and happy to visit the pixies with me.

So this we did.

～

"Suck his cock," Jasmine advised as we sat atop a bed of fallen leaves by the creek bed.

The two female pixies, Twig and Mossy, who were fluttering before us, sparkling dust drifting down from their doubled quadruple (four on each side) gossamer wings (Twig's sparkles were a gingery color mingled with a pearlescent shade, Mossy's were a buttery color with more that were the hue of a fern), burst into such gales of laughter, they wafted back several inches.

And Twig actually did an uncontrolled backflip.

In them doing so, for once, I was not captivated by their lean, pale bodies tinted much like their sparkles (in Twig's case, her skin was gingery pearl, in Mossy's case, her skin was a buttery green).

I was also not enchanted by their large, but broadly slanted eyes that had no pupil and were also colored with their magic (Twig's, a gleaming porcelain, Mossy's, a shining pear). Nor their pointed, distended ears or their thick, long, swept-back hair (Twig's, a white blonde with gold highlights, Mossy's, a shimmering chestnut, also with gold highlights)

I further was not charmed by their scant outfits that appeared to be naught but a long diaphanous strip of material expertly twisted and draped about their bodies to cover the pubis with a short skirt-like swathe with free-flowing bits. This enveloped them also at their breasts, with coils crisscrossing at their midriffs and circling their shoulders.

Nor their calf and forearm shields that looked like they were made with bits of leaves.

Nor their pixie marks of ink down the sides of their thighs, up their breastbones and the sides of their necks, and down from their hairline in the middle of their foreheads. Twig's, a contrasting shade of honey. Mossy's were marmalade.

Then again, telling them all what was happening between Cassius and I, nothing would charm me.

Not even a pixie.

"I cannot say some of the men I dally with don't get peeved with me," Jasmine went on. "But when they do, I drop to my knees," she lifted her hand and snapped her fingers, "and they get over it *just like that.*"

"Not that I would do that," I mumbled. "But just to say, I don't even know *how* to do that."

Twig's and Mossy's eyes got large.

"She's a virgin," Jasmine told them.

They twittered amongst themselves.

I regretted going to Jasmine's tent and not Hera's.

"It isn't hard," Jasmine told me. "Suction. Head bobbing. Just mind your teeth."

Was that all there was to it?

I did not ask.

"Maybe we should commune under the moon silently," I suggested.

Twig tittered at me.

"I know he had no right to send Dora away, Twig," I told her. "But maybe I shouldn't have shouted that at him."

Mossy tweeted my way.

"Yes," I agreed. "Sending your child away without your consent or even a farewell is not all right. But again, twice, I lost my temper with him and did not measure my words, and twice he's made it very clear he does not wish our discourse to go in this way."

"You want to know what I think?" Jasmine asked.

Both Twig and Mossy peeped that they did.

I said, "I'm not sure."

Jasmine disregarded me.

"I think you shouldn't let him think that he can sulk and control you in doing it. All right, so maybe you didn't handle those situations well. But at the bottom of the discussion, you're right. And that's indisputable, Ellie."

Twig and Mossy nodded while tweeting their agreement with Jasmine.

"In the midst of a melee," Jazz continued, "you do *not* toss a Nadirii from the fight and you *never* make decisions about someone's child behind their back, also behind their back carrying forward such decisions. How *you* feel badly that you've hurt his feelings, I do *not* know. He's acting like an ass. The end."

She was my friend and therefore likely prejudiced.

I could not deny, however, that she was right.

"This is the beauty of sucking his cock," she carried on to decree. "He'll get over it and you no longer have to put up with his sulking. Just give him a climax, and in future, make it clear that was a one off. So if he starts sulking again, there will be no more cock sucking. Maybe ever. That'll end the brooding right quick."

I frowned for I didn't think this was such good advice.

Mossy stretched her lips at me.

Twig appeared to be looking anywhere but at Jasmine.

They agreed with me.

In that instant, a blaze of silver and pewter pixie dust streaked by, along with one that was cinnamony and bronze.

Mossy tittered.

Twig waved at us.

And in a glittering waft of ginger, pearl, butter and fern, they flew off.

"Shaft-whipped," Jasmine muttered, watching them go. "And I've met Rocky and Timber and I can't say I was impressed with either of them."

"I thought Timber was committing to Twig," I remarked.

"Forest chatter, Ellie, you need to keep up," Jazz said, pushing to her feet. "He's got another. A female called Web. I haven't met her. She's probably lovely. But he's not, seeing as he's stringing them both along."

I pushed to my feet as well, saying, "You're joking."

She shook her head and we started back toward camp, doing this with Jasmine talking.

"I'll bet half the reason for the Night of the Fallen Masters was because our ancestors were sick to death of that very kind of rubbish." She jerked her head toward where Twig and Mossy (and Timber and Rocky) flew away. "And the kind you're dealing with from Prince Cassius."

"I doubt our foremothers slit men's throats because they were tired of having their hearts toyed with," I replied.

She stopped moving so I stopped with her.

"And how do you feel right now, Elena, when you haven't realized he knows precisely how you respond to him, because he's had that experience, my sister, and you have not? And therefore, he knows precisely how to get you to come to heel. Now you're all tangled up and worried about hurting his *feelings* when he sent Dora away and he's never even met her."

"It was for her safety, Jazz," I noted.

"How's this?" she asked. "Elena, I think it'd be best if your ward goes to The Enchantments with your mother. It's safer for her there than with us. Do you agree? Yes? Excellent. Shall we talk to your mother together, or would you wish to speak to her yourself?" She shook her head in disgust and recommenced walking. "How hard is that?"

It was not hard.

But a few words.

No resultant shouting.

I would have agreed.

Dora would be safe.

Everyone on their way to their respective destinations.

And then Cassius might hold me while we were sleeping.

Not to mention doing other things on that pallet.

Oh, and not least, we'd be getting to know each other better in other ways as we *were* destined to spend the rest of our lives together as husband and wife.

I watched my feet as we made our way back to camp and fortunately Jazz didn't press the conversation.

We were outside her tent before she spoke again.

"He's fine-looking, that's certain," she said quietly. "But he's Airenzian, Elena. Maybe he's one of the good ones, as well as one of the good-looking ones, but don't forget that, in the end, he's Airenzian, and lose yourself in the forgetting."

Now that, I had a feeling, was good advice.

I looked into her eyes and nodded.

She gave me an encouraging smile, a warm hug, then moved into her tent.

I walked to mine.

When I was inside, I saw there was one lantern still lit, the one by my trunk, which was thoughtful for I could use it to move about and prepare for bed without bumping into things in the dark.

This I did with my back to the pallet and I did it without thinking any further about how thoughtful it was that Cassius had left a lantern glowing for me (something I did not do in the times I went to bed without him).

Once changed, I blew out the light and quickly moved to the bedding because the autumn chill was claiming Wodell, and I'd learned the Firenz desert nights could be cold, but the wet Dellish chill was biting.

Cassius had not moved or made any noise while I was in the tent, so I suspected he was asleep.

This suspicion was incorrect, and he did not delay in communicating that to me for I'd barely pulled the quilt over me before his arm was about my waist and the warmth of his front lined the cool of my back.

His deep voice also vibrated into my hair, causing a trill to trace down my neck and spine.

"Did you see pixies?"

"Yes," I told the dark.

His arm about me tightened.

My, but I liked his strength.

And his warmth.

And how very *long* he was.

"I should have let you apologize the way you apologize," he shared.

This was unfortunate, for now I was wondering why I'd even apologized.

I decided not to reply.

He continued to share.

"I do not respond well to shouting."

I decided that it might not be constructive for me to reply to that either.

"I should also have let you say farewell to Dora."

Like *he* should be able to *let* me do anything.

I clenched my teeth together.

"And I see now it was hasty that I made arrangements with your mother without your participation, but although I made it clear how I feel about stipulations in such matters, I will also note that I did it not once thinking you wouldn't agree with me," he said.

So now he was making caveats while (somewhat) apologizing.

"It would be useful if you participated in this conversation, Elena," he remarked when I remained silent.

And now it would be useful if I participated in our conversation, one he instigated, when earlier he made it clear he had no desire to participate in the one I commenced.

"I wish to go home," I announced.

His arm got even tighter.

Indeed, it was near to cutting off my breath.

"Pardon?" he asked.

"I wish first, for you to let me breathe," I wheezed.

His arm loosened, though not that much, at least I could breathe.

And speak.

"I wish to go home," I repeated.

"To leave me?"

"No, you can come with me."

His body pulsed in surprise behind me.

"To The Enchantments?" he asked.

"We are delayed due to Ha-Lah and Aramus going to the sea. We have time. The sea is much farther away than The Enchantments. If we don't dally, it's but a few days ride from my home to Notting Thicket. We'd be there before Ha-Lah and Aramus, for certain."

"You could see Dora," he murmured.

"Yes."

"And I could see your home."

I felt my eyes grow round.

Had he lost his mind?

"No," I said.

"No?" he asked.

"You'll wait outside The Enchantments while I go in, see Dora and visit with my mother."

For a moment, he was completely still.

After that moment was over, neither of us were for I found myself on my back with Cassius for the most part *on me*.

"Say that again," he growled.

"I would...you would...that is..." I stammered, staring at his shadowed head and not able to think because first, he seemed suddenly to be very annoyed in a way that was concerning and second, his weight felt altogether too good. I decided to finish with, "My visit won't last long."

"You'd have me wait outside The Enchantments?" he asked.

"Um..."

"Like a dog waiting for his master to return?" he demanded.

"Not exactly like that," I mumbled.

"Not *exactly* like that?" he bit.

"Not at all like that," I amended. "Like a human male fishing and, um, practicing with your bow and, well, whatever else men do when they while away time."

"While away time waiting for *you*," he declared like I'd said, "While away a hundred years waiting for me to live my life, marry another, have dozens of children and perhaps take a trip to the heavens."

"Well...yes," I answered, before I stated the obvious. "I mean, you can't *go in*."

"Why not?"

I wasn't sure there was time to enumerate all the reasons.

I decided to prioritize.

"You're a man."

"I'm your betrothed."

"That makes you no less a man," I pointed out.

"Where you go, I go," he declared.

"Forever?" I asked, my voice pitched higher.

"That is what marriage is, Elena."

My night was not improving.

"We're not married yet," I noted.

"Let's call this practice then," he drawled.

"Cassius—"

"You can let me in," he declared. "You have that power. Am I correct?"

Oh goddess.

"Not any Nadirii can let in a male," he continued. "It has to be by agreement, sanctioned by the queen, and accomplished by a coven. But the direct royal line can. This is true, right?"

It was.

A nifty trick my many-greats grandmother had given us for reasons she wrote in her diaries had to do with emergencies.

As far as I knew, only one former queen had used it, and that had been to let in a contingent of Go'Doan to assist in healing efforts when an epidemic was threatening our sisterhood.

"Elena," he said in a warning tone.

"Cassius, I can't just let you in. Like you said, it has to be sanctioned by the queen."

"You can send a bird, informing your mother we're coming. She won't object."

"She might."

"She won't."

She wouldn't. She was very much all for Cassius and I being a *Cassius and I*.

"She might," I repeated, though not very convincingly this time.

"Does everything have to be a struggle with you?" he asked.

Truly?

"Does everything have to be a struggle *with you?*" I asked in return.

He fell silent.

I was beginning to feel somewhat pleased with myself that I might have gotten the upper hand (rightly) when he changed strategies.

"I wish to see your home," he said quietly. "Meet Dora, finally. See where you live. Where you were raised. Be amongst your people. As dire as it will be, I'll be giving all of that to you."

As dire as it would be?

Before I could recover from his quiet, cajoling tone and ask about that remark, he carried on.

"Has True seen your home?" he inquired.

"This isn't about True," I replied.

"Has he been in your home?"

I decided not to answer that.

"He's been in your home," he muttered.

"You really must stop pushing True between us," I advised.

"A man has the mother of his future children under him in their bed, there's another man who has more of her and will always have more of her if she keeps things of herself from her lover that she's given that other man, then that man will always be between them."

I could not argue that.

Though True was not between us because I wanted Cassius, Cassius, *Cassius.*

I couldn't tell him that either.

"This is actually my bed, you're just in it," I mumbled.

"Your bed *is* my bed, Elena," he gritted.

I could argue that.

I just didn't have the energy.

"Cassius, maybe we should go to sleep," I suggested.

He did not acquiesce to my suggestion.

He asked, "Why did you ask me to go see the pixies with you?"

By the mercy of the goddess.

"Elena," he prompted.

I'd had enough.

He wanted to know?

I'd tell him.

"Their flight is beautiful," I whispered, and felt his body go still over mine when he heard the reverence in my tone. "The pixie dust that soars from their wings, the contrails they leave, it's breathtaking. Especially in the dark. The magic of the forest...it's always the strongest magic. It feels like home."

I took more of his weight into me as his body relaxed into mine in a way that was less relaxing and felt more like it was...*melding.*

I needed to ignore this, and how good it felt, and I did it by carrying on speaking.

"They're this world within a world. This beautiful culture with their own clothes and music and traditions. I wished to share that with you. And we would be away. Away from the camp. Away from all these people. I like to be social, but I also like to have quiet times, to think, to reflect, to meditate. I do this in nature, staring at the moon or the sun filtering through a canopy of trees. And I thought, if you went with me, I might not be alone, but there wouldn't be so many people around. I could introduce you to the magic of the pixies and we could talk, away from the activity and all the company of the camp."

Cassius was whispering too, when he queried, "What did you wish to talk about, my princess?"

"It doesn't matter now."

"It does."

"It doesn't."

"You're very wrong."

"All right then," I said quietly. "It did matter. But you made it so it doesn't matter any longer. Now will you slide off so I can go to sleep?"

"We're not doing so very well, you and I," he stated pensively.

"I do not wish to broaden the distance between us, but I'm uncertain that has much to do with me."

As he had on earlier occasions, he shared his wisdom.

Wisdom learned from his time with his dead wife.

The problem with this was that I was not his dead wife and what he'd learned in his time with her didn't necessarily hold true with me.

"Between a man and woman, both need to take responsibility when things are not going well."

"Yes, and when one does just that, even if she's uncertain she actually should, the other should listen and not drive her into the night to commune alone with pixies."

Cassius had no reply to that.

And it could be argued I ruined my clever statement by going on to mutter, "Though I wasn't alone, I had Jasmine. Still. I think you understand my point."

"I do indeed, Elena."

"Good," I replied. "Now will you slide off?"

He did not slide off.

"Cassius," I prompted, lifting my hips a little to further communicate my request.

His response was to cup my jaw in his hand and murmur, "Cease doing that, lamb, it's stirring."

I grew very still to the point I wasn't breathing.

I forced myself to breathe.

But that was it.

That said, the breath came uneasy, especially when his thumb started to stroke the edge of my bottom lip.

He was right.

Stirring.

I took it, liking it too much, confused by how much I liked it considering the state of play between us, and just when I was about to say something to stop it because I couldn't bear it any longer without doing something about it that I might regret, he spoke.

"I'll send a bird to Queen Ophelia tomorrow, informing her of our visit."

I stared up at him through the dark.

He continued to stroke my lip, though it was no longer stirring.

Had he been present at all that night for *either* of our conversations?

Most precisely the parts about him making decisions without my consent?

"I'll tell Mars and True in the morning," he carried on making decisions. "Hera and Jasmine will ride with us, as will Mac and Ian. I'll have to leave the rest of my men behind to make certain my father doesn't do anything foolish while I'm away. But three Nadirii warriors and three Airen soldiers won't have any trouble. Not in Wodell."

Now I was not only breathing, I was deep breathing to control my anger.

"Bonus, you and I will have time to get to know one another much better without so many distractions. And you'll have opportunities to have some time to yourself, which I sense is important to you. Last, by the time we arrive, Aelia very likely might be there and I'm eager to see her as I miss her."

That first, I wasn't sure I hoped for any longer.

The second might be considerate.

And the last was sweet.

But...

In order to perhaps not shout the tent down around us, something he didn't like, but mostly something I didn't have the energy to do at that time, I focused on something else.

"You're thinking Mother will allow *three* Airenzian men into The Enchantments?"

"Yes."

"Cassius—"

I ceased speaking and his thumb ceased stroking, both as he pressed his lips hard to mine.

I pressed my head hard to the pillow.

He didn't seem to notice and ended the kiss with a wet, delicious swipe of his tongue along the crease of my mouth that made me wonder why I was pushing my head into the pillow.

Only then did he slide off, turn me to my side and press into me along my back, cocking my knees with his own.

I lay still in his arm and the curve of his body and stared into the dark.

Cassius settled in closer and settled *me* in closer by nestling me deeper into his frame using his arm about my belly.

One thing in that moment I knew for certain.

This, he and I, were *not* working.

"I should have gone to see the pixies with you," he whispered into my hair and burrowed even further into my back at the same time nuzzling my hair with his face. "I regret I did not."

Oh goddess.

And wasn't that just the crux of it?

For I would make up my mind that it wasn't working between us.

Then Cassius would say something like that, and say it holding me like that, snuggling me like that.

And then I'd think that it could.

# 47
## THE PLAN

***Farah***
*Fifty Miles Inside the Southern Border*
WODELL

True woke me with his movements.

I lay, staring into the dark, as he turned from me, and in his sleep—as he had done four times before (not including this time, this made five, and I was most assuredly counting)—he moved agitatedly.

Very agitatedly

But unconsciously.

As he had promised, we went to bed together every night since the night after my mother had been killed.

And as he had promised, in the days, he was the strong one, allowing me to be weak.

This included, after my mother's funeral...

After her body had been treated, she had been shrouded and I had laid her favorite things about her slab.

And Mars had adorned her dressings from neck to feet with long, delicate chains of gold sparkling with rubies and emeralds and onyx and amethyst.

And Elpis had carefully arranged the jeweled, intricate headdress over the wrappings on her face and head.

And last, True had surprised me after sending a bird and having a man on the fastest horse in Wodell race to Firenze so he could set the gold Dellish scepter on her chest with its large aquamarine jewel at the top. A scepter he shared any mother of a queen of Wodell would be buried with.

Then my mama had been set deep in her clan's tomb for eternity.

After all of that, we had gone back to the palace with me feeling numb.

And there, in my bed (that had in the time that had passed become True's and my bed), he'd held me close to him, silently, often rubbing my back, my arms, kneading my neck, doing this for what felt like hours.

Until him doing it made the life start to come back into me.

His patience was astounding.

And beautiful.

He was perfect.

Utterly.

But even in that perfection he was broken.

Completely.

And I had no idea what to do about it.

My mother would have known. Or at the very least, I could have talked to her about it and she would have helped me decide what to do.

But my mother was no longer here.

And it was times like these, and other times I knew would be varied and abundant in the years to come, where I missed her like it had been but moments since she had passed, not weeks.

I also wondered if this feeling would ever ease.

But I could not think of me.

I had to think of True.

I also thought about the conversation I'd had with Mars that day.

For, outside True, he was all I had left.

I knew Elpis wished to heal the breach between us. In fact, she had changed her mind and come on this trip so she could attend my wedding.

And with as little as I now had in my life, I knew it was foolish to resist her advances.

She had not been openly unkind to my mother.

But Elpis had blamed Mama for something she did not do, something Elpis knew she did not do, but she blamed her all the same.

I was having trouble coming to terms with that, and when I shared this with my intended, True advised me that I had enough to come to terms with—the loss of my mother, my impending wedding to him, the Beast rousing—Elpis could wait.

And he was right.

I would have liked to talk to True's mother about what was troubling her son, but even if I knew True had had words with her about her coldness to me, that coldness had not changed.

Which was something else concerning me for the longer his mother kept her distance from her soon-to-be daughter-in-law, the angrier True became about it.

He tried to hide this from me, and he was good at it.

He did not hide this from his mother, and I could tell she was not fond of it.

And she felt I was the cause of it.

Therefore, I had the suspicion she blamed me.

And since Silence seemed to be avoiding me for whatever reason (perhaps she wasn't good with grief, though she seemed wholly adept at handling just about everything else that came her way, and a great deal had come her way since this all began)...

And since True was in love with Elena, and he was the one I needed assistance with in the first place...

This left me with Mars.

Who, in the end, had turned out to be the perfect person, even if he did not have the answers I sought, for not only was he like an older brother to me, he was also a trained and tried soldier.

I'd broached it with him that very evening, on the rise of a moor in what I was discovering was the verdant green, gentle land that was Wodell.

After I shared my concerns, Mars was silent for a moment before he said, with no small amount of sadness, "This is common, I'm afraid, my little sister."

Although it *was* sad, I had some relief, for if this night agitation was common, perhaps there were those who knew what to do about it.

"As that is so, how do I make this unrest in the nighttime cease for him?" I'd asked.

Mars had slid his arm around my waist and looked down at me, answering carefully, "Sometimes, it never goes away."

That was not the answer I'd wished to hear.

Mars continued sharing.

"There are normally two kinds of generals, Farah. First are those who order their warriors to advance for the thrill of the battle, the desire to win at all costs. Men like this do not have trouble sleeping. They do not for they do not have the ability to count the true cost as they don't understand the severity of it. Their warriors might as well be carved of wood and adjusted on a gaming board. They are not flesh and blood. Trajan, Cassius's brother, was this kind of general."

I had heard this of Prince Trajan, and I was not a woman to wish ill on anyone, but this, as well as many other things I'd heard about him, made me not think it was so bad he was no longer among us.

"And then there are those who weigh the cost, and lament it, even before their horses advance," Mars went on. "Therefore, they do not advance unless they are assured their strategy will lead to as little loss as possible, with as much as possible to gain. These men, like Cassius, like myself, might not find sleep easy or we will face other reminders of what an order from our lips means to a soldier. It is inevitable. It cannot be escaped. It is, for a true general, yet another cost of battle."

I had stared up at him, not liking that it was clear, in some way, he faced these same things.

Also knowing he was not quite done.

He wasn't.

"True is a third type of general, *cara*. For he is forced to go into battle by men who are not soldiers at all, giving orders he knows are reckless, but he has no choice but to issue them, sustaining losses that could have been avoided. And as such, as much as it injures me to share this with you, I cannot say what you could do to help True to find some peace."

Mars was very wise. I had great hope he could assist me.

Therefore, this was a grave disappointment.

He'd then wrapped his other arm around me, held me in his brotherly embrace, and said into the top of my hair, "Though, you do have those close who know him well. My wife, for one. His lieutenants are others. I suggest you seek them out and share your concerns. Perhaps they can be more help than me."

"Silence does not wish my company so much these days," I noted carefully, for it wasn't only my company I'd noticed she was avoiding.

He sighed.

"Is all well?" I asked.

"Ah, Farah. True to you, concerning yourself with me," he replied on a squeeze of his arms. "Do not. If there was a time when you need to look after yourself, it is now."

This might be correct, but I was still worried.

I tipped my head back and caught his eyes. "But Mars—"

Another squeeze, a different one, stopped my words.

"All will be well with my new wife and I," he assured, finishing with, "In time."

I did not know if I should share what I right then wanted to share. True had told me in the privacy of our tent within days of setting off to Wodell, and I did not think he told me thinking I would tell anyone else.

But if it would help Mars, and Silence, I needed to share it.

"True has noticed this as well, Mars, and he fears she should not have accompanied you to the necropolis."

At this statement, Mars's brows drew together in puzzlement.

He then announced, "He is not correct in these fears. My queen appeared bored throughout our activities in the necropolis. Indeed, she practically fell asleep at the pits."

"I had heard this," I murmured.

"She is much stronger than True thinks," Mars declared. "In fact, all those Dellish have underestimated her, from what I can see, since she drew her first breath. This is why it is good she is now Firenz. She is with her kind now. And being with us, she will flourish."

If Mars believed that, I did too.

And at the very least, it pleased me to know he was proud of his bride.

They did not seem as happy as they had before they wed.

But Mars was like his father. He could do anything.

He'd lead their way.

Our conversation ended not long after that, with Mars again suggesting I seek one of True's men, or Silence, to discuss my qualms.

However, prior to retiring, I had not been able to do this.

Which meant, with what seemed to be my luck, True would have another episode that very night.

And that he was doing.

I waited, and his agitation did not calm, and I did not like it.

But I did like him, so I knew I had to do something about it.

I made a decision, pushed up in bed, reached to the stand beside it, and found the stick flints. I struck one, opening the cage to the lamp, and lit it.

I blew out the flint, tossed it to the stand and twisted the knob so the illumination was brighter.

That done, I turned to my intended.

I reached out tentatively and touched his shoulder.

Even with a light touch, I could feel his skin was hot, even feverish, and clammy.

"Oh, True," I whispered.

When he did not wake, even with some careful pressure, I curled my fingers around his shoulder and gave him a squeeze.

He came up so fast, his long arm flying out, I recoiled and would have toppled over the side of the bed if True had not caught my arms.

Caught them hard.

The pads of his fingers digging.

And he was staring at me through the lamplight, right at me, but also right *through* me.

It was clear he didn't see me.

I didn't know what he saw.

But I knew it was terrible.

"True," I whispered, lifting a hand between us.

He made no response, just sat there, his grip tight, his eyes haunted.

I had to stop this.

"True!" I called sharply, wrapping my fingers hard around his neck.

With a violent shake of his body, and of me in his hands, his head jerked, and I knew the moment his focus had returned.

"Farah?" He looked down, saw he had a hold on me and his grasp loosened, but he did not let go entirely. "What on—?"

"You seemed to be having an..." What word to use? "Odd dream."

He stared at my torso.

I tried not to stare at his.

True slept in loose pants made of a lightweight material that were held up by a string tied under his navel.

Although the Dellish way of men dressing—with frock coats and waistcoats and high-collared shirts, some with neckcloths (though True didn't often wear these) and frilly, lace cuffs frothing out from the sleeves of their jackets (and True did not wear these either, though I had seen a straight edge with a protruding point at the cuff and the wink of a malachite on the shirt he'd worn to Mars and Silence's wedding)—I felt was actually quite attractive (the way True wore them).

That said, his sleep pants were by far my favorite item of his attire.

Because he looked good in them.

Also because they left his chest bare.

His stomach was trim, flat and boxed.

His ribs were ridged.

His chest defined.

His shoulders dented by the deep cut of his collarbone.

And he was hairless there.

All of this was attractive.

Very attractive.

But it was the veins.

The veins that traced up his forearms and over the bulges of his upper arms.

Though mostly it was the veins that tracked from underneath his sleep pants at his pelvis up the plane of his flat stomach toward his navel.

Not to mention the deep indentations that circled his hips, something I could see as sometimes those pants rode low, and I watched avidly when they did as he walked about my room and then our tent, blowing out lamps of an evening.

He was lean and sinewy up top in a way that, even then, with all that was happening, made my mouth water.

So much, with him staring at my torso like that, my eyes could not deny themselves the opportunity to return the favor.

At first look, I bit my lower lip.

"Farah."

I forced my gaze back to his.

This was not entirely difficult.

He had the most beautiful green eyes in the world.

"The light is on," he noted. "Are you all right?"

No.

I was not all right.

My mother was dead.

I was to be made princess of a foreign land, doing this being wed to a man I was falling in love with. A man who was in love with another woman.

And he was plagued by ghosts that haunted his dreams and I had no idea what to do about it.

"I, yes...well, no. You...that is, I was sleeping and..."

It occurred to me as I blathered that this was True.

The only way to make him all right was to make him feel useful.

"We near Notting Thicket," I blurted.

"Not really," he muttered. "At this pace, we'll be there next year."

I felt my lips quirk for he was right. We were proceeding very slowly.

"We're nevertheless no longer in Firenze," I told him.

Understanding, or the understanding I wished him to believe, dawned in his eyes and they grew gentle.

"This is true," he said, falling back with his hands on me so I fell with him.

He then slid his arms around and cuddled me close.

This was not an unusual circumstance. In fact, I fell asleep in his arms every night.

But he'd never kissed me.

He hadn't even tried.

He hadn't even *appeared* like he was going to try.

"It'll be all right," he assured. "And as we're both awake, I'll share what I decided earlier. We shall delay our wedding further. At least a month. I'll speak with mother about it in the morning."

I lifted my head, which had fallen to rest on his shoulder, to look at his face.

"A month?"

He tipped his chin to catch my eyes.

"I wish you to see the Doors. I also wish you to see the Lights."

"The Doors and the Lights?"

He nodded and explained.

"The Doors are in the southern part of the Great Thicket Forest. Centuries ago, gnomes made their homes in the trees, using magic. They carved out the trunks and built up, but in so doing, their castings kept the trees alive, which they still are to this day. The gnomes still live in them, and if they allow you in," he grinned at me, "and they like me, so they allow me in, they'll show you."

"Of course they like you," I said.

He made no reply, just gave me a squeeze. But the skin around his eyes softened.

"And that sounds remarkable," I continued.

"It is," he agreed. "Mighty trees with these beautifully carved doors in the trunks, dozens upon dozens of them. I can only stick my head in and look up in most of them. Some of the bigger ones, I can enter, only crouched low. But they're extraordinary and they'd be most proud to show you."

"I would like that," I said softly. "And the Lights?"

"Direct in the middle of Great Thicket," he shared. "There's a tall rise there, and I do not know what causes it, you can't see them anywhere else in Wodell, but some nights, the skies dance with lights. Bright pinks and blues and greens and violets. The sprites have hung lights in the trees that are attuned to the dancing lights. When the skies light up, little balls illuminate in the trees. It doesn't happen every night. It doesn't even happen often. But when it does, it's magnificent."

"It sounds so," I agreed, for it did. I'd never heard of anything like it.

"We shall hope it happens when we're there. And we'll remain if they don't, for a time, to see if they will. There's a charming village close by with an inn that has warm, inviting rooms and a pub where they make delicious pies and sandwiches. There's also a bakery that makes chocolate custard swirls, the best in Wodell. And a shop that sells crystals from all over the earth. Even the Northlands and Southlands and Mystics."

"I may wish to go there just for the village."

His face grew gentle and he used the backs of his knuckles to stroke up on down my arm, murmuring, "You need some magic, sweets. And you need some time. Last, you need to fall in love with your new home."

"The Beast is rising, True," I reminded him.

"And if he rises, we shall find a temple, wed immediately and join the others. Cassius and Elena can do the same. We do not need parades and grandeur and spectacle. All we need is you and me."

*All we need is you and me.*

He was right.

But I wished it was that simple.

And that was what he truly wanted, a him and me.

"This is true," I murmured.

"In Wodell, it's my understanding a woman dreams about the man she'll marry and her wedding day from the time she's wee. As she grows older, she plans and hopes and says prayers to the gods to bring her the man who'll make those dreams come true, and a wedding that will represent the start of a life filled with joy. Do girls think of these things in Firenze?"

I nodded.

"Did you?" he asked.

I pressed my lips together, for I did.

I'd wanted a man like King Ares.

A man who was handsome and tall and strong. A man who was wise. A man who was not afraid to show affection. A man who loved his wife and son above all, but his country and his people held a powerful place in his heart. A man who did not concern himself with what others thought of him, if he believed what he was doing was right, that was all he needed.

A man like True.

His gorgeous green eyes watched me bite my lip, and he said, "You did."

I fought squirming and started, "True—"

His gaze came again to mine. "Sadly, I cannot give you the wedding of your dreams. I could not wrest the planning of this wedding from my mother if I had a thousand oxen. It will be the spectacle she set her secretaries to organizing with lists on scrolls three stories tall before we left for Firenze."

"Three stories tall?" I asked with big eyes.

He grinned again and moved his hand so his knuckles were stroking my jaw.

"I exaggerate, sweetling. Though I'll warn you, in matters such as this, my mother does not think small."

"In matters such as this, matters that involve her son who will be king."

"Precisely. Therefore, I do believe she will not demur should I say we need more time, for that gives her more time to make something grand into something ostentatious."

I wrinkled my nose.

He chuckled and said, "We will survive it. But before we have to do that, we will do something else. Something for us. I cannot give you the wedding of your dreams, but I can give you that."

He could give me that.

Gnomes and lights in the sky and chocolate custard swirls.

It sounded amazing.

"Thank you, True," I whispered.

"It will be my pleasure, darling," he whispered in reply.

I slid up a bit and asked, "Do you think your people will take to me?"

"Farah, the instant your feet crossed the Dellish border, you became the most beautiful woman in this realm. The men will love you and envy me. The women will either love you and emulate you or hate you simply because they wish they *were* you."

He sounded certain.

I was not.

"Do you think?"

"I think this is one concern you shouldn't worry yourself with for I couldn't care less what they think. You will be my wife. I will be proud to have a wife as beautiful and kind-hearted as you. And that's all that matters."

His hand at my jaw slid into my hair so he could press my cheek to his shoulder then glide his fingers through my hair.

He did this and continued speaking.

"But before, we will have time on our own. We'll leave the others behind. Take my men and a few additional guards, and I'll show you my home."

"Your home isn't Birchlire Castle?"

I felt him nod again. "Of a sort. I have rooms there. But my home is all of Wodell, and when you see it, Farah," his fingers curled around the back of my neck and gave me a squeeze, "you will understand why I claim it."

I saw the wisdom in this plan and not only because, how he described it, I wished to see his home.

But because we would be away from the others.

Mars and Silence, the latter of whom was his cousin and he worried about her, and from what I had seen, there was something to worry about.

Cassius and Elena, the latter of whom he was in love with. And although True never showed it to me, I knew it was hard for him to see the two of them together. They were not an easy match, but the sparks that flew between them were easy to interpret.

Also, his parents, both frustrating to him for his father was weak-minded and weak-willed and his mother calculating and remote. The former tried his patience, while the latter tried his temper.

We would be only amongst people who loved and respected him, his men (and, it was coming to be true in all ways it could be, *me*), traversing a land he adored.

"Shall we leave tomorrow?" I asked his chest and felt him shift before I felt his lips against my hair.

Incidentally, that kind of kiss was very nice.

But it didn't count.

He settled back and answered, "Yes."

"As we'll be traveling your realm, and there are customs here that most adhere to, and many will surely know who you are, perhaps we should find a second tent for me or if we stay at inns, I should have my own room so that—"

"Farah?"

"Yes?"

"Not another word, darling. All right?"

I closed my mouth.

True.

So protective.

So patient.

So generous.

So *everything*.

"Now, roll to blow out the lamp, and come back to me," he murmured.

I did as told, casting the tent into darkness. And when I rolled back, he wrapped both arms around me and held tight.

I sighed and snuggled closer.

I was coming close to sleep when True's voice rumbled softly under my cheek and into the tent.

"It was the assault on the palace."

My eyes opened.

"They fade," he went on. "I face battle, they return." He pulled me closer. "They'll fade again, Farah. Do not worry about me."

He was talking about his dreams.

"True—"

"Do not worry about me."

"But you said, you'll be strong when I need—"

"Farah," a jostle from his arms, "do *not* worry about me."

I nestled closer, grousing, "You can't order me not to worry."

"I'm sorry?" he asked. "Were you not listening but seconds ago?"

"I was."

"So you know I did just that."

"It's ludicrous."

"I'm a prince and a general, people do what I tell them to do."

"Well they shouldn't, if it's ludicrous."

"A royal can be as ludicrous as they want. Have you not paid any attention to my father?"

I stilled, right before I burst out laughing.

The moment I saw my mother on that bed covered in asps...

No, the moment, years ago, when I'd been told King Ares had been assassinated, even before knowing my father was the one who'd done it, I had not laughed like that or ever thought I would again.

But right then, I was, and I kept doing it when I heard True's deep chuckles accompanying me.

I lifted my head and said a shaking, "I think you just spoke treason."

"It'll be our secret."

"I hate to share this with you, my True, but I don't think you're keeping it much of a secret."

I watched his head come up and then I felt his lips press tight to mine. So tight, and he kept them to mine so long, I felt their softness that mingled with firmness and all I smelled was True.

I stilled.

Now *that*...

Oh my.

*That* was a kiss.

He lifted up farther and kissed my nose.

I stayed unmoving.

He lifted up even farther and slid a hand up my neck to cup the back of my head so he could kiss my forehead.

I remained immobile.

He fell back to the bed and pressed my cheek again to his chest.

"Now sleep, darling," he murmured. "For when we break camp and strike out on our own, we will not force our horses to walk slower than a wee babe would crawl."

"We've not been going that slow."

"It feels like it."

"I'm betrothed to a man of action," I muttered.

"You're betrothed to a man who does not wish inertia to turn him into a statue."

I started giggling again.

I felt his body relax but his mouth warned, "Farah."

"Fine. Fine." I snuggled deep. "I'll sleep."

Some time later, I was again close to slumber, when he whispered, "My True."

My eyes opened again.

He said no more.

But something about the way he said that...

No.

No.

It was foolish to hope.

I had what I had.

And it was beautiful.

The life I'd led after my father's ugly deed, even with Mama's untimely passing, I knew I was lucky.

My bones could be in a pit.

But I had True as I could have him and he gave so much.

I was greedy to want more.

I'd have Doors.

And I'd have Lights.

I'd also have chocolate custard swirls, something I didn't know what it was, but it sounded marvelous.

And eventually, if we defeated the Beast, I'd have children and grandchildren.

But I'd always have True as I could have him.

And even if it didn't include his whole heart.

With all he gave me, I couldn't ask for more.

# 48

# THE SPLENDOR

**Queen Ha-Lah**
*Deep Beneath the Triton Sea*
OFF THE WEST COAST OF FIRENZE

Rotating my fin in a corkscrew movement, I coiled through the depths of the salty sea, eyes wide, schools of glinting fish racing me.

I was free.

*Free.*

I twirled up, through the deep blue-green, feeling my fin brushed by my fellow creatures. I undulated it, speeding toward the surface, and the moonlight, murky in the depths, brightened as I got closer.

I surged up, breaking the surface, throwing back my head, the gills under my jaw sealing to invisible instantaneously, and I drew in surface breath.

"Heaven," I whispered.

I felt my darlings peck cheekily at my fin before they darted back toward the depths.

When they left me, I allowed my bottom half to float up and I drifted on the waves.

It was very late at night.

Under a guise of magic, I'd left Aramus and his men sleeping in their tents on the beach.

And I'd come home.

Home.

I did a twirl on the surface, a flip under it, pitched back up and coasted on the surf.

Aramus had been so adamant that we leave, we'd departed Fire City even before Sofia's death ceremony.

We'd arrived at the shore three days prior.

The journey was long and hot, and it was only made less of the former because Mars and his father before him had been erecting roads across Firenze that were straight and maintained—and cutting over those dunes —they probably took weeks off the journey.

And three days of walking the beach and feeling the saltwater on my feet and legs was heartening, but it wasn't what I needed.

This was what I needed.

Now I was restored.

Now I felt I could face anything.

However, the night would not last forever and I did not wish my husband, maddeningly attentive since he had injured me so greatly with his angry words after the attack on the palace, to find me gone.

And he might. The magic I'd used to keep him and his men slumbering peacefully while I departed didn't last forever either.

I had to go back.

But Aramus had told me that we would stay as long as I wished, and we'd journey to join the others in Notting Thicket only when I was ready.

So tomorrow night, I'd steal away again, to the depths and be home for a spell.

Home and free.

And the night after that, the same.

Then, I knew, we should resume our journey.

Farah was grieving.

Silence was adjusting.

And Elena had much on her plate, with a mother I perceived was quite ill (though she attempted to hide it) and with Elena herself facing a marital union with a mortal enemy that would not be taken well in his land, or possibly hers.

Not to mention, all the things Aramus wished to do when we returned home.

All of this after we defeated an apparently loath-to-surface Beast.

As much as I'd like to remain for weeks, we couldn't dally.

But Aramus had given me this. He'd gone out of his way to give me this. He'd been tremendously discourteous (leaving before the death ceremony was rude to the point of disrespectful, but he didn't care, he was on a mission). The journey had not been enjoyable (this land was *hot* and there was a great deal of it). We'd face more on the trek to Wodell.

But we were here.

Solely because I desired to be here.

I did not wish for this to cause a chink in the armor I'd erected around my heart to protect it against my husband.

He was arrogant.

He was thoughtless.

When he was angry, or overly emotional, vicious things came out of his mouth.

He clearly spent far too much time around men and had no watery clue how to handle a woman.

And he spent equally too much time being crown prince and then king, thus thinking the very earth and all its seas rotated around him.

But as I flipped my fin and glided toward the shore (dipping to swim deep on occasion), I could not deny that having this, having Aramus go so far out of his way to give me this, did not put a chink in that armor.

A wee one.

But it was there all the same.

That was, I felt that until I surfaced closer to shore and noted a lone figure standing where I left my nightclothes on the sandy beach.

A figure I knew was my husband.

I kept my fin carefully beneath the surface, and as the area between the sand and sea became narrower, the resultant prickle down my back became a slight burn in my hips all the way to the end of me, which led to a tearing sensation that caused me to gasp.

And again, I had legs.

I stopped flipping and struck out swimming toward shore.

In the shallows, when I could swim no more, nude, I stood and slowly walked through the lapping waves toward my husband.

He stood immobile in the moonlight, watching me.

We had now been married many months.

And this was the first time he'd seen me naked.

I did not wish to wonder if he liked what he saw.

But I wondered if he liked what he saw.

I stared at his face in the moonlight as I made way toward him and noted he was carrying the long sheet of toweling I'd brought to dry off when I was done.

And as I got closer, I could not tell if he enjoyed the view for his expression was naught but a frozen mask of fury.

A mask with eyes that were locked on my face.

Many months of marriage, and I could not say I knew him.

What I could say was that his temper was quick, and when he was in the grips of it, what came from his mouth could be cruel.

But he was all words and bluster.

Thus, I was not afraid. At least not physically.

I stopped before him and said, "Husband."

I barely finished the word when he moved, far faster than I would ever imagine he could, and I was wound in the toweling in a manner my arms and legs were immobilized.

I was then tossed over his shoulder.

"Aramus!" I snapped.

"I would be quiet, wife," he replied, his deep voice cold as the water at the poles.

Oh drat.

I decided it might be best to do as he suggested and have this out in our tent. I even managed to keep my silence when we made our encampment some ways away, up high on the shoreline, and I saw all his men awake and milling about the sand.

All of them.

And there were hundreds of them.

They looked as peeved as my husband.

It occurred to me then that Aramus woke to find me gone. It also occurred to me what he would do if he found me gone.

That being, he would look for me, and when he did not find me (for I was frolicking under the sea), he would wake his men to aid in the search.

This he very clearly did.

Oh dear.

Obviously, someone had spotted me swimming to shore, or found my clothing, and Aramus had sent them back to camp while he, alone, knowing I was swimming nude, waited for me.

Fortunately, he didn't loiter on the beach with his men but carried me directly into our tent.

Once inside, he put me instantly to my feet.

I struggled with the toweling until I had my arms free.

I clutched it to my chest, turned angry eyes up to his face...

And clamped my mouth shut tight.

For his enraged face was an inch from mine.

"*Have you lost your mind!*" he roared at me.

In the face of such fury, to save him from himself (and, frankly, me from whatever might come out of his mouth), I immediately became soothing. "Aramus."

"By the sirens, Ha-Lah. *By the bloody sirens, woman!*"

"If you'd—"

He moved back but an inch so he could get his finger in my face.

"I woke, you were gone," he bit. "I searched, you were nowhere to be found." He dropped his finger. "I roused the entire *fucking* camp, and no one could find a hint of you, but your bloody...*fucking...clothes.*"

I stared at his furious face.

And saw the fear behind his eyes.

And suddenly there was no armor around my heart.

It was gone.

In but an instant...

Vanished.

By Medusa.

My husband had fallen in love with me.

"My king," I whispered.

"Do you have any sirens-damned *clue* what ran through my head?" he asked.

I had a feeling I did.

It was exceptionally horrible.

And I was sorry for it.

"Please, allow me—"

"And you were fucking *swimming,*" he clipped.

I pressed my lips together, hard.

Yes, one thing I knew about my husband, when he was angry, he needed to let it out.

"Did it once occur to you to wake your fucking *husband* and share you'd like a moonlit dip?" he demanded.

When he paused long enough I thought he might actually wish my answer, I opened my mouth, but he spoke yet again.

"*No!*" he barked. "It didn't. But weeks ago, Cat had a sword run from his gut to his gullet. Sofia was magically overcome by sirens-damned *snakes.* Now *you* take off on your own with not one single guard in a foreign land and go *swimming.*"

"I'm sorry," I said softly.

"You're *sorry?*" he asked sarcastically.

"I was in no danger," I told him.

"You were in no danger," he repeated after me, again, sarcastically.

"Aramus—"

"You are beautiful."

I shut my mouth again.

"The most beautiful female of any realm. Do you know what a man would do to possess that beauty?"

I stared up at him.

He thought I was the most beautiful female of any realm?

Before his words could sink in completely, Aramus kept ranting.

"Do you know what an enemy would do to that beauty to bring the man who possesses it to his knees?"

"I—"

"And you are *queen.* The queen of the mightiest realm in Triton. If someone abducted you, I would give our entire fleet to have you back unscathed."

At this assertion, I fell back a step in shock.

"Yes, Ha-Lah," he spat. "And not because you are my queen but because you are *Ha-Lah. My* Ha-Lah. *Mine.*" He thumped his chest with his fist. "Mine to hold. Mine to *protect.* Mind to keep *whole.*"

"I didn't think—"

"No, you fucking did not."

"You'd wake," I finished.

At that, he shut his mouth and his powerful torso swung back.

He was not surprised.

No, he was angrier.

"Please listen to me, Aramus," I said urgently.

He leaned toward me. "There is not one fucking thing you can say, woman, that will make me any less furious at you for being so bloody, fucking *stupid.*"

I forced myself to breathe deep and steady, stood still and held his gaze.

He breathed visibly shallow and erratic and glowered at me.

I gave it time. Time to watch his breath even. Time to watch the fury in his expression reduce to simply very damned mad. Time to remind myself that his words came because he was afraid for me, not because he actually meant them.

Time to let it settle he thought I was the most beautiful woman in any realm.

And he was in love with me.

Then, I spoke.

Quietly.

Not soothingly.

But calmly.

"You have an exceptionally foul temper, husband."

"You terrified me, wife," he returned.

"And I am very sorry for that, Aramus."

That came quiet, and soothing.

He rocked back on his heels and crossed his arms on his chest.

I studied him.

And at what I saw, what had just transpired, and what I now understood to the depths of my soul about this man who was mine, it did not take long for me to make my decision.

"Will you come with me?" I asked.

"Come with you?"

"Yes."

"Where?" he bit off.

"Please, Aramus," I whispered, reaching a hand to him. "Just come with me."

He stared into my eyes.

He did this a long time.

I kept my arm extended toward him that entire time.

He finally dropped his gaze to my hand.

After several more moments, he reached out and took it.

As he would.

For my husband was in love with me.

Thank Medusa.

Awkwardly, with my free hand, I wrapped the toweling around me as best I could so it would stay in place and led him to the flaps of the tent and out.

"You can tell them to go back to their pallets," I said under my breath, referring to the milling soldiers.

"I will not—"

I squeezed his hand. "Trust me."

He scowled down at me before he turned to one of his lieutenants, a man named Bondi, but called simply Bond.

"You can settle. All is well. We'll return. But keep an ear out."

Bond nodded, sent a ferociously unhappy frown my way, then turned to the others.

I led my husband down the beach to where my clothes had been left.

I only let his hand go when we arrived at them.

Quickly, juggling the sheet I had around me, I pulled on my nightgown then my panties.

I wound the toweling around my arm, took my husband's hand again and led him farther down the beach.

As the distance from camp grew greater, Aramus's fingers tightened around mine and he growled a warning, "Ha-Lah."

I stopped, looked back at camp, which was not close, but it wasn't far enough away.

But my king was not comfortable with the distance.

So it would have to do.

Still holding my husband's hand, I dropped the toweling to the sand, moved so close to his front, our bodies were nearly brushing, and I tipped my head back.

"You once accused me of making you earn everything you received from me," I reminded him.

In the moonlight, I saw his expression flicker from anger, to regret, back to anger.

He opened his mouth.

But it was me who said, "This, my husband, my king, I give you for free."

And then I turned, still holding his hand, but lifting my free arm up in a wide arc.

The tingle surged from my womb to my heart to my fingertips, and a great break of water some fifty meters out and some twenty meters across rose toward the heavens on the trail of my arm, then dropped to the sea.

My arm now lowered, I lifted it up, and a gust of surf blew straight up into the air only to shower down as I again lowered my arm.

"By Triton," Aramus whispered, his gaze locked to the water.

On a tug of his hand, I moved us to the edge of the surf.

And when the waves lapped my bare toes and the leather of his boots, I tugged his hand again and made him crouch beside me.

I closed my eyes, felt the warmth overtake my insides, opened my eyes, submerged my free hand in the water and sent my request.

It did not take long for me to receive a reply.

I turned my head to my husband.

"Watch the sea, my king," I urged.

His eyes, no longer filled with fury, now filled with wonder, something that warmed me far more greatly than what I was getting from the sea, went from me to the horizon.

I turned that way too.

I heard his sharp intake of breath when four dolphins, two on each side, leapt from the waves toward each other.

"And now for a show," I said.

And they were back. This time flipping nose over fin in the air or riding above the surf on the ends of their flippers or leaping all together in formation.

They ended with just their heads above water, whistling and trilling our way.

As they sunk beneath the sea, I waved my hand still in the water, and said, "And the finale."

Aramus had not turned his eyes from the deep.

And thus he saw the great gust of water spout high before the gleaming beauty of a whale burst in a proud eruption of foam. It twisted in the air to its back, before splashing home.

*Thank you*, I sent through my hand.

The vibrations of the response tickled my fingers.

"Ha-Lah," my husband called beside me.

I turned my head his way.

"I was in no danger," I whispered.

"You don't talk to them, you command them," he whispered back.

I shook my head. "No. They're my friends. I don't command them. I sent a request. And they granted it."

"The waters?" he asked.

It took me a moment.

And then I shared.

"That I command." I inched closer to him on my toes, lifted my wet hand to wrap it around his neck, and finished, "If we are near to the sea, Aramus, nothing can harm me."

"And this is why you're a very strong swimmer," he remarked.

Well.

Not exactly.

When I didn't answer, he noted, "When first spotted, you were out very far."

"I am indeed an accomplished swimmer, husband."

"Why didn't you tell me this?"

"Because I was angry at you for hurting me."

He held my gaze.

Then he straightened, pulling me up with him.

Right into his arms, held tight to his body.

He held me at night, when we slept, never letting go.

He'd done this since he'd said the things he'd said to me in Fire City.

He'd also done this against my wishes, but in an effort, I knew, to silently ask forgiveness for the harm he'd done to me.

But when we were not abed, he rarely touched me, even before he said the things he'd said to me in Fire City.

Now I was in his arms.

And I was not certain it was conducive to my emotional health to know how good they felt around me while standing in the sand with the sea caressing my feet.

He took one from about me so he could run his finger along my hairline and detach the wet ringlets that clung there.

He watched his finger do this as if fascinated.

I watched his fascination and I did it fascinated.

"This is extraordinary," he murmured, his finger running along my jaw for no purpose as there was no hair stuck there.

I did not know if he was referring to what I had shown him, my ringlets or my jaw.

His eyes came to mine and his hand curled around my head, fingers in my hair, palm at my neck, his thumb resting along my cheek at my hairline.

An area it stroked.

"*You* are extraordinary," he said.

I felt myself melting into him with no power to stop it.

"But I do not care."

At these last words, I found the power to stop melting.

"I...pardon?" I asked.

His neck bent so his face was in mine.

"You left me."

Oh dear.

I was melting again.

"Aramus."

"You cannot even begin to imagine the terror that struck my heart when Nis found your clothes, but not you in them."

I shoved my hands between us so I could press them tight to his chest.

"My king."

"There was no sign of you. Nothing. This meant the best scenario, Ha-Lah, was you being swept out to sea. That was *the best scenario*, my wife. But even in that scenario, you were lost to me."

"But now you see I was safe and never in any danger."

"A husband could fall asleep beside a wife who commands the sea and the skies, the earth and all fire, and if he woke to find her missing, he would not roll over and fall back to sleep if she has a place in his heart."

*A place in his heart.*

Dear Medusa.

He was going to make me weep.

"Is this understood, my Ha-Lah?" he asked.

Oh yes.

It was very understood.

I nodded.

"Please say the words, my queen," he prompted.

"It is understood, Aramus."

His fingers in my hair depressed in an affectionate squeeze as his arm about me tightened in the same manner.

"You do not wish my men to know you have this power," he deduced.

"I...it is..."

"You did not wish me to know."

I decided not to answer.

"It was wise of you, Ha-Lah. I sense I've only witnessed a hint of it and I still know your power is awesome. A thing of beauty. I do not know of another who wields it. And if it was known, it would be coveted. Coveted by those who would stop at nothing to possess the one who commands it. We will need to keep it, and you, safe."

And again I felt like weeping.

For he understood.

"My closest men should know," he decreed. "But we will talk, decide how to share, and when. Not now. We have other things to sort through, you and me."

I nodded again.

When I finished, his thumb swept my cheek as his hand drew forward and he cupped my jaw.

All of this as his face got even closer.

"Do you forgive me?"

"Your temper is damaging," I whispered.

This time, he nodded, and he did it solemnly.

"Indeed," he agreed. "I have thought on this long and often during our travels here. It will be something I'll endeavor greatly to work on, though I fear I must ask your patience with this as it is a part of me and thus might prove difficult to overcome."

"You called me stupid in the tent," I reminded him and watched his full lips twitch.

"My wife, my queen, my Ha-Lah, I woke, *and you were gone.*" He hesitated for emphasis and finished, "*Swimming.*"

I pulled my lips in and bit them.

Perhaps leaving him during that particular climate of our marriage, in this particular time on Triton, not long after a massive assault on the palace where we were staying, an attack where he lost a man he cared greatly for, was stupid.

"Mm," he hummed, his eyes on my mouth, and I had a feeling he knew my thoughts.

I decided to change the subject.

"I need to be close to the sea, Aramus, for a few days."

His eyebrows drew together as his gaze lifted to mine. "Of course. This is why we're here."

"What I mean is, I wish to stay. For a few days."

"Of course, Ha-Lah, this is why we're here."

"I know that we shouldn't linger," I continued. "We should make moves to again join the others. I just need a few days."

His hand at my jaw and his arm at my waist dragged me up his big body and he rumbled, "Ha-Lah, you listen close to words I wish you would not hear, and not to words I want you to hear. We will stay as long as you like. If you desired to be here a year, I'd allow it."

I felt my eyes widen. "A year?"

"Well, perhaps not a year," he muttered. "I have a kingdom to run."

I smiled at him.

He grew still against me when I did.

Then I heard (and it must be said...*felt*) a sound that seemed to originate in his chest before it rolled out from between his lips.

And where I felt it was also at my chest.

As well as between my legs.

Which meant said legs trembled.

*Kiss me,* I begged with my eyes.

My husband was not looking in my eyes.

He was staring fixedly at my mouth.

*Kiss me!*

"We should get back," he murmured, his body moving as if he'd let me go.

"Oh, for the sirens' sakes," I snapped, took my hands from his chest, latched on to his cheeks, yanked him down to me...

And *I* kissed *him.*

I barely had my lips to his before I had my back to the sand with the great, warm weight of my husband on top of me.

His tongue was plundering my mouth.

His big hands were shoved up my nightgown at my back.

And by all the bounty of the seas, he felt good.

He tasted good.

And he kissed *magnificently*.

I clutched his bald head in both hands, holding him to me, pressing up into his body.

He tore his mouth from mine, growling, "Sirens-bloody-dammit."

Wait.

What?

Why had he stopped?

"Aramus?" I breathed.

"I'm not making love to my wife the first bloody time in the fucking sand," he groused.

I shifted my hands to either side of his head and said urgently, "We'll go back to the tent and we'll go quickly."

"I'm also not making love to my wife the first bloody time on a pallet in a tent with five hundred fucking soldiers camped close by."

I clenched my teeth in frustration.

"It's going to be you and me," he declared.

"But—"

"Just you and me."

That was very endearing.

However.

"It's just you and me right now," I pointed out.

"It's going to be special."

My frame froze solid.

Special?

"We will live our lives. We will have children. We will have grandchildren," he declared. "And through it all, you will always remember the first time we joined. The first time your husband entered your body and made us one. The time I became truly your husband, and you my wife. You will remember it as a time of splendor. Of passion. Of joy. Not with half your mind consumed with how irritating the sand feels in places it will undoubtedly get that it should not be or who might hear and what they might say."

One could definitely say, in that moment, I did not care what others might say.

Though he had a point about the sand.

"And when will this time of splendor happen, husband?" I asked.

"I don't know. I'll figure something out," he muttered irritably.

"We've been married for over—"

"I know, Ha-Lah, bloody trust me, *I know*," he rumbled, far more irritably.

Which made me, for some reason, giggle.

"This is not funny," he grumbled.

"It's sort of funny," I teased.

"It is not funny at all," he returned.

I subdued my giggles but could not stop myself from smiling up at him.

I had a place in his heart.

He knew of my powers.

He might not have moved heaven and earth, but he did move five hundred soldiers, and he did this on a direct path to the sea.

For me.

And the very thought of something harming me terrified him.

Terrified King Aramus of Mar-el.

The mightiest king in Triton.

I had a feeling I could tell him I was a mermaid and he'd care naught about it, except to do all in his power to keep that secret safe.

*Me* safe.

And I *would* tell him.

Eventually.

My auntie had told me that to win my mother, my father would have found a way to travel into the skies to gather a star to bring it to her, if this was what she desired.

I did not want a star.

I wanted to be free.

I also told my husband that.

And in a time when I did not think I would ever feel that again, Aramus had found a way to give it to me.

I stroked the back of his neck with my fingers, asking, "Can we kiss some more?"

"I would ultimately very much like to use my cock in ways both of us will enjoy. When that joyous occasion happens, it should not be out of commission due to balls being irretrievably blue," he griped.

I started giggling again.

"Now that *really* isn't funny," he clipped.

I pressed my lips together again, this time to stop laughing.

When I controlled it, I noted, "It's heartens me to know you're an exceptionally skilled kisser."

He looked above my head and complained, "I see my penance for being a massive arsehole is not complete."

"Aramus," I called quietly.

He looked down at me.

Or, he scowled down at me.

"I forgive you."

He instantly stopped scowling, though his face was no less intense, this I caught nary a second of before he started kissing me again.

It became heated very quickly, what with that talented tongue of his, those full, soft, but firm lips, and both our hunger.

He rolled us so he was on his back in the sand and I was on top (and I had the feeling I liked this positioning better, though I'd definitely try the other again, just to be certain) and both his hands dove into my panties.

Oh yes.

Aramus broke contact with our mouths, bent his head and shoved his face in my neck as his fingers dug into my arse.

"Fuck," he groaned.

"Darling," I breathed.

"Baby, this feels good," he whispered, his hands moving over my arse.

He had that right.

"We have to stop," he told me thickly.

He was right about that too.

Now that he offered it, I wanted special.

Sirens-dammit.

I kissed his jaw.

He pulled his hands from my panties, sat up so I was straddling him, but wasted no time in wrapping an arm tight around me so he could heft me up even as he got to his feet.

Mine fell to the sand.

He let me go, but took my hand, bent to snatch up the toweling, and turned us back to the camp.

We started walking.

Slowly.

"I'm not sure I'd mind a bit of sand," I murmured.

"Stop it," he replied on a squeeze of my hand.

"Truly," I said.

He looked to the sea. "All my thanks. You sent me a siren, and now I'm lost."

I smiled at his profile.

Aramus looked forward and ordered, "Stop smiling at me."

"I can't. You're being endearing."

He continued not to look at me as he noted, "You intend to torture me fully until I can find a suitable time to get you under me, don't you?"

"I was thinking I'd be astride you."

This time, his head tipped back, and he begged of the heavens, "Someone kill me."

I walked closer to him and let my head fall to his shoulder, murmuring, "Not until I get astride you."

We took several steps before I felt his lips on my hair where he kissed me.

After that, he again looked forward, but I kept my head to his shoulder, and my husband and I walked silently under the moonlight with nature's most beautiful melody of waves lapping the shore serenading us the rest of the way to the camp.

# 49
## THE BREAKFAST

**Prince True**
*Fifty Miles Inside the Southern Border*
WODELL

"This is ridiculous. An unacceptable delay," King Gallienus announced pompously as all sat around the large dining table that Mars's servants took apart to travel and put back together for them to use when they made camp of an evening.

As well as a morning.

Even a chilly morning.

The sun was bright above them.

But everyone had a rug draped over their chair to ward off the chill of the wood and six barrels of fire danced around the table to give a modicum of heat, not to mention all the women wore cloaks and the men mantles.

Except Mars, who appeared immune to cold which gave new meaning to the ancient title his ancestors bore.

The Fire King.

"This wedding nonsense needs to just be done," Gallienus concluded.

True had presently finished explaining what he'd woken early to tell his mother and father.

Something his mother was delighted about, for he had been correct, it gave her more time to build a bigger spectacle.

Something his father didn't seem to care much about.

Then again, True had known the man for thirty-one years, perhaps twenty-six of those when he was somewhat fully cogent, and he had no idea what his father cared about.

Now all at the table knew that he and Farah were off to explore Wodell and they would meet the others in Notting Thicket a month hence.

Farah, sitting at his side, shifted, and he turned his head to her to see she looked uncomfortable.

Therefore, he reached a hand to hers, and when her fingers curled around his, he brought them to the arm of his chair and held on.

"I think it's a magnificent idea," Lord Johan, Silence's father, declared. "This means my Silence can come home. To Bower Manor. And there she can spend time amongst the dells she loves so, before she has to go back to all that sand."

"*My* Silence," Mars corrected low.

Farah made a discreet noise of alarm.

"And we won't be going to Bower Manor," Mars finished, only for Silence, who sat next to her husband in the manner she often sat in the times True had seen her around her father, or really anybody, except True.

Silently.

She had been much more animated in Firenze.

She was retreating into herself again.

And Mars wasn't helping.

In fact, True worried Mars being Mars and not guiding her to an understanding of who he was and why he was that way was the reason she was doing it.

Now his cousin turned her head and stared at her husband's bearded jaw with a mutinous expression, before she wiped it clean and reached to the teacup in front of her.

Yes, Mars was not doing any guiding whatsoever.

Farah made another quiet noise of alarm.

True squeezed her hand.

"And where will you take my daughter?" Johan asked Mars, as if Mars was making off with her, instead of married to her.

True had never given much thought to Johan, except to think in a vague way he wasn't very likable and in a not-vague way he was a thoroughly poor father.

Now, True studied him.

And he did not like what he saw in the way Johan glared at his son-in-law.

"It isn't so far. We'll go back to the *sand*," Mars returned. "My queen should be amongst her people. They should come to know her. It's autumn. The crocus bloom in the north. We can visit my saffron field."

"She *is* amongst her people," Johan retorted.

Farah made a strangled noise.

Damn it.

Mars appeared curiously, and alarmingly, like he'd grown four inches simply seated in his chair as his eyes blazed fire across the table at his father-in-law.

"Silence, haven't the tenants left Cord Cottage?" True called.

His cousin looked to him.

"I'm sorry?" she asked quietly.

"Cord Cottage," he repeated. "It's vacant, is it not?"

"Yes, it is, my prince," Johan answered for his daughter, giving demonstration to one of the varied reasons why Silence had been silent much of her life. "Why do you mention it?"

"It's spacious and it's well-appointed," True answered. "One of the reasons you haven't found tenants to occupy it, I assume. It's costly. It also has a carriage house where Mars's Trusted can lodge. And land, for his men to camp. And it's but five kilometers from Bower Manor. Silence and Mars can stay there. The newlyweds can have privacy, Silence can be home, in a manner, and they would be close enough to have dinner with you and Aunt Vanka once a week or so."

"It's more like seven kilometers," Johan corrected.

"All the better," Mars stated expansively, leaning back in his chair, doing so draping his arm around the back of Silence's. "This we shall do."

"I haven't offered it," Johan spat Mars's way.

"I have," True said.

Now Johan was spitting at him, though doing it somewhat respectfully. "No offense, my prince, but it isn't yours to offer."

"Yes, it is," True's mother, Queen Mercy, put in blithely, pouring tea into Silence's now lowered cup. "All lands of Wodell are property of the crown." She set the teapot down and leveled her eyes on Johan. "When it comes down to it. Am I right, my king?"

"Right, right, indeed," his father, King Wilmer, muttered before biting into a large cut of breakfast sausage.

Johan started to get red in the face.

"And I'm sure Johan, Vanka and all the tenants, farmers and staff of the Arbor would be honored to play host to the King of Firenze and his new queen, their very own Silence," his mother carried on, sitting back, smiling a very small smile and aiming her gaze to Vanka. "Isn't that so, Vanka?"

"Of course," Vanka chirped nervously, her eyes darting to her husband.

"So that's settled." Mercy folded her hands in her lap. "Lovely."

"Is this your wish, my Silence?" Mars murmured to his bride.

She tipped her head back and replied, "Your wish is my wish, my king."

Something about her expression, her demeanor, her answer or all three caused Mars to appear impatient for a moment before he muttered, "Would that was so."

Angry pink tinged Silence's cheeks as she looked to the table.

"Ah, *mia rosa. Amo così tanto il mia rosa*," Mars whispered, but did it loud enough for others to hear.

*My pink. I so love my pink.*

Upon hearing it, that pink got pinker and Silence became very busy with smoothing her napkin in her lap even if it appeared she'd finished eating.

Mars chuckled.

Silence's head snapped up and she told the table at large. "Before the tent goes down, I'll return. I didn't sleep well last night and could do with a wee rest before we carry on with our journey."

She started to get up.

"Excellent, I'll join you," Mars announced, also making a move to rise.

She sat back down. "On second thought, Aunt Mercy just poured tea. It'd be a shame to waste."

She then reached to her tea.

Mars settled into his seat and chuckled again.

His cousin's eyes shot to True.

He gave her what he hoped was an, *I'm sorry, I can't help you* though still encouraging smile.

She turned her head to the side, a side where Mars was not, and sipped her tea, sharing she was not encouraged.

True sighed.

"Maybe, prior to us all being off, Farah, Silence and I can take a walk and have some Sisters of the Beast time before we separate," Elena forged into the breach.

Ah, Elena.

She missed nothing.

And if she could do something to help, she would, which she clearly intended to do if the speculative way she was glancing at Silence was an indication.

"Elena and I are heading to The Enchantments," Cassius told Mars.

"You are?" Melisse asked.

"We're all going," Jasmine put in. "Hera and I and Cassius's guards."

Melisse looked to Elena.

She then smiled.

"The Enchantments?" Gallienus queried with distaste.

"We have time now, and we might not prior to traveling to Sky Bay after True and Farah wed," Cassius replied. "I wish to see the home of my betrothed and it will be good for her to have some time there."

"Waste of time, Ophelia won't let you in," Gallienus returned.

"We shall see," Cassis murmured, reaching to his coffee cup.

"You will, and what you'll see is that woman not letting you in," Gallienus retorted.

"You do remember I'm marrying her daughter," Cassius asked with faux concern, as if his father might be growing addled.

"Don't patronize me," Gallienus spat. "And go," he bid. "Embark on this futile journey. With my leave. I could use the break from you and," his gaze went specifically to Elena and his supercilious tone turned cutting, "our *vaulted* company."

While Gallienus spoke, Cassius took a drink of his coffee with his eyes over the rim aimed at his father before he lowered the cup, set it aside and turned to Elena.

He then drawled, "Ah, the joys you'll know when you reach the Sky Citadel, my lamb. Family breakfasts just like this every day. And in the evenings, it's all the better, for there are dozens of courtiers Father can choose from to be an arsehole to."

Jasmine snorted.

Elena hissed, "Cassius," but her lips were twitching.

Vanka gasped in affront at the cursing.

True's mother sighed.

Farah made a noise of amusement and True squeezed her hand.

"Have you not gone yet?" Gallienus asked snidely.

Cassius's attention swept back to his father and when it did, True braced to move, he sensed Mars bracing to move, and Cassius spoke.

"As you can see, we have not, old man, and if you speak in that manner to my future wife again, I'll ascend the throne of Airen a far more direct way."

Elena repeated, "Cassius," but this time in a pacifying tone, her melodious voice wrapping around his name, making two syllables into a song.

Cassius instantly relaxed.

Watching this, True decided she'd be good for him. The man he was growing up in a den of vipers, he'd become accustomed to being quick to strike.

Elena could be lively and engaging, but for the most part she was mellow and spiritual.

True sensed Cassius could use a bit of all of that in his life.

"Good gods, people, we're all adults. Can we not get along for *one breakfast?*" Father broke in to say, exposing a rare moment where he seemed attuned to the atmosphere and an even rarer moment of wishing to do something about it. "Now, someone, hand me the preserves."

And there was the reason.

He wanted everyone to get along long enough for someone to pass him the preserves.

Vanka reached and handed the pot to her king.

"Melisse," Elena called, and received her mentor's attention. "If you'd like to come with us, you know you're more than welcome."

"Thank you, my sister," Melisse said in a manner True knew she was about to decline. "But it's been some time since I spent any in Notting Thicket. It's my favorite city outside The Enchantments. And if there's time, I'll head to Go'Doan and meet with some friends."

"I didn't know the Thicket was your favorite city outside The Enchantments," Mercy remarked to Melisse.

"Sky Bay may have the architecture, but the Thicket has all the charm," Melisse replied.

Mercy sent her a small, but genuine smile.

Gallienus clearly opened his mouth to speak, seeing as Cassius warned on a rumble, "Not one word."

True turned his attention to the Airenzian king and watched him clamp his mouth shut with defiant eyes on his son.

True then turned to Farah and said quietly, "You should have some time with the women before we go. We're in no rush. You've all grown close and I know they'll wish to make certain you're in as good of spirits as you can be before they leave you."

She smiled up at him and nodded.

She didn't often speak at the breakfast table. She preferred quiet, intimate conversations, not only with him, but, he'd noticed, with anyone.

He greatly liked this about her.

He had often, in his adult life, had thoughts of what he wished his life to include (these most frequently coming when he was in a tent, on a hopeless campaign that Carrington, through his father, had ordered him to take his men on).

True was not foolish enough to think, when he was king, he could broker a lasting peace with the other realms and sail smoothly through his reign.

Taxes needed to be paid, and people did not like paying taxes.

Services needed to be offered, and many thought they were never good enough or delivered fast enough.

And people had an alarming tendency to simply refuse to find ways to get along.

But at the end of each day, he'd hope to go up to his private rooms in the castle, to his wife, and share a quiet intimacy. Dine with their children and discuss their days. Have some small amount of normal after a lifetime of *royal*.

In this, Farah was like an answer to a dream.

So yes, he greatly liked this about her.

As he greatly liked everything about her.

Not mostly, but it must be said, gazing upon her.

Her beauty was incandescent.

And last night he'd learned her laughter was the most pleasing sound he'd ever heard.

"You also should select a servant to travel with us," he told her.

"I can see to myself."

"You need to select a servant to travel with us," he repeated.

"True, I can—"

He bent closer to her. "You are not princess in name, not yet, but you are princess. Select a servant to travel with us. I'll not have my intended not tended."

She smiled at him.

Indeed.

Incandescent.

"Can't we hire ones at the inns where we'll be staying?" she asked.

"I've no idea. I don't need a servant to unlace me."

"So you're traveling without a servant."

"Of course."

She started quietly laughing.

He tipped his head. "This is funny?"

She shook her head. "These clothes I have to wear in this land are most odd, but they're warm. However, they're not an insurmountable problem without a solution in the putting on and getting out of. If I need it, can't you lace me?"

"Of course he can't lace you," his mother snapped, bringing True's head around her way. "That's not only absurd to ask of a *prince*, it's *indecent*."

True felt Mars's energy shifting to angry, and Cassius's shifting to controlling his friend.

But for once, Cassius's aim was faulty.

"Mother, if you ever again use that tone with Farah, after we're wed, we'll move to Firenze and never return."

His mother paled.

His father's head came up.

Vanka and Johan went still.

True felt Silence's eyes shoot to him.

Farah's hand clutched his tightly.

True remained focused on his mother.

"Am I understood?" he asked.

Her jaw moved as she ground her teeth.

"Am I...*understood?*" True pressed.

"True," Farah whispered.

"Mother," True prompted.

"Son, calm," his father urged.

"I'll hear the words spoken," True said to Mercy.

"Yes," she said tightly. "You're understood."

"Excellent. Now apologize to her," True demanded.

Vanka emitted a peep.

His mother, the queen, visibly bristled at being told to apologize to an untitled foreigner.

True did not back down for this was not what he asked.

He asked his fucking *mother* to apologize for being rude to the woman who was going to be his *wife*.

"True, that's unnecessary," Farah whispered.

His mother held his gaze.

"Mother," True pushed.

"Son," Wilmer murmured.

The table sat still and silent as a son, who was a prince and a soldier, clashed with his mother, who was the invisible monarch.

"Aunt Mercy, truly, you should apologize."

True's head jerked in surprise as he felt Farah's hand in his spasm after Silence made this demand.

"Now," Silence decreed. "It's altogether unseemly you should speak thus to your soon-to-be daughter-in-law and, I mean, it's horrible to bring up considering the grave loss so recently suffered, but it's true, should you outlive Uncle Wilmer, Farah's your future queen. And this discourtesy at the breakfast table no less. So very unlike you. Goodness."

By the gods.

Silence might be stumbling in finding her way as a wife, but she was certainly finding her footing as a queen.

If he wasn't so bloody angry, he'd laugh.

"Aunt Mercy," Silence urged.

"My apologies, my soon-to-be daughter," Mercy gritted.

"That wasn't very convincing, but it'll do," Silence murmured then looked to Farah. "Yes?"

"Yes, of course. Absolutely. And Queen Mercy, I'll select a servant," Farah promised.

"You bloody will not," True bit. "I'll do your gods-damned laces if need be. If you don't wish a servant, you don't have to have one. You're going to be bloody queen. You can do whatever the fuck you want."

Jasmine chuckled.

Farah stared up at him with big eyes and said conciliatorily, "All right, my True."

"Yes," he clipped. "*Your* True."

With that, he let her hand go, pushed his chair back, got up, pulled hers out and helped her from it.

His eyes went to Silence. "She'll seek you for your stroll when she's ready."

Silence was grinning up at him. "Of course, cousin."

He noted Mars wasn't grinning up at him.

Mars was studying his wife like he'd never seen her before.

True looked to his mother. "We'll part on bad terms if you don't use the time it takes for the women to have a wander to find words to make amends. I strongly suggest you take that time and find those words, Mother."

She lifted her chin at him.

It was set stubbornly.

But she'd find a way.

It would be far from genuine, but she'd do it in a manner that was appeasing.

She had a gift with that.

He tucked Farah's hand in his elbow and moved them from the table.

When they were halfway to their tent, she noted, "I hadn't actually finished my breakfast."

He pivoted them instantly and started back until Farah broke free, laughing softly, and stood in front of him with both hands on his chest to stop him.

He stopped.

"I was joking, True," she told him, studied his face but a moment and said, "Though perhaps it's not a good time for that."

"I would have your life filled with laughter and teasing. When I'm angry, it's the best time, *my* Farah." He was sure to note that *she* noted the word he stressed, which she did, hearteningly, before he went on, "For I dislike being angry, sweetling. And your eyes alive with humor like they are right now could fill a dead man's heart with gladness."

Her lips parted.

And he watched them do so.

*Gods*, he wished to kiss her.

His mouth was dry with the need and this was becoming an affliction, this need was near fucking *constant*.

And sleeping at her side night after night...

Agony.

But her mother hadn't been entombed for even a month.

An unseemly time for a woman to be wed, thus he sought to give her more of it to mourn as well as him having some to help her fall in love with her new home.

Not to mention her future husband.

It was regrettably also an unseemly time for a gentleman to advance his affections.

When she woke him last night, and he again had to witness her in her scant, clinging nightgown—in bed, beside him, when he was vulnerable after having one of his dreams—he'd been unable even to move for fear of what he'd move to do if he did.

But he'd managed to find a moment to offer her a chaste kiss.

It was all he could have.

For some time.

And it had been *him* who had decreed they'd sleep side by side every night.

He wished to make certain she was safe. Her mother had died abed.

But it was killing him.

Fuck.

Instead of kissing her in that moment, he wrapped his arm around her neck and pulled her to his side.

She put her arm around his waist.

This was much better.

He pivoted them again and resumed their walk to the tent.

"Will you at least allow a servant to pack your bags?" he requested.

"Yes, True."

"We'll take a pack horse so bring what you wish," he told her.

"I will."

"We'll take two horses if they're needed."

"All right, True."

"And we'll get another, if you see things you wish to purchase on our journey."

"True?"

He looked down at her. "Yes, my sweet?"

She grinned up at him and put her hand to his stomach. "Stop being so marvelous."

And all of a sudden, he was no longer angry.

He bent to kiss the top of her fragrant hair, pulled away, and replied, "Never."

Her eyes grew brilliant as yellow diamonds.

They weren't exactly happy.

But they were not unhappy.

He'd take it.

For now.

He led them into their tent.

# 50

# THE FORMIDABLES

**Queen Silence**
*Fifty Miles Inside the Southern Border*
WODELL

One could say—after last night and his continued highhandedness at breakfast—I was not happy with my husband.

However, I was unhappier as he stalked (yes, *stalked*) me to our tent after breakfast.

It was entirely undignified, but he was so tall, his legs so long, in the end I was practically *running* to get to the tent before he did.

However, once I arrived, I realized I had not thought matters through for he was stalking me, which meant when I was inside, *he* was inside right behind me.

And I needed to get away from him.

Or I'd *scream*.

Unfastening the frog at my neck, I twirled my cloak from my shoulders, tossed it to some cushions in a manner I hoped appeared rather dramatic, and whirled on him remembering every detail of the night before. And in doing so remembering he'd told me if I wanted something, I should tell my husband.

Therefore, I told my husband what I wanted.

Lifting my chin, I declared, "If you wouldn't mind, my king, I would like a little alone time to rest my eyes prior to taking a wander with Elena and Farah."

"You ran from me."

"What?"

"You *ran from me*."

My frame jerked as I belatedly caught the look on his face.

No.

The look in his *eyes*.

They were aflame.

Literally.

Tiny blazes danced in his eyes.

I knew what that meant.

Oh *faith*.

"I didn't run," I told him with more bravado than bravery, also openly lying since I did just that. "I simply made my way back to the tent...quickly."

"I thought we learned a lesson last night, Silence," he said quietly.

And I was glad he did.

So very glad.

For if any fear was striking my heart, the reminder of that wiped it away.

"*We* most assuredly did," I snapped.

He took two steps toward me which, with the wideness of his gait, placed him right before me.

He then lifted his hand as if to cup my face.

Which made me wrench it away so he would not touch me.

I was about to move bodily from him when he caught me with both hands on my jaw, his movements so swift, from such a large man, it was astonishing.

It was then I was on the verge of pulling away when I felt it.

Not his touch.

The atmosphere of the tent.

It was oppressive.

Not with heat.

With air so heavy, it felt suffocating.

I lifted my eyes to his and all my breath left me at what I saw.

"Suffice it to say," he started in a sinister whisper, "if I do not wish you to run from me, if I do not wish you to avoid me, I absolutely do not wish you to evade my touch."

I should fear him. He could break me in two.

And from what I'd witnessed from him, if given reason, he would.

But in that moment, I didn't fear him.

My eyes might not be afire, but my blood was for who was *he* to tell me I could not run?

And if his touch was unwanted, who was *he* to tell me I could not deny it?

"After last night," I began bitingly, "I never want you to touch me *again*."

His brows rose in studied nonchalance. "No?"

"No," I spat.

"Shall we test this assertion, my Silence?" he asked.

"No," I denied. "You shall take your hands off me *immediately*."

"Mm," he hummed.

Then he released me.

I didn't have time to let out the breath I was holding, for in the blink of an eye, I was up, and in but three of Mars's mighty strides, I was down on the mattress with my husband on top of me.

He could not be believed!

With a great heave, I arched my back to displace him and opened my mouth to shout, only for him to claim it with his own, gliding in his studded tongue.

Of a sudden, I collapsed under him and felt like weeping.

His taste was nectar. His weight was heaven.

I tore my mouth from his, turning my head away.

His hand spanned the side of my face to pull me back, but I said, "If you do this, I'll never forgive you. If you force yourself on me, my king, there will be no coming back."

The atmosphere of the room lightened to such an extreme, it felt like the tent around us was falling to the earth.

"Force myself?" he whispered into my ear.

"You threatened it yesterday, and I could not fight you and win. I know that. I could not call out and have others come to my aid, for you are king and you can do as you wish. I know that too. But I would be lost to you in a way that could never be regained."

"I did not threaten you with this, *mia piccolina*."

I closed my eyes tight at the endearment and retorted, "You did."

"I said I would not do that."

I opened my eyes and told the side of the bed, "I would not think such a thing would even enter your mind *to* do. But obviously, since you mentioned it, it did."

"Silence," he called.

I stared at the silk of the side of the tent.

"Look at me, my queen," he whispered.

It was then I realized his hand still spanned the side of my face, but now his thumb was coasting along the apple of my cheek comfortingly.

I turned my head to glare into his eyes.

He continued whispering when he vowed, "I would never, not ever do that to you, *amore*. It is not the basest man who engages in such behavior. It is a monster. You never have to fear that from me, Silence. Not... fucking...*ever*."

I took in a shuddering breath and stared into eyes that were no longer ablaze.

They were liquid black.

"You are wanton," he shared.

No longer relieved and pacified by his vow, I blinked in affront and snapped, "I am not."

A small smile pulled at his mouth as he replied, "I have but to kiss you and you catch fire."

This was, lamentably, true.

I decided not to comment.

"I had meant to prove that point after your earlier declaration," he explained. "Sadly, it did not work. But thankfully, it led to you actually *speaking* to me and *sharing* with me what is weighing on your mind so I could do something about it."

"I am most gladdened we've worked that out," I said in a way it could not be misconstrued I was *not*, which did not anger my husband.

He looked vastly amused.

I ignored this.

"Now, if you'd get off me, I could rest my eyes for a spell before I bid farewell to my two friends."

"I will not roll off for we have other things to work out."

I aimed my eyes upward and mumbled, "Marvelous."

"Silence," he called, his deep voice trembling with laughter.

Laughter!

I aimed my eyes to glare at him again.

His hand at my cheek (still!) shifted so he could stroke the skin under my glaring eye (which felt so nice, it was difficult to keep glaring, but I managed it) as he asked, "Why were you running from me this time?"

"I was not running from you."

His thumb stopped stroking and he explained, "A husband and wife leave a breakfast table together with both their destinations the same, they stroll there...together. Not with the wife scurrying before her husband like a mouse scampering to elude a cat."

"I didn't *scurry*," I told him.

"You scurried," he replied through a brazen smile.

I had scurried.

How humiliating.

"It heartens me greatly you find this so amusing, my king."

At my tone, his smile died.

"Silence—"

"You wish me to talk. Fine. I do not like this discord between you and my father."

His face started to grow hard. "Silence—"

"But you will do as you please, I have no control, no say in anything, for example such matters as where we journey from here when everyone is scattering in all directions."

"I did ask if you approved of our plans," he reminded me.

"*After* sparring with my father and essentially determining said plans," I returned.

"If you do not wish to return to the Arbor, we will not go."

I *did* wish to return to the Arbor.

I also wished to see his saffron fields.

But the Arbor was closer than the fields and all this riding around on horses and sleeping in tents, although not fatiguing, and in the beginning most interesting, had lost its appeal and was no longer enjoyable. Further, I might not have any friends there, but Tril did and she'd be happy for a spell at home.

"I have no issue with returning to the Arbor," I shared.

"Then I do not understand your pique."

He wouldn't.

"Silence, you must explain it to me so I understand it," he instructed with apparently strained patience.

"It is not about the Arbor."

"Then share what it *is* about."

"I'd rather not."

"In manners such as this, my new wife, your tactics of speaking only when spoken to and keeping to yourself that which you'd rather not be heard do not work. And I'll hasten to add, it will never work in matters with your husband. Even if there's discord, we must have it so we can get past it."

"What you did last night was unconscionable," I blurted.

His head gave a jerk.

Since it had come out, I had to finish it.

"You used me...you used...used..." I drew in a ragged breath. "You used my response to you, my feelings for you, to...to *punish* me."

"*Amore*," he whispered, his tone quiet but heavy with remorse, and it must be noted, his eyes were drowning in it.

"You used *me* against *myself* to teach me some lesson I could not possibly understand for I have no experience being a wife, I have no experience being a queen, and I'm doing the best I can in rather trying circumstances."

His gaze moved over my face before he murmured, "I see this was not a sterling decision on my part."

"No," I agreed.

And it took not even a second for him to say his next.

"I cannot begin to express how deeply I regret this, my wee monkey," he whispered, his voice even heavier, indeed, positively dragging with repentance.

I stared up at him.

Did he just...?

*Apologize?*

And further, he had not called me his monkey in over a week.

I had missed that.

I had not wanted to.

But I had.

"I am new to being a husband as well, Silence," he reminded me. "Though not new to being a king, that is not who I am to you. I am your husband, that is all I'll truly be to you and it distresses me I have failed you so appallingly, not only in my actions, but in not understanding the entirety of the burdens you carry."

"I...erm..."

I trailed off for I knew not what to say.

Mars knew what to say.

"I have mentioned this before, though did it in times most rife, so perhaps you did not take it in. Therefore, I'll repeat it. You do not have to learn how to be a queen in but hours or days or weeks. Just be you. You are bright, and you are observant. You will find your way."

I hoped he was right.

But it made my heart glad that he thought this.

"Like earlier," he carried on. "I was brimming with pride at how you handled Mercy. It may surprise you to know, but conversations like that over a simple breakfast can lead to situations that last centuries and include conspiracies, intrigues, battles and loss of life. If Wodell lost its crown prince to Firenze, matters that, as you know, are far from peaceable between our two lands could deteriorate irrevocably. True threatened that with I believe genuine intent. And truth be told, since she met her, Mercy's behavior to Farah, who was raised beside me as my little sister, coming to a head like that over the breakfast table did not best please *me*."

Farah was raised beside him as his little sister?

I knew they were close, childhood playmates, but...

His little sister?

"You asserted yourself," Mars continued, "and reminded Mercy of her place, doing it as her niece, as well as the queen of a much more powerful realm than her own. You also reminded her of Farah's place, which it is clear she should be much quicker in learning. True wearies of her prejudice against his bride and he does this swiftly. And last, in all, you *are* a queen of a powerful realm and I'm uncertain Mercy has come to understand that is who you now are. If she hadn't, she is no longer under any illusions about that. It was firm, apparently offhand, thus a brilliant act of diplomacy."

"I was not attempting to be brilliant," I admitted on a mutter. "I was just angry Aunt Mercy was being mean to Farah and not backing down from True."

"Well then, you're a born diplomat." He dipped closer. "Which was what I was keen to tell you when we arrived...*together*...at our tent. However, prior to that, you scampered away from me which delayed me being able to compliment my wife."

He was stalking me in order to compliment me.

Now I felt like an idiot.

Maybe because I'd been one.

And perhaps, it was uncomfortable to note, I'd been thus much longer than said scampering.

"I didn't scamper either," I mumbled.

"*Amore*," he murmured, his eyes dancing.

How, precisely, could he be so vexing when he was also being lovely?

These thoughts made me do the only thing I could in that moment.

Roll my own eyes.

"Silence."

I rolled them again to him.

"Your father enjoys too much this unrest he senses between you and me," he shared gently.

When it came to my father, I could believe that.

But I didn't want to believe that.

I wanted to find other reasons for his change in attitude toward me.

"I don't think that's true," I told him with more hope than surety. "I think he's realized that the time has come he's losing his daughter to another man, that other man is a man who will take her far away, and he's utilizing the little time he has to be with her."

There was a different kind of regret in his expression when he replied, "I do not think you are right, *bellezza*, but I hope for your sake you are. And if this is what he desires, he will have more time with you as well as time to convince your husband his motivations are noble. But with the protection of your heart in mind, my love, I urge you to be on your guard if what you hope proves untrue."

This was good advice, therefore I nodded.

"Good," he murmured, his gaze drifting to my mouth as the hand not at my face which I had lost track of drifted elsewhere. "Now to correct the mistake I made last night."

Did he mean to...?

I watched a different fire light in his eyes.

He meant to.

Eep!

"My king," I called.

"Mm?" he answered, but he also didn't answer seeing as he had no intention to listen to whatever I'd meant to say, and I knew this when his lips hit my jaw just as his hand cupped my breast.

I felt the tip of his tongue trail to the skin below my ear, and this caused a delightful shiver.

Then his thumb glided over my bodice at my nipple which caused a glorious shake.

Oh my.

"My king," I whispered.

His head came up. "Right here, Silence."

He was.

Right there.

And his thumb was right then circling my nipple which had begun to ache in a strange and wonderous way.

It had also made another part of me ache in a lovely and glorious way.

My gaze dropped to his mouth.

I watched it move to ask, "Is that what you want, wife?"

"Yes," I breathed.

Apparently, he told no lies last night when he said if I wanted something, I should tell my husband for I barely finished the word before I had his mouth, his tongue, as well as his finger and thumb closing on my nipple over the bodice of my gown and then rolling.

*Magnificent.*

I mewed into his mouth, rounded him with my arms and arched up.

"Wanton," he whispered against my lips, nipping the bottom one sharply with his teeth before slanting his head and taking my mouth in a much deeper, wetter, headier kiss at the same time he angled his lower half away and yanked up my skirts.

My belly did an odd dip at these actions.

And it did another, much stronger one, as his fingers found the top edge of my panties.

But this time, he did not tease.

He did not play.

Mars dove in, firm and rough, found my nub instantly, and put delicious pressure on when he started to circle it.

Beautiful.

Oh gods.

I tore my mouth from his on a gasp and pressed into his fingers, swaying my hips frantically back and forth against his touch.

I heard his hoarse, "Ah, my Silence, yes. Ride that, *mio ardente.*"

"Mars." I clutched his back, my nails scraping against the supple leather there. Unable to find purchase as it was tight to his skin, I desperately glided them up and clamped them on the back of his neck.

"*Incantevole,*" he purred.

And I caught fire.

"Mars!" I gasped, attempting to retreat from his fingers that were suddenly too much as the blaze overtook me, all I could see was orange and red and all I could feel was heat and beauty.

When the flames receded, my husband was kissing me tenderly as his fingers played gently in the wet folds between my legs.

He must have sensed he had me back from the place he took me for he sucked on my bottom lip a moment, let it go, cupped my sex and caught my slowly opening eyes.

His were liquid again and an enchanting mixture of aroused, replete and smug.

And that look on him was so marvelous, I even liked the smug.

"All better?" he asked.

"Mm-hmm," I mumbled.

I saw his grin before I lost his hand.

He righted my skirts, slid off and rolled me to my side, then fitted himself to my back before pulling a warm hide over the both of us.

"Now, rest your eyes, my queen," he murmured into the back of my hair as he pulled me deeper into his warmth. "When Farah comes to collect you, if you fall asleep, I'll wake you. Yes?"

"Yes."

He sounded simply smug when he declared, "I would keep you in a state of post-climax at all times, this daze I create is so endearing. Except I enjoy watching you come too much." He paused as if considering before concluding, "And making you come even more."

My eyelids were drifting, and I felt I should give a response, but I couldn't catch a thought.

"And my point is proved, my wife is wanton," he teased.

I caught a thought at that.

"Be quiet, Mars."

I heard him chuckle as he pulled me even closer.

I was almost to sleep when he whispered, "I am glad to have you back, my beautiful Silence."

I wasn't back. We would never be back to the dream I'd been building about us before reality set in.

But I'd learned he could apologize.

And I had forgotten he was a good listener and did it most avidly any time I spoke.

So perhaps I was a step closer to being able to learn to live with the reality I had been dealt.

Thus, on this thought, I snuggled into his warmth.

And again, I was nearing slumber when his voice came.

This time, it was low.

But it was vibrating.

"Today proves what I suspected. You and I will be formidable, Silence. Your fortitude vigilance, tact and cunning, my strength, strategy and my father's vision, once we put down this Beast, we will leave a Firenze to our children that is strong and bold. I know it to my soul."

I closed my eyes tight, shocked he had these thoughts.

"I hope you are right, my king," I said.

"I do not hope, my queen. As I said, I know it to my soul."

I found his hand that was pressed to my breastbone with my own.

The instant I did, his fingers engulfed mine.

The way they did, so strong and true, I knew one thing.

He would be what he already was.

A good king.

As for my being a queen.

That remained to be seen.

# 51

# THE SISTERHOOD

**Princess Elena**
*Fifty Miles Inside the Southern Border*
WODELL

Hera, walking point with bow in one hand, arrow at the ready in her other, her quiver on her back, turned to me with a look that said, *Get on with it!*

Jasmine was at our right flank. True's men Wallace and Luther were at our left. And Mars's man Basil with Cassius's man Severus were at our rear.

Such was the guard one current and two future queens had while wandering a forest.

It was suffocating.

It would be good to be back home.

In the meantime, I had this situation on my hands.

Whatever *this* was.

There had been a distance growing between Silence and Farah since Firenze, and now the feel between them was so awkward, it was hard not to cringe.

This distance seemed neither of their style, but Farah had an excuse.

And perhaps Silence did too. She hadn't been immune to some traumas mixed with major changes in her life of late. Not to mention, she'd shared she'd never really had any friends so perhaps she didn't know what to do when one of them was in need.

But this had to stop.

We might be parting, though only for a while.

But in the end, the only ones who knew what we faced, what was happening, and why, were us.

I had lived my life learning how important the sisterhood was.

Standing together, we could not be defeated.

They had not learned this.

It was time to teach them.

Thus, I rushed forward from where I strode in the middle of the two of them in our line, stopped, turned to them and declared, "Enough."

They both stopped too.

Obviously, our guard stopped as well.

Silence looked guilty.

Farah looked uncomfortable.

I crossed my arms on my chest and asked, "What's going on with you two?"

Neither said anything and they avoided looking at the other.

It might not be fair, but I gave my attention to who I considered the culprit.

"Silence?" I prompted.

And the instant I did, she turned to Farah and proclaimed, "I have been awful. Not a good friend a'tall. I...I...much has happened that has taken my mind, but 'tis no excuse." She took a step toward Farah, lifted a hand, dropped it and finished, "I'm so *very* sorry you lost Sofia. I had not had the chance to know her well. But I can promise you, of what I knew, I'd been looking forward to it. And I am so *very* sorry that I was of no comfort to you when you lost a mother as lovely as she."

Farah's eyes grew bright and she pressed her lips together before she controlled her emotion, nodded to Silence and replied, "I understand. Mars is..." She seemed to be searching for words and then she found them. "*A lot.*"

"He is," Silence murmured.

"Much of it is good," Farah hastened to add.

"Yes," Silence agreed.

"But he is, well...*Mars.*"

Silence appeared to be about to start laughing and thus forced out, "He is that."

Farah smiled at her. "He's most besotted with you. I can tell he cares very deeply for you. He's never been that way, not close, not with even one of his other females."

Oh shite.

I heard Hera emit a grunt and Jasmine curse under her breath.

This because, from the look on Silence's face, this was not the right thing to say.

Farah saw it too and she took a step closer to Silence.

"Of course, they were from before," she said quickly. "Before you."

Silence lifted her chin a smidge. "Yes. Of course. Before me. He is a man, after all. And he would, erm..."

"Dally," Farah put in.

Silence nodded sharply. "Dally. Yes."

"I'm sorry, I shouldn't have mentioned that," Farah murmured.

"No need to be sorry. It is but truth. And we should always be honest between us." Silence looked to me, lifting her arm my way, then she turned to Farah, swinging her arm back. "We Sisters of the Beast."

"Yes, we should," Farah agreed.

"We should," I entered the conversation.

Both women looked my way, but it was Farah who asked hesitantly, "Is all going well with Cassius?"

"No," I said on a smile. "He's a lout."

Farah smiled back, also hesitantly.

Silence didn't smile. She regarded me not hesitantly but openly.

"Do you think you'll be able to come to some accord?" she asked with concern.

"I like him," I declared.

Both women stared at me, Farah with wide eyes, Silence was blinking.

And Severus was not far away, and I had no doubt he was listening.

So be it.

I spoke truth, and if that got into Cassius's ear, maybe he'd be less of a lout.

"You...*like* him?" Farah asked.

"He's easy to look at," Jasmine called.

"There's that," I muttered.

"There *is* that," Farah muttered too, but now she was also regarding me openly.

I stepped closer to their huddle and said my next in a way Severus would not hear.

"There is something between us that cannot be denied." I reached out and caught Farah's hand. "Something, Farah, I see now I never had with True. He was but a friend, a kind one, a good one, but we'd never even kissed."

Farah looked shocked.

"Cassius pinned her to the wall the second time he laid eyes on her," Jasmine yelled helpfully.

I sighed.

Silence giggled.

Farah smiled at me.

"He did?" she asked.

I tipped my head to the side. "As he says, we cannot keep our hands off each other, when we aren't fighting that is. He is not wrong. Alas, we fight a great deal."

That was when Farah laughed.

And I was relieved to hear it.

I brought our huddle even closer.

But my eyes were only for Farah.

"What I wish to say is, it is not True. It never really was, Farah. And the way I see him with you, he's realized this too."

Farah looked away.

"You do not see this?" Silence asked her.

Farah looked to Silence. "He is a kind man. He understands this situation is not optimal, but he wishes to make the most of it. And he helps me grieve. That is all."

"He helps you grieve while panting to get into your knickers," Jasmine hollered.

Farah's eyes grew round again.

"She has very good hearing," Silence whispered.

"She's a witch and she's using magic to eavesdrop because she's also a pain in the arse," I told her.

"I heard that!" Jasmine shouted.

I looked to my friend. "Stop listening!"

It was then I sensed movement, turned to Hera and saw she had an arm lifted. From her hand, a streak of silver and orchid sparks shot Jasmine's way.

Jasmine grunted when they hit her.

Hera looked to me and called, "Carry on."

I smiled at my friend and turned back to my Sisters of the Beast.

"You are very lucky," Farah said wistfully, eyeing both Hera and Jasmine.

My heart hurt at these words.

She might have had friends at some point in her life, but I'd noted not a one of them attended her at Catrame Palace. Therefore, it was clear she lost them due to what her father did.

She lost nearly everything because of what her father did.

The only thing she held onto was her mother.

And now she was lost too.

I squeezed her hand, reached to Silence's and took hers as well.

Silence took Farah's.

"You have lost much," I said to Farah and turned to Silence. "And you never had much." I held tight to both their hands. "And now we have each other. So we will part, but we'll always be as one. We will always have each other. And if you'll allow me to, I shall bind us together as sisters in a way that no matter where we are, if we need the others, we can call out and join together."

"How would we do that?" Silence asked.

"I would tie us to each other so we can meet through the astral plane," I told her. "We would not be together in physical form, but we would be there in mind and in heart. And that is always all that's needed."

"It is," Silence whispered.

"Let us do that," Farah said.

"Yes, let's," Silence agreed.

I nodded.

"Bring your hands up between us, all together," I instructed.

They did so, I did as well, and we pressed all our clenched fingers together.

"Now, to bind our minds. Bring in your foreheads."

We joined in that way, pressing our foreheads together over our hands, Silence needing to get up on her toes and Farah and I needing to bend to her, she was so petite, but we did it.

I held tighter.

They did too.

All we could see was our hands and the leaves and dirt beyond them.

And each other.

"I wish Ha-Lah was here," Silence murmured.

"Me too," I said. "I will reach out to her. I cannot say it will work, but hopefully it will, and it will bind her to us as well."

I felt nodding against my head.

"Let us begin," I urged. "Repeat after me. We are strong."

"We are strong," they said in unison.

The sensation gathered in my back and I sent it down my legs, to the earth.

"We are minds," I chanted.

"We are minds."

"We are hearts."

"We are hearts."

I looked between Farah and Silence, their eyes so close, topaz and silver, as I felt the swirling around our ankles.

"We are wombs."

"We are wombs."

The magic moved up, enveloping feet, ankles, calves and knees.

"We are survivors."

"We are survivors."

And up, to our thighs and hips.

"We are warriors."

"We are warriors."

And the whirlwind consumed our bodies up to our torsos.

"We are one."

"We are one."

"We are sisters."

"We are sisters."

Our hair blew and tangled together all around us as the vortex fully engulfed us.

"I have but to call, and you will be there."

"I have but to call, and you will be there," Farah repeated.

"I have but to call, and you will be there," Silence intoned.

"Nothing will break us."

"Nothing will break us."

"We are of the blood."

"We are of the blood."

"We are of the moon and stars."

"We are of the moon and stars."

"We are of the earth and seas."

"We are of the earth and seas."

"We are born of magic."

"We are born of magic."

"We are Sisters of the Beast!"

I repeated it with them, and we all cried, *"We are Sisters of the Beast!"*

The cyclone grew stronger around us, slapping our clothing against our bodies, whipping our hair in our faces.

Then it flew up, carrying us off our feet several feet up into the air.

"Hold strong!" I yelled, surprised by the strength of the spell, for it was an important casting, but I'd never experienced this kind of power when in the thralls of it.

The twister forced our bodies tight together, and my sisters and I kept hold, even as a burst of energy exploded between us. It and the maelstrom rose up to the skies, whipping the branches in a frenzy above us, tearing the dying leaves from the trees while departing us.

We dropped to the earth, and our linked hands held fast kept us together and on our feet.

"Holy goddess, what the fuck?" Jasmine asked from close.

I looked about us.

All our guards were close.

The men were scowling.

Hera was smiling.

Jasmine was eyeing me.

"Sister, you are something else," she decreed.

She was wrong.

I was not.

I looked to Silence and Farah.

*We* were something else.

With the astonishment I saw on their faces, I understood they knew it too.

We all smiled at each other before I let them go and linked arms with both of them, turning them back the way we came.

"Let us return."

The guard fanned out again and we sisters walked.

"That was...that was..." Farah stammered.

"*Amazing,*" Silence breathed.

"I wish I could take you both to The Enchantments with me," I told them. "I have a feeling you'd love it."

"I have already been there, so I know I would," Silence said. "It would just be all the better to be there with friends.

"I had never thought to journey there, but now..." Farah trailed off.

"When this is all done, we will meet there. One day," I vowed.

"We will," Silence agreed.

"Absolutely," Farah said.

"With Ha-Lah too," Silence said.

"All four. In celebration. When we vanquish the Beast," I declared.

"I hope she is all right," Silence put in. "Things did not seem a'tall well with her when she left with her king."

"I will seek her, just to sense her, make sure she is all right, and when we meet on the plane, I will share," I told them.

"If she isn't?" Silence asked.

"We'll figure it out then," I murmured.

We walked.

After a time, Farah broke our silence.

"Can I...do you mind...can I...?"

She did not finish.

"Can you what?" I asked.

"True is not sleeping well," she said on a rush.

I looked to her and Silence bent in front of me to do the same.

"There's quite a bit happening," Silence noted.

"It is a soldier's burden," Farah whispered.

I stopped, but even if I didn't, Silence did, so we all did.

"I don't know how to help him," Farah announced, sounding just that.

Helpless to help True.

It did not surprise me, but nevertheless, it broke my heart to hear that True had the battle dreams.

But I liked to see how distraught it made Farah.

Not that I wished her to be distraught, or, say, *more* distraught after all she'd endured.

But I did like that it was clear she cared that much about True.

"He is not of them," Silence told her.

I looked to Silence but it was Farah who spoke aloud my question.

"What?"

Silence shook her head and moved to form a huddle again.

"He is not of them. Uncle Wilmer. Aunt Mercy. Carrington. Courtiers. Castles. Pomp. Pageantry. Tradition. When you arrive at the castle, watch his face when someone bows to him. It..." She shook her head and finished on a whisper, "It always distressed me."

"I don't understand," Farah whispered in return.

"He would be a shepherd, if that was his lot, and be that happily," Silence shared. "A farmer. A forester. The keeper of an inn. He would have a hearth and a wife and a family and have naught even a line in a single tome in Go'Doan written to record his life and his mark on this earth after his passing. And he would do that with gladness in his heart, if he passed knowing in that life, he gave love and protected the ones he gave it to."

Farah was staring at Silence.

I was doing the same.

"But he will be the greatest king Wodell has ever known," Silence said fiercely. "And he will be *because* of this. Because he takes the hand of a farmer, he feels the callouses, and he knows the toil. Because he watches the ribbon weaving of the Day of Alabasta, the smiles on the children's faces, and he understands a day of rest needs to be proclaimed across the kingdom so his people can rejoice. Because, Farah, when he arrives home after a battle, he does not send lieutenants to share of the fallen. He travels Wodell with his men and he tells wives and mothers this news himself, he understands their suffering and it makes an indelible mark on his soul."

"Dear gods," Farah whispered.

"I didn't know he did that," I said.

"He does," Silence confirmed. "A man who is like that, I do not know." She shook her head sadly. "What I do know is that True needs to be needed. The only healing I suspect he can feel is to know he is helping someone. That they not only wish his presence but *need* it. Need him. Need *True*. Not Prince True of Wodell. True Axelsson, a good man, a kind man. And although, if it was in my power to give back to you what you have lost, I would do so, I suspect now, and it should be noted, every day in your futures together, you would be doing all you can simply needing him to be with you."

"I suspected this too," Farah said. "The weight of it seems to leave him when he feels useful."

Silence gave her a small smile. "Your instinct is right. And as such, I would not question it in future. Just keep doing what you're doing."

"It doesn't seem like much," Farah noted.

"Perhaps, but for True it would be everything," Silence replied.

"Is he...Mars is..." Farah took in a deep breath and let it out, saying. "Mars is revered in Firenze, as his father was. He is strong, and he is sure in his vision for our realm. The improvements King Ares began, and Mars continues, have made life much better for those who had very little before. Which makes those who had very much not so happy. But I believe they are coming to understand that if Mars carries the hearts of the common, they must learn to adjust, for their number is much smaller. Every coup attempt against Mars has been taken quite badly by the people, and they have been hard to control in their desires to rise up against those who wish our realm taken back to tyranny. And the assassination of Ares caused such grief across the land, I do not think even now, years later, they have recovered. It is only Mars's continued and resolute campaign to carry on his father's work that heartens them. This land…Wilmer…his counsel…and, well…*me*, a Firenz. I do not know. It is much different here, and it troubles me. It troubles me for me, and it troubles me for True."

When she was done, Silence gave her a bright smile and declared, "I am most pleased you travel our realm with True. For you will see." Her smile got bigger. "You will see."

"I'll see what?" Farah asked.

"You will see he is not revered," I chimed in.

Farah looked alarmed.

"He's beloved," Silence shared.

The alarm fled, and Farah's lips parted.

"He has but to look upon you with adoration and respect, which he already does, and the Dellish will adore you, Farah. Do not fear," Silence urged. "Aunt Mercy and Uncle Wilmer, my mother and father too, they are not like True, and the people of Wodell know it. He is of royal blood, 'tis true. But he is of *them*, and they know that too." Silence got closer to Farah. "And Mercy should heed that. You are from Firenze, but you could be from the moon, and if True wanted you, the people of Wodell would want you too."

"Truly?" Farah asked.

Silence nodded. "Truly." She smiled again. "And truly, I love this for you. You will have a grand and wonderous adventure, Farah, after all you've endured. And True will be thrilled he is the one who gets to give it to you."

"I had looked forward to this, for True seemed keen to have it, but I now look forward to it all the more," Farah said, moving them all so they'd start walking again.

"You should. The home of my birth is charming and second only to The Enchantments in being filled with magic," Silence told her. "With True as your guide, you have no hope but to fall in love."

"I already find it very beautiful," Farah decreed.

I looked to my right to see Wallace and Luther both walking, and scanning, but their backs were straighter, their chests more puffed out.

Their future queen was becoming enamored with their land.

And their future king.

And they liked it.

Brilliant.

Things had not been going all that well, I sensed, for any of us.

Or amongst all of us.

And now we were parting.

I got to go home, something I greatly looked forward to.

Silence and Farah, I had worried, were facing things they wished not to face.

I felt this way no longer.

Silence seemed again lively and engaged, as she had before the attack on the palace.

And the veil of grief had not completely subsided, as it wouldn't for some time.

But Farah's smiles were coming freer, even freer than before her mother died.

And the distance between my two sisters was gone.

So we would all be apart.

Then we would all be together, with Ha-Lah again completing us.

But at least for now, all was well.

# 52

## THE ALLIES

***Prince Cassius***
*Fifty Miles Inside the Southern Border*
WODELL

Prince Cassius stood with Macrinus and Antonius in the forest on the opposite side of the moors to the wood where the women were taking a stroll, and all three men stared at the oddly transparent witch who was upright, but equally oddly floating above the earth before them.

"They have been waiting many a year for just this chance, Your Grace," Fern promised. "They will be ready."

"It's essential this is kept completely secret, Fern," Cassius reminded her. "The new proclamations haven't yet been made. We can't begin to know how they'll be accepted. It might not be they're needed."

"They will be needed, my prince," Fern said in a dire tone. "Word has spread wide about the weddings, the identity of your intended and the preparations at the citadel for your own nuptials. There is unrest."

This was not news to him. Nero had reported much the same in the birds he'd sent.

It still did not fail to annoy him.

Fern took in his expression and went on, "Though, there is also much hope."

"We're making maneuvers to quell any unrest," he told her. "Otho is heading to you. After Nero delivers Aelia to The Enchantments, he, too, will return to Sky Bay. Soldiers loyal to me have been dispatched in squads to keep inconspicuous but close eye on the gentry. And your spies will be helpful."

She dipped her chin, ever humble.

But it could be that history would repeat itself and the arrogance of the ruling male elite would be their downfall.

Many of them didn't think twice about talking openly in front of a scullery maid, a mistress or a wife. The confidence they felt in their superiority meant they completely missed, in many cases, they were living with the enemy.

And in what was sure to come in Airen, that enemy was Cassius's ally.

He just hoped it wasn't so fucking bloody this time around.

"Mars has dispatched four regiments to the northeastern border of Firenze," he reminded her. "They will remain in their own land, but two thousand men will more than likely not be missed by Airenzian scouts. If any in Airenzian should act on this unrest, they will be sent the order to move in and keep peace, with five more regiments to follow. Not to mention, Aramus's fleet will be at the ready to blockade all ports if they're called. And I will ride with my men, and True's, entering Airen from the western borders. If any make moves, before you put your women in jeopardy, let us see if these alliances make the statement we wish them to make so arms are laid down before too many, if any, are lost."

"Please do not be mistaken, Prince Cassius. The women are ready to fight," Fern told him.

"I am not mistaken, Mistress Fern," he replied. "However, they are not trained."

"They were not trained the Night of the Fallen Masters, and they still successfully executed a revolution," Fern replied.

She was not wrong about that.

Therefore, to that, he dipped his chin to her.

"Thank you for casting your protections over Aelia and Nero," he said.

She nodded and replied, "Be safe on your journey to The Enchantments."

"And you just be safe," he ordered. "With this instability, you will naturally be under suspicion. I do not need to tell you that they do not need to know their suspicions are accurate."

Fern tipped her head to the side in acknowledgement before she blinked out of sight.

Cassius turned on his boot and started walking back to where they had camped.

His men fell in step at his sides.

The tents were down. Belongings packed. The horses loaded. And hundreds of soldiers had readied their mounts, prepared to move out.

Once the women returned, it would be time for all of them to go their separate ways.

However, now that the talk was accomplished with Fern, he needed a word with Mars and True before he and Elena started on their journey to The Enchantments.

"I don't like it," Tone muttered.

"Which part of the many things not to like that are happening are you referring to?" Cassius asked.

"You, riding solely with Mac and Ian to The Enchantments," Tone replied.

"Mac and Ian, Elena, Hera, Jasmine, and Elena tells me Hera's lover, Rosehana will also be with us," Cassius corrected him.

"Only five guards for a future king and queen?" Tone inquired.

"We will be all right," Cassius murmured.

"We're spread too thin," Antonius returned. "Nero and Otho in Airen. Me and Rus staying with your father. You heading with minimal guard to The Enchantments."

"Elena needs a respite from all our company, and it must be said, I need some time without so many bloody distractions to get to know the woman who will be my wife," Cassius replied.

"Would that the forest soon rings with much heftier groans than a Sky Citadel maid can give you as that happens," Mac entered the conversation.

"You might wish to watch what you say," Cass warned.

Mac sent him a grin. "I never wish to watch what I say."

This was regrettably true.

Cassius sighed.

"This is the most drawn-out coup in Triton history," Tone complained. "And with the comprehensiveness of our allies, it has but one conclusion. The only thing that remains to be seen is how many lives will be lost in reaching that conclusion. That is, if the man who would assume the throne doesn't get set upon by Zees, kidnapped by angry gnomes or assassinated by Airenzian traditionalists who scent change and are loathe to lose power."

"Angry gnomes," Mac chuckled.

"They are not all friendly," Antonius returned.

"They are two feet tall," Mac retorted.

"And have magic," Tone shot back.

"Were you asleep when our future queen set the night sky ablaze with but five arrows?" Mac asked. "I'll wager now, a bag of gold, Elena can best a hundred gnomes by just sneezing on them."

Bloody hell.

"Has it occurred to you that there is one realm who has not fully allied with us?" Cass asked before Tone could carry on that ludicrous conversation. "Not only will I better get to know Elena on this journey, and there is a good chance Aelia will have reached The Enchantments by the time we arrive, therefore I'll see my daughter, but also, I could make inroads with Ophelia. We have all the arms of Triton at our backs. Except the staffs of the Nadirii. I would have all arms laid down without *any* loss of life, Tone. And there is no guarantee of that. But the more I can weigh the side of a peaceful resolution to this mess, the better."

They were exiting the forest to see the rolling moors through which cut the road to Notting Thicket. The road they'd been traveling.

The camp was gone.

The royal procession was mingling about their horses.

The band that would go to the Arbor were mingling about theirs.

True and some of his men were standing with Mars and Kyril.

And the women were returned and huddled together, talking at the edge of the forest that lined the other side of the moors.

Severus noted Cassius and his men's arrival and broke from the women to move his way.

Cassius led his men toward True and Mars, as Antonius remarked, "So this is a diplomatic mission?"

"This is everything it needs to be, and in this time, every moment is everything it needs to be, or all will be lost."

Cassius saw that Severus had started jogging, which meant he had something to say before they reached Mars and True, therefore Cassius stopped walking.

He also saw that Elena was no longer paying attention to her huddle but had her eyes on Rus.

He could not see her face well enough from his distance to know her thoughts, just that her thoughts were on the direction his man was heading.

"Need a moment, Cass," Rus said when he arrived. "Alone."

Cassius looked to Mac and Tone, who caught his expression and moved away.

Severus moved closer.

"Keen to be away, Rus, and need to speak to Mars and True. What's this about?" Cassius prompted.

"She's bound them together so they can talk to each other, even if they are at some distance," Severus informed him. "A great cyclone overwhelmed them when she did. I've never seen anything like it. I thought they'd be swept to the skies. But when it was over, they just dropped to the earth like nothing happened."

He would have liked to have seen that.

"She's a witch, Rus. They can do shite like that."

"She is also no longer enamored of Prince True."

Cassius felt his body lock.

"She has realized, upon meeting you, that she never really was," Rus went on.

Cassius now felt a strangeness in his throat, around which he forced, "Pardon?"

"Princess Elena is smitten with you."

Something closed around his chest, doing this tightly, so it felt difficult to even breathe.

"Women chatter, I do not think she thought I could hear. I also do not think she cared if I did," Rus continued.

Cass's eyes drifted across the moor.

Elena was still looking their way, but when she saw she had Cassius's attention, she turned hers back to the women around her.

A womanly flirt. Wanting your attention, timid when they received it.

If the woman was comely, it was stirring.

He did not think Elena had any type of flirtation in her. But she apparently did.

And Elena was beyond comely.

Therefore, he was stirred.

"Thus, she intended me to do what I'm doing right now," Rus finished. "Telling you, so perhaps you'll do something about it."

"Thank you for this report," Cassius replied stiltedly.

"Cass—"

"I need to meet with Mars and True."

He started to move but Severus caught his arm, so he stopped.

"What just happened?" Rus asked, watching him closely.

"Naught," Cassius said through stiff lips.

"My friend, this is good, do you not see that?"

"The royal party leaves, Rus, and you need to be with them."

"If you let her in, you could be happy again, Cass. She has great beauty. She has great skill. Her confident manner is appealing. Her relationship with her lieutenants mirrors the one you've created with yours. And she watches you when you don't realize it like she wants to pounce on you, not to use her staff, but to fall on *yours*."

"Severus, we all wish to be on our way," he reminded him.

"You two suit."

"This is good, as we will be bound together for the rest of our days. Now, we need to be about our journeys."

"You're allowed to be happy, Cassius," Rus declared.

He wasn't.

He'd lived his motherless life in that dark pit of hell by the sea.

And then he'd found happiness.

He'd worshipped it.

And it didn't last.

"Go, Rus."

"You *should* be happy, Cassius," Rus pushed.

"Do I have to make that a command?" Cassius asked.

Rus's head twitched, and his hand dropped as he stepped away.

"No, Your Grace."

Cass flinched at the formality but other than that did naught but incline his head.

Severus turned to walk away, giving a dark look to Mac and Tone as he did. He cast the same expression in Ian's direction as Ian approached.

Cass ignored all of this and his men's attention coming to him as he moved toward Mars and True, feeling Mac and Ian fall in at his back. Tone would go with Rus to join the royal party.

Both True and Mars watched him as he approached but it was only Mars who spoke when he arrived.

"All right?" he asked.

No.

He wasn't.

He knew not why.

But he was not.

He had terror in his heart.

And he didn't understand it.

"Yes," he lied.

Mars studied him long moments before he glanced at True and wisely decided not to pursue it.

"Your conversation with the Airenzian witch?" Mars prompted when he looked back to Cass.

"The aristocracy of Airen sense change. They do not like it. Fern's underground of women and witches who have spent years spiriting the most afflicted females out of Airen is now at the ready to do all we need them to do, from spying to fighting. We're beginning with spying."

"And the alliance strengthens," Mars murmured.

"Indeed," Cass confirmed.

"I've had a message from Lorenz," Mars shared.

"Yes?" Cassius asked.

"He reports the Go'Doan temple in Fire City is nearly deserted."

Cassius felt his spine snap straight.

"As you suspected, they were behind the attack," he deduced.

Mars shook his head. "We cannot know. An interview with one of the few Go'Doan priests that remain made mention that this Rising that was shouted about at the pits, the priests in the Dome City believe has to do with the quakes and the return of the Beast. Why they would recruit Firenz citizens to assail my palace, he did not know. We suspect he does not know about the prophecy, which could be an explanation. Or, perhaps, not."

"And as this priest remained, it can be assumed he's not one of what appears more and more to be conspirators," Cassius remarked.

Mars nodded, but said, "Though, only assumed. Lorenz reports this man is in the dark as to why so many priests have fled. And Lorenz feels this ignorance is genuine. Before we leave, I will have a word Seph, Jell and Liam, who travel with the royal procession. It will be an antagonistic word, though I do not suspect Jell or Liam. But I never liked Seph. And if he knows something, I will sense it."

"And this priest Lorenz has in his home?" Cassius queried.

"He is healing. He is settling. But he is not talking," Mars told him. "However, the Go'Doan in Fire City pursued his whereabouts with some fervor. It was only when Guard himself visited the temple to share that he slipped away from the infirmary in the middle of the night and it could only be assumed with his other injuries that he was beset upon by someone, for possible gambling debts, or a jealous husband, thus, he has likely escaped for his own safety, did they cease demanding to know where he was."

"But Lorenz still thinks he knows something?" True entered the conversation, sharing that Mars had not fully briefed True before Cassius arrived.

Mars nodded again. "But he has patience as he believes this priest will eventually do the right thing and I have patience for I believe Lorenz knows what he's doing." Mars turned to Cassius. "I'm sending for Chu. As you know, in an effort to control her, he is dallying with Serena in Fire City. He will bring her and they both will journey to Notting Thicket to aid in keeping an eye on your father, but more, to look into the Go'Doan priests who travel with the procession."

"Control Serena?" True asked.

Both Mars and Cass looked to him. Mars then looked to Cassius to share it was up to him if he would do the same.

"Chu, one of Mars's Trusted, has made Serena his sex slave."

True stared blankly at Cass.

Then he threw his head back and roared with laughter.

Cass had never seen the man laugh at all, much less so uninhibitedly, and he couldn't stop his lips from twitching for it was not only infectious, what they were discussing was, indeed, hilarious.

"And I assume you made this happen so she would cease being such a relentless bitch to Elena," True deduced, his voice still quaking with humor.

"Yes," Cassius affirmed.

"Bloody spectacular," True muttered, still chuckling.

"Every time I am around you, I like you more and more," Mars decreed.

"Brilliant. I can sleep like a babe tonight, knowing that," True joked good-naturedly.

Mars smiled broadly at True.

True grinned back.

And it was then Cassius realized he agreed with Mars.

Every time he was around the Dellish prince, he liked him all the more.

However, they did not have time to carry on with this mutual admiration.

"Any word from Guard?" Cass inquired.

Mars shook his head. "Zosime has not delivered him their child. She is close. But I will not call on him even after their family has begun. She will need him, and his son or daughter will need time to know their father."

That had Cassius nodding, but he said, "This leaves you with few Trusted, Mars."

"Lorenz guards the throne in my absence, and Chu is an adept spy. He'll be useful in the Thicket."

"And you have but two guard, Mars," Cassius pushed.

"Two Trusted and two hundred warriors, Cass. I'll have much more guard than you."

"It is not the same."

"I have only one enemy where I'm going," Mars informed him.

He did.

Silence's father was slippery and spiteful and made no attempt to hide he disliked his son-in-law and desired to drive a wedge between husband and wife, for what aim, it was unknown.

This was also obvious to everyone, save, from appearances, Silence.

"Mind him," True put in, and both men looked his way.

"You have advice?" Mars asked.

"I have a bad feeling," True told him.

"I fear my queen is being taken in by his machinations, but the only result of that will be, when he exposes his true intentions, it will hurt her heart."

"I have a father I do not understand, and I do not respect," True returned. "Even so, it does not negate the hole that has been empty all of my life in not having that important person to fill it. Silence has never shared with me, but she has long been starved of love and affection, and now she's getting it. She is astute but matters such as these defy the logical mind when you're thinking with your heart. I do not know if she desired Johan's attention before. She never had it, so she seemed immune to its absence. I can only say if my father seemed to awaken from the trance he appears to have been in all my life and became a father to me, I might so welcome it, I'd be blind to the reasons behind it."

Mars studied True with such intensity, you could almost feel the heat coming from his gaze.

He then jerked up his chin.

True left it at that and changed the subject. "I've had words with your mother."

Mars did not like that and the line of his body shared it.

"I've asked her to work with my own to inject some modicum of Firenze into the wedding ceremony," True explained, making Mars relax. "She was eager to be of help. She rides with you now, but I'm asking you to allow her to go to Notting Thicket to do that for Farah. I've also informed my mother this will happen, and she should accord Queen Elpis every courtesy when she is at Birchlire. She has agreed."

"This is kind of you, True, and it will mean much to Farah," Mars said quietly.

"That's the goal," True murmured.

"It will also mean much to Mama for she wishes to make amends to her daughter not of the blood."

True had no response to that except to stiffly lift his chin.

Mars carried on to note, "You also travel with little guard after Farah was a target in Fire City."

"I travel with my version of Trusted, Mars," True replied.

This was all that needed to be said for Mars had no reply.

Thus, True reminded them all, "Birds. Frequently. If we do not hear from one or the other for two full days, the others ride to their last known location."

Cassius and Mars agreed to what they'd already agreed with dips of their chin.

But after Mars righted his, his expression softened when his eyes caught on something beyond them and his tone was distracted when he said, "Safe journeys to you both. We shall meet again in the Thicket."

He then cut between the two men as if they were branches to brush through.

Cassius and True turned to watch him stride to Silence, who was hurrying toward him, her cloak billowing behind her in the wind, her hands juggling her active pet monkey.

The King of Firenze arrived at his queen, took the monkey, set it on his shoulder, then swept his bride in one arm, bending her over it with great flair, even if he did it only to touch his lips to hers, lift away and smile in her face.

A blush stole into her cheeks, but she smiled back.

Well, it appeared whatever was keeping king and queen apart, Mars had made great inroads in sweeping away.

"And a stunning blow has been dealt to Johan," True murmured.

At his words, Cassius found the party that would ride to the Arbor and saw Silence's father scowling at his daughter with her husband.

"I do not think that is why he makes that show," Cassius murmured in return. "That is but Mars, the Firenz are flamboyant. And he's falling in love with her."

"I do not think that either," True replied. "I still like to see Johan back on a foot when he's been peacocking around with glee even when it's clear his daughter carries heavy burdens."

"On that, we agree."

As Mars strode off with his wife in the curve of his arm and a monkey on his shoulder, True went alert at Cassius's side.

"And there is my future bride...and yours," True said, and Cass's attention turned to Farah and Elena walking their way, arm in arm. "Thus, I shall be away. Safe journey, Cassius."

"And the same for you, True."

Cassius watched as True walked to Farah, who disengaged from Elena to meet him.

An Elena who did naught but glance at True with a small smile while continuing on her way to Cass.

He ignored that and noted True had utterly no flamboyance whatsoever, but no one witnessing the look on his face as he gazed upon Farah would miss there was no other person on Triton he would rather have close than her.

So Elena had realized it had never been True.

And for True, it might have been Elena, but he now realized he'd found the woman who was his destiny.

Thus, that band around Cassius's chest tightened.

He turned his gaze with effort to his future bride.

Tunic. Moccasins. Casings bound with crisscross straps up her thighs. Her heavy purple cloak billowing behind her in the stiff wind. Her glorious honey hair wisping across her face and catching on her full, rosy lips.

He could fuck her where he stood.

Hell, he *wanted* to fuck her where he stood.

"Are you ready?" she asked, stopping in front of him.

"Yes," he answered.

Her head tipped to the side and her gaze grew acute.

"Are you all right?" she asked.

"Yes," he lied.

Her head righted, and she declared, "I'm going to make you commune with pixies tonight."

And again, she was on about the pixies.

And...

Fuck.

*Fuck.*

Now he understood this feeling that plagued him.

He could fall in love with her.

"Cassius?" she called.

"Let us go," he muttered, moving to round her.

But he stopped when her hand fell on the center of his chest.

The touch was light, but it burned through him like a brand.

She could stop him from a charge with a touch of her hand.

She could control his mood with the tone of her voice.

She was warrior and he could not strip her of that. It was not what she was, it was who she was born to be.

It was also magnificent.

But there was a very real chance he could lose her.

In the battle with the Beast.

In the battle for Airen.

In the giving to him of children.

Fuck, she could walk down the steps of the Citadel on her way to dinner, fall and break her neck.

Danger swirled around her and would for the rest of her days.

Her hair whipped his neck and he realized she'd come closer.

He tipped his eyes down to her.

And yes, bloody hell, she was closer.

He could take her mouth simply bending his neck.

"You're not all right," she whispered. "What's on your mind?"

"Nothing. We must be away."

He made to move again, but this time, she shifted so she bodily barred his path and he had to stop, or he'd come up against her.

And he could not have that.

Thus, he stopped.

"You are changed," she noted quietly.

"I'm eager to be on our way."

"We can delay if you wish to talk."

"And what in the last two minutes of us speaking gives you the impression that is what I wish to do?" he asked.

"Well I know *this* Cassius. You're being a cad."

A cad?

He did not feel like laughing. Not at all.

But by the gods...

"A cad?"

"A cad," she affirmed.

"And what is the word for a stubborn woman who pushes a man who does not wish to talk into talking by not letting the conversation lie and then calling him names?" he asked.

Her mouth quirked. "A concerned affianced."

Oh yes.

He wanted to fuck her where they stood.

"Do pixies traverse the moors?" he inquired.

"Not often. They prefer the trees, creeks, streams, rivers, etcetera."

"So if we stand here for eternity, I won't be able to commune with them."

With that, she smiled openly.

"Your point is made."

"Excellent. Then shall we go?"

She shrugged. "Certainly."

When he moved that time, Elena allowed it.

But she fell into step beside him and walked far too close.

He could take her hand, if he wished.

He wished.

But he did not.

And when she swung astride her horse and her tunic lifted, exposing the seat of her body stocking stretched lovingly across her rounded arse, he could have pulled her off her horse, dragged her to the trees and covered her, if he wished.

And he wished.

But he did not.

However, when she looked over her shoulder at him atop his horse and her gaze was a dare before she set her moccasins into her steed's sides and bolted forward in a graceful charge, he wished to accept her dare.

So he set his boots in his horse, Caelus.

And he chased after her.

# 53
# THE DISCIPLINE

***G'Seph***
*Seventy-Five Miles Inside the Southern Border*
WODELL

Seph's delight at seeing his confederate, G'Fenn, and the four other priests with him that Seph knew were of The Rising instantly evaporated when his fellow priest was within reaching distance.

For he did indeed reach.

Doing so to strike Seph across his cheek in a slap so hard, Seph's head jerked to the side.

When he whipped it forward, his eyes were narrowed, and his temper had sparked.

"What—?" he began.

But he got no further.

Fenn slapped him again.

And again.

Seph lifted an arm to ward off the blows, only for Fenn to swipe it away and slap him again.

Seph started to retreat, his cheek stinging with pain and heat, but Fenn followed him.

One of the priests with Fenn rounded Fenn's side, caught Seph again raising his hand in an effort to protect himself, and he held Seph's wrist steady, which held Seph's body steady for Fenn to continue raining blows.

Seph jerked his head away, bending at the waist to escape, shouting, "Bloody stop!" only for Fenn to wrap his hand around Seph's throat and pull him upright.

His fingers held fast…and tight, as his brother priest put his face to Seph's.

"You fool," he hissed.

Seph realized he couldn't breathe.

He further realized he could not escape.

Fenn was taller than him, he had more weight to him, more muscle on his bones.

He was also younger.

But mostly, the hold he had on Seph made Seph fear that if he yanked away, he'd come without his throat.

"How does it feel?" Fenn asked. "To be ruled with an iron hand?"

Seph opened his mouth but no words came out.

And no breath went in.

He started gagging, lifting his free hand to the wrist at his throat, wrapping his fingers around in what he hoped was a beseeching manner.

"How does it feel, to meet a brother, an equal, and have him," Fenn tossed Seph to his knees on the forest floor, his compatriot letting Seph's wrist go, and Seph dragged in breath as Fenn finished, "bring you to your knees?"

"I—" Seph tried.

"You bloody," and Fenn's boot connected with Seph's face, causing a starburst to explode in his eyes as pain burst through his nose back into his brain and he fell hard to his side, "*fool.*"

Blinking rapidly, he pushed up to a hand in the cold leaves, turning his head, only to see Fenn's face an inch from him as the priest bent over him.

"Our temple in Fire City is all but deserted. Our priests there scattered to the winds. And thus, the king and his men are now aware that it is Go'Doan who was behind the attack on the palace," Fenn informed him.

This couldn't be.

"What?" Seph asked, feeling the blood seeping from his nose, just as he felt it drain from his face and his stomach pitched nauseatingly. "That can't be. I told them not to flee."

"You told them, and you beat them, and you whipped them," Fenn returned. "Have you not learned in the *years* of carefully carrying out our strategy that it is the carrot, *not* the stick that induces loyalty? Discipline is *only* for extremes. If you train a dog using pain, you train him only to fear and hate you, and when the time comes he has had too much, he will strike. But we are not training dogs, Seph. We are training and recruiting *men*. They have conscious thought and they have free will, and if they no longer understand and support a cause, they can," Fenn landed a vicious, closed-fist blow on Seph's cheekbone, causing him to grunt in pain, before he finished, "*walk away*."

Seph dragged himself from his fellow priest only to run into something.

He looked behind him and up.

His back was against a set of legs and another priest that had traveled with Fenn was glowering down at him.

Fenn's voice came back to him.

"You are relieved of command."

His gaze snapped toward Fenn. "You cannot relieve me of command. You don't have the authority. Only the Golden Thomas has that authority."

Fenn tipped his head to the side.

"I do not?" he asked. "That is most odd, considering I was dispatched on this journey for that purpose *by* Thom. Though not solely for that purpose as I've also been ordered to take up your command and find some way to repair the damage you have wrought."

Seph scooted away from the man who was blocking his path and pushed himself to his feet.

"I heard no word of this," he declared, his eyes on Fenn, but his attention was also on the four priests with him.

He should not have come alone.

Though how could he know he'd face such as this?

It was unthinkable.

"Yes, you did. I just told you," Fenn replied.

Seph lifted his chin. "It is not you who communicates my orders. I get them from Thom direct."

"Where's Drey?" Fenn asked suddenly, making Seph's stomach pitch again.

"Drey?" he inquired in return in order to buy some time for Seph was not heartened by this change of subject.

"Drey. G'Drey. The priest I sent to you from the gilded city to assist with The Rising. The one whose arse you whipped to the point there was no healthy skin left," Fenn explained.

Oh, but he would find the soldier who had shared so freely, and they would learn *his way* how not to betray your command.

"I do not know," Seph spat. "The last I heard was that he met an accident on the way to the school."

"Did you know he's my chosen one?" Fenn queried.

By Bedi.

This simply got worse and worse.

"No," Seph forced out his lie.

"He sends no birds. No messages," Fenn shared. "It's most peculiar. Handsome, but so needy, my Drey. His father took being Dellish to rather an extreme. And thus Drey…" He shook his head. "So misunderstood. This is a lesson for you, Seph. For it took not much effort before I had but to look upon Drey with the expression I'd trained him to read, and he'd be down on his knees, sucking my cock precisely as I enjoy it most. He did this knowing I'd then fuck him precisely how he enjoyed it most. The carrot, Seph. Almost always, it leads to satisfactory results. Sadly, it got to the point where Drey was so eager to please, I'd become weary from it and needed some distance. Therefore, I sent him to you. However, I did so knowing eventually *I'd want him back.*"

Seph swallowed and took a step away.

Fenn took that step with him.

As did the others.

Yes, this simply got worse and worse.

"And he did not participate in the mass exodus you perpetrated with the ignorance of your command," Fenn continued. "He was gone before you failed so spectacularly after being given such a *golden* opportunity. Having every important personage in Triton under one roof and hundreds of men trained and at the ready to strike a blow for The Rising that would have been felt throughout all Triton."

Seph kept moving, as did Fenn and the others, and he did it snapping, "I did not fail. It was not me who scaled the palace walls."

Fenn shook his head even as he replied, "I'm now seeing the problem. You give the command to sally into battle, success is not yours, it's your men's. But failure, G'Seph, if the men find failure, that is *always* the providence of the general."

He did not have to take a lecture from the likes of *Fenn.*

Seph was practically there that day so many years ago that The Rising was *conceived.*

Fenn was but a boy back then, not a priest, not Go'Doan.

He was nothing then.

And he was nothing *now.*

Fenn could not tell him what his *providence* was.

At his end, Seph stood still and demanded, "Cease moving."

The men did.

That was more like it.

Seph drew breath into his nose. "We shall return to the Dome City, after the assassination is carried forward on King Wilmer that I planned, an incident that will force Prince True to—"

"This attack has been abandoned," Fenn told him. "The servant you commissioned to administer the poison has been persuaded to take it instead. In the jumble of the procession breaking up into four different parties, I assume his death will not be noted for some time."

By the true gods.

"The procession breaking up?" Seph asked, and Fenn smiled.

"Ah, brother G'Seph," he said jovially, as if someone told him something he found most amusing. "Your foolishness knows no bounds. You haven't even noted how truly they all dislike you and how little they trust you. They've ridden in four separate directions. Liam and Jell know of this, and they rode with Wilmer to the castle."

"I only don't know this because *you* called upon me for this meeting," Seph informed him.

"It was decided at breakfast, *prior* to me calling upon you, and it is now well past lunch. Even Liam and Jell did not inquire as to which party you would ride with. They simply rode without you."

Seph clenched his teeth.

Liam and Jell, staunch Go'Doan, Liam worshiping at the altar of wisdom and healing, Jell simply being...*Jell*.

Both of them...

Useless.

Fenn's gaze shifted momentarily to the priest at Seph's back in a way that Seph did not like.

It then returned to him.

"And now for those extremes I was referring to," he murmured.

Seph was about to walk away as he asked, "Extremes?"

"Those that require discipline," Fenn explained.

The skin all over Seph's body electrified and this meant he did not walk away.

He prepared to flee.

However, he did not get the chance to flee.

They set upon him, and although he fought, kicked and shouted, it took frighteningly little time to drag him to an old, weathered tree stump.

They forced him to his knees beside it.

By Bedi, they intended to whip him.

He felt his cock pulse as his skin again charged in a much different manner.

But when they pressed him to bend over the stump, it was not his chest held to the grayed wood.

It was his forearms.

With one man behind him shoving down with both hands in Seph's shoulders, and two men to either side holding his forearms to the stump, Seph watched with mounting trepidation as Fenn moved off behind a tree that stood proud not too far from where he knelt.

Fenn returned with a long-handled ax.

Dearest Go'Chas.

No.

"Fenn," he whispered.

"Now," Fenn began, coming to stand before Seph at the stump, "which hand was it that you used to crop a loyal solider about the face?"

Which...

*Hand?*

"You cannot do this," Seph told him.

"It doesn't matter," Fenn replied, "as I'll be taking both."

"No!" Seph shouted, twisting savagely, but inconsequentially, against his captors. "You cannot do this, brother! We are one! We are The Rising!"

"Do not worry, *brother*," Fenn responded. "We are all trained. We will staunch the flow of blood and stitch you. You will not lose your life this crisp Dellish afternoon."

But Seph wasn't listening.

He was struggling.

The only priest not holding him down came forward to tightly tie a leather truss at the meat of Seph's forearm.

The priest to Seph's right shifted as Fenn moved into place and raised the ax.

"*No!*" he shrieked.

The next sound that came from him was also a shriek, but it was not a word, though it communicated perfectly the depths of pain that swept it out of Seph's mouth.

Oddly, losing his other hand, Seph didn't even feel.

Mostly because, seconds later, he'd lost consciousness.

# 54
# THE SIGNIFICANCE

***Tedrey***
*Receiving Chamber, Manor of Lorenz, Captain of the Trusted, Fire City*
FIRENZE

Tedrey sat on the plush cushion in the seat set in the window and stared out at the bustle of the street at the front of his master's house.

Firenz citizens moved to and fro, carrying baskets in hands, on backs, on heads, or bags in arms (or on backs). Or their hands held the hand of a little one who trotted beside them. Or they sat atop a fine, sleek Firenz steed and cantered along the road, going about their business.

There were some who were smiling. Some laughing. Some frowning. Some expressionless and deep in thought or intent on whatever they were doing.

Life went on.

But weeks ago, their king's palace was attacked. Men were executed publicly. But hours after that, their king took his queen in matrimony even more publicly and the city buzzed with excitement as the air rang with revelry.

And but a few days later, it was known and spoken about widely, of the quiet, private, but noble funeral that had been held for the wife of a traitor, a woman forgiven by a king and sent to the next realm with adoration and respect.

And today…

Nothing.

It was just any other day.

As the day before the attack on the palace was.

As the day after the royal wedding was.

And every day in between.

Life just went on.

It was all…

Insignificant.

"Tedrey."

He jumped when he heard the deep voice growling toward him and turned his head to see the warrior, his master, and the owner of the manor walk into the room.

"My lord," Tedrey replied.

Lorenz stopped and sighed heavily before he said, "You do not have to call me that, *amico*. I have shared this."

"You don't like master," Tedrey returned.

"I do not for I am not that either, until I begin to take your arse again, and you can call me that if you wish while I'm doing it."

Tedrey pressed his lips tightly together and watched Lorenz take another two steps into the room and stop.

"This," he said, lifting his heavy arm and indicating what Tedrey would understand was his lips being pressed together with what Lorenz said next, "is why I've come to speak to you."

"I don't understand."

"Faunus has called for you. You have declined."

Tedrey looked back to the street.

"Tedrey, I will have your eyes," Lorenz demanded.

He looked again to the warrior.

"You are healed and it's my understanding that this is the fourth time Faunus has called on you and you have refused," Lorenz stated.

Tedrey straightened in his seat. "If you wish to use me—"

"Stop speaking."

At the annoyed disappointment Tedrey heard in his voice, he went quiet.

"Do you still have pain?" Lorenz asked.

Tedrey shook his head.

"Do you concern yourself with the appearance of your scars?"

Tedrey again looked to the road.

"Tedrey."

His name came closer and it was said lower, with sadness, and warmth, thus Tedrey turned his head yet again, tipped it back, and saw Lorenz but a foot from him, gazing down upon him, his expression gentle.

"Faunus knows of your injuries, and he still asks for you," Lorenz reminded him.

"It's insignificant," Tedrey replied.

He watched Lorenz's brows draw together. "How so?"

"In all ways. It's insignificant. Everything." He lifted his hand and indicated the street in front of the manor. "All of it."

Lorenz turned his attention to the window, then back to Tedrey.

"I sense we are no longer speaking of Faunus wishing to take you to the Heden District to get you inebriated and fuck you until you lose consciousness," Lorenz surmised.

"There is nothing to speak of. We get up. We exist. It means nothing what we do, who we meet, what we say. We go to sleep. And repeat this until we die."

"Nyx has decided she wishes me to give her a child."

Tedrey stared up at Lorenz.

Lorenz carried on speaking.

"Zosime will give Guard a child any day now, and as it happens with women, she sees the beauty Zosime has become, the love that has grown between two lovers that were devoted to one another before, but this has bloomed beyond all imagining as her belly grows with proof of that love, and she wishes the same for her. For us. And I shall give this to her."

"I-I'm most happy for you, my lord."

"I am Lorenz unless I command you, in play, to call me otherwise," Lorenz said shortly. "And if I have to say that to you again, Tedrey, you will no longer enjoy the warmth of my home."

Tedrey felt fear bolt through him.

Lorenz did not belabor that.

He returned to his earlier subject.

"I will give my wife as many children as she feels she needs. And we will spend our days until they leave their home teaching them to do upon the world naught but what they feel is good and right. And that will be what we share with them is good and right. So it will be good and right. We will leave this world giving it something good and right. We will leave it knowing they will teach their children the same. And so on. And that is not insignificant."

"I do not lie with women. I will not give the world that."

"It does not have to be your seed to give it that. Did you not teach when you were with the Go'Doan? Did you not understand the impression you could leave on the children in your care? And I know of men who do not lie with women. I also know of children who are born into this world or find themselves without parents who need them. Men who take only men, who love only men, take these children and give them what Nyx and I will give flesh of our flesh. And what they give is no less significant."

"The palace was attacked, and no one cares," Tedrey returned. "Men lost lives. Your king was under threat. And they just go about," he flicked his hand to the window again, "with their baskets and their children or on their horses, and it is like it did not happen."

"Do you think if King Mars was harmed or killed, do you think if his queen was harmed or killed that what is outside that window would be the same?"

"And how would it be different, except perhaps a different queen some months or years in the future would be taken by your ruler? Or a different king would sit the throne? Regardless, the baskets would still be carried."

"You were not here when Ares was murdered. The city knew mourning. Windows shrouded. Heads draped in black. Horses trailing blankets of it over their rumps. Children did not play. If music rang, it was melancholy."

"And now that is over," Tedrey noted.

"Look at my face, look closely at my face," Lorenz demanded.

Tedrey did just that.

"My king, Ares, was murdered," he stated.

"You said that."

"Look at my face, Tedrey."

Tedrey watched closer.

"My king, Ares, was murdered," Lorenz repeated.

And Tedrey saw it.

Sadness.

"I mourn him still," Lorenz said quietly. "My sire is dead and has been for longer than my king. I mourn him still. My children will know of both of them and they will speak of them to their children. This is not insignificant."

"But there will come a generation when those names aren't spoken."

"This is true, but they will be of their ancestors. They will be of those who came before them. Even if the names are forgotten, the legacy of each being on this planet never disappears. It is simply the way. There is no escaping it."

Tedrey looked to Lorenz's feet, muttering, "Maybe it is only me who is insignificant."

After saying that, he watched Lorenz's sandals turn and he lifted his eyes and kept watching as the big man walked out of the room.

And that signaled to Tedrey that he was correct.

He was no king.

He would be no father.

He was part of a great collaboration that was to change the rule of all Triton, he left it and they did not care he was gone. They moved forward in their plans, which were thwarted, and it mattered not. He had brothers, ones he belonged to, and a lover, one he thought had great feeling for him. It had been weeks since he had "disappeared," and his brothers, his lover, did not care enough to search for him.

Life went on.

He started when Lorenz returned, a purpose to his gate, a leather-bound book in one hand, his fist closed over something else in his other, but there was a silver pen poking between his fingers.

"I bought these for you some days past, but my wife did not wish me to give them to you," Lorenz declared, stopping close to Tedrey in his seat. "You do not talk to her. Not of anything of import. You are gentle with her and seem to enjoy her attention, presence and prattling, but you give her nothing in return. Until now, you have not talked to me. I felt you should talk to someone, even if that someone was the pages of a book. She did not wish for you to have the opportunity to put your thoughts in a book, for it might mean you would not share with her and therefore she could not take what you give her and help you bear its burden."

He held out the book as well as his other hand, which he opened to reveal a pot of ink with that pen, which, being nearer to it, Tedrey could see was elegantly engraved all over with swirls and loops.

The book, its binding, the stamped leather, was expensive.

But that pen had to cost...

"And now I give these to you," Lorenz interrupted his thoughts and shook his hands. "Take them. Put your thoughts in these pages. Let this book bear your burdens. Then give the rest of you to your family."

Tedrey's head snapped back so fast to catch Lorenz's eyes, he felt pain at his neck.

"My family?" he asked.

"I have a vast and beautiful family, Tedrey. My wife, and the children she will one day give me. My mother still lives, and both of Nyx's parents live, as do her two sisters, and mine. My brothers, who are soldiers. My king, who is my closest brother. My lovers, Persephone, and you. If we live them right, our whole lives are filled with family and that means you will one day be uncle to my children. Does that feel insignificant?"

Tedrey's heart was beating ever faster.

Uncle?

He would be uncle?

"Take these things, Tedrey," Lorenz ordered.

"The book is leather-bound. It is costly. And the pen—"

"If these things mattered to me, I would not have handed over the coin or I would keep them for myself. They don't. *You* matter. Please pay attention. This is my point, *amico*." He shook his hands again. "And take them."

Tedrey felt his throat close.

"Tedrey…"

"They are too much and I…I do not…I could help around the house. I could—"

Lorenz's arms dropped, and his gaze grew acute as he studied Tedrey. "What manner of parent raised you?"

"I…sorry?" Tedrey asked.

"If I wanted a servant, I would hire one. If I wanted an injured man to work for his supper, I would be a beast. I am offering a gift to a friend. What manner of parent raised you that you would not accept a kindness offered with a true heart?"

Taking in these words, slowly, Tedrey reached out his hands. It was not slowly as Lorenz again extended the gifts.

Tedrey took them and felt his throat cinch.

"Thank you," Lorenz said, making Tedrey blink.

*He* was thanking *Tedrey*?

"Now I will leave you to your musings," Lorenz muttered, turning again to leave.

"I still wish to help around the house," Tedrey called to his back, making Lorenz face him.

"If you wish to help, most of the Go'Doan priests have left the city. Their schools have no teachers. If you are well, you can go back to teaching. You are needed there. It is your choice, but I would hope you did not go wearing the robes. The priests that are left, they will not turn you away, either way you return to them."

His heart leapt at the thought of being back with his students, which Tedrey found odd, but even odd, it was undeniable.

His feelings were entirely different about the Go'Doan leaving the city.

"Are you well enough to do this?" Lorenz asked.

"The Go'Doan priests have left the city?" Tedrey asked back.

"They were behind the attack. This is twice they have beset our sovereigns. It would have been ferreted out. Thus, in the end, they have shown some modicum of wisdom, for they chose flight rather than tar."

"You know it was them?" Tedrey queried nervously.

"Yes, we know it was them. And yes, I know that you were amongst the collaborators, but your heart was not true to their cause. If it was, nothing could have kept you in my home while that attack was being carried out. Not even the grave injury they did to you."

Tedrey felt heat hit his cheeks and terror burn in his chest.

"Y-you know?"

"I have known practically since I met you, *amico*."

"And you still call me *amico*?"

"Do you wish me or my wife harm?"

"No."

His answer was swift and not at all nervous.

Lorenz's lips twitched.

"And do you think I did not know this too?" he asked softly.

Tedrey looked away.

His tone was still soft when he asked, "How deeply are you in love with her?"

His gaze skittered back. "I...I don't...I don't feel that way—"

"I know it is not my wife's body you desire, but her heart that you adore," Lorenz decreed and grinned. "When I fell, I went about it the other way."

Tedrey did not doubt that and found it amusing.

However, he also found his feet and took them.

Standing and staring Lorenz right in the eyes, he declared, "I will never—"

His grand declaration didn't come to fruition.

Lorenz shook his head and again interrupted him. "I know, Tedrey. You do not love her as I do. You'll never love her as I do. Or you would not be right here, right now. But you love her, do you not?"

He did not know about love.

However.

"She, and you, are the only beings who have ever in my life shown me kindness."

Tedrey watched with no alarm as Lorenz's face grew hard.

Lorenz never liked to think of these things that had always been a way of Tedrey's life.

And so perhaps he *was* learning about love.

"I will take that as a yes," Lorenz said through gritted teeth.

"I don't know how to show it in return," Tedrey whispered.

"You will not learn, staring at the road and being morose," Lorenz replied.

This was very true.

"Do you...do you want to know about The Rising?" he offered, and Tedrey did not miss the flare in his eyes at the last two words.

However, he mistook it for the fact Lorenz already knew.

Maybe not all of it.

But he knew of The Rising.

He was surprised when Lorenz answered, "When you're ready to tell me."

"I would suspect that, if the priests have fled, it's rather in disarray," he mumbled.

"I would suspect the same, but we are not counting on that."

Tedrey continued mumbling, "That's probably wise." He drew breath into his nose and spoke more distinctly when he noted, "I do not understand why you forgive me."

"I have not said I forgive you."

These words were like a blow.

"But—" he started.

"My wife's heart bleeds for you, and as my wife owns my heart, I have little to say in the matter of her wishing to care for you. You are not a threat. You are clearly very confused. I have hope you will find your way and it will be the right way. But it is not gratitude for kindness that should guide that way. You should understand what you do is right, and that should guide your way. I will hope for this. That you learn right and how to act on it."

He'd never thought about it before.

But he wanted to learn right and not simply because every part of his life until he met these people in this house had gone so wrong.

Tedrey turned his head away again, this time so Lorenz would not see the tears that sprang to his eyes.

"Why do you not look at me as you weep, *amico*?" Lorenz asked with open curiosity, sharing that Tedrey was hiding nothing.

"It is weak," Tedrey muttered shakily.

"And again, I have proof the manner of your parents was no manner at all."

Tedrey returned his surprised attention to Lorenz.

"You are warrior," he remarked.

"I am," Lorenz agreed. "And I wept when my father died. I wept when King Ares died. I wept when my bride bound her life to mine. I felt tears sting my eyes when my king claimed his queen. I will undoubtedly weep when my wife gives me my first child, and any that come after. If she were to move to the next realm before me, I do not know if I will ever stop weeping. What I do know is I will not have the will even to try. There is no weakness in being fully you and fully feeling anything you feel. What makes us weak is when we do not celebrate all that we are, all that we feel, which is what makes us strong."

"My father did not like that I liked…"

"Men?" Lorenz guessed.

Tedrey nodded.

"A peculiar Dellish trait," Lorenz murmured.

"I was…I was very…" He cleared his throat. "I did not know how to be around people who did not take extreme issue with this."

"The Go'Doan," Lorenz stated.

Tedrey again nodded. "They…having that freedom to be who I was and be with who I wished, I was seduced by that religion."

"Religion is not seductive," Lorenz returned. "It's faith. Faith, at its heart, is pure. It is man who led you down the wrong path. Beware of laying blame on the gods, no matter which gods they are, for the actions of men, or your own. Only you are responsible for what you do and the same for any man or woman."

Tedrey stood still, struck so deeply by these words, he could not move.

"I ask one thing of this Rising," Lorenz went on, but his question was vocalized as a statement. "It is not all of the Go'Doan, is it."

Tedrey shook his head.

Lorenz nodded and continued speaking.

"Now I ask one thing of you, Tedrey. That you go speak to my wife and share some things with her I do not know for if she knows we have had this talk and she was not the one who reached you for you to offer what is in your heart, she will pout or fume and we cannot make a baby if she's pouting or fuming."

For a moment, Tedrey could do nothing but blink at him.

When he saw Lorenz's mouth quirking, Tedrey then could do nothing but smile.

Lorenz smiled back.

Then Tedrey dipped his chin at his friend.

And went in search of Nyx.

# 55

## THE PATRA

***Princess Elena***
*One Hundred Miles from The Northwest Border of The Enchantments*
WODELL

We sat around the campfire with me glaring at Cassius's back, considering the fact that I'd seen a lot of it the last three days.

The man had a fine set of shoulders and an alluring arse, but I was sick of that view.

He was walking into the wood, something he did of an eve *every* eve since we left the others.

The first night he'd gone with Mac, but Mac had returned without him.

The second night, he'd gone with both his men, and together his men had returned without him.

Neither night had he come to my tent when he'd come back.

He had promised, from that first night he joined me in my chamber at Catrame Palace, we would never sleep apart.

I had not desired this.

We were now sleeping apart.

And I did not like it and not simply because, without Cassius beside me, sleep was difficult to find, and it was restless when I finally caught it.

Further, if we stopped for lunch, he would walk away from the rest of us to enjoy his repast on his own. Or, more accurately, brood over his meal by himself.

And at breakfast, he appeared last, wolfed down some bread slathered in butter and jam, packed his horse, mounted the great steed (for Caelus was beautiful, and he had to be eighteen hands tall!), set his heels into Caelus's sides and we all had to race to catch up to him.

I could tell, at first, Mac and Ian were confused at his behavior.

After their return from their wander with their prince, this had melted into annoyance.

I'd started at annoyance.

Now I felt the beginnings of fear.

He was not being a cad or a lout. He was also not amusing or his brand of charming. He was further not attentive, not in the slightest.

He was not *anything*.

I wasn't certain our trip to The Enchantments was a good idea in the beginning. But I'd come to realize I was looking forward to it.

It would be a time where it was just him and me, riding through the beauty of Dellish forests in autumn, getting to know one another. Then being in my home, having the opportunity to *show* him my home, not to mention meet his daughter, and finally introduce him to Dora.

All right, it was just him and me, and Hera, Jazz, Rosehana, Mac and Ian.

But getting to know his men, and Cassius getting to know my women, was another form of getting to know one another.

And when he wasn't being annoying, I'd stopped denying to myself that I thought he was fascinating (and I'd found I liked his men—Mac was a scamp, wicked and mischievous, but almost always fun to be around, Ian was thoughtful and soft spoken—these traits oddly, but I found it very telling, mirroring Jasmine and Hera).

Further, Cassius was always attractive.

And I wanted more.

But now...he was nothing.

There but far away.

Distant from even his men.

But mostly, distant from me.

"So, what's up his arse?" Jazz demanded to know, her attention directed at Mac and Ian.

"Jazz," Hera said quietly.

Jasmine, being Jasmine, did not even glance at Hera.

Her gaze remained pinned on Cassius's men.

"I mean...*now*. What's up his arse *now* since it seems something is always up his arse?" Jazz amended.

"He has many things on his mind," Mac replied tetchily.

"And?" Jasmine pressed. "Who doesn't? Who," she tossed both hands toward the fire and then spread her arms wide, "sitting here under the night sky does not have many things on their minds? Not one of us is out here for an enjoyable jaunt. Change is afoot and we're all going to be facing some very serious things."

"*You* will not face assuming rule of an entire kingdom, one where the changes you intend immediately to make will not be taken well," Mac reminded her.

"*I* will be at the back of my princess, who will be queen to your new king, and her very presence in your land will not be taken well," Jasmine retorted.

"You should follow him," Rosehana said softly.

I turned my gaze her way to see hers and Hera's on me.

I focused on Hera.

She nodded, affirming she agreed with her lover.

"I agree, you should follow him," Ian added.

I turned my attention again and saw Ian watching me.

I also saw Mac studying Ian uncertainly.

Mac gave voice to this uncertainty, saying, "I'm not sure that's a good idea, brother."

"Why not?" Jasmine demanded to know.

Both Ian and Mac looked to Jazz, but it was Mac who spoke.

"This has naught to do with you," he bit. "And you'd do well to learn something it's made clear you have not learned. In matters that do not involve you, you should keep your mouth shut."

Oh no.

Man, woman, child, yeti, that was no way to speak to Jasmine.

But it must be said, especially a man.

I straightened, feeling Hera and Rosehana coming alert beside me.

"What did you just say?" Jazz whispered.

"Jasmine," I called in a firm tone.

"Cass needs some time to himself," Mac stated.

"He's had that," Jazz retorted. "Now he needs someone to help him extricate his head from his arse."

Mac straightened as well, Ian doing the same when Mac did, and I adjusted my feet, which were stretched out before me, so I could get them under me much more swiftly if need be.

"I do not like how you speak of my brother," Mac gritted.

"Macrinus," Ian murmured calmingly.

"I do not like how your brother treats my sister," Jazz returned.

"He is not treating her any way," Mac fired back.

Jazz leaned toward Macrinus. "*Exactly.*"

Mac made a growly noise in his throat.

I took my feet.

All eyes rose to me.

"I'll go to him," I said.

Hera, Rose and Ian looked relieved.

Mac and Jazz still looked angry, though not at me.

"Take your weapons," Hera advised.

I nodded.

When Cassius went rambling, he always took his broadsword and his dagger.

I could only assume he did not wander far, but I did not know.

What I did know was that in this area of Wodell, there was aught but pixies, some woodland fairies, a few clans of sprites and some harmless gnomes. There weren't even many settlements, but a hamlet here or there, which was one of the reasons we chose this meandering route. It took more time to get to The Enchantments, but there was less chance for us to run into anyone, a princess and prince journeying with a small guard, less chance of any trouble.

Of course, Zees roamed Wodell freely.

However, at this time of year, they would be traveling south, closer to the border of Firenze, in order to spend autumn and winter in milder climes.

My dagger was already tucked into its sheath at my belt.

I left my sword, which was resting on the fallen log beside me, and took up my shaft, which was laying in the leaves behind me.

I would need none of them, but when it came to fighting, I preferred the staff, mostly because I was more adept at using it.

I stepped over the log and walked to where I saw Cassius disappear into the forest.

There, I knelt, gathered my power, touched the ground, and his footsteps illuminated with a soft lilac glow.

He was a large man and thus had large feet.

Hmm.

I straightened and followed, the prints I passed disappearing behind me.

In a short amount of time, I became surprised for he had not left us long ago, but I could see his footsteps leading deep into the forest, therefore even if it had not been long, he'd gone far.

Apparently, he wished to put some distance between him and our party.

Between him and me.

I moved more swiftly, my surprise shifting to concern the deeper I got into the forest, and the farther away I became from our friends.

I then grew troubled when I searched the distance and saw his footprints continue some ways even further.

I continued on the path, the night and wood enveloping me to the point I knew, even if I called out, the others would not hear me.

After some time, I became alarmed, for the prints continued ever farther into the forest, but it appeared they came to an abrupt halt.

I quickened my pace. But the closer I got to where the glowing prints ended, the slower I moved, for Cassius's footfalls ended because he was standing in the shadows of a small glade with but spare moonlight shafting through the branches, his arms crossed on his chest, waiting for me.

I was six feet from him when he bit out, "Do not *ever* use magic to track me."

I stopped where I was.

"Do you hear me, Elena?" he demanded. "You do not ever use your tricks to seek me."

My...

*Tricks?*

I had come to talk. To ask him if he was well. To attempt to find out what was on his mind.

It was not lost on me not only was there much going on, not only was he to be wed to his mortal enemy (as such), he was simply to be wed again. He had lost the woman he loved and was forced to take another to wife. He had made it very clear I should be sensitive to that, and I had intended to be just that.

However, at his demand, that intention flew right from my mind.

"You're deep in the forest, Cassius," I told him.

"I know where I am, Elena," he returned.

"It is not safe for either of us to be this far away from the others," I went on.

"Where it is, is a distance where I can be with my own thoughts, which

I assume would communicate I do not desire company, thus do not wish to be sought for I do not wish to be found."

"It's clear you have something troubling you—"

"Oh, is it?" he asked sarcastically.

My temper frayed further but I did my best to hold on to the tattered edges.

"And as your betrothed, this concerns me."

"There's nothing to be concerned about."

"We should reach The Enchantments in but a few days and you aren't speaking to me," I pointed out.

"I don't have to speak to you to wed you. I don't have to speak to you to get you with child. Though never fear, if I need the pepper, I will not have trouble requesting it of you when we're at supper."

One moment...

He had told me that we—

"Now go back, Elena," he ordered.

I did not go back.

I took a step toward him and snapped, "But weeks ago you were on about us ruling side by side, living as husband and wife, raising our children together, and now I should expect nothing from you but your seed and knowing your desire to season your food?"

"Just return to the others, princess," he said on a harassed sigh.

"What's changed?" I asked.

"Naught has changed."

"I know of the parallel universe where we have twins who live in that different world. Between leaving the others and now, was your twin switched with you?"

"Don't be absurd."

I took another step toward him. "It's you being absurd, Cassius. What's the matter with you?"

"Naught," he clipped.

"You aren't sleeping by my side."

"You aren't far away."

I took yet another step toward him. "You haven't touched me in ages. Kissed me. Even looked upon me as if you wish to do either when before, when we were in Firenze, you seemed eager to do both...and often."

"Elena," he growled.

I took yet another step toward him, putting myself directly in front of him, and planted the end of my staff in the dirt, demanding, "What has changed?"

It took a moment, as if he needed that to make up a plausible lie, before he did not lie.

He struck.

"You are not her and with every minute I'm with you, I'm reminded of that. You are nothing like her. And I miss her. I want *her*, I do not want *you*. But I have no choice, as the whole of my life I've never had a choice. This time, the choice I do not have is that for the rest of my days I have to put up with you."

"Put up with me?" I whispered.

He opened his mouth, but I took another step, this time away from him.

His body seemed to twitch powerfully, the entire length of it, as if he were about to make a movement to reach to me and was struggling to contain that urge.

But then he grew still and said, "You asked."

"I did, indeed," I replied. I then dipped my chin and finished, "I'll leave you to your reflections."

And on that, I whirled and started to walk away, concentrating on doing only that for what I very much wished to do was run.

I didn't get a step in before I heard him hiss behind me. No words, just that hiss.

Then his arm was a tight band about my stomach, and he hauled me to his frame.

"Let me go!" I yelled.

"Quiet," he whispered harshly in my ear.

I started to struggle but stilled when I sensed it.

"Shite," he bit off right before he flung me around to his back as the first of them came barreling out of the wood.

Cassius drew his sword and dagger.

I took up my staff in both hands.

Cassius assumed a battle stance as the first got close and the second came at us from the side.

Zees.

Damn it.

When there was one, there was not two.

There were twenty.

I started to make a slow turn and heard Cassius's sword meet another sword as I saw three more rush into the clearing.

They did not all attack me, as was their way. They rarely meant harm, their intent was to intimidate and subdue.

Therefore, it was only one who approached as the others held check.

Steel clanged against steel at my back and I stepped away from Cassius, crouched low, swung around with my staff extended, and took the one charging me off his feet.

I then righted myself, twirled, lunging and thrusting, once, twice, three times, as a second Zee had come forward, I was fighting him, and he blocked each thrust, doing this grinning at me.

I swung my staff around, caught him at the arse, and when he came up to the balls of his feet, I scraped it down, hooking it at his bent knees and hauling up with great force, taking him head over feet to land on his belly in the leaves.

I swirled my staff in front of me as I faced off against the next one who was hunkered and shuffling side to side before me.

"You're surrounded, do not fight!" was shouted from the trees.

"I am Nadirii!" I yelled. "Retreat or you'll face my magic."

At that, a berry red light illuminated the glade.

I looked over my shoulder and saw the streak coming from the wood and shooting toward Cassius.

A Cassius, by the by, who was battling three Zees with dagger and sword.

Apparently, they felt it would take more to subdue him, or precisely, assure he didn't harm one of them while they were doing it.

But I could not have a mind to that. The streak was coming so fast, I had barely enough time to throw up a shield in front of him on which the streak erupted into a burst of berry and garnet sparks.

Fabulous.

These were Zees with magic.

"You cannot best Nadirii craft," I yelled, forced to engage with the next one who'd scabbarded his sword and was coming at me with a staff.

Fair of him.

I had only the time to think that thought before several streaks of red charged our way.

I erected a globe around us that deflected the streaks as I fought back the Zee, staff to staff held in both hands. But their craft was so powerful, the globe disintegrated after it fended off the Zee magic.

I heard a pained grunt, ducked on a whirl and looked back to see Cassius had dispatched a Zee coming at me from behind with a hit of his hilt to the man's skull.

Damn.

And I had only enough time to think that before I had to drop to my side, roll with knees up to my chest and come up on them with a thrust of my staff in the chest of the man charging Cassius.

The man fell back several steps.

Cassius spun and engaged him as the man who I'd been fighting came again at me.

"Enough!" I shouted, dropped to my back, kicked out both feet and used my stomach muscles to propel me onto them.

I pulled my staff back. Pivoting to the side, I thrust it, jabbing him hard in the soft part of his belly, hearing his pained "*Oof.*" Not wishing to hurt him (too much), I stopped thrusting and swung, hitting him hard in the gut, which made him bend over, then on his back, which made him drop his staff as he landed on his hands and knees.

I pushed out a hand and he went skidding on a blaze of coral into the forest.

It was then I heard the whizzing coming from all directions.

Goddess damn it!

I whirled, ran the four steps it took me to get to Cassius, staff raised like a spear at my shoulder.

A lilac shaft shot from the tip and ballooned into a wall. It wafted through Cassius, but when it hit his attackers, it sent them careening.

They did this just as I dropped the staff and tackled Cassius at his back, shouting, "Down!"

He went down on his front, me on his back.

But he instantly rolled so I was on my back in the leaves, he was lying over me, shoulders to my chest, sword raised and at the ready, as an explosion of garnet, scarlet and berry blinded us when multiple streaks collided where Cassius had been standing.

At that, Cassius spiraled around, covering me with his body, mostly my head, and for a man who did not wish anything to do with me, he certainly moved quickly to protect me from a little Zee magic.

I heard something fizzing and then Cassius's grunt. He made a movement that was jerky, and I heard his sword thud to the ground.

Shite.

I knew what that meant.

We were caged.

"Get off me," I ordered.

"Stay down," he demanded.

"Cass, get...*up,*" I snapped on a heave of his big body.

His big body moved at my heave, considering it had gone strangely inert.

I scooted out from under him, sitting up on my arse, hearing a constant low sizzle, and now seeing I was correct.

We were imprisoned in a magical red veil that sparkled in a dome all around us.

Cassius's arm captured me at my waist, dragging me on my rear across the leaves and dirt and plastering me to his side, doing this raising his sword again with his other arm, but I noted he did not raise it to the point it touched the veil.

He was also on his behind, but somehow he managed to look alert and fierce, even sitting on his arse in some leaves.

But now I had confirmation of the reason for his grunt. Touching that veil caused pain, even if you didn't do it bodily. He must have touched it with his sword.

He did not know Zees.

I sighed.

This was going to take some diplomacy and I wasn't sure Cassius was up for that.

The Zees came out in force, surrounding us.

"Fucking hell," Cassius muttered grimly.

I started counting.

I quit, still not done, when I got to thirty.

"What's this, what's this?" the voice that came earlier came now attached to a man who was standing beyond the veil right in front of us.

He wore a hat, but even so, I could see the scarf tied around his forehead under it. His hair was long, dark, and flowing over his shoulders and down his chest. His short jacket was open, the shirt beneath unbuttoned low. He had many necklaces hanging down his bare chest, some with medallions, most made of beads. His wide eyes were rounded heavily with black kohl. The sword at his back had a large jewel at the bottom of the hilt that blinked in the moonlight.

"An Airenzian soldier and a Nadirii warrior?" he asked. "Have we interrupted a spat between two forbidden lovers?"

"Be on your way," Cassius growled.

"I have not seen this in all my years," the Zee stated.

"You look naught but twenty-five," Cassius returned, and the man burst out laughing.

Through it he put his hand to his chest and said, "You flatter me."

"I'll say it only once more, be on your way," Cassius demanded.

"We shall, oh, we shall," the man replied. "After you toss your coin pouch through the veil. And I like the look of your sword and dagger, thus we shall take those too." He tipped his head my way. "Your warrior's dagger as well."

"We will not be doing that," Cassius told him.

The man quirked just one dark, arched brow. "No?"

"No," Cassius confirmed.

"You felt the magic around you through your steel," the man declared. "Please believe me, it is far worse when it contacts skin, and with a nod of my head, our witches will shrink it." He looked to me. "I respect your magic, witch. I truly do. But you are no match to ours. We Zees have been practicing far longer than you Nadirii, as you know."

This was lamentably true.

Many a Nadirii, alone, without a sister at her side, could be bested by Zee magic, if there was more than one witch in the tribe.

And they definitely had more than one witch in their tribe.

Though, lamentably for him, he had no idea who he was dealing with.

"You really should be on your way," I advised.

"Should we? Really?" the man mocked.

"You should," Cassius said in a tone I'd never heard before, and it was disquieting. "Really."

I took note.

Do not mock Cassius, even if he was arse to the leaves in a dark forest.

"We do not wish to hurt you, Airenzian, even if you are an Airenzian," the Zee replied.

"I will have no problem hurting you, Zee, and I don't give one fuck you're a Zee," Cassius retorted.

Some of the joviality shifted from the man's face as he moved closer to the veil.

The others moved closer too.

"Cass," I whispered, "be calm."

"I am fucking calm," Cassius replied, his eyes never leaving the leader of the Zees.

"You aren't."

And he wasn't.

"I bloody am."

"You aren't, Cass. Just give him your purse," I instructed, looking toward the leader. "We must keep our weapons. You understand."

"I do not," the man said, his tone having deteriorated too. "You are beaten. Give us what we ask, and we will not harm you."

"Take my man's purse and be done, and he will not harm you," I returned.

"He cannot harm me, Nadirii."

"Please do not test us," I requested.

"It is not me on my arse, caged with righteous magic."

"Lamb," Cassius growled, and I knew he didn't use my name because he didn't want them to know it.

But, damn it all, I liked it that he was calling me "lamb" again.

"Don't hurt them," I ordered Cass.

"Are you mad?" he asked.

"No," I spoke truth.

"They would not hesitate to harm us," Cassius replied.

"This isn't harm. It's just a little humiliation," I noted.

"Let us loose, my warrior," Cassius growled.

"I will if you promise not to hurt them," I returned.

The Zee was again grinning.

"One Nadirii alone? You cannot break this cage," he shared, then jerked up his chin.

The cage started to grow smaller.

And glow brighter.

Bloody hell.

"Now give us your purse and your weapons," the man ordered.

"Ellie," Cassius gritted.

Ellie.

And I liked that from Cassius far more than "lamb."

I could not dwell on that.

"Cass."

"*Ellie.*"

"*Cass!*"

"Gods damn it, Elena!" Cass shouted.

I sighed.

Then I closed my eyes.

The thrill scored up my spine and then there were shouts of surprise mingled with short screams of fear right before I heard bodies thumping to the ground.

Though, those bodies did that much farther away from us.

Right after that, I heard steel meeting steel.

I opened my eyes and shot to my feet.

"*Cassius!*" I screeched.

The cage was gone.

And worryingly, the moonlight was too.

We were surrounded in naught but night and stars.

Feet upon earth, we were in the heavens.

I'd learned what this meant.

This meant Cassius was very, *very* angry.

Proof: Cassius had beat the leader down to a knee and back on a hand. Fear was on the man's face, his sword raised in defense across his body, Cassius's braced against it. The Zee was struggling to keep Cass's weapon at bay as Cass loomed over him, a dark specter in a starry sky on earth.

I moved swiftly to him, put my hand light on his back and whispered, "Cassius."

In an instant, he stood down, taking a half step back, doing this moving into me in that protective way of his, his sword still held at the ready.

The others who had been propelled back by my bursting of the cage recovered, taking their feet, moving cautiously, and I felt every eye on us.

It took some time, but slowly, the stars drifting about us flickered out.

"Allow me to introduce myself," Cassius purred. "I am Prince Cassius of Airen, and this is my bride, Princess Elena of the Nadirii."

And on that, he swept low in a deep bow, sword arm still raised, other hand to his chest, his head tipped back, his eyes never leaving the leader, a taunting salute.

"Well," the man replied, pushing up to his feet and sheathing his sword at his back, "why didn't you just say?"

Cassius rose while growling.

I pressed my front into his side, reaching out a hand to his sword arm, wrapping my fingers around and pushing down.

It took a moment, but he finally lowered it.

I let out a breath.

However, he still did not take his eyes from the leader.

"Now, if you're assuming I'm not in the mood to be further trifled with, you would be correct," Cass informed him.

"So rumor is true. The Firenz takes a Dellish. The Dellish will take a Firenz. And day and night join in a marriage of impossibility," the man declared, sweeping a hand to Cassius and me.

"And now I can see you don't understand that by 'further trifled with,' this includes not wishing to engage in unnecessary discourse," Cassius explained.

The man ignored this, put his hand to his chest just under his throat and stated, "It is my deepest honor to meet you both. I am Silvanus. I am head of the Patra."

Cassius said nothing.

I was not surprised. It was obvious he had little to naught experience with the Zees.

I, on the other hand...

"It is our honor to meet you as well, Silvanus of the Patra," I replied.

In a bow of pure gallantry, he bent double at the waist, one foot forward, back leg cocked, and even went so far as to doff his hat and drop his head.

He came up, returned his hat and planted both hands on his hips.

He then shouted, "This demands wine!"

"Fucking hell," Cassius muttered.

I almost smiled.

Silvanus's people trilled audibly and milled about, and in no time, we could see lanterns bobbing in the wood all around and a black-haired woman rushed up to Silvanus.

She had a scarf wrapped around her forehead, it disappeared under her hair, and she was wearing a white blouse that ended under her breasts, a full red skirt with big pockets at the front and gold embroidery at the hem. Also, a thick leather belt on which hung a dagger, several pouches and a small purse. She had wide hoops in her ears, innumerable bracelets on her wrists and necklaces at her neck.

All, save probably the hoops which were not Dellish fashion, were likely stolen from unsuspecting travelers.

As the small glade lit with lanterns, she handed Silvanus a bottle with a bulbous base that was sealed at the top of the neck with red wax.

He did not peel the wax to get to the cork.

Cassius went solid at my side as he withdrew his weapon from its scabbard, and with a dramatic flourish, cut the top of the bottle off with his sword.

"We drink with royalty tonight, brothers and sisters!" he decreed loudly.

A higher pitched trill rent the air and I wondered, even at our distance, if the others would hear it and come to investigate.

"We've buffered the sound, Your Grace," Silvanus said to me, reading my thoughts as another woman approached him carrying three silver chalices (all mismatched, all lovely and all likely stolen). "We thought we could handle one Airenzian and one Nadirii. Three of the former, four of the latter would be foolhardy."

So they knew of the others.

In fact, they might have even followed me.

This was not advantageous for I'd not sensed a thing.

Zees were known to be stealthy, but I'd never been caught out.

Not once.

He shot me a wide, white smile, taking me out of my thoughts as it occurred to me I would consider lying with him, for he was shockingly good-looking.

That was, if I did not have Cassius.

Which I did not (of a sort).

Nevertheless, his smile was infectious, therefore I returned it.

Silvanus poured wine sloppily and handed me the first chalice, Cassius the next and then tossed the final chalice to a man hanging close before he raised the bottle.

"*Na zdrowie!*" he called.

To which was shouted, "*Salud!*" "*Proost!*" "*Santé*" "*Cin cin!*" "*Sláinte!*" "*Yamas!*" "*Skål!*" and "*Saúde!*"

"We travel widely," Silvanus said on a mischievous, and mysterious, wink at me, explaining without explaining some of these odd salutes, then he put the bottle to his lips and tossed his head back to take a glug.

I began to lift my glass to my lips, lips that were curving in another smile aimed toward Silvanus, when I was stopped by Cassius commanding, "Elena, do not drink from that chalice."

I looked up at him. "It's rude not to drink with a Zee."

"I do not care."

"And I do not care that you do not care," I retorted.

He turned fully to me as I continued to raise my goblet and said warningly, "Elena."

I held the vessel to the side and mimicked his tone. "Cassius."

"Do not drink."

"I'll drink if I want to drink."

"If you raise that chalice an inch higher, I'll strike it out of your hand before I turn you over my knee."

He did *not* just say that.

I felt my eyes narrow and replied, "If you try anything that ridiculous, I'll magic you straight to Sky Bay."

He bent into me. "And if you do that, I'll ride right back to you and do it again and again and again until I achieve my goal of tanning your arse so red, you won't be able to sit Diana for weeks."

I opened my mouth to retort but did not as Silvanus was right beside us, chuckling cheerfully and pounding us both on our backs.

"This is beauty!" he cried. "Magnificent!" he yelled.

He stopped pounding and looked at Cassius.

"Does she climax as magnificently as she quarrels?" he asked.

I felt my cheeks flame.

Silvanus raised both hands high and wide, bowing his back as he did so.

"Why has no one thought of this before?" he asked the heavens. "An Airenzian and Nadirii! Explosive!" He dropped his arms and smiled hugely between Cassius and me. "The Sky Citadel will crumble around you the first time you make love under its roof."

I took a small step away from Cassius and Silvanus and both men looked to me.

But only Silvanus spoke.

"What's this? What's this?" he asked, studying me closely. "Untried?"

Bloody, *bloody* hell.

He slapped Cassius on the back and shouted, "A boon! You get to train her...in *everything*." He leaned toward Cassius with a wicked grin on his face. "And the Nadirii are *very good learners*."

"You speak of my bride," Cassius said low.

Silvanus took his point, but did it still grinning unrepentantly, murmuring, "Of course. Of course. My apologies." He then tipped his head to the goblet Cassius held. "Drink, my friend. We would not poison the saviors."

"The what?" Cassius asked.

"The saviors," Silvanus repeated, bending to pick up the bottle he'd set on the ground. "You will end the quakes." He nodded between Cassius and me. "Am I correct?"

"You know of this?" I asked.

"Elena," Cassius murmured warningly.

"We are all friends here, my man," Silvanus declared, apparently forgetting not ten minutes before, he had us imprisoned under a cage of magic. His attention came to me. "And yes. We are older than the Dellish. We remember when Airen and Firenze was one vast kingdom. We remember the days when the mermaids swam the seas freely. We remember the Beast. And we have heard of the prophecy."

"What do you know of it?" Cassis demanded.

"Come!" he cried, whirling with his arm out, and more women came rushing forward, these carrying large, plush cushions they threw to the ground.

Men also moved into the glade, some with rocks, some with twigs, some with branches. They made short work of clearing away leaves and forming a large stone circle in order to build a fire.

Silvanus threw himself on three great cushions, one of which was up against a tree, and then gestured to five more, all together, which was evidently where Cassius and I were to sit.

Together.

I knew better than to spurn the hospitality of a Zee.

We had might and magic and Cassius's command of the night sky.

But Zees had very long memories.

Therefore, I sunk to the cushions, reached, grasped Cassius's hand, and tugged.

He resisted, but after another, harder tug, he dropped down beside me.

Silvanus took us in and then swung his bottle toward us.

"You will make beautiful children," he decreed.

I clenched my teeth and lifted my chalice to him.

Cassius did not do this, but he did drink with Silvanus and me.

The wine was exceptional.

"This is marvelous, Silvanus," I told him.

"Of course it is," he replied. "We took it off an Airenzian merchant on his way to the Thicket," he explained unabashedly.

"Bloody hell," Cassius muttered.

I smiled at Silvanus and took another sip.

"The prophecy," Cassius prompted.

I heard the striking of a flint, looked to my left and saw the fire was ready to spark.

Something it did, with a male Zee bending to it and blowing, dried leaves catching kindling on fire as a female Zee fed more leaves to keep the flames burning to catch the branches at the top.

"Quakes emanating from below earth, where the Beast dwells. It was not hard to put it together, Airenzian prince," Silvanus said, drawing my attention again. "And now, the mermaids and mermales have been driven away. There will be no one to stop him, if the prophesied fail."

I felt my heart skip a beat.

"The mermaids and mermales?" I asked.

"Indeed," he said on a sharp nod of his head before putting the bottle to his lips and tipping it back. He drank deeply and returned his attention to me. "They rallied all the beasts in the sea, forced him into one of their underwater caves, and created a great marine avalanche over the mouth, imprisoning him. Until, it would seem, now."

"You know this, or is it lore?" Cassius asked.

"A year ago, my friend, you asked this question," Silvanus said to him, "I would say lore. The quakes?" He shook his head. "He is surfacing. We heard of the Savage King wedding the Silent One, our True King to be wed to the Sage Bloom, the two of you. We knew."

"And the mermaids and mermales?" I pushed.

"Gone forever," Silvanus declared. "Some say they dwell in the seas around The Mystics. Some say they occupy the islands between The Mystics and the Northlands and Southlands to that west."

He shrugged, took another drink, I took another sip, and he continued.

"Some say they adapted. Over the centuries, they created magic where they formed legs spontaneously as they swam closer to the shores and could pass as legged beings, thus they walk amongst us. I do not know. I like to think the last. That in our ignorance and maltreatment of them, we did not drive them from their homes." He threw an arm out expansively. "But we Zees know of ignorance and maltreatment, so their escape? Well, that is one part of the lore I tend to believe."

"I do too," I mumbled, lifting my chalice and casting my glance up to Cassius.

He was gazing at Silvanus dubiously.

"Which part do you not believe, great prince?" Silvanus's question was directed at Cassius, showing it was not only my thoughts he could read, though Cass wasn't hiding his. "That the merfolk walk amongst us or that the Zees know ignorance and maltreatment?"

"We are drinking stolen wine," Cassius remarked.

"That we are," Silvanus replied, tipping the bottle his way.

"You are feared by many," Cassius went on.

"This is true," Silvanus replied quietly. "You do not know, and in truth, my friend, I hope you never do. It is a lesson learned with great difficulty. If you are forced to live in fear of those around you who do not understand you, do not like what they don't understand and act on it, you have but two choices. Buckle under the tyranny of their actions or find a way to make them fear *you*. Your warrior knows, do you not, princess?" he asked me.

"Perhaps we should avoid politics," I murmured into my goblet.

"She is beautiful, powerful, mighty *and* wise," Silvanus said to Cassius and I smiled at him. "You are very lucky."

Cassius grunted.

I turned my head and frowned at him.

Cassius's gaze dropped to my frown and he scowled at it.

I looked away and took a sip of wine.

"Please tell me you do not force the Airenzian wedding on this creature," Silvanus cut in. "I see her beauty blooming in pink. Perhaps blue. Maybe lavender. Not the dreaded Airenzian wedding black."

"I was going to wear my tunic," I told him.

His lids drooped.

My belly swooped.

"And you should, for you wear it well," he hummed to me.

Cassius suddenly reclined against the cushions at our backs which were up against a boulder.

And he took me with him with his arm snaking about me so that I ended up mostly reclining against *him*.

Silvanus smiled a knowing smile.

I turned my head again and shot my betrothed an annoyed glare.

He endured that but half a second before he turned, set his goblet to the ground and then came back to me.

I held my breath as he used the very tips of his fingers to trail my cheekbone before they sifted into my hair at the side and his face came very close.

"In mourning, the Firenz shroud everything in black," he murmured. "Windows, mirrors, murals, fountains, doorways, horses, heads, covering anything they see that could bring joy and depicts beauty, for they cannot bear to gaze upon it in their despair." He shifted just his eyes in the direction of Silvanus before he said in a louder voice. "Apropos an Airenzian bride should wed in that color, don't you think?"

"Indeed," I heard Silvanus agree softly.

Cassius's attention returned to me, he was again murmuring, and I was again holding my breath at the expression on his face.

"The Dellish bride wears white, pale pink, pale green. The Firenz bride wears whatever color she wishes."

My lungs started burning so I dragged in a breath but held it again when his hand in my hair shifted to cup the back of my head and his beard scraped my cheek as he put his lips to my ear.

I could feel them brushing my skin as he said, "You, my lamb, will wear pale lilac. You will herald a new beginning for all Airenzian women by wearing a color of light and hope. By showing them through your reign as their princess, and then their queen that they face a future where they will know choice."

His arm about me curled tighter, drawing me nearer.

I gasped softly when his teeth nipped my earlobe before he growled, "And if you flirt one more time with that Zee, before the night is over, you will know the stroke of my cock so you will have no doubt who you belong to."

It was then I realized I was panting and pressing my until-then forgotten goblet tight to the leather at his chest.

"Am I understood, my princess?" he asked.

"I'm not flirting," I whispered.

He drew his head back and the firelight danced on his face.

But I saw nothing but the night sky in his eyes.

Oh my.

Prince Cassius was furious.

Those night eyes moved over my face and then he murmured, "You do not know the allure of your smiles, and thus you did not understand their potency or your actions." His gaze captured mine. "Now you do. So I will ask again. Am I understood?"

I felt it wise in that moment to answer, "Yes, Cassius."

"Good," he whispered, the stars blinked out of his eyes and he drew farther away, but still held me close as he reached for his chalice.

I dragged in deep breaths, lifting my goblet to my lips to hide doing so.

"And I shall repeat, you are very lucky, dark prince," Silvanus said low.

"We shall see," Cassius replied before taking in some wine.

"Ah yes!" Silvanus suddenly shouted. "Now we dance."

And as if he willed it, music filled the air from guitars and fiddles playing across the glade.

Three women approached me.

Cass's arm disappeared as one woman took the chalice from my hand and set it aside then the other two took my hands and pulled me to my feet.

"Music! Wine! Dance! Beautiful women!" Silvanus cried while the women dragged me away from the cushions. "Life is for the living! Thus, we must *live!*"

One woman lifted her arms in arcs over her head, keeping eye contact with me as much as she could as she whirled, her skirt swirling out in a wide circle around her, then she stopped, stepping forward side to side, before lifting her arms and twirling again.

"You! You!" the other women called, clapping and pointing at me while stepping and swirling.

I did not look back at Cassius and Silvanus.

I was confused.

He told me he did not wish to be with me and then moved to protect me, behaved with jealousy and shared in no uncertain terms I belonged to him.

I did not understand him, and I had a strong feeling it had little to do with the fact I had not lived amongst men and I had little contact with them throughout my life.

He was naught like True.

He was also naught like what I had noted of Mars, or any of Cassius's men (or True's).

But as I swayed to the music, caught up in the bright skirts, firelight, clapping and laughing, I emulated the movements of the women around me, heartened by their encouraging smiles, and lost myself to the dance, deciding not to think on this.

For Silvanus was right.

Life was for the living.

And in that moment, I decided to let all that was happening go.

And just live.

***Prince Cassius***
*In a Glade, One Hundred Miles from The Northwest Border of The Enchantments*
*WODELL*

"WE CANNOT STAY LONG," Cassius said into his goblet, though the words were directed to Silvanus, his eyes were on Elena dancing with the women by the fire. "Our party will grow concerned."

"Ah, but you should let her have a few dances," Silvanus urged.

Cassius took a sip, tore his gaze from Elena's supple movements, and looked to Silvanus, noting a number of male Zees were dropping cushions about them in order to join them.

He again looked to Elena.

His intended was still dancing.

She was also smiling.

He turned to Silvanus.

"A few," Cassius allowed.

Silvanus grinned.

But through it, his eyes were strangely intent.

"I know of lost loves," he declared abruptly.

The men assuming cushions glanced about each other.

Cassius braced.

Silvanus sat back, drawing a hefty swig off the bottle before he lowered it, his attention now on the dancers.

"I am surrounded by beautiful women. I have been all my life, and this did not change after I found the one who was the only one for me nor did it change after she was lost," Silvanus said. "When I had her, and then after she was gone, I did not even see them."

Cassius watched him closely and therefore saw the Zee's face get soft.

At that, Cass turned his head and looked to the dancers to see the one who had brought him the wine, the one who had showed Elena their dance, was smiling at the leader of the Zees not brightly, not widely, but contentedly.

"Until I did," he heard Silvanus finish.

Cassius turned back to the Zee.

"I felt guilt," he said in the direction of his woman. His eyes moved to Cassius. "And then I did not."

Cassius drew breath into his nose.

"I felt fear," Silvanus carried on.

Cassius's chest started burning.

"And then I did not," Silvanus went on. "I learned. Happiness is very powerful, my man. I understand you fighting it. It is instinct. A protection of ourselves. A defense. Something we men know very well how to do. But as I said, life is for the living. And happiness always wins. You shall see."

"She's a warrior," Cassius reminded him.

"And a good one." Silvanus also did some reminding.

Cassius turned his attention to his chalice.

"We will speak no more of it," Silvanus said.

"I would be obliged," Cassius muttered.

"Except..." Silvanus continued.

Cassius sighed and looked to the man.

"Do not hurt her in your quest to protect yourself. This is important advice, dark prince. A fragile, precious thing broken can never be mended. It will never have the beauty it had when it was whole. Heed this, I urge you. Regardless of what lies in your future, I can promise you, if you listen to my words and take them to heart, you'll be glad you did."

He had been cruel to Elena earlier.

Purposefully.

His intent, to drive her away.

Silvanus had heard it.

And now, after witnessing them together, knowing who they were, he understood it.

Cassius held his gaze a long moment.

And then he nodded.

More wine was brought, and the men did not avoid discussing politics now that Elena was not with them.

They argued agreeably, if at times heatedly, for some time, alternately watching the women dance or glancing to where they had set up their own cocoon of cushions to laze upon, drink wine and chat when the music slowed after much more wine had flowed.

Cassius did not miss Elena drooping.

He also did not miss when her eyes closed.

Silvanus's woman gently took the chalice she still held in her hand away, and still Elena did not wake.

"My bride needs her tent," Cassius murmured.

"And mine needs my cock," Silvanus replied.

The men stood, and when Cassius offered his hand, Silvanus looked at it, seeming perplexed for a moment, before he grasped Cassius's forearm in a tight grip.

Cassius returned the odd clasp.

"I do not know king or prince, outside our True, who would extend his royal hand to a Zee," Silvanus said, not letting go.

"I am not prince or king you have met, until now," Cassius replied.

"And I am glad of the meeting." Silvanus extended his free arm wide over his head. "It has been our pleasure to host you in our home." He gripped tighter, dropping his other arm "And I hope we meet again, my friend."

"That pleasure was mine, and I have the same hope, my brother," Cassius returned, meaning it and seeing Silvanus knew it.

Thus Silvanus, quick to do so often, did it again, this being smiling broadly.

They gripped each other's flesh for another moment before they let go.

He walked to the women, who did not appear ready to break up as the men did, going directly to Elena, though doing it nodding respectfully to the others.

He received their return nods, and when Elena didn't wake, simply mewed when he gently shook her shoulder, he equally gently lifted her in his arms.

A true warrior would not allow this, even after wine, battle, dancing and worry.

Unless she was entirely comfortable in the company she kept.

She knew the Zees were no real threat from the start.

She knew a great many things.

Including how to handle herself in a variety of situations.

Many of them, much better than even he.

Her head fell on his shoulder, sliding forward, so her forehead rested against the side of his neck.

She felt heavy at the same time light in his arms.

Warm against his chest.

And her smell was bloody heaven.

One of the women came to him, and careful not to wake Elena in the doing, put his princess's staff in Cass's hand.

Ready to go, he turned to Silvanus and bent slightly at the waist.

Silvanus affected yet another grand bow and Cassius's lips were twitching as he turned and walked out of the glade.

Elena did not stir during the long walk back.

And she did not stir when he made their camp and immediately faced three of their infuriated party, all standing, ready to confront him.

Though two of that party shifted instantly to alarm.

Hera took a step forward, asking urgently, "Is she—?"

"Shh," Cass hushed her quietly, but sharply. "She's asleep."

Hera stopped dead and stared up at him in shock. "Asleep?"

He had been correct.

Elena would not allow what was currently happening.

Unless she was completely comfortable in her company.

His gut got tight at the thought, and it was a feeling like the one he felt at the weight he held in his arms.

Heavy.

And light.

"We encountered Zees," Cass explained, still speaking quietly.

Her face lighted as she hummed, "Ah."

Rosehana was grinning.

"Are you joking with that?" Ian bit.

"No," Cassius answered.

"You were set upon by Zees?" Ian demanded.

"'Set upon' might be strong wording," Cassius prevaricated, for they were, and then they were not.

"You've been gone hours."

"We have. But it was clear from Elena's behavior you do not spurn a Zee's hospitality."

"You don't," Rosehana affirmed.

"And they had good wine," Cassius added.

"They always have good wine. They don't bother robbing the merchants who transport poor-quality grape," Hera muttered.

"Wine? Zee hospitality? Again, are you joking with that?" Ian demanded.

He looked to his friend. "I am not. We were fine, but I understand your concern and I apologize for causing it."

At this, it was Ian who was staring up at him.

"Did Mac and Jasmine go looking—?" he began.

Cassius did not finish this as he heard a low, long, feminine moan coming from Mac's tent.

He narrowed his eyes on the tent.

Then he did the same at Ian.

"They've been at it all night, practically since Elena followed you," Ian informed him. "Though, I will note, it began with them wrestling an entirely different way. It just changed, not surprisingly, as they rolled closer to his tent."

Bloody Mac.

Cass nearly smiled.

"Which I hope means he'll tire her out and soon so the rest of us can sleep," Hera muttered.

"Hmm," Rosehana hummed, catching Hera's attention.

She took one look at her lover's face before she turned to Cassius.

"You're here. You're fine. We're to bed," she declared, then, sliding Elena's staff from his fingers and taking Rosehana's hand, they headed that way.

Cassius watched them go before looking to Ian.

"Mac and Jazz?" he asked.

"This journey is going to kill me, Rose and Hera at each other nightly, now Mac and Jazz in on the act. I hope there are some Nadirii who do not hate men in the trees we seek, or I'll need to stop in a market along the way to buy some balm."

Cassius chuckled.

Ian stared at him again, not angrily, or frustratedly.

With surprise.

"To your tent, brother," Cassius said, having risked too long waking Elena with this conversation, he was not going to get into why his mood had been dark for days, and now he was chuckling.

He moved toward Elena's tent.

"Cass," Ian called, and Cassius turned back. "You are well?"

He had good friends.

"Better," he murmured.

Ian nodded, his face in the firelight showing relief.

Yes.

He had good friends.

Ian moved to the fire to bank it and Cassius resumed walking to Elena's tent.

For their journey to The Enchantments, their tents were much smaller, thus much lighter. They were meant for single occupancy, though two could sleep in one, but without much room to spare.

With one of those two being an Airenzian soldier, there would be no room to spare.

This, Cassius thought, would not be an issue.

He bent low, also crouching, in order to scoot in.

He set Elena on her blankets and removed her moccasins, found the ties over her casings and loosened them, pulling the casings away.

Exposing the lengths of smooth flesh on her legs, Cass swiftly looked away, stowed his sword and dagger close at hand, took off his boots, unbuttoned and shirked his shirt. He was then even more careful in taking off her belt and removing it with her dagger.

That done, he arranged the two of them fitted closely together under the fold of the blanket, both their heads on her rolled-up saddle rug.

Sadly, he awoke his princess doing this last.

However, all she did was press closer and whisper sleepily but with unhidden relief, "You're back."

And she again fell fast asleep.

He held her in his arms tight to his frame and breathed her in.

She rode like she was born in the saddle. She bantered with her friends with affection, humor and respect. She had a small tent with but a blanket on the ground, and did not go to it, or rise from it, with even a single complaint. Indeed, she erected it herself without request for assistance.

She could build a fire. She could cook over it.

Her use of her staff was strong, sure and swift.

Her magic was awe-inspiring.

And she learned Zee dancing in no time, which foretold her learning how to do other things with her body, and his, with great ease.

A female moan muted by distance drifted to the tent, but it was drowned out by a loud, long male groan.

And Cassius found himself smiling into Elena's hair.

Silvanus was right.

Until that night, Cassius would not have described Princess Elena of the Nadirii as fragile in any way.

But when he spoke his cutting words, he knew she was.

He did not believe the slightest in the power of happiness.

Happiness was weak and fickle and transient.

However, what he had come to understand that night was that Elena had not learned this.

And something else Cassius had come to understand that night, and he understood it the moment she first called him Cass.

He would do all in his power to make sure she never did.

# 56
## THE DOORS

***Farah***
*Just Outside The Doors, South Center of the Great Thicket Forest*
Wodell

"It wasn't me, it was you."

"It bloody was *not* me, it was *you*."

"I remember it like it was yesterday."

"I remember it like it was two minutes ago."

As our horses walked slowly, the steady sway of their gait relaxing, I looked to the side to see True's face gentle, a small curve on his lips as he listened to Luther and Wallace bicker, something they did a good deal.

It was affable and based in mutual fondness, oftentimes could be amusing and sometimes Bram or Florian would join in (never Alfie, he was far too serious, though he would make them quiet down if it started to get agitated).

I was not right then amused.

It had been days we slowly traversed this beautiful countryside with its rolling patchwork of fields and herds upon herds of fluffy, black-faced sheep.

Intermingled in these were small hamlets or slightly larger villages with cream stone buildings that had tiled roofs covered in moss or were topped in thatch. These buildings were cut with packed earth or cobbled roads winding through and surrounded by grass that was a green so green, it was like blankets of emerald.

Then there were the mighty forests, the colors of the falling leaves ranging from green to brown with stark yellows, bright reds and a plethora of oranges mixed in.

And there was such fauna, it was difficult to believe it was real. An abundance of deer, hare and rabbits, squirrels, hedgehogs, pine martens and badgers. We even saw fox, and once, a pack of wolves in the distance.

And the air sang with the flocks of birds heading south for the winter.

In fact, the night before had started warm, but True had risen in the middle of it from the bed we shared at the inn where we'd stayed. He did this in order to close the window he'd left open after the chill set in.

But before he closed it, I'd heard the hoots of owls.

Thus, I hoped I'd see an owl. They'd fascinated me from the very first drawing I'd seen of one.

It was known Wodell was full of magic and I wondered if all of this was what people meant when they spoke of it.

But I had seen the shimmering dust of a pixie's flight.

And True had pointed out a fairy with leaves tangled artfully in her hair, a garland of them adorning the waist and wide skirts of her gown, her gossamer wings fluttering behind her. She was leading a lost fawn—who was only perhaps a few inches shorter than her—back to its mother.

So there was even more magic to this bountiful, beautiful land.

Indeed, True had told me not half an hour before that we neared The Doors so I hoped soon to see gnomes.

My mother, like many Firenz, was not admiring of anything Dellish (save its wool).

But I could not help but think she would have adored this journey through this land so very different from our own, for it was impossible not to fall in love with it.

I wished to be looking forward to The Doors and meeting gnomes, as I had all the many things True told me he wanted to show me.

But I was not looking forward to this.

For it had dawned on me, as Wallace and Luther bickered about hijinks they'd participated in, all the stories all the men spoke about of women they'd pursued (sometimes the same one at the same time), follies they'd attempted, evenings of inebriation, song, fisticuffs and games of chance they'd had...

True had not been among them.

They were his men and they were not hiding from me True's participation in these shenanigans for fear of what I might think.

I could tell by the smile on True's face that it was grounded in gladness his men had these adventures, not nostalgia at memories of times shared.

I twisted on my steed to look back at Alfie, who was riding at our rear.

He caught my gaze and his head tipped to the side in inquiry.

I could not ask, not then, of course, maybe not ever. It would not be right to speak of True behind his back. Especially with one of his men.

I turned forward and again gave my attention to True.

"Did you ever try to ride a greased pig?" I asked after what Wallace and Luther were squabbling about.

He smiled at me. "No."

"Even as a child?" I pressed hopefully.

He shook his head.

Of course he had not.

Because, from what I could ascertain, he had not had a childhood.

He had been too busy being trained by his mother to be king.

I faced forward, feeling my jaw set.

"You seem disappointed in hearing the information that I was not foolish enough to try to mount a greased pig, my sweet," True teased.

"It *was* foolish, ask Luther," Wallace said.

"I would not know, ask Wallace," Luther added.

I did not respond to their gibing because I was what True thought I was.

Disappointed.

I had never tried to ride a greased pig, for that was lunacy. And the poor pig. Why would anyone do such a thing to an animal? It was bad enough they were raised only to be slaughtered and eaten. Forcing that indignity on them?

But I wished True had stories of *something* that was fun (even if it was also lunacy).

"Farah?" True interrupted my thoughts.

"Mars and I played at the paints," I shared suddenly.

"The paints?"

"Bows with arrows tipped in small bags filled with cotton saturated in paint. If an arrow struck you, it stung, but did not wound. What it did do was brand you with a splotch of paint. I beat him. Often. It made him very angry."

True chuckled. "I can imagine."

I looked to True. "Did you do something like that?"

He nodded.

I was heartened.

"I began my archery practice at six," he stated.

I felt my face fall. "Your archery practice?"

"Mother desired I hit a bulls-eye by seven. I achieved that."

I was in no doubt.

I looked again forward but then twisted and scowled behind me at Alfie.

True's captain was serious-minded.

He was also smart.

I had a feeling he was understanding my scowl for his gaze darted to True before he returned my scowl and the sentiment behind it.

"Is something amiss?" True asked as I righted myself in the saddle, and I glanced out the sides of my eyes to see him looking back at Alfie.

"No," I lied.

"Why do you look at Alfie?"

I did not want to lie again.

Therefore, I didn't.

"It does not seem you had much of a childhood."

I didn't know if True desired to answer, but it didn't matter for I forged on.

"Or adulthood, for that matter."

"I don't understand."

I looked to True. "Tell me one story where you had fun."

"Fun?"

By the gods.

My heart lurched for it appeared he didn't even understand the word.

"Fun, True," I said softly. "Something silly or trivial or frivolous that had no reason but to make you laugh or make you happy."

"I'm taking you to see The Doors."

"That doesn't count."

He turned his attention forward, but I could see he felt awkward.

And I immediately felt badly.

"I do not wish to—" I began.

"When I was younger, whenever we visited Bower Manor, or her parents brought her to the castle, I would play hide and seek with Silence. She was wicked good at it. I could search for hours and not find her, and I would swear, when I did, she made herself be seen because she felt pity on me."

"That's lovely, I think," I murmured.

"I'm eight years older than her, and for the most part, it was felt I was looking after her while the adults did adult things."

"It's still lovely."

"It did not take long before my mother shared she thought it was beneath me to play such childish games."

"Even doing it with a child?" I asked.

He did not answer my question.

He said pensively, "Silence was devastated. Though she never spoke a word, certainly no childish tantrums, she just went back to playing with her dolls, but it was a ruse. She had no interest in them. She loved her cousin and spending time with me. She also had no friends."

"That's heartbreaking, True," I whispered.

"I think I was more upset." His voice dropped. "A boy of fourteen, stripped of his only playmate. A six-year-old girl."

I stared at him, the gentle sway of the horse, the beauty of the trees around us not relaxing me in the slightest.

"Farah."

And I continued staring at him, eyes burning, throat prickly, something I had not felt or called upon in many years scratching at my spine.

"Farah!" True clipped. "Halt!" he ordered.

We halted, even my horse did so, though I didn't pull the reins as I could not tear my eyes from True, or my thoughts from his last words.

"Farah."

I swallowed hard so I would not wail my fury for who knew what would happen if I did that.

"*Farah!*" True barked.

It was his voice in that tone that made me blink.

And when I did, a vast shower of leaves that were floating all around fell to the ground about us.

The horses shifted with agitation.

Oh dear.

"Was that you?" he asked, and I noted his men had closed ranks and drawn swords.

They were concerned there was other magic out there and they did not know who wielded it.

"Yes," I told him. "I'm sorry. My magic comes to me through emotion. I've..." I drew in breath. "I've kept a very tight control over it since, well, since my father..."

"Yes, I understand," True muttered.

Yes.

Somehow True always did.

His men sheathed their swords.

"I did not want to make matters worse because sometimes, I can control it and sometimes," I lifted a hand and let it fall, indicating my control of the leaves, "I cannot."

"You do not have to feel sorry for me, sweetling," True said gently.

"I do not feel sorry for you, *caro*. I feel fury, and I do not mean to offend or show disrespect, but it is aimed at your mother." As I'd started this, I decided to give him it all. "And your father."

I heard a "huh" coming from Florian and a grunt from Wallace.

I cast my eyes down. "I'm again so very sorry, saying these things is disrespectful to your queen and king."

"They agree with you," True stated and I lifted my gaze to him. "I just tired of hearing them complain about my parents so I asked them to stop." True shifted his horse nearer to mine. "Father, I cannot say. But Mother... she has her faults, but she is loyal to me and I believe, in her way, loves me."

"I will not love our children as she loves you," I informed him.

His beautiful mouth quirked. "I'm counting on that."

"And when I am queen, when I am mother to the future king, I will not allow her to love *our* children as she loved you," I went on.

"Finally, the fiery Firenz is coming out of her," Luther declared.

"About time," Wallace muttered.

I looked between them.

They had not much engaged me at all. Not due to rudeness or dislike, my sense was that it was due to me being in mourning.

Now that they had, I felt a wonderful warmth at their vocal approval.

At this point, True asked bizarrely, "Is he closer?"

"He is, True," Alfie answered.

"And in the trees?" True went on.

"Yup," Alfie said.

"Well, hullo!" Florian called.

I gave my attention to him then turned it to where he was staring into the woods.

The instant I did, a male slid out of a tree, doing this down a stout vine, on which he stopped, holding onto it, at least seven feet from the ground.

He had a long white beard, a long mustache that curled at the tips, and was wearing trousers and boots that laced up the front, a cloak on his shoulders with the hood up over his head, shadowing his eyes.

And he was maybe, at most, two feet tall.

Another popped up from behind a fallen log, then climbed up on it.

Both of them stared at us.

Or...

It appeared...

*Me.*

"Is that your bride, my prince?" the one on the log called, his voice a little tinny, and I was shocked he spoke thus without first giving a greeting and a bow.

"It is," True answered.

"Our apologies, mistress," the one hanging from the vine said, his voice somewhat squeaky. "Your great beauty everlastingly tied to this ugly mug," and he arched his body to push off, swaying his vine toward True. "Tragic," he finished.

I felt my lips part.

True laughed out loud.

I felt my mouth drop open.

I had never heard him laugh like that.

"Does she speak?" the one on the log asked True.

"She does when she's not frozen in astonishment at displays of shocking insolence toward the crown prince," True answered. "I've a mind to send to Birchlire for the royal tormentor and have you both flogged."

"Is there a royal tormenter?" the one on the log asked the one on the vine.

"No," the one on the vine said.

"I'm recruiting," True told them.

"I'm good with a whip," the one on the log returned.

All the men laughed, even the male gnomes.

"Come, meet Farah, your future princess," True bid. "She wishes to see The Doors."

"It's good she wishes it," the vine gnome said as he slid down to the ground and both of them approached. "We often say yes to beautiful women. Ugly princelings, no."

True chuckled.

He also dismounted, rounded his magnificent horse (aptly named Majesty) at the rear and came to me. He put his hands to my waist and pulled me down, then held my hand as he walked us back around and stopped us in front of the little ones.

"Farah, meet Welbrix and Galbdor."

He indicated each with his hand as he said their names. Welbrix was the one who came from behind the log. Galbdor was the one who came from the tree.

"Hello," I said.

"If wedlock with this lummox doesn't work," Galbdor jerked a thumb to True, "I'm happy to carve a higher door into my tree so you can get through without bumping your head."

"My tree already has a high door," Welbrix said.

Galbdor looked to Welbrix. "Not high enough for this statuesque beauty."

"The point is to make her *bend over*, stupid," Welbrix retorted.

I started laughing.

Both males looked up, and I could see coming from under their hoods that they had long hair, Galbdor's white, Welbrix's gray, though, curiously, their faces appeared unlined with age.

And they were grinning at me.

"It is true what your *handsome* prince has told you," I said. "I would be most grateful if you would honor me with showing me your home."

"The honor would be all ours, princess," Galbdor replied on a bow.

I was struck with the title, something True referred to often regarding me, but not anything anyone else had ever called me.

And it was then I realized this would be real. In a month's time, I would be a princess.

I knew this, but it had not penetrated.

Two months ago, I lived in exile.

Now, I was to be princess. Then queen.

And I would live my life beside a handsome prince, who would become a gentle and benevolent king.

My mother had not lived to hear me called princess. She had not lived to see me spend even a day as wife at the side of a handsome prince.

And she would have loved that for me.

"Farah?" True called softly.

I looked up to him.

"No one has referred to me as princess before," I whispered.

That tender smile of his returned. "I would get used to that, darling."

I felt a tender smile of my own forming.

"Are we to endure you two staring, starry-eyed at each other for eternity, or can we go find some ale?" Welbrix asked.

True glanced at Welbrix before he looked to Alfie. "The horses?"

"We've got them," Alfie assured.

This must have meant something to all for Welbrix and Galbdor immediately turned and started moving through the leaves and fallen boughs between the trees, and with a tug of my hand, True and I followed.

"Watch your step," True murmured.

I often went barefoot in Firenze, and only if necessary, wore sandals.

Here, footwear was essential, as was warmer clothing.

Thus, Mars had had an extensive wardrobe crafted for me, and that day, I was wearing a gown made of the deepest green velvet with an overskirt at the back made stiff green taffeta embroidered in gold. It had a square neckline that showed the cleft of my breasts (but barely) that was edged in a thin ribbon of gold lace. And the overskirt was held in place by a crisscross of sage-green satin ribbons that started beneath my breasts and went down to my waist.

My feet were in slippers, something that True frowned upon, stating I needed boots, especially while riding.

However, as not many wore boots in Firenze, this was not thought of (in fact, I was grateful to Mars for even considering my need for a warmer wardrobe at all for that would not have crossed my mind), and by the time it was, it was too late.

True shared that in our wanderings, we would traverse through a village that had the finest cobbler in all of Wodell, and we would order several pairs while we were there.

We had not yet been to that village.

So I now wore sage satin slippers with gold embroidery around the rims and soles of supple but thick suede.

Even though I'd found the soles proved hearty protection against damp, dirt, twigs and even stones, the slippers were not warm.

And they were definitely not the footwear to traverse a forest floor.

True, as was his nature, held strong to my hand and walked slowly beside me with great patience.

Welbrix and Galbdor did not have the same patience.

"You should carry her on your back," Welbrix suggested crabbily to True.

"I will help you ride the vines, my princess," Galbdor offered.

"I would like to learn to ride the vines," I told Galbdor.

His faced brightened.

"You are not swinging from vines," True growled.

I liked my True. This was because he was likeable. Kind-hearted. Attentive. Solicitous. Chivalrous.

But it must be said, I liked he had that part in him—the growly, decisive, manly part.

It gave me *such* a lovely shiver every time that came out.

"Touchy, touchy," Welbrix muttered.

I heard the men fall in behind us, signaling the horses had been secured.

And a little distance later, I jumped when I caught unusual movement out the periphery of my vision.

Another gnome was swinging vine to vine.

He alighted on a branch, stared down at us with hands on his hips, his cloak held out at his elbows, before he tipped his head back, cupped a hand around his mouth and shouted, "We have True!"

There was nothing for several steps.

And then the entire forest came alive.

Vines swinging. Branches shaking. Leaves rustling.

Gnomes approaching from every side.

And that was when I witnessed what Silence told me I'd see.

We had been treated with deference by everyone we met throughout our journey so far.

And outside me thinking that True's guard was rather small for his personage (yet I never felt concern we were in danger due to the manner in which True interacted with people, and the way they reacted to him) I had not seen this.

Welbrix and Galbdor might tease their prince and further do so by flirting with his woman.

But the rest did not, it would seem, even notice I was there.

By the time two or three had arrived at him, True was swept away from me by gnomes crowding him, touching him, clasping his hands and dragging him, with many more joining them as they went.

He smiled down at them, greeted many by name, shook hands, and often glanced back at me, only ceasing in doing this when he saw Alfie and Wallace take places at my sides, grips on my hands, and continue to help me across the damp leaves at my feet.

In fact, I was so fascinated by watching True with his people, the way they greeted him, chattered at him, welcoming him into their place like he was a favored son returning from a long adventure and they missed him, I did not notice we'd entered The Doors.

But when I did, I stopped short and stared about me in awe.

The trees here were far stouter and much taller than elsewhere.

And I knew then that I had not yet encountered the magic that was Wodell.

*This* was the magic that was Wodell.

The sunlight shafted down, seeming diffused, softened, and I did not know how.

And there were doors.

Doors everywhere.

Some seemed hidden, like the mouths of caves, in a tangle of vines.

Some were majestic, with grand, sweeping steps carved in the expanse of great roots at the base of the trees, guiding you to elegant double doors in the trunk.

Others had simple stepping stones leading to extraordinary wooden doors shafted with curlicue iron hinges.

And still others had shallow, hewn-stone steps that time had covered with moss and dusted with packed dirt and leaves that led up to the door in the tree.

One had a wide, studded wooden door, a lantern at the side, and a window protruding from the tree above it with diamond panes in the glass.

Indeed, there were many iron lanterns lit against the dim of the forest floor that did not see shafts of sunlight. These were overhanging a web of paths between the trees, but they stood perhaps only four feet high (thus I made note to keep track of them as I walked, for I didn't want to run into any of them).

The earth was a tangle of great exposed roots as well as dirt, turf, and fallen autumn leaves.

And the earth was not flat but held gentle, undulating swells that in the end rose up relatively high so all you could see was the homes built in nature speared with sunlight and dotted with lanterns, cut by earthen paths.

I took it all in, slowly pivoting to do so, Alfie and Wallace stepping away to give me an unhindered view.

And when I finished, I whispered, "It's simply magnificent."

I sought True with my eyes, only to find him again smiling at me (as it seemed this was one of True's most favorite things to do).

"I've never seen anything this beautiful, True," I told him where he stood some fifteen feet away, thus I had to raise my voice. "And I've seen the sun rise over Fire Lake. I thought I'd never see anything as beautiful as that. But this..." I swung my hand out. "Nothing is more wonderful than this."

When I stopped speaking, it took some moments to realize there was a hush in the forest.

And when I realized that, I again became aware that True and I were very much not alone.

I felt a tug on my skirts and looked down to see Galbdor.

"You need ale," he declared.

And a cheer rang up. It was not great, but it was jolly, and that was when I found myself swept in a sea of gnomes.

It nearly swept me past True, but he caught me in his arms and held me there, awarding me that beautiful smile on his handsome face, but this time, up close.

However, something else was there too.

I felt my breath catch at that something else.

Right before I felt my belly dip when he bent his head and pressed his lips hard to mine.

Another cheer rang up, but this one was loud, and True released my lips.

"I'm pleased you like it, darling," he whispered.

Still feeling his lips against mine, smelling the musk of him mixed with forest, a scent that was the perfect combination, and truly the most beautiful thing I'd ever smelled, I could do nothing but gaze up at him.

But then our clothing was tugged in a way that could not be ignored (sadly).

Therefore, True let me go but swung an arm around my shoulders, which meant I received the delight of winding mine around his waist, and with an escort of gnomes, he walked us deeper into The Doors.

"It is hard not to be concerned about it, True," Baldrick said.

Baldrick was a gnome I had met earlier, and he was introduced as the Grand Fell, the leader of the gnomes of The Doors.

He also had white hair, but his face was full of lines, heralding his age. And he had a big belly, something which most of the others, men and women, did not.

They were diminutive, but they were fit.

And I'd noted that age did not factor in hair color. There were a few gnomes with brown hair, but most had hair in shades of gray or white.

We were sitting on a bench made of artfully woven and arched shoots and stems, some of them still having green leaves on them (for the bench grew out of the earth).

We were also surrounded by gnomes who sat perched on stone slabs set in the soil or on tri-legged stools, cushions or rugs they'd brought out, these set on the roots, leaves and turf.

True and I had tankards of ale (practically everyone had tankards of ale in their hands, though True had set his aside on the arm of the bench so he could hold my hand). They were smaller than ones found in the pubs of this land, but they were not *that* small (gnomes, I'd learned, like their ale).

I had investigated some of what lay behind The Doors (as much as I could, the doors were small, the ceilings were low, but I'd been invited into a few of the homes). It was quaint, interesting, homey and appealing.

But nothing rivaled what lay without.

Now we were settled into one of the only areas that seemed designed for non-gnomes (which meant True's men were sitting on rugs on the ground with their tankards of ale) and visiting.

"I did not say you shouldn't be concerned, Baldrick," True replied peaceably. "I simply told you not to be too alarmed and asked you to lead your people to that same place. All nations are aware, and all are moving to do something about it."

We were talking about the quakes.

True had not shared that they heralded the return of the Beast, something I knew that all the sovereigns wished to keep quiet for fear of mass panic and what might come of that.

However, unusually, that seemed to be the only thing True wasn't sharing.

"So the quakes come from magic," Baldrick deduced.

"We're assured this is the case by the Great Coven," True told him.

At mention of that coven, Baldrick noted, "It is rumored Ophelia is unwell."

True had his arm across the back of the bench, but at its end, it was curved around my shoulder.

I had decided, after that kiss, to rest my hand on his thigh.

It had, at first, been a mistake for what lay under my hand was hard as steel and thus, far too affecting.

But at that point, True had set his tankard aside, curled the fingers of his freed hand around mine and held it there, so I did not pull away.

And at Baldrick's remark, I twisted mine in order I could curl my fingers around his and give them a squeeze.

"I do not know," True evaded.

"You've just been with her," Baldrick pointed out.

"You know of Ophelia," True replied. "If she is, she would not say. And you know of Serena, if you mentioned anything of the like, she'd slit your throat. You also know of Elena, if her mother is ill, she'd be doing something about it."

"With Elena bound to Airen, if something happens to Ophelia—" Baldrick began.

"Much change is happening across Triton, Baldrick. We've made peaceful treaties with Firenze and Mar-el that will open great trade for the people of Wodell. And Gallienus feels it's time for his son to have more responsibility. Cassius has much different sensibilities than his father, and this means good change will be happening in Airen as well."

"This is promising news, True. Most especially the alliances forming between Wodell and Firenze," Baldrick remarked, glancing briefly with an equally brief nod at me before he turned back to True. "But a Nadirii led by Serena would not be welcome to any land."

"Ophelia is not blind to her daughter's flaws, Baldrick."

"She is also not old enough to leave this earth, but if she is ill..." He shook his head. "Even a witch as powerful as Ophelia does not have power over all. And she cannot see all, including the future. Anything can befall anyone at any time. The only hope was that Elena would be heralded the successor, but now she is to be Queen of Airen, of all places."

"I have a good rapport with Ophelia. The same with Elena. And in truth, I am one of the few who has such with Serena," True told him.

"You are not yet ruler of our land, my prince," Baldrick retorted. "Which brings us to Carrington."

I stiffened at mention of King Wilmer's advisor who did not have Wodell's best interests at heart, nor his king's. Indeed, it was unknown *what* his interests were, except they were not good.

True squeezed my hand reassuringly.

"You speak of treaties, but there are whisperings across Wodell of more campaigns," Baldrick finished.

"This will not happen," True told him inflexibly.

Baldrick's expression grew kind. "I want to believe you, True, but your peoples have lived under a capricious king for some time."

"It will not happen, Baldrick," True repeated, and this time it was steely.

Baldrick grew silent.

I sat silent as well, half concerned about the topic, half marveling at how openly True discussed such matters with his subjects.

Of course, this was the Grand Fell of the Gnomes of The Doors. But Baldrick's constituency probably numbered around one hundred and fifty, maybe two hundred gnomes.

And many of those had gathered around and were listening too.

But True treated Baldrick, and in turn the others, as if they were equals, deserving of all the information that was safe to share direct from the lips of the crown prince.

Not only sharing it.

But discussing it with them.

"Silence has bewitched the Firenz king," True said quietly. "He cares for her deeply already and shows it openly. Your future queen will be Firenz. Our ties with Firenze now are unbreakable. Thus, I can assure you, Baldrick, there will be no future campaigns. I would be called on to lead them, and I will not. And as I will not, any other who would be called on to do so in my stead will refuse."

"Sedition?" Baldrick asked with surprise.

"Wisdom," True answered.

It took a moment, but Baldrick smiled.

It faltered when he noted, "Carrington is still a problem."

And this was a marvel too, for Baldrick knew much, beyond what he might learn from gossip, proclamations or heralds.

This meant he either made it his business to know, regardless he resided in a wood at the southern regions of the Great Thicket Forest, or someone, probably True, or agents of True, kept certain personages in the know about matters he thought it important they be apprised of.

I had the sense it was the latter.

"This is not unknown to the people who need to know it," True assured. "That is a fact you can trust, dear friend."

Baldrick nodded, seemingly appeased by this cryptic answer.

I let out the breath I had not realized I was holding and took a sip of my ale.

The ale was as was everything about this land, earthy and hearty and wonderful.

There was a low whistle, which made Baldrick turn his head.

He turned it back to us, his attention lighting on True but a moment before it came to me.

"It is not our intention to bring to the fore what must be weighing heavy on your heart and mind, but we have taken advantage of this surprise visit, and it would be our deepest privilege if you allowed us to bestow a gift on you, our princess."

"I..." I did not know what to say, so I peeked up at True.

He did not look happy.

"What would be coming to the fore, Baldrick?" he asked brusquely.

"It's a veneration, True," Baldrick answered.

True relaxed and looked down on me.

"You should allow it, sweetling," he murmured.

"Allow what?" I asked.

His arm about me pulled me closer. "Just allow it, Farah."

I gazed into his eyes, but I knew I needn't search.

True would not let anything harm me.

I turned to Baldrick. "It would be my privilege to receive your gift, sir."

He smiled kindly before nodding to someone else.

A lady gnome walked up to me, her face also lined, her hair snow white as well, and I remembered we'd been introduced, but her name escaped me.

I panicked briefly about this rudeness, but this feeling blew away when she raised her hand, and in it, I saw a locket made of filigreed pewter that rounded two small ovals of glass.

And in the glass seemed a hodgepodge of ash, sand and...

Dirt.

"My princess," she began, "this is a tradition amongst gnome bands when one is lost. We had not much from your land, nor the time to create a proper veneration, but some of our people had visited one of your beaches and brought back some sand. And we know of the Firenz use of incense, and thus we added some dust from a burnt cone bought from a traveling Firenz merchant. Last, we put in some ground leaves from here, with some dirt, for the daughter of the great mother who birthed our future queen has walked over our earth. So this, we give to you to hold close so—"

She spoke no more for the sob that tore from my throat stopped her.

True turned me into his arms.

I pressed my face into his neck.

"It was a mistake, True," Baldrick said hurriedly. "Too soon. We'll take it away. We're so very—"

"No. Nonononono," I said urgently, and huskily, pulling my face out of True's neck and turning to them. "No. Please, no." I reached out to the female who had shrunk back. "I will receive it. With gladness. And carry it with me always, with love for my mother and appreciation to you for this show of such profound kindness to a stranger in your land."

With a tremulous smile, the female placed the locket in my palm.

I closed my fingers around it instantly.

"We do not have a chain long enough for your neck," she said quietly.

"I'll get her one," True replied.

Of course he would.

I lifted my fist clenched around the cool glass to my chest, my eyes still on the female, tears trailing my cheeks.

"I will treasure it," I whispered. "Thank you."

She had wet in her eyes too as she nodded and backed away.

"I hope this is indication," Baldrick began gently, "of how sorry we were when we heard of your loss, Your Grace."

I looked to him and nodded.

True tucked me closer to his side.

I pressed my hand harder to my chest.

"Thank you," I repeated to Baldrick.

He smiled a smile of deep compassion.

"She would have liked you and your people," I told him.

"She would have been welcome here," he replied.

I tried to swallow the sob that came from that.

And I failed.

True turned me back into his arms.

After I got some control, I stammered into his chest, "I-I'm not b-being very p-p-princess-like."

True did not respond.

Baldrick did.

"As far as I can see, you're exhibiting traits that suggest you'll be the finest princess this land has ever known."

I peeked out from True's chest and noted Baldrick's expression shared he meant those words.

And as such, it made me continue weeping.

**Prince True**
*The Doors, South Center of the Great Thicket Forest*
WODELL

"She's comely."

"That she is," True murmured to Baldrick with a smile aimed across the clearing to where Farah sat with three female gnomes shifting about her, working at weaving late-season forest blooms in her hair, the four of them amicably chatting.

"She feels deeply," Baldrick went on.

"This she does," True agreed.

"For you."

He looked to Baldrick.

"I thought she'd walk right into a tree, so intent was she in watching you with your people," Baldrick noted.

True had noted the same.

He had also noted the look on her face, as if he was some fantastical being beyond gnomes or pixies or fairies.

Beyond anything she'd seen.

He had never had anyone gaze at him like that, and he was a prince, for the gods' sakes.

It gave him the most extraordinary feeling.

A feeling a hard kiss on the mouth with his men and two hundred gnomes in attendance meant he could not take said kiss where it needed to go to do that feeling justice.

"I cannot tell you, True, how happy I was to see you move over our roots with that woman at your side," Baldrick declared.

"She's magnificent, isn't she?" True agreed, his attention drifting back to Farah. "She'll make an excellent queen."

"She'll make an excellent wife."

True again turned to Baldrick.

"I will tell you something I have desired to tell you for many years, my prince," Baldrick continued. "With an amendment, for before, I wished to say you should seek this. But now, you have found it. Therefore, allow it to happen. Allow someone, finally, to look after you. You will never stop worrying about every soldier, their wives, their children. Every shepherd and head of sheep in their flock. Every pixie that grazes the surface of the Dellish rivers with their wings. This all too much to bear without someone at the end of the day to take some of the weight."

"Farah has borne enough weight," True returned.

Baldrick tipped his head sharply in Farah's direction. "That one could hold a mountain high, and would, if she felt it would make it easier for you to pass through."

True stared at the male.

"Do not underestimate her, True," Baldrick warned. "Brix and Gal told me, they followed you for some time, and witnessed the beauty of her magic. They also reported to me why it came forth. This means she shares many a trait with you, my prince. She is at her happiest when she sees the ones she loves are happy. She is at her most powerful when she's protecting the ones she loves from something that might cause harm. Stop treating her like the substance that holds the sand of her land and the dirt of ours in her veneration. She is not made of glass. She is far less fragile than you think. And you do her a disservice by giving her too much, and not allowing her to return it. Allow her to return it, True. Let her make you happy."

Again, True's gaze drifted to Farah.

She was now, along with having her hair arranged, playing pattycake with a little gnome girlchild.

True felt warmth hit his stomach.

He thought of the flight of the leaves all around them, how they rose up and hovered, as if waiting for a command, and wondered if she actually *could* hold up a mountain.

And then he thought of why they rose up.

He'd never given much consideration to his life, how he'd lived it, who had been around him when he did and how they'd treated him.

It was his life, it had been lived as it had been lived, and there was no changing that now.

It had always been his future he'd looked forward to. Something, eventually, he hoped to control.

Something he'd hoped to fill with peace and goodness.

Something that wasn't within his grasp.

He already possessed it.

It was sleeping by his side every night.

And right then, playing pattycake with a child.

"Oh yes, I'm very happy for you, True," Baldrick muttered.

"Carrington plans to subvert the treaties by attempting to claim the northern border of Firenze and push south when the royal procession moves to Airen," True announced abruptly

He and Baldrick were now alone, the others going about their business.

However, his men stood at the ready some ways away, telling him without words that it was time to go.

And it was.

The day was getting short and they had ten miles to traverse before they made the village where they intended to stay that night. They had a tent, and it might have grown warm for the final spell before the depths of autumn and the biting chill of winter set in, but the nights were cold, and he did not want Farah far from a fire iron.

Thus, it was time to finish briefing his friend so they could move on.

"This doesn't surprise me," Baldrick said on a sigh.

True turned to him. "Matters are in hand."

"Will this finally be done?" Baldrick asked.

"The proclamations have not been heralded, but they will, shortly after Cassius returns to Sky Bay. He's assuming rule as regent."

Baldrick's eyes grew wide.

"There's concern there'll be a revolt. The other realms will move to ally with Cassius should that happen, and Carrington thinks to slip in and find victory when the rest have their attention turned to Airen," True continued.

"By the gods," Baldrick whispered.

"Although King Mars has sent troops to his northeastern borders, and their presence will be made known the instant Cassius makes his proclamations, freeing their women from oppression, Mars has also sent troops to his northwestern borders. Carrington doesn't know this last. Though, this is only a precaution. He won't need them."

"I feel great gladness for the women of Airen. It is about time and was around three hundred years ago. I also feel great anger at the avarice of our royal advisor," Baldrick declared.

He was not the only one.

"I will expect you to keep that to yourself," True told him.

"It goes without saying," Baldrick replied.

"I will do the same if need be, Baldrick. Cassius is done with half of his subjects living under tyranny. I am done with all of mine living under whim."

With that, Baldrick's face grew firm with resolution.

"Is there aught you need of us?" Baldrick asked.

"Not aught that isn't likely dangerous," True answered.

"Do not offend me," Baldrick warned.

"I came to show my intended The Doors, introduce her to your band. This is not why I'm here, friend."

"I believe you, True, but we are Dellish and we are loyal to the crown, the one *you* wear. So I will repeat, is there aught you need of us?"

"Are Welbrix and Galbdor still skilled with seeing things even as they remain unseen?"

"The best of any gnome band."

"My men noted them following us."

"If that is true, it is only because they didn't mind you did."

True nodded. "I have eyes and ears in Notting Thicket, but Brix and Gal could see things, hear things, and follow up in ways others cannot. This would be useful, and at this juncture in relations, could even be crucial."

This time, Baldrick nodded. "It is done. They'll leave in the morning."

"You have my gratitude."

"If that is so, invite me to your wedding to that lovely girl."

True felt his brows draw together. "You haven't received your summons yet?"

Baldrick looked away. "You know how your mother feels about gnomes."

True felt a muscle pulse in his cheek. "That will be rectified."

Baldrick again caught his eyes. "True—"

True interrupted him. "The others?"

Baldrick didn't answer.

"Baldrick," he prompted.

"There is talk, and no. None have received the royal summons. She might have invited the Keepers of the Lights, but I don't know. No one talks to them. They're ridiculous in their pretention."

This feud with the fairies of the Keepers of the Lights was centuries old and True wished the charmed folk would settle it.

Though he had to admit, the Keepers made it difficult for they *were* pretentious.

He'd have a word with them when he and Farah made the Lights.

For now, he had to concentrate on not getting angry that his mother had apparently not invited representatives of gnome bands, sprite clans, pixie families or any fairies Baldrick was speaking to (for all the fairies leaned toward arrogance, and because of that, feuds often broke out, particularly with the gnomes).

"You've now been invited, and I'll send a bird to the Thicket on the morrow to demand moves are made to make that official," True declared. "Wodell will be represented at my wedding, Baldrick, *all* of it."

Baldrick held his gaze and dipped his chin.

True sensed approach and turned his attention that way, seeing Farah, her shining black hair twisted and braided around blooms of ginger, gold and rust, moving to them.

"Sadly, it's time for us to go," True murmured, pushing up from the bench.

"Stay longer next time, True, and be sure to bring her," Baldrick invited.

He looked down to the gnome. "If we can, we will."

Baldrick lifted his chin.

Farah made it to them with a smile Baldrick's way.

She transferred it to True and turned her head side to side.

"Is it as beautiful as it felt when they did it?" she asked.

Everything about her was stunning.

"Yes," he answered.

Her smile brightened.

"We must be away, my sweet," he told her.

Her face fell.

He hated to take her away, for she did not hide she felt peace and comfort here, something he'd hoped she'd find.

But there was more Wodell to show her and not much time to do it.

Not to mention, the gnomes of The Doors had no beds that were long enough for them.

"Night comes. You need a warm meal and a soft bed," he went on.

"All right, True," she agreed quietly and looked down to Baldrick before bending to him and offering her hand. "It's been a pleasure. Thank you for having me."

He took her hand in both of his, turned it palm down and patted the back. "It was *our* pleasure, indeed."

Farah straightened from the Grand Fell and True bent to him. "Until we meet again."

"Yes, True, would that time is short," Baldrick replied.

They shook, and after True righted himself, he tucked Farah's hand in the bend of his arm, guiding her toward where his men were waiting.

She went, waving, smiling and calling farewells.

True did the same.

It was unknown to them that all around watched with happiness and hope, for the only thing better than benevolent rulers was budding love.

Not to mention, Prince True and his lady Farah were an exceptionally striking couple.

They were away from The Doors, and Farah had lifted her skirts, but even held close to his side, she watched where her feet fell as they made their way through the forest back to their horses.

"Can we go there again someday, True?" she requested.

"Absolutely," he granted.

She shot him a luminous smile.

*That one could hold a mountain high, and would, if she felt it would make it easier for you to pass through.*

That was *his* duty.

But he could not deny he felt warmth deep in his chest at thinking she might feel the same.

"Thank you for taking me there, it was even better than you described," she told him.

He lifted her hand from his elbow, bending to it and kissing her knuckles before he tucked it back to where it was, all the while he kept their gait slow, but steady, toward their mounts.

When he again looked forward, Farah dropped her head to his shoulder.

"And thank you for the loveliest day I've had in a very long time," she went on softly.

With that, True turned his head to kiss her hair.

He heard her gentle sigh.

It was not holding a mountain high for her to pass under.

But she was happy.

Which meant, so was he.

~

**Baldrick, Grand Fell of the Gnomes of The Doors**
*The Doors, South Center of the Great Thicket Forest*
WODELL

"EXPECT A SUMMONS. FROM TRUE."

Glenda, Empress of the Pixies, nodded while looking unsurprised.

As she wouldn't.

They all suspected, upon True's return, if he heard they had not been included in the royal nuptials, this would happen.

"Is she as marvelous as tales are telling?" she asked.

"Better."

Her little pixie eyebrows rose into the pink markings at her forehead. "Better?"

"Their love will move mountains."

"And defeat Beasts?" Glenda inquired.

Baldrick held her eyes. "I felt fear, Your Grace. Now I have only hope."

"Then she *is* better than marvelous."

"We will still need to be ready," he warned.

"As ever, Baldrick, of course," she drawled.

With that, and without another word, as was her wont, she buzzed away, only to turn back to look at him from the distance.

"Does she make him happy?" she called.

"He does not know it quite yet, but she is his world."

"It's about time he got one," she replied.

She then swooped a loop in the air on a trail of taffy-pink pixie dust and darted out of sight, glittering dust drifting to the earth in her wake.

Baldrick moved to his tree and into it, ready to put up his feet and drink more ale.

And later, when he lay down in his bed, he slept easy for the first time since he felt a quake.

# 57

## THE FINNIE

**Queen Ha-Lah**
*Beach Beside the Triton Sea*
OFF THE WEST COAST OF FIRENZE

Pecking at them with my fingers, I pulled at my curls, giving them more volume around my face as I stared into the looking glass that hung from a post in Aramus and my tent.

After nightly swims and daily showers in fresh water, I was going through my supply of oils and essences to keep them healthy, bouncy, separated and tamed, as I liked them.

This meant we'd have to find an apothecary along our journey to Wodell so I could blend some more.

Although Aramus had received a bird saying that we had much longer to make our way to Notting Thicket than we'd previously thought, we still had to leave. And soon. We'd dallied more than a few days and we'd been told the journey would take at least three weeks at a quick pace. From the beginning, we had little time to linger.

Therefore, we were leaving in the morning.

I would need far less oil and essence for my hair once we were inland.

I still needed to blend.

I sighed, turned away, and my skirts that had a number of loose, filmy panels that drifted like kelp around my thighs twirled about my legs as I did so.

I grabbed a short piece of toweling that was resting on our pallet as I made my way to the flaps of the tent that were tied back, giving me a wide view of the magnificent sea. I walked through the opening and stepped out onto the sand.

And felt my foot hit *home*.

I could not stop my smile.

Xi was wandering in front of our tent. He looked to me and I turned my smile to him.

"Good day, Xi," I called.

"My queen," he replied on a return smile and stopped.

"Where is he?" I asked.

"Attempting to murder a squad of soldiers he's drilling in sand maneuvers," he answered, jerking his head back down the beach.

I turned that way to see perhaps twenty men doing things with Aramus standing before them, shouting.

"Mind," Xi went on, and I looked back at him. "They've already drilled in these maneuvers about five hundred times. But I suppose you can never be too ready."

I really should not laugh but I was having difficulty not doing just that.

"Has that rider I asked you to send returned?" I inquired.

He shook his head, but his brown eyes were dancing. "Though I expect him this afternoon. I'll find you the minute he arrives."

"I'd appreciate that, Xi."

"I'd appreciate if my rider finds there's some remote inn or luxury Firenz tent, I don't give a damn what it is, except that whatever it is, is within but a few miles of this beach. Just as long as Cap can take you there and take care of business before there's a mutiny. Who would have thought we'd be *less* happy when you two started to *get* happy? Though, the point is, you need to really *get happy* so the rest of us don't consider regicide."

"I'll do my best to see if I can make things ..." I searched for words. "Calm down sooner than that."

He dipped his chin. "I would be forever grateful, my queen. As would Nis. Tint. Bond. Ore. Nav. And about five hundred other men."

I started quietly laughing.

He gave me a wink and began to continue in the direction he'd been heading (which, I would note, was away from his king) when I stopped him.

Xi again looked to me.

"I hate for you to have to go back, so perhaps you can send a sailor in your stead. But could you get word to my husband I'd like to speak to him when he has a moment?" I requested.

"I'll send the one I least like," Xi offered.

I started laughing again and nodded. "It would be appreciated."

He gave a slight bow and murmured, "Anything for my queen."

He then resumed on his path away from my husband and I watched him eventually call out to a man who rushed to him. Xi spoke some words, the man did not look happy, but he nodded to his superior officer and started to trudge toward his king.

I avoided his eyes as he got near me, pressed my lips together in order not to smile, and made my way over the sand to the lapping sea.

In the ensuing days since I showed my husband my magic, I had made many overtures to his men, most especially his closest lieutenants, and had been rewarded beyond my wildest dreams.

They were good men and their fun-loving, close nature that I'd been witness to these last many weeks being something I, myself, finally could enjoy was like being awarded a precious gift.

Though I did not kid myself.

The joviality and courteous attention I now enjoyed had naught to do with these overtures and everything to do with the fact that Aramus and I were not only getting along, he often held my hand when we'd stroll the beach. I also endeavored greatly to make him laugh as often as I could (and succeeded frequently). Further, we had all our meals together, and when he left me, I'd made a habit of pressing my body to his as well as my lips.

This had the result of, in the beginning, making Aramus cheerful, and his men, attuned greatly to him, noticed it.

However, more recently, with many a night spent together, this had the result of making Aramus noticeably frustrated, and this Aramus made noticeable by being increasingly irritable.

In the resultant confusion (for Aramus was good-humored with me and our tent rang with his laughter in the evenings), I had taken a chance and shared with Xi and Bond what was occurring (or not, as this case was). Further, I shared what was their king's wish to do about it. And lastly, how I wanted to rectify this as soon as possible when we resumed our journey.

Including forward planning.

The men were all in hearty accord.

Thus, the rider Xi had sent to scope a spot where my husband and I could consummate our marriage (finally) and do it in a manner that would make him happy.

Though I had plans, that evening, to do what I could to ease the tension, as it were.

Who knew how long it would take to find something that Aramus approved of for our "splendor?"

Something had to be done.

For him.

For his men.

And for *me*.

When I made the edge of the waves, I flicked out the toweling in order to set it on the sand, thinking I probably should stop cuddling my husband with intent when we were abed in the evenings. Kissing his neck. His chest. Pressing to him. Making him groan and roll into me so my hands could roam him as his roamed me. Offering my mouth to his enjoyable plunder.

But I couldn't help myself.

My king was just that delicious.

I settled my rear on the toweling, my knees to my chest, arms around them, and gazed at the sea, the breeze ruffling my curls and wafting the thin material of my dress about my thighs.

I did this smiling at my thoughts.

This smile faded as I realized the sea would be behind us tomorrow.

No more night swims.

But it was more.

I had not yet told my husband I was mermaid.

He knew I had Mer blood, but he did not know the fullness of that.

When he was with his men, doing captain things and kingly things, outside of thinking how handsome he was, how much I was coming to like his lieutenants, how much I enjoyed my husband's company and how it seemed I would very much enjoy the "splendor" we would share, I thought about that.

About how beautifully Aramus had reacted to learning of my magic.

But he did not know the half of it.

He would ask questions of my father, my auntie, my village, the things I did in Nautilus when he was at sea, and he would listen to my answers with the utmost attention, as if learning every morsel of my life was as delicious as his kisses.

And I shared with him even the minutest morsel.

But as each day passed into the next, and I withheld that from him, it felt just like that.

As if I was withholding something, something important, from my husband.

Keeping it a secret.

Not trusting it to him.

For he gave me his laughter freely. His attention admiringly. Time with his men. Tales of his father. His mother. His grandparents. His exploits on the sea. He did it openly, weaving rich stories that would have me enthralled.

But I was keeping the most important part of me from him.

I needed to share all of me with him.

I had decided the best way to share was to show. To find a boat, row out, tell him and dive into the sea, surfacing as mermaid.

But we were leaving tomorrow. If I did it, it would have to be tonight. And I had other activities planned for that night.

Could I do both?

*Should* I do both?

Would he allow me to do both (precisely, the second part) once he found out who I truly was? Would he wish his wife, his lover, his queen, the mother of his children to be a mermaid?

Or would he find me fantastical and abhorrent in some way because of it?

He'd mention mermaids before and told me, if I was one of them, he would protect that knowledge and me. Like he said he would do with my magic.

But speaking of it when he did not think that it was the case, and it *being* the case, were two different things.

My mother and father and auntie and grandmother and all of our people held this truth about ourselves as the utmost of secrets. No one around us knew who we were, what we were.

We'd learned.

But now, could I trust my husband?

A husband who was also king of the seas?

I started when I heard a thump in the sand beside me.

I looked that way to see Aramus's boots there. His socks landed on them before I tipped my head back and then twisted my neck, for he was moving behind me.

He settled in there, his long, muscled legs on either side of me bent, his heels in the sand in front of the toweling, his arms snaking about me to pull me back against his body.

Thus, I settled into *him*, turning to face the sea and resting my head on his shoulder.

"You'll miss it," he said in my ear.

He was speaking of the sea.

"Yes," I answered.

"Notting Thicket is far inland. But Sky Bay isn't. We will make our way there immediately, once True and Farah are wed," he promised.

I smiled a small smile at the waves before I changed our subject.

"You're being too hard on your men."

"They must keep sharp. If this bloody Beast ever appears, it'll be the mightiest thing they've fought. In the meantime, whatever happens in Cassius's realm will likely not be pretty. It's important they're ready."

I had never been to Sky Bay.

I'd heard the beaches of Airen were black.

But what I knew of Sky Bay, it was all rock.

They did not need to be drilled on the beach.

I twisted to catch his gaze.

"I know nothing about soldiering, but my impression is that this is not normal drilling."

His brows drew together. "Have my men been complaining?"

"No," I somewhat lied.

"They best not," he muttered, his attention drifting to the waves.

I twisted even farther in his arms and put my hand on his chest.

"Husband," I called.

His eyes tipped down to me. "Wife."

I grinned up at him because I liked that I was that...to him.

Though I was not *that*, not yet, not entirely.

It was time to get on with that.

The "entirety" part.

Thus, hesitantly, I began, "I think that tonight we should ask the men who have tents closer to us to move them a bit away so—"

"No," Aramus denied, before I even got my suggestion completely out.

"But—"

"No, Ha-Lah. We leave tomorrow. I'm sure there will be some settlement or village or *something* along the way that will prove fit for our needs."

"But we can—"

"No."

"What I mean to say is, not going through with the whole—"

"My queen," he gave me a squeeze, "*no*."

I felt my face screw up. "You aren't even listening."

"Will what you say make me hard?"

I paused to consider that.

"Right," he muttered.

"Aramus!" I snapped, also slapping him lightly on his chest.

"Ha-Lah," he replied.

I persevered, "I could just…with my mouth. And then you could, er… with your mouth. Or fingers. Or, say…*both*."

He tilted his head back and said to the skies. "She wants to kill me. She actually does. My wife wishes my death."

I turned fully in his arms so that I was sitting on a hip between his thighs and thus could press both hands to his chest, hard.

"Husband, we need to ease the tension."

He again looked to me. "And we will…*properly*."

"I do not know. I have not had much experience. The fumblings of youth. But I'm relatively certain I can suck your shaft…*properly*," I stated as he glowered at me. "With a little supervision," I ended on a mutter.

"Can we make a pact?"

"A pact?" I asked warily.

"A pact," he asserted. "This pact including you not mentioning your experience, however not much there was. And I will do the same, even though mine could not be construed in any way as 'not much.'"

Considering his simply sharing his "could not be construed in any way as 'not much,'" made my blood get hot, I felt it wise to reply, "Absolutely."

"Now, if my men are such ninnies they cannot handle sand drills from an exacting captain without making their discontent known to their queen, I will meet you in bed this eve after I've found some privacy and taken care of things."

I shifted against him as a very certain visualization consumed my mind at how he would go about doing that.

"Ha-Lah, stop staring at me like you want to take a bite out of me," he grunted.

"I sort of do," I whispered, staring at his mouth.

"Months, she's a cold fish. When I can't bed her, she's a hot tart. I cannot win," he groused.

I ignored that and asked, "Can I watch you take care of things?"

Aramus was back to grunting. "No."

I pouted.

He pressed a swift kiss on my mouth, lifted away a few inches and declared, "There is much we need to talk about, and this is not it."

"And what would be it?"

"Tonight, we must show my men your magic."

I grew stiff in his arms.

Those arms tightened, and his voice lowered. "Ha-Lah, you can trust them."

I knew this, for Aramus trusted them. I also knew this, for they'd been showing me I could from the moment we started our voyage to Firenze with their service and regard of my king.

It still worried me.

"Is it only the sea, or all waters that you command?" he asked.

"All waters, though my power, all my magics, Aramus, are stronger when I'm close to the sea."

He nodded.

"Saltwater," he deduced.

"Yes," I confirmed.

"But you still command fresh," he went on.

"I cannot call down the rain. But yes, a lake, a pond, river or stream, there is power there for me."

"Therefore, should we see a lake or pond, we can separate from the other men and you can show my brothers, when you are ready."

I gazed at my husband.

That was it?

I'd stiffened, I didn't make even one verbal protest, and he decided we would wait?

"Aramus—"

"And now, I must ask about your powers. I felt your magic on the way to Fire City. Does it debilitate you to use it when you are not close to water, fresh or sea?"

I took us back to our previous subject, saying softly, "Aramus, we can show them tonight."

He shook his head. "No. You aren't ready. We will do it when you're ready."

"Do you trust them?" I queried.

"Yes," he told me. "With my life. But more, with yours."

Then it was decided.

"We will show them tonight."

"Ha-Lah, if—"

"Aramus," I pressed into his chest with my hands, "we have no idea what the future will bring. If it is needed that I call upon my magics, they should not be surprised by them. If you trust them, then I trust them and tonight, they will learn about me."

His face gentled and he bent to give me another swift kiss.

"If you're ready, we shall," he said when he pulled away. "If the night comes and you find you are not, then we shan't. It is your magic, your gift, your choice, Ha-Lah."

"Thank you, husband."

He shook his head again. "It is naught for you to express gratitude for, my queen. It's yours to give and it is you who must feel comfortable in the giving."

Somewhere along this journey, I had earned the love of my husband. He had not told me this, but I knew.

And it must be said, he was earning mine in return.

Very swiftly.

Especially when he said things like that.

I pressed to him and it was me this time who touched my lips to his.

When I slid away, I answered his earlier question.

"And no. It does not debilitate me to use my magic when I'm not close to water. Though, it is not as strong when I'm not close. And like any witch, the more I use it, the less of it I have. It has to regenerate, and it does, but if I'm not close to water, not very swiftly. This happens faster when I am near lake, pond, river, or stream. And even faster, when I'm close to the sea. Indeed, it's almost immediate and the magic is nearly indefatigable when I'm *in* the sea. It would take great works and onerous feats for it to dim when I am in the sea."

Something passed over his face as I said this, making it appear as if he was not looking at me even when he was.

"Aramus," I called.

"That is very Mer."

By Medusa.

How did he know that?

"Pardon?" I whispered.

"The merfolk. Their magic comes from the sea, so when they're in it, it's nearly inexhaustible."

"How d-do you..." I cleared my throat, "know that? The merfolk have been gone for centuries."

Something shifted in his eyes I could not read before he gave me a squeeze, straightened me in his arms and said, "I am King of Mar-el. King of the Sea. My father passed on to me many things others do not know, as his father shared these with him, and his with him, and so on for millennia."

I did not think that was it.

Or not *all* of it.

"My king—"

I said no more for something else changed about him and his head jerked to the side.

It was then I felt it.

And heard it.

There was a restless feeling about the beach and loud murmurings of the men farther up the shore.

I heard a call.

Then a shout.

And more shouting.

After that, I was up.

All the way up, in Aramus's arms, and it seemed he was intent on running up the beach with me.

I understood why. There was a great shadow coasting down the beach, blocking the sun.

By the seas, what could that be?

There were even more shouts, and as Aramus started running up the beach, Xi, Nav and Bond were suddenly there, surrounding us, all with their sabers unsheathed.

"Get the bounden under the trees!" Aramus bellowed, and I looked where he'd directed this order and saw Nis turn on his boot in the sand and go running back up the beach.

We'd almost made our tent when I heard what came next.

Aramus heard it too but he did the strangest thing.

And the craziest.

He halted.

"Aramus!" I shouted. "Put me down! We need to run!"

From what, I did not know.

I just knew we had to run from *that sound*.

I squirmed in his arms and he released my legs, but he did not release me.

He held me close to his body with one arm.

"Aramus!" I struggled against his hold, terror filling me. "We need to *run!*" I screamed.

He was looking up to the skies.

I tried to pull him with me but noticed his men around us were all also looking to the skies.

And they were all smiling.

The others, not his closest brothers, were not smiling. There was a good deal of shouting mostly drowned out by the noise coming from above. And I could feel the frantic activity.

That noise was getting louder.

Closer.

The shadow all but covering the beach.

The noise was flapping.

I heard the screams and may have done the same myself when the first showed over the horizon.

And then another.

And another.

More.

Dozens.

By the sirens.

*Dragons.*

"Aramus," I whispered pitifully, pulling at his hold.

He looked down at me, still smiling.

"Frey arrives."

I stopped pulling and blinked.

"Calm them," Aramus ordered, Xi nodded, and he and the others jogged up the beach to what seemed like chaos.

As it would.

Because...

*Dragons!*

Aramus did not jog us up the beach (not that trees were going to be of any assistance, I'd never seen a dragon, but I'd heard stories, and their fire could melt iron and disintegrate stone).

He moved us down it, toward the water, as colossal, mighty dragons filled the sky, their flapping wings a cacophony of terror. And those wings were so strong, I could feel the stiff breeze wafting down from their command of the air about them.

I fought my husband's hold, as we were headed where the dragons were going, though it didn't matter where they were headed since now they were *everywhere.* They filled the skies, blocking out the sun.

"*Aramus!*" I shrieked.

He stopped, pulled me close, wrapped his arms around me and coaxed, "Baby, calm. It's all right. Frey is friend and Frey commands the dragons. He must have heard word about the Beast and comes to our aid...with *his own* beasts."

Oh.

Well then.

We were close to the water, and after my husband shared this with me and sensed I had taken it in, he tipped his head back to watch the dragons.

I did as well, and considering they were not going to rain dragonfire on us at any random moment their dragon brains told them they should do this, it struck me they were rather magnificent beasts.

They flew well out to sea, until, as one, they made a graceful turn, flapping back.

Aramus and I turned with them and thus we were prized with the opportunity to watch, as in formation they shifted their heads and shoulders back, extending their powerful legs with those fearsome claws. Then massive sprays of sand rose up as they landed one after another after another on the beach.

We watched this spectacle, and we continued to watch even after the last dragon landed and some of them had sat, hind quarters bent, front claws to the ground, their long, thin, forked tongues drifting out of their mouths, their reptilian eyes blinking.

Some even settled all the way to the sand to lie down, their mighty tails curled around a flank, their webbed wings standing proud at their backs.

"They're incredible," I whispered, for even if they seemed tranquil, and they were at least one hundred meters way, I didn't wish to rile them. "Have you seen them before?"

"Never, but I'm glad of the seeing," Aramus replied before he turned us, and we saw what I was surprised to see, but apparently, my husband was not.

A handsome, four-masted galleon sailing around an outcropping of sand, stone and trees some five hundred meters up the beach.

Aramus chuckled.

"She's almost prettier than your ship," I breathed.

Aramus stopped chuckling and his arm about my shoulders gave me an unhappy squeeze.

I looked up at him. "I said 'almost.'"

"Nothing is remotely close to the beauty of the *Siren's Scream*."

I scrunched my nose, not because he wasn't right, his ship was gorgeous, but because…

That *name*.

"I have long-since decided she'll be rechristened *Her Majesty's Beauty* when we return to Nautilus, does that make you more loyal to her?" he asked.

I felt my chin go back in my neck in shock.

"You're rechristening her?" I whispered.

"Of course," he said like my question was ridiculous. "I am a seaman with three mistresses. One is the sea. One is my ship. The last is my wife. I cannot rename the seas of Triton, or I would, so they all would be one. But I can rechristen my ship."

Oh dear.

I might weep.

And oh yes.

He was earning my love.

Aramus stared at me.

He then noted, "Ha-Lah, my father's ship was called the *King's Dream*, this after my mother. And my grandfather's was called *Crystal Magic*, for my grandmother had eyes much like your own."

"I did not know this."

"I told you about my grandmother's eyes some nights ago."

"I mean, about the ships."

"Well, now you know."

Now I knew.

There was an army of dragons on the beach behind me. A beautiful galleon heralding a surprise visit from an apparently powerful man who was a friend of my husband's. A welcome visit, with what we might be facing.

But all I could think was *"Her Majesty's Beauty"* had a lovely ring to it.

"I see this makes you happy," Aramus remarked.

"It's the highest honor I've ever been given," I replied.

His brows shot together. "Wife, you married *a king*."

I smiled up at him as I pressed into his body. "The *second* highest honor, I mean."

He scowled down at me.

I kept smiling up at him.

"As heartening as many might think witnessing your style of flirtation," Ore said from close, and both my husband and I looked his way, "it's making me ill. Not to mention, Frey is hailing. Shall we hail back? Or perhaps give him a bent arm fist. Right before, of course, he orders his dragons to annihilate us."

I suppressed a giggle.

The bent arm fist, when you clap your other hand into your elbow while doing it, was rather rude.

Though it didn't invite dragonfire, in my opinion.

"Hail him," Aramus gave the obvious order.

Ore strode off.

I tipped my head to again look up at my husband, stating, "This is exciting."

"This is exceptional," he returned. "I sent our remaining ships to Sky Bay. One had gone home to ready our fleet should Cassius need our aid. Another had done the same to transport Cat's body so he could be at rest. I did not expect the delay in True and Farah's wedding, so by the time the other ships arrived to us and we sailed to the River Fae to take it down to Notting Thicket, it would be longer than riding. Now, we can board *The Finnie* and sail with Frey and the rest of the men can ride through that sand and heat until they meet the wet and chill. I was not looking forward to that and more, not looking forward to putting you through it."

And I was not looking forward to doing that.

"Thus, my Ha-Lah," he carried on, "you do not have to leave the sea."

And again, yes.

My husband was earning my love.

Swiftly.

However, I had plans for that eve, or one in the not too distant future.

"And Frey will likely give us a cabin," Aramus continued. "And although there will be men around, there will be a proper bed and I can think of only one more suitable place to make my wife *my wife*. That being in my bed on the *Scream*. But this will do."

To that, I shot him a blinding smile because I agreed.

This would do.

I turned my gaze away from the soft look my husband was giving me to the ship that was apparently called *The Finnie*.

Yes, it would do.

Absolutely.

~

"Oh...my...God, I am *so totally* having gowns made like that for me," the white-haired woman proclaimed about two seconds after she alighted from the boat that had been rowed from *The Finnie*.

Two very tall, very built, very handsome men had jumped into the surf to guide the boat to the shore, the only passengers two women.

One was wearing a shirt much like my husband often wore (and like one of the men with her wore, though his was brown). It was white with billowing sleeves and unlaced at the neck. On the bottom, she wore breeches and boots.

The other woman was a redhead in a pretty, peach gown with cap sleeves and an empire waist.

I did not think much on this.

I thought it odd, the white-haired one's vernacular.

"I am *too*. Holy *crap*. It's *fab*," the redheaded woman said as she flipped off her slippers without thought, dragged her skirts up to her thighs and jumped out of the boat after her companion.

"Hey, I'm Finnie," the white-haired one said to me, extending a hand like we would shake.

Did she not know I was queen?

"And this is Maddie," she went on, tipping her head to the side to indicate the redhead.

"Um…" I mumbled.

"Wee wife, this is Queen Ha-Lah of the Mar-el," one of the big, built men informed her.

"Oh, right, yeah, the royal rigmarole," the white-haired one muttered. She dropped her hand, dipped a perfunctory curtsy that was amusing, considering she had no skirts, and said, "I'm Seoafin, Ice Princess of Lunwyn. And this is Lady Madeleine, wife of Lord Apollo," she jerked her head back to the other man, "Head of the House of Ulfr. And this is my husband, Frey, commander of dragons and elves and all-around hot guy that is impervious to age, which is kinda annoying since every day, I get a new wrinkle."

"You do not," the redhead snapped.

"I *so* do, look," the white-haired one demanded, jabbing a finger at her forehead.

The redhead squinted at her forehead and stated, "I see nothing."

"It's there," the white-haired one stressed.

"It isn't, Finnie. It's in your imagination."

"I'm in the sun all the time and we're almost out of sunblock," the white-haired one said, then turned to me. "I need to get a message to Valentine. She'll stock us up."

"Er…" I murmured.

The big man at Finnie's side moved forward, casting her a glance that looked part beleaguered, part besotted, before he turned his attention to me, swept down in a somewhat respectful (but not entirely) bow and rose.

"As my wife said, I am Frey, and it is an honor to meet you, Queen Ha-Lah."

"It is indeed. And you, King Aramus," said the other man, who might not be as big as Frey, but he was still large, and dark headed, as was Frey, though there was just a hint of silver in each man's hair. This one swept a low, respectful bow and came up, declaring in a deep voice, "Apollo Ulfr."

I nodded, fascinated, for *he* had the most extraordinary green eyes.

Even greener than Prince True's.

True's reminded me of the forest.

This man's looked like jade.

"We forget, we've been together so long," the redhead batted a hand between herself and Finnie, "it's good to be around someone from home that, we, uh...that is..." She faltered then smiled. "I'm so honored to meet you."

She then curtsied much like her husband, that being properly.

I dipped my head, fascinated by these two bizarre-acting females.

"Aramus," Frey stated, moving to my husband and clasping his hand.

"Frey," my husband replied, clasping back and then they pounded each other stoutly on their shoulders.

They broke, and Frey threw out a hand. "As noted, my wife and my friends."

My husband nodded to the others and looked back to Frey.

"Should I deduce the elves have been talking?" he asked, tipping his head toward the dragons.

Frey's face grew serious. "We were warned and did not delay taking our voyage."

"And how did you find us?" Aramus asked. "We're far from home."

"We were headed to Nautilus but received a message from a witch we know. She guided our way," Frey answered.

I wondered what witch knew of us but did not get the chance to ask.

"It is good you're here," Aramus said low.

"I'm glad you think so, for it isn't only us. I've sent for Lahn and Tor," Frey informed him.

I felt grave surprise.

"Dax Lahn?" I asked. "The mightiest warrior of The Southlands?"

"The mightiest warrior anywhere, I'd say," Apollo entered the conversation.

"And King Noctorno of Hawkvale and Bellebryn," Frey noted, and his attention shifted to Aramus. "They're some weeks behind, but they're coming."

"It's our understanding we'll need all the might we can get. Therefore, they'll be most welcome additions. If the Beast ever surfaces," my husband said.

"I had noticed things seem peaceful," Finnie remarked. "We were expecting pandemonium."

"The last quake we had was the mightiest of all," Aramus told her.

"I expect it was," Frey replied. "At sail, we felt it as a swell we nearly did not navigate."

Aramus nodded, his face grim, and he looked down at me.

I moved closer to him.

If they felt it as a swell at sea, it would have been a fierce tidal that hit Mar-el.

"We have not received any birds that communicated devastation," I reminded him, sliding an arm around his waist. "Our people are hearty. They will endure."

He curved his arm around my shoulders and nodded, though he looked no less grim at my assurances.

"Nothing since, King Aramus, and it's been weeks," Apollo put in.

My husband gave the man his attention. "It has gone off schedule. We cannot know if this is good, or if it is bad. With the last quake, we also heard a mighty roar. It was made clear with that, not only is he closer to the surface, he is angry. He's been imprisoned under the earth for millennia. We are on guard."

"There is a prophecy—" Frey began.

"We know of it," Aramus told him, pulling me even closer. "And it's in hand. Mars, the king of Firenze, has wed Silence, Countess of the Arbor of Wodell. In roughly a month's time, Prince True of Wodell will marry Farah of Firenze. After that, we're to Airen in order that Prince Cassius can marry Princess Elena of the Nadirii."

Frey cast a satisfied glance at Apollo. "So love has prevailed. Excellent news."

"Love has prevailed?" I asked.

Frey looked to me and stated simply, "The prophecy."

"Yes," I said. "The unions of these nations through marriage will give additional power to the men and women wed."

"Through love," Frey amended.

"I'm sorry, I don't understand," I told him.

Frey looked from me, to Apollo, his wife then to Aramus.

"These are not love matches you speak of?" he inquired.

"No. Arranged marriages, to fulfill the prophecy," my husband answered, but I could feel the stiffness in his frame.

The others shifted uncomfortably as they gazed about each other in the same manner.

"What have the elves told you?" Aramus demanded.

Frey sighed before he replied, "The power the united will wield does not come from the union of nations. Or the union of flesh. It comes from love."

Love?

I tipped my head back to look at my husband just as he tipped his down to look at me.

Mars and Silence, I could see that happening.

Aramus and me, it was definitely happening.

Cassius and Elena and True and Farah?

"Shite," Aramus spoke my thoughts out loud.

Shite, indeed.

～

"WELL, this is lovely. Just, er, well...lovely," I blathered as I walked into the captain's cabin aboard *The Finnie*, my husband following me.

We had all taken a meal together on the beach, Aramus and his men briefing Frey and his men about all the goings-on, Frey and his men sharing news from across the Green Sea, the women listening intently.

My husband had then asked if we might ride with them up the coast, turning east from the Triton Sea along the north coast of Wodell, through the Seil Sea, into the River Fae, which would lead us inland and right to Notting Thicket.

Frey had immediately agreed.

However, Finnie and Maddie had begged for some time with their feet on land to have the opportunity to relax, "sunbathe" and "maybe find something we can make into a Frisbee."

I found both these women quite odd, though engaging.

What was odder was that their men did not seem odd.

I'd met people from The Northlands.

These men acted like that.

The women did not.

At least, not exactly.

The way they spoke was often very strange and on occasion they said things that mystified me.

I saw my husband casting curious glances their way as well, but like me, he said naught.

Though considering sailing to Notting Thicket would take half the time as riding, he agreed to a delay in leaving, but requested, "Time aboard your ship for my wife and I. We have not had much privacy since leaving Fire City."

I found the wide grins the women gave me and knowing smiles the men gave Aramus vaguely embarrassing. However, I was so tuned for Frey's response, I did not pay that feeling much attention.

"Of course," Frey agreed. "We'll change cabin for tent. Do you have accommodation for Maddie and Apollo?"

"If we don't, we'll make it," Aramus answered.

I was instantly relieved, thrilled, ecstatic.

And then I was petrified.

It would happen...tonight.

I would become my husband's wife...*tonight*.

My husband would be my true husband...

*Tonight*.

He had experience that could not be construed as "not much."

I had the fumblings of youth and then some other fumblings that were just...not much.

I was no longer virgin, but although I had felt desire, and excitement (most of this happening with what I'd done with Aramus), beyond that...well...

That was it.

Not much.

What if that was about me, and not as I had thought, that it was about my partner?

What if Aramus enjoyed my touch and kisses, but when things became more ardent, he did not enjoy what I did not know how to do?

What if it was *I* who was fumbling?

I hid my anxiety as best I could as Finnie demanded to row back to the ship to retrieve some things and "make the cabin presentable," upon which a heated discussion that could easily be termed an argument broke out about how Frey would row her, how Finnie was quite capable of rowing herself, thank you, and how Frey knew that but he did not care, etcetera.

"They do this a lot," Maddie muttered after leaning toward me. "Married for decades, Frey will not get it into his head that 'me, Tarzan, you Jane' thing doesn't work with Finnie."

"Tarzan and Jane?" I asked.

"You know, he's all alpha man looking after his woman and she's all for alpha in bed, but the rest, not so much."

"Alpha man?" I inquired.

"Do you have wolves in this land?" she queried.

"The mainland does, but..." What she was saying dawned on me and I smiled. "Alpha. I see. Clever."

"My husband commands the wolves," she shared.

Apollo commanded wolves?

She turned to Apollo. "Do you think that will work here, honey?"

"Regrettably, my poppy, I have the feeling we shall see," he answered heavily.

She turned again to me, now curiously not concerned in the slightest that her husband might have to command wolves due to our circumstances which might be dire. "He might not command dragons and elves, but he's still badass."

Badass?

Maddie studied my face then asked, "Have you heard of Minerva?"

I reared back. "The malevolent she-god of Hawkvale who was vanquished some years ago?"

She smiled. "Yes. Her. Well me and Finnie vanquished her. With Circe and Cora, who are on their way with Lahn and Tor, and a little more help from friends."

I stared at her, mouth agape.

"We're pretty badass too," she shared.

"You're witches?" I whispered.

"Well, I wouldn't call myself a witch. But if the shoe fits..." She shrugged.

I had heard tales of these powerful witches who had vanquished the she-god Minerva and her triumvirate of evil-doers.

And now one of them was bickering with her man three feet from me and the other one was babbling at me.

I thought this should be good.

But they were so odd, I worried it was bad.

"I am also witch," I shared.

She smiled largely. "Awesome!"

"If you want to row, row, for heaven's sake!" Finnie cried, got up, cast a longsuffering glance at Maddie, then stomped down the beach to their boat.

"We'll be back," Frey murmured, rising and following her much more slowly.

"Do you have any more of this mango juice?" Maddie asked. "It's delicious!"

I had a servant bring her more juice. I then asked another to change the sheets and tidy Aramus and my tent for Finnie and Frey and see to it that Maddie and Apollo had appropriate accommodation. Last, I had another bounden pack a small bag with things for myself and my husband that we could take to *The Finnie*.

Frey and Finnie came back and Aramus loaded up the bag and rowed us to *The Finnie*.

And now we were there.

In the captain's cabin.

After nearly a year of marriage.

Ready to consummate it.

I had the desire to rush back up the steps onto the deck and jump into the sea.

I quelled this by staring out of the paned window at the back of the cabin. Aramus had one like that on the *Siren's Scream*, including the bench under it covered in pillows and cushions for lounging.

"Princess Seoafin and Lady Madeleine are lovely, aren't they?" I asked.

"Ha-Lah."

"Though odd. I can't put my finger on it—"

"Ha-Lah."

"But they're charming. Just... peculiar. Though not in a bad way."

"They're from a parallel universe."

My head swiveled around to my husband.

"Pardon?"

"They are not of this world. They're of another one. A world that has all the same people as here, but different. Twins. All of the witches who defeated Minerva are from that other world. I did not know this, but while you were seeing to our tent, Apollo shared he'd noted our reactions and he told me."

"They...they're from another world?" I whispered.

"Yes," he confirmed impatiently.

"By the seas," I breathed.

"I have promised Apollo, thus we cannot speak a word of it to anyone. Particularly about Finnie. She is not strictly of royal blood. It would put the whole House of Wilde, which is the ruling House of Lunwyn, in disarray, and her son, who is to assume rule very shortly, in peril."

"Those Lunwynian Houses don't seem to get along very well," I muttered, for I had heard some stories and not many of them were fairytales.

"I do not care about Lunwynian Houses. I care that my wife has situated herself all the way across the cabin and gives every appearance of wishing to avoid me while alone in a room with me, this along with being terrified of me."

I realized then that I had done just that.

Far from him.

And far from the cozy, cocoon of a bed that was situated against the side wall.

A bed my husband was standing in front of.

I drew in breath and found his gaze.

Then I drew in courage.

When I had it, I said quietly, "I am not terrified of you, Aramus. I'm terrified that I will not please you."

His powerful body gave a sudden jerk.

And then his face grew gentle.

So gentle, the very air in the cabin felt a velvet.

"I fear I must break our pact, my Ha-Lah, even though we have not had it for long," he said in a voice as gentle as his face. "Thus, I must ask, how much is your 'not much?'"

"Very much not much, my husband," I whispered.

And at that, his face grew downright tender.

"Come here, my queen."

On slow feet, I walked to him.

When I came near, with careful arms, like he was gathering a wounded kitten close, he pulled me to him and held me there.

"I very much wish to end what has felt like years of wanting you and not having you, and do it swiftly," he said softly. "But instead, first, and I will warn you, it might take all night, I will endeavor to enumerate the many, *many* ways you please me, my queen."

"Aramus," I breathed, his words causing me to melt into his big, strong, solid, warm frame.

And thus, he began.

"Your beauty. I could gaze on you for hours, days, years, millennia, until this planet falls from the sky, and I would not tire of it."

By Medusa.

"Husband."

"Your wit. The way you tease me. It makes me smile and entices me, all at once."

I slid my arms around his waist and whispered, "Darling."

"You have the voice of a siren."

He thought that?

"I could lose my sight, and just be able to listen to you and be a very happy man."

He thought that.

But he was wrong.

This would not take all night.

For already, I could not take more.

"Please, you must—" I tried.

"Your power," he continued "Knowing you, I should have known it would be naught but the magnificence it is. And it is, my queen. It's magnificent."

I felt tears welling in my eyes. "My king, you really must—"

"And you found it in your heart to forgive me. I spoke cruel words, lashing out in a way that was worse than feeling the tip of a whip. Unforgiveable. But you did not make me go to the ends of the earth to prove my remorse. You did not make me shower you with jewels and gold. You did not force me to my knees and make me beg and kiss your feet. You took yourself away, as I deserved, and gave yourself back, because your heart is just that kind."

Now I'd definitely could take no more.

"Please be quiet, my husband, and—"

"I will hunt no more whale, for they are your friends and you please me so much, my queen, I would never harm a creature who is friend to you."

I stood frozen in his arms, staring up at his beautiful face.

He took one hand from about me in order to cup my jaw and he dipped his head close to mine.

"Would you like more?" he queried.

I could not imagine he had more.

I did not mention that.

I asked, "You will not hunt the whales?"

"It will be added to the proclamations. It will be forbidden. No one will hunt the whales, for they are Companions of the Queen. If they do, they'll answer to the King of the Sea."

I could not believe he was saying this, and it meant so very much that he was, I felt a tear trace down my cheek.

Aramus captured it with his thumb and dipped his face even closer.

"You could never *not* please me, Ha-Lah, that's how much you please me," he whispered.

"Do you love me?" I asked.

"I did not know it, until recently, but I fell in love with you kneeling at your side in the sanctuary of Leuthea. I fell more in love with you when you appeared before me in your wedding gown, so regal, it was not like you were not yet queen, but you had been for centuries. And I fell more in love with you later, when you were standing by our marital bed and you stated your case with passion and strength, utterly unafraid of me."

I stared up at my husband.

He grinned. "Though, I would have preferred you stated your case in the morning over breakfast after we'd had a night where we were both very naked and we did very pleasant things to each other while were that. Not to mention, done it in a much quieter tone."

I felt a tremulous smile hit my lips.

Then I admitted, "I'm falling in love with you too."

His head dipped that much nearer so when he said the words, "Thank the gods, I know," his lips brushed mine.

Another tear traced down my opposite cheek as a frisson chased up my spine.

"Let us make magic together, wife, aboard *The Finnie*," he whispered.

I nodded, and with us so close, my nose brushed against his.

That was when my husband kissed me.

It was gentle, and it was sweet. He took a great deal of time exploring my mouth, then gave more, allowing me to explore his.

The taste of him…

Sublime.

Then he turned us, so I had my back to the bed, and slowly he lowered me there, lowering himself on top of me.

His weight was like the heavens had landed atop me.

He rolled us though, so I was on top, as if he feared his weight would frighten me.

I showed him by kissing his mouth, his jaw, his neck, his throat that I was not afraid.

But kissing his mouth, his jaw, his neck, his throat, I smelled the salt of him, the aroma of sea and man and husband.

And I tasted the same things too.

Therefore, when I kissed his mouth again, I tried plundering.

It worked.

I was rolled, and my efforts ceased for my husband was plundering me with mouth *and* with hands.

That frisson I had felt strengthened. My skin felt strange. Needy for his touch just as my hands itched to give the same to him.

I pulled at his shirt to free it from his trousers in order to find skin.

Stymied by his waistcoat, I mentally cursed it, planted my foot in the bed and heaved him.

Now I was on top and he was on the bottom. I shifted to straddle him, but my damnable fingers did not work for desperation at trying to release the dratted, confounding buttons.

"You wear too many clothes," I complained.

"You wear just enough," he murmured, his fingers gripping my short gown and pulling up, my arms going with it.

Leaving me in nothing but panties.

He tossed it to the floor, his eyes hit my body and grew hungry.

Thus, there I had it.

He very much liked what he saw.

That expression on his face, I felt a spasm at the core of me, and I grew wetter.

"Sirens, your beauty," he growled.

I then gasped, for Aramus flipped me and got to his knees between my legs.

In a trice, gone was his waistcoat.

In a blink, he'd pulled off his shirt.

His wide chest with that expanse of smooth, dark skin, the swells, the dips, the peaks of his nipples.

Phenomenal.

But too far away.

I pushed up to take a nipple in my mouth.

Before I succeeded in this endeavor, my husband pushed me down and did what I wanted to do to him to me. He fed my nipple into his mouth with a stroke of his tongue and then he *drew*.

The searing sensation that fired from nipple to between my legs had me arching off the bed, lacing my fingers at the back of his head, holding him to me, demanding *more*.

"Aramus," I moaned.

He lifted up, taking possession of my mouth, his tongue sweeping inside, as he grabbed my hand and pressed it flat against his crotch.

Oh.

My.

All of that was *mine*?

I whimpered into his mouth.

"See what you do to me," he growled in mine.

I didn't see.

I felt.

But I wanted to see.

And *so much more*.

"Aramus—"

"Yes."

"I want to see—"

"*Yes*," he grunted.

He then pulled away and I scrambled to my knees, raining kisses on his shoulders, the back of his neck, running my hands down his sturdy arms as he sat on the edge of the bed and tugged off boots, socks...

He stood and turned to me, his hands at the belt of his trousers.

I reached out, running my fingers over the silken, heated skin of his chest, but my head was bent.

I so very much wanted to see.

He unbuckled then unbuttoned his trousers...

And then he sprang free, long, thick, proud.

By *Medusa*.

So, *so* beautiful.

And all *mine*.

The heat of me saturated, my mouth watered, my head dipped...

He kicked his trousers away and I had his hands under my arms.

I gave a mew of protest when I was up for nary a second before I landed on my back.

And my panties were gone.

I stopped protesting.

His hands ran down the insides of my thighs, spreading them, and I quivered, staring at the hunger on his face as his eyes roved all over me.

"Please, please, please," I chanted.

"Please, fuck, please," he gritted, his fingers drifting back up and trailing through my wet.

Oh, that felt *nice*.

I whimpered.

At the feel of me ready, the hunger in his face bloomed and I hooked the back of his thigh with my heel in an effort to bring him to me.

He put a hand to the bed beside me, arm straight...

And his eyes to mine.

"I wanted to make this more," he grunted.

"It's perfect," I assured.

"I want to make it splendor."

"Aramus—"

"Ha-Lah, it needs to be—"

I lifted both hands and caught him at the back of his neck, pulling myself up, my eyes locked to his.

"Husband, take...your...wife," I commanded.

He growled unintelligibly, I felt that noise drive up inside me like a physical thing, and thankfully I also felt him shift.

He was at my entrance.

So close.

So very close.

And then with a sure, smooth glide, he filled me.

Oh, how he *filled me.*

And we were one.

One.

Complete.

*Perfect.*

"*Yes,*" I breathed, using my hands to pull him down to me.

He lowered at my pull, took my mouth, and I had his shaft *and* his tongue.

Divine.

He glided in and out, oh gods, beauty, and I wrapped my legs around his arse, digging in, holding on.

He glided faster, harder.

Better.

"More," I begged against his lips.

He nipped my bottom one and growled, "I live to please my queen."

He was doing that.

By the all the bounty of the seas, he was doing that.

He gave me more.

"Faster, darling," I entreated.

My husband went faster.

By the gods.

Faster.

*By the gods.*

With one hand clamped to the back of his neck, my nails on the other one digging into his spine, the walls of me pulsing around his shaft as I took him and took him, and more, and faster, I heard the animal noise he made just as I cried out, all that he'd built inside cresting.

And I broke through, surfing an ecstasy I did not know was to be had.

And then it scoured through me, like a cleansing, sheer bliss so pure, so intense, it was excruciating, it was rapture, and it felt like the entire boat rocked with it.

"Husband," I whispered, clenching him to me every way I could.

"Wife," he grunted, thrusting fiercely, then his head jerked back, teeth gritted.

He seethed between them before his hips pounded into mine, stayed there, grinding deeply.

And the King of the Sea roared.

**Frey Drakkar**
*Beach Beside the Triton Sea*
Off the West Coast of Firenze

"What on…"?

Frey Drakkar turned his head to his wife.

He then turned his head to the direction where his wife was staring.

That was when he stared.

It started with drifters.

But then it became crowds.

Finnie and he joined them.

He felt Apollo and Maddie fall in step at his side.

They stopped with the others at the tips of the waves and stared in awe at *The Finnie*, surrounded by dolphins, multiple pods of them, leaping and flipping all around his ship.

He felt another presence on their other side, and Frey looked that way to see Aramus's man Tintagel standing there.

"Should we be worried about this?" he inquired, even though he knew he needn't.

Tint was grinning like a madman.

"No," Tint gave him the response he expected.

"Does this happen every time they make love?" Finnie asked, awe in her voice.

"I hope we'll see," Tint replied, and when his eyes got wide, Frey looked back to the galleon.

He did this just in time to see two whales some ways farther out than *The Finnie* break the surface, leap entirely out of the water, and land with massive splashes on their sides.

"Not expecting there'll be sand drills tomorrow," Tint noted strangely, and still grinning, he turned and walked up the beach.

The rest stayed where they were, and it started slow, but then it built until the cheering and clapping rent the air.

He felt his wee wife's eyes and looked down into their ice-blue beauty.

"I think I like it here," Finnie declared.

His Finnie. His adventuress.

She found something to like everywhere.

He smiled at her.

Then he decided he didn't care how close the other tents were.

So he took her hand and led her back up the beach.

**Queen Ha-Lah**

*Aboard* The Finnie

*Off the West Coast of Firenze*

ARAMUS WAS NUZZLING my neck and I was stroking his back when the cheer rent the air.

We both stilled completely.

Then my husband lifted his head and looked down at me.

My, but he was handsome.

"Do you think they—?" I began.

"No."

"But the timing can't be a coincidence."

"None of my men can see through wood, baby," he murmured, but his head twitched just as I heard it.

The high-pitched, happy shriek of dolphins.

A goodly number of them.

He slid out, I did not like losing him (in the slightest), but I did like how he gathered me to him, wrapping a blanket around us both, and pulled us to a porthole.

We looked out and saw a large pod of dolphins flirting with the surface of the sea as they swam away.

"Right, well then, I guess they know," Aramus muttered, humor in his tone.

I looked at his profile. "Should I be mortified?"

He turned his head to gaze at me. "No."

"I feel like I should be mortified."

His big body started shaking my body when he started laughing.

Then his big body covered mine since he pulled me down to the bed with him on top of me.

And he was still shaking with laughter.

"So, apparently, the dolphins will keep us company when I join with my wife," he remarked.

"Apparently," I mumbled.

He was still laughing, his eyes warm and dancing.

I loved to see that in his gaze.

Nevertheless, I rolled my own eyes.

When I rolled them back, he was no longer laughing, and he'd lifted his hand to tangle it in the curls by the side of my head.

"It was not the splendor I had hoped, my love. It went too fast. But next time—"

I felt my eyes narrow. "What words are these you say?"

He closed his mouth.

"I will never forget it," I vowed.

His expression gentled. "Ha-Lah."

"Never, not in my life."

"My Ha-Lah," he whispered.

"You are more beautiful out of clothes than in them," I declared.

At that, my husband grinned an arrogant grin.

"Though next time, I would like to maybe get my hand around what is mine before you flip me on my back and take over," I shared.

"I'll remind you that you did not protest that maneuver in the slightest, wife."

"I'd had my breath knocked out of me."

His laughter this time was audible, and he forced through it, "Liar."

"It's true!" I kept lying.

"My queen commanded me to take her. She did not command me to let her grab hold of my cock."

"You're too handsome and your body is too pleasing. We'll never go slowly if you take your clothes off."

"Shall I get dressed?" he offered.

"No," I snapped.

He kissed me, light, but wet, doing it through a smile, and I liked all that very much.

Especially the smile.

Well, no, especially the kiss.

Actually, both equally.

I did not like it when he stopped, therefore I frowned at him.

He was not frowning at me, he was gazing at me tenderly.

"Now, my queen, do you doubt you please me in all ways?" he asked quietly.

It was my turn to feel warm and good humored and tender.

And arrogant.

And powerful.

And *everything*.

I did not gloat.

I said, "Thank you for the splendor, my husband."

He appeared perplexed.

"Do you think we're done?" he queried.

"We aren't?"

"Very much no."

I stretched out under him.

His eyes flared.

And I lied yet again, "But I feel most lethargic."

"That's all right," he replied, then he buried his face in my neck, and under my ear, he whispered, "I'll do all the work."

He ran his teeth down my neck.

And then he did as he promised.

# 58

# THE FINAL CHOICE

**Queen Mercy**
*The Bark Parlor, Formal Receiving Rooms, First Floor, Birchlire Castle, Notting Thicket*
Wodell

"Well, if that wouldn't be appropriate, I really can't say."

Queen Elpis was in a snit, Mercy saw.

But really, *incense?*

In a *temple?*

Revolting.

"There must be something else that would make this more...*homely* to Farah," she remarked, ignoring their other companion in the room, Melisse, studying her with disapproving eyes.

But...please.

Censure from a Nadirii?

The woman resided in a realm where no men were allowed. There was a reason for that, of course, but Nadirii lived in a culture defined by bias. She could hardly cast judgement against Mercy wishing to abide by Dellish traditions at a bloody royal wedding, for the gods' sakes.

"As I explained," Elpis replied impatiently, "most Firenz wedding ceremonies take place in nature. A favorite spot of the couple, or of the bride, or the groom. The bride chooses colors she enjoys and decorates in those as she sees fit. A priest or priestess presides, the one closest to the bride, or the couple. Though normally, it is a priest or priestess of The Grace."

"A priest of Wohden will reside over True's nuptials," Mercy stated implacably. "A future king of Wodell is married under the eyes of our god of power."

"Of course," Elpis murmured.

"So obviously, that will not change," Mercy decreed.

"As, I will note, I did not suggest it should. I simply suggested, since this will be an affair of some pageantry, which is not the Firenz way, perhaps some rose or cedar incense could be burned, a tribute to The Grace. Either scent most assuredly reminding Farah of home."

"We will have *roses*," Mercy pointed out, and they would, tens of thousands of them. "Won't that do?"

"Roses are not considered a tribute to our gods," Elpis explained. "But a gift *from* them."

Mercy fought sniffing her disapproval.

"I suggest you reconsider her gown, Your Grace," Melisse suggested...*again*.

"That would be highly inappropriate," Mercy retorted...*again*.

"Farah is very beautiful, and many hues I'm sure suit her," Melisse stated. "But I would think something more robust, and Firenz, like wine or currant, would not only be reminiscent of home, but of her king. Not to mention, it would be more suitable for her coloring."

"Every future queen of Wodell wears pale green," Mercy returned.

"All right then, as green is the color of the royal standard, then perhaps something deeper, say juniper," Melisse proposed. "Or something richer, for instance, emerald or jade."

"The tradition of royal weddings is centuries old," Mercy replied. "*Not to mention*," she went on acidly, "the gown has been weeks in the making and still is not finished. We cannot start a new one now. There's not enough time."

And, *not to mention*, there wasn't enough money.

Her husband was going to announce an increase on taxes as it was in order to pay for the flowers, and the bunting, the ribbons, the catering, the wine, etcetera.

The cake that was being made as an exact replica of Birchlire Castle cost nearly as much as the gown, the bodice of which was crusted with seed pearls, for bloody sakes.

Fortunately, the common folk enjoyed the pomp of a royal wedding, for somehow, it did not occur to them that they paid for it.

Indeed, the city was teeming with excitement, something that shocked Mercy, for they knew their new princess would be Firenz.

And more shocking, as the days went on, this excitement seemed to grow exponentially.

She could not imagine why.

Though she was glad it was, for that would soften the blow of tax increases.

Elpis drew a sharp, audible breath through her nose, gaining Mercy's attention, and Mercy watched her look out the window, her hands folded in her lap, her back straight, her face composed, but Mercy still knew she was seething.

She did not care.

How True could have arranged this rubbish was beyond her.

"Then the wedding portrait," Melisse pressed doggedly. "They could sit for it at one of Prince True's favorite spots in the gardens. That's in nature, as is Firenz tradition."

Was she mad?

"The wedding portrait *always* depicts the future king seated in his *throne* in the *throne room* with his bride standing behind him, as is the place for any princess and definitely *queen*."

Melisse sighed.

A servant walked in.

Mercy turned irate eyes to the man.

He blanched at her expression but bowed low, holding out a gleaming, intricately carved wooden tray.

"A message from His Grace, the Royal Highness, Prince True," he announced.

She lifted her hand his way.

The man came forward, head still bowed, arm out proffering the tray.

She took the folded message on top, and he backed away, leaving the room.

She unfolded it and stared at the words.

True had sent a bird.

There was an established shorthand for use in such messages, as birds could not carry missives that were paragraphs long.

Even so, this message was unusually short.

Even for a bird.

*Send a royal summons to the charmed folk immediately.*

He meant, invite them to the wedding.

She clenched her teeth.

Now, her son would allow incense.

She was wondering, as she had since that scene at the breakfast table some days ago, where she had gone wrong with her boy.

He was sleeping with that harlot, perhaps that was it.

She had him drunk on her cunt.

"Perhaps we can resume these discussions tomorrow," Melisse said, breaking into Mercy's annoyed thoughts.

"I cannot tomorrow," Elpis replied. "Silence has arranged for a docent at the library to take me on a tour of some murals my daughter-in-law particularly likes in the city."

*Well, bully for you,* Mercy thought.

But of course Silence would do that.

Elpis had a daughter-in-law who was proper, respectful and did not endeavor to bewitch her son with her charms and then turn him against his mother.

Elpis pinned Mercy with her eyes. "And I'm glad for some entertainment arranged by *my* queen."

Her point was not veiled.

Mercy hadn't exactly been spending her days regaling the Relict Queen Elpis of Firenze with amusements.

But Mercy did not care about that either.

She had a great deal to do, and it wasn't all planning a wedding. She didn't have time to entertain a guest *she* did not invite to the castle.

"I'm sure you'll enjoy that greatly," she said.

"I'm sure I will," Elpis murmured, rising gracefully from her chair. She dipped her chin to Melisse as she moved across the room. "Always a pleasure." Her gaze came to Mercy and she simply said, "Mercy," as her farewell.

Gods.

The Firenz.

She would be happy when this was all over, and she only had one of them to deal with.

Elpis wasn't two steps out of the room before Melisse spoke.

"Have you seen G'Seph?"

"No," Mercy answered.

"Curious," Melisse said quietly.

Hardly.

"When those priests are in the city, they like to go to their temples," Mercy informed her.

And they did.

To collect their tithes to take to Go'Doan.

"Hmm," Melisse hummed while rising. "Your Grace, I'm sorry to say I shall need to leave you as well."

Mercy nodded.

Melisse then moved closer to Mercy, not the door, and she felt her brows draw together as the woman did so.

"You have," she said quietly, "singlehandedly, for years, kept this realm safe from rack and ruin."

Mercy stared up at her in shock.

Melisse carried on, "It is not only a shame, it is shameful that your subtle, brave, intelligent, quiet, but in times heroic efforts will not be recorded. In generations to come, no one will know who held Wodell safe for the reign of King True. Alas, this has been the lot of many women throughout history."

Mercy found she was having difficulty with her breathing, considering it had escalated alarmingly.

"But regardless of that, you must know you leave a legacy. A legacy of a kingdom that is whole, if not thriving as it should, to your son." Her voice dipped. "And you have left a son who will make it thrive."

Mercy said not a word as she concentrated on regulating her breath.

And concentrating on every syllable from Melisse's lips.

No one, not a single soul, had remarked on what she had done.

"You have not nurtured love and devotion from your son," she went on. "You have built respect and loyalty. Do nothing to prejudice that, Your Grace. He is who he is, but he is also who you made him. There is a great deal to take pride in that. You have given your country everything, Queen Mercy, *everything*," she stressed, her message clear.

She had sacrificed much.

Including being a mother to her son.

All so Wodell would have a good and just king.

No one had ever commented on this either.

What she had given.

And what she had lost.

"Do not make that for naught now," Melisse advised. "For soon, the fates willing, you will enjoy your efforts."

She bent slightly, holding Mercy's eyes.

"He is who he is," she repeated, "and also who you made him. Let him be that and rejoice."

Mercy remained silent as Melisse tipped her head respectfully and moved to the door.

She stopped in it and turned.

And there, she delivered her parting shot.

"It's just incense. There," her hand flittered out in front of her, "and then ash."

With that, she walked out.

Mercy continued to breathe heavily as she stared at the door, and did it feeling something peculiar happening behind her eyes.

They felt prickly and hot.

She thought no more on this when her woman, Helga, appeared in the door.

Helga shot her a look, dipped a short curtsy, then dashed away.

Gods damn it.

It never ended.

Reading Helga's silent message loud and clear, for Helga was her eyes and ears in this castle and had sent such messages repeatedly over the years, Mercy herself rose and moved out of the room, rushing in the practiced way she did this.

This being, walking very fast but without the appearance of doing so.

She sought, and found, her husband.

He was not in his formal study, a grand room with rich appointments and an extraordinary view of where the River Fae met the Great Wohd.

He was in his informal study, a small, intimate room with rich appointments (though they did not rival that of his formal study) and a view of a minute corner of the gardens.

He was in a chair by the fire, a book held open on its arm, but he looked as if he was about to nod off.

"Husband," she said sharply.

Wilmer started, coughed, slapped his book closed and turned to his wife.

"Must you sound like a harridan?" he asked.

*Must you behave like an imbecile?* she thought. *Not a month ago, Prince Cassius stole his father's rule right from under him whilst sitting at the same table as the man. Your son has arranged opened trade routes and advantageous alliances that you could take credit for and the people would be whispering your name with excitement, not your son's as they prepare to watch him atop his horse as they ride through the city to his nuptials. And in the middle of the afternoon, you are at sleep in front of the fire.*

"Well?" Wilmer prompted, and Mercy realized her internal rant meant she missed something he said.

Considering it was likely not important, she didn't ask after it, but instead dispensed with her usual subtlety and inquired outright, "Has Carrington just gone?"

He sighed.

"My king," she pressed.

Knowing, in this mood, she would have what she wished, he gave it to her.

"We've decided to increase the tax another coin."

Her eyes narrowed. "What kind of coin? Gold? Silver? Pewter? Brass? Copper?"

"Gold."

Mercy's torso drifted back.

The shepherds, they could afford this (perhaps). The wheat farmers as well. A good few of the larger orchardists.

The rest...

"Why?" she inquired.

He waved a hand at her and muttered, "Carrington has some plans." His gaze then focused on her face and it did it more sharply than normal. "He's also suggested I demand an accounting of the tithes the Go'Doan temples receive and then demand a taxation from them. And to this I agree heartily, wife. They have long argued these funds go for the good of our people, and thus should have an exception. We have long known much of them go to the polishing of the domes in that city. Not to mention, they rose up in Firenze against the king, proving at least some of them are what we expected...not trustworthy. They've enjoyed an exemption for far too long. That ends now."

For once, she could not disagree.

So she didn't.

She focused on something else.

"And these plans of Carrington's?"

"Wife."

"Husband."

"Mercy."

"Wilmer."

"We need a standing army."

As she suspected.

"We have a standing army," she reminded him.

"No," he said firmly. "*True* has a standing army."

Her heart clenched.

"It is of Wodell," she stated.

"It is *for* True," he returned. "And you know it."

She did.

Their army would follow True to certain death if he asked it.

And they had.

However, they knew who truly asked it.

"Carrington seeks to bolster against *our son*?" she asked.

He straightened in his chair. "I will not have my son take my reign as Gallienus suffered."

"I will not have my husband pit himself against my son," she retorted.

"You speak to your king," he bit.

"You speak to your wife and the mother of your son and, I'll remind you, Your Grace, *your queen*."

"Carrington said you'd have words against this," he muttered.

"For once, Carrington was correct," she snapped.

At that, his head twitched.

And then he rose.

She stood straight and still and stared at him.

"You'd do well to remember who you are and *who I am*," he stated softly.

Mercy made no reply.

"You know, the streets ring with excitement for his wedding," he shared unnecessarily, for she did know.

Unlike her husband, she knew everything.

"I was wed in this very city, *to you*, not some Firenz hussy, and shops did not put signs in their windows to say they would be closed," he went on bitterly. "Pubs did not put signs in their windows to say they'd be celebrating with free leaf cakes and sparkles. There are people already *camping* outside the steps of the *temple* to catch a glimpse of their prince and his new princess and the ceremony isn't for *weeks*."

"You can learn from this, my husband," she told him carefully.

"I can, indeed," he spat. "They adore him. They *worship* him. And I returned home from weeks away, raised my standard above the castle, and not a flower fell at the castle gates."

They hadn't.

But if he'd announced that Mar-el were allowing ships laden with wool through the seas instead of there being murmurs of increased taxes upon his return, they would have.

"And you make of this that you need to raise an army?" she queried.

"I make of this that I'd do well to do as Carrington advises. *Protect my rule*," he replied.

They held each other's gazes.

It was Mercy who broke the silence.

"You do this, you make me choose."

"Choose wisely," he advised.

She stared her husband in his eyes.

And she answered, "I will."

With that, she swept from the room.

She then located her secretary, or one of them, the one who was in charge of her correspondence.

And she ordered the royal summonses.

She then found her other secretary, the one keeping track of the wedding plans.

And she ordered rose and cedar incense.

She then called for the royal seamstresses.

For they were making a different wedding gown.

# 59

# THE WORTH

**Queen Silence**
*The Corridor, Cord Cottage, The Arbor*
WODELL

I carried the tray bearing the tea service myself, for the servants had again gone missing.

Or, not missing, precisely.

I knew where they were.

I was just ignoring it.

(Or trying to do so.)

An endeavor destined to fail, I realized, when I walked into the drawing room and saw my father standing, gazing out the window.

"The tea is ready," I called false brightly.

He turned and scowled at me, continuing to do so as he watched me set the service down on the table between the two leather chesterfields that were positioned perpendicular to the fire.

I'd always loved Cord Cottage, especially the drawing room.

And particularly the fireplace.

The dark, shining wood above it had carvings of ancient Dellish soldiers at war with Firenze (something Mars had smiled most amusedly at when he saw it). The stone columns that held these protruding friezes up with their carved-stone panels at the sides. The recessed fireplace with its heavy irons that heated the room so well.

When we'd arrived, I'd remembered something I had forgotten.

This being, I had, at one point in my life, when I was much, much younger, daydreamed about marrying a wealthy shepherd or arborist and moving here, away from Bower Manor (and my father).

And now I was here, with a king as husband.

And I was not away from my father.

"You've been gone ages. Did you actually *make* the tea?" he demanded crossly.

"I'm enjoying doing some domesticated things, Father," I lied.

Well, it wasn't truly a lie. There was something relaxing about making tea, letting your mind blank as you waited for the kettle to boil, watching the water brown as it ran through the strainer.

Accomplishing something, even something as small as making tea.

It was something.

I'd never really done that, I realized, after the servants Father had employed to look after us at the cottage found other things to occupy their time, so it was up to me to do a few things for myself.

Tril had told me repeatedly to get the maids in hand.

And she'd be furious if she knew I did not call on them to make tea (fortunately, right then she was in the village, finding some material to make a gown for me for True and Farah's wedding, as well as visiting some friends).

And I really should do that. I'd have a whole palace to manage when we returned to Firenze.

But at that juncture, I just...couldn't.

"I understand why you're ignoring that," Father stated, jerking his head haughtily to the window. "But you really shouldn't, even if *he* seems to *vastly* enjoy it."

I heard the noise drifting in through the closed window.

Speaking of domesticated things, my husband had taken to chopping wood.

We needed a good deal of it to heat the cottage.

That said, we had a groom who took care of the horses, the stables and manly things around the house, like fire starting and wood stocking.

When I inquired after it, Mars said it kept him fit.

I did not think this was why he did it.

I allowed my eyes to glance out the window.

Yes, there were our servant girls, all three of them, admiring the King of

Firenze as he chopped wood at the same time they were babbling at Kyril who stood near.

I had noted these past few days, these girls didn't care whose attention they caught, including any one of the hundreds of handsome, brawny Firenz warriors camped around the wood.

But if given the choice, they clearly wished to have their skirts tossed by a king.

It was ludicrous.

Mars.

Chopping wood.

For an audience!

It was more ludicrous Mars allowed it.

I sat on the edge of a chesterfield and turned my attention to pouring tea.

"Come, Father, before it gets cold," I urged.

"You should come," he replied, moving my way. "*Home*," he finished. "At least for dinner. If that barbarian wishes to sit at our table, he is my daughter's husband, I'll allow it. But seeing as he enjoys attention so very much, letting you spend time in your home with your mother and father, it will give *him* the time to have as much attention as he likes without the distraction of *his wife*."

I miraculously kept my hand from shaking as I offered him his cup and saucer after he'd seated himself across from me, and I did this murmuring, "I wish you wouldn't call Mars a barbarian."

"He's shirtless outside, Silence," he declared.

"Chopping wood is onerous work. Even the men at Bower Manor take off their shirts when they do it."

"Not when I'm home."

This was, thinking back, correct.

"And not," he continued, "now as I know they're doing it."

"His people do not wear very many clothes," I reminded him.

"And the man crossed the Dellish border some time ago, daughter," he reminded me. "We put up with his idiosyncrasies when we were in his country. He's in ours and should show some respect."

I finished pouring my own cup and sat back with it, sighing.

"And it's chilly out there," Father continued. "Even chopping wood."

I could not imagine my father ever chopped wood, thus he would not know the effort it would take or how that might fight back a chill.

But he was not wrong about the cold.

After a short warm spell, the nip had set in.

At first, this was delightful, cuddling with Mars in our tent as we journeyed here.

And then it continued to be delightful, cuddling with Mars in front of the fire, or in bed before we slept, after we arrived here.

Then it became less delightful.

We cuddled, and Mars kissed me and embraced me and did things to me with his mouth and his fingers that were extraordinary.

Once he gave me a climax, however, he'd then hold me, this lasting less and less time, before, eventually, he began to sigh heavily, as if he was annoyed, and if it was in the night, he would turn away from me, but if it was in the morning, he would get out of bed and leave me.

Marriage, I was finding, was not a'tall easy.

Marriage to Mars, I was finding, was like being in a carriage with the shades drawn on a ride on a very bumpy road when you could not see the dips until you felt them.

"If I were you, I'd get on giving him a child," my father declared.

I blinked at him.

"A son, if you can manage it, so you wouldn't have the bother of needing to give him another," he continued. "I heard those Nadirii can magic the sex of a child in the womb. You can ask one of your new friends to cast a spell. Then you can leave him with it and come home."

Leave?

My husband?

With "it?"

That "it" being my *child*?

I did not get into that.

I got into something he might understand.

"Father, I am queen."

"His mother still lives. She can supervise the palace in your stead. She knows how. She's been doing it for years."

I put my cup in its saucer and lied, "I think I'm getting a headache."

"This does not surprise me," he muttered.

I looked out the window.

Mars was no longer chopping.

He had the ax resting on its head, he was leaning a hand into the end, and he was chatting.

To our servants.

There were servant boys everywhere at Catrame Palace.

Did I see him chat to any of them?

No.

Not once!

Before I looked away, I saw Kyril peer through the window at me and he did this frowning.

Lamentably, my husband saw him do it and he looked over his (bare!) shoulder at me.

Then, without even dipping his chin to acknowledge he had my attention, he turned back to a servant girl and resumed chatting.

Her name was Pegeen.

And she was very comely.

In fact, all the girls my father had employed were young.

And very comely.

"Silence," my father called my focus, unfortunately for him.

For I'd had enough.

Of him.

Of Mars.

Of marriage.

Of prophecies.

Of beasts.

Of bloody Kyril frowning.

I wanted a fire, a rug, a cup of tea, a book, my wee Piccola, my own company…

And peace.

I set my cup down and stood.

My father looked up at me.

"I'm sorry if you feel this is rude, but much has happened, and in this time where I can unwind before it all starts up again, I'm going to find my book and do just that."

"You shouldn't read if you have a headache," my father advised.

"And you should stand when a queen stands," I returned.

My father stared up at me in shock.

"And not question what she wishes to do with her time," I carried on.

He moved to the edge of his seat, saying conciliatorily, "Silence, I can imagine, a new bride, infatuated with her husband, finding it difficult to adjust to his culture's mores of faithlessness and serial dalliances—"

"Stop speaking," I hissed.

This time, he blinked in shock.

"My marriage is not your concern, you will not speak of it again. My husband is not your concern either. He is also not a barbarian. If you refer to him that way again, Father, we will no longer enjoy these visits. If you truly wish to spend time with me before all is said and done and I return to my new home, endeavor to make that time agreeable. Do *not* endeavor to drive distance between my husband and myself. I can assure you, if you pit the home and hearth you gave me at Bower Manor against the grandeur and serenity my husband offered at Catrame Palace, you...will...*lose*."

He stood, sharing, "You might be Queen of Firenze, but you are still Countess of the Arbor and *my daughter*."

"There's but one of those titles that has meaning."

He recoiled in insult.

I glared up at him.

"It seems I have bad timing, no?"

I started when I heard my husband's deep voice.

He was leaning a shoulder against the doorjamb, deceptively casually.

He'd donned his shirt, thank the gods.

He'd also donned an expression of benign inquiry.

But his eyes flamed so he did not fool me.

And those eyes were aimed at my father.

"I believe I'll take my leave," Father muttered furiously.

"I would too," Mars said.

Father cast him a scorching look, but no one could beat my husband with the scorch.

He then looked to me. "I will accept your apology at Bower Manor when you're ready to offer it."

"I will send word to the servants there to be sure to sweep away the cobwebs while you're waiting for that," I returned.

His face hardened, before, without a backward glance, he stormed from the room.

I heard the front door slam and then I whirled on my husband.

"You will be sacking Pegeen," I demanded.

His brows went up.

"Sorry?" he asked.

"The maid. The fair one. You'll be sacking her. Today. I want her out of this house by supper."

"It is not my place to manage servants."

"You have no problem flirting with them."

I felt the room begin to heat and it was not the excellent irons under the fire that made it do so.

"If my wife is at issue with the company I keep, I would suggest she keep me company."

"I have no interest in chopping wood."

"Neither do I," Mars returned smoothly. "However, it is a better use of my time than taking my mood out on my men, or, say, shaking some sense into my wife, no?"

Shaking some sense into *me*?

What sense did I need?

And...

*His* mood?

"And how are *you* in a mood?" I asked.

"I don't know, Silence, perhaps it's because I don't have a spouse seeing to *my* needs," he answered.

"By watching you chop wood?" I queried incredulously.

"Fuck no," he bit, his temper snapping. "You are not daft, don't pretend to be."

"What on earth are you talking about?" I demanded.

"Maybe you are daft," he muttered.

I reared back as if he struck a blow.

"Daft?"

"Daft," he clipped.

And again.

I'd had enough.

More than enough.

It was time to have this out.

And be done with it.

"You know, I know," I whispered.

"It seems to me you do not know much, so please. Tell me. What is it you know, wife?"

"I know I have to share."

His head jerked. "Share?"

"That is the way and I know it is the way. I know it's something I'll have to endure. And I promise, I'll find it in me to do just that. For you. For our marriage. But even if it's not your custom, I just ask, and please, I beg of you, regardless that it is how you are, who you are, what you expect of our marriage, of *me*, I beg of you to grant this. That you go about doing the things you need to do, but don't make me participate and don't make me watch."

His manner was entirely changed when he asked quietly, "Watch what?"

"Pegeen?"

"The maid?"

"Yes."

"Silence, *piccolina*, you're making no sense."

"When you do the things to her that you do to me."

That did not get me fire.

At that, in but an instant, he straightened from the jamb only for his body to go statue still.

And his face seemed made of stone.

Thus, his voice was gravelly when he asked, "Are you accusing me of infidelity?"

"It is your way, I know—"

"It is whose way?"

"Yours."

That got me fire, and it appeared, alarmingly, that he'd grown inches.

In all directions.

Indeed, it felt the very air was aflame when he asked, "Mine?"

"Firenze!" I cried wildly. "You told me, after the first time, the first time you made me..." I shook my head. "That when we brought others to our bed, we would choose carefully. I know it's not infidelity to you. I understand how it is in Firenze. But it is not," I pressed my hand to my chest and leaned toward him, "*my* way. I do not wish to share you. I do not wish to see you with other women. I want no other man but you."

"Silence—"

"And I heard, I *listened*, it was important to you, so it was important to me, and so I listened to *every word* of the piercing ceremony, Mars. And it was about vowing to give you my ear and my thoughts and my words, but not *my body*. And thus, you wear the chain and I know I have your ear and your thoughts and your words, but I have to share *your body*."

"*Amore*," he said gently, "you haven't actually had my body."

"What?"

"You haven't taken my body."

"We sleep together every night."

Mars grew still again, but this wasn't stony.

He looked stunned.

I had no chance to ask after why he looked that way.

He spoke.

"Do you know what sex is?"

I felt my cheeks flame and answered tersely, "Yes."

"You are certain?"

"Yes," I snapped.

"So you're aware that what I give you with my mouth and fingers, you can give me with your mouth, or fingers, or more importantly, other parts of your anatomy, and I can give the same to you using other parts of mine?"

The sound of my teeth clacking together rattled in my brain, I shut my mouth so fast.

"When I climax, I produce seed—" he went on.

"I know, I know, I know," I interrupted him, waving a hand his way.

"Do you?" he asked. "Do you know that happens when I orgasm?"

Orgasm?

Oh...

*Balls.*

This was mortifying.

More, it was *horrifying*.

My husband had been seeing to me.

But I had not been seeing to my husband.

Good gods.

I knew he grew hard.

And I knew what came of that.

And I had an idea of how babies were made, his parts, my parts, what went where.

I just did not know, until he made it happen, that I could climax.

So I did not know that he could...

Gods.

But of course, he could. He'd even mentioned how difficult he found it, sleeping next to me night after night without "release."

That was what he meant by "release."

I just did not put it together.

I did not think.

And now that I was thinking, what I thought was I needed to get out of that room.

I sought to do this immediately.

I ran in the opposite direction of Mars.

I did not even make it to the door.

Both his arms closed around me, I was pulled back and held fitted against his frame.

I also had his mouth at my ear.

I closed my eyes tight.

And again felt the room.

Not aflame this time.

It was in inferno.

"By the fucking *gods*, those two should have every joint disconnected with how they raised you."

I opened my eyes and stared, unseeing.

What?

"Your mother did not tell you of this?" he rumbled.

"N-no," I stammered.

"She was with you, on your journey to Firenze, for weeks, and in my palace, for days, knowing you were to wed me imminently, and she did not sit down with you in all that time and share this?" he demanded.

"No, Mars," I whispered.

"By the fucking *gods*," he growled on a fierce squeeze.

"Mars, you...you're holding on too tight."

He relaxed his grasp.

Slightly.

"I do not want that maid," he kept growling.

"All right."

"I want my wife."

"All right," I continued whispering.

"I was giving you time to get used to me and our play, waiting for you to give indication you were ready to take it further, something you did not do."

Oh *balls*.

"Because, apparently, not only didn't you fucking know *how*," he went on, "but because you also didn't know there was anything further *to do*."

I did not confirm what he'd already discovered.

I noted, "I-I'm sure this is not the easiest thing to discuss with your child."

"We will be open and honest about the pleasures of the flesh with our children, Silence. They will know of it, they will know to expect to enjoy it, *both* sexes, and they will not be ashamed of it."

"All right," I repeated.

"And incidentally, you are not a child. You're an adult. One who, those weeks ago, would imminently be wed."

I could not argue that.

"Are you taking pennyrium?" he asked abruptly.

"Pennyrium?" I asked in return, stupidly.

He turned me in his arms but instantly imprisoned me in them again with my body held cinched to his.

"Pennyrium is a draught you can take—" he began to explain with reined impatience.

"I know what it is, Mars, I just..." Gods, I *was* daft. "There was no reason to take it."

And there wasn't, not because we weren't having sex, but because I hadn't thought of it, for I'd never had to before (pennyrium being the draught a woman took daily which (I had heard) was very good at guarding against pregnancy).

"Prior to sacking her, we'll ask that maid to procure some so you can begin taking it immediately," he declared.

I did not wish to be this type of person.

But she was the type of person who flirted with a woman's husband.

So I did not have very many qualms in making this the last (and one of the only) chores Pegeen did before she was on her way.

However…

"But don't you want a child?" I queried.

"Yes, I want several, but first, I want time to enjoy my wife, and also, if this Beast ever rises, I do not want her pregnant when we fight it."

"Oh, right," I mumbled.

He jostled me. "Silence."

My gaze had fallen to his throat, so I lifted it to his face.

"The salute of the Trusted Ones, do you remember it?" he asked.

I was confused.

"The salute of the Trusted?"

"When you met my men and they pressed your hand to their heart and their stomach," he explained.

I nodded. "Yes, I remember."

"I ordered that salute altered when the men gave it to you."

When he went no further, I asked, "Altered?"

"With another woman, or a man, in that instance, they would have had their hands pressed to my men's hearts, and their cocks."

"Oh," I breathed.

"Yes," he replied. "In other words, Silence, I do not want your hand anywhere near another man's cock."

Oh my.

"All right," I said quietly.

"You are exceedingly responsive during bedplay."

I pressed my lips together as my eyes got big.

"Because of this, it was my assumption, one I now know was mistaken, that you would greatly enjoy sex in its myriad varieties."

Oh faith.

"There are women like Zosime who wants naught but Guard and he knows this, so he would never take another but his wife," he shared. "This is why they suit, as Guard is a man who does not want another woman, but his wife. And there are women like Nyx who enjoys exploring different things. This is good, for Lorenz enjoys giving this to her. They also suit. I had no idea what kind of husband I would be, until I knew you'd had no one before me, which meant when I had you, you would never have anyone but me. And Silence," he squeezed me, *hard*, and did this dipping his face to mine, "now that I know this is also your wish, *you will have no other but me.*"

I would have no other but him.

My heart squeezed.

And it did this with gladness.

"All right," I breathed.

"And as it is your wish, I will have no one but you, and that suits me."

But he'd just been flirting.

Thus, tentatively, I asked, "Are you sure?"

"I don't know, I've not been inside you yet, but unless you suffer from a heretofore unknown condition that renders you catatonic the instant you take a cock, all evidence suggests I will not ever be disappointed."

This made me so glad, if I could jump with joy, I would.

Mars was holding me pinned to him, so I couldn't.

Thus, instead, I muttered, "I don't think that condition exists."

"Let's bloody hope not," he grunted.

I wanted to laugh but was afraid to do so at that juncture for he appeared still to be cranky.

Therefore, I fell silent.

Mars also fell silent.

I eventually had to break it or start squirming under his stare.

"Are we done talking?" I asked.

"No," he answered. "You should know, infidelity might be defined differently in Firenze, but it exists. No husband or wife takes a lover that is not known to the other or without the other present, either participating, or watching. It matters not to you. We have our accord. But you should know this as this will be your world, your way, and the way of the people around you."

I nodded, for I agreed, I should know this.

"Further, an accusation of infidelity is taken *very* badly, my wife. Our society is such that this doesn't happen often, for it needn't, with this openness between lovers, between husband and wife. However, what is *not* different amongst our two realms is the understanding, to those who have shared vows, this act is considered the height of an abuse of trust. Thus, if an innocent is accused, it is the deepest affront. And in some clans and tribes, infidelity, if proved, can go punished. Depending on the clan or tribe, this punishment can range from a baron or chieftain granting the severance of a marriage to parts of a body being shorn free."

"Oh my goodness," I whispered.

"Yes," he agreed, and then carried on, "And from this point forward, if you ever have any question about the ways of your people that you do not completely understand, you ask me, or Mama, so you do not make a blunder that will upset or embarrass you, or, say, make your husband very, very angry."

I nodded again while biting my lip, for he was definitely right about that.

"At least this time it was but days I had to deal with what was eating at you before you shared it with me," he declared. "Though, from the words you hurled at me, I would say this was what had actually taken you away from me all the way back in Firenze."

What he said was right.

However...

Just a moment.

"You were chopping wood," I reminded him.

"My ears still worked," he returned.

"No, Mars, you were in a mood because you were angry at me and *you* said nothing to *me* about it."

He appeared astonished for a moment before his face grew gentle.

"I did do that," he murmured.

"And I didn't *hurl* words. I was just upset."

His lips twitched, and he kept murmuring when he said, "A poor choice of *my* words, *amore*."

I huffed.

He gave me a squeeze.

And then he whispered, "I'm very sorry, *mia bellezza*. I should have spoken to you about what was troubling me."

I loved it that he could apologize like that.

So quickly.

So sweetly.

"You're forgiven," I whispered in return.

"You are too, though I would have done that anyway, after what you said to your father."

Balls and begorrah.

I had a feeling he had not just appeared in that doorway.

"How much did you hear?" I asked.

"It started around, 'Do *not* endeavor to drive distance between my husband and myself.'"

"He was being vexing," I muttered.

"I do not know what he'd been saying, but our conversation started with you demanding I dismiss that maid, so I could guess, and that is not vexing. That is him trying to drive distance between you and me, and that, my Silence, will not be tolerated."

"I did share that with him, Mars," I reminded him.

"There is a grave difference, my kindhearted wife, of how you will not tolerate something and how *I* won't. You understand this, no?"

Eep!

"I wouldn't like it if you separated all his joints," I whispered.

"I would not do this to your father, but I would ruin him," he returned unemotionally. "I would take everything from him that matters, and as much as I hate to share this with you, what matters to him is not you. But I would find it, whatever it is. And I would take it. And I would leave him knowing I had it, I took it, and he'll never have it again. This conversation we're having, the whole of it, is very important, including this. So I must know, is this something you understand?"

"He's my father, Mars," I told him.

"He is the man who sired you, Silence, there's a vast fucking difference. You will not know this until you see how I will love and treasure our children. So now, no matter his ways and wiles in trying to convince you differently, you will simply have to trust me."

I decided not to say anything further.

Mars didn't say anything either.

We stared at each other.

It was me again who put a stop to it.

"Now are we done talking?"

"Indeed, we are, my queen, for now, although I will not enter you until you're protected against conceiving, I will teach you how to pleasure me."

I felt my eyes grow huge.

His face got close.

It had changed.

His voice had changed.

The feel of the room had changed.

I would not be surprised if the whole world had changed.

This as he whispered to me, "You have much to make up for, *mio ardente.*"

Oh *faith.*

I had no other thought or got no word in before he was kissing me.

And with that, I had no other thoughts but my husband's mouth on mine and how much I liked it.

I was returning his embrace, enthusiastically, when he broke it.

I would have protested this, but I was too shocked to do so when he bent low, put a shoulder in my belly and hefted me up on it.

"Mars!" I exclaimed.

He did not reply to me.

He carried me across the room, saying, "You, the fair one. My wife needs a three-month supply of pennyrium. Go to the village and see to that," right before he made a turn toward the stairs.

I lifted my head to see Pegeen (and Bernadette…and Olive) standing in the doorway Mars had lounged in earlier, staring at us with wide eyes.

I tried not to smirk.

I had a feeling I failed.

It was when he made the top landing that it came back to me where I was, where I was going and why.

Before I could comment on this, Mars made his own comment.

"It is good you'll be doing all the work, *piccolina*, as I have tired myself out, chopping all that wood."

I did not believe him for a second.

I did not have the opportunity to share that for he bumped me off his shoulder, I landed on my back on our bed, but my husband immediately grabbed my hips and flipped me to my belly.

That belly dipped, I felt my breasts swell in a pleasing manner, and both of these things happened again when I felt him tug sharply at the laces at the back of my gown.

"Mars," I whispered.

They came loose, and I was flipped again to my back, then my skirts were tossed over my head.

Oh my.

I had a feeling I was going to find that it was rather fabulous to have your skirts tossed by a king.

If that king was your husband.

And that husband was Mars.

I felt his hands at my hips again, sliding up, taking my dress with it.

I lifted my arms, the dress was gone, and I was in nothing but my chemise, my corset and my panties.

Though, with a great sweep of his arm, I lost the panties.

I shivered in delight.

However...

I thought I was going to be pleasing him.

"Mars," I whispered again, lifting my head from the pillows and watching him press a kiss to the skin under my navel.

His beard tickled but that wasn't the only reason why I trembled as he slid farther up, and I had his weight when he captured my lips.

I thought no more of pleasing him.

I thought only of kissing him and touching him, and this was what I did.

I heard his boots clunk to the floor as he toed them off, ignored it, and continued to kiss my husband.

I could not ignore his fingers curling into the material of the chemise that covered my breast, nor could I ignore him pulling it down.

Nor did I want to.

I gasped against his lips.

His lips disappeared, and he moved down so they could capture my nipple and draw deep.

At that, I whimpered, sliding my fingers into his hair and squirming beneath him.

"Mars, my love," I breathed.

And felt his growl rumble against my nipple before I lost his mouth there and his face was in mine.

"What did you just call me?" he demanded.

I wasn't listening.

I was fumbling with the laces at his waist on each side of his long-sleeved leather shirt.

"Silence," he called.

"This must go," I mumbled desperately.

He pushed up, yanked at the laces, then tore off the shirt.

All that skin.

The muscle.

Oh, yes.

I put my hands to it, rising, pressing and twisting to take him down to his back.

"Silence," he gritted.

"Lie down," I ordered.

"*Bellezza.*"

I squinted at his face and snapped, "You aren't being very accommodating, my king."

He lay down.

I climbed on top of him.

His large hands spanned my hips where they straddled his belly, and he whispered, "My Silence."

I was again not listening.

All that skin available to me?

A *feast*.

I dipped in and went right for a nipple, like he'd done.

I lost a hand on my hip and got fingers clenched in my hair as he grunted, "Silence."

Oh no.

My head shot up.

"Was that wrong?" I asked.

He lifted his head from the pillow and ordered roughly, "Do not stop."

I stared at the expression on his face, the heat in his eyes, and something swept through me.

Something beautiful.

Something powerful.

No.

Something *invincible*.

I mewed my triumph and moved up, taking his mouth.

He kept his fingers in my hair and wrapped an arm around me, giving it.

That studded tongue.

His taste.

I drank. I explored. I ravaged.

And then I got greedy, wanting more.

I took that too, tugging at his beard with my teeth, licking his neck, nipping his collarbone, drawing deep at his nipples, tracing the boxes at his belly with my fingertips.

I had made it to the waistband of his leather trousers with my lips before he hauled me up, guided my mouth to his and it was he who ravaged my mouth as he took possession of my hand.

And without delay, he pressed it into the waistband of his trousers and wrapped my fingers around his rigid shaft.

He grunted.

I gasped and broke our kiss, resting my forehead against his and gazing hazily in his flaming eyes as he steered my hand in stroking.

"It feels like steel," I whispered in wonder.

And it did, solid and *hefty*.

He made a low, animal noise and took control of my thumb, rolling it over the tip.

"And silk," I breathed.

I felt his other hand shift, and suddenly we had room to move for he'd unbuttoned and freed himself.

As well as our hands.

I peered down and watched us stroking his magnificent shaft.

"And beautiful," I finished in marvel.

Done with his errand, Mars snaked his hand around the back of my thigh and in, gliding his fingers through my wet folds and tweaking my nub.

I gasped and pressed into his touch, even as I protested, "I'm supposed to—"

"Quiet, wife," he grunted, his hand over mine at his shaft tightening.

I felt every ridge and vein, I felt his powerful body tighten and strain under me, I watched from close as his expression darkened gorgeously.

And I wanted more.

I also realized that he'd shown me the way.

So I took it.

I slithered down his body, losing his touch, to his annoyed, "Silence."

I ignored that too.

Also, when he'd realized my destination, I ignored his soft, "Wife."

And on a downward glide of our hands, I drew him into my mouth.

He made a noise so splendid, I nearly climaxed just hearing it.

Oh yes.

I was invincible.

His hand went way from mine as he slid both of them into my hair and he rumbled, "Stroke, *piccolina*, and suck."

I did both, happily.

"Bob," he grunted, his hips raising and lowering, showing me what he wanted.

I gave it to him.

"*Fuck*," he clipped.

I slid him out and looked to his face, unsure.

"Yes?" I asked.

The boxes of his stomach contracted, coming out in sharp relief as he lifted up, reached beneath my arms and pulled me with him as he slid up the headboard.

But he didn't shift my position.

He only put us in one where he could more easily watch.

He then directed with a thick, "*Yes.*"

I smiled at him.

The flames in his eyes raged.

The area between my legs quivered, and I dipped my head and went back to work on his beautiful shaft.

I felt him straining, I heard his noises deepening, these causing a quickening in me, and I thought vaguely how magnificent it was that I would climax with him just giving him this when I lost purchase on him seeing as I was dragged up his body.

He shifted his legs so I was straddling his hips.

I protested, "Mars!"

His hand again wrapped itself around mine at his shaft and his other hand delved between my legs.

I gasped, my head falling back, my hips rocking.

And he whispered, "Yes, Silence. That's it, *amore*."

I fought the sensation he was causing, righted my head and said, "You."

"And you," he replied.

His fingers so skilled, my hips became frenzied, my hand clenched his cock tightly, and my husband built the heat in both of us.

"I-I need something," I whimpered.

"You'll have it soon, *amore*. But take this now."

We worked his tip with our thumbs and then he deepened our strokes as he pressed the silk of it to me and rubbed.

Oh yes.

I needed something.

Something *more*.

Him.

"Gods," I breathed.

"You must finish, Silence," he grunted.

"Mars."

"Finish," he growled.

"Mars!" I cried, trembling above him as my climax consumed me.

"*Fuck*," he bit, shifted me slightly away, and I felt the violent jerks of his body as he changed the strokes of our hands to deep, tight, swift tugs.

I wanted to watch, but I was dancing in the flames, so I couldn't.

They faded, leaving me panting.

Mars was breathing heavily and inquiring, "Do you wish to rest on me?"

I had no idea why he was asking that, for I was only able to hold myself away from him because he was doing the holding.

"Why would I not?"

"My seed is all over my stomach, *piccolina*," he said gently.

I tugged from his hold and collapsed on his body.

I felt it relax under me as his arms curved around me.

I snuggled deeper.

He was a little slippery, but he felt *divine*, all of him, particularly the hardness still there that I felt pressing against the moist, sensitive part of me.

Still, even as I nuzzled his chest with my cheek, I said, "Not fair."

He sounded bewildered (and his voice had a pleasing note of gruff), when he asked, "Not fair?"

I tipped my head up to look at him, seeing his bearded chin deep in his throat to look down at me, all his many piercings winking in the sunlight coming through the windows.

"I was supposed to please you."

"You might have been climaxing when it happened, my queen, so perhaps you missed it. But you can rest assured that happened."

"Yes, with *you* doing it to yourself as well as me."

His mouth quirked. "Trust me, it was you doing it."

"Was not."

His lips curved. "It was."

"Was not."

He smiled blinding white. "It was, Silence."

"It was supposed to be me making up for things," I reminded him.

"I see you need to understand something," he murmured.

Oh balls.

Not me understanding something *more*.

He drew me up his body so we were face to face and cupped the back of my head to bring us even closer.

"If there is ever a time when we are intimate, and I do not pleasure you, I have failed you," he told me.

That was quite lovely.

Actually, beautiful.

However...

"There have been a number of times when we were intimate that I did not pleasure you, Mars," I pointed out miserably.

"For you did not know how."

"You were right earlier. I was being daft, thus thoughtless. I should have put it together."

"You've had things on your mind."

"And *you* are making excuses for me," I grumbled.

"Silence."

He said no more, so I asked, "What?"

"You must cease being so hard on yourself. You are glorious just the way you are. Those around you who are not blinded by their own faults see it clearly. It is only you who does not. I urge you to see yourself as I see you, *amore*, and have patience with yourself as I do, for I know you will be worth it. And I know this because you already are."

I felt the need to weep at his words, but I did not give into it.

I lifted my hand to lay it against his bearded cheek and asked, "How is it that the fates gave me someone so marvelous?"

"I do not know the answer to that, even though I've often been asking myself the same thing."

I felt my face crumble, and to hide it, I tucked it in his neck.

To fight back the tears, I mumbled, "Thank you for understanding."

"Thank *you*, my bride, for liking my cock so much."

I knew he was saying that to release the heaviness of our conversation.

And it worked.

I giggled.

He reached out and pulled a rug over us.

He then reached out and tugged the cord for a servant.

I moved my head out of his neck at that.

"What are you doing?" I asked.

"Calling a servant," he told me what I already knew.

"I know, but why?"

"I do not feel like getting up, and the fire needs stirred and fed," he answered. "What I do feel like is eating my wife's cunt, which I will do, once the fire is stirred and fed."

I squirmed against him, shocked at his frank language, but nevertheless aroused by it.

I saw the satisfaction hit his face at my response, but he did not make note of it.

He continued, "Then we will nap. After that, we will have dinner abed. And after that, you will please me again, while I please you. And a servant needs to know our plans as they will be required to feed us."

"I'm not sure they know how to cook," I muttered.

"The fare they've provided I have noted has been substandard. Your father does not have skills in hiring staff."

What he had skills at was hiring staff that he thought might turn a king's eye.

A knock sounded at the door.

"Come!" Mars commanded.

The door opened, and I pressed closer to him, not looking in that direction.

His arms held me tighter.

"The fire needs stirred and fed," he ordered. "And my queen and I will be enjoying our bed for the rest of the day. Bring wine, cheese and bread now. Fresh water and cloths in the queen's boudoir. Later, we will be requiring supper. We shall ring when this is desired."

"Yes, Your Grace," I heard, and I recognized the voice. It was Olive.

She didn't sound happy.

She would be less happy after Mars went on.

"I would suggest whoever cooks does so with the heretofore undemonstrated desire to please us, for if we dislike the fare we're offered, whoever made it will be dismissed."

"Yes, Your Grace," came from the direction of the fire.

Hmm.

Definitely unhappy.

I grinned.

"Don't dally," Mars finished.

"Of course, Your Grace."

She did not dally for, shortly after, I heard the door close.

The minute it did, Mars pushed us down in the bed and rolled me to my back on the mattress with him atop me.

"I must clean us up," he murmured. "Hopefully there's still water in my cabinet."

"All right."

He touched his lips to mine and made to pull away.

But I moved quickly to wrap my fingers around either side of his neck and he stopped.

"Thank you for being so understanding," I said softly.

His expression grew tender (or more so).

"If I am ever not this, Silence, that would be a failure as well," he replied. "One that you should not abide, no?"

I had a choice to kiss him or shed a tear.

It took no time a'tall to make the decision.

My husband approved of my decision.

And thus, it took some time for him to clean us up for we got lost in the embrace.

# 60

## THE CHALK

***Chu of the Trusted***
*Northwestern Dune Dessert, by the Tebes River*
FIRENZE

Serena washed in the river while Chu watched, recalling again the unsettling occurrence that happened between them some days before.

He had called her to him, not to their usual room in the Heden District, but to an *osteria* there.

He had then shared what his king had told him to share, not as a Master to his slave, but as a Trusted of the King of Firenze to a general in the Nadirii army.

What he found unsettling was her reaction.

Her appealing face took on an efficient expression.

She then asked a series of swift, succinct questions about the evidence they had to support their suspicions.

After that, she said, "Carrington is a fool and half the Go'Doan I find shifty. How do you wish to proceed?"

And at this, that unsettled feeling bloomed.

"We will work together, on both," he told her.

She, Serena of the Nadirii, a known firebrand who had only one use for men and was not particularly fond of team efforts, simply nodded.

And that unsettled feeling grew.

But she asked, "What do you wish Heloise and Genia to do?"

"I do not know who they are, so I don't wish them to do anything."

"They're my lieutenants. They remained behind in Firenze with me."

"Then, as they are your lieutenants, you clearly trust them, thus I wish you to brief them, we will introduce them to Lorenz and Guard, and they will assist here in keeping watch over the Go'Doan that are left and searching for the priests who escaped while we travel to Wodell."

This she did not support, and she verbalized that.

"I'd prefer they stay with me."

"We're going to be spying, mouse. That endeavor is much more successful when it is not attempted by a battalion."

"Two warriors is not a battalion, and I am not your mouse when we are not at play."

He leaned to her, touched her tunic at the side of her breast, watched her eyelids go heavy, and he pointed out the obvious.

"You are my mouse at all times, Serena. Now have you ever acted spy?"

She shook her head, and he knew she was more attuned to his finger lightly caressing her over her tunic than his words.

"Would you like to learn?" he asked.

She nodded.

He sat back and removed his hand.

She looked disappointed.

Chu allowed himself to enjoy that look for a moment before he ordered, "Give direction to your women. I will send a message to you when we will all meet. It will not be long, little mouse, so do this packing. And pack light. We must make haste to Wodell and we don't need our horses heavy. Yes?"

She nodded again.

"Go," he commanded.

She did not go.

She took a moment to study him and he could not read her face as she did.

She then went.

He watched her walk away, and after she was gone was when Chu realized he remained unsettled by her manner.

It was trusting. Attentive. Businesslike.

And none of those were known traits of Serena of the Nadirii.

However, she had fought in the attack on the palace alongside the rest of them, so it could be she wished vengeance, and assisting in finding out who was behind that would take her closer to that aim. That said, she was allowing the Firenz to take the lead for it was their palace that was attacked.

Not to mention, there was an alliance between the Nadirii and Wodell, Wodell opening its mercantiles to the Nadirii to sell their wares (mostly woven baskets, other artisanal works, health tonics and liniments, and magical potions, brews and implements), which was important revenue for The Enchantments.

And although Wilmer was an unpredictable ruler who might, or might not, support the abolition of oppression in Airen, and sustain alliances depending on that decision, True was not so unpredictable.

Therefore, it could be she wished to be certain to keep that secure for her people.

However, the reason he was unnerved by her behavior was that it appeared she was simply what her manner suggested.

Trusting.

Attentive.

Businesslike.

She was a fierce warrior, and a very skilled one.

And Chu was not mistaken about her reputation. It was known widely she was so unpleasant and hostile as to be reviled by many, and it was feared Ophelia would leave the Nadirii to her rule, which many considered, with her disposition, would be catastrophic.

His king did not trust Serena with the information he'd trusted Chu to give to her.

He trusted Chu to have her in hand.

And Chu had her in hand, in play.

What Chu did not trust was that he had her *in hand.*

She detested her sister, did not hide it and took every opportunity to share this with her sibling.

And as far as she knew, they were riding to where her sister was, which was why Chu suspected Serena was behaving reasonably.

In order that the bully would be closer to her favorite prey.

But in the days that followed, as they rode, she was quiet and demonstrated (further, for he already knew this) that she was an immensely competent horsewoman, and openly enamored and caring of her steed. She did not complain that they rode under the hot sun. She did not protest that they bedded on blankets in the sand with no cover but the stars. She did not worry about insects and snakes attacking her in the night. She did not bemoan the chill that invaded the air when the sun left the sky. She did not take issue with infrequent meals, less frequent baths, and she wasted no time on her appearance.

They were on a mission and she, seemingly, was absorbed in getting on with it.

This was a problem for Chu.

For he admired all of this.

And, his mission, with Serena, was to make her slave to his cock, and onward from that, his command, and she might have been an inadequate lover in routine bedplay, but she was an exceptional submissive.

This, as well as being very easy to gaze upon. So much so, she needn't take time on her appearance. This came naturally.

Now, he knew more of her, and like most men, Chu enjoyed sex in a variety of incarnations, particularly Master and slave, but he had always selected partners who were explicitly feminine and acquiescent in aspects of life, as well as play.

Serena was not that and he found the duality more intriguing than he should.

She rose from the water, wearing nothing, her lithe body slick and glistening in the moonlight.

She cast a glance his way as she did so, sharing she would be open to his command, something he had not given her since they embarked on their journey, except for him to share he did not wish for her to wear her bodystocking in sleep, just her tunic.

He knew, at first, she found this indication he would call upon her in the night, but as yet, he hadn't.

To regain his equilibrium, he decided that night, he would.

He did not make note of that then.

He rose, disrobed, and moved to the water to bathe himself.

He knew she had her eyes on him as he did so, but he didn't even glance her way.

He fully dressed again after.

Chu then went to his blanket which was spread three feet from hers, his saddle rug rolled up at the top to act as a pillow.

She was sitting on her blanket, knees up, arms loose around her calves, staring at the gentle flowing Tebes.

He sat, then fell to his side, head toward the river so he could see her face, torso up on a forearm. He stretched out his legs.

"Tell me about your sister," he ordered.

"Elena is not my favorite subject," she replied.

"This was not a request, my mouse," he said softly.

She did not turn her head, but her eyes darted to him.

He also watched her body come alert.

Hmm, yes.

She was ready to play.

"I don't wish to discuss her," she shared.

"I don't care."

She looked back to the river, mumbling, "She's perfect."

"Is she?"

She fully turned her head then and stated, "Yes. Have you not noticed? Are you one of the very few who does not think she commands the sun and dapples the leaves with golden rays?"

"I cannot say I did not watch with some awe, her performance at the coliseum," he shared.

Serena continued to mumble. "You and all of Fire City."

"Though, otherwise, I do not know her."

She again turned away.

"I pity you. She's *extraordinary*," she told the river sarcastically.

"And you envy her, rather than being proud someone of your direct blood is remarkable, negating a possibility for *you* to be remarkable, as there is very little that is more so than someone who could be dimmed by another's light, having the strength of will and goodness of heart to exalt in that light and shine their own because of love."

She looked at him again, her arresting face having grown hard.

"With respect, *Master*," she bit, "but as you are not in my position, you couldn't possibly know."

"I disagree, mouse, for my older brother was taller, stronger, more agile, swifter, and he was the oldest of us all, thus born to be king."

Her eyes grew round.

"And I loved him greatly," he finished.

"By the goddess," she whispered.

"Unfortunately, in my culture, when multiple boys are born to the royal family, it is customary, when they begin to come of age, for the younger ones to be murdered so that they do not dispute or connive to circumvent the ascendency, something that, through history, happened with great frequency."

At that, she twisted her whole upper body to him, saying, "Bloody hell."

"Indeed. Making this story all the more heartwarming is that it is the mother of the boy who would be king who ensures her other offspring do not stand in his way. While the father casts his gaze elsewhere and ignores what is happening, the mother hires the assassins who will slaughter her children. That is, if one has not shown in his training that he won't be a better ruler. Unfortunately for the three of us, but I hope fortunate for the realm of my birth, my brother was extraordinary."

"You're a prince?"

"No, I am a Trusted."

"But you were born a prince."

"In a meaningless way," he allowed.

"That's never meaningless," she said softly.

"No, it was," Chu disagreed. "What was *not* meaningless was my brother, who would be king, who loved me as much as I loved him. Thus, he helped me to escape so when the assassins were to come to take my life, and those of his other brothers, we were not there. Instead, I am here, alive, in the service of another great king, and my life has meaning."

"I'm *her* older sister," she reminded him.

"Then act it."

She looked to the river.

He gave her time to think on that.

Before he was done giving her that time, she asked the river, "What happened to your other brothers?"

"During our escape, one was felled with a spear. After it, the other connived to go back, take vengeance and seize power. However, to do that and not leave any loose strings, he would have to dispatch me. We fought. He did not win."

That earned him her attention. "So where is he now?"

"At the bottom of the sea."

Her eyes were again large. "You killed him?"

"I preferred to be the one left breathing, but more, to be certain that my older brother would not eventually face the same test."

"You killed your brother so he would not kill your other brother?"

He shrugged.

"Chu," she whispered.

In the beginning, she did not remember his name.

She had come to learn it.

And he had learned to like it on her lips.

"As you can see, I come from a fond and affectionate family."

He watched in the moonlight as something moved over her face. She seemed disconcerted and suddenly awkward, as if she did not know what to say, to do or to think.

This reaction did not surprise him.

It was that way, Chu had found, when you'd spent your life concerning yourself only with yourself, and suddenly, you thought of the feelings of another.

And it was not in his character, not in the role he played with a partner, definitely not in the role he was meant to play with her, but he felt the need to alleviate this for her.

"Come, mouse," he murmured. "Bring your saddle rug and blanket. I will tell you a tale of the land of my birth."

All awkwardness left, alertness suffused her frame, and she tried not to appear eager, but she failed as she moved to do as she was told.

He took the saddle rug and propped it against his own, leaning back to it, before he set her blanket aside.

He then opened and cocked his legs, tipping his head to his lap to share where she would position.

She moved there immediately, settling down on a hip between his legs.

"Slide down and free me," he murmured, watching her face grow hungry. "Then get comfortable and draw my sac in your mouth."

That hunger grew, stirring him, though he'd been hard before, this beginning when he gave her the order to join him.

She again did as told, and he watched her, stirred all the more.

Absolutely.

She was an exceptional submissive.

Her warm wet mouth around his balls, he leisurely stroked his hard cock as he looked into her eyes.

And he began.

"This tale is known as the Emperor of Dust. But it is about the lady of the chalk. Not surprisingly, she lived on the chalk, alone, and lonely. From her home on the chalk, or the moon, she watched the earth, pining for company. She witnessed men and women falling in love, and she yearned for a lover. The emperors along the ages knew of the lady of the chalk. They knew it was she that appeared, lighting the night sky. They had heard her beauty was the greatest of all throughout eternity. And they knew her power was even greater. Generation after generation, they plotted and planned to find a way to build a bridge into the night sky, to the chalk, in order to claim her, possess her, make her beauty their own. But mostly, they schemed to take her magic that shone through the dark." He lowered his voice. "Suckle, mouse, gently."

She did that.

He enjoyed it as she did.

He also shifted so his legs were wider, the cushion of his thigh steadier for her head, and he carried on.

"One day, while watching the earth, the lady of the chalk noticed a warrior. He was the mightiest of all. His spear always hit true. His bamboo staff was never broken. He was also the most handsome she'd ever seen over her thousands of years on the chalk. She fell in love with him and sent down her magic to grace his sword, for it never to be broken in battle, for him never to be harmed when he faced a foe. She did this as he slept, but he woke, and on the beam of her magic, he saw her face and fell madly in love with her. He sent a promise through her beam that he would find a way to get to her. He would then wed her, keep her safe and make her happy for the rest of her days. Release, Serena."

She let loose his balls.

Chu shifted his cock and she took his cue, repositioning.

He slid in her sweet, hot mouth.

"Hold me, my slave princess," he murmured. "No suckling."

She nodded carefully, her eyes locked on his.

With his cock in her mouth, Chu stroked her jaw and recommenced his story.

"The emperor at that time had a powerful sorcerer who he had ordered to find a way to the lady of the chalk. In his magical mirror, this sorcerer saw the beam, heard the warrior's message, and warned the emperor that the lady of the chalk had fallen in love with the mightiest warrior of the realm. He also warned the emperor that he had had a dream that this warrior was so strong and stout, their love so true, the warrior could build a bridge and he would not only steal the lady of the chalk from the emperor, he would also leave the emperor empty." He cupped her jaw and warned, "I said, no suckling, Serena."

She stopped what she'd started doing.

"Good girl," he murmured and continued, "Worried about his reign, the emperor vowed no one would have her but he, so he gathered them all and ordered every warrior in his realm to attack the warrior. He found the sorcerer was right. This warrior was so strong and stout, his sword indomitable, one after the other, hundreds, then thousands of warriors fell as the lady of the chalk watched in fear and horror. And when her love defeated the last one, she rejoiced, and he roared his triumph to the sky. He threw up his sword in victory and a bridge formed on the arc of its path, straight to the chalk. So delighted was he that the bridge had formed, he ran there, without sword or shield, the emperor running after him with his royal bow and arrow. The warrior arrived, took his love in his arms, but before he could bestow on her a kiss, he took an arrow to his back, right through the heart. As he fell, the lady of the chalk held tight to her beloved and fell with him, into the dark sky, falling and falling through the nothingness, together forever. At their loss, the moon grew cold and stark, and the bridge crumbled away. The emperor perished there and dissolved into dust, known only for eternity as the Emperor of Dust."

As he finished, he saw Serena staring up at him, his cock in her mouth, but her eyes again were bemused, feeling something and not understanding it.

"Slide me out, Serena, then on your hand and knees, arse to me, I wish it reddened before I fuck you."

She knew how to feel about that and did not delay in carrying out his instructions.

Chu took his knees beside her, allowing his hand to roam the pale skin of her arse. Also allowing himself to enjoy the delicate trembling of her long limbs as she felt her Master's touch and awaited his intentions. This he did before he spanked her, not lightly, but not too much. She'd be in a saddle for days and he wanted her in every moment to be aware of her Master and his dominion over her, but not suffering.

He then positioned behind her and drove into her slick, greedy cunt. He listened to her deep, needy moans as he used her until he pulled her up by her hair, sitting her on his cock, straddling his lap.

He petted her clit.

She whimpered.

"Who's inside you?" he whispered in her ear.

"My Master."

"Did you enjoy your spanking?"

"Yes."

"Did you enjoy the story?"

"No."

"Why?"

"I don't...I-I don't know."

"Why don't you know?"

"I don't know the answer to that either, Master."

"Because it was unhappy?"

"Was she alive?"

Her question threw him.

"I'm sorry?"

"Her lover was dead, she held him, falling forever. Was she alive while she held him, the lady of the chalk?"

"What do you think?"

"I want her to be dead."

"Why?"

"Because it is far too awful to think of her forever alive, holding her dead lover."

It was.

It was far too awful to think of it like that.

He just didn't think Serena had it in her to consider that.

But he liked it that she did.

And as she did, this deserved a reward.

"Climb off, turn, and climb back on, Serena," he growled.

She twitched in surprise, for after their very first time, he'd never taken her facing him.

But she did as told.

When he had her sleek pussy again, he ordered, "Tunic off."

She did that as well.

And he liked her like this, naked and vulnerable astride him, while he was fully clothed.

He held her eyes and commanded, "Now ride me until I come, if you come as you do, do it freely, but do not lose my gaze."

Serena rode him, hard and rough, and Chu dug his fingers into the heated flesh of her arse as she did so.

He lost her gaze when she came, still bouncing on his cock, but he allowed that for she carried on bouncing on his cock.

He took his hand from her arse to grip her hair and yank her head back, feeling her pussy tighten around him and hearing her cry of pleasure when he did this.

He then shot his seed deep inside her.

"Don your tunic," he ordered hoarsely, still drifting down from his climax.

With shaking hands, she complied.

"You've pleased me," he shared.

"This makes me happy, Master," she whispered.

"Did you miss our play?"

"Yes."

"How much?"

"Very much, Master."

"Show me how much, little mouse."

She looked confused again.

And Chu took pity on her again.

"Offer me your mouth, beautiful slave," he murmured.

That earned him surprise but she tipped her head back, her lips parted.

He took what he wanted until she squirmed in his lap, then he took it away.

"Grab hold of the blanket, shake it out behind you and hold it to your shoulders," he commanded, and she obeyed, now with trembling hands.

He lay back, bringing her with him so she was atop him, astride him, his seed mixed with her juices dripping between them, the blanket over them.

"You sleep here," he said.

"Master?"

She was confused again.

This time, he did naught to enlighten her.

"As your reward for pleasing me and sharing your need for your Master's attention, if you wake before me, you will wake me with your mouth at my cock. If I wake before you, you will wake with my cock sliding in your mouth. Now relax and sleep."

"Yes, Master."

It took her some time, but she relaxed, and he felt her body start to get heavy.

Only then did he say, "She was alive, the lady of the chalk, for that is our fate, a life of yearning and then heartbreak. But in the end, she had what she wanted in her arms for eternity."

"I don't like that, Chu," she whispered.

"Tell my mother that."

It was then she did something that was most unsettling of all.

After making a mew of what sounded like pain, Princess Serena of the Nadirii nuzzled his neck with her face, tightened her hold on him with her thighs, and tucked her arms against the outside of his in an effort to hold him.

This hold loosened as she found sleep.

But Chu didn't.

He lay under her, his body warmed by a confounding woman, his eyes aimed at the cold desolation of chalk.

# 61
# THE UNICORNS

***Prince Cassius***
*Ten Miles from The Northwest Border of The Enchantments*
*WODELL*

Night had fallen, and Cassius sat on a log by the fire, his eyes to Elena, his ears trying not to hear the whispered murmurings and soft noises being made by Mac and Jasmine where they were sitting on their own log not far away.

He realized that Elena, seated across the fire from him, was doing the same —trying to ignore the lovers, and failing —when she stood and announced, "I'm going to go sit by the brook for a while."

She then went to their tent, came out of it with a blanket, and he watched her head in the direction of the brook.

"Do you want me to follow her?" Ian asked.

"No," he answered and stood, turning his attention to the nuzzling lovers. "Take it to a tent," he ordered.

Mac broke it off to look up at him and say, "Grand idea."

He then stood, dragging Jazz up with him and heading toward his tent.

Cass watched them disappear inside, then he glanced about the others.

"I'm joining Elena," he stated.

"Grand idea," Hera muttered.

He speared her with his gaze and then turned to Ian. "It's not far. We'll be all right but keep an ear out."

Ian nodded.

Cassius moved but headed to his and Elena's tent first, nabbing the other blanket, for the night was cold, colder not near the fire, before he traced her steps.

In the days (and nights) since they'd met the Zees, he'd spent time with her and slept at her side, holding her as he did so.

But he knew she'd grown frustrated.

She had, first, because during their days riding beside each other, she'd attempted to get to know him better. But although her questions about him and his life in Sky Bay were thoughtful and delicately stated, any answers he could give were dark and bleak, and he did not wish to burden her with them.

So he didn't.

Which he knew, the longer this lasted, the more it seemed he was being closed from her. Distant.

She was also frustrated because he knew she wished his attentions in another way, these physically, in the night, and she communicated this through tentative touch and a tortuous amount of her long-limbed body restlessly shifting against his.

But he didn't give these attentions to her.

This was mostly because he *wished* to give them to her, very much so.

Indeed, *too* much so.

In fact, it was all he could bloody think about when he wasn't thinking about how to share about himself, without burdening her with what he was sharing.

However, what he didn't wish was for her first time to be in a small tent without a lot of room to move, thus room for him to be certain to see to her, as well as no light, so he could not see with his eyes if he *was* seeing to her, and last, with too many people close by.

This event should be special.

His first time had not been.

At fifteen, he'd fucked a whore his brother had forced him to go see, doing so while his brother and his brother's mates shouted raunchy encouragement through the door.

He wanted different for Ellie.

Better.

Much better.

And that was what she would have.

Further, Cass had no idea if he would cause her pain, even make her bleed, and he didn't want them to be where they'd been if those eventualities occurred.

He also knew his response to her enough to know that he couldn't give her even a little, for if he did, it would spin out of control.

Because he wanted it all.

And as the days slid by, he wanted her more and more.

However, watching what stunningly seemed to be blooming between Mac and Jazz, who bickered a great deal, and fucked even more, was putting right in front of Elena's face what she did not have with Cassius.

They'd make The Enchantments mid-morning the next day. She said the ride to the center, where her mother was, Dora was, Aelia was (they'd heard word she had arrived), and Elena's treehome was located was about half a day's ride farther.

Once there, they'd have a good deal to occupy their attention and very little time alone.

He'd wasted what they'd had, for a reason, but their time was nearly gone.

He had to give her that reason.

And to do that, he had to burden her with it.

He saw her golden hair in the moonlight where she sat beside the brook, watching the lazy but colorful flight of the pixies, these streams of bright Cassius had noted were getting fewer in the evenings as the leaves fell and the temperatures cooled.

She but glanced over her shoulder at him when she heard his approach, then turned back to the brook.

He sighed, carried on toward her, and when he arrived, he dropped his blanket to the still-green, lush, thick grass by the water and joined her on the blanket she'd set out.

He cocked his knees, rested his wrists on them and said quietly, "I must explain something to you."

"Hmm?" she hummed, pretending not to care when he knew she cared a great deal.

She'd grown fond of him.

He had no idea how.

But she had.

"I do not wish to do it," he went on.

She turned her head at that, and her voice was sharp to hide the hurt when she replied, "Then don't."

"I do not wish to do it, Ellie, because it is vastly unpleasant and the knowing of it is a burden I do not want you to bear."

He saw the surprise light on her features before they softened.

Yes, as he was finding with Elena, she did not hold her pique. She did not make him work to gain her attentions after he'd (somewhat) spurned them these past days.

She opened immediately to him.

For she was Elena.

"I keep telling you, I'm stronger than you think," she replied with the softness he saw in her face.

"You do not know, my lamb," he replied.

"Tell me."

His eyes moved over her beautiful face and his lips whispered, "I hate this."

It was then, her expression grew alert, as did the air about her.

"By the goddess, Cassius," she whispered back, twisting to him and reaching out to wrap her fingers around his thigh. "What is it? Tell me," she urged again.

He looked to her hand, felt her touch hot as a brand, left it as it was because he liked the feel, then he turned his gaze to the slowly rolling brook.

"You know my mother is dead," he said.

"Yes," she replied.

"She died of a chill."

"I'm so sorry."

"That was what I was told."

Elena did not reply, but the awareness he felt from her enhanced.

"It was a lie."

Her hand spasmed on his leg.

"I remember, nights and nights of hearing the noises," he shared. "I remember, lying abed, listening, fear paralyzing me, my mind a turmoil, not understanding, but knowing those noises were not right. I remember, the night before it happened, Trajan screaming in the middle of the night. I remember, the day after he did that, we were moved from our chambers to ones far away from my mother and father in another area of the castle. I remember, lying awake then, not able to sleep for fear of it happening without me there, as if my closeness to her was some balm. So I remember getting out of bed so I could go to their room. I wanted her to know I was close. I only intended to open the door enough she could see me and know I was there. But I saw them."

"You saw them...what?" she prompted when he stopped talking.

He looked to her then. "I saw my father raping my mother."

She swayed back, then forward, her hand clutching his thigh.

"Cassius."

"I was six."

And then he saw what he'd feared he'd see.

The dread in her face that he so wanted to protect her from.

"*Cassius*," she breathed in horror.

"I knew, even then, it was not an act of love between partners. The violence. It was obscene."

She moved closer, taking her hand from his thigh to press it to his chest.

"That was why Trajan was screaming," he explained. "He told me, later, in whispers, for we knew better than to talk about it openly. He'd had enough. He was older. Understood what was happening. He'd gone to save her. To stop it. Father forced him out and had us moved."

"I hate that for him," she said. "I hate that *for you*."

"She saw me. In the door."

"Oh goddess," she breathed.

"He was in the act, forcing himself upon her, and her face was twisted in pain, but nothing like how she looked when she saw that I saw. That pain..." He blew out a breath. "Ellie, there is no word to describe the depths of that pain."

Elena moved again, pressing herself to his side, wrapping her arm around his stomach.

"She was dead the next morning," he declared.

"No." This came out almost silently.

"Killed herself, drowned herself in her bath. Not because she couldn't take it, because she did not want her sons to see her like that. Not again. And she had no control over it, nowhere to turn, no one who would help her. It would happen again and again and again, and we would know it did."

He closed his eyes, opened them and continued speaking.

"But she was already dead inside, Elena. I knew it. I saw it in her eyes that night. Because when she saw me, she knew she'd failed at giving us the only thing she could give us, keeping that from us."

Elena trailed her hand up his chest, his neck, to cup his jaw.

"By the mercy of the goddess, that's the most tragic thing I've ever heard."

"I'm born of rape, Ellie."

She dropped her head, resting her forehead against his shoulder.

"So was Trajan. *Gods*," he groaned, seeing his mother in his mind's eye. "She was beautiful, Ellie. So lovely."

She lifted her head and stared into his eyes.

Hers were bright with tears.

Cassius kept talking.

"She loved us both, so fucking much. I still hear her voice reading us stories or singing me to sleep. I still feel her arms around me and how she would hold me tight. I see her expression when we were brought down to the breakfast table. Her face lit up with such gladness at the sight of her two boys."

"I'm glad she at least had you."

He had always wondered about that.

It seemed he and Trajan were the only things that gave her joy.

But how could they with the way they'd been conceived?

He did not ask Ellie about that.

He told her, "It was not a love match from the beginning. Father coveted her beauty, and as king, he could have it. So he took it. She hated him. She feared him. She recoiled every time he was near. She always seemed to move to protect us from him. And I knew nothing but her cuts and scrapes, bruises and swelling, limping and holding herself carefully. I wouldn't know, until much later, that it was he who made her so. That it was not normal for a woman to be like that. It was just, then, all that I knew."

He lifted his hand and curled his fingers around hers at his jaw.

"My stories do not get worse than that, lamb," he said. "But they are not much better. Now, do you understand why I did not wish you to carry this weight?"

"I do, and so now, do you see that I have not broken under it?" she asked.

He shook his head. "Elena, more grows from that. This kind of atrocity, this kind of evil, it breeds and spreads and infects everything around it. For me, I'm angry at her almost as much as I hate him. She fought him in the act. Years she'd endured that, and she still fought. Why did she not *continue* to fight? Why did she not try to get away? Perhaps she could have escaped. To The Enchantments. To Mar-el. Being a bounden, she'd have more rights and protections than she did in that bloody citadel."

"She still would have had to leave you."

"But eventually, I could have found her."

"Oh, Cass," she whispered, her fingers moving under his to stroke his jaw.

"I also failed her," he stated.

She appeared perplexed. "How?"

"I wanted no part of him, of my birth, of that castle, of his reign. I removed myself from it as much as I could when I could not actually remove myself. I watched my brother turn into him, and I did nothing to stop it. And I knew women all over my realm faced the same and I did nothing to stop that either."

"You were the second son. This is a precarious position, Cassius, I know that. You knew it better than me for you lived it."

"I still did nothing to stop it."

"You're doing something now."

"Do not think this will be easy, Elena. There will be a revolt. It's inevitable."

"And you'll best it."

"I want to kill him."

She pressed closer at his declaration.

"I have to remove myself from that too, from the feelings I have," he told her. "I have to close them down, freeze them out. If I do not, if I let free that rein, I will murder my father."

"You do know this is not an unreasonable reaction," she replied, and he let out a bark of disgusted laughter. "It isn't, Cass," she pushed.

"The lifelong urge to commit patricide?" he asked disbelievingly. "What kind of man does that make me?"

"You're asking the wrong question."

"What is the right one?"

"What kind of son does that make you?"

Was she mad?

"That I want to kill my father?"

"That you want to avenge your mother."

He closed his mouth.

"And you will do that, by freeing those like her from similar tyranny," she declared. "She will not witness it, but do you not think she is in the beyond, watching you and proud of you and knowing that *she* made you? Knowing that, through *you*, part of *her* will liberate her sisters? How beautiful a legacy is that, Cassius? What *beauty* she has created, my warrior. What a *precious gift* she has given our world."

Gods damn it, he had to have her.

He could no longer hold his need at bay.

He didn't want her.

He needed her.

*Now.*

So he took her, starting with her mouth.

He also took her down to the blanket, with him over her.

And feeling her under him, Cass was as he expected he would be.

Lost to her.

He simply couldn't get enough.

Her lips and tongue, his hands on her body.

She responded eagerly, hungrily, spurring him on.

He pulled at her tunic.

She tugged at his leathers.

He yanked off her moccasins.

She wrenched off his boots.

Every inch of her skin he exposed, he consumed. Gorging on her taste. Reeling at her touch. Intoxicated by her smell. Triumphing at the sounds he earned from her. Drunk at the sight of her.

Every sensation demanding he take more.

And he did.

A nuance of the haze shifted away when he found himself on his back, naked, with a naked Elena, her smooth skin radiant in the moonlight, tracking her lips swiftly down his stomach to his stiff cock.

He moved to stop her.

But before he could, the warm moist of her sweet mouth closed around him and he lost all reason.

His hips surged up, seeking more, and she moaned around his shaft, giving it. Sucking deeply. Bobbing greedily. She released him only to lave at his balls while stroking his cock with her hand, his fingers in her hair, encouraging her to give more so he could have it, possess it, have her, *possess her.*

Then she moved back to his cock, swallowing it down, humming around it with a reverence that bordered on worship.

He was close to climax, he could feel the pressure build, his balls drawing up, and only then did a small amount of reason return.

Cass knifed up, pulling her away to her noise of angry protest.

He flipped her to her back, repositioned, opening her legs, using his fingers to spread her, then he bent and fed from her.

*Gods,* she was nectar.

Her back arched, driving her pussy into his mouth, as her low moan rose, drifting through the trees.

He took and took, starved for her, savoring her, unable to get enough, driving her to a frenzy, pulling her legs over his shoulders, feeling his cock ache as she dug her heels into his back, rocking against his mouth.

Her noises were now desperate whimpers, unintelligible pleas.

Before he heard, "No. With you."

Cassius kept at her, his mind consumed with the desire to taste her climax on his tongue as it sang in his ears.

She tugged at his head. "Cass, please. *With you.*"

He knew what she wanted and angled over her, putting his mouth to her ear, his fingers toying in the wet between her legs to keep her primed, as he whispered, "I need to prepare you. You must be ready to take me."

"I'm ready," she breathed, her hands moving on him, nails scraping, her teeth sinking into his neck.

*Fuck.*

He groaned at the bite before saying, "I don't want to hurt you."

"You won't hurt me."

"Ellie—"

She was reaching for his cock.

He tried to slant it away.

Both her hands clamped on his cheeks, she pulled his face above hers and whispered, "Cass, sweetheart, *please.*"

The passion in her eyes, the longing in her face, he was no match to fight it.

He wrapped a hand around his cock, guided it to her, and slowly, carefully, watching her face closely, he slid inside.

There was no barrier. No tearing. No sound of pain.

The more of him she took, the more her lids drifted closed. Her back bowed, her arms lifted over her head, her chin tipped back, and she stretched beneath him, receiving his cock like an offering, glorying in the act.

He watched, mesmerized by the beauty of her, until her slick tight closed around him to the root.

Then, with an iron will he did not know he possessed, he held immobile in her snug embrace, giving her the opportunity to get used to him.

Her eyes opened, her arms came down, her nails dug into his arse, and she whispered, "You're perfect."

At these words, Cassius completely snapped.

He growled, took her mouth, and fucked his princess.

She gloried in that too, grazing him with her nails, milking him with her pussy, wrapping her legs around his thighs to lift her hips to receive more.

She moaned, and he grunted.

She whimpered, and within but strokes, her head flew back, her mouth disconnecting from his, and her cry of release rang through the forest, spurring him on to take her harder, faster, the sleek walls of her pulsing around him.

He held tight to what little control he had left as her climax carried on because he drove it on, thrusting into her, triumphant in watching the magnificence wash over her and not let go.

And he did this until he could take no more.

He then buried himself inside Elena, his head snapping back, the shout of his impeccable release cracking through the wood like thunder as he poured his seed inside his princess.

When it was done, he collapsed atop her, mindless—her smell, the wet fist of her cunt, the feel of her hair tangled in his beard all he knew.

All he wanted to know.

It was the soft touch of her fingertips drifting along the small of his back that brought him into the present.

He instantly shifted his weight to a forearm to take some of it from her, turning his head so his nose brushed her neck, trying to find the words to ask her forgiveness for his loss of control, the feverish passion he unleashed, the hard fucking he'd forced on her.

Her first time.

He'd made her endure that her first time.

He'd made her climax, but he'd done it like *that* her first time.

He did not find those words before she whispered wondrously, "You gave me stars."

Stunned, he lifted his head and saw a soft darkness all around them, blinking pinpricks of light floating about, like they'd risen into the heavens and were coasting in the night sky.

Cass lost his fascination at that when she said, "I'm very angry at you."

It sounded pouty and playful, but the words made his eyes shaft to her.

"For not doing that to me a whole lot sooner," she finished.

He blinked down at her.

"Oh, and for stopping me suckling you. I was enjoying that," she went on.

He continued to stare down at her.

She tugged at his beard and teased, "Do you lose the ability to speak after you climax?"

"No," he grunted.

Her cheeky mood dissolved, and instead of tugging his beard, she was stroking it when she whispered, "Thank you."

Lost in her new mood, as well as her eyes, he asked, "For what?"

"For making that so beautiful."

*Fuck.*

Thank the gods.

He pressed his forehead to hers and closed his eyes, groaning, "Elena."

She shifted her head so his cheek slid down hers and she had her lips at his ear.

"I now know why they leave," she said there quietly.

"Why who leave?"

"The sisters who leave The Enchantments when they find a man who touches their soul."

He closed his eyes tighter.

"I now know why they leave," she repeated.

"Lamb."

She kissed his neck and said again, "Thank you, Cassius."

He kissed hers then lifted his head and kissed her mouth before he broke from her and said, "My pleasure. *Very* much my pleasure, my princess."

She grinned up at him. "I sort of noticed that."

He couldn't stop himself from smiling down at her.

"And *hearing* that," she teased. She began to appear thoughtful when she remarked, "Odd, how it's almost more pleasurable to know I gave you pleasure than to have my own."

He did not find that odd at all.

He also did not find it odd Elena thought just like that.

She came back to him. "Though, only *almost.*"

He wrapped his hand under her jaw, sweeping his thumb along her lower lip, watching his movement, murmuring, "I know this feeling."

Even though she felt this, and he was relieved she did, with her inexperience, he had to share that there was another way.

He looked into her eyes. "That was rough, Ellie. I had hoped to go more gently the first time we were together."

"Maybe we can try that sometime," she suggested. "In a few months, or perhaps a few years."

His relief increased, he grinned at her, trailed his thumb across her lip again, his eyes watching, and murmured, "Mm."

"Oh my goddess," she breathed.

At the tone of her voice and the understanding from it she was no longer in their conversation, Cassius shifted his gaze to her eyes and felt his whole body tense.

She was glancing to the side.

"What?" he demanded, his head jerking that way.

And that was when his entire body stilled.

He felt her head move as she turned it to better see and she repeated a thunderstruck, "Oh my *goddess*."

He could not believe his eyes.

And thus, he asked, "Elena, are you seeing what I'm seeing?"

"I think so, unless your lovemaking is so good, we're both having delusions."

He did not think it was that.

They moved, and Cassius tensed again, dipping his shoulder toward the unknown in an effort to afford her some sort of protection, wondering where his bloody clothes were.

"It's okay, Cass, they're harmless," she whispered. "But skittish. No sudden moves."

He warily eyed the one in the lead, thinking that horn was not harmless.

"Elena," he growled.

"They come closer."

He watched, alert but altogether fascinated as the two unicorns moved slowly, making their way toward he and his princess.

"I wonder what they're doing here. They only dwell in The Enchantments." She was still whispering.

"Fucking hell," he muttered as they got even closer.

"Just, rise up...but *slowly*," she instructed.

He did, pushing up on a hand, disconnecting from her, which was bloody disappointing, but he had two unicorns on his hands, no clothes on, his woman was also nude, there wasn't a pixie in the sky and not a sound in the forest.

It was eerie.

Odd.

Not right.

Elena came up with him so they were both on their knees, front to front, and he twisted her so he was between her and the unicorns, his back to them. He turned his head as he did this so he did not lose sight of the creatures.

The lead one halted, drew back, dropped his head, so that long, glittering, spiraled horn was aimed their way.

"Fuck," he bit.

"It's all right. Just be still," she urged.

They were unknowns, but they were beyond exquisite. Their white coats gleamed almost opalescent. The front one, the bigger one, casting more purples and blues, the back one, the smaller one, casting more corals and pinks.

They shifted closer, closer, Cass's body getting more and more taut, his arms around Elena, holding her tight to him, but ready to toss her away if need be.

And then he saw Elena's arm drift out.

"Ellie," he clipped.

"It's all right. I promise."

She held her hand low, palm up.

The front unicorn got closer, dropping his head lower, and Cassius got stiffer.

And then he gripped her tight as the unicorn bent even lower.

Only to snuffle her hand.

"That's it, boy. Get a good sniff in. Hullo," she cooed.

The unicorn jerked his head back.

Cass braced to lift her into his arms and run.

Then he realized he'd lost track of the other one and therefore started when he felt a delicate snort in his neck on the other side.

His head whipped around, and the other unicorn took a step back.

"She's flirting with you," Ellie said happily. "Put your hand out. Let her get used to you."

Gods, the mare was beautiful.

That thick white mane. Her intelligent black eyes. The dove gray fur that shadowed her nose.

He did as Elena had and reached out, slowly, his hand low, palm up.

The mare bent to it, sniffled, then drew her lips back and nipped.

The stallion butted her with his head, almost like he was jealous.

"Definitely flirting," Ellie decreed.

The mare butted back, then nuzzled under the stallion's neck.

He whinnied softly.

"By the gods," Cassius murmured.

"Hand me my tunic, Cass, but I don't think they're used to us yet, so continue to move slow."

He saw her tunic in the grass, and moving carefully, he reached to it.

He gave it to Elena and then found his trousers.

By the time he had them up and fastened, Ellie was on her feet, close to the stallion, holding his stately neck in her arms and stroking him.

The mare whinnied and stepped to him and Cass mimicked Elena, cautiously moving close then stroking her neck as she leaned into his touch.

It was then he noticed her horn, and he must have exuded his emotion, for she reared a bit, the stallion's head came around and he brayed his warning at Cassius.

Cass forced himself to relax, but did it stating, "Her horn has been shorn."

"No, sweetheart. The mare has a shorter one than the stallion. As it seems is nature's wont," she joked.

The stallion left Ellie, butted the mare from Cass, but they didn't go far, perhaps a few feet, before they both bent and started tugging at the grass with their teeth.

They finished dressing, and when they were clothed, Elena pulled him down to their arses on the blanket, falling into him and resting her head on his shoulder after they were seated.

Cass dislodged her to reach for the free blanket and wrap it around them, the chill pervading now that their activities no longer produced heat.

Once they were in their cocoon, Elena replaced her head to his shoulder, but this time also reached out to take control of his hand. When she had it, she fiddled with is fingers absently as she watched the creatures.

She had never done this, for they had never done this, sat together with nothing to do but just...

Be together.

And Cass realized he felt more at peace than he had in longer than he could remember.

Elena broke their quiet, but she did it in a tone that sustained the serenity.

"Earlier, you granted me a gift that was terrible, but beautiful, for the trust behind the giving of it is most dear to me. And now, I'll return that."

Cassius said nothing.

Elena linked her fingers with his, and her gaze on the unicorns, she spoke again.

"It was centuries ago that the realms agreed that the taking of a unicorn horn was forbidden. Sadly, it was not the maiming of these magnificent creatures, and the terrible pain it caused them to have it removed, that was behind this accord. It was that the magic that could be extracted from a horn was thought too much for any witch or sorcerer of any given realm to possess."

When she paused for a lengthy time, Cassius murmured, "I learned this from my tutors, lamb."

"Did you learn why most of the charmed folk left Airen?"

"No," he muttered.

"Can you guess?" she asked gently.

"Yes," he sighed.

"There is a reason naught but the trolls and yeti, griffin and gogma-goggs reside in Airen while Wodell and The Enchantments are rife with pixies, sprites, gnomes, fairies, and as for The Enchantments, unicorns."

Cassius stared at the animals, wondering what would possess someone to mutilate that beauty.

His attention was taken when Elena's fingers tightened around his.

"My many-times great grandmother learned to speak with a goodly number of creatures. And this she did with the unicorns. When it came close to the time the sisters would take action against their masters, she made a pact with them. The unicorns would forever be safe in her land of female warriors. And in return, they would give us that land."

Cassius's head shot to the side so sharply, Elena lifted hers to catch his gaze.

"The unicorns built The Enchantments?" he asked.

She nodded.

"It was not your grandmother?"

"It was her spell, the craft of my bloodline, but it was the unicorns' magic."

"By the gods," he whispered.

"Yes," she whispered in return. "It is also why they now reside only in The Enchantments. It's where they're safe, for regardless if it is forbidden, there were many who coveted the horn of a unicorn and thus they took them. So it's not only Nadirii magic that keeps The Enchantments hidden to all but our sisters. It is also the unicorns. The unicorns united with my bloodline, my queen."

"What other man knows of this?" he demanded.

"None," she admitted.

He turned to her. "Elena, you should not have told me."

Her brows drew together, tiny lines forming between them. "Can I not trust you with this?"

"If something were to happen to the unicorns..."

She held his gaze steady and finished for him, "The Enchantments would fall. We could possibly keep them strong for a time, but it would take much magic. It would deplete us and eventually…" she trailed off and shrugged.

"This is why you shouldn't have told me," he growled.

"Cassius—"

"Intelligence that crucial to your defense must be protected at all costs."

"You're to be my husband," she reminded him.

He had no response to that.

Liviana, his dead wife, had not had state secrets that needed to be guarded by any means necessary.

He had never in his life experienced this level of confidence shared.

Her expression assumed a look of concern, even fear. She started to draw away, and Cassius felt her withdrawal.

He also took measures to stop it for the moment he felt it, he could not bear it.

Tightening his fingers around hers, he pressed them to his stomach.

"I have never…no one has ever…" He couldn't seem to find the words. "Even my father shares only what I need to know for the safety of our land and I'm his top general."

Elena stared into his eyes.

He dropped his voice. "The confidence I gave you is nowhere near the one you gifted me."

"Cassius—"

"I have nothing to give you that has that level of beauty."

Her eyes grew large and her mouth clamped shut.

His did not.

"There must be balance in a marriage, Elena, and we can never have that. And I must admit to you that this troubles me, and it has for some time."

"What do you mean?"

"You have much to give, I have nothing."

The concern came back to her features, but not the fear, before she said, "How on earth can you utter those words?"

"They are but truth."

"They are so false as to be laughable," she retorted.

That was when Cassius shut his mouth.

"You are beautiful," she snapped.

He opened his mouth at that.

"My appearance is inherited, not of my making."

"You could be slovenly, and you are not," she retorted.

He could not argue that.

"I like your beard," she declared.

He suddenly felt like smiling, but he did not smile.

"I, personally, have naught to do with the growing of my beard either, my princess," he pointed out. "Just the decision not to shear it."

She went on as if he did not speak.

"You are mighty. You are fierce. You are loyal to your men. You engender loyalty *from* them. You are a very good kisser. You are an exceptional lover, and I have no experience, but I still know that. You are protective of your daughter. Against all that is rational with how you were raised, you understand the importance of family. And even if the burden of responsibility you carry is unwanted by you, you don it with no complaint and wear it like a mantle made for only you. You had the strength of character *not* to become your father, like your brother did. And...and...I like your ink."

She would be inked into him, he vowed in that moment.

She would be inked all over him.

But he knew where he'd put her first.

"Elena—"

"By the goddess, Cassius, your sense of compassion is so strong, you wished to shield me from knowledge of your life you thought would harm me. Your protective instinct is so...so...*instinctive*, you moved to shield me from *unicorns*. It is your first thought in any uncertain situation. That thought being not about *you* but about *me*. How can you even begin to say you have naught to give? I've never heard anything so preposterous in my *entire* life."

So heated was she in this tirade, he could see the pink in her cheeks in the moonlight, the fierceness in her violet eyes making them appear to glow amethyst.

He could also feel the attention of the unicorns, but they did not move away.

Nor did Cassius.

He moved closer, taking her to her back and covering her again.

"What are you—?" she began.

"It won't be gentle this time either, my warrior," he growled against her lips.

He watched her eyes grow wide and then he saw them grow hooded when he kept his own open as he took her mouth.

He did not give in this time when he eventually got his mouth between her legs.

He made her come that way and learned the taste of her climax was glorious.

Though he did give in when she wished to ride him.

However, he sat up as she did so in order that he could watch from close as she enjoyed his cock.

He vaguely heard the unicorns whinny when they both climaxed.

And in the end, he liked it much better when he collapsed to his back with Ellie draped on him.

Cassius did not limit the exploration of her skin to the small of her back. He perused her arse too.

And Elena showed she liked it by shoving her face in his neck, sighing and trembling against his touch.

He wished to prolong it, and he did as long as he could.

But eventually he had to say, "We must return to camp."

"I know."

"The camp is not far, thus, it is likely they will have heard us," he warned.

"I know."

"If Mac was not enthralled in his own pursuits, there will be ribbing," he continued.

"Same with Jazz."

He drew in breath and let it go. After, he rolled her up and took them to their feet. They dressed.

And as if knowing they intended to rejoin the others, the unicorn stallion brayed at them before both creatures turned and gracefully galloped into the forest.

He and Elena watched them go until they could be seen no longer.

Then Elena offered to carry the blankets, Cassius refused, tossing them over an arm and taking her hand with his free one.

They started back that way and Cassius asked, "Do you know why they left The Enchantments to be here in Wodell?"

"The unicorns?"

"Yes."

"Because they're ours."

He stopped them to look down at her. "Pardon?"

"Unicorns mate for life," she told him.

This knowledge was interesting, but it did not answer his question.

Therefore, he prompted, "And?"

"Do you remember that card you drew? In the garden at Catrame Palace when I did your reading?"

"Yes."

"I drew a unicorn as well, some weeks earlier, the day I was told I was to wed you."

He stared at her.

"I did not understand it," she muttered. "Now I think I do."

"Would you like to share?" he requested when she did not go on.

She continued to mutter when she said, "I don't know."

"I do," he stated firmly.

She hesitated, took in his expression, then bit her lip.

"Elena," he warned.

"There are tales of yore. Tales of lovers," she began, but said no more.

"Yes?" he prompted yet again.

"True love, destined for one another," she whispered.

He grew solid.

She carried on.

"In those days, before it was known the magic a unicorn possessed, that it could be had by taking their horns. Before the unicorns learned to evade our kind. That if two lovers who were destined for one another found each other, they would know this for their unicorn mates would find them. Then man and woman, stallion and mare would be bound together in love and magic. And if the woman should perish, so would the mare, so the stallion and male could have the other close in their mourning. And, er...vice versa."

When he made no reply, she rushed to fill the silence.

"This does not mean what you had with your —"

"It is not surprising, Elena," he stated gruffly. "We *are* destined for the other."

She peered up at him hesitantly.

To take the hesitance out of her gaze, he bent and touched his mouth to hers and then murmured, "I have received many gifts tonight."

She smiled a smile of blinding beauty.

He allowed himself a moment to enjoy it before he tugged on her hand to get them moving again.

When they arrived, they saw the fire was banked, the campsite deserted, and Cassius thanked the gods for this as he led Elena to their tent.

They were curled together under their blanket when Mac called out, "About bloody time," which was followed by Jasmine's husky laughter, a loud giggle from Rose and an annoyed shout from Ian of "You just couldn't keep your mouth shut, could you?"

Mac chose not to reply.

"Bloody hell," Cassius muttered.

Elena did naught but laugh softly and cuddle closer.

When no more came from any of the others, Cassius relaxed.

"You see?" Elena asked confusingly.

"See what?"

"You were tense, waiting for someone to say something else, when you don't care. You think *I* care. And only when you knew it would be all right for me did you find calm."

He was incorrect.

She had not grown fond of him.

It was much more.

A great deal more.

And Cassius could not deny having this from her was warming.

He did not give her that knowledge.

He curled her closer and murmured, "Be quiet and go to sleep, princess."

"Can we have more sex in the morning?" she requested.

If she talked about it further with that eagerness, she'd get it right then.

"Yes," he answered. "Now quiet."

"All right, sweetheart," she muttered contentedly and burrowed closer.

Cassius did not think he would find sleep with ease.

Mere moments after he felt Elena find it, which was mere moment after she spoke her words, he followed her there.

# 62
## THE DANCE

**Prince True**
*The Antlers Pub and Inn, Five Miles from the Lights*
WODELL

"The royal summons has been received, and we shall go, but only if the gnomes do not sit in front."

True did not hear Áine speak.

He was busy sitting in his chair at the back of the pub, as away from the music as they could get (which was not very far), watching Farah twirl around with Wallace, Luther and Florian.

The beat of the drums, the quick notes of the flutes, pipes and strings meaning the tempo of the dance was lively, bringing color to her cheeks. Her eyes were lit, and her smile was bright.

She had lost her cares in that moment and was simply...

Happy.

"My prince, did you hear my words?"

He turned his head and looked down to Áine, the fairy spokeswoman of the Keeper of the Lights, who sat beside him. Her copper hair flamed in the bright lanternlight of the pub, the glittering ribbons in it twinkling, all of this framed by the iridescent wings that shown gold and honey that she had opened behind her. But her brown eyes were sharp on him.

"No, I'm sorry," he admitted his rudeness. "What did you say?"

She glanced at the dancing then back to True. "I said that we shall go to your wedding, but only if the gnomes do not sit in front."

He fought back a heavy sigh. "Áine, your peoples are two to three feet taller than the gnomes. They would not be able to see if they were not sat in front."

"You can give them cushions."

"Is it really that important where you're seated?"

She straightened her shoulders and he knew her well enough to know what was coming.

"The fairies—"

He interrupted her. "I know the fairies have stronger magic. I know the fairies consider the sacred places they keep safe to be more important than that of the gnomes, pixies and sprites. I know the fairies were brought forth by the Green Men, the gods who created the forests that are Wodell. Though I'll remind you, the gnomes, pixies and sprites also came of the Green Men, just after the fairies. And last, I know that the gnomes are at least *two feet shorter* than you, the pixies even smaller and an elderly person with bad sight might not even be able to see a sprite. What I also know is that, in the end, we are all one in Wodell and it matters not who sits where at a wedding."

"You say this, and the gnomes will hold it over our heads for a century."

"Áine, the gnomes can't *reach* over your head."

Her eyes grew wide and then she tipped her head back and laughed her bell laugh.

True grinned at her but felt it as Farah's attention came to him.

Therefore, he turned his to her.

She was still dancing, but doing it smiling in his direction.

He felt his grin turn into a smile and tipped his chin up at her.

"Her beauty is great."

As Farah was whirled away by Bram joining the dancing, he looked back at Áine.

"Firenz women are known for their beauty, but I'll tell you true, Farah is the greatest I've ever seen," he shared.

She tilted her head to the side and her face turned from shrewd to kind. "I'm not talking about that kind of beauty, my prince." Her chin dipped, she looked under her lashes at him and murmured, "And here she is, to demonstrate the beauty I'm talking about."

And just then, he felt his hand taken up and pulled.

He looked that way and saw Farah had hold of him, her happy face now close, warming True to his core.

"Come. Dance," she urged when he resisted her pull.

"I must finish speaking with Áine, my sweet," he denied.

She turned her gaze to Áine and pleaded, "Just one song...or three. Then you can have him back."

He chuckled, and Áine replied, "It would give me great gladness if you danced with your prince the rest of the night."

Farah instantly pounced on her words.

"There you have it, True," she said, pulling harder.

He looked to Áine, intent to resist, but he didn't get his mouth open to say that first word.

"We will sit behind the gnomes, and pixies and sprites," she declared. "If we get to be in attendance to witness our prince find his happiness, we will sit wherever we're placed. Now go. Dance."

"You are my favorite being in the land," Farah avowed to Áine.

"Even above Baldrick?" Áine asked drolly. "For you must know, he boasts broadly that you are partial to the gnomes of The Doors. I know this for the pixies are spreading that tale throughout the land."

"All right, then at least tonight you are my favorite," Farah admitted.

The bells of Áine's laughter rose above the music, and the fairies were so sensitive to any perceived slight, True was taken aback she showed no offense.

Through her amusement, Áine urged True, "Dance with your bride, my prince."

Only then did he allow himself to be pulled out of his seat and led to the dancefloor. Males and females of the human and fairy varieties cheered and made room as Farah and he came close.

But he felt immediately strange, for they were not dancing any dance he knew and was adept at doing. There were no waltzes. No structured minuets.

There seemed a lot of hopping, skipping, jogging without getting much of anywhere and twirling, all of this without any rhyme or reason, though there was rhythm.

This was how the countryfolk danced. He'd seen it before, but never participated in it. And they did not give lessons on such in the city, lessons such as his mother had him start taking when he was twelve to learn the courtly dances of the gentry.

He started to take Farah in his arms in order to try to do his best, considering she seemed to wish to dance with him quite badly, but instead she wrapped her arm along his stomach and tucked her hip to his at his side, starting to turn him as she walked one way, and he the other.

"I don't know this dance, sweets," he told her.

"There is no dance to know," she replied, continuing to guide him with pressure at his middle. "Just move to the music however you see fit."

He gazed through the crowd, watching eyes quickly shift away before he would catch them, and he felt less strange and more awkward.

He also felt, acutely, that he was their prince, their future king, and inept hopping, skipping and twirling was not at all what they should witness their future king doing.

Farah suddenly stood in front of him and took both of his hands. She shook them, vigorously, which in turn stirred his arms.

"Don't think about steps or what you're supposed to do," she instructed. "Don't think about anyone watching you, for they aren't dancing and thinking of anyone watching *them*. They're simply enjoying themselves through the music. So, True, just listen to the music, do what you wish and do it *enjoying* yourself."

She had no idea.

She had no idea they *were* watching him, they always did, and they always would. Thus, he must be circumspect in everything he did, every word spoken, every action taken.

Everything needed to befit a king.

Before he could find some way to communicate this, Farah held their arms out and stepped to his side, bumping her hip to his. She stepped back and did the same on the other side. She then moved from foot to foot for a few beats of the tempo as if showing him what it was before she stepped back, lengthening their arms between them, and moved quickly forward, nearly brushing his body, pulling their arms out to the side.

She then abruptly let him go and hooked an elbow in his and forced him to spin.

And spin.

But suddenly, she let go and True was reeling, searching for her, only to be caught by another woman, elbow in elbow, and twirled.

And twirled.

He had not managed to get his wits about him before he looked down on the curvy woman who had hold of him. Her bust was nearly bursting from her bodice, and she was beaming up at him with what appeared to be unadulterated glee, her face red and shining from exertion.

"It is my deepest honor to be dancing with you, Your Grace!" she cried excitedly, before she let him go, and he was caught by another woman.

This woman whirled him, also beaming, and further shouting to the room, "Look at me! I'm dancing with our handsome Prince True!" Her head twisted this way and that with the twirl as she yelled, "I shall steal him from you, my lady."

"Never!" Farah called, breaking from the man who was spinning her to come and lay claim on True.

The woman spun away with a delighted laugh.

"No one comes between a fair maiden and her prince!" someone shouted.

"Hear, hear!" someone else called.

Farah reeled him around and around, smiling up at him happily before she stopped their turning and caught his hands. She did some maneuver over their heads that took their arms behind their necks before she let go and fell back.

True nearly cursed, moving to catch her, but before she fell, it was she who caught his hand, their arms long. Then she twirled in, holding hands, so she banged into him, her back to his front, their arms wrapped around her middle.

She tipped her head and again caught his eyes.

"Just listen to the music, *bello*," she urged. "And *let go*."

She then whirled out again, still holding his hand so he caught her before she would fly away.

After that, using their hands and arms and legs and hips, she spun and twisted, skipped and swayed, as well as did a good deal of jogging without getting much of anywhere.

Watching her, glancing at the others, listening to the music (but it must be said, mostly watching Farah and how joyful she seemed, not to mention the atmosphere of the same that charged the air around them), True fell into it.

Indeed, after a spell, True got lost in it, his blood moving, warming his body, his heart beating pleasantly harder, the joviality about him, the cheers and clapping, the stomping of feet and encouraging calls, the bursts of ringing laughter, the constant accompaniment of cheerful music.

The light growing in Farah's eyes as he fell into the dance.

All of this driving him ever onward.

He laughed with her when she ran into a man who then took her away and True moved directly to the partner he had left behind, spinning her, twisting her, whirling her.

She, too, appeared openly gleeful as he did this before he twirled her away and caught another woman.

And when she spun away, he found himself with a female fairy.

He bent low, took her elbow, and they moved about the floor before she flapped her wings, taking herself off her feet so she was at his height, something that made the fairy laugh, thus, True did too.

This she did before she also spun off (or flew off), and he found himself confronted with Florian, who immediately curved an arm around his stomach, bowed low, lifted and then caught True's arm and spun him around.

Everyone about them shouted with laughter and True grinned at his man before a comely woman laid claim to Florian.

True was pulled around and Farah was there.

When the music started building to a crescendo, she took both his hands and moved to the side, forcing him to move to the other. She took them faster and faster, doing this leaning back. He had no choice but to do the same, watching her long, shining hair flying to the side, her skirts billowing, her face gleaming, her laughter never ending.

It made him feel odd.

Dizzy.

Out of control.

And he liked it.

Because he also felt strangely more alive than he'd ever felt. His heartbeat in his chest escalating not due to a frustrating conversation with his father, infuriating news about Carrington, deep concern about an order to send his men into battle, his blood spiking because he was leading them there.

No, it wasn't any of that.

He felt...

Uninhibited.

Free.

As the music sounded like it was going to die away, he tugged sharply on Farah's hands, which meant she flew forward and slammed into his body.

He wrapped his arms around her, lifted her well off her feet, holding her at her thighs under the curve of her behind, and kept twirling around and around.

True watched her head fall back, her fingers linked around the back of his neck and her laughter rang through the room as he kept his head tipped, a grin stamped on his lips, and exalted in her glee.

He did this until the music stopped, and when it did, he wished it hadn't.

But only then did True cease whirling and let her slide down his body.

That was a liberty he should not have taken, but he could not have stopped himself even if he'd been thinking.

But he was not.

He was captivated by her happiness.

Farah did not keep her hands linked at his neck.

She wrapped her arms around it, pulling him down to her.

Lost in her, feeling the warm softness of her body, her breast heaving against his chest, more aware of her than he'd ever been—and he'd been very aware of her for some time. Indeed, more aware of her than he had ever been of *anyone*, True bent to her, watching her eyes heat, glittering like topaz.

And then his gaze dropped, and he saw nothing but her lips.

"To the Prince and Princess of Wodell! Farah and True!" someone shouted right before his mouth would find hers.

A cheer split the air. *"Farah and True!"*

His eyes rose to hers and he saw frustration before she blinked it away and whispered, "Farah and True."

"Farah and True," he whispered back.

She smiled at him right before she was whisked away.

He went to reach for her, but he could not.

For he was whisked away too.

"THANK YOU FOR THE DANCE, my prince," a woman called as her man pulled her to the door.

"My pleasure, Edwina," True called back.

Edwina waved and waved as she was dragged along, her eyes moving to Farah.

"Lovely to meet you, Lady Farah!" she yelled, almost out the door.

"And you!" Farah yelled back just as Edwina was pulled out.

His mother would be cross for months if she'd seen anything that night, specifically True (and Farah) shouting across a pub at a commoner.

But after that night, all True could think was...

Fuck his mother.

He looked to Bruce and Simon, who were sitting with them, enjoying an end-of-evening port, and he smiled at the men.

They returned his smile.

The band had stopped playing perhaps twenty minutes before. Half of them were gone, the other half were enjoying well-earned ales or whiskies at the bar.

Other than that, most of the rest of the folk in the pub had cleared out, including Florian and Luther, who had both found maids to share the remainder of their evenings with.

In fact, Bram was chatting one up a few tables away, and True suspected he soon would be enjoying the warmth of her bed.

Alfie and Wallace were sitting at the table with Farah and True, Bruce and Simon.

Although Farah was at the table, she would more aptly be described as sitting on his lap.

This had started with her lifting her feet there, for they were "killing her," and as others joined and left them at the table, it somehow naturally progressed to her having her arse in his lap.

It fit perfectly there.

But having it was killing *him*.

"It will be talked about for decades to come, when Prince True and the Lady Farah danced the night away at The Antlers," Bruce declared, contentedly eyeing True with Farah perched in his lap.

"I would prefer it talked about, providing lumber from this region to the ports cities in the north and west to build ships so our wool and wheat and pewter can sail across the Green Sea, now that King Aramus has given us leave for ships to sail, selling our goods to the Northlands and Southlands," True replied quietly.

"Oh, that will be talked about as well, Your Grace," Simon replied.

"We had already heard of it," Bruce shared. "Birds are flying. And you know how they like to gossip, so pixies are late to finding their trees. They have so much to talk about, they're flitting all over Wodell."

He did know this, and in this instance, he was glad the pixies had this penchant.

"The quakes are concerning. Though they seem to be coming less now, the last one was very powerful," Simon noted.

"We are told these are borne of magic," True informed them of what he'd been telling others along their journey, and as the pixies and birds were flying, they probably knew. "And we are hard at work with the Great Coven to put an end to them."

The men nodded, seemingly appeased by this information, as had been all the others.

Bruce looked to Farah before he nudged Simon and remarked, "We shouldn't keep you from your bed any longer, my prince. Thank you for gracing us with your presence and thank you for the honor of meeting our future queen."

"The honor was mine," Farah murmured, catching True's attention, for her tone sounded sleepy.

Yes, it was time for bed.

"Kind to say, milady, but trust me, 'tis untrue. The honor is all ours," Simon replied to Farah before pushing out of his chair.

Bruce followed him.

True tightened his arms around Farah as he made to do the same, but both men held hands up to him as Simon urged, "Please, keep your seat. We hope the Lights shine for you while you're here and we hope to see you again in our village soon."

True remained seated, nodded to the men and watched as they took their leave.

When they were gone, he turned again to Farah.

"Is it time to find our room?" he asked.

"Are there others you wish to speak to?" she asked in return.

He scanned the pub.

All that were left were in the final throes of flirting with intent, doubled over drafts they would probably pass out before finishing, or already passed out.

He also caught Bram's chin lift to Alfie as he led his maid out the door.

True gave his attention again to Farah.

"No."

She grinned and slid off his lap, grabbing his hand and feebly beginning to pull him out of his seat.

He did not make her work at this and came up, glancing over his shoulder at his men.

Both nodded as he led Farah to the stairs that would take them up to their room.

"Are Bruce and Simon important personages in this village?" she asked after they were up three steps.

"Not that I know of. Indeed, I've never met either until tonight."

She seemed to startle, and he pulled her closer with her hand at his elbow as she did so, looking down at her.

"All right?" he asked.

"You usually talk to leaders," she said instead of answering.

He was bewildered.

"I do?"

She appeared just as bewildered.

"You don't? You are friendly to all around you, but sitting and having serious chats like the one you just had with Bruce and Simon about affairs of the realm, they are not chieftains or barons or…whatever you call them in this land? What is it? Lords?"

"In the second village where we stayed, I spoke to a member of the gentry," he informed her as they made the top landing and he guided them down the hall.

"That is it?" she inquired.

"Yes." He was still confused. "Does this surprise you?"

"I, well…I…" She said no more as he stopped them outside the door to their room and produced the key from his trousers.

But he didn't open it.

"It does surprise you," he noted.

She looked up at him. "Mars deals with barons and chieftains."

"Yes," he said when she spoke no more.

"Baldrick was a leader," she remarked.

"He was. But I'm still not understanding your surprise," he said.

"Does your father mingle with his subjects as you do?" she asked.

He nearly roared with laughter, thus, his one-word answer was shaking with it.

"No."

"And he does not dance with them."

"Bloody hell, no," he replied, putting the key to the lock and letting them in.

He was closing and locking the door behind them when she spoke again.

"Mars is removed. We have many celebrations and he's seen reveling with his people, but not *amongst* them. He is on the royal podium at the coliseum. If marquees are erected, his will be easily seen, but apart. There are instances, such as dancing, feasts and other revelries, where there will be those of the populace invited to be close to the king, but it is a special honor, usually for a feat accomplished or a service provided to the realm. And there are times that Mars, as had his father, travels the realm to speak directly to the people. Not to give speeches, to sit with local teachers or healers or priests to hear what they have to say about what is happening in the land. And in those times, he will be with his people at feasts they make for him or celebrations to honor him. But he is always held in a position of distinction, for instance, at a high table, or separated and sitting with the leaders of the clan."

True had thrown the key down on a table and was walking to the fire when Farah finished talking, after which he murmured, "My father doesn't do even that."

He'd bent to feed some logs on the banked fire and stir it when she said, "I know of no realm where a prince can ride the countryside with five guards and be safe."

He straightened and looked to her. "I know this will also surprise you, my sweet, but the Dellish are a peaceable people. Many here do not leave their villages their whole lives, and that is not because they want to do so and cannot. It is because they have no desire to. This is a land of home and hearth. Farm and forest. We have one large city inland, and four port cities that do not come close to rivaling the size or populace of Notting Thicket. And as you have seen, many villages and hamlets much like the one we're in. Thus, we are not cosmopolitan or sophisticated. Intrigues might not be reviled, but they are not often sought and are considered mostly a curiosity."

He placed the screen carefully back in front of the fire before he moved to the bed and sat at its end in order to pull off his boots.

And he did this as he continued speaking.

"This does not mean that the Dellish are unambitious. That they do not wish better or more for themselves and their loved ones. Thick thatch for their roofs to keep them dry and warm in the winter. More fashionable clothing. Fine pewter or china to use to serve when they have guests. Everyone wishes comfort and a higher standard of living. To give the best they can to their children and leave them with better lives than the ones they'd had. The Dellish work hard and not all are unassuming."

Done with his boots and socks, he stood to unbutton his waistcoat and carried on sharing.

"Many speak of the university in Go'Doan. The high academics of Airen that produce such extraordinary architects and engineers. The exemplary military training in Firenze that is practiced by all the clans and tribes. But the law is studied in Wodell, this being the laws of all the lands, and the advocates who earn their credentials here can practice in any realm. And Dellish counsellors are the most sought after on the continent. And the Go'Doan aren't the only ones who produce fine educators. Our teachers who are trained in our universities then go on to teach in our schools are exceptional. I would pit any school in Wodell against any other in any realm. The one thing the Dellish won't abide the king not funding through their taxes is education for their children and it is no boast to say it's the best in all of Triton. And it is obvious our training and constant advancements in agriculture and forestry are outstanding."

He noticed out of the corners of his eyes that Farah had barely moved from the door as he swung his waistcoat over a chair by the window, put his fingers to the buttons on his shirt and went on.

"What I mean to say with all of this is that it is often confused by those in other lands, but the majority of the Dellish may wish only a simple life, but they are not simple."

True stopped unbuttoning and looked to her.

"They do not want ruby mines and saffron fields," he shared. "They want delicious food on their tables, their wives in silk petticoats and the ability to gift her with a precious bauble on not an infrequent occasion. And when my reign is all said and done, I do not care if my entry in the Go'Doan tomes of history has one sentence. 'King True kept the nation of Wodell peaceful and prosperous until his son wore the crown.'"

He threw a hand up and finished with a confession.

"I do not wish to be a great king, my Farah. I simply wish to do right by my people. And to do that, I must know them and what they want. Therefore, I sit with men like Bruce and Simon, and it matters not what they do or what station they have. I tell them decisions made amongst princes and kings so I can watch their reactions and know if these decisions were the right ones."

True had barely stopped talking when she started.

"You very much love your country," she said in a soft voice.

He was even further confused.

"Of course," he replied.

"You do know, my prince, that if your reign is naught but peaceful and prosperous for your people, that is the very definition of a great king."

Abruptly, as if struck with a blow to the gut, True stopped breathing and stared at his intended.

"And you do not travel safe because yours are a peaceable people," she continued. "You travel safe because you are as loved by the people of your country as you love this green realm. And this is because you do not care the station of the man who sits at your table. It is also because you listen to them. Tonight, it was because you danced with them, even if that is not why you danced. You did that for me. And last, it is because, due to all of this, they know you will be a great king who will lead them to a time of peace and prosperity."

By the gods, he needed to make love to her.

At the very least kiss her.

Properly.

But he could not.

That day he had only seen but a few moments of melancholy steal over her features when he knew her thoughts turned to the mother she lost. He had kept her busy in this charming village outside the Lights so her mind did not turn to maudlin things. And he felt a very real triumph in giving her that.

But even so, it still was not the time for ungentlemanly advances, even if it appeared she wished his kiss after their first dance.

It was the time to get his tired queen-to-be to bed and hope on the morrow when they did not drink ale and dance in a pub but instead traveled in an effort to see the Lights, the night sky showed her its wonders.

"Would you like to use the screen, darling? Or shall I turn my back?" he offered her the choice of how to prepare for bed.

She dropped her head and appeared to studiously examine the floor as she moved toward the screen.

"Those young men put my bags behind the screen. I'll use that," she murmured.

"Farah," he called when she was almost behind the tapestry-covered screen in the corner.

She stopped and gave him her eyes. "Yes?"

"I enjoyed the dancing," he said quietly.

"Did you find it fun?" she asked.

"Fun?" he asked in return.

Suddenly, she appeared very sad, and not about the loss of her mother.

Therefore, he hastened to say, "Of course I found it fun, sweetling."

She lifted her chin just the slightest bit. "Your desire is to be a king who provides a peaceful, prosperous nation to the people of Wodell. My desire is to live my life beside a happy True Axelsson."

True felt his heart clutch.

"I am happy, Farah," he said gently.

"*Mio amore*, you don't know what happiness is," she whispered. "You've never felt it. And I have never had a mission in my life."

She lifted her chin further and her voice was much stronger when she spoke on.

"There is one thing in the now I am glad about. I have a mission. To make True Axelsson happy. And I vow I will not die until I accomplish it. And neither will you."

And with that, his Farah disappeared behind the screen.

# 63

## THE VOWS

***King Mars***
*The Master Bedroom, Cord Cottage, The Arbor*
WODELL

Mars awoke without his queen in his arms.

His immediate instinct was to growl his displeasure, find her and drag her back to bed.

He did the first part of that.

But upon turning his head, he saw her lying at his side, on her belly, her long, black hair a tumble over the pillows and sheets, face turned away, covers down to her waist, one arm thrown out, the other buried under her body, the ivory skin of her back bared for the rest of her was nude, and even unconscious, she appeared worn out.

Something he knew she was.

For he had made her that way.

No longer annoyed, he grinned to himself, reached and pulled the cord that would call a maid.

He then rose, moved to the fire that was dying and fed it some kindling and logs.

Not that he felt the cold. He was not immune to it, but it was rare it was a concern for him.

However, Silence felt it.

He then moved out of the room and into his cabinet.

There, he splashed cold water on his face, took some in his mouth to rinse, spat that out, dried his face and pulled on a pair of his *ante* pants, these black.

He moved out the door to his cabinet that led to the hall and saw the maid, Pegeen, hurrying toward the master bedroom, thus he stopped.

His wife had found a much more benevolent mood of late. Thus, she had not directed him to let go of any of the maids.

Then again, the women had begun to do their duties, if only adequately.

"You," he called to her.

She stuttered to a halt, her eyes darting his way, then falling instantly to his chest. An avid look filled them, before she shot them back up to his.

It was an annoyance, but he made a note to don a shirt around others in this land. They, or at least the maids, acted like a bare chest was an invitation to pounce.

"The queen's draught, *caffé*, rolls and fruit. Also, fresh warm water for my bride and start the fire in her boudoir. Immediately," he ordered.

"Yes, Your Grace," she said with a bow, walking backwards several steps, and he did not wait to see if she turned before she backed away so far, she fell down the stairs.

He backtracked into his cabinet, closing the door behind him, then walked through it, closing the door to the bedroom so the chill from one room would not invade another he was trying to heat.

He checked the fire, saw it was dancing, before he returned to bed.

He slid under the covers carefully, in order not to wake his wife.

He did not wish for her to wake.

Yet.

He studied her glorious hair and flawless skin and he did this thinking at the same time capturing a tendril of her hair and twirling its softness around his finger in a way she would not feel, but he could enjoy touching something that was her.

Mars could not say that he was familiar with all there was to know about pennyrium.

However, he was a man who wanted to father only children he wished to have, so the basics were known well by him.

It was said the effects were nearly instant, and upon but a few hours of drinking the first draught, a woman would be protected from conceiving.

Though if there was a margin of error, this was the point where that was at its greatest, and he had not heard frequent stories when conception occurred in this time, but he'd heard them.

Silence had taken a draught with dinner the evening they first began to communicate much more freely in their marriage, both verbally and physically.

She'd also taken one yesterday.

This morning would be her third.

It was time.

With this thought Mars slid down in bed, released her hair, but took hold of her, pulling her over his chest and drawing the covers up her back after he had her where he wanted her.

She nuzzled her face into his neck sleepily for a moment before she became dead weight.

He again grinned.

"Silence," he called, shifting her hair off her shoulder and neck.

She did not stir.

"Silence," he said louder, tightening the arm he had about her.

She stirred, then mumbled, "'Tis not morning."

Mars smiled "It is, *bellezza*."

"Buh," she stated.

"You must wake," he declared.

"I mustn't. We are a king and queen at leisure. We can sleep the day away."

"I have ordered *caffé* and rolls," he informed her.

"Ugh," she grumbled, pressing closer.

He started chuckling, through it saying, "We have not left our bed in over a day, Silence."

She said nothing for a moment, before she asked, "And?"

He continued to chuckle as he pulled her up, forcing her to be face to face with him, before he rolled her so he mostly covered her, but they were still face to face.

"I have also ordered your draught," he told her.

"Oh," she whispered, getting that quicksilver look in her eyes he was becoming accustomed to and liked very much.

This time he liked it for the same reasons as he always did, including the fact it shared how much she liked his weight on her.

"It will be your third dose," he reminded her.

"Oh." She continued to whisper, now shifting under him in a way his cock took notice.

"I do not tire of your hands or your mouth, my queen." He dipped his head so his lips were nearly on hers, and whispered, "But I wish to come inside."

"Oh," she breathed, that lovely syllable hardening his shaft fully, and as she'd earned it, he pressed it against her leg and the noise came again. "*Oh*."

He grinned, brushed his lips to hers and rolled, pulling her fully on top of him.

She looked adorably dazed as he stated, "First *caffé* and rolls."

She then appeared adorably perturbed and he found he could not stop smiling that morning.

He tucked her hair behind her ear and asked, "Did you sleep well?"

She nodded. "Did you?"

"Oh yes."

Her little white teeth came out and scored her lower lip, her eyes telling him her thoughts were on why they both slept so well, and he wondered how discomfited she would get if the maid served their rolls while his mouth was between her legs.

"What are the different stamps for?"

Her bizarre question effectively took his mind from her taste.

"Sorry?"

"You have two stamps on your desk in your quarters upstairs in your palace. Stamps for sealing letters. One is a snake. The other is a lick of fire."

It would seem she wished to get to know him better in ways that did not make him groan.

He like that very much too.

His wife had not asked much about him. They not only had not had the time, when they did, she'd had other things plaguing her mind.

Mars had not realized, until that moment, that he'd felt it hurtful that she had not.

"I wasn't snooping," she said quickly. "I saw them that night that I was, uh…"

"There is nothing of me you cannot know," he said gently.

The worry transforming her features disappeared.

"And nothing of me you cannot ask," he went on.

"Thank you, husband," she said softly.

"The snake is for personal matters. The fire is official," he shared.

"And the wax?"

"The wax?"

"You have four colors of wax. Green, red, black and gold."

He found this question intensely interesting.

"You remember well matters which are not significant," he noted.

"Everything about you is, um...significant."

This made Mars growl again, give her a squeeze and he lifted his head to press a hard kiss on her mouth.

When he settled back, she'd assumed her slightly dazed look, and it was then he gave her answers, doing so settling into the knowledge that his Silence might not have asked, but from nearly the beginning, she'd been interested in knowing her king.

"The green is for personal correspondence. The black indicates military matters. The gold is a royal summons. The red is governmental. Such as endorsements. Sanctions. Proclamations. In short, general, but official, correspondence from the king."

"That's very...orderly," she remarked, and he again grinned.

"For a savage?" he teased.

"No, Mars," she said. "But maybe...yes."

"It was all red under my grandfather's reign," he explained. "It was my father who created the system."

"But...why?" she asked.

"Why?"

"Every missive from a king is important," she explained.

"It is, *amore*, and none of this indicates that it should be ignored. But the clans, specifically, and some tribes, have structures. There are barons, but in many cases, they will have a man that is head of their warriors. They will have another man, or sometimes a woman, who is in charge of sharing information with their people. They will further have a secretary who handles their diary. Gold will be opened by secretaries. Black should be seen by no one but the chieftain, baron or their top general. Red would be understood to bear information that will be distributed. It allows leaders to delegate and it makes the demands of a king seem less demanding, even if they are still demands."

"That is very clever," she murmured.

"My father was that," he replied.

"You speak of him with much respect," she said searchingly.

"I wish you would have known him. He would have come to care for you greatly."

This brightened her eyes exorbitantly. "Do you think?"

For the first time that morning, Mars did not feel bright, for the fact she asked that question like it was impossible for her to believe his remark, did not make him feel bright in the slightest.

He did not comment on this.

He'd deal with her father, and her mother, at another time.

He answered, "Papa suffered no fool. He was well-read. And he, like you, valued silence and listening over pontificating. When he spoke, people listened, not only because of his manner, but because I cannot say I know of a time when he spoke just to speak instead of speaking when he had something important to say."

Her fingers drifted through his beard as she murmured, "I'm sorry you lost him."

His voice dropped deeper when he replied, "I, as well."

Her hand moved, and her thumb trailed over his cheekbone as she gazed into his eyes and whispered, "Why is it that a great man like Ares is lost to this world and men like Wilmer and my father live on to be at least, ineffectual, and at worst, whatever my father is?"

"It is rare a great man, or woman, in all of history lives long, *piccolina*," Mars replied. "Study your history books. A man, or woman, of vision or will, whose efforts and strategies might affect progress, comes to tragic ends and they do this early. This is because people do not like change, especially those who will have to share riches or power they have kept to themselves while also keeping those around them under their thumbs in order to ascertain they cannot take those riches away, or worse, lessen their power. I can think of only one in all of history who lived long, and that is because she created The Enchantments to protect herself and her sisters."

He felt his arms about her tighten automatically when he saw the look on her face after he spoke.

"Silence?" he asked after the fear she now wore stark in her expression.

"You are great," she said.

He relaxed, and although pleased she thought this, she was not right.

"I walk in the footsteps of a giant," he told her.

"We will defeat the Beast."

He was glad at her positivity.

"That is not greatness, *bellezza*, it is destiny."

"You could *not* have walked in your father's footsteps. You could have erased everything he did," she pointed out.

"This is but a decision, not a mission."

"You are great, Mars," she declared stubbornly.

He fought back his smile and murmured, "All right, wife. I am great."

If she wished to think that, he would not continue to argue the point.

"Do not humor me," she demanded, appearing cross.

"This is hard when you are being humorous."

She glared at him for long moments before her thumb again moved over his cheek and her eyes shifted there.

Her mood shifted as well, and Mars watched it happen, fascinated.

"How did you get your scars?" she asked.

Ah.

The question she had asked what seemed so long ago. On their wedding night.

And at hearing it, Mars felt the best he had in weeks, indeed, since the loss of Sofia.

For this question demonstrated to him he finally *truly* had his Silence back.

"As is custom, my father sent me to Airen to train," he began. "It is what, over the centuries, after the war that tore our one country into two, has kept the peace. Trajan, and Cassius, trained in Firenze and knew our ways and strategies. And I, as did all princes of Firenze before me, trained in Airen to know theirs."

Silence nodded.

Mars carried on.

"It was not long after I arrived that Trajan challenged me."

"Oh no," she said.

"It is fine, Silence. As you can see, I am here, no worse for the experience."

"But you have scars."

He tipped his head on the pillow. "Do you want to hear the story?"

His wife shut her mouth.

He fought another smile and continued.

"Future king to future king, Trajan said. I was younger than him by five years, but Laches men grow fast, and I was his height, if I did not yet have a powerful build. I was also young, and most full of myself, so I accepted."

"This story isn't getting better," she mumbled.

He ignored her and kept telling said story.

"Cassius was alarmed. Not that he didn't know my skill, and that I could look after myself, but that he knew his brother was a cheat."

"And still, no better."

"I unhorsed him, Silence. And when we persisted on our feet, I disarmed him."

"Oh," she whispered.

And there was that noise he liked so much.

Mars ignored that too.

"Trajan was not a bad soldier, but he was a terrible loser. I offered to shake hands and embrace, he turned his back on me and walked off the field. Cassius felt this made matters worse. He followed me like a shadow for weeks. He remained so close, the others began to call us lovers, thinking this was an insult, when it was not. They stopped doing that when Cass, nor I, appeared to be offended by these comments."

"Are the Airenzian not free sexually, like the Firenz are?" she asked.

"No one is quite as free as the Firenz, little monkey," he told her. "But although it is not hidden and considered debauched, as it is in Wodell, it is not spoken of openly and there are some of a certain bent, bullies and bigots, who attempt to use their antipathy toward it as a weapon."

"Airen seems a most unpleasant place," Silence mumbled.

"It is a land of great beauty and great bleakness. If you ever visit a battlefield, even years after the battle is done, you will feel the pain and despair. If there is enough of it, it taints the very soil and does not let go until the last who knows of the atrocities that happened there perishes. Airen's soil is tainted with centuries of pain and despair. So much so, it rises up and dulls the very air."

She studied him with intent eyes.

He continued speaking.

"It was some time after the challenge I bested against Trajan when Cassius relaxed his vigil. It was the dead of night and I was in the barracks, asleep. There were five of them. Six with Trajan. The five held me down. Trajan cut me. They would have raped me, but one of my bunkmates was Cassius's now-lieutenant, Macrinus. He ran to inform Cassius and Cass came with Macrinus, Otho and Nero. Numbers more balanced, the tide was turned, and I did the first thing my father ever expressed disappointment in me for doing."

"What was that?" she asked, her voice somewhat breathless.

"I cut him as he cut me, and then I took one of his testicles."

Silence gasped.

Mars spoke through it.

"I did the former in vengeance. I did the latter as a lesson. Man or woman chooses to take cock. It is not forced upon them. King Gallienus was infuriated and called for my father immediately. Papa came, and he was not angry that this occurrence strained relations between two nations, for even Gallienus could see the cuts on my face and he knew his son had acted in a craven manner, without a hint of honor. Both future kings had been disfigured, one more monumentally, but it was Trajan's actions that made it so. Thus, this was smoothed out relatively quickly. Father was also not angry at the lesson. He was angry at the vengeance. He said vengeance is meted over a lifetime of living above pettiness, and he considered lashing out in anger petty. He said it is the man who walks the high road who sees the best view. The climb to that road is often arduous. But the view is worth it. And regardless, even the climb is better than wallowing in the mud."

"All I have heard, including this, it is clear your father was, indeed, very wise," she noted quietly.

She was not wrong, so Mars did not remark on that.

"This is how I got my scars," he finished.

"It wasn't just retribution. It was also envy. Prince Trajan sought to sully your handsomeness," she remarked.

"Perhaps," he allowed.

"No. He did. I have heard Prince Trajan took after his mother in looks and was not near as handsome as his brother."

Mars chose to ignore the fact she found Cassius handsome.

Instead, he shared, "His mother was a great beauty. Trajan simply had bad luck and he did not make it better by being interesting or amusing or good-natured and pleasant to be around, but instead he was simply an arsehole."

"He did not succeed," she declared.

Mars was confused.

"In being an arsehole?" he asked.

"In sullying your handsomeness."

At this announcement, Mars growled again and lifted his head to kiss her, but she pulled away.

"Why did you not act before to save the women of Airen?" she queried.

His wife asked this fraught question as a knock sounded on the door.

He called for the maid to come in, and Silence, having begun to get used to being served while naked and abed with her husband, simply pressed up to sitting on a hip and wrapped the sheet around her.

He liked this progression too.

Very much.

The maid put the tray at the side of the bed Silence was not occupying, as had been their wont over the last day, and after asking if there was more required, and learning there was not, she took her leave.

Silence had served his coffee, swallowed down the draught and was nibbling a roll when he addressed her question.

"With Gallienus, and with Trajan, it would have meant war, my queen."

"Does it not mean war now?" she asked.

"A revolt is different from a war. Especially with strong allies that will significantly decrease the chance of bloodshed."

"Do you offer women from Airen asylum?"

He did not answer that.

"Mars," she pressed.

He sighed before giving her what she desired.

"The clans and tribes very much did not want to get drawn into this unpleasantness, my monkey. They will gladly and stalwartly defend Firenze, but they are often embroiled in clan clashes when not united to fight for Firenze, and even if fighting is a way of life, few of them had an interest in shedding blood for another realm's problems."

"So, what you're saying is, you don't," she whispered with obvious disenchantment.

"It is known to me there is a secret system that several tribes abet, offering succor and safe travel to The Enchantments, or deeper into Firenze where the dunes spread for many miles and only the most hearty and nomadic of our tribes reside. Once delivered upon them, they take in these women who have escaped, and it is the same as them disappearing from the face of this earth."

"And you do nothing to stop these tribes from their endeavors," she said.

"I do not. Nor did my father."

"And that is all."

She continued to appear disappointed.

He drew in breath.

He then shared, "It is not, for these women need food, they need horses, and they need clothing, and they must go to the tribes in the dunes with an offering of an amount that will make it worth it to them to take these women on. And it is not the wealthiest of tribes who assist them. So they receive generous funding." He paused. "Anonymously."

Her eyes widened before she surmised, "So the other clans and tribes who might be against this do not know of royal involvement, and neither does Gallienus."

"Precisely."

She smiled at him contentedly and took a bite out of her roll.

"It is a great secret and has been for decades this is happening, Silence," he warned. "The decisions have been made, but the proclamations have not been heralded and there is already growing unrest in Airen as word has spread Cassius will take Elena as bride. They know what will come of that. If it is known peremptorily that Firenz kings, for two generations, have been aiding in the escape of Airenzian refugees, we will not be attending True's wedding nor having days in bed for I'll be on a horse with my sword, leading my warriors in battle, and you will be at Catrame Palace, shadowed every step you take by a guard of at least fifty."

She waved her roll at him and spoke with her mouth full. "I will not breathe a word."

Truly, his queen was a marvel, for he could not understand how she could be so impeccably fuckable sitting abed, chewing on a roll.

And since now, at long last, he could actually fuck her, she could resume chewing on her roll later.

Thus, he reached out a hand and plucked it from hers.

"I was enjoying that," she declared as he tossed it on the tray.

Mars reached long, took hold of the lip of the tray and dragged it across the bed until he could take full control of it.

He then moved it to the nightstand.

After that, he turned to his wife. "You will enjoy this more."

She protested no further as he reached out again and pulled her to him.

He took her mouth in a wet kiss.

Her response was instantaneous, and heated.

He had learned through their play that it was crucial to get the upper hand with his queen, and do it from the start, for she learned speedily.

And thus, if she got her mouth or even her fingers wrapped around his cock, he would consider decrying his country and his crown in hopes she would not let it go until she was thoroughly done with it.

The key was using his mouth and fingers on her first so she felt the same way.

This he did, until her movements and noises told him she was about to give over to climax.

Only then did he roll onto his arse and drag her to her knees astride his lap.

She clamped onto his head under his ears at both sides and breathed a fiery, "Yes," against his mouth, moving her hips to seek his shaft.

"Silence."

"Mars."

"Silence."

"*Mars.*"

It was a plea, and her squirming was nearly his undoing.

But this was it.

Their consummation.

He was husband about to truly take his wife.

He was king about to truly claim his queen.

And he was Mars, she was Silence, and therefore he was intent on giving her more.

With this in mind, carefully, and slowly, he did something he had never done to his bride.

He slid a finger inside her.

He felt his cock twitch.

Gods, that sleek clutch.

Her head fell back, a moan escaped her throat and somewhere in the back of his mind he thanked all his gods she enjoyed riding.

"My wife, look at me."

She didn't look at him.

Instinctively, she was riding his finger.

Fuck, she felt *extraordinary*.

He needed to get inside.

"*Wife*," he bit, using his free hand to right her head and control her movements. "Look at me."

She focused on him hazily.

"Grasp my cock," he ordered.

His greedy queen did not delay in that. Her little hand wrapped around what was hers with a possession that made his balls swell and his aching shaft bead.

He drew his finger out of her slick tightness and then shoved two of them back in.

She gasped.

"I vow to give my body to no other but you," he growled.

Silence stilled.

Completely.

"Say it," he demanded.

"I vow to give my body to no other but you," she whispered reverently.

"And I vow to take no other body but yours," he went on.

"And I vow to take no other body but yours," she parroted, her eyes filling with wet.

He started stroking her pussy with his fingers.

She licked her lips and took his cue, stroking his cock.

He moved his hand from her hair to wrap it around hers on his shaft and stroked up, covering her thumb and pressing it to the underside of the head.

"I will be pierced here, for you."

The wet in her eyes trembled.

"Mars," she breathed.

"You will not be pierced, wife," he rumbled. "You will be pristine and untouched...by anyone but me."

"I don't want anyone touching you either."

"Basil will do it," he grunted.

"Oh."

Fuck.

That word on his woman's lips.

He needed to finish this and have her.

"I want you pierced at your navel for me."

"All right," she agreed immediately.

Mars smiled, it died before he growled, "I will do that piercing."

"Shall we do it today?"

Ah yes, his greedy little queen.

Sadly, he had to deny her.

"I do not have a gem worthy for your body in the now, *mio ardente*."

She pouted.

He pulled her hand away, slid his fingers out of her and positioned.

She lost her pout, her tears, and her face grew ravening.

So very greedy. If there wasn't so much about her to like, he'd like that most of all.

"Mars," she panted, shifting impatiently.

"If I cause hurt, you tell me immediately," he commanded.

"Yes, all right, I will," she assured quickly.

"My wife wants my cock," he murmured.

Her lips came to his, her eyes open, and she whispered, "Please."

If she wanted something, he would give it to her.

Always.

And this was no exception.

Mars wrapped an arm around her waist and moved her down, filling her slowly, watching from near her eyes fill with surprise, then astonishment and finally, that quicksilver hunger.

For his part, he'd never felt anything near as resplendent as her tight, wet, hot sheath.

"Fuck," he groaned.

"Yes," she whimpered.

"*Fuck*," he bit.

"*Yes*," she breathed as she settled atop him, taking him to the root.

They held each other's eyes.

"You're perfect," he whispered.

"I was going to say the same thing," she replied.

He smiled yet again then drifted his hands up from her waist to her ribs and ordered, "Now, wife, take your king."

She needed no further encouragement.

She rode him, back arching, offering her full, beautiful breasts with their rosy tips for his taking, and he accepted her offer.

Silence then rode him harder.

Thus, Mars sucked deeper.

Her fingers went into his hair and fisted.

"My love," she gasped.

Oh yes.

*That* deserved a reward.

Mars flipped her so he was on top, hooked the back of her knee at the bend of one of his elbows, wrapped her other leg around his arse, and he stared down at her as he did the riding.

"*Yes,*" she cried, her tight cunt undulating around his cock, her hips lifting to take more, her hands frantic on his skin. "Oh, by the gods, Mars. Oh, *faith. Mars.*"

Gods, she was beautiful, her hair everywhere, her body jolting with his thrusts.

"I can't...I don't..." she stammered.

"Then don't," he grunted, rolling his hips and driving in again.

She whimpered then moaned, tightening her hold with her leg, grasping the back of his neck with a hand, the nails of her other scoring up his spine.

He arched into her at the exquisite pain, and she cried out, slamming her hips into his with each pound, meeting his passion artlessly.

He noted the room turning red.

And he ignored it.

He was fucking his queen.

He saw the flames erupt in midair.

And he gloried in it.

Because he was finally *fucking his queen*.

"Silence, let go," he demanded.

"I don't want...this...to...*stop*," she returned laboriously, her words interrupted by his thrusts.

She'd begun to do this, his stubborn wanton. She held onto her climax like she wanted to draw it out for a century.

It was tortuous.

And magnificent.

"Wife," he slid a hand between them and tweaked her clit, "*let go.*"

She cried out, her pussy gripping his cock with her orgasm, and only then did he let go, roaring his climax, bucking into her, filling her with his seed, and through this, soft explosions lit the air all around them.

Nearly spent, he fell to her and rolled them, his hips twitching under hers, hers doing the same against his, her heavy breaths caressing his neck as he wrapped her hair around his fist and lifted her head.

He dipped his chin to catch her eyes while their combined fire still burst all over the room.

She was just noticing it, he could tell by the awe in which she was taking it in.

"Silence," he rumbled to get her attention.

He got it as she breathed, "Mars, the room is on fire."

"That is us," he decreed.

She stared at him.

He pulsed up inside her and her lips parted as her eyes grew hooded and a flame erupted behind her body.

Proof.

"That...is...*us*," he repeated.

"My love—" she began.

"Yes," he bit, claiming those two words forcefully. "I was wrong, and you were right. But it is not about me. It is about we. *We* will be legend, Silence, Queen of Firenze."

"I...I just want to be a good wife and a good mother...and maybe, if I can manage it, a good queen," she replied.

The flames died out, the red receded, and they did this as Mars Laches stared at his bride.

This he did right before he burst into laughter, doing that wrapping his arms tight around her.

Eventually, Mars slid a hand up to cup the back of her head and he shoved her face in his neck.

But he was still laughing.

It took him a moment to feel her finger, which was trailing over his pectoral.

It did not take him any time at all to feel it circling his nipple.

"If you make me get out of this bed today, my king," she muttered, "I won't speak to you for a week."

Smiling, he rolled them and looked down at his Silence.

"We will finish our breakfast. We will have the maids bring your wee monkey to us for a visit. We will have them take Piccola away when you have had your fill. And then I'll fuck you for the rest of the day. Is that plan to your liking?"

"You seem to need, um…rest periods," she noted.

He tipped his head. "Is that a challenge?"

"I don't, well…know," she replied, gazing up at him questioningly.

"It is a challenge," he confirmed.

And then he smiled yet again before dipping closer.

"And I accept," he drawled.

His wife's extraordinary eyes went quicksilver.

This they did…

Right before he kissed her.

# 64

## THE ENCHANTMENTS

*Prince Cassius*
*Ten Miles from The Northwest Border of The Enchantments*
WODELL

She was killing him.

"Elena," he bucked his hips up into hers, "*move*," he growled.

"Mm," she murmured, bending to him and using her lips and tongue on his neck.

That felt nice.

Her wet snugness wrapped around his cock felt nicer.

But she seemed content to sit on it and do nothing but squirm every once in a while, while gazing down upon him, drinking him in with her eyes and tracing his ink with her fingertips.

Yes.

Fucking killing him.

Though, all that was before she started taking him in with her lips.

"You feel very nice," she said into his neck.

"You feel very nice too," he said to the roof of the tent. "And if you don't mind, I'd like to feel all that nice riding my cock."

She lifted her head and smiled down at him impertinently.

Then she squirmed her hips on his.

He groaned.

Bloody hell.

He scowled up at her.

And then it hit him.

"Are you teasing me?" he whispered.

"Hmm?" she asked, her brows drawing up lazily as she licked her lower lip with the tip of her tongue and grazed the ridges of his ribs in a touch so light, he could convince himself it hadn't happened even though every inch of his body knew it had.

"You're teasing me," he murmured.

She squeezed him with the walls of her pussy before saying, "I don't know what you're talking about."

"You bloody do," he growled and bucked powerfully, throwing her off.

Not expecting that, she cried out and lost track of her limbs.

But before he could get her into position on her belly to do his own teasing, she recovered and came at him.

Cassius could not say he'd ever wrestled in the confines of a one-person tent, with a beautiful naked woman, or other.

What he could say was that it was a highly delectable experience.

Especially when his superior strength and the close confines merged to give him an advantage, and he won.

This winning meant Elena was on her knees before him, his hand wrapped around the back of her neck pressing her cheek to the blankets, so her moan was muffled when he drove into her with his cock.

"Yes," he grunted.

"Yes," she breathed.

Cassius let her neck go and gripped her hips, forcing them forward and then slamming them back to take his thrusts.

Elena found the rhythm, and embraced it heartily, panting and whimpering.

He was getting close, but she seemed to be able to take his fucking the rest of the day, and enjoy it, therefore he realized something had to be done.

He fell back, arse to his heels, pulled her up on his cock, satisfied by her pleasured gasp, and continued pulsing up into her as he put the finger of one hand to her clit, the fingers of the other to her nipple, and with all, he rolled.

Her head fell back to his shoulder.

"I think...I like...morning sex," Elena panted.

Cassius tugged at her nipple, and she turned her head, biting into his jaw through his beard.

"I'm thinking you just like sex," he grunted.

"Yes," she whispered into his neck. "With you."

Fucking Elena.

He turned his head with meaning, a meaning she read.

He then took her mouth, fucked it with his tongue, pulling at her nipple, rolling tight at her clit and thrusting inside, fast and deep.

She came, her moan drifting down his throat.

He wrapped an arm around her chest, the other around her belly, and he planted her on his cock, coming too, his groan driving down hers.

She was nibbling at his lips when he stopped feeling nothing but enjoying being buried inside her and he took over, not nibbling, claiming her lips for a deep kiss.

He ended it to give her the chance to breathe, for if they had the time, he could fuck her all day, but if it was all he could have, he could kiss her all day as well.

He had allowed her to drop her head back and was exploring the skin at her throat with his lips, at the same time he shifted his hands back to where they'd been, one cupping her breast, the other doing the same between her legs, when it came to him.

The unicorns last night.

And now, they were in the same position as the lovers had been on the Eros card he had turned from her deck in the gardens of Catrame Palace.

Both of these direct from that reading.

Fucking hell.

He didn't know what to make of that.

But his arms did.

Of their own accord, they moved again so he was holding her to him around her middle, as if he was giving her a hug.

An intimate one.

But a hug nonetheless.

Her arms wrapped around his, and the only way she could in their position, Elena hugged him back.

Unadulterated Elena.

If she could find a way to give, or give back, she did it.

They stayed right where they were until they heard Jazz shout, "Since you two are done going at each other, maybe we can pack up and get home?"

Cass sighed, Elena doing the same with him.

"We should get moving," she whispered.

She was correct.

But when she started to pull away, Cassius held her fast.

Her neck twisted as he lifted his head and caught her eyes.

"I enjoy having sex with you as well, my warrior," he murmured.

She grinned. "It is lovely to have the words, Cass, and I might not have a great deal of experience, and all of what I have is with you, but I'd gathered that."

"I enjoy being intimate with you, Elena," he somewhat repeated.

The humor swept out of her violet eyes and she stared at him.

"There is a lightness and freedom to it that I..." he trailed off.

"Cass—" she whispered.

"Have never experienced," he finished.

"You don't have to do this," she told him gently.

He was not going to say his next still mostly hard inside her.

Not for her.

Not for Liviana.

So he pulled her off his cock and turned her so he could take her in his arms, on their knees, front to front.

"It is not about her, it is about us," he shared. "And that's what I want you to know. That being with you has meaning to me. It is not just something that is enjoyable. It is not simply a release. It is not a natural progression of what destiny has thrown in our laps. It is you. It is what you give me. I do not know if I have ever felt light in my life. I know I never felt free. There's a playfulness to you I do not know what to do with, for I have never felt playful. But I feel it is important as well for you to know you give that to me, and that, too, has meaning."

"You've never had a childhood, so I'm not surprised you don't understand how to take teasing."

"Oh no," he rumbled. "The kind of teasing you did earlier, I invite you to try at your whim. Just know you'll suffer the consequences."

"Hmm...I'm wondering if we both have the same definition of the word 'consequences,'" she...bloody...*teased*.

Fucking hell, he was going to laugh.

Which was what he did, clutching her to him and shoving his face in her neck to do it.

He felt her hands roaming his back and realized she was not laughing with him when he stopped.

He lifted his head.

Instantly, she curled her hand around his jaw.

"I'm not certain we'll find a lot of time to be playful in the coming months, Cass, but I'll do my best."

He could not stop himself from taking her mouth.

So he didn't.

"If you two don't get a bloody move on," Mac shouted, "the Beast will have devoured Triton while you cavort in your tent."

Cass broke the kiss.

And when he did, Elena asked, "Did Mac just use the word 'cavort?'"

Cassius felt his lips twitching as he answered, "Yes."

Elena burst out laughing.

Holding her close, enjoying the feel, Cass laughed with her.

"ALL RIGHT, someone remind me why the Nadirii have been our enemies for nearly three hundred years," Mac demanded as they all rode side by side behind the women in front of them.

Not five minutes ago, they'd entered The Enchantments.

Before they did this, on a somewhat gray, blustery day in Wodell, the women stopped them in a perfectly ordinary area of the forest.

Elena, Jasmine and Hera had dismounted.

They'd then walked in a line, though separated about ten feet between them, and they did this humming.

Cass could make out Elena's lyrical lilt from his place in his saddle.

And he'd been mesmerized by her.

She seemed to be doing naught but striding, and then when they ceased moving, standing, however there was an energy emanating from her that was enthralling.

The hum increased in volume, but it did not take long before all three women arched back, their hair flying, their arms extending behind them, when a stiff wind blew as great rifts formed in the air before them.

Three domed openings some two feet taller than a man on a horse and just wide enough for that horse to walk inside could be seen, like rents in the very air, these rents appearing to separate one world from another.

Cass had lost his breath.

For beyond these openings, as they sat astride their horses on a dreary day in Wodell where the leaves were mostly gone from the trees and the landscape was barren and dull (save the green of the grass that never quite went away in Wodell), before them was bright sunlight shafting golden rays through colossal trees that had leaves bright as shamrocks, others as striking as limes, still others as bold as a parakeet's breast.

The grass was a sea of emerald and Kelly and apple green.

The dark bark of the trees was a stunning contrast to this feast of verdant green with the only backdrop being a sky of pure blue without even a single cloud to mark its flawlessness.

Cassius realized he'd been sitting in stunned silence, staring at his first glimpse of The Enchantments when Jazz called, "All right, men, ride on and welcome to The Enchantments!"

Rose rode through first, Ian following her through the opening Hera had made.

Mac rode through next, using the opening Jasmine had created, Jazz moving back to swing atop her mare and follow him.

Cass rode through last, tearing his gaze from the view to watch Elena as he passed her on her way back to her mount.

She was grinning up at him.

He shook his head down at her in disbelief at what she had just shown him, and that she was so damned cheeky in doing it.

Once inside, the women took lead, mostly because the men slowed their steeds in order to take it all in.

The openings had closed behind them directly after Hera, Jasmine and Elena rode through.

And Cass had noted instantly, the moment Caelus's hooves struck enchanted soil, the temperature of the air was at least twenty degrees warmer.

It was not balmy. It was not hot. It was not chilly either.

It was perfection.

"I'm not sleeping with one of them, but I have to admit, that show rivaled the parade in Fire City and I had never seen anything that magnificent," Ian replied to Mac's comment. "In other words, I understand what you're saying. Anything of that marvel should not be enemy."

Cass turned his attention to Elena's back.

Her frame seemed more relaxed in the saddle. She was chatting amicably to Hera at her side. And the sound of her voice carrying back to him was beyond lyrical. There was no wariness, no tenseness.

It was poetic.

She felt safe.

She was home.

"What do you think our reception is going to be?" Mac asked.

"I don't care if we have to ride through a barrage of arrows, just as long as I get to dodge them with this view," Ian said as answer.

"There won't be a barrage of arrows, Hadrian," Mac returned. "Triton is advancing, don't you know. Peace is at hand. And we're us. They'll love us."

Bloody Mac.

"What I know is that I'd aim a barrage of arrows at any being that might even come close to endangering this realm, I wouldn't care if they were guests of the queen," Ian retorted.

"I can't say I disagree," Mac muttered, upon which Jazz turned.

"You like it, possum?" she called to Mac, her face bright and her carriage relaxed as well.

"I'm never leaving," he called back.

She smiled brilliantly at him.

Elena turned in her saddle too, her eyes catching Cassius's.

She did not say a word.

He still read her expression.

Most especially the challenging grin quirking her lips.

And so, when she dug her heels into Diana, he was already doing the same to Caelus.

Female warrior and steed burst forward.

And the male equivalent chased after her.

Cass's amazement of the lush, clement surroundings had not paled when he saw his first treehouse, the wide sweep of its steps that started at the ground adorned with the first flowers he'd seen in The Enchantments, and these were as rich and abundant as the leaves in the trees.

The wooden treehouse it led to had several levels, various balconies, blinking diamond-paned windows, and a droopy thatched roof that made it look as if it was from a gnome settlement in Wodell, except crafted for larger beings.

However, Elena did not slow the gallop of her horse, either keen to get home or keen to take him there, so he also could not slow and fully take it in.

Or any of the others they passed, which were not uniform in the slightest.

There were slate roofs and tin roofs painted green and shingled roofs, and tile.

The windows were square or arched or round.

The levels were stacked one on top of the other or had ladders or stairways leading up expanses of trunk to get to the next, or set away, farther down a branch.

Some of the structures were spherical, others square, others a jumble of shapes that fit amongst the tree where it resided.

There were barrels or colorful pots or wicker baskets filled with flowers adorning the ground below or the decks of balconies, or hanging off their railings.

And there were benches and forest stools and swayback chairs also in both places, some around firepits, others set beside meandering streams.

But there was not a single structure on land.

It was visually charming.

It was also, from a defense perspective, incredibly clever.

As they rode, Elena in the lead, Cassius behind her, the others pounding after them, he noted they were receiving attention as Nadirii came out of their homes to their balconies, or appeared on foot or mounted, coming from the trees.

And the sisters watched them ride.

The calls began to sound that he'd heard when in battle with them (as well as at the Nadirii parade at the coliseum in Fire City) as Nadirii upon Nadirii shared their princess was home.

And warned they had visitors.

Cassius had his sword in its hilt on his saddle, his daggers at his belt, another in his boot, but he did naught but keep his gaze on Elena's back and follow her into what, with the significant increase in treehomes, was clearly the heart of The Enchantments.

He did not expect they'd have any reception but a wary one. Ophelia would see to that.

And he did not think at all about the fact that he, Macrinus and Hadrian were the first Airenzian males to ever be on Nadirii soil.

But if this startling event that made history was going to occur to him, it did not when Elena reined in her mount with Cassius following suit close to the largest and grandest treehome of them all.

And he heard, "*Papa!*"

His eyes went directly to the sound and his leg instantly moved to swing off Caelus as he saw his daughter's auburn hair shining in the sunlight while she raced down the steps of the grand treehouse toward her father.

His sole focus his girl, he had enough time to get his boots on the ground, take two quick strides toward her and get into a crouch with his arms extended before Aelia was in them and he was up, lifting her with him and holding his daughter tight to his chest.

"My darling girl," he murmured, his face stuffed in her hair.

"My darling papa!" she cried, her arms tight around his neck.

As was their way, for he took pains to make certain she had no idea that moments of preciousness would one day be hard to come by, so you should take the time to savor them when you had them, she pulled away first and demanded to know, "Isn't this land *splendid*?"

"It is, indeed, my little beauty," he agreed.

"They live in the *trees*!" she cried.

He smiled at her. "As I've seen."

"And everywhere is so *green*," she carried on.

"I've noted that as well, my darling."

"And you would really not believe what these ladies can do with their bows and swords and staffs," she shared excitedly.

He actually would.

"Is that so," he replied.

"It is! It is so!" she exclaimed. "It's no wonder they always beat Uncle Trajan."

He grinned at her. "Yes, they are most fearsome."

"No, they aren't. They're lovely to me," she contradicted.

"I am most glad to hear that."

And he was. He would never imagine Ophelia or the Sisterhood would be anything less to his daughter.

But he was still pleased to hear, and see from her behavior, that she had been treated well. And he made note to express his gratitude to Ophelia for that.

"I think it was Uncle Trajan they didn't like," she decided. "I was only four when he was gone but I do remember him being in a foul mood most of the time. Unless he was being mean to somebody," she remarked. "He quite enjoyed that."

And that was his wee Aelia.

She didn't miss a trick.

Even when she was four.

She abruptly changed subjects, as was her way.

"Did you get me a present?"

"Are you my dearest daughter?"

She giggled and patted his beard. "I'm your only daughter, silly."

Before he could reply to that, his body locked when he heard the words she spoke as she carried on.

"No, wait! That's my new sister!" she yelled, twisting in his arms and pointing to the pretty blonde girl he'd seen with Elena many weeks before.

"Her name is Theodora and she can already ride a *real horse*, not just a pony." She twisted back to Cassius. "And she's my friend!"

"Well, isn't that grand," he muttered, keeping his emotions carefully in check, for he had not informed his daughter any of this was happening.

Though his gaze sliced to Elena, who was standing not close, but not far.

He saw her eyes on him and she appeared torn between some soft emotion that was strong enough not to let go even though the emotion warring with it was the fact that she was exceptionally angry.

He would know why when she looked away and growled, actually *growled*, "Mother."

"She needed to know," a stately voice came from behind his daughter from a person he could not see, but he knew was Ophelia.

"Do you not think it should be her father who told her?" Elena demanded.

It was at this demand, on his behalf about his communication with his daughter, when Cassius stopped thinking he could fall in love with Elena, Princess of the Nadirii.

Instead he realized that was already happening.

On this staggering thought, Aelia chimed in.

"Hullo. Are you the lady that's marrying my papa?" she asked Elena.

Cassius froze again.

But he did not do this for long when Elena's head turned Aelia's way and the fierce warrior who could split the shaft of an arrow at twenty paces, ride like the wind and fearlessly fight Zees stared at a little, red-headed girl appearing terrified.

At her expression, he burst out laughing.

Aelia studied him quizzically as he put her down but took her hand and led her to his betrothed.

"Princess Elena, I would like you to officially meet my daughter, Princess Aelia of Airen. She likes chocolate pots, detests playing with dolls, started demanding to ride a horse, *not* a pony, when she was three, she can be a rascal and she is far too intelligent for my sanity."

He looked down at his daughter and continued.

"Princess Aelia, this is Princess Elena of the Nadirii, the woman who will soon be my wife and your mother. She rides like the wind, something I suspect she will teach you. She can charm Zees with a smile. And her aim is so true with an arrow, she can probably shoot a walnut off your head at one hundred paces." He paused when he saw his daughter's eyes light, then warned severely, "But she will not be doing that."

Aelia looked from him to Ellie, back to her father.

"She is most lovely," she shared.

"In visage and in heart, my daughter," he replied quietly.

Aelia looked between them again before she leaned to him and got up on her toes.

"Can she speak?" she whispered loudly.

He bent to his girl and whispered loudly in return, "I believe she wishes to make a good impression on you. I should have told her to come charging into the area making starbursts in the sky with her arrows."

Aelia's eyes got large and her whisper turned reverent. "She can do that?"

"She can, indeed." Cass straightened, put his hand to his daughter's shoulder and pulled her to his legs, murmuring, "I'm learning Princess Elena can do most anything."

Aelia turned her gaze from her father to Ellie.

"Will you do that for me?" she asked shyly.

Finally, Elena's musical voice came forth and it did this as she swept a low bow, saying, "It would be my honor, Princess Aelia."

Aelia giggled.

Elena lost her fright and smiled down at Cass's girl.

She turned that smile to her side and called, "No hug for me?"

"Did you bring *me* a present?" Dora called in return.

"You were in Fire City with me, darling," Elena reminded her.

"I wasn't in Wodell with you," Dora pointed out.

"Hmm..." Elena hummed, looked down at Aelia, then lifted her hand, palm up, as she turned Dora's way.

She bent to her hand and blew lightly.

From her palm swept a stream of sparkling purple and coral dust that turned green the closer it got to Dora.

And when it was right in front of her, it bloomed into a beautiful tree about three feet tall and two feet wide with lush green leaves that faded to red, then orange, then yellow, and finally brown before they fell from the tree leaving it barren for but a moment before the tree disappeared into miniature doves that wafted away into nothing.

"Golly," Aelia breathed.

"Showoff," Jazz murmured from close.

Elena winked down at Aelia before she gave her attention again to Dora.

"Will that do?" she asked.

Dora appeared unimpressed and solidified this impression by crossing her little girl arms on her chest.

"Are you going to leave me behind ever, ever, *ever* again?" she demanded to know.

It was at that, Cassius was stunned that Elena did not seek her mother's eyes.

She looked to Cass.

And he was further stunned when she did this not as censure for the decision he made in Firenze as pertained to Dora, but to read the expression he gave her.

Thus, she turned back to Theodora to say, "Maybe. If there's danger."

Dora was unsurprisingly not mollified by this answer and thus continued her hostile interrogation.

"Is he sleeping in our treehome?" she asked with a jerk of her head Cassius's way.

Bloody hell.

"As I told you, Theodora, he is." Ophelia entered the conversation.

Bloody *hell*.

"Just you wait, Papa," Aelia told him excitedly, shaking his leg as she did so. "You get to sleep with the princess in her *eyrie*. Dora's taken me there. We *play* there. It's all high up in the *highest heights* of her tree. *High*. Like the citadel, except, well...*nice*."

Apparently, this new situation with her father having a woman in his life was not going to faze his daughter.

At least that was some relief.

Cass grinned at his girl as he heard Mac, Jazz, Ian, Hera and Rose laugh quietly around him.

His grin did not last long when his attention went back to Elena to see she was in a silent contest of wills with her ward.

"We don't have to—" he began.

"You do. You will," Elena cut him off not taking her gaze from her girl. "Theodora, are you going to come here so I can introduce you to Prince Cassius?"

Dora didn't move.

Elena tensed.

Cass was about to say something.

Then Theodora stomped down to Elena.

But she did not allow Elena to introduce her.

In a defiant, but wounded and even perhaps frightened voice, she admitted, "I don't like being away from you."

Elena instantly melted (this not at all surprising) and smoothed the girl's golden hair from crown to the back of her neck.

"I go on patrol all the time," she reminded her.

"But that's close," Dora muttered.

Cassius was realizing, belatedly, even more than he already had, the mistake he made in sending Dora away without letting Elena see to her.

He again was about to say something, take responsibility for his decision, but as if she was attuned to him, Elena's eyes darted his way and she gave a short shake of her head.

He remained quiet.

"If Cassius and I think it is safe, you and Aelia can come to Prince True's wedding with us."

"Really, Papa?" Aelia asked excitedly.

He nodded down to her.

"All right, Dora?" Elena prompted.

"All right," Dora mumbled to the toes of her moccasins.

"Speak clearly," Elena ordered gently. "And look at me when you do."

Dora lifted her head. "All right, Ellie."

Ellie.

Evidently, hostilities were at an end.

"Now, can I have a hug?" Elena requested.

Theodora wrapped her arms around Elena's hips for a brief moment and let go.

But Cass noticed when she had a hold, she held hard and closed her eyes tight.

"Right, shall we meet the future king of Airen?" Elena suggested.

"I 'spose," Dora muttered, glancing at him from under her lashes.

Elena, wisely, Cassius suspected, let that one go.

Upon introduction, he swept a low bow as Elena had done to Aelia, which he was pleased to see made her lips tick, though she tried to hide it.

Aelia boisterously greeted his men, further introductions were performed, and Theodora seemed unimpressed with Mac, but captivated by Ian.

And after Ophelia announced they were to take tea in her receiving room, with an audience of many silently watching, they moved to the stairs of the grand treehome, the girls walking before Elena and Cassius, Mac and Ian behind them, and he heard Mac say to Ian, "Well, you caught the eye of at least one Nadirii."

"Shut up, mate," Ian retorted.

Mac chuckled.

Cass looked to Elena.

He was again not surprised her mind was no longer on her ward.

Her gaze was riveted to her mother's back.

Ophelia's health had worsened visibly in the weeks since they left her. She was thin to the point of gaunt and her battle with pain was beginning to contort her attractive features.

He took Elena's hand and murmured, "We'll talk later, lamb."

Her gaze drifted to him and she nodded up at him silently.

"Hear that Dora?" Aelia whispered loudly. "'Lamb.' I told you Papa was dreamy."

"He would be dreamy, he's moonshine," Dora replied.

"And you were right!" Aelia cried. "He's moonshine, and Princess Elena is sunshine!"

Cass looked down at Ellie.

She kept ascending the stairs, murmuring, "I'll tell you later."

This meant, but moments after she spoke her words, Prince Cassius of Airen did something he never thought he'd do in his life.

He entered the Nadirii Queen's home.

And he did it smiling.

❧

"Do you think they're asleep?" Elena whispered.

"No," Cass only sort of whispered.

"Do you find this odd?"

"Yes."

"Do you think they find this odd?"

"Perhaps. However, Aelia is in fits of glee. She's not stuck in a lifeless castle with no one to play with. The woman who will help raise her can make doves fly from her hand. And she has a sister." He dropped his voice lower. "Dora's mother left her once, and didn't come home, and I'm an arsehole for sending her away from you after an attack on the castle and the worst quake we've felt without you getting the chance to explain things to her."

Ellie, resting her chin to her crossed arms on his chest, his back to her bed, head up on her pillows, pushed down with her arms and replied, "It's done. We're moving on."

Cass sighed.

He then brushed the backs of his finger against her cheek and changed their subject, going gently.

"Your mother has worsened."

She turned her head so she could rest her cheek to her arms.

He curved his hand along her jaw.

"Ellie."

"I have that medicine that G'Liam gave me. I shall ask one of our healers to test it, and if it is all right, give it to her."

"This is probably wise," he murmured.

"Are you offended?"

He was not.

But at her question, he was perplexed.

"Offended?"

She put her chin to her arms again to catch his gaze.

"There was no fanfare. No great parade. No grand celebration the Prince of Airen had arrived. Just tea and cakes and we were sent off home so I could make you a humble dinner of hearty vegetable pie and treacle tarts."

He smiled at her. "It was good tea and cakes."

"Cass."

"And you're an excellent cook, which is surprising."

At that, Elena appeared perplexed.

"Why is that surprising?"

"A woman handy with a staff *and* a wooden spoon? You're every man's dream. While I sit back and get fat, you can feed me *and* defend my citadel."

She lifted up in order to slap his bare chest but did this grinning.

"Not to mention, that pie was delicious and there was not a measure of meat in it," he went on.

"I shall make you swear off meat," she declared.

"You shall not," he returned.

She gave him a stubborn look.

Cass had one arm about her, he wrapped the other one around, dragged her up his chest then rolled her to her back with him now pressed chest to chest to her.

When he had her as he wished, he whispered, "I am not a fanfare type of prince."

"Well, that is good, for the Nadirii lack fanfare."

"You are at ease here," he noted.

"I'm home," she replied.

"When all is said and done, lamb, if it is allowed for me to accompany you, we will find times to make certain you can be in your land where you feel home."

He could tell what this meant to her when she breathed, "Cassius."

"And even if I cannot accompany you. You will need to come home regardless, with Theodora, and if she wishes it, Aelia."

Her expression softened, her hands came to his face, and he knew what *that* meant to her when she asked in a very low whisper, "Do you think we can have sex silently?"

"No."

She frowned.

"Papa!" Aelia shouted from her fluffy pallet that was the level below, one Dora—apparently happily—shared that was Dora's own. This shouting demonstrating why they could not have sex at all. "When you marry Elena, will Dora be a princess?"

"Yes!" Cass shouted in return.

"Yippee!" Aelia cried and went on loudly. "See, Dora! I told you!"

"She will?" Elena queried.

"Yes," he repeated.

"Is that standard royal procedure?"

He raised his brows. "Do I care? I'll be king. The only good thing I learned from my father, I can do what the fuck I want when I am king."

She smiled up at him and through it said, "Are you absolutely *certain* we can't have sex silently?"

He very much wished he could answer differently.

Alas, he could not.

"Yes."

"Papa!" Aelia yelled.

"My darling girl!" Cass yelled back. "In fifteen minutes, if I go down there and I don't find two sleeping beauties, I shall be most cross."

A moment of silence before...

"We're going to sleep *right now*!" Aelia assured.

"Is she going to go to sleep?" Elena whispered.

"Hell no," Cassius muttered. "But she *will* stop shouting."

Elena stifled a giggle.

Cass smiled at her as she did.

His smile faded, and his hand lifted so he could again stroke her cheek.

As he did this, his mind also wandered.

"Sweetheart," Elena called gently, and when he focused on her again, he knew where his mind wandered could be read easily.

"I don't wish to—" he started.

"I thought we learned about sharing."

"We never had this," he admitted. "She died giving birth. We never had—"

Ellie wrapped her hands around either side of his neck and stated firmly, "Her name was Liviana. She lived. She loved you. You loved her. She gave you a daughter. She is a part of our lives, a part of you, a part of your girl. Her name is Liviana, Cass. And it will not harm me at all if you speak it to me."

They could not have sex.

But he could press a hard kiss on her lips.

And after she gave him her gift, this he did.

When he lifted away, he shared, "I never held Liviana in my arms and shouted at our daughter to go to sleep."

She stroked the skin at the back of his ears with both thumbs, murmuring, "You've lost so very much. It would break a weaker man."

"Make no mistake, I am broken, Ellie."

"You appear quite whole to me."

"It's an illusion."

"Then you are a master illusionist."

"Ellie—"

"Cass, a broken man does not let the world melt away when confronted with the beloved daughter he has not seen in some time. There was no one for miles when you first held her in your arms. A broken man would be lost to her. He would be lost to everybody."

She paused, as if reflecting, before she continued to speak.

"I would say you were lost after your mother was gone, though more, it was about never really having a home or a family. And Liviana found you. In her, you had both. And you thought you were lost after Liviana was gone. But you haven't been. Aelia's had a hold on you while you've been drifting. You just need to find your feet again, and you'll be fine."

He was uncertain Aelia had a hold on him, that was a burden he refused to consider he forced his young daughter to bear.

But he was beginning to feel that Elena did.

And not simply literally.

To communicate a modicum of what this made him feel, he dipped to her, grazing her cheek with his until he found her ear with his lips.

"As I am a stranger in this land, it will be up to you to find someone to look after the girls while I take you somewhere in this sun-drenched haven where no one can hear how much you enjoy all the things I'm going to do to you."

She trembled beneath him, and at the feel, he fought getting hard.

She also whispered, "I can manage that."

"That's good," he muttered, kissed the skin below her ear and then rolled off her, pulling her to her side and wrapping both arms around her so he could fit her to his front. "Now go to sleep," he ordered.

"As you wish, my prince."

He closed his eyes. He heard hoots of owls. He felt Ellie's soft warmth. Her steady breathing.

He also felt her living space all around them, which was not simple, nor sparse, or even small, but was filled with personality and colors, comfortable nooks and inviting furniture.

Last, he felt the night envelope them, here, in The Enchantments, where it was not just dark, but like a soft blanket holding the sun at bay so there could be rest.

And he opened his eyes when Dora yelled, "Ellie, can Aelia try riding a horse tomorrow?"

The team up.

Aelia had successfully been silenced, so Theodora became the mouthpiece.

"Not if you both don't go right to sleep," Elena yelled back. She cuddled closer to him and mumbled, "I fear we're going to have our hands full, sweetheart."

He didn't.

He didn't fear it in the slightest.

He hoped they added two, three, even four more before all was said and done.

He had never wished for anything, not a thing.

But a family.

Cassius didn't share that.

He just pulled her closer, drew in the fragrance of her hair, and in the soothing calm of The Enchantments, he fell right to sleep.

# 65

## THE SURPRISE



That night, in The Enchantments, many a stool was taken, many a staircase was ascended.

The Sisterhood was talking.

A number of them had met Prince Cassius of Airen on the battlefield.

He was the enemy.

But even so, it was known wide he was not like his brother.

Even in battle, a fair fight was understood.

As was the dirty.

Cassius had been fair—honorable in victory, and defeat.

Trajan had been neither.

That said, it was with great surprise the sisters watched Cassius ride behind their princess into The Enchantments, and not simply because he was a male, an *Airenzian* male, an Airenzian *prince* in their realm.

But because he rode behind their princess into The Enchantments.

A woman in Airen rode in a carriage at the back of a procession.

In the rare instance she was astride a horse, again, she rode at the back.

A man did not follow a woman.

Never.

Not ever.

Prince Cassius seemed unbothered by this.

In fact, it seemed he took no note of it at all.

And this, the Sisterhood thought, was very strange.

Not bad.

But very strange.

The talk in treehomes, around fire pits and beside streams was not solely about this.

No.

For the ones who had witnessed it were speaking widely about how Prince Cassius of Airen had greeted his daughter.

A girl-child born to an Airenzian male, especially those of the aristocracy, was disregarded to the point that this event went so far as to be ignored.

If a boy-child had not already been sired, or if another one was desired, the male set upon his wife as soon as he wished in order to beget one, as if his daughter had not been born.

Therefore, it was with great surprise that the Sisterhood watched Prince Cassius lift his daughter in his arms, hold her, smile at her, talk to her and *listen to her* as if what she said did not mean something.

It meant everything.

Equally surprising was how close the girl seemed to his men.

Prince Cassius clearly doted on his daughter.

All those men did.

Of course, it was not unknown that Cassius had loved his deceased wife.

But this...

Further discussed was how he was with their princess.

Elena was a skilled warrior. She also was an exceptionally powerful witch. She held more power than her sister, definitely. There were even those who believed she held more power than her mother.

Elena loved and respected her queen.

She loved and respected her mentor.

She loved and respected her lieutenants.

And she loved and respected her sisters.

They loved and respected her.

She was easy-going, spiritual, observant, focused and attentive.

Most hoped that Ophelia would name her second born as her successor.

Thus, most were troubled when it became known she would not be Queen of the Nadirii, but Queen of Airen.

Perhaps troubled wasn't the word for it.

Perhaps worried was.

Serena had not demonstrated the traits needed to lead a realm. She was quick-tempered and vengeful and often would allow emotions to color her thinking, and her actions.

It was thought by a fair few that Elena would be an even better queen than Ophelia, and Ophelia held much respect from her sisters.

However, there was not a great deal of warmth to Ophelia.

She was not officious, though she was often remote.

She was also level-headed, introspective, diplomatic, loyal and fair.

But she was not warm.

So the loss of Elena to Airen was worrisome, not only that one of their own would be forced to live in the land of their enemy.

But that the Sisterhood would lose the woman who should be queen.

More happened that night that surprised the Sisterhood.

There had been laughter in Elena's treehome that evening, and the anomalous sound of the deep tones of a masculine voice.

The same could be heard in Jasmine's treehome, until other sounds were heard.

And the same could be heard in the queen's treehome, where the last Airenzian lieutenant had been quartered, as if the queen sat at her leisure to have a chat with an Airenzian soldier.

It was most clear that Elena did not seem put off by her intended.

Indeed, as they walked from the queen's residence to Elena's, they'd been seen holding hands.

The Sisterhood did not know what to think of any of this.

They were all trained in the art of war. Even those who did not have the inclination for it, from a young age, were required to learn basic skills with staff, daggers, bow and arrow, sword and hand-to-hand combat.

They were also all trained in witchcraft.

This requirement was much more strictly enforced. Even those who did not show talent with a spell, a potion, scrying, astral travel or the like were obliged to practice what they could and attempt to better what they lacked.

But for the most part, a woman was free to do what she wished, as long as it strengthened the Sisterhood.

Be it fighting.

Or patrolling.

Or training.

Or teaching.

Or healing.

Or weaving baskets or concocting lotions or elixirs or stitching tapestries or knitting blankets or jumpers to sell at Dellish markets to trade for things needed in The Enchantments or to gather coin for the same.

It was for the most part a social community, duties were paid by those who earned so those who fought or patrolled, trained, taught or healed were remunerated for their efforts on behalf of the Sisterhood.

Although this had worked for centuries, the Nadirii were not a nation without troubles.

There were those (albeit they were few) who were lazy, and the others looked down on them.

There were those who wished for more aggression against the male aggressors, there were those who wished for less.

There were those who did not much like the many refugees they took in, there were those who were happy for greater numbers to strengthen the Sisterhood or felt it was their duty as Nadirii to welcome any woman into their company.

There were those who intensely detested all males and wished nothing to do with them. There were those who often journeyed out of The Enchantments to seek male company, or to meet long-time lovers, or simply because they enjoyed a variety of companionship.

But all, being in touch with the magical veil, knew that the quakes were a bad omen.

And in an uncertain situation, you needed strong leadership to guide the way.

Ophelia was wasting.

Serena was problematic.

Elena seemed to be lost to them.

And now, Prince Cassius (and his men) appeared to be full of surprises.

And not bad ones.

But in all, the only thing that was known was the Sisterhood had no clear leader for the future.

So, no.

As the talk wore on well into the night their princess returned, the Nadirii did not know what to make of any of this.

They didn't know at all.

# 66

# THE TRICK

***Melisse of the Nadirii Sisterhood***
*Some Ways South of Notting Thicket*
WODELL

She was getting nowhere and seeing nothing.

This was not right.

She had naught of his, of course.

The path would be far easier to see if she did.

Thus, now she had only her magic and the knowledge he'd been to Notting Thicket a number of times, therefore he spent much time in or around the Go'Doan temple there, as well as being invited to Birchlire Castle.

So she had taken up a variety of pebbles she found in both places, cast over them, and followed where they led.

But she was far out of the city.

Quite far.

Every time she stopped to toss a pebble, she followed the direction it pointed to her, but she felt nothing more, saw nothing more, not a hint he'd been there recently.

The sun was getting low. Shadows were claiming the forest. Night would fall fully soon.

Melisse needed to make camp.

Even so, she stopped her horse, swung off and pulled a pebble out of the pouch at her belt, just to make sure she was on the right track.

She threw it and watched it skitter down the narrow, not-oft traveled road through a thick forest. The road where she'd been traveling for some hours now.

But her eyes narrowed beyond it.

Was that…?

She stared.

It couldn't be.

She clicked her tongue to tell her horse, Fortune, to follow her. She put one hand to the hilt of the dagger on her belt and opened her senses before she moved forward slowly.

Very slowly.

The glow in front of her did not get stronger, but it also did not waver.

A healthy, fit being would glow much brighter should she send a seeking pebble in its direction anywhere near it.

She could not be twenty meters away, but that glow was barely lit.

And it couldn't be anyone else.

No one.

But G'Seph.

That kind of glow could only mean…

She began to move more swiftly, staying alert and aware of her surroundings, both through her actual senses, as well as her magical ones.

She felt nothing.

Except the life force coming from the direction of that glow.

He was hurt.

Badly.

Perhaps even dying.

And he'd been left in this wood.

Who would do such a thing?

Melisse got closer.

And closer.

He was lying in the leaves, a thin blanket pulled over him, held tight to his chest by his arms.

"G'Seph?" she called softly, feeling Fortune shift uncomfortably at her back. "G'Seph?" she asked more firmly when he did not answer.

She cast a spell to light the area about him and gasped.

Her horse whinnied and shifted again.

"Good goddess, what happened to your hands?" she whispered,

reaching out to him, staring at the bloody stumps expertly bound where his hands should have been.

When he didn't answer, just seemed to be attempting to slide away from her, she lifted her gaze to his face.

He smiled, and it was grotesque.

Fortune neighed, and Melisse sensed her steed starting to rear.

It was then the warning her Dellish sister Rebecca gave her—a warning in all that was happening she had not remembered—came to the forefront of her mind.

Unfortunately, it did this right before the pain exploded at the back of her head.

# 67

# THE CONFRONTATION

**Queen Mercy**
*Grand Corridor, Second Floor, Birchlire Castle, Notting Thicket*
WODELL

"Queen Mercy!"

Mercy pretended not to hear him and kept moving.

"Your Grace, Queen Mercy! One moment!" Carrington called.

She carried on walking, not rapidly, but decisively away from him.

"My queen!" he snapped loudly, much closer, as if he were running, and she sadly could no longer pretend her thoughts were elsewhere and she hadn't heard him.

Therefore, with resignation, she turned, pretended to look surprised and remarked, "Why, Carrington."

"I've been chasing after you since Stand Hall," he noted irritably.

"Have you?" she asked. "I'm sorry. I didn't notice. I've much on my mind."

"We must speak," he declared.

"Of course," she agreed.

He opened his mouth to do that.

However, she continued.

"Talk to my secretary. Find a time. Much is going on, but I'll have a word with her and make certain she fits you in."

His face grew hard. "I meant now."

Mercy put her hand to her chest in apparent astonishment. "Now?"

"Yes, now. I have urgent matters to discuss with you."

"Well, then, first thing in the morning," she stated. "I have things on my schedule at that time, but I'll see if I can shift them around."

His expression changed again, this time to one she did not like.

It was smug.

"My queen, the things I wish to discuss are messages from your king. And as you know, there is nothing more urgent than that."

Of course, he would be smug about this, for he knew Mercy was no longer sleeping in the same bed with Wilmer. Not only that, they weren't even speaking.

So now, Carrington thought he had the upper hand, for if there was something Wilmer wished to share with her, Carrington would be sent to share it, thus whatever it was, he would know it before her.

And whatever it was, he likely had a say in the message itself.

"*Your* king," she returned blithely and watched shock hit his eyes at the inference he thought she was making. "*My* husband," she finished.

He frowned and took the decision to ignore that.

"It's come to our attention that you've ordered a new wedding gown."

"I have," she confirmed.

"You must demand the seamstresses cease production on it immediately."

She showed no reaction to this declaration except curiosity. "And why would I do that?"

"You've been given a strict budget for this wedding, my queen. No more, no less. The figure was astronomical to start with—"

"Hardly astronomical," she interrupted him to say. "The crown prince of Wodell is getting married. The king's own nuptials had the same budget and that was thirty-three years ago."

"Regardless, it was what you have to work with and what we could *afford*, and you do not have permission to go above it."

Permission?

*She* did not have *permission*?

Mercy stood completely still and stared at him.

The superciliousness returned to his expression, for with this message, and the fact he'd been sent to deliver it, it was clear he thought he finally had a firm grasp on the upper hand.

"And we've learned you've hired twelve new seamstresses," he remarked.

She responded to that.

"I have. The two royal seamstresses we have on staff could hardly finish a new wedding gown on time, not to mention what I am to wear, which they hadn't even started, *and* build a trousseau fitting Lady Farah when she is princess."

"*Lady* Farah?" he asked in shock.

"That is what I said," she replied.

"When did that whore become a lady?"

Even if the feel was wafting from her, Mercy herself slightly shivered at the coldness she was exuding toward him.

She did not think about the fact she'd had these same thoughts about her soon-to-be daughter-in-law.

She did not, for not only had she decided to change her way of thinking, it was not to be borne *he* would make such a remark, to her or anyone (but it must be said, mostly to her).

"You are speaking of my son's betrothed, the woman who, in a very short period of time, will be crowned princess of this very realm and *your future queen*," she reminded him coldly.

"Of course," he murmured, and even this foolish toad knew he'd stepped over the line with that, therefore he swiftly changed the subject. "You've also ordered a trousseau?"

She stared at him like he was daft. "Farah will be traveling almost immediately with True to Airen for Prince Cassius and Princess Elena's nuptials. She can hardly go across an autumn Wodell into the brisk sea winds of Sky Bay wearing Firenz sheers. And she *shouldn't* for she'll be the Princess of *Wodell*."

He shook his head.

"We simply don't have the money for that," he retorted.

"I'm sorry, did you not just send the heralds *with* the collectors to spread the word another coin was expected from our citizenry, due immediately, for their levies to the crown?" she queried.

"That is to strengthen your husband's coffers, which you know are running frightfully low, not for overages in costs of the wedding."

It was not for that and it was an insult he was pretending she didn't know it.

"That's interesting," she noted. "For I've read the proclamation with my own eyes and the king seemed to make a point of mentioning his son's upcoming ceremony in the announcement of the latest tax increase."

At that, Carrington was silent.

Mercy was not.

"It would seem to me the peoples of this realm will have a very clear impression the gold coin they must offer the collector was for that precise thing. At least, it seemed clear to me when I read the proclamation."

Carrington's mouth grew tight and he continued not to speak.

"So," Mercy sniffed, "obviously, after meeting my son's intended, I realized the dress I ordered to be made would not suit her. Considering her station and the historical event that's about to occur, she obviously must have a dress that suits her, and she will. She'll also have a wardrobe that suits a Dellish princess for a royal journey. And gold coins will be falling into our chests very shortly. In fact, I saw the guards bringing those already collected in the Thicket just this afternoon. So many of them, it would cover ten new wedding gowns and a wardrobe that would last years. Thus, I'm afraid there really isn't much to discuss. Therefore, if you don't mind, I'll continue to be on my way."

She began to make a turn when Carrington bit, "Mercy."

Very slowly, she again gave her gaze to the horrible man.

"Mercy?" she asked quietly.

"We've known each other for over two decades," he spat.

"And in that time, I have not given you leave to address me as such."

"You should," he returned.

"I believe it's my decision whether I should or should not."

He gave up on that and went on to something less enjoyable to discuss.

"You seem to view me as the enemy when I further detain you to share helpful advice. That being you are choosing the wrong side."

"Side in what?" she asked, feigning ignorance.

"You know in what," he returned.

"Carrington, if you wish to natter in riddles, really, can we do it sometime after all this wedding brouhaha is over and I can put my feet up by a fire and perhaps enjoy unraveling them?"

"This..." he hesitated as if searching for a word, "*estrangement* between you and the king will not go well for you. You may be queen, and my last wish would be to cause the least offense, but I feel it is in your best interests to share you are no longer young and not the renowned beauty you once were."

She thought it impossible for him to get more obnoxious.

She had been wrong.

"As you say, I am queen, but I am also mother to the heir to the throne."

"If you do not have the favor of the king—"

Mercy interrupted him.

"It is known wide Wilmer is prone to vacillating, it will shock no one I fall out of his favor for a time. Indeed, they're probably surprised that hasn't already happened a dozen times over throughout our marriage. Though I cannot imagine, for the Dellish who prize the faithfulness of a devoted spouse, should his eye wander, that will be well taken by the people. If, perchance, something like that were to happen, and then it was to get out."

Carrington actually appeared stymied by that, proving he could get even *more* obnoxious.

But he was always obvious.

She wondered if he was already trying to tempt her husband with courtesans.

She could not think long on that.

She was angry with her husband. She was often frustrated by her husband.

But she loved her husband.

If he strayed, in her heart, she would no longer have a husband.

Just a king.

"However, I will *always* be mother to the heir to the throne," she finished.

"I'm uncertain how important that is when we have a robust sitting king," he retorted.

"Really?" she inquired. "This surprises me as you're always so keen to share with my husband how well you read the pulse of the people."

None of his points had been veiled for he lacked the skill to do such a thing.

None of hers had either, for he lacked the intelligence to gather her meaning if she did.

They stared into each other's eyes.

She couldn't do that all night, not only because it was ridiculous, but because she actually did have a number of things to do.

Thus, she queried, "Are you quite done?"

"I have a feeling you are," he replied, the double meaning behind this also not veiled.

"We shall see," she murmured, dipped her chin and turned away.

Fortunately, he didn't call out to her.

Unfortunately, their chat meant she had to seek her chamber, and not go to check the progress of the seamstresses before she returned to her study to read through the updated response list and continue to devise and revise the seating in the temple and at the reception for the wedding.

Opportunely, Helga was in Mercy's boudoir, seeing to some mending of lace on one of Mercy's gowns.

Her maid's attention came to her the moment Mercy entered the room, but Mercy did not speak until she had the door closed behind her and she and her maid were close.

"The ravens were sent to Prince True yesterday, yes?" she asked.

"Of course, milady, as you requested."

"And Sir Bram?" she went on.

Helga nodded. "The messages direct from your hand, written twice each. Two birds for each message sent to two men. Four birds. I watched them fly away myself."

Mercy nodded.

"I need you to bring paper and pen, Helga. I'll need another message sent tonight. Not a bird, a messenger on a steed," she instructed.

"Oh no," Helga whispered.

"Yes, my friend," Mercy muttered. "As my son is far away, we need reinforcements. I need to send for Silence," she paused. "And Mars."

Helga held her mistress's gaze for but a moment before she nodded, dipped a curtsy and then strode off quickly to do as she was asked.

Mercy stared at the gown Helga had left behind on a fainting couch upholstered in forest-green velvet.

The nap of the couch was worn and at the bottom lip, there was a fray.

Her gaze wandered around the cozy, warm room with its merry fire.

She saw the intricate carvings in the dark wood panels on the walls and in the cornices. The once-thick, vibrantly-hued, now thinning and fading wool rugs on the floor. The beautifully crafted furniture that appeared feminine and delicate but was indeed stout and comfortable. Furniture that was tended well but needed reupholstered.

They could not afford reupholstery.

They could barely afford the staff it took to keep the wood gleaming.

In the king's castle.

Another five years of Carrington, they were headed for ruin.

She closed her eyes tight.

*You are no longer young and not the renowned beauty you once were.*

As if the only measure of a woman was her youth and beauty.

She did not go to the looking glass to see the veracity of Carrington's words.

She knew she was still attractive. She took pains with Nadirii and Firenz elixirs on her skin and hair, and not simply to make certain her husband didn't grow a wandering eye. This, she did mostly for herself.

It was, in her life, her only treat.

She also knew after she caught the eye, and won the heart, of the prince who would be her husband and then her king, that her youth and beauty began to fade from importance because she took pains to make that so.

However, that did not mean Carrington's words did not wound.

Mercy drew in breath.

The tax proclamation that implied the people were paying for True's wedding with their hard-earned gold (which they *were*, but they didn't need to be told that directly) could easily put a pall on the celebratory air of the capital and even turn public sentiment away from her son.

And she could not let that happen.

She stared at the fray in her fainting couch and another thought came to her.

Where was all the tax money going?

The seemingly incessant campaigns to re-secure the southern border of Firenz land weren't actually *incessant*.

Wodell was not a wealthy nation, they weren't a poor one either.

Why was there such a huge concern about her spending on the wedding?

She could not say she oversaw the budget for the realm (just the castle), but it was her understanding their coffers were low, not empty.

Even before the tax increases, she should be able to hire seamstresses.

Definitely after them.

Further, she should be able to reupholster a couch.

These thoughts meant she added a visit to the royal auditor to have a look over the treasury accounts onto her list of things to do that evening.

She had already sent birds to True, suggesting matters were such that he should come home as soon as possible, as well as to Bram, ordering him to take pains to bring her son home.

However, they were not near. It would take ages for them to get to the Thicket.

But Silence and her beast of a husband were only a day's ride away.

And King Mars might be a savage, but he was not difficult to look at, and even Mercy thought he had an engaging manner.

He was wealthy.

He was now their ally.

And he was besotted with his Dellish countess-now-queen.

If paraded about the city, that tall, dark, dynamic king with his petite, pretty, pale Dellish queen on his arm would at least set the women's thoughts to swooning.

That was, until their own handsome Prince True returned with his (Mercy had to admit), exotically beautiful future princess at his side

And Mercy knew, if played correctly, a woman could control the sentiments of an entire family, certainly her husband.

Romance was in the air, and there was something Mercy also knew, and she knew it very well.

Romance equaled hope.

And hope was worth a million gold coins.

# 68
## THE HONESTY

**King Mars**
*The Study, Cord Cottage, The Arbor*
Wodell

Sitting behind the desk, Mars studied the dispatch that had just arrived from Lorenz in Fire City.

The Go'Doan were being circumspect. But even so, Lorenz was not convinced that all the conspirators had fled from the city.

Further, the city-state of Go'Doan had officially denied any knowledge of and definitely any collaboration in regards to the attack on Catrame Palace. They went so far as to denounce it, and anyone behind it, with "all due potency."

Mars wondered what potency they thought was due this denouncement.

They went on to request to continue their "vital" work in that "region" and shared they had already sent new priests to take up the posts of the "wayward" ones that had "gone missing."

In his last years, his father had kept Mars close to his side in order that Mars could witness the king at work, and they could discuss communications received, decisions made, and strategy taken.

Therefore, Mars did not have to consider long what his father would think of the Go'Doan official statement.

What Ares would think was…

It was bloody rubbish.

He turned his attention to studying the second missive received that morning, this given to Silence and bearing the royal seal of Wodell.

It was from Queen Mercy.

Silence had read it, then handed it to him, saying, "I'd love to show you around our capital. It's really very pretty. And it'd be nice to spend time with your mother."

To which he'd replied, "We shall leave in two days."

And then he'd received her smile.

However, looking at it now, he found some of the language interesting.

*It would be most beneficial if you and King Mars could arrive early. The wedding planning is taking up much of my time, and I'm afraid Queen Elpis is at odds for things to do.*

*Most beneficial* was unusual wording.

And if his mother didn't have enough to do—something she'd never suffered from in her life—then she would either find something to do or ride back to the Arbor and be with them.

They did not need to leave the Arbor to be with her.

Something was amiss, and Mars did not have a good feeling about it.

His head came up before she appeared in the doorway.

When the maid saw she had his attention, she blathered, "Sir, Your Grace, uh, sir, you have a visitor."

Mars fought back a sigh when she offered no further information, before he prompted, "And that visitor would be?"

"Lady Vanka."

Silence's mother?

Why was the maid announcing a visit from Silence's mother to him?

Mars felt his brows draw together. "My wife is reading in the drawing room."

"Lady Vanka is here for you, um…sir, and she's asked that, well, erm… uh, her, uh, your wife, that is—"

For fuck's sake.

"Her Grace," Mars bit. "She is queen, even if she is not your queen. As I am king. We are 'Your Grace' if you're speaking to us, and she is 'Her Grace' if you are referring to her. Or 'the queen,' 'Her Highness,' or 'Her

Majesty.' You know this, therefore your hesitancy in speaking is inexplicable. And I'll take this opportunity to note that from this point on, anything else will not be considered impertinence. It'll be considered insubordination and your time in our service will be terminated. Is this understood?"

"Yes, Your Grace," she whispered.

"Now finish what Lady Vanka wished you to say."

"She wants to speak to you without Her Grace knowing she's here until after she speaks with you."

Mars tipped his head to the side and demanded, "Was that that difficult?"

"No, Your Grace," she murmured.

"Bring the lady to me," he ordered.

"Yes, Your Grace." She dipped a curtsy and disappeared out the door.

It was the second time in five minutes he did not have good feelings, this about Vanka seeking him, and only him.

Fortunately, his wife was now *his wife*.

She, as had he, had much enjoyed making up for lost time in their bed.

Therefore, he was in a very good mood.

Further lighting his mood, over the past days, Silence had grown open and honest and curious, and if not consistently talkative (which was not her way), the bonds they'd been forming since nearly the moment they met (in his consideration) were fortifying.

Rapidly.

He was falling in love with her.

And she him.

For his part, this was a surprise. He would not have foreseen falling in love with a wee, quiet, pale, reflective Dellish woman, no matter she was a great beauty.

She was still wee, quiet, pale, reflective.

And Dellish.

But now, he could not consider a future without the daily opportunity to look in those silver eyes, to listen to her thoughtful words, to experience the profoundness of her passion, to gaze upon her pale skin beside him in bed or be buried in her wet cunt.

But oddly, of all that, her contradictory demeanor was what he found most attractive.

She was independent, but due to her upbringing, she brought out a protective instinct in him the likes he had not known existed. He was prone to protect the ones he loved, but the maltreatment she endured and the machinations they both were now having to put up with he found intolerable.

She did not need him.

And yet she did.

She gave every impression that she could live her life with her books, her other pursuits, her maid Tril, and that was all, and she would be perfectly content.

But that was not what life gave her.

Life gave her Mars.

As well as a rearing that was abusive in its neglect.

So in the end, she did have need of him.

And one of the reasons why appeared right in that moment at his study door.

He looked at Vanka then past her to the maid.

"Close the door behind the lady," he ordered.

The maid nodded, curtsied and did as asked.

Vanka had taken two steps in and stopped.

She began it with, "Mars, I cannot say how relieved I am that you agreed to speak to me."

"You're my wife's mother," he pointed out, coming up from his seat behind the desk. "Though, I will note, I'm not much comfortable with having a conversation without Silence knowing you're here, so I would suggest you get on with it before what minimal comfort I have vanishes."

She took his words to heart, two more steps into the room, and stated, "It's my understanding harsh words were spoken with my husband."

"Only to the extent such words were returned," he replied. "It is clear Johan made no effort to know his daughter while he raised her, and thus it is no surprise that he underestimates her."

Vanka winced at this statement, but she did not deny it.

Mars continued, "He was attempting to drive a wedge between husband and wife, for reasons I do not understand, though in the end, I do not care. Such won't be abided, no matter the reason. Silence read his intent and made it clear she won't abide it either."

"This is...it is...somewhat what I wish to discuss with you."

He was not following.

"What is? My desire to further strengthen my marriage to a woman who is my queen and will be the mother of my children, a woman I've come to care for deeply, rather than having it undermined when it's barely over a month old? Or your husband's conniving to make certain that does not happen?"

"You care deeply for her?" she asked quietly, staring at him intently.

His brows shot together in annoyance. "I must warn you that minimal comfort I had with our conversation is swiftly vanishing."

She shook her head, started to lift a hand, dropped it and said quickly, "I wish to discuss, that is…it's been reported…" She drew in a deep breath. "What I mean to say is, you are in Wodell. We are a certain way here. And…and…"

Her cheeks pinked, much like her daughter's, which was a fortunate reminder or his reaction to what she said next would have been far more explosive.

"I understand how it is between a new husband and wife. But the forcing upon servants of the, erm, that is to say, a certain…*decadence* is considered unacceptable in this realm. I know it is much different in your land, but it is not the same way here. Obviously spending the day in each other's presence is suitable, especially at this point in your marriage and most especially since you did not have a proper courtship. But, erm…in a bedchamber." She said no more on that and finished, "It reflects badly on Silence and—"

She spoke no further as Mars strode around the desk, across the room, past his mother-in-law, out the door and down the hall.

The first maid he saw, which happened to be in the corridor outside the drawing room, he stopped.

"Pack your things," he commanded, ignoring her eyes growing huge and her face turning ashen. "You're relieved of your duties. As are the other two. Tell them immediately and I want all of you gone from this manor in an hour."

Her eyes flitted beyond Mars, where he knew Vanka, who had followed him, stood, then back to Mars.

And thus, he read on her face she knew that he was now aware that she was running to the lord of Bower Manor and sharing intimacies she had no business sharing.

"But, sir—" she began.

She was the one he'd very recently finished giving a lecture, though she was not referring to him how he'd told her to do so.

Which was irritating, but it was a moot point at this juncture.

"An hour," he declared.

"We were only doing what we were told," she whispered.

Mars had his temper in check.

But at this pronouncement, that was slipping.

"Mars, what on earth—?" Silence asked from the doorway.

She'd joined them, which he thought was good, even if, for his wife, it was bad.

He glanced at his queen briefly, saw her juggling her monkey, surprise stamped on her beautiful face.

He'd explain to her later.

He had to deal with this now.

He turned toward Vanka and again lifted his brows.

"They were doing what they were told?" he asked.

Vanka's cheeks flamed.

"Mother, what are you—?"

Mars turned and interrupted his wife again to say to the maid, "Leave us, gather the others, go to your quarters and await my decision on this matter." When she hesitated, he finished on a lean, "*Now.*"

The girl nodded, bobbed a curtsy and rushed away.

"Mars—" Silence murmured.

Mars did not respond to his wife.

He turned to her mother.

"Johan hired servants that would spy and report on his daughter and her husband?" he asked.

"Oh, my goodness," Silence whispered in horror.

"It is—" Vanka began.

"You do know, this being discovered, it could be construed as a conspiracy of Wodell against the Firenz king and his queen," Mars remarked.

"Dear gods," Vanka breathed, her hand coming up to her throat.

"Mars," Silence said soothingly, and he felt her come close and wrap her fingers around his upper arm.

"It was meant nothing like that," Vanka stated quickly.

"No, I find it no surprise it was not," Mars retorted. "Tell me, Vanka, has a maid or valet ever entered your bedchamber when you were abed with your husband?"

Vanka's face remained flushed.

"Mars," Silence whispered, her fingers tightening on his arm.

Now understanding this situation to its fullness, especially the fact Silence's own parents were behind it, his control snapped when Vanka made no reply.

"*Tell me!*" he barked.

Silence pressed close to his side.

Piccola, her monkey, took that opportunity to transfer herself from her mama to her papa but Mars completely ignored the monkey crawling up his chest and positioning on his shoulder with its little hands clutching Mars's neck.

"There has been occasion—" Vanka started.

"Of course there has," he clipped. "You are wed, and you are gentry and your servants have the running of the household, but they do not dictate what happens within its walls. Your husband installed spies in his daughter's home to report on what happens here so he could have any information he could acquire to utilize in order to undermine her marriage. And when Silence made it clear she would not fall prey to his personal attempts to do this, he sent you here to do the same. That is, after realizing his efforts had come to naught to get them to whore themselves in hopes of gaining my attention and causing a rift in my marriage I would not have been able to repair should I have been of the character to do such a revolting thing to my wife."

Silence pressed closer.

"A revolting thing?" Vanka asked, appearing stunned he would find it revolting to cheat on his gods-damned *wife*.

The bloody, fucking *Dellish*.

"You clearly have utterly *no* understanding of a Firenz husband, just wed or wed for forty years," he shared with strained patience. "That is a prejudice of ignorance that does not matter at this juncture. What matters at this juncture is that I do not have to say my marriage is not your concern. What I will make very clear is that *your daughter's* marriage is not your concern."

"I...it would seem there's been a misunderstanding," Vanka tried.

"There's been no misunderstanding," Mars retorted. "Another prejudice is that you think my people are savage. Uneducated. Dimwitted. We eat, sleep, fuck and war. This is not true. You and your husband have underestimated your daughter her entire life. You underestimating me comes as no surprise. Though, to bring matters in hand, it's important you know that you have. And last, before you leave, you must know that Silence and I will be having a long conversation about what part you play in her future. Once we come to an understanding, you and your husband will be informed of our decision. Until then, neither of us will see you, and if Silence does not convince me to allow her to keep you a part of her life, you will never see her again, is that understood?"

"But—" Vanka started, no color in her face, none at all.

However, as far as he was concerned, for the moment, this matter was concluded.

"You may now leave, and if you don't, I'll have my men remove you."

With that, he took hold of his wife and moved her into the drawing room.

Once there, he shut the door.

It took a moment before Silence spoke, and when she did, it was in a careful tone.

"Perhaps you could have allowed her to have her say?"

"And what do you think she would say, *piccolina*?" he demanded, crossing his arms on his chest.

Silence, her head tipped far back to keep hold on his eyes, pressed her lips tight.

She knew what her mother would have to say and that was nothing good, for it might be a surprise the maids were spying on them and reporting back to her father, but it was not a surprise why they'd been chosen and what they'd preliminarily been asked to achieve.

In fact, those three were such bloody awful maids, it would further not surprise Mars to learn they were not maids at all, and maybe they were even prostitutes, before they came to Cord Cottage.

"I wish you to be done with them and never see them again," Mars shared his thoughts on the matter of her parents. "However, they are not my mother and father, so I will now listen to your feelings on the subject."

She tipped her head to the side. "Is now a good time for us to discuss this?"

"It isn't, for I am livid, and it is, for I am *livid*, and as such, I feel quite strongly about arguing to get my way."

They had not stopped far from each other.

But she came closer, pressing the front of her body to his, and she lifted a hand to take Piccola from his shoulder.

Her eyes were dancing through these movements, and although he enjoyed that dance, he found nothing amusing about this situation in the slightest.

And in order to communicate this to his wife, although he very much wished to wrap his arms around her, he kept them crossed.

Piccola dashed under his hair and around the back of Mars's neck to perch on his other shoulder, stating quite clearly she did not want to be taken from her papa.

Silence let their pet have her way and rested both hands on his chest above his arms in a way, Mars did not fail to miss, she seemed not to care he was set on communicating his irritation.

He much liked that his queen showed no fear when he was angry.

And it was tremendously annoying.

"I would like, at least, my mother to have a say," she told him quietly.

"I will grant that."

Her face softened.

"The maids were doing as instructed," he went on. "They are not overly skilled, but we will only remain in these lodgings for a short time. Finding, hiring and training new to be in our employ would be a waste of time for the two days we will stay in this cottage. Further, it would take from other pursuits and you having this boon to be in your element and enjoy it. You won't be back here for a very long time. I will have a word with them. I will pay them from my own purse, something I should have done from the bloody beginning. And their loyalties should then revert to us. But in the end, this is your decision. If you don't feel safe around them, they will be dismissed."

"I was thinking of possibly giving Tril the run of them," she told him. "She'll keep them in line and watch them like a hawk."

"This is your decision, so it will be."

She studied him closely before asking, "How angry are you still?"

"Insanely."

"My darling king," she murmured, her eyes warm on him, her words treasured, even if her lips were quirking.

And suddenly, he was angry no more.

He uncrossed his arms, slid them around her and pulled her nearer.

Only then did Piccola dash down his chest to disappear in Silence's hair.

"What did she say to you that set this off?" she asked.

"She told me we were not to be intimate around the maids. That it was not done in this realm, for servants to see us abed."

Silence appeared baffled. "She came to tell *you* that?"

"Well, as you know, she didn't tell you, *bellezza*."

"He sent her to tell me that," she whispered.

"Sorry?"

"If she told me that, I would hesitate to call upon the maids when we were in that state. My father knows that. And as we have to eat and need wood and the like, we have need of the servants. Father also knows if I refused freer relations with you, it would hinder said relations on a variety of levels." She lifted one shoulder and murmured, "I hate to think this way, but I think the maids told him we were happy and enjoying each other's, erm...*company*, and for whatever reason, Father sent my mother to do something about it."

He did not think that was the case at all.

He knew it was.

"I do not think your mother is cunning enough to understand she could adhere to her husband's demands and thwart them at the same time by taking a different tack."

"I know you won't believe this, but I think my mother loves both Father and I, is torn between doing what is right for the both of us, and I think she selected you to discover the measure of the man who married her daughter, for you two do not know one another well. And as you are correct, she is not cunning, she felt she could still carry out Father's wishes either way."

"I did not read the same, my queen," he said carefully.

"Perhaps I'm wrong," she mumbled.

"But you hope you're right," he deduced.

She scrunched her nose and gave a small shrug.

At her scrunching her nose, Mars's good mood was restored.

Therefore, he grinned and bent to kiss that nose.

Her expression was even gentler when he lifted away.

"Whatever comes of this, continue to be wary of them, my love," he warned. "Both of them. No?"

She nodded.

"Go back to reading," he ordered. "I'll deal with the maids and speak with Tril."

"I can speak with Tril."

"You shared this book is one you're enjoying."

She did not reply.

He gave her a squeeze. "Enjoy it. I'll manage this issue, finish my work and join you after a while."

She nodded.

Mars bent to touch his mouth to hers, which was the only thing he allowed himself to do. If he tasted her, he'd have her on her back on the carpets and there would be no reading of books.

He had no idea how the Dellish felt about such a thing.

He also didn't care.

But Silence was enjoying her book.

*That*, he cared about.

Once he touched their lips, he put his to her hair before he began to let her go.

Clearly needing a change of scenery, Piccola leapt to him as he did.

"I'll take her," Silence said, lifting a hand.

"She can accompany me on my errands," he murmured, lifting a hand to stroke the tiny, furry back of the monkey now grasping his shirt as he moved away.

"Only you," he heard her whisper.

This made him turn before opening the door.

"Only me?" he inquired.

He saw she had not moved, and her eyes were on their pet before they lifted to his face.

"Only you would go to possibly sack, possibly employ three maids who were involved in a ludicrous conspiracy to destabilize a marriage then go about royal duties, all with a wee monkey in tow."

"When we have them, if our babes aren't toddling around the rugs underfoot in my study at the palace while I work, I will find this very upsetting."

Something moved over her face when he spoke those words.

Something of such power, it blasted across the room, struck him in the chest, and robbed him of the ability to breathe.

Something of such importance, Mars knew he'd never forget the vision of Silence standing in that room wearing that grape-colored Dellish gown he did not like, but he liked it on her.

No.

He would not forget that vision of his wife for the rest of his life.

"You scared me," she said in a voice so low, he could almost not make out her words.

"Scared you?" he asked in much the same tone.

"At the Necropolis. In Fire City. When you were torturing those men. And during the attack. Your ferocity. The violence you displayed that seemed second nature."

Fucking hell.

"Silence," he whispered.

"It was terrifying."

He began to make a move toward her when she spoke again.

"My hands struck fire."

"Sorry?"

"During the attack on the palace. Elena did not save me from the man who was strangling me. She hadn't made it to me yet. I had my fingers around his wrists to pull them away, and he let go right before his hands burst into flame. I did that. I...I...it was *I* who did that. Elena arrived after and dispatched him, but I made his hands catch fire."

She grew silent.

Mars stared at her across the room, his hand now cupping the monkey at his chest, and he said nothing, waiting for her to go on, freely sharing her mysteries.

"I can disappear," she whispered this admission. "That night, in your bedchamber, when you discovered me, when you saw me, I was surprised, for when I do not wish to be seen, I can pull my shadow over me and no one will see me. This is how I could eavesdrop on King Wilmer, Queen Mercy and Carrington. This is how I went unseen at our wedding reception. You see through it, but no one else does, which I think is part of our destiny. It is my magic. It has always been my magic. And it is my secret. No one knows. Not True. Not even Tril. Not anyone, but you. But the...the...fire thing has never been my magic. Until I had you."

His wife again grew silent.

When she did not break it as she had before, he asked, "Are you done?"

She nodded.

She then shook her head.

"I can also...*hear* very well. Better than anyone I know. This is also how I knew Wilmer and Mercy and Carrington were speaking about True."

And when she again spoke no more, he asked gently, "Now, are you done, my queen?"

"I...I...you cannot...cannot know..." she trailed off, wet in her eyes.

Mars did not prompt her.

It took everything he had, but he gave her the time she needed to offer more treasure.

As a tear slid down her cheek, she carried on.

"I have never, except True, and as best she could, Tril, had anyone who looked after me."

His chest was burning.

His throat was burning.

It felt like every inch of his skin was burning.

"And...and...I am happy to be taking the pennyrium so we have time together and we will be at our greatest strength to defeat the Beast, but I cannot wait to give you children, Mars. The way you speak of the family we will have, I cannot wait to watch you be a father to our babes. To...to share my love for them with you. I find I long for something I never longed for. Something I didn't know I could have, until you spoke of it. I long for what I will have with you. I long for the life I will build with you. I want it to happen yesterday, which means for the first time in my life, I am happy in my now, but even so, I cannot wait for the morrow."

"Come here," he growled and watched her body start. "Come, my wife.

Take Piccola. Call Tril. Give her our pet and tell her to deal with the maids as she sees fit. I'll meet you in our chamber."

"Mars—"

"You will do this, Silence, or the maids will be sequestered for hours and Piccola will watch our activities without supervision, and she's a good girl, but she is not yet fully trained, so who knows what she'll get up to."

She hesitated no further, moved to him and took their monkey.

She did not move away for he caught her with one hand on her neck.

His queen lifted wet eyes to his.

He would never wish tears in her eyes.

But for this, this emotion she shared with him, this honesty.

He cherished them.

He forced his voice to a whisper when what he wanted to do was howl with elation.

"We will discuss all of this in much more depth after I reward you for giving yourself fully to me and after I thoroughly celebrate being given that precious gift."

Her hand fell light at the base of his throat as she breathed, "My love."

He needed her to do as told or things would swiftly get out of hand.

"Do as I bid, Silence, or be carried from the room."

"I quite liked it when you carried me from the room," she admitted softly.

And thus, she was carried from the room.

The maids were sequestered longer than he'd intended.

And Tril did not give that first damn at being summoned to their chamber while Silence was lounging abed, spent, and Mars stood at the door in nothing but his *ante* pants.

Indeed, Tril was as she had been for the last several days.

Beaming.

And her eyes didn't once fall to his chest.

Piccola chirruped her dissatisfaction at being taken from her mama and papa.

But Mars would have her brought back.

Later.

He'd learned his wife was docile for a period of time after an orgasm which meant he could play with her at will without having his control tested as his little wanton sought to get her fill.

And it was after he spent a good deal of time doing that, when his Silence was nearly catatonic in his arms, that he murmured, "We will discuss the Necropolis and why that is the way in Firenze at another time. Now, *mia piccolina*, tell me about your shadow."

She snuggled deeper, rubbing her face on his chest, and he felt the scrape of her marital chain on his skin there, an eloquent statement that its meaning in their marriage had been fully realized.

She did this before she tipped her head back, aimed a contented smile at him—and further sharing the priceless gift of her secrets—she told him all about her shadow.

# 69

## THE KISS

***Prince True***
*The Antlers Pub and Inn, Five Miles from the Lights*
Wodell

"We've got men on him all the time," Bram reported as True, Farah and all his men sat around a table at the back of the pub over a late luncheon of sandwiches made of hearty slabs of beef with their juices soaking into the thick-cut bread.

This was accompanied by a strong ale, which True thought was needed for this discussion.

"We've had men search his office, his rooms, others following him," Florian took up the thread. "They've found nothing. They've seen nothing."

As True and Bram had just received birds from True's mother, pressing him to return home, the men were reporting on efforts with Carrington, about which they received daily dispatches from the capital.

"He cannot possibly be acting in his own interests," True noted. "He's subverting my father's reign. With this new tax, now he's targeting Farah and me. It seems his intent is to weaken the power structure of the realm. He can't be doing this just for jollies."

"We've had a man loyal to you intercept all his missives and read them before sending them on. We've had men following him wherever he goes. He says nothing of concern, he meets with no one suspect," Wallace said.

"You are sure they've not been noticed in these endeavors," True inquired.

Wallace shook his head. "Not a chance. They're skilled, True. You know that."

He did. It would be a great surprise if the men chosen for these tasks were noted in carrying them out.

"And Carrington's secretary?" True queried.

Wallace shook his head. "The same."

True turned his attention to Luther. "His history?"

But it wasn't Luther who answered, it was Alfie.

"He studied at the university in Go'Doan, True."

True locked eyes with his captain.

"They were behind the attack in Fire City," Alfie reminded him. "And our men in the Thicket report G'Seph disappeared somewhere along the journey from Firenze. This cannot be a coincidence."

No, it could not.

And on the scale of where someone stood regarding the Go'Doan, Alfie had always been firmly planted in the zone where he did not trust them.

Not in the least.

"And he studied there," Alfie repeated. "There's nothing of concern in his background, except that. He has a mistress who he rarely visits who is paid well for services she doesn't often render. She lives in apartments even more palatial than most accommodation at Birchlire. But this only shares your father pays him too much. As you know, we have a man on her as well, and she enjoys shopping and lunching with friends, evenings at the theater to show off the gowns she's able to purchase. Nothing in her communications, activities or acquaintances causes alarm. Other than that, the man spends his time with his nose up your father's arse and treating his secretary like a dog."

Alfie leaned toward True and finished.

"He is being circumspect now, after the attack in Firenze. This is why we're finding nothing. But whatever his agenda, it stems from his link to Go'Doan, True. I'd stake my life on it."

These words, from Alfie, carried a lot of weight.

Therefore, True nodded to his captain and looked around the table, asking, "We have men on the temples?"

"Yes," Bram answered. "Business as usual. Thus, I'd like to send them in for a search. Though to do that, the edict has to come from your father. That said, this is risky. If it's done overtly, they would be aware we're onto them. If it's done covertly and the crown doesn't know about it, and our man was discovered, we'd be hard-pressed to explain why we acted without the knowledge of the king. Thus, putting the realm at odds with a nation of priests who most think are harmless, but others subscribe to their beliefs."

"And what about Gal and Brix?" True pressed on. "Any word from them? Could they infiltrate the Go'Doan temples?"

"No word. According to a pixie sent by Baldrick, they're 'deep under,'" Wallace shared. "I don't know what that means, but I can send a message to Baldrick, see if he can get one to them and set them on the temples."

True nodded his acceptance of that suggestion, drew in breath, let it out, and sat back.

It was glaringly apparent with his recent proclamation his father would not wish to entertain a request to search the temples from True. Even if the attack in Firenze made it expedient to do so, and the Go'Doan would understand why it was done, and if they had nothing to hide, they would have no protest.

True didn't endorse the idea that every temple and every priest in every realm should be under suspicion, watched or searched.

But that didn't mean questions shouldn't be asked.

And those questions should have been asked in Wodell already.

They had not.

Carrington had used Cassius's regency to his advantage and True had inadvertently fallen in with this plan by taking this journey for Farah.

He would not change his decision about the journey for Farah.

He'd change the advisor his father trusted.

True had never been "in," as such, with his father.

Now it was clear, in very important ways, he'd been cast out at the worst possible time for his realm.

"We have a much more immediate problem," Florian put in. "This gold being demanded, ostensibly for your wedding, is not being taken very well. The pixies report there was a great deal of excitement in the city. Now there's a great deal of grumbling. So much, it could turn and quickly. Against you."

"Taxes having been raised steadily every year over the last five years, though income has not seen the same increases," Luther added. "This addition to royal levies that had already increased this year, I'm not surprised there's grumbling."

"For the first time in your life, you have an image problem," Wallace said to True. "And the first time in Carrington's career, he's made a subtle strategic move that will have long-lasting ramifications that will strengthen his hold on your father and his control of the throne, all this accomplished by weakening you."

"And we know he's raising an army," True stated.

"Quietly, but yes," Bram replied. "He's dispatched recruiters across the realm, and they are at work. And it's my understanding through missives from the queen that the king knows this and sanctions it."

Bloody hell.

He had definitely been cast out.

As had, it would seem, his mother.

"You need to be regent," Alfie stated quietly.

"I need to form a parliament," True replied.

He felt Farah stiffen beside him.

"That would be impossible, unless you're regent," Alfie returned.

Alfie was correct, as his friend had been correct in the many times they'd discussed this, even before Cassius became regent.

"You wish to give up your rule?" Farah asked softly.

He looked to his intended. "I wish to give my people a say in how their land and their lives are governed. I would be the final voice. If I felt what was decided was not for the good of the realm, I would have last right of refusal. And my name would need to be signed to any law, tax, treaty, proclamation for it to be valid and put into effect. But that would not happen unless my people have spoken through their representatives about how it should be done."

"That would mean it could take ages for decisions to be made, and it might even be mayhem, no?" she replied.

"It is better than an entire country at the whims of whatever personality the gods bestow on their monarch and whatever choices he makes for his advisors," he said.

She held his gaze for a long moment before she whispered, "You are a marvel, Prince True of Wodell."

He felt relief she was not against this idea.

In fact, it appeared she championed it.

"He is a man of his people," Alfie declared.

"Not in the now," Bram noted. "He's a man who's besotted with his Firenz bride and wishes to give her a lavish wedding to be paid for by every thatcher, blacksmith, wealthy orchard owner and shepherd. This is a blow, True. And you need a swift recovery. Your mother expects a good deal from you, but I agree with her in this stead. Carrington has taken advantage of your absence. You need to go home."

"Do you have coin?" Farah asked abruptly.

True turned to her. "Pardon?"

"Of your own. Do you have currency of your own?"

His men grew alert at this question but True simply answered, "My maternal grandmother left me an inheritance. I've not needed to touch it. So yes, I have coin."

"Is it substantial?" she inquired.

"Why do you ask, milady?" Alfie demanded in a low tone, using the words "milady" to express he didn't like her line of questioning, for she'd long since insisted they all call her Farah, and they'd long since acquiesced to this demand.

She looked to Alfie. "Because regardless what that proclamation said, it is signed by the king. It might infer that it is True demanding this new levy at his fancy and the whim of a betrothed who desires an extravagant wedding, but it was *signed by the king*."

She turned again to True and spoke on.

"You are known, and you are loved. This proclamation has to come as a surprise not to some, but to many. If *you* do something that is very much *you*, such as give a substantial donation to an orphanage, or a hospital, or a school, and declare it a gift in celebration of your wedding, this will *not* be a surprise. It will be very in character of Prince True of Wodell. King Wilmer taxes his people. Prince True gives from the heart to his land."

"Bloody hell, that's genius," Wallace muttered.

And bloody *hell*.

It was.

Farah glanced about all of them. "Further, I am naught but a citizen of my realm, but I would expect my monarch has the intelligence to acquire staff to manage his resources so that a wedding ceremony, no matter how lavish, would not require an extra duty." Her attention returned to True. "I would ask, in the case of an additional tax, where the rest of my taxes went. Especially if where they went is not readily apparent. That would not be attributed to you. That would be an assessment of the decisions and supervision of the king and his advisors."

True grinned at her.

She was not quite finished.

"Furthermore," Farah continued, "of note is the fact that you're wedding a woman from a realm with whom this one does not get along. This could have been an issue, more so after this tax was proclaimed. But I can request Mars makes his own substantial donation, perhaps to someplace in the Arbor, a library or museum that is oft-visited or otherwise cherished by Silence. Mars making this donation in his new queen's name, an alliance through marriage with Firenze would not seem such a bad thing. The king of Wodell will be seen as taxing, the prince and his beloved cousin with their Firenz spouses have the best of the realm deep in their hearts and are willing to act on that."

"Fucking brilliant," Bram said. "I'll send a bird to Mars immediately."

"I'm not done," Farah told him quietly.

Bram didn't move.

None of them did.

She turned again to True.

"And we need to invite real people to the wedding, True. You have the charmed folk represented. But who you are, what you represent, we need more. A trusted soldier you know and his family. A tutor from your childhood you particularly liked. A servant of the castle who is close to you, someone day to day who gives their loyalty to the crown, and to you, in ways otherwise unseen, and not often honored."

She scooted closer and carried on.

"None of these invitations will be questioned or considered strategic. If they have touched your life, it is not out of character for you that they have your regard and for you to make a point of that on what is considered by the Dellish the most important union you'll make in your life. This will be a small gesture, but I have no doubt it will be noted and spoken about."

She was absolutely correct.

It would.

And that would spread wide.

"In this case, it's advantageous," she continued. "But in truth, if True Axelsson was being wed, and not Prince True, you would have done this from the beginning. In fact, these would be the first invitations, outside family, that you'd send."

He loved it that she knew that about him.

Farah reached out and wrapped her fingers over his hand where it rested on the table.

"You are the prince of the people, True," she said. "You wish to give them a voice in the governing of their land. Start that by having them represented at your wedding. I do not think this will alleviate their indignation at having to pay further taxes. But I think it will definitely state who you are and what you're about and even might be considered your response to your father's decision to require more of his people without giving anything in return. He has foolishly, for reasons I don't understand, not made it known what boons have been negotiated for Wodell in Firenze. But *you* have. He's taxing, but you are making arrangements to put *more* coin in their purses at the same time giving generously and honoring those who serve the realm. Your father can't counter that. And should you wish to press regency, he might even be pushed into the position by the will of the people to accept it."

"How is it that you are this perfect?" True asked the instant she stopped speaking, and when he did, he watched her eyes grow large. "Beautiful, gregarious, kind *and* sage," he murmured. "You are an impossibility."

He saw the blush rise on her cheeks and was enjoying it when Alfie interrupted.

"We send birds now, to the queen and to Mars. As well as Bram riding immediately with the fullness of our message and making sure it's carried out. We follow on the morrow and make haste to Notting Thicket. Once there, you and Farah are seen in the city, not only attending the opera, but also visiting an orphanage."

True turned his hand, captured Farah's fingers and brought them down to his thigh as he nodded to Alfie then to Bram.

"Do it," he bid.

Bram was out of his chair instantly.

"Your mother might not like having to find extra chairs for extra guests in your temple," Farah murmured.

"Mother will do what's best for the realm," he replied, for he knew she would.

She always did.

What was best for Wodell.

And what was best for True.

He looked to Alfie. "Carrington's secretary."

"Yes?" Alfie asked.

"If Carrington does not treat him well, could we possibly recruit him in our endeavors?"

Alfie nodded. "I'll grab Bram before he rides. He'll need to attempt that personally."

True lifted his chin. "Before you go, give him these names to give to my mother to add to the wedding list."

True recited the names as Alfie listened. True knew his captain needed to take nothing down. He'd remember.

His friend might not be jocular and talkative, but he was observant, exceptionally loyal and wickedly smart.

Alfie left their company.

"I'll order us more ale," Luther muttered, and got up to do that.

"If we leave on the morrow, I have a lass to say farewell to, so I best get on doing that," Florian shared, and then he was gone.

"And I best get on that message to Baldrick," Wallace declared, and on a grin, he left Farah and True alone at the table.

"I hope the Lights play tonight," Farah said. "We have not had luck while we've been here, and although this village is very charming and the people in it more so, it would make me sad we came here but have to leave without seeing the Lights."

Although he agreed with her, True did not comment on that.

He said, "You think I am a marvel, but you are a wonder."

Her head gave a slight jerk before she asked, "Hardly. Why would you say such a thing?"

"Because upon meeting you, and with every moment I've shared with you since, I have come more and more to know down to my soul you will be the perfect wife for me."

Her lips parted, and a look of astonishment moved over her features.

However, he was not finished.

"But now I have learned you will also be the perfect queen for my country. That is not more important, but as you know well, it means a great deal to me."

She looked away, but he still noted her eyes grew bright with tears.

True allowed her the limited privacy she could have but did it rubbing his thumb over her knuckles.

When she looked back, she had control, but he could see it cost her.

"I wish my mother had been able to know you better before we lost her," she said softly.

"And as you know, I wish I'd been able to know her better as well," he replied.

"She would be very happy that destiny choose you for me."

"She would not be alone."

Farah pressed her lips together to again gain control.

True continued stroking her knuckles.

When she appeared to be ready, he offered, "Do you wish another sandwich?"

"I will not be able to eat again for a week after the last."

"I'll accept that as a no."

She smiled.

He leaned closer to her. "We'll come back and see the Lights, darling. We'll then bring our children to see the Lights. I will make sure you won't miss them. That is a promise."

Her face grew soft and she nodded.

Her eyes then fell to his mouth.

And thus, he sat back, for he was ready for that, but he feared she wasn't.

Not yet.

She turned her attention to the table, her jaw working, and he knew she thought he was wrong.

Perhaps going home to the Thicket was a good thing. There would be much more to take her attention, more to keep her mind off her loss, and distractions for them both so neither did anything earlier than was healthy for her state of mind.

"Shall we walk off our sandwiches by getting some of that taffy from the candy maker down the lane?" he suggested. "She would never admit it out loud, but Mother loves that taffy and will be glad we brought some to her."

Farah drew breath into her nose, turned to him and smiled brightly. "Yes, and more chocolate custard swirls."

"I thought you were full up."

"They're for the men," she told him.

"That was what you said last time, before eating three of them and we had to go back and buy more so two men weren't left without."

"It's only four doors down the lane, True, it's hardly trekking back to Firenze to buy some *cioccolato al caffé*."

He stood, helping her out of her chair as he did, murmuring, "You speak of this *cioccolato al caffé* often and I'm wondering why you did not offer it to me all that time I was in in Firenze with you."

"I'll remind you, True, we'd just met, and it's safe to say you had a number of other things going on."

He led them toward the door where her cloak and his mantle were hanging on hooks, saying, "It sounds like this *cioccolato al caffé* was worth an interruption."

She let out an exasperated sigh. "I'll make some for you. Mama taught me how."

"And that I will look forward to, my beloved, for I can just imagine how the kitchen staff at Birchlire Castle will react to my bride taking over while I sit a stool like a besotted fool, watching her make candy."

She shot him a grin.

He returned it reaching for her cloak.

"Oi!" Luther shouted, and they both looked his way to see he had the handles of four tankards of ale in his grasp. "Where did everyone go? I got us ales."

"We're getting taffy for the queen. And chocolate custard swirls. We'll be back in a bit," Farah told him, sharing this bit of news loudly with an avid audience of the pub luncheon crowd.

"Get me three swirls," Luther ordered, not like he was talking to his future queen, like he was ordering about his little sister.

"Will do," Farah said, latching her cloak that True had settled on her shoulders at her throat.

"We'll order more ale in when we return," True told Luther, dipping his head to the tankards. "You can have those."

"Don't mind if I do," Luther replied, moving back to the table they vacated.

True clasped his mantle, took his lady's arm and led her to candy and custard swirls.

One half day where they were allowed to be mostly just True and Farah and their friends.

Then it would be back to reality.

It was not a great deal of time.

But he intended to make the most of it.

"TRUE," Farah called urgently, shaking his shoulder.

He was up and out of bed in a trice, his sword, which always rested against his night table, in his hand, his pulse spiking, his skin tightening.

"By the gods, I'm so sorry," she whispered.

He was scanning the room by the dim light coming from the fireplace, his heart now racing, searching for a threat.

He flinched when he felt her hand on his back and heard her soothing voice.

"True, all is well. It's just fine. I'm so *so* sorry. I just woke you because... look, *caro*. To the window."

Noting no one was in the room but them, he drew in a deep breath and turned his head to the window.

Around the drapes, green light was dancing.

"I think the skies have cooperated," she finished.

He strode over to the window and peered around the side of the curtain.

There were trees in the way, but it couldn't be hidden.

The Lights were dancing.

He turned to his betrothed.

"You're right," he shared. "Hurry, my love. Dress. Let us go."

She was out of bed almost as quickly as he'd left it moments ago.

"Dress warm," he warned.

"I've no other choice. All my gowns weigh twenty pounds," she replied from behind the screen.

This was an utter lie.

He still smiled.

As had become their way, he dressed in the room, she behind the screen.

She came out when she needed him to tighten her laces, something he did.

They then both sat on the bed, side by side, to put on their boots.

He helped her with her cloak before he swung on his mantle.

She was pulling on her gloves as they moved into the hall.

He immediately started toward Alfie's room.

She caught his arm.

He looked down at her.

"Just us," she whispered.

"Farah—"

"Please, witnessing this magic?" she beseeched. "Just us, True."

He looked into her topaz eyes.

He then gave in.

He guided her to the stairs, down them, and through the still-crowded pub, both of them calling greetings as they went.

He flipped a silver coin to the stable boy, which was so far above the boy's normal token, his eyes nearly popped out of his head when he caught it.

It was nowhere near the worth of gold, but it'd likely keep his family fed for a week.

"Just the prince's steed, please," Farah called after him then looked up at True. "I'd like to ride with you. It would be warmer."

It would be hell, her arse in his crotch for five miles.

He thought this.

He said, "If that is your wish, sweets."

When the boy had brought a saddled Majesty, True swung up and then leaned low to the side to catch Farah about the waist and pull her up before him.

He dipped his chin when the boy gave a bow, then he clicked his teeth, dug the heels of his boots into the sides of his mount, and they galloped out of the stables.

Majesty's hooves clattered on the cobbles as the wind blew Farah's soft hair in his face, its fragrance stirring him deeply.

To combat that, he bent into her, pressing his cheek against the side of her head.

They left the village and took the winding path that led up the wooded hill, and it seemed with every strike of Majesty's hooves, the air lit more brightly about them.

They were but a mile away when he heard Farah's joyous laugh.

"What is funny?" he asked in her ear.

"Nothing," she answered, turning her head and catching his eye, also catching his heart with the joy he saw in hers. "Nothing. It's just so beautiful, I cannot process it. All I can do is laugh."

She looked forward and tipped her head back to better see the streaks of lights that could be seen through the tops of the trees, swirling in the sky.

They were making the clearing when the lights that came from the magic of the sprites could be seen in the trees, globes glowing golden as the very air around them turned hues of pink, green, violet and blue, these last the hues that swirled in the night sky.

"By the gods, True, by the gods," Farah chanted before musical laughter erupted from her. "It is impossible!" she cried. "Such beauty."

True couldn't stop himself smiling as they made the top of the rise, the trees glowing, the skies glowing, the air glowing.

He had seen it several times before.

But gazing at it now with Farah in his arms, somehow it felt as if it was the first time he experienced the enormity of the beauty.

He also saw, with gratitude, that although the rise under the Lights could get crowded with onlookers, tonight there were only a few.

But the sprites were zinging here and there, holding court, showing off, their glistening wings that were bigger than their bodies sometimes the only thing to be seen.

He'd barely reined in Majesty when he lost hold of Farah as she slid off.

True dismounted only to see her head tipped all the way back and she was whirling, arms out, like a dance, but not.

"By the gods, True!" she exclaimed to the skies. "*Such beauty.*"

He crossed his arms on his chest, his eyes never leaving her, and whole-heartedly agreed.

"This land!" she cried. "This land is magic from rich soil to regal trees to the very *heavens.*"

True noted some of the sprites had stopped zinging in order to watch Farah, and some of the others that were there for the Lights did the same.

She was not behaving in a queenly manner, not even the manner of a princess.

And he didn't give a good gods damn.

Suddenly, she stopped twirling and looked to him, "I never wish to leave here. Must we leave here?"

"I'm afraid in just over a week we're to be married, my love, and that's happening in a temple in Notting Thicket," he reminded her. "I think the guests who are traveling from all over Wodell would be cross if we didn't show up."

"You can get married here, Your Grace!" someone shouted. "We'll be happy to stand as witness!"

True looked in that direction to see a man, a woman, and two children of about twelve and ten, all of them smiling at him and Farah, and he shouted back, "I'm very much looking forward to seeing my bride in whatever gown she'll be wearing."

"'Twill be the most beautiful bride in history, I'll wager," the wife called.

Farah clapped her hands together, leaned forward for some reason to tuck them between her knees, before she called back, "Thank you! That is so kind!"

"You are a great beauty, Lady Farah!" the woman yelled.

Farah righted and threw her arms out to her sides.

"And *you* are most lovely and demonstrating why my prince and I can *never* leave this *glorious place*," Farah yelled back.

Watching this byplay, True felt something happen in his stomach he did not recognize.

"There's a cottage for sale at the end of Tuck Lane," another man across the rise shared loudly.

"Do not tell me that," Farah returned, swinging his way. "We must be away to the Thicket tomorrow and if I know of a cottage that could be ours, I'll chain my prince there, and since he'll be noted missing, I'll end up in a cell in the capital for princenapping, not in a temple wearing a heavy gown getting married."

That feeling surged up True's gullet.

"I'm not sure you can princenap your own prince," another woman called.

"I'm not sure I want to find out, no matter how good the beef sandwiches are at The Antlers," Farah replied.

And then it happened.

True burst out laughing.

It was not simply an expression of humor.

It was something more.

Something deeper.

Something preposterous.

Absurd.

Outlandish.

Something *remarkable*.

She was just being...

Funny.

That was it.

She had no care in that moment.

So *he* had no care in that moment.

He had no thought.

He just found his Farah funny.

And was happy she was happy.

As if sensing a difference in the timbre of his laugh, Farah whirled to look up at him with eyes that made it seem his amusement was even more marvelous than the beauty that illuminated all around.

"Princenapping?" he asked on a snicker, and he was uncertain he'd ever snickered in his life.

She smiled tentatively and noted, "I'm relatively certain that's illegal."

His waning laughter waxed.

She moved to him and took both of his hands.

He watched her, chuckling.

When his hilarity had begun to fade, she said softly, "You are the most handsome man I have ever known, but there is no compare when you're laughing like that."

He pulled one hand from hers, ran the backs of his fingers down her cheek, and smiling at her, said, "I'm delighted I please you."

"You do. From the beginning."

Any amusement died.

"Farah," he whispered.

"Please, I know you don't wish to, but here, in this place, please, in all your kindnesses to me, I must beg one more. Please, True, kiss me. Not a press of the lips. *Really* kiss me."

At her words, his amusement wasn't even remembered.

"You don't think I wish to kiss you?" he asked.

She looked away.

"Look at me," he demanded.

She turned her eyes again to him.

"I wish to kiss you," he told her.

She shook her head. "You don't have to—"

He cupped her cheek and bent his face to hers.

"Farah, I've been fighting the desire to take you in my arms for so long, it's like it's become a new limb. An unwanted one. And unwieldy one. But one I have to bear."

She blinked up at him.

"But...Elena," she whispered.

"What about Elena?" he inquired.

"What about Elena?" she breathed, her eyes enormous, glowing more golden than the globes around them.

"That's what I asked."

"You're in love with her."

"I was. And then I met you."

She swayed into his body to such an extent, he had no choice but to do what he'd have done anyway.

He caught her in his arms.

She felt good there.

As always.

"Really?" she asked, not hiding her shock.

He was not shocked.

He was annoyed.

"I've hardly been hiding it."

"I thought you were...to be nice, well...faking it. For me."

Yes.

Annoyed.

"I would not fake finding you irresistibly attractive, incredibly good company, endearing, kind, intelligent—"

"All right," she interrupted him. "So why—?" she stopped herself speaking, slid a hand up his chest to his neck and whispered, "Oh, True."

She did not need him to tell her why he had held himself back.

"You needed time," he muttered.

"Thank you, *bello*. But please trust my assessment of my own self when I assure you, I don't need any more time."

"We have an audience."

She was coming up on her toes, pressing closer, her other hand gliding up his chest toward his neck.

"Who cares," she murmured.

"Farah."

"Kiss me."

Her hand had made his neck, and both were sliding into his hair, her fingers putting pressure on.

"Farah," he warned.

"*Kiss me*, True," she demanded.

Bloody hell.

He couldn't deny her.

And he couldn't deny himself.

Not with her being like this.

Not just with her being *her*.

Not any longer.

He kissed her.

The moment his lips touched hers, his entire body came alert and his gut started to warm.

When her lips parted under his, and his tongue instinctively snaked out, joining their mouths, his skin tightened all over his frame and his gut and chest started to burn.

He pulled her closer, angling his head, his tongue dancing with hers, not like it was the first time they danced, like they'd known the other for eternity.

Her smell.

Sublime.

Her taste.

Outstanding.

The feel of her soft body pressed to his.

Superlative.

It was the best kiss he'd ever had.

She was the taste of destiny.

Destiny mixed with love.

To end, it was bloody, fucking *fantastic*.

He broke their lips, murmuring, "Darling."

"I think maybe," she breathed, "if you do not wish to..." She didn't finish that. She concluded, "You should sleep in another room tonight."

It was good to know the kiss affected her the same.

And fucking frustrating as all hell.

"I think this wise."

"And *I* think it's important you know I do not mind if you wish to stay with me."

"We will join on our wedding night, Farah. That might not be the way of the Firenz, but it is the respect a Dellish man gives his future wife."

"You being Dellish is usually quite charming. Now it is not," she groused.

He grinned.

She narrowed her eyes at him and warned, "We will be kissing much on our way to Notting Thicket."

"That will make it difficult to make haste," he teased.

"Do not kiss me like that," she whispered, suddenly very serious. "Do not make me feel like this. Do not make me this happy, True Axelsson, and then take it away from me."

*This happy?*

He became serious too.

Deathly.

And he locked his arms about her and dropped his head so close, all he could see was her eyes.

"Never," he vowed.

Her hand still in his hair put pressure there.

So True made her happy again and he kissed his Farah, thoroughly.

So thoroughly, a cheer of encouragement filled the air as the Lights danced in the sky and the sprites zinged through the golden globes.

Prince True didn't hear it.

Because True Axelsson was finally kissing, *really* kissing, the woman he loved.

# 70

## THE CALL

*Lady Farah*
*Room above The Antlers Pub and Inn, Five Miles from the Lights*
WODELL

"Silence," I called into the air, feeling silly. "Silence, are you there?"

There was no reply, which I did not find surprising, but I found it frustrating.

I didn't have a good deal of time, True wished to be away and soon.

But I had to do this, and it had to be fast.

"Silence," I whispered urgently. "Can you hear me? Are you there?"

"Farah?"

Thank the gods.

"Silence," I answered. "Can you...?"

I trailed off when I saw a vision of her shimmering before me, slowly coming into focus.

What *wonder*.

"Faith!" she exclaimed. "Look at you. You're right there."

I smiled.

"What is this?" a deep voice that seemed as if it came through a tunnel could be heard and then a hazy arm could be seen and Silence, who had grown distinct, suddenly disappeared.

"Mars!" she snapped, and I could focus on her shimmering some five feet to the left from where she'd been.

She was standing, appearing to push against a hold and glaring up at something.

"What is this sorcery?" he demanded, and although I heard Mars's voice, and there was a large area close to Silence that was wavy, his frame was obscure.

"Farah is calling," Silence told him.

"I see nothing but sinister particles," he retorted.

"They're not sinister, they're *Farah*. I see her perfectly well," Silence returned.

"Well, I do not, thus you will leave this place."

"*Mars!*" she cried, now appearing to struggle. "It's Elena's magic. So we can talk to each other when we're far away. It is fine. I am safe. Go. Go on." She seemed to be pushing at something. "Go, Mars. It's girl time."

"I do not like this for I do not trust this so I shall *not* go. If you are so certain this is fine, then speak to my little sister. But if I do not have a good feeling about it, we will leave this place."

Mars.

Always protective.

"Silence," I called. "It's all right. Mars should probably hear this too."

"Hear what?" he demanded.

"You can hear me?" I asked.

"I can hear you, but I cannot see you," Mars answered. "And what I wish to hear is what you feel I should."

"She's right there," Silence informed him, pointing at me.

"I can see you looking at glittering air, wife, but I cannot see Farah."

"How odd," Silence murmured.

They were being adorable, something I never thought I'd think about Mars, and it made me very happy to witness...for the both of them.

But as happy as it made me, I did not have time for this.

"Please hold," I said. "I'm going to try Elena."

"For fuck's sake," Mars muttered.

I watched Silence roll her eyes at me.

I ignored that (but did it smiling) and called, "Elena. Elena, we must speak. Are you there?"

When nothing happened, Silence queried, "Should I try too?"

"Perhaps that would help," I told her.

We both called, and called, and when Mars was heard saying, "Bloody hell," Elena started to form.

"Farah, Silence?" she asked.

"What the fuck?"

Cassius.

"It's all right, Cass," Elena told him.

"Elena, you have Silence and I and, well, Mars. I have something you all need to know. Please hold while we try to raise Ha-Lah," I said to her.

"Bloody hell, why can I hear Farah coming from nowhere in your eyrie?" Cassius demanded.

"Just calm down, warrior, we have a link," Elena said to the indistinct figure hovering over her shoulder. "I'll call to Ha-Lah. I know what I'm doing," Elena said to me.

"Excellent," I replied.

She did that while Mars said, "Cassius."

"Gods, *Mars*?" Cassius replied.

"I am here, with my wife, staring at glittering air and talking to a nothing, feeling like a bloody fool," Mars told him.

"As am I," Cassius replied.

"Would you two be quiet, I can't concentrate," Elena snapped.

Silence started giggling.

"By Medusa!" Ha-Lah could be heard.

"What the hell?" Aramus could also be heard.

"Please, do not be alarmed," Elena stated quickly. "It is my craft. Farah is calling. She has something to tell all of us. And, as you should see, Ha-Lah, Silence, is also here."

"Wife, why am I hearing Elena's voice drifting about our cabin?" Aramus asked as Ha-Lah came fully into focus.

"She just told you," Ha-Lah answered, appearing to be sitting on a bed, but looking to the side at something. "It's her craft."

"Aramus, I'm here too," Cassius told him. "However that 'here' might be."

"I as well," Mars declared.

"Bloody hell," Aramus muttered.

"Would you men be quiet?" Elena demanded. "Farah has something to say." She looked between the women with an exasperated, "This is why I did not include the men in my spell. It's bad enough they are linked to us so we can hear them. I fear it would be worse if we could actually *see* them."

Silence giggled again, and I smiled.

"Is True well?" Aramus asked. "For I do not hear him."

"He is of good health, but he is not well, and I think he wishes to deal with this amongst his men, though Mars will be receiving a bird very short-ly," I reported.

"Talk," Cassius ordered.

"Carrington is raising an army," I told them.

"Damn," Cassius murmured.

"And the king has proclaimed a new tax for True and my wedding," I shared.

"Fuck," Mars muttered.

I suspected the message intended by this tax was not lost on anybody, so I did not get into that.

"And True and I are leaving imminently to make haste to Notting Thicket in an attempt to repair the damage. But I think we're going to need all of your help," I told them.

"What you need to be done will be done, little sister," Mars declared.

"It will be asking much of you, and as I have asked so much already—" I began.

"You've asked nothing," Mars stated. "What is it you need?"

"The bird will share, and I will further request that you make a dona-tion in Silence's name to some public service she enjoys in the Arbor."

"What a lovely idea," Silence murmured.

"It is," I agreed. "But it also needs to be done in a way it is known Silence is True's beloved cousin and the alliance between Wodell and Firenze will mean good things for the Dellish people."

"This will be done today," Mars replied.

Oh, but I loved my king.

"And you'll be asked to go to Notting Thicket—" I began.

"We leave on the morrow," Silence shared. "Queen Mercy has already requested we come."

Mercy, as I suspected, was no fool.

But I was glad, as well as astonished, she was thinking on the same lines as me.

"Excellent," I said. "But you'll need to be seen amongst the people."

"This will not be difficult. My bride wishes to show me her capital," Mars returned.

That gave me relief.

All right.

Onward.

"Alfie thinks Carrington is in cahoots with the Go'Doan," I informed them.

This was met with total silence.

Until Cassius asked bewilderingly, "What word is there from Chu?"

"Chu?" Elena inquired.

"He has made the Thicket," Mars answered Cassius. "And as he will be engaged in his duties, I will not be able to contact him for fear of such communication being noted which might mean he's discovered. But he will be in regular contact with me if he discovers anything."

"Chu?" Silence asked after Elena's query.

"I shall tell you later, *piccolina*," Mars murmured.

"For the rest of you," I butted in, "I need to request you cut your forays short and head to Notting Thicket with all due haste. From what I'm hearing, True will need allies, the more, the faster, the better."

"We're already on our way," Ha-Lah said, and when she continued, the smile on her face came through in her words. "And we bring dragons."

"Dragons?" Silence breathed.

"Men," Aramus boomed. "Frey Drakkar has heard word about the Beast and has come to our aid. We sail with him right now toward Notting Thicket. And he says the Dax of Korwahk and the king of Hawkvale are in route."

"You're joking," Cassius said.

"This is a boon," Mars added.

"Have you noticed it is *we* who have the link and it is *the males* who are doing most of the talking?" Elena asked tetchily.

"It is the way," Ha-Lah murmured.

"It is so lovely to see you, Ha-Lah," Silence said. "You have been missed."

"That is kind, Silence," Ha-Lah replied. "You have been missed too. Are you well?"

"Very!" Silence chirped, which made me, as well as Elena and Ha-Lah, smile.

"Farah?" Ha-Lah asked, her smile less bright when it came to me, and her voice was heavier.

"True and his men have been taking care of me," I told her quietly.

"For this, I am glad," she said softly.

"I am glad for this too," Mars put in, not softly.

"You seem happy," Elena noted to Ha-Lah.

Ha-Lah smiled a certain kind of smile.

Aramus could be heard grunting.

Enough said on that.

I started grinning again.

"There are things to do, are we done chatting?" Cassius asked.

"No one asked you to be in this conversation, Cass," Elena pointed out.

"Wodell is raising an army to thwart an alliance and wage war on one of my allies. Their king's counsellor is possibly colluding with the Go'Doan who were behind an attack on a palace *you* and *I* as well as *all our friends* had to take up swords to rout. And considering all of this, we have to make the decisions about whether or not to take our daughters into an uncertain situation, and my vote would be *hell no*. This means I'll have to argue with you about that and then tell the girls they aren't coming and deal with their tantrums. We don't have time to chat," Cassius returned.

"You finished that by assuming you'd get your way about the girls," Elena retorted.

"I will, for there's no way *in hell* I'm allowing our girls to go into an uncertain situation," Cassius shot back.

"They'll be devasted and we've already been separated from them for too long. Especially you and Aelia," Elena argued.

"Perhaps we can discuss this without an audience," Cassius suggested.

"Perhaps we can discuss this instead of using Melisse's treehome for alone time," Elena replied.

Well, it seemed things had advanced between those two, even if they'd stayed the same.

Something about that made me feel most pleased.

"I have a donation to make," Mars announced, then demanded, "Release my queen and myself from this summons."

"But I wish to chat, my husband," Silence said.

"As you wish," Mars murmured.

And that made me feel *most* pleased.

But I had to share, "I can't chat. They're packing the horses now and we must be away. I'm so sorry."

"It was lovely to see you and ascertain you are well, even if for a short time," Ha-Lah said.

"You as well," I replied.

"You *all* as well," Silence put in. "And when we meet again, I have so much to share. And I look forward to hearing about all of your adventures."

"I cannot wait," Elena said.

"Me either," Ha-Lah agreed.

"Until we meet again," I bid as farewell.

Silence waved.

Ha-Lah blew a kiss.
And Elena swept her arm in front of herself.
Then they were all gone.
My work was done.
Now it was time to head to the Thicket.

# 71

# THE DECISION

**Prince Cassius**
*The Queen's Palace*
THE ENCHANTMENTS

Some hours after that odd conversation with the destined others, and a long argument with his woman about the girls, Cassius was summoned.

Now he stood on the scrollwork rugs amongst the woven furniture of Ophelia's receiving room, staring unseeing at the carved panels that adorned her walls.

There was an embargo on any Nadirii goods in Airen. In fact, it was illegal even to own them and the penalties were severe if caught trying to smuggle them in from Wodell, Firenze or Go'Doan.

However, he had seen their artwork in his travels, and found it distinctive and attractive, but being amongst it these past days, he was glad that embargo would soon come to an end and that Nadirii beauty would be easily had throughout his land.

"Cassius," Ophelia said.

He turned, watched her walk down the stairs and did it keeping in check the impulse to move to assist her.

He dipped his head. "Your Grace."

She came to a stop at the foot of the stairs, most likely to rest, but appearing to do so in order to emphasize what she said next.

"You sleep by my daughter's side. You and your daughter break bread with she and hers. It is most unexpected, but it is also indisputable. You are my son. I believe it is time to call me Ophelia."

He dipped his head again.

She motioned to a davenport with a woven dome above it.

He moved there, even if he did not wish to sit in that contraption, as she walked to a hanging chair of the same shape.

She climbed into it.

He waited until she was settled before he sat at the edge of the cushion.

When she did not say anything, he did.

"You asked to speak with me without your daughter present, and I am here, but I must share, I'm not comfortable with her not."

Something moved over her face, a face that seemed to have aged years in the days they'd been there.

It was not hard to read it was relief.

What was hard was to realize she had shown that emotion so openly.

Ophelia was not one to share her thoughts in any way, unless it was intended.

"Also unexpected," she said quietly, "is how well you two suit."

Cassius did not respond.

She squared her shoulders and lifted her chin before she hit him with a verbal brick.

"I am dying, my son."

He had the unusual instinct to burst from his seat.

He did not.

"Ophelia—"

She waved her hand and spoke over him.

"There is nothing to do but plan for that eventuality."

"I think you should speak to your daughter. She was approached by a Go'Doan priest at Catrame Palace. She has—"

Ophelia nodded. "Elena discussed this medicine with one of our healers. And that healer, Joan, discussed it with me. I cannot say in this moment my trust in the Go'Doan is at its highest. But if Joan feels it is safe, I will take it. She's studying it now. But even if it is safe, it will not but perhaps prolong the inevitable."

"I find I have nothing to say," he replied. "Except this saddens me, for my princess, for your Sisterhood, for my daughter, who I would wish to know you better, and for myself, for you have my respect."

"Thank you, Cassius," she murmured. "And I did not ask you here to make you speak. I asked you here to request you listen. For I have made a decision and it's important that the Prince Regent of Airen, as well as the future husband of my daughter, is understanding of it, and supportive."

Cassius nodded.

"I will be naming Elena my successor."

Every inch of Cassius's body froze.

"It will be up to you," she went on, "and she, how you will rule different lands side by side."

"What you suggest is an impossibility," he said in a tone heavy with incredulity.

"What I have decided is an imperative."

"She will rule by my side," Cassius shared. "I will need her engaged. I will need her counsel. What we wish to achieve in Airen I cannot possibly foster without Elena's aid."

"You are a good man," she said softly, studying him contemplatively. "It is most odd, do you not think, how a strong and stalwart tree can grow from the seed of a gnarled and diseased one."

Cassius had no reply, but even if he had nothing to say, that didn't mean he had no feeling at hearing her words.

He did.

And it was a rare sense of pride, that this great queen would think this of him.

"What you do not understand is that she is quite like you in many ways," Ophelia carried on. "Especially her skill in selecting those she trusts. You need her to rule by your side, and she will be able to do that. She will not need you to rule by hers, but she'll need assistance. And she will find that in Hera and Jasmine, specifically Hera. As well as my lieutenants, primarily Melisse. The balance will be hard fought, but from what I know of my daughter, and what I see of you, in the end, it will be won."

"I see I will not be able to change your mind," Cass admitted. "And I mean no offense, but as difficult as this will be for my princess and I, I also see no alternative."

Ophelia gave a single nod, but said, "Serena will need a role, and as to that, I have not decided. Her last communication to me shared she allies with a Firenz Trusted to spy for that country, which caused such deep surprise in me, I cannot express it. So all I can do is hope that such change in all the realms has brought change in my eldest daughter and that I have time to read what that is and make the right decision for her future."

He could not imagine any change in Serena, but if Chu was affecting that, he was more of a miracle worker than Cassius thought.

"I urge you to take pains to stay well for as long as you can, Ophelia. As you know, we have no idea what we will face. War. The Beast. Go'Doan treachery. Which will come first, and what will come of it."

She gave a slight shrug. "I have the time I'll have."

"Your daughter needs you."

"I'll have the time I'll have, my son," she said quietly. "No more, no less. When the goddesses call to me, I cannot evade their summons. Now I need to know I have your support. But more, I need to know she will have it."

"For what it will be worth, you have it," he promised. "As will Elena."

Her head tipped to the side.

"These words," she whispered. "They surprise me. For a man of such skill and intellect, you do not know your own worth. I hope my daughter can help you find your way to understanding the magnitude of that."

Again, Cassius made no reply, but that feeling of pride came back.

"I have one other thing to discuss with you," she said.

"Please go on," Cassius bid.

"You must take Aelia and Theodora with you to Notting Thicket."

His princess being his princess and the future queen of another nation, he had no say. Only Elena could abdicate, if that was her wish, and he could not imagine, how she was in her realm, how clear her devotion was to it, that she would.

His daughter, and Theodora, he, and Elena, had the only say.

Therefore, he shook his head. "Elena and I have discussed this, and we're told there's much unrest—"

"They must not be in The Enchantments."

The way she spoke those words made Cassius's mouth snap shut.

"I do not know, I cannot say, but I do not like what I feel in the veil," she told him. "And I know one thing as a mother. No daughter is safer anywhere than with her parents."

"If you feel The Enchantments are in danger, we will not leave," he declared.

She shook her head.

"Wodell is on the precipice of greatness. The like Ares cultivated in Firenze, and Mars has continued to nurture. This must not be imperiled, for it is also on the precipice of ruin. It must be given every opportunity to fall the right way. And it goes without saying the plans for Airen must move forward. The Enchantments might be shaken, but we will survive."

"You understand if they don't, if *you* don't, I will have a woman and a daughter on my hands who will be inconsolable."

"Ah," she murmured.

"Ah?" he asked.

She smiled a small smile. "And there you will find your worth, Cassius, for this is wholly untrue. They will be, for they will be consoled by you."

Cassius felt these words like a punch in the chest, so much, they left him winded.

"I *will* be gone, Cassius, it may be weeks, it may be months, but it will happen. And now...now..." She drew in a delicate breath and released it. "Now I can go in peace, knowing I have left my Elena to you."

"Ophelia—"

"I am tired," she muttered, maneuvering out of her hanging chair.

She couldn't expect to leave it at that.

He stood. "Ophelia—"

She was moving slowly across the room, but she stopped and looked at him.

"When my babies were young, I taught them to read the cards," she whispered.

Her words, the look on her face, Cassius braced.

"Every morning as wee girls, they turned a card," she shared. "And I told them the meanings, day after day, until they could read them themselves and understand the omens."

"Elena does this still," he told her quietly.

Her face softened, her eyes grew sad, and she smiled.

"I turned the Dragon this morning," she told him.

He had no idea what that meant, but from her demeanor, she thought it was not good.

But he knew it was.

"And Frey Drakkar comes with dragons," he informed her.

"No." She shook her head. "The Dragon means fire, power..." She paused. "Endings."

Yes, she thought it was not good.

"And The Drakkar comes with dragons," he said through his teeth. "Bringing fire *and* power."

"So I turned another card," she went on as if he did not speak.

Cassius was silent.

"It was the Pegasus card. Astral travel. Flight." She held his gaze and finished, "Freedom."

"You're giving up," he accused.

"I'm giving over," she returned.

"Which is the same as giving up," he clipped.

"You know loss, my son, help her through it."

"Ophelia—"

He stopped speaking when suddenly, a tear raced down her cheek and the word she spoke was as weak as her visage.

"Please."

Cassius swallowed.

Then he declared, his voice gruff, "A great woman begot a woman who will be great."

"I find myself annoyed with you," she replied, "for I was ready, with no regrets, and now I am not quite ready, for I know regret, and this is that I will not know my son."

Another punch in the chest.

"Your granddaughters will know you as if you supped with us nightly," he swore.

"And that regret strengthens."

Cassius fell quiet.

"You will live with love and you will die with love, that is my gift to you, my son," she whispered.

"It will be cherished, and it will be protected, that is my promise to you, my mother," he vowed.

She stared right in his eyes, the weakness in hers gone, all he saw was strength.

And then she said, "I'm counting on that."

# 72

## THE DUO

***Princess Serena***
*In an Alley, Outside the Go'Doan Temple, Notting Thicket*
WODELL

Serena watched Chu run down the narrow alleyway, leap toward the wall, land halfway up it, press off it with his foot, and fly across to the wall opposite, reaching out to catch a beam under a roof.

She did this thinking she must ask him to teach her that leaping thing.

She then watched him swing from the beam until he'd rotated over it, his body disappearing under the eaves.

For her part, she was crouching under a moldy, holey blanket, the edge pulled well over her forehead. However, her visage could remain hidden and she could still see beyond it with her head dipped, looking out from under her brows.

They both stayed in place as the minutes dragged on, and not many people moved by at this time in the eve.

She was patient.

Not because it would please her Master (all right, partly because of that).

Not because it would please Chu (though it was partly because of that too).

But because this spy business was *everything.*

"Zsst, zsst," she heard Chu's low signal.

She adjusted her place, her gaze, and saw them coming down the alley in the white robes and golden belts of the Go'Doan.

She positioned, kept the blanket about her, and shuffled out when they got close.

"A piece for a pauper," she muttered, affecting the Dellish accent to hide her Nadirii birth, and keeping her head ducked under the blanket.

"Begone, woman," one of the priests spat, kicking out at her with his foot.

*So much for their god Go'Vicee, who demanded service,* she thought, avoiding his kick, staying low, and maneuvering around him, pulling at his robe, as was her directive.

This was to get their attention, and keep it, so that Chu could drop down in that utterly silent, stealthy, remarkably appealing way of his, whereupon he would pick from their robes whatever they carried and be away before they even knew he was there.

"A piece for pauper who has not eaten in a week," she begged.

The one who had addressed her stopped, turned, aimed a kick that she allowed to land, expelling a surprised and pained, "*Oof,*" for the arsehole packed some power.

"*Begone, bitch,*" he hissed.

She crawled back toward him, grasping the hems of his robes, beginning to chant, "Piece for a pauper, piece for a pauper..."

But she barely got that out before Chu ruined their ploy by dropping soundlessly from the eaves, taking the priest who had kicked her by the head, and slamming it viciously into the stone wall.

He fell unconscious to the cobbles as the other one started to whirl, saying, "What on—?"

That priest got no more out as his head was slammed into the opposite wall and he dropped, out cold, to the ground.

Chu swiftly started searching the folds of the priest's robes as Serena took her feet, dashing off the blanket and pressing it into a ball, snapping under her breath, "That was practical, but hardly our plan, Chu."

He tipped his head back to look up at her from his squat, and she saw his face.

Therefore, she fell quiet.

He found nothing of worth on the one priest, but he took his purse, she knew, so this would appear as a robbery, and not what it was.

He then moved quickly to the other, searched him, and she saw him take some missives bound together with silver string.

Silver was not the color of Go'Doan.

Gold was.

A frisson slid over her skin.

The letters disappeared in Chu's cloak, along with both priests' purses, and before she could say anything, he had her hand and was dragging her down the alley.

She decided to remain quiet as he pulled her out of that lane, down a wider road, into a narrower passageway, and finally he shoved her under the lintel of an unlit doorway.

"You might want to give me a warning if you're going to change...*ho!*" She ended on a cry as he shoved up the skirts of the tatty Dellish gown she wore as a disguise.

"Silence," he bit.

She said nothing as he continued to push up the skirts, his actions not meant to be titillating, and he kept pushing, even the loose bodice of the too-large dress, until he exposed what he wished to expose.

He then bent to the side and studied her ribs.

"Chu," she whispered as what he was doing penetrated. "I am all right," she promised quietly.

He straightened abruptly while dropping her skirts and catching her gaze.

"He kicked you," he ground out.

"I am all right," she repeated.

"He called you a bitch."

Dear goddess.

She moved closer to him, feeling awkward, not understanding what her instincts were saying and how her body was complying.

Only knowing in her soul it was right.

She then wrapped her fingers around the side of his neck and squeezed, saying firmly, "Chu, I am *all right*."

He scowled into her face.

"We will not be able to gather the information needed if you attack every person who might harm me," she told him.

"There was no 'might' about that, Serena, he *kicked you*."

"Shh," she hushed, stroking his skin with her thumb. "I am fine, my Master."

He relaxed at that.

"And you really can't be going about smashing Go'Doan heads into walls," she told him. "Or we'll be found out in a flash."

"Those weren't Go'Doan."

She blinked.

"What?"

"Those weren't Go'Doan," he repeated. "There is faith in that religion. The conspirators might have earned their robes, but they are not of that religion, no matter what they say. A zealot is not holy, except in the sense he has wholly lost his way."

"You're annoying when you're being wise," she muttered.

He grinned at her.

And something fluttered in her belly.

Good goddess.

What was happening to her?

Then he took her hand again and they were snaking through the shadows on silent feet until they made their lodgings.

He opened the door and pulled her in, locking the door behind her.

She tossed the blanket aside and went direct to the banked fire to stir it, for they were nowhere near Birchlire Castle or the luxuries it provided, it was bloody cold, and the stone needed repointed for she would vow she felt the wind sweeping through that place.

Thank the goddess Chu slept practically on top of her or she would have frozen to death.

Still, she was demanding they put blankets up over the walls to keep the draught out if they had to stay here much longer.

He swept off his cloak and lit some lanterns. She pulled a slab of meat and a cake of cheese out of the larder.

They sat at the rickety table close to the fire, and they did this side by side as he threw the coin pouches and missives on the table.

They both ignored the pouches.

"Silver?" she asked.

"The Rising?" he asked in return.

She shrugged, for all they'd taken off priests they had hit thus far had come to nothing.

Chu reached for the missives, untied them and they saw there were only two.

He broke the seal on the first and, heads together, they read,

> *Instruct C to continue efforts with W. Recent plan is working. Unrest brewing. The brothers have made FC. New strategy commencing there. But they have been told to hold until after we AM.*

"C, Carrington. W, Wilmer," Serena said. "FC, Fire City? I have no idea about AM."

When Chu didn't reply, she turned her gaze to him to see him studying her.

"You decipher that in but a second?" he asked.

"It isn't hard," she replied, feeling a strange warmth hit her cheeks.

"No, I would have gotten it as well, but not in but a second."

She had no idea how to respond, so she didn't.

She looked away and urged, "The next."

Chu set the first aside and broke the seal on the second, which was short enough to be sent by bird.

They read,

> *C reports M a growing threat. Plan to commence has been ordered. LLTR.*

"C, Carrington. M, Mercy. Long live The Rising," she whispered.

"Fuck," he muttered.

She again looked to him. "Mercy's a threat?"

He was still studying the note. "I do not know."

"How can she be a threat?" Serena asked, her eyes straying back to the missive, until she felt his on her and she again turned to Chu.

"Ask my mother."

A chill slithered down her spine.

"Women outside The Enchantments are not as powerless as you think, mouse," he murmured. "You don't have to swing a staff to make your point."

He was being wise again.

And annoying.

She decided to ignore that.

"I think this proves Carrington is working with this Rising."

"I think this proves nothing to King Wilmer. He is under a spell many weak men fall prey to."

"What spell is that?"

"Compulsive stupidity."

Serena started laughing.

Chu grinned at her as she did.

She reached out to the cheese, taking up a knife, cutting a slice and handing it to Chu, before reaching to cut her own slice, muttering, "We have to figure out what AM means. That's the plan. But we need to report what we have to True, Cassius and Mars, and you need to send a bird to your brother in Fire City. This isn't just proof Carrington is in on it. It proves this Rising faction of the Go'Doan is also at work in Wodell, and it would stand to reason they have agents in Airen."

"Serena," he called.

She munched her cheese and looked to him.

"I will be the beggar from now on."

Oh no, he didn't.

"Chu, I can take a kick from a Go'Doan priest."

"I will be the beggar from now on," he repeated.

"When are you going to take it in that I'm fine?"

"I know you are fine. I don't care you are fine. No man kicks my woman."

She stilled.

He didn't seem to notice.

"I will play beggar and I'll teach you to pick pockets. You're a swift learner. But we'll find a better disguise for you as well if they feel your work and notice you before you're able to get away. But that might be moot as we know at least the priest with these letters is part of the plot. So he will be our focus in hopes we can uncover what AM means."

When she opened her mouth to protest, he kept speaking.

"It is decided and there will not be a discussion. Now, do you wish to fuck normal tonight, or do you want to play?"

She had wanted a discussion.

Until he offered an alternative.

"You're giving me a choice?"

"I was, but you wasted it," he shared, surging up, taking her with him so she was held to his front.

Fighting material, she wrapped her legs around his hips (bloody skirts on these gowns, she'd be glad to be back in her tunic), but fortunately freely winding her arms around his neck.

"Normal fucking," he muttered as he walked them to their pallet. "Too bloody cold in this realm to play. I want you trembling, not shivering."

Serena smiled in his face.

Right before she landed on her back with Chu on top of her.

# 73
# THE WRONGS

***Tedrey***
*Private Play Suite, Carmine Rooms, Heden District, Fire City*
*FIRENZE*

Tedrey lounged, and watched, with a side view (the best there was) as Faunus took Saturn on his hands and knees.

Tedrey's shaft was so hard, it was aching, but whenever they invited him to the Carmine Rooms, all he did was watch.

Later, in his chamber at home, with his groan muffled by a pillow, he'd see to himself.

But all he could do for the now was enjoy watching.

They did not disappoint as Faunus reached out, clutched Saturn's hair and yanked his head back.

The ferocious look on Faunus's face.

The look of pain and pleasure on Saturn's.

Tedrey shifted on his cushions.

Faunus's eyes turned to him.

Tedrey bit his lip.

Faunus pulled out to Saturn's delicious grunt, and then he let his hair go in order to smack his arse.

"Go suckle him," he ordered.

Saturn turned his head to Tedrey and his expression remained hungry even as he grinned.

"No," Tedrey said.

"You are hard, I can see," Faunus noted, taking his feet as Saturn crawled in a predatory way toward Tedrey.

He wanted to watch Saturn move.

But, by the gods, the man standing was beautiful.

He particularly liked his scattering of chest hair.

His long, muscular legs.

And his enormous cock.

"I just wish to watch," Tedrey said.

"You gulped down my seed greedily enough those many weeks ago," Saturn noted as he came closer. He finished, saying, "The only time you took my cock."

Too late, Tedrey started to scramble away.

Saturn caught his ankles and dragged Tedrey toward him.

"No, really, I'm not ready," Tedrey protested.

Saturn kept one hand clamped on an ankle and gripped Tedrey hard between the legs.

Tedrey groaned in sumptuous agony.

And the smile was back.

"Not ready?" he asked.

Faunus dropped again to his knees between Saturn's calves and grasped Saturn's buttocks, kneading them.

Saturn had amazing buttocks and Faunus had long, strong fingers.

Tedrey swallowed.

"You only wish to watch?" Faunus whispered.

Saturn dragged Tedrey closer so his face was hovering over Tedrey's crotch.

By the gods, that move made him bead.

He started trembling.

Faunus smacked Saturn's arse, Saturn's big body twitched, and he groaned.

"You wish to watch?" he continued to whisper, his attention aimed at Tedrey.

"Y-yes."

Faunus landed another strike.

"Fuck yes," Saturn gritted.

Faunus went back to kneading, clearly much harder now, for Saturn's head arched back.

Faunus then reached between Saturn's legs and did something Tedrey could not see, but it made Saturn's back curve, his chest dipping toward the floor, his neck arching further, and his eyes went hooded.

Faunus then used his free hand to slap Saturn on both buttocks repeatedly, and hard, the smacks cracking through the room, driving through Tedrey's balls, and his cock, before Faunus ceased what he was doing between Saturn's legs. He gripped his arse cheeks, spread him, then drove his cock inside.

Tedrey moaned.

Faunus fucked.

Saturn groaned, shoving his face in Tedrey's crotch and burrowing.

"I want to be inside you," Faunus grunted, and Tedrey's eyes shot from his cock driving inside Saturn to Faunus's face.

He was looking at Tedrey.

He was referring to *Tedrey*.

"I do too," Saturn gritted.

"I am marked," Tedrey admitted.

"I...don't...care," Faunus replied, each word coming on an inward thrust.

"I don't either," Saturn said.

Faunus pulled out again, reached long, grasping a smooth wooden toy that was at the ready, and slid it inside Saturn.

"Get naked," Faunus growled to Tedrey, taking his feet.

Saturn pushed up and stood too.

When Tedrey didn't move, Faunus tipped his head to the side.

"You can take us, or we will take you," he didn't quite suggest. "Your choice."

Tedrey stared at Faunus, his big muscled body, his huge, beautiful shaft.

He then stared at Saturn, his bigger muscled body, his fantastic cock.

Then he looked at Faunus.

"I want you to take me," he said so low, he worried they didn't hear him.

Faunus smiled a wolfish smile.

Saturn just lunged.

In the end, he took them both at the same time, Saturn at the front, Faunus at the back.

He didn't even think about his marks.

Not once.

He swallowed Saturn's seed down his throat and then Faunus pulled him up, still taking his arse, but doing it with his strapping arms wrapped around Tedrey's chest, as Saturn stayed at the front, pumping his shaft.

Suddenly, Faunus took over at Tedrey's cock.

"Give me your seed, Tedrey," Faunus growled in his ear, stroking with a tight fist, and fucking with an otherworldly skill.

Tedrey did as told, his world exploding in an ecstasy the likes he had never experienced (not even close) as he jetted up his chest, jerking in Faunus's hold, the seed coming, and coming, and coming some more. It finally lessened, and he could focus on the strokes up his arse as Saturn again took over and milked him dry.

Glorying in the deep groan that rumbled in his ear, Tedrey took Faunus's offering not a minute later.

When they were done, Saturn tweaked his nipple making Tedrey's body jolt pleasantly, before he winked at him, took his feet, slid free the toy that was inside him and sauntered to the door, tossing it to some toweling.

He opened the door, whistled, and when the servant in the hall came forth, he ordered refreshments.

He then closed the door.

But through this, Tedrey didn't move.

For Faunus held him impaled.

And Tedrey didn't wish to move.

But not simply because Faunus held him impaled, and being full of this man, particularly this man, he did not want to lose, even if Tedrey did not understand why this man felt so right.

Also, because Faunus *held him*, and he didn't want to lose that most of all.

Which was likely why he felt so right.

"I have scars, you have seen them," Faunus said quietly in his ear.

"From battle, training, manly pursuits."

"What does it matter?"

Tedrey turned his head to the side.

Because it mattered.

Faunus licked him from shoulder up the tendons of his neck to under his ear before he whispered there, "I was right. You were beautiful shooting before me with me deep inside."

Tedrey shivered.

Faunus sunk his teeth into Tedrey's neck before he lifted him off.

When Tedrey lost him, he knew he was right, for he suddenly felt profoundly bereft.

He did not want to lose him.

Not any part of him.

He was taken from these thoughts when Saturn tossed them both wet towels before he dropped to the large, plush, fluffy, richly-colored cushions and stretched in a lounge.

Faunus cursorily cleaned his shaft and joined him there.

Tedrey was more furtive (and thorough) in his cleansing, and when he dropped his used towel in the basket that was there for that purpose, he met them on the abundant silk-covered cushions that littered the floor.

He then swiftly draped a loose silk over his hips.

Both men noted this with their eyes but neither said anything.

The wine, cheese, almonds, dates and olives Saturn ordered were served promptly, the servant backing out after he made the delivery, and Tedrey again grew uncomfortable.

For Nyx and Lorenz had talked him into meeting Faunus and Saturn, something he did on a now regular occasion.

But he'd always just watched.

So when they lazed after climax and chatted to each other and him, he was dressed, removed.

His cock needed attention, but he felt safely distant even if he was but feet away.

Tedrey was so lost in his feelings of awkwardness, it took Faunus shoving his calf with a foot to get his attention.

"Are you here or am I still up your arse?" he asked.

It was a joke, and Saturn chuckled, but Tedrey saw Faunus's face was serious.

"I can eat a cunt, and fuck it," Faunus announced apropos of nothing. "And I like it. But it will be a man I give my marital chain."

Tedrey felt his insides seize.

Faunus had no way of knowing his words caused this, but even if he did, Tedrey had a sense he wouldn't have stopped sharing.

And he didn't.

"That man will have to understand I need pussy on occasion, but he'll understand it knowing he owns my cock."

Tedrey had to clamp his legs together so they wouldn't visibly shake.

"I do not know why you're sharing this with me," Tedrey said quietly.

Saturn made a low noise that was part amusement, part exasperation, so Tedrey looked to him.

"What?" he asked.

"A woman will take my martial chain knowing I need my arse fucked.

And I'll need arse to fuck," he shared. "I want a Nyx," he grinned. "But randier."

Tedrey could not imagine a randier Nyx.

"That's just so you know where we stand," Saturn finished.

"All right," Tedrey muttered.

"And still, you are completely missing it, *amico*," Saturn declared.

Tedrey was confused.

"Missing what?"

Saturn shook his head and looked to Faunus.

Tedrey also looked to Faunus and he nearly recoiled at the barbarous expression on his face.

"I like looking at you and I liked fucking you and I liked watching you come," he rumbled.

"I'm, well...*glad?*" Tedrey asked, like Faunus could tell him how he was feeling.

"He doesn't ask you here because he enjoys an audience, Teddy," Saturn put in.

*Teddy?*

Saturn started laughing, shaking his head again, and through both, stated, "He asks you here because he's wanted to fuck you since he met you and because he just *likes you*, stupid."

Tedrey's gaze darted to Faunus who continued to look savage.

Or savagely annoyed.

"You like me?" he asked.

"For fuck's sake," Saturn muttered, still laughing.

"I'd like to get to know you, and not just the part of you that likes watching me fuck Saturn," Faunus answered. "Though now, I know I like fucking you, so I like that part too. That said, I wouldn't mind learning more to see if I like *that*."

"I'm but a school teacher," Tedrey reminded him.

"So?" Faunus asked. "Basil's a Trusted and his current chosen one crafts mosaics. I suppose they're attractive mosaics, people pay a good deal of coin for them. But he's not a warrior or even a school teacher."

"But he's got a fine arse," Saturn muttered.

Faunus looked to the ceiling and said, "Any hole, and every hole, that's all my brother has on his mind."

"This is true." Saturn was still muttering.

"I am...well, this is not the way where I come from," Tedrey said to Faunus.

Faunus dropped his chin and scowled at Tedrey. "Go'Doan?"

"Wodell," Tedrey shared.

"And thus, after weeks of trying to win him by showing him my skill with my cock, he gives me a morsel," Faunus grumbled. "He hails from Wodell."

Tedrey started to smile.

"You think this funny?" Faunus asked.

"I think you feel better inside me than you look inside him," Tedrey answered.

Saturn hooted.

It came slow, but when he was finished, Faunus smiled a smile Tedrey felt tighten his balls.

To evade that smile, Tedrey looked to Saturn. "No offense. You take cock well."

Saturn grinned hugely at him, reaching for some almonds. "None taken, *amico*. But just so you know, you do too."

"So, you escaped the dogmatic Wodell," Faunus remarked, regaining Tedrey's attention so he saw him reaching for the carafe of wine to fill their glasses. "And you saw the error of your ways with the Go'Doan."

Tedrey shot him a look.

Faunus grinned at him unrepentantly, set the carafe aside, took hold of his wineglass and brought it to his lips, but instead of sipping, he asked, "What else makes you, Teddy?"

His deep voice wrapping around Tedrey's new pet name was almost more beautiful than hearing Nyx humming in the mornings.

"I left for Go'Doan after my father found me with a farm boy who was not as good as you with his cock, but he had almost as good a body as you."

"Trying to make me jealous?" Faunus murmured into his wineglass, but his eyes were still on Tedrey.

"Then he beat me nearly senseless and ordered me to leave and never return. And I did as he asked," Tedrey concluded.

He knew his mistake instantly for Faunus suddenly grew so immobile, he appeared made of stone, and Tedrey was too scared to glance at Saturn, for he felt the oppressiveness of the room and he knew he was the same.

None of them moved.

None of them spoke,

Until Saturn broke it.

"Faunus," Saturn whispered when Faunus seemed incapable of breaking the hold his emotion had on him. "Faunus," Saturn said louder.

Faunus's voice was a sinister whisper when he said, "If I make you mine, I will find your sire and I will make him regret this betrayal of his flesh."

*If I make you mine.*

"I have forgotten him," Tedrey assured on a lie.

"Then why do you hide your body from us?" Faunus asked.

"My marks," Tedrey explained.

"Bullshite," Faunus spat. "It is the mark your sire made in your head." He leaned toward Tedrey, only slightly, but the movement still held great power. "I will erase that mark, Teddy. If I am for you, or not. If you are for me, or not. That is what I will leave you. I will erase the mark he left on you and leave you free to be."

Tedrey found he was not breathing.

Faunus's voice dropped low. "But mark this now, *bello*, if you become mine, he will pay. There is no word you can say against it that I will hear. It will be my right to claim that vengeance for you. And I will claim it, make no mistake. Before this goes further between you and I, you must understand that."

Tedrey just stared at him.

"Nod if you understand that, Teddy," he prompted, now speaking gently.

Tedrey nodded.

Faunus leaned back, took a sip of his wine and reached for an olive.

The spell he'd cast over Tedrey was broken, but Tedrey's hand was shaking when he took his own sip of wine.

Faunus looked to Saturn. "When I recover, Teddy's going to suckle me. Do you want my mouth around your cock, or yours around his?"

"Start with you, end with him," Saturn answered.

"This works," Faunus murmured then looked to Tedrey. "Now, Teddy, come closer, get rid of that gods-damned silk, rest your head on my chest, and tell us about the children in your class."

At this order, the subject change and the swift shift in mood, Tedrey couldn't help it.

He burst out laughing.

He had not done that since...

Maybe.

Ever.

He wasn't sure if that was right.

What he was sure about...

It felt good.

~

FAUNUS RODE beside him all the way back to Lorenz's home.

He also rode with him to the back of the house.

And he dismounted when Tedrey did.

After they handed the reins to Tedrey's horse to the stable boy and secured Faunus's mount, Faunus walked Tedrey to the back door.

There, they stopped.

"We will go to an *osteria* tomorrow, not one in Heden. The one I like most in the city. The woman who cooks there, she is a goddess. And she will like you, but do not feel too proud. She is friendly. She likes everybody," Faunus said.

Tedrey shook his head and crossed his arms on his chest, smiling up at him.

"Saturn will not be joining us," he stated.

Tedrey stopped smiling and bit his lip.

Faunus lifted his large hand, slid it along Tedrey's neck, and took hold of his hair at the back in a grip that Tedrey felt stir him, even if after their thorough play that evening, he did not think he had it in him to be stirred.

"I will warn you, Teddy," he said after he dipped his face to Tedrey's. "I am at the call of my captain. New Go'Doan have recently arrived in town and I'm one of a squad who is to watch them around the clock. If another cannot make their duty, I would be called to it. But if that should happen and we cannot go to that *osteria* tomorrow, we will the next eve. And I would like you to return to my home with me after."

But Tedrey was no longer listening.

"New Go'Doan have arrived in town?" he asked.

"You are safe at the school, *caro*," Faunus murmured. "Lorenz has seen to it."

He was not.

Not anymore.

"What Go'Doan have arrived in town? Do you know names?"

Faunus was watching him closely.

"Yes," he answered.

"G'Fenn?" Tedrey asked.

Faunus hesitated.

Tedrey wrapped his fingers around Faunus's throat and demanded, "G'Fenn?"

"Why do you ask after this name?"

It was Fenn.

He was there because G'Seph failed, or he was there for Tedrey, or both.

But he was there.

Tedrey pulled away, turned and swiftly entered the house.

He felt Faunus on his heels.

They were in an informal chamber at the back, and Tedrey and Faunus were heard before they arrived.

He knew this when Nyx called out, "Did you have a good time with the men, *tesoro?*"

He made the doorway and saw them on the divan. Lorenz in dark yellow *ante* pants on his back, Nyx snuggled down his side, and it appeared they were reading from the same book propped on Lorenz's flat stomach.

Both of their eyes came to him.

"Well, allo, Faunus," Nyx greeted with a smile, pushing up to an arm.

But Lorenz's gaze had come to Tedrey, it moved to Faunus, and then returned to Tedrey.

"What's happened?" he asked.

"Is there a priest called G'Fenn at the temple?" Tedrey demanded tersely.

Lorenz looked to Faunus again and back to Tedrey.

But he said nothing.

"You don't trust me," Tedrey declared.

"*Amico*," Lorenz murmured.

Tedrey lifted his chin and declared, "He is of The Rising. It is a secret faction of the Go'Doan that most priests don't know about. But it is large. It is strong. Its followers are devout. And they plan to destabilize all realms, utilizing carefully positioned people who hold local power, or troops they have indoctrinated to their cause to take over and force everyone to adhere to their religion."

Slowly, Lorenz curled up so he was sitting on the side of the divan with his feet to the ground and his wife pressed to his back.

"And I will go back to them," Tedrey announced.

The air in the room went flat before it electrified.

"This is your lover," Lorenz said low.

"It was. Now he is just a general in The Rising. An important one. And I have been gone for a long time. I do not know their plans after the attack on the palace was thwarted. But he will trust me. So I can find out. And when I do, I will tell you."

Lorenz's chin jerked back.

"That's not going to bloody happen," Faunus growled from beside him.

"You are known in that school as having the protection of the captain of the Trusted," Lorenz pointed out.

"And when he seeks me out, I will share with Fenn that I fled due to the abuse of the leader he has obviously replaced. I have the proof of the extent of that abuse that he can see with his own eyes. And believe me, Fenn will not like it. That is not his way. He will think he knows why I left, for he knows my ways. And he will not be surprised I hurried back the minute I heard he was here. He will also have me back, I know it. Last, he will believe I *am* back, for I was foolishly infatuated with him."

Lorenz took his wife's hand from his shoulder, squeezed it, turned his head to kiss it, all this before removing it.

Then he stood.

"Again, you are known to have the protection of the captain of the Trusted," he repeated. "You bloody live with me, Tedrey."

"And thus, I will share with him information you wish me to share, as I glean from him information you will need to bring down The Rising."

Lorenz's brows drew up. "A two-way spy?"

"Ostensibly," Tedrey confirmed. "Though the information from you will be false and eventually lead to a trap."

At these words, Nyx scurried from the divan, stating, "Absolutely *not*. I will not allow this madness."

Tedrey didn't take his eyes from Lorenz.

Lorenz didn't take his eyes from Tedrey.

"He is untrained in espionage, my captain," Faunus put in.

Nyx rushed to her husband's front and put a beseeching hand to his chest until his eyes dropped to her. "If he is found out, what will they do?"

"I won't be found out," Tedrey said.

Her long, beautiful, dark hair flew as she shot an angry look his way, hissing, "Shush!" She went back to her husband. "You saw what they did last time and he did nothing wrong then."

"I saw it too, my brother," Faunus growled to Lorenz.

"I'm going, I don't need your permission." Tedrey chose Faunus to say these words to, for he'd never speak them to Nyx.

"You are not going," Faunus returned.

"I am," Tedrey shot back.

Faunus got nose to nose with him. "You are *not*."

Tedrey butted noses with him. "I *am*."

"I won't allow it," Faunus rumbled.

"I gave you my arse tonight, Faunus, not my leash."

Faunus's dark eyes flared.

It was incredibly appealing.

But Tedrey did not back down.

"Oh, *caro*, you allowed Faunus to have you?" Nyx cooed. "This makes me very happy. I was so worried there was a block you could not get around."

Tedrey took his face out of Faunus's in order to stare at the ceiling and wonder why he shared so much with Nyx.

At the same time he knew precisely why he shared with Nyx.

Because she listened.

Because she cared.

And because he loved her.

"And by the way, you were fooling nobody, groaning into your pillow," she finished. "Why do you think I left that oil by your bed? No one likes chafing."

Good gods.

"You so very much wanted my cock," Faunus murmured, and when Tedrey again looked to him, he was looking arrogant.

That was incredibly appealing too.

"And I want it again. And I want to get to know you. And I wish to go to that *osteria* with you. But I must right wrongs. And that is what I'm going to do, Faunus," he vowed.

"Tedrey," Lorenz called, and both a now-glowering Faunus and Tedrey looked to him. "You did not actually commit any wrongs, *amico*."

"I treated my Go'Ella abysmally. I participated in a plot against four realms. And I was under your care, receiving your kindness, and I did not share there would be an imminent attack that occurred, and when it did, it took many lives. I committed wrongs, my friend, and I must be allowed to right them."

"Gods dammit," Faunus bit.

"No, *amore*," Nyx whispered, staring at her husband's profile. "No, *mio amore!*" she cried, her voice turning frantic. "He could be hurt, and he has *your* protection."

A muscle jumped in Lorenz's jaw.

"Nyx," Tedrey called.

She whirled on him.

"I don't belong here," he told her.

"You do!" she spat.

"And I won't until I do right."

She shut her mouth and closed her eyes tight, dropping her head.

Lorenz noted his wife's capitulation and slid an arm around her, pulling her close to his side.

She turned into him and rested a cheek to his chest.

"Saturn will be your contact for your assignment," Lorenz decreed.

"He will not, I will," Faunus declared.

Lorenz shook his head. "You are too close."

"And Saturn is not?"

"You know he isn't, brother," Lorenz said quietly. "Not the way you are."

It was now Faunus's jaw where a muscle worked, before he looked down at Tedrey.

"Are you going to fuck him?"

"Faunus," Tedrey murmured.

"You're going to fuck him."

"He will expect me to do so."

At that, Faunus took hold of his throat, pulled Tedrey to him and claimed his mouth.

It was their first true kiss.

His tongue was as assertive as the way he used his cock.

He broke the kiss and scowled into Tedrey's face. "You take him, you think of me."

"It would be impossible not to," Tedrey muttered dazedly.

"It best be, for when you come back to me...*when*, Teddy," he stressed, "and I have even the barest suspicion it was not, I'm binding your cock and balls and playing with you for a week with no release."

"Well, if the kiss didn't work, which it did," he quickly assured at the flash in Faunus's eyes, "that will."

Faunus continued scowling at him until he bent, bit Tedrey's lower lip until he tasted blood, yanked his head to the side and bit his neck so hard Tedrey knew he broke the skin (and he liked both), then he released him and prowled way.

"He calls you Teddy?" Nyx asked. "Oh, *mio piccolo buco*, much must have happened tonight. Come. I'll get wine. You must share *it all*."

"I'm not sure he's *il tuo buco* anymore, *mia gazella*," Lorenz remarked.

"Oh, poo," Nyx scoffed, moving toward Tedrey. She stopped at him, slapped him lightly on the cheek and asked softly, "You'll always be mine, won't you, *caro*?"

"I will always be yours, Nyx," he replied, just as softly. "Always."

Her eyes brightened with wet, but she looked away quickly and moved away the same, murmuring, "I shall get the wine."

Tedrey turned back to Lorenz.

He had his arms crossed on his chest and his eyes locked to Tedrey.

"Maybe I'll be significant yet," Tedrey whispered and watched Lorenz's handsome face gentle.

"You already were, but if you need this to understand that's true, *amico*, then you must do it," Lorenz replied.

"Do you trust me?" Tedrey asked.

With no hesitation, Lorenz answered, "Yes."

Tedrey pressed his lips together.

These people had given him a lot since they'd saved him from The Rising.

But that was the most precious of all.

"Promise, standing in my home, looking right into my face, if you ever feel in danger, you will come to me immediately," Lorenz demanded.

"I will...*amico*," he agreed.

Tedrey then smiled.

His eyes full of disquiet, Lorenz did not smile back.

Instead, he murmured, "Come, I have a feeling there is much you wish to share with me."

Tedrey went to his friend.

For he was right.

# 74

## THE NEW ADVISOR

**Queen Mercy**

*The Queen's Solar, Birchlire Castle, Notting Thicket*

WODELL

Mercy was standing at the window, looking down from the great height of her solar at Notting Thicket.

She had traveled widely with her husband, but Melisse had been correct those many weeks ago.

Her city was the most beautiful of all.

By far.

The Great Wohd River and the delicate River Fae meeting under that very castle—a grand, turreted bridge spanning the junction—was the magnificent focal point to a rich abundance of charm and even whimsy.

The expansive, regal castle rising upon its hill in the center of the capital was the heart. Its many high spires and towers reaching to the skies. Its arched windows, carved stone, bold balconies, regal entries and elegant fancies, all of which climbed high and spread wide, was in and of itself something out of a fantasy.

Then there was the city with its cobbled streets, mellow-stoned buildings and moss-covered tiled roofs spread out over gently rolling rises or hugging the shores of the rivers.

And beyond that, spreading as far as the eye could see, vast forests now in a riot of autumn color mixed with fields of brilliant green and cut by the calmly flowing rivers that ran through the city.

It was, all of it, every inch, not just the Thicket, but *all of it*—from the cliffs at the Seil Sea to the north, to the border with Firenze in the south, to the beaches of the Triton Sea to the west, to the border with Airen to the east— property of the king. And it had been, by royal edict, after centuries ago, Wilmer's many-times great grandfather battled his two brothers and two cousins in the Quinate War.

And won.

Now, it would be her son's.

"My queen."

She turned at the deep voice and saw Bram at the door with Wallace.

Her son's lieutenants were all nearly as handsome as True.

Bram was tall, quite muscular and dark-headed.

Wallace had dark blond hair, was shorter, stockier, but no less appealing of visage.

If she could have hand selected her son's men, she would have.

True would never allow that.

However, in the end, it didn't matter.

She would have selected the men he had.

In fact, she had considered these very choices indication that not only had she taught him well, he had *learned* well.

Although, Wallace seemed a little bedraggled at the present.

Then again, he'd been traveling.

"Come," she invited.

They moved in and her gaze remained fixed on Wallace as they did.

He bowed when he arrived, straightened and announced, "I rode ahead to share the news in order that you could be prepared. True, Farah and their party are an hour out of the Thicket."

Her heart skipped a little at knowing her son was close.

"Thank you, Wallace," she replied, then bid, "Now please, I'm certain that was an arduous journey. Take the time before the prince arrives to refresh, have a decent meal, rest."

"Thank you, Your Grace," he murmured, bowed, and after a glance at Bram, walked out.

Mercy glanced at Bram as well, before turning back to the window.

"Cassius and Elena?" she asked.

"They should arrive on the morrow," Bram answered.

Excellent.

"Aramus and Ha-Lah?" she continued.

"We received word that their ship meets with part of Aramus's armada at the mouth of Great Wohd. They should sail down it and be here no later than the day after tomorrow. Along with The Drakkar of Lunwyn, his Winter Princess and their dragons."

*Most* excellent.

She looked forward to meeting The Drakkar and his Ice Princess. She'd heard much of them both.

More, she looked forward to seeing his dragons.

"Mars and Silence?" she carried on.

"They are at a show some children are performing for them today at a school."

This surprised her, so she turned her head to look at Bram who stood to her right, but behind her.

"A children's performance?"

Bram's lips twitched. "Word got 'round that they've been busy in the city these past days. The children's teacher put forward the invitation. Silence accepted. And what Silence wishes, Mars provides."

That large, fearsome man *did* seem to be incredibly smitten with her niece.

And they had, indeed, been busy.

Bram, just the day before, had to ask Mars to *stop* deluging every museum and library they visited with donations. That king and his queen had even stopped at a place that looked after stray dogs, of all things, and had given them three gold coins out of his own purse, for the gods' sakes.

He was overshadowing the donation True had made to the hospital that looked after Wodell's wounded soldiers, and True's support had not been insignificant in the slightest.

"King Mars, sitting and watching children sing," she murmured, allowing some amusement to sound in her voice.

Bram did not hide his amusement. He grinned widely.

"They are the talk of the town, or will be, until True and Farah arrive."

True.

And Farah.

She turned her attention again to the window.

"Is all in place?" she asked quietly.

"Yes."

"It has been checked?"

"And double checked, and triple, my queen. It took me about five minutes to turn Carrington's secretary. He detests his superior. Told me he'd been hoping for years someone would cotton on to this and ask about it."

"Would that he hoped so much he came forward with the knowledge," she noted.

"And be sacked or worse?" Bram asked, before he explained, "For as you know, the king has not ever given indication he'd wish to hear a word said against his advisor."

This was a good point.

Mercy did not belabor it.

Bram went on, "There is no evidence of a link to the Go'Doan. But there is a solid trace of embezzlement. It's indisputable. He's been stealing for ten years."

"The royal auditors?"

"I looked at the documents myself, Your Grace. They had no idea it was happening. Every chit is signed by the king. They could only assume each withdrawal was at the request of their monarch. Carrington could be forging his signature, and I am no expert, but I looked closely, and if he is, he has a skilled forger's hand. Regardless, they are so true to the king's own mark, if I were an auditor, I would not question it and not only because it's not my place to question the king."

Mercy drew in a delicate breath.

Then she nodded.

"In other words, all is in place. It is time," she said.

"Yes," Bram agreed, and she could feel him preparing to move with her.

She waylaid him with, "One thing."

"Yes, Your Grace."

She hesitated, staring at the beauty of her realm, the gently rolling waters of the river. The winding lanes and jumble of quaint buildings. The hustle of carts and carriages, horses and foot traffic.

All her son's.

All Mercy's.

And soon to be...

All *hers*.

"Do you like her?"

"Sorry?"

She turned fully to her son's man.

"Do you like her?" she repeated.

Bram studied his queen's face.

Then he said, "Yes. She is funny, and she is kind. She is also savvy. Her grief for her mother was quiet and reflective, not dramatic and attention-seeking. However, it stated clearly she has a large capacity to love." He paused before he stated, "And she loves him, Your Majesty. It is budding, but it is true. She looks upon him as if he is her whole world, and in a way, with the loss of her mother, he is. Even so, she gives in a way she does not wish to take. She makes him laugh." Another pause before he concluded, "She is perfect for him, my queen."

"And my son?" she whispered.

He gave her a small smile. "He's been lost to her since Firenze."

"She will make him happy." It was a statement meant as a question.

"She will," Bram confirmed. "But more, she will give him peace."

That was what she needed to hear.

Therefore, she nodded smartly.

It was time to move on.

"Let us go," she decreed.

It was Bram who nodded at that, stepped aside and allowed her to precede him.

This she did, even though he murmured, "He's in the royal study, not his personal one," as she passed him.

Of course he was.

Making a statement now.

He was king.

And would remain king.

Wilmer was correct about that.

He was king and would remain king.

But things were going to change.

Today.

When she arrived at the door to her husband's study, she looked up at her son's lieutenant, saw him dip his chin, step away and position himself at the side of the door.

He had his hand on the hilt of his sword at his belt.

He would not need it.

She had no idea what her husband's reaction would be, but it would not be violence.

Though, she knew her son had ordered his lieutenant to protect his queen, even against their king.

It just was not going to get to that.

Mercy knocked.

"Come!" Wilmer called.

She turned the handle and moved in.

He was sitting behind his desk, staring at it as if he didn't know what it was, when she walked in.

His head came up, his slightly jowly but still handsome face registered surprise, then it softened.

She memorized that look even if she steeled herself against his display of clear affection.

"My wife," he whispered as she stopped in front of his desk.

"My king," she replied.

"Mercy," he said, standing. "I am so very pleased you sought me out."

"I am glad to hear it."

"This estrangement, my love..." He moved around the desk, approached her, took both her hands when he arrived and held them tight in his. "I do not like it," he finished gently.

She was glad to hear that too.

However, she had the feeling he would like less that she did not seek him to put their rift behind them.

Indeed, what she was about to do could very well drive them further apart.

Or break them altogether.

It was a shame.

She would grieve this.

But it was unavoidable.

"You will see, in time, as will True, who will also find times where he must make maneuvers to protect his reign, that this is a valuable lesson Carrington and I have taught you," he declared.

A valuable lesson was about to be learned.

It was just not that one.

"I have heard word that True and his party are an hour out. Will you be greeting them at the castle gates with me?" she inquired.

"Of course," he mumbled.

"I must inform the staff he arrives. They are prepared, but I wish them to be presented to the new princess upon their arrival," she said.

"As you know, I leave these matters to you. Simply have someone inform me when he nears or come yourself. We will walk down together."

"I'll see to that. In the meantime, we must arrange to have Carrington arrested on charges of embezzlement, fraud and treason."

His hands spasmed in hers before he dropped them like they were afire and took a step back, his face a mask of shock.

"What is this you say?" he hissed.

"Carrington has been stealing from the royal treasury for the last ten years. Small amounts at first, though they became larger as his activities went forward without question or investigation. Thus far, we've been able to ascertain that he's stolen twelve million, seven hundred and twenty-two thousand, four hundred and nine pieces of gold. Twice that in silver. And equal amounts in pewter and copper. We have not been able to trace where these funds have gone, but we believe it is to Go'Doan, or this Rising that was behind the attack at Catrame Palace in Firenze. Further investigation is needed and has been ordered."

"Is this a joke?" he spat.

"It is absolutely not," Mercy replied, low and firm.

His eyes rounded as he saw her gravity.

Then his face set in stubbornness.

"I cannot believe this," he declared and began to turn away from her.

"You can, and you will. The evidence will be presented to you and unfortunately, it will include your very signature on every single voucher for withdrawal."

Wilmer went completely still.

"You sign whatever he puts in front of you," she reminded him. "I warned you about that. You did not heed my warning. And thus, *you*... personally...signed away the royal treasury." She paused before she finished, "And you did this repeatedly."

He remained still, but now his face was ashen.

"Now," she said, turning and moving around the desk, "we are in the position where we must control the damage."

She stopped beside his chair.

She studied it.

She then drew in breath before she situated herself in front of it.

And she sat.

Looking up at him from the king's chair, the only time she had ever sat there, and likely the only time she ever would, she continued speaking.

"Fortunately, this comes at a time when our people have something to celebrate and thus, they have something to occupy their minds. And they will have more. We will also, with gratitude to Carrington," she said with some irony, "have a full treasury. Therefore, on the morrow, we can announce much joyous news which I believe will drown out the din that the king's chief counsellor has been arrested for theft and treason and any further rumblings of discontent at this new levy that has been waged."

She clasped her hands over her skirts in her lap and sat back.

"For on the morrow," she began steadily, "you, your son at your side, will announce that you have discovered your counsellor's perfidy. The moment you did, you had him immediately arrested. After the wedding, he will be tried. After his trial, when his guilt is ascertained, he will be hung."

"Mercy," Wilmer whispered.

She ignored him and continued.

"You will follow this with the jubilant news that you are naming your son, Prince True, as your new chief counsellor. He has proved his loyalty to you and his realm repeatedly in his adult life. And he did the same very recently in Firenze at the diplomatic table, negotiating an alliance with Firenze that will mean an end to the strife with our southern neighbors, *and* open trade routes on the seas, as well as trade directly with Mar-El, which will mean Dellish wares will reach ports on this continent much more expediently, and others abroad we have rarely been able to attain."

Her husband had lost his pallor.

He now was red in the face and looked ready to explode.

Mercy ignored this too.

"And last, you will declare that the recent tax will be utilized to assist port authorities and ship builders to handle much more significant traffic and custom, for the seas have been open to Firenze and Airen too, though tariffs will be assessed to their imports. This, as well as you and your new counsellor will be open to applications for funding credits to small merchants, farmers and shepherds who wish to increase their operations in order to supply what we hope will be significantly amplified demand."

"This is all very tidy for you," he sniped.

"Actually, True made it all very tidy for *you*," she replied calmly.

"He is again the hero, Mercy," Willmer pointed out.

"Did it not occur to you to wonder, even a little bit, why Carrington did not advise you to herald loud and wide the agreements True made in Fire City?"

"I didn't wonder," he retorted. "I asked. And I agreed with Carrington that this, as with much else, would make True stronger and me weaker."

Mercy shook her head. "True is not separate from you, Wilmer. He's your son and heir. He is *a part* of you and your reign in a very literal sense. It is Carrington that made you question that. And he had no care that True would appear stronger because of these negotiations. What he could not allow is that *you* would appear stronger because of them."

After sharing that, she put her hands flat on the desk and spoke in order to end this.

"He has compromised you, and you have allowed it. We must all, every one of us, understand our weaknesses so we can bolster them. You have never, not once in my knowing of you, demonstrated an interest in governing your land. True doesn't relish it either, but he understands it's his responsibility and it is in his nature to assume it. It is not in yours. It's in yours to delegate it. Therefore, appear in the throne room to knight the knights. Inspect the troops. Preside over arbitration, and announce the rulings, but allow True to decide them. Do what it is in your nature to do, delegate, but this time do it *wisely*."

"This is essentially making my son regent," he remarked.

"It is making your son *counsellor*. It is paving the way to make your *heir*, flesh of your flesh, equipped with the experience to be king. You did not wish him to be regent and you do not wish to rule. You get both. You get what you want. *All* you want. But this time, with a strong realm that has strong leadership. How can you protest that?"

"And you have investigated Carrington without my consent?" he demanded. "That is not your place, Mercy. With that, you have stepped over the line to such an extent, it, too, could be considered treason."

She sat immobile, such was her affront.

"It is the *king* who decides his counsel," he spat. "And it is the *king* who sits in that chair." He rapped his knuckles on his desk and commanded, "Arise."

She stared at him and did not move.

He leaned toward her. "*Arise*."

"You have two choices," she said softly. "We can walk out that door and direct Sir Bram to find Carrington and arrest him. Or I will walk out that door and direct Sir Bram to share that the king has signed the vouchers for the man who pilfered his treasury, and as such, he relinquishes his rule but as figurehead. And the Crown Prince, True, of Wodell, has become regent. It's your choice. Make it now."

His expression was the definition of thunderstruck.

"Blackmail?"

"It is your choice, Wilmer, make it now."

His incredulity melted, he glared at her and snapped, "This will be the finish of us, wife."

She felt her heart stutter, but she did not take her gaze from his.

"It is your choice, my king, *make it now*."

"And have this hanging over my head so my wife and son can use it at will and play me like a puppet?"

"At least your new puppet masters will have the good of the people of Wodell in mind, not, at best, greed, and at worse, involvement in insurrection."

He drew back in insult.

"You speak these words to me?" he asked.

"You yourself said this will be the finish of us, husband," she reminded him. "I no longer have the wifely duty of managing your delicate sensibilities."

Wilmer's temper visibly snapped.

"Arise from my chair and get out," he demanded hotly.

"Is that your answer?"

"Tell the people what you want," he decreed, throwing his hands up. "I made a mistake. I have many responsibilities. I am king, but I am also a man. Mistakes are made. They will understand."

"Will they? Will they, Wilmer?" she asked. "With Carrington's counsel you have repeatedly led them to war against a superior force which not only ended in defeat, but to the deaths of our native sons. You have foolishly signed away *their* hard-earned monies. You have taken the counsel of a man who might be colluding with enemies of the state and you've done it for *years*. Every...single...thing Carrington has advised you to do has been with the goal of making you appear weak, dithering and greedy. His intent is not hard to read, just hard to prove. He wishes to destabilize your throne and you *let him*. So tell me, Wilmer, will they truly understand?"

His eyes narrowed, and his lips whispered, "I think I hate you."

Her heart sank.

She gave no indication of that.

"What is your choice, my king?" she pressed.

He looked to the side, teeth clenched.

He looked back to her, nothing but cold in his eyes.

"Have him arrested," he ordered.

"Do you wish to see the evidence?" she offered.

"I don't care anymore."

Mercy was not surprised at this.

For he never did.

"As you wish, my king," she murmured, pushing up from her hands on the desk and rising from his chair.

"Right," he mumbled sullenly.

She moved to the door.

She also stopped at it and turned.

Quietly, she said, "I hope sometime in the future, be it far, or near, that you understand I did this because I love you."

"Really?" he asked, not having moved from his position in front of his desk, but he no longer appeared sullen or cold.

He looked upon her with distaste.

And somehow, that wounded her most of all.

"Really," she whispered.

She then turned, stepped out of his study, closed the door and looked to Bram.

She then gave the king's order.

# 75

## THE WELCOME

**King Noctorno**
*The Maiden's Breast Inn and Public House, Dunlyn, North Coast*
AIREN

"Oy, oy," the man behind the reception bench called the moment they walked over the threshold. "Wenches to the back."

Tor looked to Lahn who was studying the man curiously.

Though "curious" for Lahn appeared threatening.

The man was either blind, or stupid, because he aimed his next directly to Lahn.

"And you, we don't want any instigators. You don't keep yourself to yourself and toe the line, you can go back to Firenze, but before that, you can get your arse out of here."

After the innkeeper delivered that, Lahn slowly turned his head to Tor and lifted his brows.

"I said, wenches to the back!" the man shouted, as Cora and Circe moved to their men's sides.

Tor's gaze shifted back to the keep to see, within seconds, he'd shot from unfriendly to dangerously hostile.

Tor further felt his wife's bemusement, her mood matching his.

508

He also sensed attention coming their way from their right, opposite where the inn's reception was.

This being where the tables and bar of the pub were.

Tor looked that way.

Yes.

They had the attention of the entirety of the pub.

All of the patrons being men.

"You can send them to the back or you can get your lunch elsewhere," the man warned.

Tor looked again at the innkeeper. "Send who to the back?"

"What's the matter with you?" the man queried in return.

"Not a thing," Tor answered.

The keep gave him a look up and down and demanded, "You Airenzian?"

"I'm Valerian," Tor shared, deciding not to share he was *the* Valerian, that being that country's king.

The man reared back, making an "oof" of surprise.

"Long way away for you," he stated something Tor did not need reminding of as this was the first time his boots had hit solid ground since they left Korwahk weeks ago.

"Yes," he agreed unnecessarily.

"How'd you make it through those bloody Mar-el pirates?" he asked.

Tor had no wish to enter into a discussion with him, so he simply said, "Luck."

"Best know our ways, Valerian," the man instructed. "Your women, if they travel with you, they enter at the back. They go straight to their rooms. And they stay there."

"No."

Oh shite.

That came from Lahn.

The innkeeper's face went hard.

"Lahn, let's go somewhere else," Tor suggested.

"Won't matter where you go, 'less you find one of them agitator's places that'll let you in," the innkeeper advised. "Got our women locked down. We feel the cold winds blowin'. Not gon' let some Nadirii put ideas in their heads."

As they all processed this information, most of which none of them understood, some of it they didn't want to understand, the innkeeper, and it would seem some patrons, became impatient.

There was shifting.

Tor went alert.

Lahn didn't twitch.

"Best go, Valerian, and get your women outta here or they'll be removed and so will you," the keep warned.

"A man touches my queen, I'll tear his arms from his body," Lahn declared.

*Fuck.*

The feel of the room worsened.

Significantly.

"Lahn," Tor said.

"Let's just go, baby," Circe urged quietly.

Unfortunately, one of the patrons was positioning either to better watch the byplay, or to do something about it.

And his positioning took him closer to Circe, something she noted.

"I'd back off if I were you," Circe advised him.

"I'd keep my fuckin' trap shut if I were *you*," the man sneered, and, after sweeping her up and down with his gaze, very stupidly finished, "*whore*."

A moment later, his face was slammed into the wall, and after that, he was flying across the room.

Not careening.

*Flying*.

Bloody hell.

Lahn.

When the onslaught came, that being the rest of the patrons (*and* the innkeeper) on attack, Tor did not draw his sword.

He kept his wife close behind him and fought with his fists.

He was capable with fists.

Lahn was a monster.

The twenty-odd patrons (and innkeeper) were littering the floor, some moaning, all bleeding, most unconscious within ten minutes.

Fortunately, there were no arms torn from bodies.

Tor could not say there were no fractured limbs.

Tor and Cora, Lahn and Circe stood amongst the carnage.

Cora was looking at Circe.

"Well...hell," she said.

"Mm-hmm," Circe agreed.

Tor was looking at Lahn.

"That wasn't much of a welcome," Lahn noted.

"Agreed," Tor replied.

"Maybe we should go back to the ship," Cora suggested.

Tor thought there was no maybe about it.

They exited the inn and moved down the paved street, all four of them agreeing without words to abandon their idea to escape the ship and spend a night or two on land before continuing on to meet Frey and Apollo in Notting Thicket.

Tor was surprised.

He'd never been to Airen, and although the eastern shores were a wonder of black sand beaches that were breathtaking, the northern coast was made of stark, craggy black cliffs that were as welcoming as that innkeeper.

Nevertheless, the port city was a veritable marvel. He'd wished to study the tidy pavings of the streets, because he'd never seen anything so smooth. And the architecture was austere, but undeniably impressive.

The city seemed modern and was clearly advanced.

Its people were not.

"I think it'd be best if I send a man to have a conversation or two and find out what the fuck is going on," Tor said to Lahn as they moved back to the dock. "Apparently, you look Firenz and that seems only slightly better than being female."

"This is a good plan," Lahn muttered.

People stared at them as they moved through the streets and it wasn't simply because Lahn was enormous and wearing the native hide clothing of Korwahk, except with a long-sleeved leather shirt with a long, amber-yellow wool mantle that went to his heels at the back (usually, he wore no shirt and definitely no mantle for it rarely got cold in Korwahk).

On their return journey to their galleon, Tor noted that there were far more men on the streets than women.

And the women scurried along, heads bowed, and if on their way they approached a man on the pavements, they got out of the man's way, not the other way around.

His queen noticed this too. He knew it when she got nearer to the point she was practically walking sideways. She tucked herself so close to him, she no longer held him around his elbow, but he was forced to slide his arm protectively along her shoulders.

"I don't like it here," she murmured.

"I don't either, love," Tor replied.

They made their ship and made their way up the gangway.

Bain, Lahn's man, was the first they saw.

"Refresh supplies quickly. We leave in the morning," he ordered.

"I thought we were staying a few days," Bain said.

"This is no place for us."

Bain took in his king's face, then looked to Tor's split knuckles and finally at the expressions the women were wearing.

Then he quickly prowled away.

"I'm going to get you a cold cloth for your hand," Cora announced, gave him a squeeze, got up on her toes and kissed his jaw, and then she made haste in doing that.

She was shaken.

Tor felt his jaw harden, because he wasn't fond of his Cora feeling shaken.

"I'm just going to go below. I don't even want to look at that city," Circe declared, shot Lahn a glare, he returned it with a scowl, definitely a husband and wife of one mind, and she followed Cora.

Tor turned to the railing and stared at the city that seemed to have been built of the black stone that covered the coast.

The structures might be extraordinary, but the overall sense was gloomy.

Lahn came up on his left side.

"I do not have a good feeling, my friend," Lahn stated.

"I don't either," Tor replied.

The two kings studied the unwelcoming city.

If this was their first taste of Triton, neither were looking forward to what was to come.

# 76

## THE PET

*The Priest*
*Ancient Ritual Ground, Lesser Thicket Forest*
WODELL

Finally, they were back on track.

They had the men.

The new recruit had been trained.

They'd retaken their vows.

They had the sacrifice.

They had the moon in the sky.

And tonight, the Beast would be appeased.

Their sacrifice was staked to the ground, and his nemesis, who was also, regrettably, his brother in their undertaking was undoing his trousers in order to use her when the ground shook.

The priest smiled.

He'd been missed.

So much so, the Beast couldn't even wait for the offering to share his gladness to have his master back.

His smile began to fade as the quake didn't stop and it was not the same as the last ones. It did not seem to shake the trees beyond, meaning it could be felt from sea to sea.

It was just there.

At the Ritual Ground.

More to the point, right where they were standing.

The moist dirt seemed to be breaking apart all around them.

He braced to run but got not that first step in as he cried out, the men also emitting shouts and grunts of surprise, the sacrifice screaming (again), and they all started falling.

Not sinking.

Falling.

But through the dirt.

As he dropped, the soil was all around his body and face, thus, he could not pull in breath for fear of getting a lung full of loam.

He tried to fight it, scratching and clawing at the dirt above him to cease falling and start climbing, but it only proved to take energy he needed to keep holding his breath.

The priest did not know if it was fortunate, or other, when he stopped dropping through the earth and seemed to be tumbling through air.

He gulped in a huge breath right before he landed in a heap on a hard floor.

"Not that one, he can go," he heard a woman say.

Lifting a hand to his face, the priest brushed away dirt.

And then froze.

For they were in an underground chamber that seemed to be made of stone lit well by an abundance of torches on the walls.

And there was a fair-haired, ludicrously attractive and ridiculously well-built man approaching his nemesis who had landed about six feet from the priest.

His brother in the cause, but also his foe began to try to take his feet.

He did not make it before his body dropped to the ground.

Without its head.

That fell to the ground where the fair one tossed it unceremoniously.

The priest gulped down bile.

By the gods.

That man had torn a head from a body *with his bare hands*.

*What was happening?*

"Not that one either," the female voice came again.

The priest started scooting away as the fair one approached their new recruit, who was scampering clumsily, making mewing noises of terror.

The fair man seemed unhurried, but he moved eerily swiftly.

The new recruit had his back to the priest when that…not a man, it had to be a *creature*, caught hold of him, again at the head.

Lifting him up by said head.

But he did not tear it from his body.

He twisted it so that his brother's back was still to the priest, but a ghastly crunch sounded, and the recruit's head was facing the priest at his back, eyes still filled with fear.

But now lifeless.

"Not him, or him," the female voice said.

She was indicating the last two, and the priest sought to escape, when suddenly he froze again for the woman's face was an inch from his.

"I don't think so," she whispered.

He daren't move.

Vaguely, he saw she was attractive (he supposed). Voluptuous, but petite. Very thick chestnut hair. Brown eyes.

He heard a scream, a grunt and his eyes jerked in that direction.

One of his brothers had his throat torn out, the bloody gaping maw where it had been a vision of gore the sight of which made his innards shrink.

The other was lying on his side, but his vacant gaze sat above his chin that was resting on the back of his shoulder.

The creature did this in but seconds.

Barely a blink.

"There, there, dear," the woman cooed, moving to the sniveling, scuttling offering who began cowering against the stone wall when she had the woman's attention. "You're safe. Come!" she called, and the girl they would have sacrificed that night jumped. "See to our new sister."

The priest had shifted carefully away, but his back struck stone, and he realized he was stuck with no escape as a gaggle of women came forth out of an opening in the wall of this strange cave.

And dear gods, some of them were wearing Go'Ella shifts.

They started clucking and cooing over the terrified sacrifice as they helped her to her feet and took her back where they came.

"Now, you," the woman stated.

On his arse, back to stone, he darted his eyes up to the woman.

The fair one was standing behind her but just to the side.

His face was sheer beauty.

His expression was chilling.

They both were looking at the priest.

"I should introduce myself," she said, and he looked immediately back to her. "I am Marian. Mistress of the Beast."

"Oh, my gods," he breathed.

"Yes," she grinned sassily "Didn't see it playing out that way, did you?"

"Are you...did you...how...?" He couldn't finish, and he couldn't decide who to focus on.

Her.

Or his Beast.

Not his Beast, no.

*Hers.*

"Now, where shall I start?" she began, crossing her arms on her ample chest and leaning back a bit as if settling in to tell a long tale. "I hail from Wodell. We won't talk about my early years. They're miserable. I entered a profession I didn't care for, opening my legs for men for a few coins. We won't speak about that, as it's dismal as well. I made the excruciatingly *stupid* decision to attempt to escape that life by becoming a Go'Ella."

Oh no.

She suddenly threw her arms out to the sides and the priest flinched in fear at the abrupt movement.

"And now here I am," she declared. She then lifted a hand and tapped the side of her chin with a finger before adding, "Oh, yes. And I'm a witch." She indicated the creature behind her with a flick of her hand. "Apparently, a powerful one."

"We are...these men you just murdered, we are servants of the Beast," he shared.

"Oh," she whispered, a gleam in her eye he did not like, "you will serve the Beast."

After uttering that, she turned, dipped her chin, and said softly, "You may have him, my *brutum.*"

The man-like creature smiled an unnerving smile, turned his attention to the priest and started moving toward him.

He scuttled to the side, twisted to his hands and knees in a mindless attempt at escape, and this was a grave mistake.

He was caught, and he was such in the wrong position.

He was not killed.

His robes were torn from him.

And he was used.

Brutally.

The creature was very tall, but lean.

And his member was enormous.

And the priest was not ready nor were precautions taken against harm.

But regardless, this was not something he wished.

Not at all, but especially having it happen to him with *her* watching.

In the end, when the creature had finished on a mighty roar that seemed to shake the stone all around, collapsed atop him for so long, he thought he'd suffocate from the weight, and then pulled out, the priest lay naked on his belly in the dirt, used, in pain, and feeling a sense of humiliation so strong, it quite suddenly simply defined him.

He curled into himself, feeling the trickle of blood coming from his arse, pain so intense there, he worried he'd never be the same there again.

He closed his eyes tight, wrapped his arms around his calves and clenched his teeth when he sensed her draw near.

"You didn't enjoy that?" she taunted. "He *is* very large, I will admit. It took me some time to get used to that big cock. But he and I enjoyed the time it took. Then again, I have natural lubrication." She paused. "Oh, and I was willing."

He said nothing.

"Doesn't feel good, does it?" she asked quietly. "When it's not something you want. When it's the last thing you ever wish to happen to you."

He remained silent.

"He's told me," she went on. "My precious darling has shared much this glorious time we've spent together, getting to know one another, him showing me all his many special talents, me sharing what is happening above, some planning, some plotting, etcetera. And I did the math. Over six thousand, five hundred."

He had no idea what she was talking about.

"But that was only the number of women you and your kind raped and murdered over the centuries," she said.

Oh *gods*.

"They were each used four times, well, at least in your reign of terror. Prior to that, it was five before they were relieved of their pain...and their lives. That's over thirty-two thousand times." He heard her take in a sharp breath before she said in a much less conversational tone. "Over *thirty-two thousand rapes.*"

"It is the ritual," he whispered.

"It is *savagery*," she hissed.

He needed to focus.

He needed to find his magic.

He needed to cast a spell. Any spell. Some distraction, so he could get his bearings and find a way to leave this place.

He had no idea if he could move, but he would it if it meant escape.

"We've decided to wait," she shared. "You foolishly notified everyone up there that he has roused, annoying him with your 'rituals.' They must come to think this idiotic prophecy has been fulfilled and it will keep them safe. So we will wait."

He felt her get nearer to him before she spoke on.

"I had wanted to take their vengeance. Those women you violated. Those women you slaughtered. Giving him use of your flesh as many times as your people took their flesh. But we can't wait *that* long. Violating you thirty-two thousand times would take years. It might take *centuries*."

He released a hand to start to draw in the dirt, the beginnings of a spell.

"Don't be stupid," she murmured, and he could tell she was drifting away from him. "Do you think your magic works here? The merfolk have bound him and bound his magic. I can sink to his lair, and I can rise to the surface, and take him with me, or the girls, but we don't know how. He's been powerless for millennia. Until me."

"We were only doing what—"

All of a sudden, her hand snaked out and caught him by the jaw.

She forced his neck into a painful twist so he would look at her.

She was crouching behind him.

"Don't," she snapped. "There is no excuse for what you've done. There are no words you can speak. Do you think its these *rituals* that roused him? How bloody *man* of you. They had nothing to do with it."

"Wh-what did?"

She pushed him off and his cheek struck stone.

"It was time. He wakes, he sleeps. He wakes, he sleeps. It's just that he sleeps for over a thousand years. And he needs someone, that someone being *me*, to bring him to the surface. We've had a few forays, just for him to get the lay of the land and for us to recruit some helpers. But our base will remain down here. At least for a spell."

He carefully began to drag himself away from her, but when her eyes narrowed, he stopped.

"If you can get to the surface, then I have great power up there," he informed her. "I'm sure I can rise too. I can help you up there. I know people. And you know I know people who serve the Beast. I have connec—"

"Oh no," she murmured, reaching out again, and he quailed, but she only stroked his hair. "We're keeping you. Our little pet. When you aren't serving him, you'll serve his harem." She tipped her head. "Do you know how to cook? They're mostly quite lovely, but none of those ninnies knows how to cook."

"I don't," he cleared his throat, "I don't know how to cook."

"That's all right." Her gaze moved down his body, and a sick smile curved her lips. "You have other uses."

"I want his mouth," the creatures deep, velvet voice sounded.

He was like a godly seraph.

And yet, he was a monster.

That smile remained in place as she studied the priest. "He has a quick recovery. And he can come, and come, and *come*." She rolled her eyes with exaggeration before she bent over him. "And wait until you see what else he can do when he is not bound to this under-realm. He has such power, such *awesome power*. And not just with his cock."

"You are wasting a great resource," he tried. "I am—"

"Yes," she sat back on her heels, "who are you?"

"G'Jell of the Go'Doan."

"No, you aren't. That's the name they gave you when they stripped you of who you were so you could be theirs. Who are you?"

"Jellan of Airen," he whispered a name he hadn't spoken in decades.

"And you are a great sorcerer?" she asked.

"Yes. Yes, I am. I have much power," he told her fervently.

"No." She shook her head. "No, you don't. You *did*. But like those girls, all those many girls over the centuries, you have nothing anymore, Jellan. As they were pushed to the point they wished they were dead, you will be pushed to the same. Except your torment will last a great deal longer."

She then stood, nodded to the Beast, moved toward the opening the other women disappeared through, and *he* moved toward G'Jell.

Jell scuttled away, but he was caught by the hair at the top of his head, yanked up in a way that caused excruciating pain in his scalp, and then he was force fed cock.

And thus, his torment continued.

# 77

# THE SACRED HORN

***Melisse***
*Northwestern Border of the Veil of The Enchantments*
WODELL

Gagged, bound, her shoulder having been dislocated somewhere along the way, not having had but minimal water or food for days, Melisse was tossed to the ground within feet of the veil of The Enchantments.

There were a number of men in this party.

Too many of them.

By the goddess, how had they missed this many Go'Doan conspirators?

She was woozy. Concerned about her head wound, dehydrated and ravening, often traveling belly down on the back of a horse, and when she wasn't, she'd been sequestered with a guard.

Thus, she couldn't get a lock on how many there were.

One hundred?

Two?

"We are ready?"

"Yes, sir."

"Torches?"

"Yes."

Torches?

Did they think they would burn The Enchantments?

Did they think they could even breach them?

They could not.

Not even with her, for she would not open them, even upon threat of the certain death.

And they might have bound her hands, her mouth, and weakened her focus so she could not cast, but they could not steal her magic.

"The last Nadirii patrol?"

"Moved out of this area six hours ago."

"They'll be quite far by now. Send the order. Men in positions."

"Yes, sir."

Melisse searched the area as best she could from where she lay with only waning light to see by in hopes to observe, well...*anything*.

She had not seen Seph since he'd lured her to that place.

Though she'd thought often of his hands.

How had he lost his hands?

And if it was this faction who took them, why was he still allied with them?

She could not think on that now, nor should she have thought of it then.

Ophelia had always told her, mind the curiosity of a cat. Cats were agile and limber. The scrapes they could escape were vast.

People were not the same.

She should have listened to her queen.

Or at least brought backup.

She should also have listened to Rebecca, who told her Fern of the Great Coven had sensed bad omens for Melisse.

So intent was she on the safety of the prophesied, she did not dwell on her own.

She could not think on this either.

Melisse attempted to focus on clearing her mind so she could endeavor a spell to loosen her binds. Or communicate with the veil to send a warning, no matter how weak. Those in treehomes close to this location, and the patrol, even six hours away, might sense it and come to her aid.

But...

What did they think they could achieve?

This was no small operation.

One, two hundred men?

On a fool's errand of violating The Enchantments?

"Men are in position, sir."

Damn it, she'd lost focus.

She closed her eyes, sought the veil.

And lost her concentration at the tone of voice of the leader.

"Excellent," he whispered, sounding nearly feverish with anticipation.

Hundreds of years, The Enchantments had never been breached.

Why did he sound so...*certain*?

She felt movement close and she ignored the pain in her shoulder as she twisted to her back to better her position so she could put her heels in the turf and push away.

Or kick out.

But she stopped dead when she saw him, the leader, a priest she had not, before her capture, met.

They called him Nath, G'Nath, which meant his born name was probably Nathan.

He was tall, likely in the middle of his third decade on earth.

And right then, he was holding a unicorn horn.

He had a sacred horn.

Oh, by the great goddesses, how had he gotten hold of a sacred unicorn horn?

They were forbidden in every realm!

"Ungag her, we will need her pain," Nath ordered.

Another one came up behind her, and she twisted her head this way and that, not believing she wished to keep the gag, but now she had an inkling of what they were up to.

She would almost certainly not survive it.

But that wasn't the only reason she had to fight it.

Using every ounce of strength she had left, she struggled, twisting her body, kicking out with her bound feet.

Another man had to come to assist, and another.

"Control her, hold her down, and *take the gag*!" Nath shouted.

She was too weak, she could not fight them physically.

She gave up and closed her eyes in order to attempt magic.

The gag was released.

Immediately, she was struck across the face, closed fist.

And again.

A third time.

She shook her head, blinking away the stars, and ended with her eyes open.

He was standing above her, a foot planted at each side, the horn raised.

"No," she whispered.

He brought it down in a vicious stab.

"*NO!*" she shouted.

It pierced the flesh and her breastbone, driving through.

Agonizing pain scattered from wound throughout her frame as she screamed her anguish and glittering white sparks mixed with the amethyst hue of Melisse's own magic shot high and wide, lighting the area all around, all the way to the dusk sky.

"*Yes!*" G'Nath bellowed.

Through the draining pain, Melisse heard hoots, hollers, cheers.

She turned her head and her agony magnified as she saw the rift form in the veil from where she lay. Its edges sizzled white hot as it rose from the earth where she lay and expanded.

Up.

"No," she whispered.

Out.

"No," she breathed, her lids drooping as a weakness so profound, she knew she had no hope to fight it pervaded.

Up and out, she watched a rough two-foot square of the veil open.

Then three.

Four.

Five.

Seven.

No.

And then...

Melisse blinked at what she saw beyond the disintegrating barrier.

"What—?" G'Nath started in shock.

The gap was ten feet square and expanding.

But beyond it, Melisse clearly saw Ophelia sitting her steed.

Behind her, at least five battalions of Nadirii warriors.

Her eyes drifting open and shut, Melisse's lips curled just as Ophelia released the Nadirii yell.

It was echoed by five hundred Nadirii sisters.

And the call of the Sisterhood rent the air.

It was the sweetest sound she'd ever heard.

And then they rode.

Even fading, she noticed that, as the Nadirii attacked, charging through the rift into Wodell, pressing the Go'Doan collaborators back and into disarray at this surprise attack, the hooves of every sisters' horse flew over her, not a single one striking.

They sensed her.

They might be sacrificing her.

But she would do the same.

Their home must be defended at all costs.

Death was close, she knew as her blood seeped into the soil, and all she wished was to drag herself a few feet so she'd die in her beloved home.

Instead, before she could begin her last endeavor on this earth, she felt herself dragged farther away from the melee, but on the Wodell side.

She was then lifted.

Put on a stretcher.

A man ordered a terse, "Go. *Fast.*"

She blinked up at him as he jogged beside the stretcher.

She knew him.

"Please, I wish—" she began.

G'Liam of the Go'Doan, their Education Minister, looked down at her.

"Don't speak. Save your strength," he ordered. "I am uncertain I can repair the damage. This effort will be impossible if you do not help me."

She was near to losing consciousness, therefore she'd have no choice but to "help."

She was also confused.

"You wish to repair the—?"

"We are not all like them, and we are not all ignorant of their intrigues. Last, there are some of us who do not fear them, but instead are intent to do something about it. Now be quiet. I have a makeshift operating theater up ahead. It is not the best, but it will have to do."

Melisse had no choice but to be quiet.

She'd blacked out.

# 78

## THE DECRYPTION

***Princess Serena***
*Go'Doan Temple, East Side, Notting Thicket*
WODELL

Chu had managed to find Serena a better-fitting disguise, but still, she would be glad to see the back of that heavy gown with its tight bodice and never-ending skirts.

This thought was only vaguely on her mind.

Mostly, she was considering those notes they'd stolen.

She was doing this with her hands on the handle of a broom, her hair bound up and hidden under a kerchief, not doing very well sweeping a hall in a Go'Doan temple.

In disguise, she had approached the priests, declaring her desire to become a Go'Ella.

They had explained that, before she could be initiated into the sect, she would have to demonstrate her faith in all three of their gods as well as her desire to serve its priests.

And wouldn't you know it...

The way they expected her to do this was by sweeping floors, polishing candlesticks, cleaning windows, and the like.

This was not surprising.

But it was annoying.

Though it had to be done for her to get close enough to overhear.

So it was done.

Chu had likely become one with a wall somewhere, such was his ability to grow invisible.

But he was never far.

Not ever.

And not because he didn't trust her.

Also not because he had a mission he wished to see through (or not only because of that).

But because the bloody man was intent at all times—and in all ways he could—to protect her.

She was a goddess-damned Nadirii for fuck's sake.

But would Chu let her take the risk and not risk himself, or instead, divide their efforts and go find someone else to spy on?

No.

So he was there.

She couldn't see him.

Fortunately, no Go'Doan could see him either.

But she knew he was there.

She also knew she found this protective bent endearing.

She had no idea why. It made no sense in the slightest.

But it made her feel like she felt when she was home, by herself, next to a creek after she'd had a swim, and she was lazing in the sun.

It was a romantic notion, and she wished to hate the very fact she had it.

She simply...

Didn't.

This was only partially on her mind for also on her mind was trying to listen, since the priest they'd ambushed was in a chamber just beyond where she was sweeping.

But the bloody door, not to mention the walls, were too thick.

She couldn't hear a thing.

She suspected the other priest he was with in that chamber, which was the one he'd been walking with the night they'd set upon them, was also of The Rising.

She suspected this because, outside of those two, the temple was vacant.

It was Prince True's wedding day.

It seemed the entire city was festooned with streamers, the air had smelled for days of leaf cakes baking, and excitement was heightened day to day with extraordinary occurrences so now it was at a fever pitch.

First, there was Mars and Silence arriving in the city to great fanfare then proceeding to take it by storm, appearing so often (to the glee of the citizens of the Thicket), it seemed they had to have been cloned.

And then there was her bloody sister and Cassius coming with a parade of Nadirii warriors behind them. The spectacle of a contingent of the Nadirii Sisterhood with its princess and the Prince of Airen at the lead was blathered about like the Great Goddess herself had led that parade.

Not to mention Aramus and Ha-Lah arriving at sail down the Great Wohd with an impressive armada in tow under a sun darkened by a sky filled with dragons.

Bloody *dragons*!

Where had they gotten *dragons*!

The town was agog and remained so, unsurprisingly, for the dragons were lolling about on a sparsely forested rise north of the city and you could see them from anywhere in the capital. Not to mention, one, or two, or twelve would often take flight apparently just to spread their wings. And when they did, it didn't matter who you were or what you were doing, they were dragons, they were magnificent, so you stopped, looked to the skies and watched.

In awe.

That was, all did this, save Serena and Chu.

Serena and Chu couldn't think of kings and queens, princes and princesses, royal weddings and dragons.

They had a mission.

And it had been a big shock along this journey to come to the understanding that they both were of one mind about a variety of things.

Most especially the fact that, when you had a mission, even if dragons were on offer, you focused on that mission.

So they were not with the revelers in the streets. They also had not rushed to the parade route to jostle with the crowds lining it in order to garner a glimpse of the wedding procession. Nor had they booked their table at a pub for a wedding feast followed with a slice of leaf cake and sparkles. Further, they had not made their way to the rise to see if they could view the dragons from up close (as scores of others had done).

They were at work.

And Serena wondered why she'd spent so much time fighting Trajan of Airen.

She should have found a disguise, infiltrated the Sky Citadel, and spied on the bastard.

Then toyed with his mind.

It would have been a lot more fun.

Unless, of course, to do that she'd had to do the sweeping.

Whilst debating whether or not to use her magic to hear what was happening in the chamber beyond, in that moment, mostly her thoughts were on something that had been nagging at her for days.

Those notes.

And the mention of AM.

What was AM?

She swept, she tried to listen, and she went over those missives in her head, which she now had read so many times, she had them memorized.

AM.

*But they have been told to hold until after we AM.*

*C reports M a growing threat. Plan to commence has been ordered. LLTR.*

*M*, was Mercy, they were sure of it. *After we AM* had to be an event. Or an action. Or...

Their plan, whatever it was, had commenced.

If *M* was Mercy...

It hit her like a bolt, and she shot upright, dropping the broom.

"Zsst, zsst," she hissed, quickly moving down the hall.

Chu did not materialize.

"Zsst, zsst!" she called.

Goddess damn it, he was always close to her and he needed to—

"Ssst!" she heard and saw him (or part of him) hidden in a doorframe some ten feet away.

She hurried there.

"We have to go," she whispered urgently.

"Did you hear something?"

"I decrypted it," she said.

He knew to what she was referring, for he ordered immediately, "Talk."

"If M is Mercy, then AM is..."

It hit him then too.

"Assassinate Mercy," he whispered in a dire tone.

They stared in each other's eyes.

Chu then took command.

"You, to Birchlire, warn them. I'll work those priests."

Without a word in protest, Serena nodded.

And without thought of who might see, she tore that damned kerchief off her head and raced out of the temple, her copper hair flying.

# 79

# THE ROYAL WEDDING

***Prince True***
*Quarters of the Crown Prince, Western Turret, Birchlire Castle, Notting Thicket*
W*ODELL*

"Your mother," Luther murmured.

True turned from the full-length, oval looking glass where he was inspecting himself in his dress greens, what he'd be married in, toward the double doors to his bedchamber, where Luther stood.

He nodded.

Luther looked over his shoulder and nodded to Wallace, who was in the sitting room.

Luther then disappeared, and True's mother walked through.

She was dressed for the ceremony in a russet-colored gown that was subtly extravagant. The top was made entirely of a delicate lace with a demure V-neck and stitched minimally throughout with something that sparkled. The skirts were yards and yards of shining satin.

Her hair, the color which she had given him (though hers was beginning to silver), was a wonder of swirls and poofs, the poof being bunched at her nape.

She was wearing one of many sets of royal jewels. These, her amber and emeralds surrounded by diamonds. A large round amber at her lobe falling into an even larger tear of an emerald. The same in a curve adorning her neck.

And the same as a tiara threaded into her hair.

It was not the first time he thought this, and it probably wouldn't be the last, but his mother was a beautiful woman.

He and she had not had a great deal of time together since his return.

He had been busy with his father, or more to the point, the business of his realm for his father just sat petulantly and watched as True struggled his way through meetings with auditors and ministers and guild leaders, talking about everything from budgets to school syllabi to setting a minimum wage (something, until then, his father—meaning Carrington— flatly refused to do) and establishing a college to train mariners.

When he was not at this pursuit, he was meeting with Mars, Cassius and Aramus, as well as Frey and Apollo, to catch up about what had happened since they parted, what had been learned, what had not, and discuss what was to come.

In his rare free times, he couldn't often find Farah, for she was off in the city with the women or in her own engagements with his mother to meet the castle staff, learn how it was run, go over the plans of the wedding in detail and be educated on being a princess of Wodell.

They'd caught snatches of time, mostly in passing, and some of this they spent in minimal whispers, but most of it they spent in maximum embraces.

They managed to have only one dinner together, a pompous affair held the night before attended by five hundred guests.

He had not been surprised to learn that Farah had been spectacular holding court. Her natural calmness and ability to see humor in a variety of situations had transferred to him and something the like he detested—an official royal reception—was something he learned to enjoy.

Regardless of that, he found the past days exceptionally frustrating.

She was in the same bloody building as he, but that building had over six hundred rooms, and her chambers were in an eastern turret.

She had an amazing view of the bridge over the rivers.

But she was as far away from him as she could get.

He missed her.

And he would be glad when this day was done.

For a number of reasons.

One of them being, while they were being wed, the servants would move her to his bloody rooms.

"I have just come from your bride," Mercy announced.

Oh fuck.

"Mother—"

"She is a vision," she declared smartly. "The most beautiful creature I've ever seen."

True blinked.

Slowly.

"Well," he started carefully, "thank you for arranging that. I'm certain the gown is—"

"The gown is divine, but it pales in comparison with its wearer."

He stared at her in surprise.

"I was concerned when she demanded the gnomes of The Doors do her hair, but I shouldn't have been. She knows what suits her."

He was not surprised at all Farah had made that demand.

She'd bestowed a great honor on those charmed ones.

However, that wasn't why she did it.

Yes.

She would be the perfect queen.

"How is she otherwise, outside of stunning, which she always is?" he asked.

"Nervous as a rabbit."

Damn.

"Mother—"

She waved her hand in front of her face. "Elena, Silence and Ha-Lah are with her. After Elena's suggestion that she do something called 'meditate' didn't work, they've plied her wine."

His brows shot up. "So my bride is going to be inebriated at our wedding ceremony?"

"Never fear. Queen Ha-Lah has a head on her shoulders. I have every faith she'll stop things before they get out of hand," she assured.

She moved from where she'd stopped just inside the room, coming to him.

When she arrived, she lifted a hand to brush nonexistent lint from his sleeve.

She also spoke on.

"Though that lieutenant of Elena's, I believe her name is Jasmine, was there and that was a concern, for there is something not right about that girl. But Elena sent her off to find her seat in the sanctuary, therefore that should not be a problem either."

Of course she would think Jasmine was not right.

Jasmine knew duty.

But once it was done, she devoted her life to fun.

Mercy ran her finger over the ribbons on his chest while her eyes watched.

"So all is well," he noted.

She dropped her hand and clasped it with the other in front of her, lifting her eyes to his.

"All is well, my son."

"You and father—"

She shook her head. "Let us not talk about such things on a joyous day."

She thought this was a joyous day?

He studied her.

By the gods, she actually thought this was a joyous day.

"You and Farah—" he began.

"I've come to the decision, after some very good advice from a very wise woman, and words of support for your soon-to-be princess from your own man, to open my heart and see what comes in. And, just so you know, I thanked her for the taffy."

She thanked Farah for the taffy.

She thus had some understanding of what would come into her heart.

His mother was making an effort.

A mammoth one.

For him.

As usual.

He did not have a warm and affectionate mother.

But he absolutely had a devoted and loving one.

He unclasped her hands by taking them in his own.

"Mother—"

"Now, you should start making your way. There is much traffic in the city. The capital guard has lined the streets and they're keeping the parade route open, but you'll need to allow your people plenty of time to take in their prince on his way to his wedding, so the ride will be slow."

"Are you going to let me finish a sentence?" he asked.

"No," she answered, giving his hands the barest squeeze before pulling away and moving toward the door. "I'm off now. Meeting your father at our carriage," she said as she went.

She turned at the door, expertly flicking her voluminous skirts behind her when she did.

"Majesty is saddled and blanketed and waiting for you when you're ready," she declared.

"Thank you, Mother."

"I didn't saddle him, the royal groom did."

"No," he said, his voice heavy. "*Thank you*, Mother."

She tipped her head to the side, and in response to that, oddly said, "Your father wanted to name you Frederick. Did you know that?"

"I didn't," he replied quietly.

Then he braced as her voice matched his and a thread of molten gold ran through it when she spoke her next.

"But it was as if I was a seer," she whispered. "We discussed it for days and days. He put his foot down, but I was adamant. I knew what you should be named. And in the end, I was right. You turned out so handsome."

He stared at her, his throat feeling thick.

"And true," she finished, her tone now an ache of pride.

Then, with another expert flick of her skirts, her head held high, True's beloved mother walked out of the room.

$\sim$

**The People of Wodell**
*Royal Wedding Parade Route, Notting Thicket*
WODELL

THERE CAME the marching guard first.

All in dress greens.

Their hats with the long drifting feathers wrapped around the wide brims were set upon their heads.

Swords were unsheathed, and at the command of their captain, they thrust them high above, or at another command, they rested them on their shoulders.

This way, they marched in precise lines, ten across, fifty rows.

They were followed by the military drummers.

Ten across.

Five lines.

There came the mounted guard next, the rumps of their horses dressed with the blankets fashioned of the Dellish flag, a sea of green in the middle of which was an acorn, the nut in brown, the stem in yellow, the cupule a patchwork of reds, oranges and butterscotch.

This delegation was followed by the pipers.

Ten across.

Five lines.

After the pipers came the king's carriage.

Open-topped, festooned in Dellish silver-pewter with a shiny forest-green lacquer, the doors of the carriage denoting the royal standard of the Wodell line. A shield cut in quarters, acorn to the top left, oak leaf under it, a tree in full bloom to the top right, a barren tree under it.

It was noted by all that the queen's gown and jewels were resplendent, as was her visage and hair. She looked stately, but opulent, and most felt great pride viewing her as she waved regally at the crowd from her seat.

The king wore the dress greens of the Dellish military with a hat that had a dramatic flourish of a feather.

And it was noted by a fair few that he wore this uniform even if he'd never seen a single battle.

Mostly, though, they didn't pay any mind to him, just his wife.

And then craned their necks to see what came next.

For this was when the crowd perked up and the excited cheering began to grow from constant...

To frenzied.

He was getting closer.

As was she.

For after the king was a procession of marching flag bearers.

Ten across.

Four rows.

The first row the flag of the acorn, second of the leaf, third of the blooming tree, last of its skeleton.

And after that, Prince True's chosen lieutenants, Sir Alfie in the lead, followed by Sir Bram and Sir Luther side by side, and then Sir Florian and Sir Wallace.

That was when the cheers went deafening.

For behind them, on his esteemed chestnut charge Majesty, his horse's rump covered in the royal standard, sitting straight and riding hatless, was their most handsome Prince True.

Men cheered. Women screamed (and some swooned). Children ran along the parade route beside him. Leaves flew in the air.

He turned and dipped his chin this way, that.

He caught eyes.

If those eyes were of a child, he smiled.

He was handsome beyond compare.

He was beloved beyond measure.

Following their prince came the dark-skinned, daunting, but appealing King Aramus of Mar-El and his extraordinarily beautiful queen, both mounted on horses that had their necks hung with sea-blue silks that undulated like water.

Next to them rode the large and fearsome, but attractive King Mars of Firenze and the new pride of Wodell, his Dellish queen, Silence. They, too, were mounted, with their horses' necks draped in crimson that was edged with green.

Behind them, also side by side, rode the beautiful and proud Princess Elena of the Nadirii with the ferociously handsome Cassius, the Prince of Airen.

The rump of her horse was blanketed with a purple silk edged in coral with a white oak leaf in the middle.

And it was noted widely, Prince Cassius's horse had his neck draped with two silks.

One the black of Airen.

The other...

Coral.

Following them were the surprise guests at the wedding, the Ice Princess of faraway Lunwyn and The Drakkar, her husband and the most powerful man of that realm. This power was proved, for as they rode, a lone dragon soared over their heads.

At their sides were those some had heard were Lord Apollo and Lady Madeleine, Lunwyn's top general and his wife.

Behind them rode three lines, five across, of harpists who played while sitting in low carts pulled by manned horses.

And this was when they knew the grand finale was near.

*She* would soon be there.

And the frenzy grew fevered.

Following the harpist were ten lines of ten girls aged from eight to twelve, these selected from schools across Wodell in honor of their educational aptitude. They tossed splendiferous autumn leaves to the cobbles.

And behind them, as the crowd grew nearly silent in expectation, a long pause in the route many figured was designed in order to increase that expectation (and it was).

But eventually, it came.

And the din was deafening when it did.

The Wedding Carriage.

An extravagant conveyance made of brass and gold, lacquered in yellow and orange, the royal shield on the doors. Covered, it had two liveried footmen at the back, two at the front, four Dellish soldiers in dress greens marching at each side, and the liveried driver with his forest-green, velvet top hat sat on a bench festooned with orange fringe and gold ribbons and tassels.

Through the windows they could see her.

Her dark hair up and away from her lovely face in curls threaded in lace ribbon the color of juniper, this tumbling over her left shoulder.

She wore extravagant earrings and an intricate necklace of green tourmaline and diamonds.

They could not see her gown, except it was the color of the ribbon in her hair and off-shoulder. They could see, as she waved through the windows, her long sleeves were studded with sequins, but the green material there was sheer. They could also glimpse that the sweetheart neckline was tufted with tulle, the bodice covered in a nuanced appliqué and subtle green glitter.

It was those closest to the temple, those who had camped outside its sweeping steps for weeks, who got the best show.

For they saw the troops and the mounts and the drummers and the pipers take formation in the park opposite the temple.

They also had witnessed the arrival (though separate) of King Gallienus of Airen, as well as Relict Queen Elpis of Firenze earlier. Not to mention, Lord Johan and Lady Vanka of the Arbor.

But then they watched their king and queen, their prince's lieutenants, their prince, and the kings and queens and prince and princess of all the nations of Triton and one of the Northlands enter the temple.

Most of all, they watched the footmen rush forth and open the door to the Wedding Carriage when it came to a gently swaying stop at the foot of the steps.

And out alighted Prince True's betrothed.

Their future princess.

Their future queen.

Her skirts burst from the carriage, and when she stepped down on a beaded green slipper, they fell in wide, graceful folds from a densely adorned midriff and neckline, the appliqué and sequins smaller at the top, but becoming larger all around the skirt.

As she alighted and moved forward, her train spread out behind her, five feet long and at least that wide.

She was not a vision.

She was resplendent.

She was a miracle.

Even more so as she seemed to gaze side to side with endearing timidity, a small, nervous, but nevertheless striking smile on her lips.

To the clamor of a cheering crowd, gracefully, she lifted her ample skirts and walked alone up the steps to the temple but was met at the top by King Mars.

He offered his elbow with an adoring smile.

She took it with a brave one.

And it was then she won the hearts of a nation when the king of her land, gaze aimed forward, led her to the temple doors.

But Princess Farah turned back and looked over her shoulder, that smile still on her lips.

She lifted her elegant hand...

And waved to her people.

∼

***Prince True***
*The Altar, Temple to Wohden, Notting Thicket*
WODELL

"GOOD GODS," Alfie muttered.

"Bloody hell," Bram whispered.

"I have never wanted to be you, until right now," Florian murmured.

True heard them.

And didn't.

For Farah was walking down the aisle toward him.

There were flutists playing, with the accompaniment of strings.

Sprites were resting on the railing in front of the gnomes who sat in front of the fairies who sat in front of people, behind whom floated pixies, this on his left side at the pews flanking the aisle.

Aramus, Ha-Lah, Elena, Cassius, Mars, Silence, her parents, Frey, Seoafin, Apollo, Madeleine, Elpis and Gallienus as well as his parents sat in the pews to his right.

There were pompom chrysanthemums of cream and bronze and gold bunched with autumn leaves in remarkable arrangements everywhere, including at the tips of bunting in hues of marigold, amber and juniper that lined the fronts of the pews.

And when you entered the temple, the outer sanctum smelled of cedar from the incense burning, while the inner smelled of rose.

It was not, as he feared, ostentatious.

Though it was abundant.

It was also celebratory and beautiful.

But nothing compared to her.

Nothing.

She was nervous, he could see it.

But with every step she took to him. Every second she gazed at his face as she came closer.

That disappeared.

When Mars arrived with her at the altar, True did not look to her protector to hear his message, as tradition dictated.

He said to Farah, "I didn't think you could be more beautiful, but every day, you prove me wrong."

Her smile lit up the vast space.

"I think that's enough said," Mars remarked in a low voice, and True tore his eyes from his bride to look to his friend. "Except this," he went on. "There is not a man in any realm I would offer her to without some sense of unease."

A king then dipped his chin to a prince and finished.

"Except you. Be happy."

True accepted this honor with a silent nod.

Mars turned to Farah to see her beaming up at him.

He bent to kiss her cheek then put her hand in True's proffered elbow.

That done, Mars walked away to join his wife in the pews.

"Is this really finally happening?" she asked.

"It is, my love."

"It's like a dream."

She was not wrong.

His mother had given them a beautiful wedding gift.

So beautiful, it was like a dream.

He wrapped his free hand around her fingers at his elbow.

"Mercy had the most beautiful gown made for me," she shared.

He felt his lips quirk. "I did not miss that."

"Apparently, this color is not tradition," she told him.

"It isn't."

"But it very much suits me."

"It does."

"The incense, True, that was so kind. Remind me to thank her."

He thought he might start laughing.

He did not.

He answered, "I will."

"You look most handsome."

His lips quirked again. "Thank you, darling."

"Are you as nervous as me?" she queried.

"No," he answered. "I'm impatient."

She got his meaning and her eyes gleamed.

They heard a throat clear and both looked to the Wohden priest standing before them.

"By your leave, Your Majesty, if I could start the ceremony?" he requested.

Hell yes, he could start the ceremony.

For then it would be done.

And Farah would be his princess.

His wife.

His future.

One he was finally looking forward to.

With pleasure.

"Please do," he bid.

Farah shifted, pressing closer to his side.

True locked his frame to support her weight.

The priest smiled in amusement, drew in breath, lifted his hands palms up.

And he began.

True kept his fingers curled around Farah's the entire ceremony.

He was unsure he heard a word.

He smelled her perfume.

He felt her presence at his side with such acuteness, he knew he would not forget, standing right there with her pressed against him, not for the rest of his life.

But mostly, he didn't hear the words to the ceremony because he was keen to have her pronounced his wife.

Not to mention, he was very ready for their wedding kiss.

# 80

## THE PLAN COMMENCES

**Prince True**
*Temple to Wohden, Notting Thicket*
WODELL

The first indication that something was wrong was when Prince Cassius's lieutenant, Macrinus, made a stealthy exit for reasons unknown.

However, he was seen by a few people, a few fairies, some sprites and several gnomes catching sight of something at a side entrance to the temple.

Macrinus then left his seat silently, but with haste, and disappeared through there.

True, focused on his bride, focused on his future, focused on the fact that it was for once bright, missed this.

Completely.

Thus, he missed that the man Macrinus saw there was Nero, another of Cassius's lieutenants. A man sent to Airen over a month ago to see to its defense against a probable revolt.

And missing it, he missed Nero was travel worn and his face was a mask of foreboding.

The second indication that something was wrong was when Cassius caught site of something at the entrance of the temple.

There was a quiet altercation happening there. A common woman with copper hair appeared determined to gain entry but was being held back by Dellish guards.

She fought like a warrior. However, her tact was as a warrior that didn't wish to harm anybody.

And thus, six guards to one woman, she was losing.

Cassius's eyes narrowed on it.

He then brought Elena's attention to it.

She looked that way and her head jerked in surprise.

True missed this as well.

For it was only moments before Farah would be declared his wife.

And he was not going to miss that.

The final indication that something was wrong, True could not miss.

No one could.

And as Macrinus rushed back into the sanctuary, moving swiftly toward his prince, and Cassius seemed to be attempting to stop Elena from coming up from her seat, at the back of the balcony, twenty men wearing dark-gray robes, black hoods with eyeholes and carrying longbows rushed in and lined the back aisle.

There was barely time for the murmurs and frissons of surprise of those seated in the balcony to register on the rest of the congregation before, as one, the assailants raised their bows aimed toward the front of the sanctuary.

And as the Wohden priest declared the joyous news that the Crowned Prince, True Axelsson of Wodell was now married under the gods and in the eyes of all in the land to the Lady Farah of Firenze, now Princess Royal of Wodell, Macrinus reached Cassius and told him something with great urgency.

Cassius's face turned to stone.

Elena's expression registered grave shock.

Aramus, Ha-Lah, Mars, Silence, Frey, Finnie, Apollo and Maddie looked on grimly.

Gallienus, however, looked smug.

And a shout was heard from the balcony.

*"Long live The Rising!"*

True turned instantly.

But it was too late.

The arrows were threaded, the strings pulled back.

Swiftly, he turned his back to the archers and fell on his wife, taking her to the ground with him on top.

In a flash, Alfie saw the aim and began to race across the nave.

True's other men raced to Farah and True.

Wilmer noted the threat and threw himself to the floor behind the railing of the pew.

Screams were heard.

Shouts.

Mars, also noting the aim, and after shoving his wife to the floor, attempted to leap from his place in the pew just down and behind the King and Queen of Wodell.

But the arrows had flown.

One struck Sir Bram in his back right side.

One rooted in the side of Sir Florian's left thigh.

Two hit Sir Alfie in the back.

One hit Queen Mercy in the clavicle.

Four hit her in the chest.

One struck her in the neck.

One seared through the shoulder of True's dress greens.

And embedded itself in his bride.

The plan had commenced.

Its mission accomplished.

**The End of Part Two**
*The Rising Series continues with The Dawn of the End.*

# THE RISING SERIES GLOSSARY

**Terms, Words, Places**

Abhainn Mouth – (AH-been) (n/place): Harbor city in the north of Airen located at the mouth of the Dunleth Abhainn (river).

Abyss (the) – (n/place): Large "bottomless" hole in the rock of a cliff on the coast of Mar-el fifteen miles down the coast from Nautilus, the capital city of Mar-el.

Airen – (Air-EN) (n/place): Country of Airen located in the northeast of the Triton mainland. The northernmost area is barren and craggy and made up of great boulders of black rock. The rest is mountainous or fertile and green, mostly pastureland, forests and rolling hills.

Airenzian – (Air-EN-zee-an) (adj.): Of Airen.

Alabasta – (Al-ah-BASS-tah) (goddess): Of Wodell. Goddess of Wisdom and the Earth. A goddess shared with Lunwyn in The Northlands.

Amphite – (Am-FITE) (n/place): Underwater capital of the Mer. Location of royal palace of King of the Mer.

Ancient Ritual Ground – (n/place): Area in the Lesser Thicket Forest of the country of Wodell where rituals were (are) conducted, including human sacrifice.

Argyll Forest – (n/place): Forest on the western border of Airen, butting The Enchantments, the city-state of Go'Doan and Wodell. The parts of it in Wodell are known as the Lesser Thicket Forest. Location of the Silbury Henge.

*Ashesh* – (Ash-EHSH) (n): Drug akin to opium. Available throughout Triton. Grown in Firenze.

*Angmostros* – (Aing-MO-stros) (n/creature): Sea creatures in the shape of enormous eels, some one hundred yards long, with two heads with long necks, very large mouths and very sharp teeth.

Aviast – (Ay-VEE-ast) (n): Keeper of a loft of ravens used for sending messages.

Bayzian – (Bay-ZEE-an) (n): Citizens of Sky Bay, the capital of Airen.

Birchlire Castle – (Birch-LEER) (n/place): Home of the King of Wodell. Located in Notting Thicket.

Bishop Cross – (n/island): Island off the southeast coast of the country of Airen. Temperate, but barren and very remote.

Bloody Boy Cove – (n/place): Deep cove to the north, across the wide bay (and hidden from sight) from Nautilus, in Mar-el.

Body stocking – (n): Worn by the Nadirii under tunics. More like a leotard or bathing suit. Can be tank/spaghetti strap/long-sleeved/strapless at top. Regular cut or high cut at the hips.

Bounden (The) – (n): Those taken into service on Mar-el as punishment for sailing the Triton seas without permission from the Mar-el king. This punishment is known and anyone who sails the seas risks it if caught doing so. The service of the bounden lasts a specified amount of time and those taken into it are guarded under significant strictures as by law as to their treatment. Once service is done, many of the bounden remain on Mar-el to make their lives there.

Cairngorn Lake – (KAREN-gorn) (n/lake): Very large lake located in the southeast of the country of Airen.

Carleigh Manor – (Car-LAY) (n/place): Royal manor house about thirty-five kilometers south of Sky Bay in the country of Airen.

Catrame Palace – (Cah-TRAME) (n/place): Royal palace of the King of Firenze. Located in Fire City.

Cells – (n): The room or rooms of a Go'Doan priest. In Go'Doan, they are quarters, with more than one room. For new priests or those in Go'Doan temples in other countries, the cell could be one room. However, they are not spartan, ranging from very comfortable (for a Go'Tish, a new priest) to luxurious (for a Go'En, a high priest).

Close – (n): A narrow, dead-end alleyway in a city. Mostly a footpath and not used for carriages or horses, etc. Opposite of "wynd" [see below].

Collected (The) – (n): Old or ancient books gathered and translated by the Go'Doan from all the realms of Triton. These were protected and kept safe in the Narration Hall (main library) of the Dome City.

Crittich Keep – (Crid-ITCH) (n/place): Royal prison and dungeons of Wodell, located in the capital of Notting Thicket. Also contains administration offices of the constabulary, prison and guard system in Wodell, interrogation rooms, cells for those held for questioning, and in the bowels of its depths, ancient torture chambers. Outside the Keep is the Lawn, where executions take place.

Cyrus – (SEAR-us) (n/place): Large merchant town to the northeast of Silbury Henge on the outskirts of the Argyll Forest.

*Dahksahna* – (Dahk-SAH-nah) (n/title): Means "queen" in Korwahkian, the language of Korwahk in The Southlands.

Dahlia Rooms – (n/place): Sex palace in the Heden District of Fire City in Firenze.

*Dax* – (n/title): Means "king" in Korwahkian, the language of Korwahk in The Southlands.

Dellish – (Del-ISH) (adj): Of Wodell (akin to English, Spanish, etc.).

Dome City – (n/place): Another name for the city-state of Go'Doan, named as such as it's known for its plentiful gold domes.

Doors (The) – (n/place): A magical gnome settlement in the Great Thicket Forest of Wodell where the gnomes live in the trees, the name referring to the many doors carved into the trunks.

Dune Desert – (n/place): Desert north of the Sheeonee Mountain range in Firenze.

Dunleth Abhainn – (DONE-leth AH-been) (n/river): Long, wide river running from an inlet in the northern shore of the country of Airen, southeast all the way to Cairngorn Lake. At the town of Kilcree Break, the Dunleth forks into Westfork River, which runs southwest to the Argyll Forest. (Abhainn means "river" in Gaelic).

Emerald Oil Asps – (n): Snakes in Firenze. Black with emerald-colored eyes. Highly venomous.

Enchantments (The) – (n/place): Forest in the center of the mainland of Triton with trees made magically tall and stout in order to house the Nadirii Sisterhood in their treehouses. Protected by fierce magic, The Enchantments cannot be breached by anyone other than one of the Sisterhood or unless given Nadirii permission. Regardless of the intensity of magic that protects it, it is patrolled constantly by Nadirii warriors.

Fire City – (n/place): Capital city of Firenze. Located to the north of the Sheeonee Mountain range that takes up the center of Firenze. Fire City is close to Fire Lake, the largest lake in Firenze.

Fire Lake – (n/lake): Very large lake to the east of Fire City in the country of Firenze formed by runoff of melted snow from the Sheeonee Mountains.

Firenz – (Fir-EHNZ) (adj): Meaning, of the country of Firenze.

Firenze – (Fir-ehn-ZAY) (n/place): Country of Firenze situated across the south of the Triton mainland. The largest country in Triton. Most of the country is desert or sand dunes with the middle of the country having a very large mountain range with high peaks that get great amounts of snow. When this snow melts, it floods Fire Lake, close to Fire City, and leads off into a large number of rivers and tributaries that cut through the desert and dunes with strips of fertile oases.

Firenzii – (Fir-ehn-ZEE) (n): Language of Firenze (much like Italian).

Fotiá Sea – (Foh-SHAH) (n/ocean): Body of water to the south of the continent of Triton.

*Fumeria* – (Foo-mare-EE-ah) (n): Water pipe. Akin to a marijuana bong but much more elegant and ornate.

Gairn Plain – (n/place): A stretch of plain southeast of Sky Bay and west of the Dunleth Abhainn in the country of Airen.

Go'Doan – (Go'Dōn) (n/place/religion):
    (1) City-state of priests, scholars and healers with temples, archives of the history Triton and a university. Also known as Dome City.
    a.   Go'Da (Go'DAH) (n): University in Go'Doan

    (2) Religion in Triton with temples across the continent where people worship:
    a.   Go'Bedi (Go'bed-EE) (god of obedience)
    b.   Go'Vicee (Go'vee-SEE) (god of service)
    c.   Go'Chas (god of faithfulness)

    (3) Orders of Go'Doan:
    a.   Go'Fell (order of priests as a whole)
    b.   Go'En (high priests)
    c.   Go'Ar (Advanced priests, often are sent to do missionary work or teach in Go'Doan schools across Triton)
    d.   Go'Tish (new priests/trainee priests)
    e.   Go'Tec (priests who teach/scholars in the city-state)
    f.   Go'Nis ("Keepers of the Records," priests who record history)
    g.   Go'Ella (female acolytes that serve priests and the city-state)

Great Thicket Forest – (n/place): Massive forest in the middle of the country of Wodell, to the east of which is Notting Thicket, the capital city of Wodell.

Great Wohd (River) – (n/river): A very wide, very long river separating from the River Dorian in the north which runs from the Seil Sea. The Great Wohd cuts through the eastern part of Wodell, meeting the River Fae at Notting Thicket, the capital of Wodell, and continuing westerly nearly to the border of Wodell.

Green Sea – (n/ocean): Body of water to the east of the continent of Triton.

Gulliver – (n/place): Town in the south of Wodell located seventy-five miles from the Firenz boarder.

Hawkvale – (n/place): Country in the middle of The Northlands, south of Lunwyn, north of Fleuridia, ruled by King Noctorno and Queen Cora.

Heden District – (HEE-den) (n/place): Red light district of Fire City, Firenze. Where to find prostitutes (male and female), participate in orgies or other sexual games and play, consume smoke or *ashesh* or *koekah* and other forms of decadence.

Highgate – (n/place): Large gate at the top of the cliffs protecting Sky Bay, the capital city of Airen. Situated slightly to the southeast at the highest heights of the mountains that surround the capital city.

Ibex-whales – (EYE-bex whales) (n): Whales of which the bulls have enormous, ridged tusks that look like that of an ibex.

Irons – (n): Used in fireplaces or freestanding in rooms in Airen, Mar-el and Wodell, wood or other burning fuel in them or piled on them to heat them in order to heat a room.

*kah rahna fauna* – (n): Loosely means "my golden doe" in Korwahkian, the language of Korwahk in The Southlands.

Keel Castle – (n/place): Home of the king of Mar-el. Located in Nautilus, the capital city.

Keeper of The Lights – (group): A group of fairies who oversee and protect the area where The Lights (see: Lights (The)) can be viewed in the Greater Thicket Forest of Wodell.

Keerian Name – (description): The way Lunwynians (people of Lunwyn in the Northlands) describe a given name or as we know it Christian or first name.

Kilcree Break – (Kill-KREE Break) (n/place): Town in the middle of the country of Airen located at the break of the Dunleth Abhainn (river) where the Dunleth continues on to Cairngorn Lake and the Westfork River begins, running toward the Argyll Forest. A gentry seat.

*Koekah* – (koe-KAH) (n): Drug akin to cocaine. Available throughout Triton. Grown and manufactured in Firenze.

Korwahk – (n/place): Country taking up the northern part of the continent, The Southlands. Ruled by *Dax* (King) Lahn and *Dahksahna* (Queen) Circe of the Golden Dynasty.

Korwahn – (n/place): Capital city of Korwahk in The Southlands.

Lawn (The) – (n/place): Grassy area outside Crittich Keep, the royal prison and dungeons of Wodell, where executions take place. Located in Notting Thicket.

Lesser Thicket Forest – (n/place): Forest on the east border of the country of Wodell, west border of Airen. The parts of it in Airen are known as the Argyll Forest. Within it in Wodell is the Ancient Ritual Ground.

Leuthea – (LOU-thee-ah) (n): Sea goddess of sailors in distress. Worshiped by Mar-el.

Lights (The) (n/place): Atop the highest hill in the center of the Great Thicket Forest of Wodell where, on occasion, the sky illuminates with colored lights (akin to the Northern Lights). The reason for the phenomenon is unknown.

Lotus Den – (n/place): Bar and drug den with rooms for rent for a variety of hedonistic activities in the Heden District of Fire City in Firenze.

Lowgate – (n/place): Large gate in the downslope of the cliffs that protect Sky Bay, the capital city of Airen. Situated to the northwest in the lowest area where the cliffs meets the sea at Twilight Harbor.

Lunwyn – (n/place): Country taking up the northern part of The Northlands. Ruled by Queen Aurora.

Mar-el – (n/place): Country of Mar-el, island nation situated to the northeast of Triton (off the coast of Airen). Made up of dark rock around the shores, beaches, fertile land inland. Most of population works in some form of sea trade.

Marital Chain – (n): Firenz form of a wedding ring. It starts at upper ear, threads down to the lobe, across to the nostril and down to end at a hoop at the side of the mouth. In most cases, if it indicates marriage, it's worn on the right side. It's meant to signify listening to your mate, keeping them in mind, and communicating honestly with them.

McGarrity's Teahouse – (n/place): A brothel in Wodell.

Medusa – (n): Goddess of the sea. Worshipped by Mar-el.

Medusa's Gate – (n): Large, ornate monument to the goddess Medusa in which is the gate to the lane to Keel Castle in Nautilus, the home of the King of Mar-el.

Mer (The) – (n/people): Race of underwater charmed folk, including mermaids and mermales. Their fins split into legs and their gills disappear when they swim close to land so they can "pass" as human and move about on land.

*Miet* – (n/celebration/holiday): The celebration of the crop yield in Firenze, held as autumn subsides to winter. Celebrations mostly center around planned orgies, but they also include copious intake of liquor, food and drugs.

Mystics (The/the) – (n/place/spiritual practice):
(1) The continent to the west of Triton across the Triton Sea. Referred to with capitalized "The."

(2) Spiritual practice that includes personal reflection, transcendent study and deep training in various physical skills of defense and attack. Referred to with a lowercase "the."

Nadirii – (Nah-DEER-ee) (n): Sisterhood of warriors who live in an enchanted forest (The Enchantments) with no men. The veil around this forest was raised after the women of Airen revolted against their oppressors, magicking them to sleep, slitting their throats and escaping by stealing into the night to the newly established enchanted forest. No one can enter without Nadirii permission.
    (1) "Nadirii" means "oppressed" in the old tongue.
    (2) "Nadirii" means "sisterhood" in the ancient tongue.

Narration Hall – (n/building): Very large library that is very tall as well as built down deep in the earth in the Dome City where the tomes of history are recorded and kept, as well as all other books the Go'Doan have collected.

Nautilus – (n/place): Capital city of Mar-el, located on the southwest coast.

Night Heights – (n/mountain range): Range of mountains to the east of Sky Bay, the capital city of the country of Airen.

Nippenlas – (n/festival/holiday): A festival held midwinter in Wodell for the sole purpose of drawing the citizens out of their homes and to break the monotony of long nights and cold winters.

Northlands (The) – (n/place): One of two continents to the east of Triton across the Green Sea.

Notting Thicket – (n/place): Capital city of the country of Wodell, located to the east of the Great Thicket Forest.

Our Lady the Queen's Orphanage – (n/place): National orphanage in Notting Thicket, Wodell. Under patronage of the Queen of Wodell.

Pennyrium – (Pen-EER-ee-um) (n): A drug a woman can take through dissolving a powder in water in order to protect against conception.

Piercing Ceremony – (event): Done at age thirteen to boys and girls in Firenze, it is the ceremony where the right ear is pierced at the top and lobe, as well as the nostril and the side of the top lip. It is where the marital chain is threaded after a Firenz is wedded. Small hoops are worn in these piercings until a person is married and takes their chain.

*Rayloo* – (command): A Korwahkian word meaning [as it is in the imperative conjunction] "be quiet."

River Dorian – (n/river): Long, wide river running from Seil Sea through the eastern region of the country of Wodell, through the Lesser Thicket Forest, to the city-state of Go'Doan.

River Fae – (n/river): A river running from mountains to the north of the country of Wodell, through the mid-eastern part of the country to join with the Great Wohd at Notting Thicket, the capital of Wodell.

Royal Service Infirmary – (n/place): National hospital in Notting Thicket, the capital of Wodell, that treats all, but was created and caters to Dellish soldiers.

Seil Sea – (n/ocean): Body of water north of the continent of Triton.

Sheeonee Mountain Range – (SHE-oh-nee) (n/place): Large mountain range that makes up most of the central part of the country of Firenze. Very high peaks that get a great deal of snow. Snow melt feeds Fire Lake (outside Fire City) and five large rivers that run through the country, including the widest that flows north toward Wodell, the Tebes River.

Smoke – (n): Marijuana. Used mostly in Firenze but available throughout Triton.

Silbury Henge – (n/place): Standing stone henge in the forest on the western border of Airen where it meets The Enchantments and the city-state of Go'Doan. Made up of five standing stones and a sacrificial/ritual slab.

Sky Bay – (n/place): Capital city of Airen, located in a northwesternmost bay of Airen, close to the border of Wodell.

Sky Citadel – (n/place): Home of the King of Airen. Located in Sky Bay.

Slán Bailey – (SLAHN) (n/place): Royal prison in Airen, the building of which takes up a full, small island off the coast of Twilight Harbor in Sky Bay.

Soldier's Poison – (ritual): If a soldier is wounded gravely in the service of Airen or Wodell, he can request to be relieved of his life. This request is made of his commanding officer, and that officer can grant or refuse it. The ritual allows for a farewell from any loved one the soldier selects and making peace with his gods, before he's given a fast-acting, painless poison of a dense concentration of undiluted *taibac* to take, or if he's unable to drink it himself, it is administered to him by his commanding officer.

Southlands (The) – (n/place): One of two continents to the east of Triton across the Green Sea.

Strait of Medusa – (n/waterway): Narrow body of water that separates Mar-el from Airen.

Sparkles – (n): (When referring to a beverage) Champagne.

*Taibac* – (TIE-back) (n): Tobacco. Not smoked. Used as a poison to induce cardiac arrest. Can go undetected if poison is administered in small doses for a long time.

Tebes River – (TEH-behz) (n/river): Large river that flows from the Sheeonee Mountain range in Firenze, north toward the country of Wodell.

Temple to Wohden – (WOE-den) (n/place): National cathedral in Notting Thicket, Wodell where parishioners worship the god Wohden, the Dellish god of power and war. Also, where all royals are wed.

Trevor's Gorge – (n/place):
(1)  A gorge south of Notting Thicket in Wodell that runs through a small, ancient mountain range (thus not high). It was formed by a narrow, but strong tributary that breaks off the Great Wohd River in Wodell.

(2)  Also, the name of the large town situated at the west end of the

gorge. This town is known for the making of sharp, but rich, goat's cheese that is renown throughout Triton.

    a.   Trevor cheese (n/food): Cheese from this region.

Triton – (n/place):

    (1)  The continent to the west of the Northlands and Southlands, and to the east of The Mystics. It is surrounded by the Green Sea to the east, the Triton Sea to the west, Seil Sea to the north and Fotiá Sea to the south. It consists of one large land mass about the size of Australia and one large island (Mar-el) to the northeast. Countries include Airen, The Enchantments, Firenze, Mar-el, Wodell and the city-state of the Go'Doan.

    (2)  (n/god): God of the sea, worshiped by Mar-el.

Triton Sea – (n/ocean): Body of water to the west of the continent of Triton.

Trusted Ones (The) – (n): The elite guard that is commissioned with the safety of the King and Queen of Firenze. Also known as "The Trusted."

Twilight Harbor – (n/place): Wharf/dock in Sky Bay, the capital city of Airen.

Westfork River – (n/river): Short, narrow river in the country of Airen running from a break in the great Dunleth Abhainn at the town of Kilcree Break. The Westfork River runs southwest to the Argyll Forest.

Wodell – (n/place): Country of Wodell situated at the northwest of the Triton mainland. Very fertile and green, consisting of mainly farmland, forests, hills, dells and moors.

Wynd – (pronounced like "to wind your way") (n): A narrow, open-ended alley. Mostly a footpath and not used for carriages or horses, etc. Opposite of "close" [see above].

Zees – (people): A race of wanderers. Mostly in Wodell, but also some would travel around the westernmost border of Airen.

*Full glossary, including character lists, tarot meanings, and gods and goddesses can be found on The Rising Series page at KristenAshley.net*

# KEEP READING FOR MORE OF THE RISING

**The Dawn of the End**

Once upon a time, in a parallel universe, there existed the continent of Triton...

The queen has been assassinated. The Enchantments are under attack. The plot is unfolding. And our lovers, Silence and Mars, Cassius and Elena, True and Farah and Aramus and Ha-Lah are forced to separate as treachery and civil war sweep Triton.

Not to mention, the Beast is still a threat to every breathing being on the continent, and it is the destined warriors and witches who must stop him.

The attention of the fated mates is scattered and weighed down with bereavement and heartbreak as some leave Wodell to go to Airen, Mar-el and Firenze.

But they must amass their powers....

**The Beast is rising.**

**Keep reading for more of The Dawn of the End.**

# THE DAWN OF THE END
## CHAPTER 81 - THE SCHEMER

**Jellan**
*Underground Lair of the Beast*
*Wodell*

He felt it, even in his weakened state.

The veil, it was growing strong.

The prophecy, it was advancing.

When he also felt he had company in this dark hole where they allowed him to go when they weren't using him or making him serve, Jellan curled deeper into himself, pressing his abused body closer to the stone wall.

He could tell them.

He could use his knowledge of the prophecy, his feel for the veil, to better his circumstances down in that dirty, cold, ugly hole.

"Hungry?"

It was *her*.

Marian.

The Mistress of the Beast.

*His* Beast.

That fiendish creature should be *his*.

Not *hers*.

The thing liked using him.

Perhaps Jellan could turn that around, gain control of...

She kicked him in the back, and Jellan tasted blood as he bit the insides of his mouth to stop from crying out.

He'd given them his tears. His pleas. His moans of agony.

They would have no more.

They would take no more from him than what they could force from him.

"I asked, *are you hungry*?" she demanded.

He needed to keep his strength.

"Y-yes," he answered.

He heard something drop to the ground close to him and turned carefully, battling the pain that seemed to infuse every inch of his body.

He could not make out what it was in the dark, a joint of some animal, not very much meat, lying in the dirt.

He took it up anyway, thinking he had to plan.

He had to *plan*.

And he had to have strength to plan.

He had power.

He was a Go'En priest, for Bedi's sake. A member of the Society of the Beast. One, if not *the* most powerful sorcerer in all of Triton.

He was born to master the Beast.

He was *made* to master the Beast.

He had to find a way.

He had to *plan*.

She started to move away, but he called to her, forcing timidity into his tone.

"C-can I ask you a question, Mistress?" he requested.

She turned, moved back to him, and he braced.

Like a woman, her moods were inconstant and sometimes volatile. He could not know if she'd kick him, call to the Beast and demand Jellan be used again or stroke his hair and coo to him.

In the end, he would lash her to the ritual ground, Jellan vowed it. He'd call the entire Society to have their way with her. He'd stand over and watch her take each cock and then he'd stand over her and watch her take each blade. And finally, when she was beaten and humiliated to the core of her soul and praying death would come fast, he'd give her that by drawing the final blade across her throat.

All of this looking right in her eyes.

All of this with the Beast at his back.

"What is your question, pet?" she asked.

So it was his benevolent mistress this time.

"I...the last quake, there was a demanding cry from the creature. I thought that he...I was not at that ritual, I thought that he—"

"Was calling to you?"

He nodded, gazing up at her but not meeting her eyes.

Fearful.

Submissive.

Beaten.

She needn't know he was none of that.

"He wasn't, he was calling out to me," she explained. "He sensed me. I'd been visiting him. And he was tired of your vicious shenanigans. Thus, he was calling me home."

"But, if he has no power down here, how does he make the earth quake? How did he call out like that? How does he pull you down? Me? The other women?"

"He has no magic, but he does have feelings. And just like everything with him, his feelings are stronger, more powerful, more sweeping than anything a mere mortal would have. They move the earth. When he makes the surface, if he should not get his way, they'll probably shake the heavens."

Jellan shuddered at that thought.

"But how does he pull you down?" he pressed.

"He doesn't. I did that."

He blinked up at her.

"I brought you," she went on, "and your *brothers*, our girls. That is *my* power. He reached to me, but my magic gave him that power. And my power brings him to the surface. But once there, the merfolk's binds on his magic are erased. And once we feel the time is right, we will surface and make all of Triton bow to us."

**The Dawn of the End is available now.**

# ABOUT THE AUTHOR

Kristen Ashley is the *New York Times* bestselling author of over eighty romance novels including the *Rock Chick, Colorado Mountain, Dream Man, Chaos, Unfinished Heroes, The 'Burg, Magdalene, Fantasyland, The Three, Ghost and Reincarnation, The Rising, Dream Team, Moonlight and Motor Oil, River Rain, Wild West MC, Misted Pines* and *Honey* series along with several stand-alone novels. She's a hybrid author, publishing titles both independently and traditionally, her books have been translated in fourteen languages and she's sold over five million books.

Kristen's novel, *Law Man*, won the *RT Book Reviews* Reviewer's Choice Award for best Romantic Suspense, her independently published title *Hold On* was nominated for *RT Book Reviews* best Independent Contemporary Romance and her traditionally published title *Breathe* was nominated for best Contemporary Romance. Kristen's titles *Motorcycle Man, The Will*, and *Ride Steady* (which won the Reader's Choice award from *Romance Reviews*) all made the final rounds for Goodreads Choice Awards in the Romance category.

Kristen, born in Gary and raised in Brownsburg, Indiana, is a fourth-generation graduate of Purdue University. Since, she's lived in Denver, the West Country of England, and she now resides in Phoenix. She worked as a charity executive for eighteen years prior to beginning her independent publishing career. She now writes full-time.

Although romance is her genre, the prevailing themes running through all of Kristen's novels are friendship, family and a strong sisterhood. To this end, and as a way to thank her readers for their support, Kristen has created the Rock Chick Nation, a series of programs that are designed to give back to her readers and promote a strong female community.

The mission of the Rock Chick Nation is to live your best life, be true to your true self, recognize your beauty, and take your sister's back whether they're at your side as friends and family or if they're thousands of miles away and you don't know who they are.

The programs of the RC Nation include Rock Chick Rendezvous, weekends Kristen organizes full of parties and get-togethers to bring the sisterhood together, Rock Chick Recharges, evenings Kristen arranges for women who have been nominated to receive a special night, and Rock Chick Rewards, an ongoing program that raises funds for nonprofit women's organizations Kristen's readers nominate. Kristen's Rock Chick Rewards have donated hundreds of thousands of dollars to charity and this number continues to rise.

You can read more about Kristen, her titles and the Rock Chick Nation at KristenAshley.net.

facebook.com/kristenashleybooks

twitter.com/KristenAshley68

instagram.com/kristenashleybooks

pinterest.com/KristenAshleyBooks

goodreads.com/kristenashleybooks

bookbub.com/authors/kristen-ashley

# ALSO BY KRISTEN ASHLEY

**Rock Chick Series:**

*Rock Chick*

*Rock Chick Rescue*

*Rock Chick Redemption*

*Rock Chick Renegade*

*Rock Chick Revenge*

*Rock Chick Reckoning*

*Rock Chick Regret*

*Rock Chick Revolution*

*Rock Chick Reawakening*

*Rock Chick Reborn*


**The 'Burg Series:**

*For You*

*At Peace*

*Golden Trail*

*Games of the Heart*

*The Promise*

*Hold On*


**The Chaos Series:**

*Own the Wind*

*Fire Inside*

*Ride Steady*

*Walk Through Fire*

*A Christmas to Remember*

*Rough Ride*

*Wild Like the Wind*

*Free*

*Wild Fire*

*Wild Wind*


**The Colorado Mountain Series:**

*The Gamble*

*Sweet Dreams*

*Lady Luck*

*Breathe*

*Jagged*

*Kaleidoscope*

*Bounty*


**Dream Man Series:**

*Mystery Man*

*Wild Man*

*Law Man*

*Motorcycle Man*

*Quiet Man*


**Dream Team Series:**

*Dream Maker*

*Dream Chaser*

*Dream Bites Cookbook*

*Dream Spinner*

*Dream Keeper*


**The Fantasyland Series:**

*Wildest Dreams*

*The Golden Dynasty*

*Fantastical*

*Broken Dove*

*Midnight Soul*

*Gossamer in the Darkness*

**Ghosts and Reincarnation Series:**

*Sommersgate House*

*Lacybourne Manor*

*Penmort Castle*

*Fairytale Come Alive*

*Lucky Stars*

**The Honey Series:**

*The Deep End*

*The Farthest Edge*

*The Greatest Risk*

**The Magdalene Series:**

*The Will*

*Soaring*

*The Time in Between*

**Mathilda, SuperWitch:**

*Mathilda's Book of Shadows*

*Mathilda The Rise of the Dark Lord*

**Misted Pines Series**

*The Girl in the Mist*

*The Girl in the Woods*

**Moonlight and Motor Oil Series:**

*The Hookup*

*The Slow Burn*

**The Rising Series:**

*The Beginning of Everything*

*The Plan Commences*

*The Dawn of the End*

*The Rising*

**The River Rain Series:**

*After the Climb*

*After the Climb Special Edition*

*Chasing Serenity*

*Taking the Leap*

*Making the Match*

**The Three Series:**

*Until the Sun Falls from the Sky*

*With Everything I Am*

*Wild and Free*

**The Unfinished Hero Series:**

*Knight*

*Creed*

*Raid*

*Deacon*

*Sebring*

**Wild West MC Series:**

*Still Standing*

*Smoke and Steel*

**Other Titles by Kristen Ashley:**

*Heaven and Hell*

*Play It Safe*

*Three Wishes*

*Complicated*

*Loose Ends*

*Fast Lane*

*Perfect Together*

*Too Good To Be True*

www.ingramcontent.com/pod-product-compliance
Lightning Source LLC
Chambersburg PA
CBHW061607210726

48287CB00001B/29